The Whalebone Theatre

JOANNA QUINN

FIG TREE
an imprint of
PENGUIN BOOKS

FIG TREE

UK | USA | Canada | Ireland | Australia
India | New Zealand | South Africa

Fig Tree is part of the Penguin Random House group of companies
whose addresses can be found at global.penguinrandomhouse.com.

Penguin
Random House
UK

First published 2022
001

Copyright © Joanna Quinn, 2022

The moral right of the author has been asserted

Set in 12/14.75pt Dante MT Std
Typeset by Jouve (UK), Milton Keynes
Printed and bound in Great Britain by Clays Ltd, Elcograf S.p.A.

The authorized representative in the EEA is Penguin Random House Ireland,
Morrison Chambers, 32 Nassau Street, Dublin D02 YH68

A CIP catalogue record for this book is available from the British Library

ISBN: 978-0-241-54283-5

www.greenpenguin.co.uk

The Whalebone Theatre

'Magnificent. As capacious, surprising and magical as the whale that lends its bones to Cristabel's theatre: a tale of intertwined lives and braided fates as deftly managed and heartbreaking as a Dickens novel' Rebecca Stott, author of *In the Days of Rain*

'Playful, inventive, sharp, funny . . . sheer, undiluted delight from start to finish. It breathes fresh, bracing air into the lungs of the multi-generational saga – and the very form of the novel itself. Few people writing today can match Quinn for the energy and precision of her prose: sentences begin boldly, proceed to hit every nail on their path, then land, gorgeously, in a totally unexpected place. In Quinn's hands, archetypes are re-born: characters damaged by the usual unsavoury traditions of the British aristocracy are depicted with piercing efficiency, then found to be loveable despite it all. Catchphrases from the past are dug up, tossed wittily around, and suddenly understood for the very first time. Most importantly of all, perhaps, Quinn gives us Cristabel, the sort of intelligent heroine that has been sorely missing from every other classic since *Middlemarch*: disinterested in marriage yet capable of immense love. It's impossible not to be charmed by this book, its cast of characters, and Quinn's constantly striking prose. It is both reassuringly familiar, and startlingly new: a big fat Victorian novel written by someone from the post #metoo years' Susan Elderkin, author of *Voices*

'I defy any reader not to fall in love . . . it transported me wholesale to another time and place and while I wandered its pages, I forgot the world for a while' Wyl Menmuir, author of *Fox Fires*

'A beautifully written, completely immersive read that I can't quite believe is a debut. Very highly recommended' *Bookseller*

'Can there be a better proscenium arch than the salvaged ribs of a beached whale? Framed by these giant bones, Quinn's story passes like a fabulous pageant, richly coloured and packed with incident, taking us from the lonely and orthodox Dorset childhood of the extraordinary Cristabel to the poignant aftermath of her heroic Second World War' Frances Liardet, author of *We Must Be Brave*

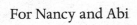

For Nancy and Abi

What cares these roarers for the name of king?

William Shakespeare, *The Tempest*

Contents

ACT FIVE: 1944–1945

ENCORE

ACT ONE

1919–1920

The Last Day of the Year

31st December, 1919
Dorset

Cristabel picks up the stick. It fits well in her hand. She is in the garden, waiting with the rest of the household for her father to return with her new mother. Uniformed servants blow on cold fingers. Rooks caw half-heartedly from the trees surrounding the house. It is the last day of December, the dregs of the year. The afternoon is fading and the lawn a quagmire of mud and old snow, which three-year-old Cristabel stamps across in her lace-up leather boots, holding the stick like a sword, a miniature sentry in a brass-buttoned winter coat.

She swishes the stick to and fro, enjoying the *vvvp vvp* sound it makes, uses it to spoon a piece of grubby snow to her mouth. The snow is as chilly on her tongue as the frost flowers that form on her attic window, but less clinging. It tastes disappointingly nothingy. Somewhere too far away to be bothered about, her nanny is calling her name. Cristabel puts the noise away from her with a blink. She spies snowdrops simpering at the edge of the garden. *Vvvvp vvp.*

Cristabel's father, Jasper Seagrave, and his new bride are, at that moment, seated side by side in a horse-drawn carriage, travelling up the driveway towards Jasper's family home: Chilcombe, a many-gabled, many-chimneyed, ivy-covered manor house with an elephantine air of weary grandeur. In outline, it is a series of sagging triangles and tall chimney stacks, and it has huddled on a wooded cliff overhanging the ocean for four hundred years, its leaded windows narrowed against sea winds and historical progress, its general appearance one of gradual subsidence.

The staff at Chilcombe say today will be a special day, but Cristabel is finding it dull. There is too much waiting. Too much straightening up. It is not a day that would make a good story. Cristabel likes stories that feature blunderbusses and dogs, not brides and waiting. *Vvvp*. As she picks up the remains of the snowdrops, she hears the bone crunch of gravel beneath wheels.

Her father is the first to disembark from the carriage, as round and satisfied as a broad bean popped from a pod. Then a single foot in a button-boot appears, followed by a velvet hat, which tilts upwards to look at the house. Cristabel watches her father's whiskery face. He too is looking upwards, gazing at the young woman in the hat, who, while still balanced on the step of the carriage, is significantly taller than him.

Cristabel marches towards them through the snow. She is almost there when her nanny grabs her, hissing, 'What have you got in your hands? Where are your gloves?'

Jasper turns. 'Why is the child so dirty?'

The dirty child ignores her father. She is not interested in him. Grumpy, angry man. Instead, she approaches the new mother, offering a handful of soil and snowdrop petals. But the new mother is adept at receiving clumsy gifts; she has, after all, accepted the blustering proposal of Jasper Seagrave, a rotund widower with an unmanageable beard and a limp.

'For me,' says the new mother, and it is not a question. 'How novel.' She steps down from the carriage and smiles, floating about her a hand which comes to rest on Cristabel's head, as if that were what the child is for. Beneath her velvet hat, the new mother is wrapped in a smart wool travelling suit and a mink fur stole.

Jasper turns to the staff and announces, 'Allow me to present my new wife: Mrs Rosalind Seagrave.'

There is a ripple of applause.

Cristabel finds it odd that the new mother should have the name Seagrave, which is her name. She looks at the soil in her hand, then turns it over, allowing it to fall on to the new mother's boots, to see what happens then.

Rosalind moves away from the unsmiling girl. A motherless child, she reminds herself, lacking in feminine guidance. She wonders if she should have brought some ribbons for its tangled black hair, or a tortoiseshell comb, but then Jasper is at her side, leading her to the doorway.

'Finally got you here,' he says. 'Chilcombe's not quite at its best. Used to have a splendid set of iron gates at the entrance.'

As they cross the threshold, he is talking about the coming evening's celebrations. He says the villagers are delighted by her arrival. A marquee has been erected behind the house, a pig will be roasted, and everyone will toast the nuptials with tankards of ale. He winks at her now, bristling in his tweed suit, and she is unsure what is meant by this covering and uncovering of one eye, this stagey wince.

Rosalind Seagrave, née Elliot, twenty-three years old, described in the April 1914 edition of *Tatler* magazine as 'a poised London debutante', walks through the stone entranceway of Chilcombe into a wood-panelled galleried room that extends upwards like a medieval knights' hall. It is a hollow funnel, dimly lit by flickering candles in brass wall brackets, and the air has the unused quality of empty chapels in out-of-the-way places.

It is a peculiar feeling, to enter a strange house knowing it contains her future. Rosalind looks around, trying to take it in before it notices her. There is a fireplace at the back of the hall: large, stone and unlit. Crossed swords hang above it. There is not much in the way of furniture and it does not attract her as she hoped. A carved oak coffer with an iron hinge. A suit of armour holding a spear in its metal hand. A grandfather clock, a moulting Christmas tree, and a grand piano topped by a vase of lilies.

The piano, she knows, is a wedding present from her husband, but it has been put to one side beneath the stuffed head of a stag. Around the walls droop more mounted animal heads, glass-eyed lions and antelopes, along with ancient tapestries showing people in profile gesticulating with arrows. As blue is the last colour to fade in tapestry, what were once cheerful depictions of battle are now mournful, undersea scenes.

To the right of the fireplace is a curving wooden staircase leading to the upper floors of the house, while on either side of her, worn Persian rugs lead through arched doorways into dark rooms that lead to more doorways to dark rooms, and so it goes on, like an illustration of infinity. The heel of her boot catches on a rug as she steps forward. They will have to move the rugs, she thinks, when they have parties.

Jasper appears beside her, talking to the butler. 'Tell me, Blythe, has my errant brother arrived? Couldn't be bothered to show his face at the wedding.'

The butler gives an almost imperceptible shake of his head, for this is how Chilcombe is run, with gestures so familiar and worn down they have become the absence of gestures – the impression of something that used to be there; the shape of the fossil left in the stone.

Jasper sniffs, addresses his wife. 'The maids will show you to your room.'

Rosalind is escorted up the staircase, passing a series of paintings depicting men in ruffs pausing mid-hunt to have their portraits done, resting stockinged calves on the still-warm bodies of boars.

Cristabel watches from a corner. She has tucked herself behind a wooden umbrella stand in the shape of a little Indian boy; his out-stretched arms make a circle to hold umbrellas, riding crops and her father's walking sticks. She waits until the new mother is out of sight, then runs across the hall to the back staircase, which is concealed from view behind the main staircase. This takes her down to below stairs, the servants' realm: the kitchen, scullery, storerooms and cellars. Here, in the roots of the house, she can find a hiding place and examine her new treasures: the stick and the crescents of soil beneath her fingernails.

On this day, below stairs is a clamorous place, the tiled kitchen echoing with activity. The servants are excited about the evening celebrations, anxious about hosting the wedding party, and full of gossip about the new wife. Cristabel crawls under the kitchen table and listens. Items of interest spark like lightning across her consciousness: favourite words like 'horse' and 'pudding'; voices she recognizes surfacing in the melee.

Her attention is caught by Maudie Kitcat, the youngest kitchen maid, saying, 'Maybe Miss Cristabel will be getting a little brother soon.' Cristabel hadn't seen a little brother get out of the carriage, but perhaps one would be coming later. She would like a brother very much. For games and battles.

She also likes the kitchen maid Maudie Kitcat. They both sleep in the attic and practise their letters together. Cristabel often asks Maudie to write the names of people she knows in the condensation on the attic windows, and Maudie will comply, squeakingly shaping the words with a single finger – M-A-U-D-I-E, D-O-G, N-A-N-N-Y, C-O-O-K – so Cristabel can trace her own small finger along them or rub them out if they have displeased her. Sometimes, Maudie will visit her in the night if Cristabel has one of the dreams that make her shout, and Maudie will stroke her head and say shhh, little one, shhh now, don't cry.

In the kitchen, Cook is saying, 'An heir to the estate, eh? Let's hope Jasper Seagrave's still got it in him.' Bellows of laughter follow. A male voice shouts, 'If he can't manage it, I'll step in and have a go.' There is more laughter, then a crash, something thrown. The sound of servants roaring at this incomprehensible exchange is a thunderous wave washing over Cristabel. She decides to use her stick to write her letters, tracing a circle in the flour on the flagstone floor, round and round. O. O. O. O. Time away from her interfering nanny is rare, she must not waste it. O. O. O.

O for 'oh'. O for 'ohnoCristabelwhathaveyoudonenow'.

Upstairs on the first floor, Rosalind sits at the dressing table in her new bedroom, although she hardly can call it new, for everything in it appears to be ancient. It is a room of aggressively creaking floorboards and fragile mahogany furniture lit by smoke-stained oil lamps: a collection of items that cannot bear to be touched. She hears laughter coming from elsewhere in the house and feels it as a rising tension in her shoulders. A maid stands behind her, brushing out Rosalind's ink-dark hair, while another unpacks her cases, carefully extracting items of lingerie that have been folded into perfumed satin pads. Rosalind is aware of being examined, assessed. She wishes she could open her own luggage.

Rosalind checks her reflection in the dressing table mirror; composes herself. She has the pert face of a favoured child. Wide eyes, an upturned nose. This is complemented by her self-taught habit of clasping her hands beneath her chin, as if delighted by unexpected gifts. She does this now.

She has done well, despite everything; she must believe this. There had been sharp talk in London. Intimations of unwise dalliances. Suggestions she'd ruined her chances fraternizing with one too many beaux. But all those men had gone now. One by one, all the charming boys she had danced with and strolled with and dined with had disappeared. At first, it was awful, and then it was usual, which was worse than awful, but less tiring. After a while, it was simply what happened. They left, waving, on trains and went into the ground in places with foreign names that became increasingly familiar: Ypres, Arras, the Somme.

The years of the war became an achingly monotonous time, with Rosalind perched on a stiff armchair, trying to finish a piece of embroidery while her mother intoned the names of eligible young men listed in *The Times* as dead or missing. There were stories in the newspapers about 'surplus women' – millions of spinsters who would never marry due to the shortage of suitable husbands. Rosalind cut out magazine pictures of society brides and glued them into a scrapbook: an album of lucky escapees. She was fearful she would become a black-clad relic like her widowed mother, a woman alone, fussing over teacups and miniature monkey-faced dogs, entrapped by knitting baskets and petulant footstools.

Even when the Great War ended, there was nobody left to celebrate with. The handful of passable men who did come home spent parties swapping battle stories with hearty girls who had been in uniform, while Rosalind stood against a wall, her dance card empty. So when she met Jasper Seagrave, a widower looking for a young wife to provide a son and heir, it seemed a space had been made for her, a tiny passage she could crawl through into the orange blossom light of a wedding day, where a house of her own would await her.

And here she is. She has made it through. A winter wedding, not ideal, but still a wedding. Despite the sinus problems of the groom.

Despite his insistence on the jolting carriage ride. Despite the view from the rattling carriage windows jerking backwards and forwards like scenery waved about by amateurish stagehands. Despite the clamping, clawing feeling in her heart. It could all be rectified.

Rosalind lifts her new diamond earrings to her ears. She watches in the mirror as one of the maids lays out her ivory chiffon peignoir, arranging it with respectfully covetous hands on the four-poster bed, which has a high mattress like the one in the story of the princess and the pea. Outside the darkening window, there is the crackle of a bonfire, the murmur of voices as the villagers arrive, and the rich, burnt smell of roasting meat.

Cristabel is standing in the garden by the fire, closely observing the suckling pig hung over the flames on a spit, a red apple jammed in its rotating mouth. She holds her stick in her right hand. Her left hand is in her coat pocket, fingers running over other newly acquired treasures found below stairs: a scrap of newspaper and a pencil stub. It is a kind of reassurance, to have these small things she can touch.

She can hear her nanny crashing through the house looking for her, her angry nanny voice running ahead of her like a baying pack of hounds. Cristabel knows what will happen next. She will be taken upstairs to her bedroom without supper as a punishment for disappearing. The candle will be blown out and the door locked. The attic will become shadowy and endlessly cornered: a shifting blackness raked by the slow-moving searchlight of the moon, a great lidless eye.

Cristabel runs her thumb backwards and forwards over the stick's rippled bark, as she will later on, when she is lying in her narrow bed – as a way of turning over the time when she is not allowed to make a silly fuss. When she was a little baby she made a fuss, and her nanny made her wear the jacket with the arms that tied round to stop her climbing out of bed. She does not intend to make a fuss again.

Beneath her pillow, she keeps various sticks, several stones that have faces, and an old picture postcard of a dog owned by a king, which she found under a rug and named Dog. She can line them up, feed them supper, have them act out a story, and put them to bed. She can protect them and stroke their heads if they have shouting dreams, and make sure they don't get out on the cold wooden floor.

She crouches down next to a patch of snow, uses her stick to write her letters. O. O. O. She hears her nanny saying: 'For pity's sake, there she is. Digging in the snow, getting herself filthy.'

Cristabel likes the word snow. She whispers it to herself, then continues her work, her daily practice: shaping letters, making words, taking names.

S-N-O.

The Morning After

1st January, 1920

New year, new decade, new house, new husband. New as a new pin. Didn't her mother always say something about new pins? Rosalind feels pinned beneath the sheets of the marital bed. There is a rigidity to her spine that recalls the dinosaur skeletons in the London museums. She is fixed in place. An exhibit. White-capped maids come and go, lighting the fire and drawing the curtains, as busy and remote as gulls. Through the window, Rosalind can see bare trees flailing.

Jasper has said it may take time for her to adjust to the role of wife. He says she is young and that being with a man is new to her. (An image flits into her mind – an August evening near the boat shed with Rupert, his moustache scratching against her neck like wire wool – she shakes it away.) Jasper believes she will become familiar with her marital duties in time. She will become familiar with the unfamiliar. She is holding herself very still because it does not seem possible for these unfamiliar acts to exist in this room, alongside such steadfastly ordinary items as her silver hairbrush, the bedside lamp.

The maids bring her breakfast, balancing it on a tray on her eiderdown so she is presented with an unappealing display: a heap of gelatinous scrambled eggs cupped by the curving gristle of a sausage. She covers the tray with a napkin and reaches for her glass atomizer: pff, *pfffff*, and Yardley Eau de Cologne hazes the air.

The maids pass and call, pass and call. Rosalind hears her own voice producing suitable words for them. 'Not much appetite. Thank you so much.' The maids take the words and the uneaten food away with them. There is a discreet spiral staircase hidden behind a Chinese screen in the corner of the room that allows them to come and go without using the door.

Soon she must attend to things. She must dress appropriately and do what is expected of her. She must be a – what was it Jasper said? His voice so horribly loud in her ear in the darkness, like the voice of a giant – she must be a sport. Rosalind looks up at the tapestry canopy hanging over the bed to find the pattern she had studied last night. It is hidden in the larger design, a sort of lopsided face looking back at her, repeated many times over.

The maids reappear, swooping about with garments and undergarments; they want to dress her and make her beautiful. Men used to tell her she was beautiful. They admired her and talked of their beating hearts, and she felt this as an exultation, an adoration. She never believed that what they called love would involve such obscene exertions. Brute weight and panting effort. A pile of flesh smelling of port and tobacco, pressing the air from her body until she could not breathe. And the pain: pure white pain, flashing like stars behind her eyelids. No, this has nothing to do with love.

A maid approaches. 'Mr Seagrave has gone to Exeter on horse business, ma'am. He hopes you enjoy your first day in Chilcombe.'

Rosalind nods. She has no words left. She is blank as paper in her stiff sheets.

The maid comes closer, crossing the creaky floorboards. 'We met yesterday, ma'am. You may not remember. I'm Betty Bemrose. I'm to be your lady's maid.' Rosalind glances down to find that, most surprisingly, the maid has placed a hand on her own. 'Perhaps a bath, ma'am? You look wrung out.'

Rosalind looks at Betty's concerned face beneath her white maid's cap. It is round and freckled, and there is the unexpectedly reassuring pressure of her hand.

Betty continues, 'There are some bath oils, ma'am. Believe you brought them with you. That'd get you back on your feet.'

'Rose,' Rosalind says. 'There is a rose oil.'

'Lovely.'

'A dear friend gave it to me. He was an officer. Died in France.'

'So many gone,' says Betty, heading into the adjoining bathroom.

'My sister's husband was lost at Gallipoli. They never even found him. I had them bring up some hot water for you earlier, ma'am, so I only need add the oil.'

'My friend – he had freckles like yours.'

'No!'

'He was charming.'

Betty reappears in the bathroom doorway. 'When you're having a bath, I'll get the bed linen changed. Put some more coal on the fire. We only light the upstairs fires when there's people staying so they do take their time to get going.'

'He took me to The Waldorf once. Have you heard of it?'

'Can't say that I have, ma'am.'

'Simply everybody goes there.'

Betty comes to the bed and gently pulls back the covers. 'Let me help you, ma'am.'

Rosalind grips the young woman's arms and allows herself to be navigated to the adjoining room, where a cast iron hip-bath waits in front of a low fire, holding a shallow layer of still water, scented with roses.

Sitting on a step outside the kitchen door, Cristabel grips her stick firmly in her fist and writes in the dust: B-R-U-T-H-E. B-R-O-H-E-R.

'Try again,' says Maudie Kitcat, passing with a basket of dirty bed linen. 'You are near enough getting it though.'

The new Mrs Jasper Seagrave, bathed and anointed, leaves her bedroom and makes her way downstairs. She is unsure what is expected of her. Her husband is away, and she does not know how to find out when he might return. A letter from her mother has arrived, reminding her of the importance of establishing her authority with the staff, and Rosalind fears enquiring about her husband's whereabouts will not improve her standing in the eyes of the household.

However, she does make authoritative decisions on several matters: that sausages are repellent and fit only for dogs; that a modern bathtub must be installed; that the Christmas tree should be thrown out, along with the lilies (her mother always says lilies remind her of very *obvious* women). Also: a gramophone is to be purchased post-haste, and her husband's sullen daughter should have a French governess. *You,* writes Rosalind's mother in a forward-leaning hand, *are a new broom in the household! Brisk and firm!*

Despite her mother's instructions, Rosalind finds it difficult to issue orders to the male staff, many of whom, such as Blythe the butler, are old enough to be her father. But it seems apt that she, the young bride, should be unknowing. Hadn't she read in *The Lady* that 'men can't help but respond to the feminine charms of the innocent ingénue'? 'Be elegant,' continued the magazine, 'and a little spoiled, but not bored.'

Rosalind leans on the piano near a framed photograph of her new husband. She likes the words 'new husband', they have an exciting feel to them, like a gift box rustling with tissue paper. She likes to use the words even as she avoids looking at the photograph. *New husband. Elegant, not bored.*

The day passes. Other very similar days pass.

Rosalind subscribes to magazines and cuts out pictures of items necessary to her new life – hats, furniture, people – or notes them in a list. Next door to her bedroom is a small room, a boudoir, containing all the lady of the house might need: a decorative table at which to serve tea, a roll-top writing desk, an ivory letter opener. Rosalind sits at the desk and sifts through her magazine cuttings like a miner panning for gold.

With the help of Mrs Hardcastle the housekeeper, she orders a few essentials – silk pillowcases, hand creams – and waits for them. If she stands on the gallery landing, she can look down into the entrance hall, known as the Oak Hall, to see if anything is arriving. She discovers saying 'I'm having a little wander' will usually remove hovering servants. But if they continue to linger, she will then feel obliged to embark on a little wander.

Chilcombe is only modestly sized, nine bedrooms in all, but has been built and added to in such an arcane way that each part seems difficult to reach. Its residents and staff must make long excursions along convoluted corridors with a variable camber, sloping like a ship's deck. There are often unexpected steps, sudden landings. The windows are narrow as arrow slits and the stone walls damp to the touch.

Rosalind would go out, but the outside world seems unapproachable. In London, the outdoors had been tidied up into parks. At dusk, the lamplighters with their long poles would light the gas lamps lining the pathways, golden circles flickering into life across the city. But in Dorset, the darkness descends so completely it is like falling into a coal cellar. There are no bandstands or statues. Merely ominous woods and a few acres of estate land, home only to ancient trees with fencing round their trunks, as if each were the last of its kind. One wizened oak is so decrepit its branches are propped up with metal staves. Why do they not let it die? Rosalind wonders, for it is very ugly; a bark shell of itself, strung up like a man shackled to a dungeon wall.

The back of the house overlooks a courtyard edged by brick outbuildings: a laundry, tool sheds and stables. Adjacent to the outbuildings is a walled kitchen garden tended by a gardener trundling back and forth with a wheelbarrow. Sometimes there are dead pheasants or hares hanging from the door handles. There are murmured, laughing conversations between servants. Rosalind watches from a landing window, careful not to be seen.

There is a village about a mile away, Chilcombe Mell, but when Rosalind and Jasper passed through on their journey from the train station, she had seen only a handful of thatched cottages, a few shops, a church and a pub. It seemed a half-abandoned place; the buildings all slumped together at the base of a valley as if they had slithered downwards in an avalanche. Beyond the village is a ridge of high land running parallel with the coast, a steep escarpment topped with straggly trees and prehistoric burial mounds. It is known as the Ridgeway and shuts out the world quite succinctly. Who will ever find her here?

Jasper had told her, during their courtship, that the Ridgeway was thought to be the hill the Grand Old Duke of York had marched his 10,000 men up and down. 'Why on earth did he do that?' she'd replied, knowing that this was not the desired response. His wooing of her had largely consisted of him presenting her with historical facts in the way a cat continually brings its owner dead mice, despite their perplexing lack of success. Even at the beginning of their relationship, there had been this awkwardness: a sense of tight smiles and small unpleasant acts of disposal.

When, one morning, there is a knock on the door of her boudoir, Rosalind is quick to respond, expecting Betty bringing her latest purchase. Instead, it is a stout, bearded man in tweed plus fours. Rosalind's surprise is considerable, as she has managed to entirely divorce the physical being of Jasper Seagrave from the words 'new husband'.

'Hear you've been shopping,' says Jasper.

'A few items. Heavens, why did you knock? Does a husband need to knock?'

'If you prefer, I won't.'

'It merely seems –' Rosalind finds she has envisaged a different reunion between husband and wife. Shouldn't he sweep in, declaring he has missed her terribly? Shouldn't there be trinkets? Wouldn't that make this all much better?

'Taking Guinevere out this afternoon,' says Jasper. 'Don't suppose you fancy coming along?'

'Is that a horse? Isn't it raining?'

'Not much. No matter. See you at dinner.'

'I've never been good with horses –' and here she hesitates, uncertain how to address him, 'Jasper. Dear.'

Jasper tugs his beard, then leans forward to plant a bristly kiss on her cheek. 'No matter,' he says again, before heading downstairs.

She calls for Betty to draw her bath before dinner. Betty natters away as she lays out Rosalind's eau-de-Nil silk evening gown – long lines, finely pleated, beaded side-seam – and Rosalind is grateful. It helps settle her mind, which has become agitated since Jasper's arrival. She reclines in the perfumed water and enjoys Betty's talk as background noise: a sister's engagement, plans for her upcoming birthday.

'Your birthday – how old will you be, Betty?'

'Twenty-three, ma'am.'

'The same age as me.'

'Wish I was the same size as you, ma'am. You'll be pretty as a picture in this gown.'

Rosalind glances at her own white arms. 'We may have to take the gown in, Betty.'

'Have you been off your food again, ma'am? That's a pity. I suppose you miss your London life. I know your mother writes to you often.'

Rosalind suspects her mother would disapprove of such intimate conversation with staff. She pictures her hunched over her writing bureau, scribbling: *A wife's role is to submit to her husband! To be helpmeet, inspiration and guide!*

'My mother writes every day,' she says. 'I'm her only child.'

'She must be proud of you, doing so well for yourself,' says Betty.

A wife's role, thinks Rosalind. To submit. Elegant. Not bored. She spins these words in her mind through the silences of dinner in the dark red dining room and the waiting in the bedroom afterwards and the time after that, when she looks up at the canopy to find the lopsided face watching her in her wife's role, and there is something in that which allows her a little distance while it goes on: the unspeakable intrusion, the nightshirt he never takes off bundled between their bodies like something he is trying to smother, and even though there is a part of her mind that fights, that baulks and resists, she does not move a muscle, she never cries out, she simply remains there, gripping the bed sheet with both hands, staring up past him.

How is she to believe it? That this violence is done to her nightly, and all around her, people sleep soundly in their beds, happy it is being done.

And a small finger in the attic traces B-R-O-T-H-E-R, B-R-O-T-H-E-R, B-R-O-T-H-E-R.

Prodigal Brother

A distant *putt-putt-putt* is the first sign that the long-absent Willoughby Seagrave, Jasper's younger brother and only sibling, is returning to Chilcombe. Cristabel, crossing the lawn with her newly appointed French governess, stops to listen. It is an entirely new sound that reaches her ears from across the full distance of twenty centuries; one that has never been heard on the estate before. Cristabel drops the dead snail she is carrying in order to concentrate. The French governess also pauses. *Mon Dieu, petite Cristabel. C'est une automobile! Oui, Madame, c'est vrai.* It is a motor car.

As it approaches, the noise of the vehicle clarifies: it becomes a rattling, rapid *dug-dug-dug-dug*. To a few of the men cleaning out the stables behind the house, the sound is chillingly reminiscent of German guns. But to Maudie Kitcat and Betty Bemrose, the servants tripping over themselves to reach the front door first, it is the sound of glamour and escape, of day trips and freedom, of London and Brighton, of Swanage and Weymouth. It is the sound of the future. It is Willoughby Seagrave.

Betty and Maudie are both ardent fans of Willoughby. Between them, they make sure they receive the letters he sends to Cristabel, the wartime niece he has never seen due to his military service in Egypt. Betty was taught to read by her father, who runs the pub in the village, so she is able to read Willoughby's letters out loud to Maudie and Cristabel, and what letters they are, full of deadly scorpions, desert moons and nomadic tribes. All recounted in Willoughby's looping handwriting with its upward-rising dashes and lavish capitalization; his voice both confiding and dramatic (*Mark my words, little Cristabel – this was an Adventure of the Highest sort!*).

His letters always begin *My dearest youngest Lady*, then launch headlong into a continuation of an escapade from a previous letter, so his correspondence becomes a never-ending tale of derring-do (*You will no doubt remember I had leapt from the bad-tempered Dromedary, lest Muhammad think me a fearful wobbler, and together we were pursuing the Senussi on foot through the Dunes – my men following, fatigued but resolute!*). At the end of every letter, Cristabel commands, 'Again. Again.' And so they must.

Why Willoughby is still galloping about the desert while everyone else has come home from the war is not entirely clear to them, but they have seen a photograph of him in his cream uniform that Jasper has put in a drawer, and he is just as dashing as the film stars in Rosalind's magazines. Twenty-three-year-old Betty enjoys Willoughby's adventures in the same way she enjoys a gossipy newspaper story about the Bright Young Things and their London parties. But for fourteen-year-old Maudie, Willoughby is overwhelming. When Betty reads out his letters, a violent flush creeps over Maudie's face, colonizing her features.

Maudie, the youngest kitchen maid and Cristabel's companion in the attic, is an orphan with a tendency towards intensity. She once locked a delivery boy in the laundry after he teased her about her wayward hair. There are rumours her family were smugglers. There are rumours the delivery boy found a headless rat in his bicycle basket. Maudie has grabbed Betty's hand and is now scrambling with her towards the front door as the vehicle containing Willoughby and a pile of battered luggage roars up the drive. They cannot miss his opening scene. For this is the promise of Willoughby: he is a performance.

The noise is such that Jasper, breakfasting in the dining room, pauses mid-kipper, and asks, 'Are we being invaded?'

Rosalind, at the far end of the dining table, sets down her teacup and holds a hand to her throat. From outside comes the bang of someone slamming a car door, followed by the cacophony of all the rooks that nest in the surrounding trees taking to the sky at once.

Blythe the butler performs a neat half-bow and is about to seek out the noise-maker, but the noise-maker is already with them, striding into the room, his face sooty with dirt, and a pair of driving goggles pushed on top of his wavy copper-coloured hair. Somehow, the space is jammed with people who weren't there a moment ago, a mass of them pressing in behind Willoughby, a crowd that includes Betty and Maudie, Mrs Hardcastle the housekeeper, the new French governess, and Cristabel, carrying a stick.

'Well,' says Willoughby, his voice warm and reassuring, with a slight laugh to it. 'Hello, everyone.'

His audience giggles and gabbles their replies, talking over the top of one another; nervous participants.

Cristabel pushes through the onlookers and solemnly raises her stick. Willoughby bows deeply as a pantomime prince, saying, 'You must be Cristabel. I can see your mother in you. What an honour to finally make your acquaintance.' Then he addresses Jasper and Rosalind, still seated at the table, 'Although, I heard a rumour in London that my brother is keen to extend his family – and why wouldn't he be?'

Rosalind blushes. Jasper opens his mouth but misses his cue, as Willoughby turns back to his audience.

'Betty Bemrose, I have missed you. How I longed for your capable hands in the desert. Nobody in Egypt darns a sock like you. I was threadbare and bereft.'

'Mr Willoughby,' replies Betty, bobbing up and down, both mortified and delighted.

Willoughby's tone moves so smoothly between registers, it is hard to determine whether he is starring in a romantic film, a Shakespearian comedy or a West End farce, and therefore difficult to know whether to be offended by him. Most give him the benefit of the doubt, as there is a line that curves upwards around one corner of his mouth that speaks of his pleasure in ambiguity and his enjoyment of all the benefits of all the doubts that have already been given to him – and his generous willingness to accept more.

Jasper sniffs. 'I presume from that terrible racket you've bought some ludicrous vehicle.'

'Wonderful to see you too, brother,' says Willoughby. 'I do have a ludicrous vehicle. Perhaps I could take you for a drive?'

'Might have told us what time you were arriving. Given us time to kill the fatted calf,' says Jasper, pulling his napkin from his collar.

'Spoil this lovely surprise? Heavens, no,' says Willoughby, although he is now smiling at the French governess. 'I rather fancy this young lady would enjoy a ludicrous vehicle.'

'Monsieur Willoughby –'

'I can see you as a racing driver, mademoiselle. Leather gloves on. Ripping along at thirty.' He pulls the goggles from his head and tosses them towards her. 'Give those a try.'

'Mr Willoughby, you'll be wanting a bath no doubt,' says Mrs Hardcastle, but Willoughby has taken the governess by the arm and is leading her back through the Oak Hall, saying, 'A quick spin. Just to get a feel for it.' Maudie's face, as she watches them pass, is as agape as a desert moon.

When Rosalind makes her way to the dining room window, she sees, in the pale light of a February morning: Willoughby, a French governess in driving goggles, an unsmiling housekeeper, and a child wielding a stick, all seated in an enormous open-top car that is chugging slowly along the drive, occasionally veering on to the edge of the lawn. This unusual activity is overlooked by Jasper, who is not quite smiling but not quite not, along with Betty, Maudie and a cluster of servants. Rosalind watches as the car accelerates, kicking up gravel, its French passenger screaming, and Willoughby shouting over his shoulder, 'We'll be back for lunch.'

Rosalind hears Jasper come in and retreat to his study at the back of the house. She wanders to the drawing room but cannot settle. She is disturbed by the servants, who are fluttering from room to room, window to window, like a flock of birds trapped in the house. In the end, she simply folds her hands, closes her eyes and waits. She is getting better at waiting.

The driving party returns to Chilcombe three hours later, dust-covered and bearing streaks of what looks like strawberry jam. Cristabel is fast asleep, still clutching her stick, and being carried by Mrs Hardcastle. Rosalind is in the Oak Hall to meet them.

'Goodness,' she says, 'somebody take that child upstairs and give her a good wash. I can hardly bear to look at her.'

She hears her mother in her voice and finds it reassuring. The disruption of Willoughby's arrival has allowed her to step into a role that has thus far eluded her: the lady of the house. She straightens her back as the windswept motorists troop past. The French governess has a pink carnation tucked behind one ear. At the rear of the party, Willoughby lingers in the doorway, holding his motoring cap in his hand, ruefully stroking his moustache.

'Why don't you come in?' Rosalind asks.

'I fear I've made a dreadful first impression.'

'It certainly isn't usual for guests to take half the household off on a jaunt.'

'No. It isn't on,' he says.

'Whatever must the villagers think. Seeing you careering about like that.'

'Do you care what they think?'

Rosalind frowns. 'Of course.'

He shrugs. 'I believe they rather enjoyed it. We stopped at the pub so they could have a good look at the motor.'

'You went to the pub in the village?'

'We did. Do you object?'

'No. Yes,' says Rosalind. 'I mean, I might not have objected. Had I been asked.'

'That's what I hoped. Can we start again? On a proper footing this time. After I've had a bath. I'll be so shinily clean and perfectly mannered you won't recognize me.' He smiles and it is the blinding burst of a photographer's flash powder.

'That sounds – acceptable,' says Rosalind.

'You are a good egg. I knew you would be.'

'Did you? Why did you think that?'

But he is already moving past her, pulling his shirt from his trousers and bounding up the stairs two at a time, calling, 'Is there hot water for me, Betty?'

Rosalind is left waiting by the door, holding her unanswered questions, her handful of lines.

Circling and Re-circling

March, 1920

Chilcombe is different with Willoughby in it. Even before Cristabel opens her eyes, she can sense a tingling shift in the air. She creeps out of bed at the same dark hour as Maudie, before anyone else is awake, and while Maudie heads to the scullery to begin her morning chores, Cristabel tiptoes down to the kitchen and heads outside to find Willoughby's motor car.

Maudie has told her the only good thing about getting up horribly early is that the last day has gone, but the new one not yet begun, and in that gap, the house belongs to Maudie. Cristabel feels the truth of this as she steps out under a deep blue-black sky, where the only sound is a blackbird's chirruping call, a run of silver stitches through the darkness. This breathless, shadowy world is full of possibility. Everything she touches now will be hers.

The motor car has been parked by the stables and covered with a tarpaulin, which is easy enough to climb under. Hoicking up her nightgown, Cristabel clambers into the driver's seat and examines the steering wheel, the polished wooden dashboard, and the glass-covered dials, very tappable. She moves the steering wheel from side to side. She says, 'Hold on to your hats, ladies.'

Sometimes, she looks at the back seat to see where she was when Uncle Willoughby gave her a jam tart, to be eaten with fingers, no plate or napkin, as he drove through puddles, making everyone shriek. 'Just for you,' he had said, 'no sharing allowed.'

'I don't share,' she replied, and he laughed so much she hadn't bothered to explain she wasn't given things, so she couldn't. She likes to hear him laugh. That irrepressible sound, bursting through the ordinary run of things like a cannonball. Cristabel kneels up on the leather seat and reaches for the rubber bulb of the brass car horn.

Rosalind wakes early, jolted from sleep by a loud noise from outside. Surely Willoughby isn't leaving already? Whenever he is with them, the house has a sense of exciting, preparatory activity – as if it were the start of a holiday – but there is always the accompanying fear he might suddenly depart.

She has Betty dress her quickly in order to be at the breakfast table as fast as she can, but she is the first to arrive. Willoughby and Jasper appear an hour later, demanding large quantities of food. Rosalind rarely manages to eat anything at breakfast, or even say anything beyond the usual pleasantries, but watches as the brothers bicker while devouring whatever is placed in front of them, overlooked by portraits of stern Seagrave ancestors.

Jasper's method of feeding is base and agricultural, the resolute troughing of a man who has long since eaten his way past culinary enjoyment, whereas Willoughby eats like a flamboyant painter – sweeping swathes of marmalade across crumbling toast, pouring milk into his teacup from a jug held so high the liquid becomes a single thin torrent, and licking butter from his fingers while waving down Blythe to request more bacon.

'Sister-in-law Rosalind, the current Mrs Seagrave,' says Willoughby, helping himself to the last of the eggs. 'What are your plans for the coming weeks?'

'Willoughby,' growls Jasper, from deep within his kedgeree-dotted beard.

'Well –' says Rosalind.

'Because I'm off to Brighton for a few days, so you won't have to feed me, and you'll save on candles. I'm staggered you're still holding out against electrical lights, Jasper. My bedroom is black as the very grave.'

'Oil lamps are perfectly adequate,' says Jasper. 'I will not have unsightly cables strung across my land.'

'What are you doing in Brighton, Willoughby?' asks Rosalind. 'I've been to Brighton.'

'I'm to meet a man about an aeronautical adventure.'

Jasper sighs. 'Do be sensible, Willoughby. Our family funds are not a bottomless pit. As I keep telling you, there are good positions in the colonies for ex-military men. Saw your friend Perry Drake at the club last month – he's off to Ceylon to keep the locals in line.'

'Perry will be a credit to the Empire, I'm sure. But I don't want to do that. Mother and Father left me money to do whatever I want.'

'You can't fritter away your allowance on foolishness,' says Jasper.

'Why not?' says Willoughby. 'Don't you read the papers? The great estates are all being sold off. Why not spend our pennies on something enjoyable before we lose the lot? When's the last time you bought anything other than a horse? Why this pettifogging insistence on things being done as they've always been done?'

'I bought a piano. For Rosalind. For my wife.'

'Does anyone ever play it?'

'One has responsibilities –'

'The future's coming for you, brother, whether you like it or not,' says Willoughby. 'Talking of Perry, you've reminded me he met a chap in the army who would make a decent land agent for Chilcombe. Fellow called Brewer. Practical sort with a keen eye for a balance sheet. You'll need one of those soon.'

But Jasper is continuing along the conversational path he started on before there was any mention of land agents. 'One has responsibilities. We have staff who rely on us.'

Willoughby turns to Rosalind. 'Let me tell you about my aeronautical adventures, Mrs Seagrave. A newspaper is offering an obscene amount of money for the first aviator to fly non-stop from New York to Paris.'

'Wouldn't that be dangerous?' asks Rosalind.

'One might lose one's hat. But it's exhilarating up there, gazing down on the clouds. A white feather bed stretching all the way to the horizon.'

'Fatuous nonsense,' says Jasper.

'I've never been in an aeroplane,' says his wife.

'I'll fly down here. Land on the lawn,' says Willoughby.

'You'll do no such bloody thing,' says Jasper.

'Cristabel would be delighted,' says Willoughby.

'You should not be encouraging a love of aviation in an impressionable young girl.'

'Might be a little late there, Jasper. I've ordered a toy aeroplane for her and, do you know, I found one of those wooden swords we had as boys hidden in the stables – I've cleaned that up for her too.'

'Heaven's sake, Willoughby, that was my sword,' says Jasper.

'You couldn't land an aeroplane on the lawn, could you?' says Rosalind.

Willoughby smiles. 'Is that a dare?'

'I will not allow you to flap around on my lawn like a pheasant,' says Jasper.

'Eagle, surely.'

'I will not be provoked at my own breakfast table, do you hear?' barks Jasper, yanking the napkin from his collar.

'Everybody can hear, brother.'

Jasper stamps from the room, slamming the door. The tableware rattles: a thin silvery peal of cutlery versus crockery. Willoughby leans across the table to pull his brother's breakfast plate towards him. They hear a shout from the hall – 'The child's left her bloody twigs everywhere!' – Cristabel's voice crying, 'Retreat to the barricades!' then the sound of small feet running up the stairs.

Rosalind waits for the table to compose itself. 'Willoughby, surely we won't have to sell off Chilcombe? Jasper says it's been in the Seagrave family for generations.'

'You're a Seagrave now. What do you think?'

'I'm never sure what I think.'

'You need to have a son, then you can start to sound more confident. Two sons, ideally. An heir and a spare. No need for blushing, dear sister.'

'Don't you care what happens?'

'Mrs Seagrave, I'm the spare. None of this is mine, as far as the eye can see.' Willoughby gestures widely, then returns to Jasper's leftovers.

Blythe the butler enters, adjusting his white gloves. 'Will you be requiring anything else, sir?'

'Nothing at all,' says Willoughby. 'Have someone bring my car round.'

'Off so soon?' says Rosalind, but Willoughby is already leaving, taking Jasper's toast with him.

Breakfast with both Seagrave brothers in attendance often ends in this way, with food thievery and napkins thrown to the ground and dramatic exits, and the current Mrs Seagrave left alone at the dining table, staring at the sugar bowl for want of anything else to do. Whenever Willoughby goes, she feels she has missed a chance. She is eager to show him that she too is familiar with the wider world, conversant with the latest society news. She wishes she knew how to capture his interest, how to slow his bright carousel long enough that she might join in.

The more she studies him, the more Rosalind notices that the rules of behaviour do not seem to apply to Willoughby. His attendance at meals is haphazard; his handkerchiefs are Egyptian silk and jewel-coloured. He never joins the household when they dutifully troop off to Chilcombe Mell church on Sunday mornings, but Rosalind has seen him chatting cheerfully to men from the village. Jasper chastised him about it once and Willoughby replied he'd fought alongside such men and wasn't about to start talking down to them now.

After her afternoon rests, Rosalind often opens her bedroom curtains to see Willoughby's tall figure disappearing into the trees at the edge of the lawn, with Cristabel trotting at his side clutching a wooden sword. Betty tells her that they go down to the beach, that Willoughby is teaching his niece to catch crabs. She wonders who has allowed this. She wonders what the French governess she has employed is doing.

She has the sense there are no boundaries in Willoughby's life. It is so enviably free in contrast to her own, so adroitly nonchalant. Rosalind's life, first with her widowed mother and now with Jasper, seems an endless succession of Sundays: clock-marked, rule-bound days of manners and luncheons. How thrilling to discover that the rigid particularity of things – fish knives, tablecloths, topics of conversation – is as arbitrary as deciding that one day should be called Sunday and treated differently to all the rest. If Sunday is only Sunday because we call it Sunday, then why not call it Friday instead?

One morning, she meets Willoughby in the Oak Hall. He is on his way out; she is having a little wander. He nods towards the list she holds in her hand.

'Anything of importance, Mrs Seagrave?'

Rosalind looks down at the list. 'Oh. It's nothing.'

Willoughby frowns. 'Is it a shopping list? I'm off to London today.'

'No, this is my list of the shops I want to visit. When I go to London.'

He takes the list from her hand. 'Do you need anything from these shops?'

'I won't know until I visit them. I don't know what's in them as I've only read about them. In magazines. They are new shops and I want to see everything they have. Then I'll choose. A hat perhaps. Or a bracelet. Something unique. I have very particular tastes.' These nine sentences are the most she has ever said to him.

'Right you are.' He glances at the list, hands it back to her, then leaves the house with a wave.

Two days later, Betty brings a parcel to Rosalind. 'Came in the second post for you, ma'am.'

Inside, Rosalind finds a beribboned gift box from the hat shop that was at the top of her list. It contains an illustrated colour catalogue describing every style of hat they sell, along with a note in looping handwriting that reads: *For Mrs Seagrave & her Very Particular Tastes. W.* It hums in her hands.

Rosalind wanders the gallery landing, absent-mindedly touching her throat, watching dusty columns of light fall through high windows into the hall, where the grandfather clock ticks and tocks. In her boudoir, she cuts pictures from her magazines, lets them float to the floor. She goes through her catalogue, circling and re-circling.

The catalogue. The note. The catalogue. The note. Her turn coming round.

It becomes a habit then. Whenever Willoughby leaves for London, he visits Rosalind beforehand to enquire whether he should pay a visit to one of her shops.

Willoughby is practised in the art of being attentive to women, but he enjoys this diversion, primarily because of the specificity of Rosalind's requests – 'A soliflore scent from an established French house, but not eau de toilette, it should be eau de parfum or nothing at all' – so unexpected, coming from his brother's demure young wife.

He enjoys too the ceremonial return to Chilcombe: carrying in a pile of boxes and watching as Rosalind examines their contents, intent and focused as a jeweller, her acceptance or rejection of items entire and irreversible. It is the only time he sees her make decisions without deferring to Jasper, and he finds it captivating.

Sometimes, he will pick out an item himself, testing his eye against her own. He will tell her the shop manager suggested it, and wait for her reaction. It amuses him that his choices are consistently rejected; he feels sure if he offered them as gifts, she would claim to adore them.

Only one of his secret purchases – the new Guerlain women's scent Mitsouko – passes her test. She tips a drop on to her wrist, sniffs it, then screws up her nose. 'Awfully heavy.' But as he is about to re-seal the elegant square bottle, which has as its stopper a glass heart, she takes it back from him. 'No, I'll keep it. It's not altogether vulgar.' When he leaves, her face is at her wrist, breathing it in, with an absorbed expression.

These moments come back to him at odd times. Her delight at the arrival of the items, her glee in the unwrapping. The lilac veins in her wrists. The shadows beneath her eyes. How she stared. She seemed to be looking at more than a few items in gift boxes: it was as if she saw the whole world in miniature; the eye of the botanist trained on the microscope.

★

29

One afternoon, Willoughby passes Cristabel on the gallery as he is carrying a stack of parcels to her stepmother.

Cristabel brandishes her wooden sword and says, 'Halt, stranger. I'm waiting for a brother. Is he in there?'

'Afraid not,' Willoughby replies. 'Both hands used on a broadsword, by the way.'

'He will be here soon. Maudie told me what wives do.'

'Darling girl, don't listen to the maids' silly chatter.'

'Maudie isn't silly. Why don't you have a wife?'

'I haven't found one that wasn't already taken. Besides, they seem like hard work. Expensive too. I prefer to spend my money on motors.'

'When will I have a motor?'

'When you stop frowning at your favourite uncle. We'll go for a spin tomorrow, shall we? You can bring that French governess of yours. I do enjoy her company.'

'I can't bring her.'

'Why ever not?'

'New mother has sacked the governess.'

'*Quel dommage.*'

'Maudie says new mother doesn't like anyone prettier than she is.'

'Maudie isn't silly at all, is she? What is this ferocious scowl for now?'

'I'm not pretty. But new mother still doesn't like me. But I don't care about that.'

'You shouldn't. Pretty girls can be terrifically dull. Remember, two hands on the hilt. Weight on the back foot. Better.'

Entreaties

March, 1920

Weymouth is full of sand. A chilly easterly wind is blowing across the wide expanse of the bay, skittering over the white tops of waves and whisking fine sand from the beach, so it gusts in stinging flurries towards the seafront hotels, neglected after years of diminished wartime trade. A line of vacant faces squinting out at a battleship-grey sea. To Jasper, the seaside town feels deserted, a final outpost.

He walks the length of the Esplanade, a broad walkway curving along the beach. In the previous century, it was promenaded upon by royalty, but now there are only wounded Anzacs – soldiers from Australia and New Zealand stationed in the Dorset town to recuperate, pushed along in blanketed wheelchairs, with empty sleeves or trouser legs tucked up and neatly pinned. Jasper considers it a cruel twist of fate that brave men used to the Southern Ocean's azure seas should wind up on England's insipid South Coast, the ocean's limpest handshake.

Scattered among the leftover Anzacs are a few early season visitors, gripping their hats on this blowy day, and down on the beach a handful of children are paddling, skinny limbs pinking with the cold. A pair of old-fashioned bathing machines stand empty at the water's edge. A sign saying 'Back Soon' is propped against the striped tent housing the Punch and Judy puppet show.

At the far end of the Esplanade, there is a red-brick terrace of guest houses, backing on to the town's harbour. Ships' masts are visible above the rooftops, like a series of crucifixes. The penultimate building has a wooden billboard propped by its front door, which proclaims it to be the residence of MADAME CAMILLE, MYSTICAL PSYCHIC adviser to KINGS AND QUEENS, TELLER OF

FORTUNES – SHE SEES ALL! SHE KNOWS ALL! This is followed by a chalk illustration of a single eye.

Brushing sand from his beard, Jasper knocks on the door. A young boy lets him in and points up a dark staircase. Madame Camille has a narrow room on the first floor. Something red and gauzy has been draped over a standard lamp, giving the space a rouged, infernal glow. Madame Camille herself is seated at a baize card table by a window overlooking the harbour, her hands resting on a glass ball. Jasper presumes it is meant to be a crystal ball, although it could be a ship's buoy scooped from the harbour for all he knows.

He sits down opposite her and places three coins on the table. Madame Camille's eyes flicker over them, quick as a lizard's tongue. She is thin-faced, with a fringed scarf draped over scraggly hair.

'You've come for someone you've lost,' she says, her accent unfamiliar. Irish perhaps. Or pretending to be.

Jasper is startled by the informality of her address. 'I have. My wife. My first wife, Annabel. I overheard a servant of mine saying you contacted her late husband, and I –'

'Annabel. A strong woman. They don't always want to be contacted, the strong ones. Reluctant to accept it themselves, you see.' Madame Camille rubs the glass ball.

'I see.' He isn't sure he does.

'Do you have an item of hers that still remembers her touch? Something she always kept with her?'

Me, he thinks. I still remember her touch. He frowns, then reaches into his pocket to find Annabel's accounting notebook, each page filled with the miniature Sanskrit of her pencilled numbers. Madame Camille takes the notebook, closes her eyes, breathes loudly through her nose. Outside, a paddle steamer lets go a brassy hoot from its funnel as it makes its way out to sea.

'I hear voices,' says Madame Camille.

Jasper whispers, 'Is she there? May I speak to her? I wanted to explain about Rosalind. A sense of duty compelled –'

'A spirited lady.'

'Is she cross with me?'

Madame Camille frowns. 'She's distracted. Keeps searching about. Did she lose something dear to her? Jewellery? A set of keys?'

'Nothing springs to mind.'

'It can be the most unlikely item – a window left open – it bothers them awfully.'

'I keep the windows closed as a rule. May I speak to her now?'

'She's calling out, bless her heart.'

'For heaven's sake, why can't you tell her I'm here? Or at least give me some proof that this woman is truly my Annabel.'

Madame Camille half opens her eyes. 'Not in the business of proof, mister. I gives you what they gives me.'

'Ridiculous!' Jasper exhales, spittle ricocheting through his whiskers.

Her eyes are fully on him now, undiluted, sharp as a fox. 'Perhaps that's all then.'

'This is what I get for my money?' says Jasper, noticing at that moment the money he placed on the table is no longer on the table.

'It comes as it will,' she says, infuriatingly unconcerned.

From the corridor comes a deep masculine cough.

Jasper stands up and barrels furiously from the room, past the young boy who let him in, now accompanied by a large man in vest and braces with great hams for arms, and rushes back down the stairs, into the daylight, and the sudden shock of garish seaside life is nauseating: the limbless Australians, the discordant jangle of a pipe-organ in the pleasure gardens, and the nasal cries of Mr Punch grappling with his wife. *Thwack, thwack, thwack. That's the way to do it.*

Jasper hurries along the Esplanade, his face repeatedly crumpling in a kind of agony. How stupid to think he could talk to Annabel. Utterly idiotic to go to that fraudulent gypsy. He finds a handkerchief. Blows his nose loudly. Plonks himself down on a wooden bench. Looks out along the shore.

He is heartily sick of Dorset. Every morning, reading the newspaper, he will seek out advertisements describing land for sale in Cumberland, in the north of England, where he and Annabel had spent their honeymoon. Hadn't honeymooned with Rosalind. Hadn't seen the point.

In Cumberland, everywhere you looked, you faced the kind of epic landscape that could make a man take up religion or watercolour painting. But Jasper is trapped on the crumbling bottom edge of England, constantly badgered by disgruntled tenants and staff, all wanting more from him when he has increasingly little to give. He thinks of the accounting notebook in his pocket, how it changes from Annabel's neat numbers to his own chaotic scribble, dotted with question marks.

Rising taxes have forced him to sell off two tenant farms and he is only clinging on to the last having agreed to fix the rent at pre-war rates. His own family are more of a hindrance than a help. Rosalind has eye-wateringly expensive tastes, and although she is due to inherit a hefty amount when her mother dies, said mother refuses to shuffle off. Meanwhile, Willoughby is burning through his allowance at a flagrant rate. Whenever Mr Bill Brewer, his new land agent, shows him the household ledger, Jasper can see – for the first time in his life – gaps, debts, vacancies. Just last week, his one remaining gardener had gone off to work in a Torquay hotel.

There are only a few of Jasper's original staff left. Barely a handful had returned from the war, and most had left something of themselves behind on the battlefield, if not a foot or an arm, then whatever it was that controlled their emotions. Jasper recognized the flighty look in their eyes as that of a horse after a thunderstorm: there could be no talking reason to them. They would have to come round in their own time, if they ever did.

In an attempt to balance the books, he had sold a few family portraits. He felt a twinge of sadness as Great-Aunt Sylvia was carried away, but then a diminuendo of that feeling, as if her solemn face were watching him from a train moving into the distance. When housed in Chilcombe, the portraits had been part of a reassuring continuum, but once given a price, something of them vanished. The train containing Great-Aunt Sylvia rounded a bend; the smoke from its chimney rose up and merged with the clouds.

Jasper blows his nose again, a mournful bugle call. The sea is still grey, the wind still cold. Somewhere along the diminishing coastline lies his home. His ancient home containing a wife he doesn't love and a child he doesn't know how to love and an empty space where his love used to be.

Sometimes, when Cristabel wakes in the night, she cries, 'I'm up here!' as if answering a question about her whereabouts, but nobody in the house has asked the question, nobody in the house has called for her. From her tiny bedroom on the other side of the roof space, Maudie hears Cristabel shout out once, twice, then a mumbled version and then nothing, just the silence of children, held high in the pitch-black attic, listening, waiting.

Every morning, after breakfast, Rosalind will go to her writing desk to compose charming letters of invitation, hoping to begin the life she imagined when she said her wedding vows. Each missive she sends out she imagines as a plucky messenger pigeon flying over the great wall of the Ridgeway. Every letter includes an enticing mention of *Jasper's brother Willoughby – a war hero!* – and folding him into an envelope gives her a strange pleasure, as if she were sealing Willoughby inside her future plans. *Do come!* she writes. *Do!*

But replies to her entreaties are few.

One evening at dinner, she says, 'Jasper, perhaps we could consider taking a house in London for the season?'

'I stay at the club if I need a bed,' he replies.

'What about when your daughter comes out? It would be useful then.'

Jasper coughs. 'Long way off.' He pushes back his chair and leaves the room.

Left alone at the long table, Rosalind senses the scuttling approach of servants and lifts her smile in readiness.

'Everything satisfactory, ma'am?'

'Perfect. Thank you.'

Later, lying in her newly installed bathtub, Rosalind calls to Betty, 'The child, Jasper's child, how old is she?'

Betty's freckled face appears in the doorway. 'Just turned four, ma'am. Had her birthday last week, in fact.'

'Is she coming on all right, do you know?'

'I believe so, ma'am. They say she is a bright girl. Already learnt her letters. She's a funny one, Cristabel. The other day –'

'Could you fetch a towel, Betty?'

'Right away, ma'am.'

Rosalind swooshes gently to and fro, luxuriating in her new tub, until Betty arrives with the towel, then she heaves herself from the suction of water, rejoining gravity.

At her dressing table, she idly plays with the contents of her jewellery box while Betty brushes her hair. 'Betty, does the girl Cristabel resemble her mother? I've never seen a photograph.'

Betty pulls a face. 'Hard to tell, ma'am. Mrs Annabel, God rest her soul, had what you might call strong features.'

'Ah,' says Rosalind, meeting her own gaze in the mirror. The reassurance of her face. Its fine planes. Its surety.

Betty says, 'I've let out your red gown as you asked, ma'am. It was tight at the waist, wasn't it? Good to see you've got your appetite back.'

So First, the Primroses

April, 1920

Betty was the one to tell Rosalind. Pragmatic Betty with her numerous sisters and accumulated knowledge of what goes on within the mysterious, treacherous innards of women.

Rosalind was in her rose-scented bath, casting an assessing eye over her floating Ophelia body. 'I must stop eating rich desserts, Betty. I'm developing a paunch.'

Betty paused in her folding of towels. 'Well, ma'am. I was meaning to say. My eldest sister gets a bump there when she's expecting.'

'Expecting what?'

'Expecting a baby, ma'am. When she's in the family way.' Betty kept her attention on the towel in her hands. 'Forgive my impertinence, ma'am, but do you – have you noticed any change to – has your monthly visitor arrived of late?'

Rosalind said nothing. There had been the word 'baby' and then her ears had tucked themselves shut, neat as an otter's, so Betty's voice had become an unintelligible *wurble, wurble, wurble*. She held herself very still. There was something in her. They had put something in her. How dare they intrude upon her like that.

Betty looked at her. 'Ma'am?'

'I won't be joining my husband for dinner tonight,' Rosalind heard herself say, and was surprised at the civility of her voice. 'Would you be so kind as to let Mrs Hardcastle know? That will be all.'

Rosalind stayed in the claw-footed bathtub until the water went cold, only her face, knees and breasts poking above the surface: a pale archipelago. Floating in the filmy water, held up by it, she hung suspended above the rest of the house. She listened to the continuation of evening activity: the patter of servants on staircases; the chiming of the grandfather clock; a rook cawing outside, jawing companionably on like an after-dinner speaker. Everything was as it should be, as it always would be.

When she sank a little, so her ears were submerged, she heard her own heartbeat very close by. Lying there, goosebumped and shivering, Rosalind wished, for the first time in her adult life, that she could see her mother, but then she remembered how her mother was, and wished instead she had been given a different mother. One like Betty's, perhaps, who ran the pub with her husband and was prone to being overly generous with the gin but was someone you could tell your troubles to. But how foolish to think in such a way. Your mother was your mother, whether you liked it or not. You had no choice in the matter. If she had a gin-swilling mother who worked in a village pub, where on earth would she be now? Certainly not in a claw-footed bathtub. Certainly not in possession of pure rose bath oil. And Rosalind watched the light on the bathroom wall shift in slow degrees from gold to peach to grey.

The following morning, a doctor came into her bedroom.

Rosalind presumed Betty had told Mrs Hardcastle about her body's new bulge, and this information had been passed on to both a doctor and to Jasper, as there was a posy of primroses on her breakfast tray. She was relieved by this, as she could not think how to tell Jasper herself. So first, the primroses, and then the doctor, all before she was out of bed. Now she was the carrier of a possible Seagrave son and heir, her husband would give her flowers and allow strange men into her room to examine her.

Dr Harold Rutledge was his name. A friend of Jasper's. Stout and ruddy as a toby jug. Rosalind kept her eyes on the canopy above the bed as he ran his hands over her abdomen, leaning close enough that she could smell last night's brandy on his breath.

'All seems tip-top. Plenty of rest, no horse-riding, but normal marital relations can continue,' Dr Rutledge said, then laughed, an oddly triumphant noise. 'Good old Jasper,' he added, pulling aside the top of her nightgown to press a cold stethoscope to her breast.

Rosalind wondered what he could hear through his metal instrument. She imagined a hollow hissing of reeds. She was aware of a crowded, desperate feeling in her mind that only abated when she concentrated on a far corner of the canopy.

The doctor removed the stethoscope and closed her nightgown as casually as a man turning the page of a newspaper. 'Excellent, excellent,' he said.

Everybody seemed very pleased, and, despite the fact Rosalind didn't tell a single soul, everybody seemed to know, almost immediately. Village children appeared with bouquets. The butcher's boy arrived with a parcel of meat. Even the vicar in Chilcombe Mell church beamed benevolently at her from the pulpit while speaking of fruitfulness. It was as if they had been waiting for this all along.

She remembered how welcoming they had been when she arrived. Their eager hands opening doors, carrying bags, offering tea. They had pressed her clothes, poured her wine, and she had felt rather royal, as if she were someone of importance. But they hadn't wanted her at all, had they? They had wanted it.

Rosalind retired to her bedroom, pleading nervous strain, admitting only visits from Betty or Mrs Hardcastle or Willoughby, if he came with things from London. Jasper, surprisingly acquiescent, retreated, muttering, 'Whatever you wish.'

Dr Rutledge called occasionally to examine her expanding stomach. He advised she take up cigarettes, saying women were prone to hysteria when with child. 'Brain's starved of nutrients. Try a few every day after meals and you'll be right as rain.'

The cigarettes (provided by Jasper) (in a silver case engraved with her initials provided by Willoughby) were vile, but she persevered. There was something about the way they set her head spinning she almost enjoyed. She imagined herself with a stylish cigarette holder, at a party in Belgravia. She didn't like to look down at her body any more. She preferred the version of herself she was ordering clothes for: the society hostess with the twenty-one-inch waist.

Deep in her belly, the implanted creature grew. She did her best to ignore it, but she was hot and tired, a bloated vessel. At night, even with the windows wide open, she tossed and turned in her own sweat, her body generating heat like a smelting furnace. Every morning she woke exhausted, with a sour metallic taste in her mouth, as if she had spent the night sucking coins.

Of course, they had not thought to tell Cristabel. The thought did not enter their minds. It remained outside their minds, along with most matters pertaining to Cristabel. Such thoughts were items left uncollected, of little value. And, as often happens, these forgotten items were picked up by servants.

Maudie Kitcat peered into Cristabel's attic bedroom one evening and said, 'You're to have a brother or sister, have they told you?'

Cristabel looked up from her bed where her collection of stones with faces were building themselves a home under her pillow to protect themselves against the ravaging attacks of the postcard of a dog called Dog. 'The brother?'

'Could be.'

The stones with faces came rushing out of their pillow shelter, their expressions twisted cries of joy and relief, and the postcard of a dog called Dog was tipped over, like a great wall.

Maudie watched, with her curiously fixed stare, and continued, 'Betty says if they don't have a boy, they'll keep going till they do.'

'Where is the brother living now?' asked Cristabel.

'In Mrs Seagrave's belly. That's why she's gone fat.'

Cristabel reached under her bed to grab a few sticks from her stick pile to build a little bonfire. She carefully leant the sticks against each other, then said, 'I didn't live in her belly.'

'You didn't.'

'I lived here. In this place. This is my place.'

'That's right.'

'The brother will live here too. With me. I will look after him.' She looked at Maudie who nodded, then walked away down the attic corridor.

Cristabel placed the postcard called Dog on the bonfire and put the stones with faces in a circle around it. There would be a great feast tonight. A postcard of a dog called Dog would be roasted with a red apple in its mouth. There would be fresh snow. And jam tarts. And everyone would have seconds. And no one would go to bed.

Under Beds

Under Cristabel's Bed

Feathers, sticks, sheep's wool, a seagull skull, a dried ball of glue, one large lobster claw.

Three snails in a jar.

A trench lighter.

A wooden sword.

A toy aeroplane.

Drawings of soldiers, sometimes accompanied by dogs, camels or bears, captioned: HOLD FAST FOR ENGLAND and BROTHERS UNITE and LOYAL PALS and SHE-BEAR SUCKLED THEM.

Lists of names, some crossed out.

One toffee, half eaten, rewrapped.

Under Maudie's Bed

Four of Willoughby's letters to Cristabel.

An old piece of soap found in a guest bedroom.

A book about hunting African wild beasts taken from the study.

A pocketknife.

Lumps of chalk found on the Ridgeway.

A slate on which the letters of the alphabet are practised.

A diary.

A pencil.

Shoe boxes containing the following:

Invitations and dance cards for events held during June and July 1914.

A napkin taken from the Café Royal, London, during the early hours of 17th July, 1914.

Six theatre tickets.

Two cinema tickets.

A daisy chain, pressed and dried.

Thirty-seven illustrations of bridal wear cut from magazines between 1913 and 1918.

One hundred and fifty-two magazine clippings depicting items including: Victrola gramophones, anti-wrinkle turtle oil creams, illustrations of correct dining etiquette, Sioux Indian ornaments, electrical reading lamps, croquet mallets, Turkish cigarettes, camphorated reducing creams, luxury hosiery, Royal Worcester teacups, and revitalizing health tonics to restore natural vigour to body and mind after times of great strain.

An article entitled 'Which Kind of Marriage Turns Out Best?' cut from *Woman's Weekly*, February 1919, following sections underlined:

> *He has a horror of the lip-salving, opinionated girl of today. He*
>   *just wants a wife with one or two ideas in her head and a home*
> *A woman who is loved has no need of ambition*
> *A man may run straight – but a woman must!*
> *Without passionate love*
> *Magnetic spark*

Photographs cut from various women's magazines captioned:

> *The tide of progress that leaves a woman with the vote in her hand*
>   *but scarcely any clothes on her back must now ebb and return her*
>   *to her femininity.*

A free art plate of Florence La Badie, effervescent star of
    Thanhouser Film Corporation.
Off to the Paris fashion parades in a giant aeroplane from Croydon!

Articles entitled:

'The Latest Ways of Warming Homes'
'A Loving Wife's Burden'
'Life Stories: At the Crossroads!'

An advertisement: *Maternity Corset: in all the latest designs, giving a*
Quite Ordinary Appearance *to the wearer – a physical as well as a mental*
comfort. Spotted broche, ribbon trim, side lacing allows for adjustment.

A Sleeping Woman

August, 1920

One summer afternoon, Willoughby says, 'This used to be my mother's bedroom. It was very different then.'

'How so?' Rosalind looks up from leafing through fabric samples. Now seven months pregnant, she is propped up in bed wearing a floral nightgown and matching bed jacket.

Willoughby has draped his long frame across the delicate chair that sits beside her dressing table. Betty is in the adjoining bathroom, cleaning the new sink. A gift box lies on the floor, its lid half off, something chartreuse and silky spilling out of one corner like liquid.

He says, 'Mama favoured a funereal style of decor. Windows closed against contagions. Curtains drawn to protect the furniture. I had to sit by her bed in the gloaming while she read the Bible.'

'The only books my mother considers acceptable are the Bible and Debrett's,' replies Rosalind. 'She thinks reading unbecoming in a woman. Told me I should never develop a taste for fiction.'

'You're fond of magazines,' says Willoughby, smoothing his moustache.

'I prefer the pictures to the stories.'

'So do I.'

'I'm grateful to my mother, of course,' says Rosalind, after a pause.

'I'm not. I couldn't breathe around her. I'm talking of my mother, you understand.' Willoughby ruffles his hair, looks about the room. 'I much prefer it now. Even with this flowery wallpaper.'

Rosalind blinks. 'Rose damask. From Haynes of Paddington. I'm glad you approve. Do you approve?'

Willoughby laughs, a rich, dark sound. 'I do. The room's inhabit-ant is also much improved. Although I rarely see her outside of this room.'

'I hope to be up on my feet soon, but Dr Rutledge tells me I should rest,' says Rosalind. 'It's not unpleasant though. Quite sopor-ific. I lie here and I imagine the parties I will have, in the autumn, and at Christmas. I lie here and picture the parties and what I will wear and absolutely everything to do with them. After that, I close my eyes and think of nothing. I simply stop for a while, and every-thing continues about me, almost as if I weren't here at all. Isn't that strange.' During the course of this speech, her hands become rest-less, her fingers twisting into her hair.

Willoughby shifts in his seat. 'I look forward to these imaginary parties.'

In the bathroom, Betty turns on the taps in the new sink. The pipes give a great clanking boom.

Willoughby smiles a little downward smile as he stands up. 'I should let you rest.'

Rosalind watches him leave.

During the last weeks of her pregnancy, Willoughby continues to visit Rosalind, bringing requested items from Mayfair boutiques. After examining the purchases, Rosalind often falls asleep. It occurs to Willoughby that he has never seen a woman sleep in this way before. When next to a sleeping woman, he is usually asleep him-self. Or picking up his clothes on the way to the door. He remains in the chair by the dressing table, murmuring to Betty, 'I'll sit here a while, see if she comes to. Perhaps you could fix her some fresh flowers.'

He likes to observe Rosalind's face, which is like a child's as she sleeps, both innocent and furious. Sometimes she frowns, as if con-centrating; sometimes a smile repeatedly twitches the corners of her mouth, as if she were greeting a line of people. Sometimes, most peculiarly of all, he can see the movement of the baby in her belly, her nightgown briefly distended by a miniature foot or fist pushing outwards.

Mrs Hardcastle had given him a hard stare when she met him emerging from Rosalind's room one afternoon, carefully closing the door behind him. 'Mrs Seagrave needs her sleep, Mr Willoughby.'

'That's precisely what she's getting,' he replied, hands held up in innocence.

He isn't unaware, of course, of the body beneath the nightgown, still slender despite its protruding stomach. A sleeping woman is not conscious of the ways her buttons can gape, or how her bed sheets can wind about her legs.

But there is something else too: he is enjoying this time because it is unlike any other time he has spent with a woman. He is a man for whom doors and nightgowns have opened easily. The world, for Willoughby, is entirely accessible; it lies about like the spoils of war, waiting for him to take it. But his exchanges with Rosalind are bound about with restrictions and propriety. They feel decorous, courtly, soothing. The presentation of gifts in a quiet room. The pulling of a ribbon on a parcel. Nothing more.

Behind the veil of her eyelids, Rosalind roams the darkness. She has noticed a peculiar thing. She feels the presence of Willoughby most intensely if she closes her eyes. She feels he is somewhere in the darkness with her, and they are drifting around each other like balloons. There is a sense that if she presses forward, pushes through the darkness, she will come upon him, sprawled in an armchair by a dressing table, swinging one leg to and fro like a pendulum, waiting in a room much like the one she is in now.

Increasingly, she cannot sleep when he is in the room with her, although she dutifully tries to. She focuses on the black behind her eyes and wills it to let her through, concentrating on limiting her movements, controlling her breathing. Sometimes she drifts into a doze and then returns, drifts then returns, like a tethered boat on a moving tide.

Outside, the summer burns on. The sunlight through the floral curtains tinges the room warm pink like the inside of a conch shell

46

or the fleshy glow of the world as seen by a child with its fingers pressed over its eyes.

One day in the last week of August, Rosalind is lying on her high bed, elegantly draped in a masquerade of sleep. Betty has gone to the kitchen, dispatched by Willoughby to fetch a jug of water. Suddenly, Rosalind hears his chair creak. He is moving. And she knows, with a tightening of breath in her throat, that he knows she is not asleep. His voice, when it comes, is close to her ear, soft. 'Stay just as you are.'

She hears the sound of a chair being pulled across the wooden floor, then the sound of him sitting down near her. She remains perfectly still, unable to admit to her charade, even though he has spoken to her. The darkness behind her eyes has shrunk to nothing. She exists only in her throat, the tips of her nostrils. She could exist in this single moment for ever – then the chair scrapes back and she hears him leave the room.

He comes again the next day. Betty is dispatched. The chair next to the bed.

He comes again a few days later. Betty leaves. The chair pulled closer.

He comes again and it is the first day of September and he places his hand on her torso at the place where her stomach begins to swell. He leaves it there for a moment, as if monitoring something, then briefly stretches out his fingers like a pianist reaching for an octave so that his thumb touches the underside of her breast. They remain like this for a while, neither of them moving, before he takes his hand away. But a moment later, it returns, landing on her side, then moving to her wrist, her waist, her throat.

Rosalind, lying back under the weight of her belly with her eyes closed, is unaware of his movements until they arrive fleetingly on her body. It is as if she were a great mountain range and his hands the tiny, feathery touches of explorers with their charts and compasses, slowly making their way across the slumbering earth, casting their ropes about her.

(But where is
Jasper? He is
at the stables,
the races, the
auction, the
church, the one
decent restaurant
in Sherborne, the
gentlemen's club
in Marylebone:
he is anywhere
at all that is
nowhere near
a wife within
weeks of
childbirth. He
exists in a thin
seam of usual
haunts that allow
him the luxury of
looking neither
up nor down nor
side to side but
simply straight
ahead, most
often through
the bottom of
a brandy glass,
because he
cannot look
anywhere else.)

And when her waters break, when Willoughby is above her in her
airless bedroom on a warm September afternoon, it is as if Rosalind
has become molten; turned from flesh into liquid and left her own
body behind.

Cristabel and the Stories

There is much for Cristabel to do before the arrival of the brother. Maudie says babies are tiresome and she'd as soon leave them on the lawn for the rooks to have at their eyes, but Cristabel feels this is because Maudie does not have any brothers. Or sisters, for that matter, but brothers are the main thing.

A brother, according to the books Cristabel has read, is a plucky lad full of life and go, ripe for adventure. Uncle Willoughby is a brother, and he is much more adventurous than her father. Cristabel's brother will need a wooden sword like hers, and she has put some of her stones with faces into his cradle to act as companions, for on windy nights there is a howling in the attic that even a plucky brother might find alarming.

She is also planning to tell the brother stories. Her current charges – the stones and the postcard called Dog – are always hungry for stories. She reads to them from discarded newspapers or Uncle Willoughby's letters. Sometimes, she even manages to steal a book from her father's study. She is forbidden to enter the study or touch the books, but if she ever sees the room unattended, she will dart in and stuff a book under her dress. Only one at a time though, and returned quickly, so there are no telltale gaps left on the shelves.

The study contains collections of Greek myths; leather-bound volumes of *The Iliad* and *The Odyssey*; a book called *Moonfleet* about smugglers, and, best of all, a row of adventure stories by someone called G. A. Henty, with titles like *At the Point of the Bayonet* and *The Bravest of the Brave*. According to the author's introductions, they are based on true episodes in England's glorious history. It is from these books she has learnt the ways of brothers.

The Henty books are cloth-bound, with gold-lettered titles and illustrated covers bearing crossed rifles and jousting knights. Each is carefully inscribed with the same scribbly name on the frontispiece – *J. Seagrave Esq.* – and the pages repeatedly marked with greasy fingerprints. When Cristabel first opened Henty's *The Dash for Khartoum*, a shower of old pie crumbs fell from its pages into her lap. They turned out to be edible.

Cristabel has enjoyed every one of these books and memorized as much of them as she can, but she would like the brother to have something new, not stolen. A story to keep.

'Do you have any stories?' she asks the French governess, who rolls her eyes and says, '*Non.*'

'Do you have any stories, Betty?'

'What do I want with stories?' replies Betty, who is on her knees, blacking the grate in the attic.

'You read the stories in the new mother's magazines.'

'They're romance, Miss Cristabel. Not fitting for the likes of you.'

'Why? What's in them?'

Betty sits back heavily on her haunches, her face red and perspiring. 'They're about weddings and that.'

Cristabel frowns. The brother will not want stories about weddings. He will no doubt find them as tedious as she does, so she resolves to make the best of what she has. She can read him the letter from Uncle Willoughby about discovering a scorpion in his boot in Constantinople, and it can be followed by the newspaper report she found about the hanging of an Ontario man who took hours to die, and she can finish with Henty's account of an Englishman leading a band of peasants to victory against the blood-stain'd sons of France. Maybe after that, she can do it backwards.

'Maudie, does a story always have to go from beginning to end? Can it go the other way?'

'However you prefers it, Miss Cristabel,' says Maudie, carefully sharpening her pencil with a pocketknife. 'In my diary, sometimes I go back and read a bit from last year, and it don't matter. All headed to the same place. It's pleasant to drop in on yourself unexpectedly –'

Maudie Kitcat's Diary
25th December, 1918

> *frost*
> *church*
> *plum pudding*
> *member when I kisst Clive in the last stabel on the left after church that time an how he shook*

'– and find yourself still there. But when you're reading it, you know more than you did then. So you feel clever. Cleverer than that Betty Bemrose, at any rate.'

'What's in your diary, Maudie?'

'Never you mind.'

'Can I see it?'

Maudie shakes her head. 'Not ever. I'd have to slit your throat while you was sleeping.'

'With that very knife?'

'Very same.'

Maudie is an excellent mentor in so many ways, and Cristabel is extremely gratified to take her advice regarding stories. Forwards or backwards, it doesn't matter a jot.

Waiting, Wanting

25th August, 1890
Thirty years earlier

It was the first day in months his parents had even glanced at him, and Jasper was ballsing it all up. Forced into a sailor suit that strained over his sixteen-year-old tubbiness and trying not to drop his baby brother in a stuffy photographic studio in Dorchester as a man hidden beneath a black cloth peered through the lens of a wooden contraption and shouted at Jasper if he breathed too visibly. Every time the photographer shouted, Jasper's father shouted, his mother sighed, and the photographer's assistant also sighed. An echo chamber of shouts and sighs. All his fault.

But his parents – Robert and Elizabeth – couldn't raise themselves to scold him properly. They were too busy adoring nine-month-old Willoughby in his voluminous christening gown, and continued to do so all the way home, cooing like idiots at the baby as they bounced about in the horse-drawn carriage. Jasper pressed his forehead to the rattling window and watched the sky pass by. The stately clouds proceeding over the water meadows outside the town looked solid, habitable. Great white clouds. Great white myths.

Baby Willoughby was a miracle. Everybody thought so. For almost the whole of Jasper's life, his mother Elizabeth had been pregnant, but every Seagrave child born after Jasper died, usually immediately. Others survived just long enough to be given weighty ancestral names, which they took down with them into the Seagrave crypt at the village church, where their small coffins were lined up on a shelf like parcels waiting to be posted.

It did not do to make a fuss, but it was felt as an affliction; this repeated boxing up of tiny bodies, this shutting up, this muffling. Chilcombe was a mute place of closed doors where red-eyed maids pressed handkerchiefs to their mouths. At the end of every meal, Elizabeth would lay her cutlery precisely in the centre of her bone china plate without a single sound.

One of the footmen told Jasper that babies were made because 'married folk do what cows and bulls do'. Jasper had seen this: the snorting bull lurching on top of the cow; the cow staring ahead, fatalistically chewing its cud. His body recognized such activity as known, as possible, but he could not imagine his parents behaving in such a way, for they hardly seemed aware of each other.

His mother wore black dresses that extended from chin to floor, and drifted about like a ghost, whereas his father existed somewhere beyond the walls, charging about the Empire. If Robert ever returned, it was a brief, blustery visit, in which he would blow through the building in a flurry of discarded boots and shouted orders to servants, like a localized tornado: a great deal of flattening; no real contact. Sometimes the only sign that his father had returned home was a new stuffed animal appearing in the Oak Hall.

How the babies were produced seemed unlikely, but that they died seemed inevitable. Jasper was the sole survivor: all-conquering and monstrous. From his bed at night, he sometimes heard an ailing infant crying and transformed these sounds into the screams of the vanquished Arabs in Khartoum. He imagined himself leading the victorious British troops; national acclaim quick to follow, his proud father slapping him on the back. When the screaming finally stopped, silence hung on the quivering air, long and expectant.

Then Willoughby was born. Jasper barely gave him a thought, expecting this baby to go the way of the others, but Willoughby, with his copper hair and bow-lipped mouth, did not die. And one day, Elizabeth unexpectedly dropped her cutlery in the middle of breakfast and asked for the baby in the nursery to be brought to her. Jasper, up in the attic schoolroom reciting Latin verbs with his tutor, heard footsteps running by, then Willoughby being borne past like a young maharajah in an elephant parade.

The following day, an even more surprising event occurred. His mother appeared in the schoolroom. She had never been there before. Previously, the schoolroom was merely the name of a place that existed somewhere above her, remote as heaven.

'One of the maids suggested Willoughby might like a toy,' Elizabeth said.

A maid appeared brandishing two of Jasper's tin soldiers. 'Will these do, ma'am?'

'Perfect,' said his mother and away the raiding party went, leaving Jasper with nothing but *amo, amas, amat, amamus, amatis, amant*.

From then on, it was as if there were some sort of celebration going on in the house that Jasper was not permitted to attend. When he walked through the house with his tutor, heading out for his daily march along the coast, he would see people arriving to view the miracle baby, guests gathering in the drawing room, and his mother holding Willoughby, her face strained with anxious hope. It was an expression Jasper had previously seen on Cook, whenever she had created a new meal for his parents.

(Jasper would often lurk in a corner of the kitchen as Cook waited to hear how her creation had been received, because if she caught him watching, she would wink and say, 'Now you'll eat anything I give you, Master Jasper,' and this would be followed by a tasty morsel: a chunk of cheese or an apple briskly polished on her apron. It was also true. Jasper would eat anything Cook gave him, primarily because she was one of the few people to speak to him without being obliged to do so. Besides, it satisfied something in him, to take food and eat it, it didn't matter what it was. He was neglected and peevish; peevish and neglected. It was hard to tell which came first.)

'Chop chop, Jasper,' his tutor would say, ushering him out of the house, and Jasper would spend the walk slashing at plants with his wooden sword.

In the evening, when the time came for Jasper to greet his parents before their meal, he would descend the staircase, hair flattened with saliva, and lurk in the hall until permitted to enter the dining room; somewhere he only saw in glances, as he was not allowed to gawp about like a fish. The walls were painted blood red, to show off the meat served on the family china, while his parents were lit by candles, their long shadows looming behind them. In discreet corners, servants waited to serve; just as the dining room waited for Jasper every day, waited to find him wanting.

One evening, Robert, a man who began conversations somewhere in the middle, said, 'Time for you to learn more than Latin, boy. Need to set an example for Willoughby. You'll be coming with me tomorrow.'

At the mention of Willoughby, Elizabeth smiled down at the dining table, as if admiring her reflection in a pond. Jasper looked at the paintings on the walls. Portraits of Seagraves with alabaster skin, from a time when both men and women favoured ringlets. All seemed to be pressing a single hand to their chests, one finger splayed apart as if attempting to subtly point to something: the lustrous fabric they were wearing, perhaps, or the faux classical landscape behind them – *Look! In the trees! A little domed temple!* – or even the alarmingly high forehead of the person in the portrait next to them. At the far end of the room hung the photograph of surly Jasper in his sailor suit, holding Willoughby in his gown.

'That wooden sword of yours,' said Robert. 'It's a child's toy. Give it to your brother. That will be all.'

Dismissed, Jasper went upstairs and got into bed, where he retrieved a biscuit stored under his pillow and picked up his King Arthur book. Then he put them down again. He should read less. Eat less. He should buck up his ideas. Jasper stared at the ceiling.

The following morning – in fact, all of the following mornings, of all of the following years, throughout his youth and then his twenties and his thirties – Jasper glumly followed his father out of the house to learn about his responsibilities as heir, while inside, his younger brother blossomed effortlessly. Willoughby learnt to walk in a single afternoon; Jasper stole whisky from his father's liquor cabinet, went swimming in the sea late at night, slipped on the pebbles and broke his ankle so badly he was left with a limp. Willoughby gambolled everywhere with his favourite wooden sword; Jasper hobbled about, weaponless, waiting for his father to die so he might be able to prove himself to his father.

The limp did not help matters. Jasper felt uncomfortable when visiting tenant farmers. He preferred doing the rounds on horseback. Up there, he was far enough removed from the *populace* to achieve benevolence. On foot, lumbering along, he was cumbersome as a circus bear. He noticed the sharp eyes of the estate workers as he approached; their smirks as he lurched across uneven fields like a man moving a wardrobe.

His social life was similarly limited. He wanted very much to be a fine English gentleman, but he could not dance, as his weak ankle gave way beneath him. He sat at the side of assembly rooms, imagining grisly deaths for young bachelors who could waltz. His poems remained in his pockets. He comforted himself with the thought that noble Hector never bloody well waltzed. During the night, if he had consumed too much food at dinner (and he usually had), he could hear himself breaking wind in his sleep, the helplessly escaping air a sort of continuation of his inept attempts at making small talk, a smattering of half-hearted repartee.

Sometimes, while following his still-very-much-alive father about the place, Jasper came up with schemes for how he might change life at Chilcombe if he were in charge. In reality, there was no space left for his ideas, given the scale of his father's. Robert Seagrave's booming Victorian confidence dominated the future like the grand avenue of beech trees he was planning. Robert would never live to see the trees grow, but he had no doubt that in hundreds of years, Seagraves like himself would be parading beneath them.

It was a curious thing, that Jasper's father's life served as impediment to his own. Occasionally – on November afternoons, for example, the low sun glinting over the cobalt sea – the ocean inspired huge, inexpressible sensations that reduced Jasper's thoughts to broken half-sentences.

I love the –

How can we not believe that –

To meet someone who –

What would it be –

Sentences snapped in two before they had the chance to become clichéd, before his gloomy mind could dismiss them as claptrap, as impossible nonsense.

'Jasper, pay attention, for pity's sake,' his father would bark.

There was cheese to be eaten in the kitchen. Cake too. Apple dumplings. Peppermint creams. Turkish delight. The jelly-covered crust of an old pork pie.

The Boxing Day Hunt

December, 1914
Six years earlier

Willoughby. Willoughby! Jasper did his best to ignore his brother. It was the first and, God willing, last Christmas of the war, and the younger Seagrave son was home on leave. Taking a break from soldiering, Willoughby bestrode the front lawn wearing white jodhpurs, a scarlet jacket and a top hat, while knocking back a glass of port and holding a frisking horse for a pneumatic blonde heiress. Jasper heard the heiress exclaim, 'Such bravery! We all think of you,' and knew it was not the massed troops of Britannia that she and the other women of England held in their minds as they knelt to pray in village churches or gazed across the sea towards battle-scarred France – it was bollocking Willoughby.

Willoughby Seagrave was the toast of society and, most gallingly, the toast of women. Jasper had seen even the dowdiest of old maids gazing lustfully after his long-legged brother. The boss-eyed spinsters Jasper escorted to county balls never looked at him that way. Catching his reflection in silver-framed mirrors, he knew why. He was a sobersided man in his forties, with a haggis for a face, and he was forever peering about, as if trying to puzzle out the answer to something everybody else knew.

Jasper had hoped when he became head of the family, matters might be different. That he might be respected. It was true that once his father finally had the good grace to expire – toppling over like a tree after Sunday lunch, as if to show them how an Englishman should die – things started to look up.

The whole village lined the route to the church on the snowy day of the funeral, just before Christmas 1913, and Jasper walked behind the men carrying the coffin, aware of the villagers' eyes following him. As he paced behind his father's body, he heard in his mind the carol 'Good King Wenceslas'. *In his master's steps he trod, where the snow lay dinted.*

It would be wrong to say he was happy at the funeral; he felt his father's absence as a vast, whistling space. But as the mourning party left the churchyard, having deposited Robert in the crypt next to his wife and all their babies, Jasper found himself humming the tune – *Bring me flesh and bring me wine* – and by the time he was back in the house (the house that was now his), pouring himself a brandy, he was softly singing. *Thou shalt find the winter's rage, freeze thy blood less coooo-ooooold-leeee.*

But it soon transpired that matters hadn't changed. Whenever Jasper met local people, they only wanted to talk about his father and how there would never be another of his like. Robert had been blessed with the gift of obliviousness and the villagers appeared to admire him for it. Whenever Robert cantered by on horseback, he would wave at them so very generally, it was as if he were blind and simply gesturing in the direction of people he had been told were nearby. If he ever appeared on foot, there would be a flurry of hat-tipping and curtsies that he would stride through, like an explorer through jungle undergrowth. On the rare occasions when Robert did notice an individual among the masses – an especially pretty child, a pleasingly capable groom – then that person felt the very eye of God had turned upon them.

Jasper was not, is not, never will be God.

'Everything all right, sir?' said the stable boy holding Jasper's horse.

'I Imph,' replied Jasper, watching the fulsome heiress leaning from her horse to take a sip from Willoughby's glass. Their father had never allowed women to join the hunt, believing their erratic reactions spoiled the sport, but Willoughby was welcoming them with open arms.

One booted foot into the strong hands of the stable boy, and Jasper is hoisted into the saddle, immediately kicking his horse Guinevere away from the rest of the pack.

★

Thankfully, Willoughby didn't last long. After an hour of riding, he declared the fox they were chasing to be an unbeatable beast, bellowed, 'A port, a port, my kingdom for a port!' and led his followers and the panting hounds back across the fields to the house.

It took Jasper another hour of determined hacking before he could take solace in the countryside: the clockwork clatter of a pheasant's wings as it burst from a hedgerow; the sea in the distance, the same washed-out white as the sky.

Faithful Guinevere carried him on until they were quite alone. He was almost starting to feel equable when a woman cantered up, wearing a black riding jacket and a hat with a veil. She was not riding side-saddle; she was riding square in the saddle as men do.

'Trying to escape?' she asked, slowing to a steady trot.

Jasper grunted.

'Precocious, isn't he? Your brother,' she said. 'I had been warned.'

'Bloody going to ride his bloody horse into the bloody ground,' said Jasper.

'Shame we couldn't warn the horse. I say, what a field for a gallop – come on.'

She was off. Guinevere gave a skip of delight and Jasper found himself following. They thundered across the hard winter earth like jockeys.

At the far end of the field, the woman pulled her horse to a halt. Her hands, Jasper noticed, were firm but gentle with the bit. She didn't go in for the yanking that Willoughby and his boorish friends were prone to.

'There's a respectable inn near here,' she said. 'We could let these fine creatures have a well-deserved rest.'

She led him there, swinging herself from the saddle with a boyish leap. Jasper dismounted, feeling, as he always did, the drop in status that accompanied his drop to earth. His weak ankle buckled as soon as his feet hit the ground.

The woman looked up from where she was scraping her boots. 'Riding accident?'

Jasper rifled through his usual list of suitably manly excuses for his limp, but her flushed face, friendly as a Labrador, caused him to say unexpectedly, 'Pebbly beach. Whisky.'

'Bad luck,' she winced, tying their horses to a fence. 'Hamper you at all?'

'Nuisance when deerstalking. Gives way on occasions.'

'I've a horse with a gammy leg,' she said, pushing open the door to the pub, which was hunched low beneath a thatched roof. 'Used to pitch me off in the most unlikely places, but then he learnt to watch where he put his feet. You know how useful that can be in a hunter. Looking to breed him next year.'

'Is that so? I'm looking for a sire for Guinevere.'

Jasper could hardly hobble to the bar fast enough. A pair of brandies and they were soon sitting by the fireplace in the snug, cantering through his favourite subjects: horses, hunts, bloodlines, breeding. Her name was Annabel Agnew. She had black hair escaping in wiry coils from her hairnet and a trace of mud across one cheekbone. He ought to tell her to wipe it off, but perhaps not yet.

'Didn't think the fairer sex went in for horses,' said Jasper, with what he hoped was a jocular air.

'Always loved them. Get to ride more now as I'm helping my father run our estate. My older brother was killed in France, so until my younger brother learns the ropes, I'll still be running it. He's at Harrow. Hoping he'll stay there until the war is over.'

'Awful business. But the Germans won't hold out for long. England will always come up to the mark. What brings you to Chilcombe?'

'I have a younger sister too. The one who fell off her horse before she'd even mounted it. I'm under strict instructions to keep her away from your brother. Which – it now occurs to me – I'm failing to do. She's terribly smitten with anyone in a uniform.'

'You're the chaperone, eh?'

'The spinster sister is often required to prevent their siblings contributing a little too much to the war effort.'

Jasper guffawed. 'Should get back to the house then.'

Annabel frowned and leant back in her chair. 'Just how fast can he be, this ruinous brother of yours?'

'Well. I suppose there are several young women back at the house.'

'All of whom he probably needs to charm.'

'Quite right.'

'Could take him about as long as it takes us to have another drink.'

'You might well be correct.'

'So, this Guinevere – tell me where you found her. She's an impressive beast.'

Later, three brandies later, when they were trotting back to Chilcombe, Jasper noticed that, on horseback, she didn't seem so tall. In the pub, when they stood up in the inglenook, she had rather towered over him, but in the saddle, thanks to Guinevere, he had at least half a hand on her.

Jasper and Annabel dismounted in front of the house, leaving their horses to the stable boy. Jasper limped quickly to the entrance, keen to escort her inside, but as he pushed open the front door, he heard riotous laughter.

Arriving in the Oak Hall, he saw Willoughby in an armchair by the fireplace – an armchair he had presumably dragged out of the drawing room – surrounded by his acolytes, who were drinking port and carelessly chucking logs on to a ferocious fire. There was a woman slumped next to Willoughby, wearing the bottom half of the suit of armour and inexpertly sounding a bugle. The other parts of the armour were scattered about the floor like dismembered limbs.

'Nearly had it that time, darling,' said Willoughby.

'That armour is not for dressing up,' snapped Jasper. At the sound of his voice, servants lurking on the gallery vanished into bedrooms.

'Only just got back, Jasper? Must have been a very wily fox,' said Willoughby, without looking round.

The woman attempted to sit upright, hiccupping loudly. She was the blonde heiress.

'That woman should be taken to her room,' said Jasper, feeling his face redden. 'We have guest rooms for our guests. She should be lying down in one of those.'

Willoughby used the spear belonging to the suit of armour to push a log on to the fire. 'Is that what we do, brother? Do we ask our guests to remain in their rooms?'

'That is not what I said, Willoughby.'

'Jasper, we are back, all too briefly, from a bloody business, fighting the good fight. Surely even you can't begrudge us a few drinks?'

Jasper was about to give them a sizeable piece of his mind, when he heard the strangest noise. Annabel was laughing uproariously. He should have guessed there would be something wrong with her. She must be one of those lunatic spinsters. He was wondering if she would ever stop, when she slapped her hands against her sides, and said, 'You won't believe it, but that's exactly what Jasper said.'

'What did I say?' said Jasper.

'I was adamant that if we came back here and found a scene of gallivanting, that Jasper should kick you out, you insolent buggers,' said Annabel. 'But he said I couldn't begrudge boys back from the front a few drinks.'

Jasper glanced at Willoughby, who had turned to look at Annabel.

'He's even put some money behind the bar at the pub in the village so you chaps can have a pint or two before dinner,' she continued. 'Isn't that right, Jasper?'

Jasper opened his mouth, Annabel supplied the words. 'What do you think, chaps, drinks in the local hostelry?'

The men looked at each other, then the one called Perry said, 'Splendid idea, Jasper old boy.' Soon they were all putting on their hats and trooping out, leaving the heiress to be helped by Mrs Hardcastle.

Willoughby, bringing up the rear, paused in front of Annabel. 'I don't think I've had the pleasure,' he murmured, carefully buttoning his jacket.

'Annabel Agnew,' she said, extending a hand. From the side, Jasper noticed she had the profile of a Roman emperor.

'Knew a girl by that name in Hampshire,' said Willoughby, taking her hand in his. 'She preferred to be called Belle.'

'Annabel,' said Annabel.

'Friend of Jasper's, are you?'

'Very much so,' she replied, her voice brisk as a whip. 'Don't think I caught your name.'

Willoughby smiled. 'Willoughby Seagrave, at your command.'

'Jolly good,' she said.

Jasper caught a look passing between them, that of the strict schoolteacher to the wilful pupil: a steady reckoning of each other's strengths.

After Willoughby had left, Annabel turned to Jasper. 'There is a village pub, isn't there?'

'Yes. Place called The Shipwreck.'

'Thank the saints. I was rather banking on that. Best send a boy down there with instructions for the landlord, or that motley rabble will turn up to find no drinks available.'

'Bloody hell. Yes, we must.'

'No hurry though. None of them looked capable of anything more than a saunter.'

Jasper called in the youngest footman and sent him down to The Shipwreck with orders to give Willoughby and his friends everything they wanted. It pleased him in an unexpected way, this act of munificence. He wondered whether he ought to do something similar for the staff on special occasions. He considered musing out loud about this idea in front of Annabel Agnew. He decided he would do this as he gave her a tour of the house.

Summoning up the courage to do so took him through the study, the dining room, the garden and the stables, but eventually, when they arrived back in the drawing room, he said, 'Might borrow that idea of yours. Drinks at The Shipwreck. For the staff, I mean. New Year's Day. Perhaps a show of fireworks for the village children.'

'Capital notion,' she said.

'Thank you for stepping in earlier,' he mumbled. 'I went off half-cocked.'

'My pleasure.'

'Willoughby makes my blood boil.'

'Best keep him out of the house then,' she said, and were this statement coming from anyone other than the straightforward

Annabel, Jasper might wonder if it was meant flirtatiously, but with her, it seemed simply an honest assessment of the situation. Although, he couldn't be sure that there wasn't a slight sparkle in her eyes. Then he realized he had been studying her face for some time while half chewing on his moustache.

'I chew it, when I'm thinking,' he said, smoothing his moustache back into place.

Annabel held up one of the loose strands of hair that had escaped from her hairnet – the ends were broken and split. 'Snap.'

One of Jasper's hands was still attending to his facial hair; the other suddenly felt agitated and empty. There was only the sound of logs in the fireplace burning, their crackling and sighs, and his own breathing.

Annabel was still holding her own hair. 'Always been envious of dogs. Having bones to chew.'

'Yes,' replied Jasper. He could hear her breath now, as well as his own, and the silence seemed even larger.

'Always wanted lots of dogs,' she said, looking at him with a frankness that was astonishing.

'Very fond,' he said, and felt, at that moment, that somehow each of his breaths drew her closer to him, though he could not remember either of them moving.

Then a maid came in carrying a coal scuttle. 'Beg pardon, Mr Seagrave,' she said. 'I thought everyone had left.'

'Not everyone,' said Jasper, swallowing. 'Could you bring us some tea?'

'And cake,' added Annabel.

Jasper found he was beaming at the remarkable Miss Agnew. 'Yes. Yes, yes. Lots of cake.'

Jasper and Annabel spent the afternoon by the fire in the drawing room. It was a quiet room, north facing, with a cool light, the walls heather green, hung with paintings of rural landscapes: cattle in snow, cattle fording a river, cattle come to a river at twilight. They drank tea and ate cake and talked about horses and dogs, dogs and horses. He told her some of his favourite historical facts about the region and it transpired she had some fascinating ones of her own.

Time appeared to do extraordinary things. At one point, Jasper glanced at the clock on the mantlepiece, and it was four o'clock, but when he looked again a second later, it was gone six. Then, when he was watching Annabel efficiently demolish a slice of fruit-cake, her cheeks glowing pink in the heat from the fire, and she looked up to catch his gaze, he found he was aware of each and every second as it passed. When Willoughby's boisterous party returned from the pub and Annabel got up, saying she must check on her sister before dinner, Jasper was suddenly disconsolate.

As she was leaving the room, Annabel turned back. 'Fancy a ride out tomorrow?'

Jasper nodded. Annabel waved a strand of hair at him and disappeared.

Dinner that night was not as hideous as he feared, despite having two of Willoughby's brainless friends seated next to him. He could suffer their nonsense because every time he looked up, he could see Annabel in a blue silk evening gown, at the other end of the table. In the candlelight, her hair shone black as oil.

The men around him were talking of war. They couldn't wait to get back to France, to get stuck into the Boche. They would be home by springtime. Willoughby was boasting to the blonde heiress about being posted to Egypt, promising to bring her back a pyramid.

This is my house, thought Jasper. Tomorrow, these people will leave, and this will still be my house. Annabel Agnew lives in Wiltshire. Wiltshire is not that far away.

In the midst of the clamour and battle of the dining room, he raised his glass to her across the table.

His

'Naturally, my sister is heartbroken,' Annabel had said, relaxing into an armchair in the drawing room. 'Ever since she heard the notorious Willoughby was off to Egypt, she's been reading the news-papers, and now the Ottomans have invaded, she's beside herself.'

'She needn't worry,' said Jasper, pouring brandy into two glasses. 'My brother has a knack of avoiding anything resembling hard work. Last I heard, he was learning to ride a camel.'

Annabel laughed. 'Thank goodness you're nothing at all like him.'

Jasper paused in front of the drinks cabinet. From there, he could see out of a window overlooking the lawn to where a rook paced to and fro, its considered manner suggesting a man with his arms held behind his back, filling time, waiting for news. The February wea-ther was grey and dismal, a thick fog had rolled in from the sea. There was just the rook, the lawn, the fog, and the room Jasper was standing in.

What he meant to say as he turned round to offer her a glass was, 'Would you care for a drink?' but Jasper Seagrave had never been good at public speaking, and the words came out quite differently. What he said was, 'Would you care to marry me?'

Annabel took the drink from his hand and said, 'Let me get this one down me.'

Jasper turned to pace, to regret, to rue, to stew, but Annabel had drunk the brandy in a single gulp and was placing the glass on a side table, saying, 'I think I would, you know. Yes, I think I rather would.'

★

When they married, one month later in the village church, it was a modest celebration, as so many were away fighting. They honeymooned in the Lake District, in beautiful Cumberland. Afterwards, Jasper would remember that day, those first weeks, in bright flashes, like scenes glimpsed from a moving train. It seemed remarkable to have such happiness when news from abroad was increasingly dark and worrying, but Annabel Agnew – Annabel Seagrave – made everything remarkable.

Returning to Dorset, he felt somehow taller. He was sure the servants looked at him differently. Annabel was so practical, so cheerful: her strong hands flicking through the household accounts or knitting mufflers for the troops or tightening a stirrup on Guinevere or checking the teeth of one of their new dogs. She proved perfectly capable.

They were unsure if she would ever be able to have a child. The riding accident that meant she always rode square in the saddle, never side-saddle, had damaged her pelvis. There were concerns. Annabel over thirty and Jasper in his forties. Some days, he believed he would be happy to die heirless simply because she was there every morning when he woke up. There, frowning through her reading glasses at her notebook, a pencil behind her ear, then turning to him with a smile. She was larkish at times, but always concentrated when he spoke. 'Got it,' she would say, and she always had.

They trained their horses together, talked about entering a few in races. They even went up to Ascot that year, and thought it was the new corset beneath her dress that made her faint after the first race. She wasn't used to being out of her riding breeches and, when they got home, announced she didn't want to go anywhere that required corsets again. They didn't know she had fainted because she was with child. A month later, when it had become clear that Mrs Seagrave was pregnant, they had laughed and wept until Annabel insisted they stop because they were upsetting the dogs.

She suffered throughout her pregnancy. Her damaged pelvis gave her great pain. 'It better be a boy,' said Jasper, carrying in one of the new puppies to show her, 'can't let you go through this again.'

Willoughby was surprisingly admiring. His telegram from Cairo read:

Jasper suspected Willoughby was worried about what might happen if Jasper never produced an heir, because then the great weight of the family name would shift on its axis and slide towards Willoughby, and all the camels in Persia couldn't gallop fast enough for him to escape being buried beneath that.

But what did that matter, because Chilcombe was truly Jasper's now, in a way it had never been before. When he and Annabel, his wife (his wife!), walked arm in arm across the lawn, he felt he was returning to his rightful place. He would follow her as she walked through the house, watching as she opened doors, opened windows, opened cupboards, finding the most unlikely things: a harp (which she could (almost) play); a stuffed baby elephant (which she had mounted on wheels for their child to ride), and Jasper's old copy of *The Iliad*, which they read together to the baby in her stomach.

Annabel. She was bracing: she was the wind that smacked you in the face when you set your horse at a gallop, and she was the warming brandy waiting for you by the fire at home. They were to have a child in the spring. A son, he was certain. Everything was coming towards him now.

They Won't Let Him

They won't let Jasper in the room. They won't let him in the room. Three men, four men, have to heave him away. He tries to break down the door, he wants to see her, but they say not now, sir, not now, sir, you wouldn't want to, sir, the doctor says there was a great deal of blood, sir, it's for the best, sir, but he had only just found her, he had only just found her, he needs to get to her, he needs to see her, he needs to tell her, she was going to help him, she was going to make him, she was his, she was his smart sparkling Annabel, a thoroughbred, that's what she was, and she would have him, she would have him, she accepted him, she took his hand, she kept everything in order, she did the books, she could account like a marvel, and when she turned to him from her writing desk to ask if there was anything he needed, he would say that everything was perfectly satisfactory, that he would sit and read the papers, but the day's news would slip through his fingers to the floor and all he could do was watch the concentration concentrated in the nape of her neck, where wiry wisps of hair fell over her collar, and he never thought he would admire brains in a woman, but she had the brains of a good hunter, she knew when to take the fence and when to stall, where the ground was boggy, where the turf was firm, she made it look easy, that leggy stride of hers, a woman who could break the neck of a pheasant without blinking because it was kinder to be quick, and in the evenings, he would sit before the fire and watch her laughing as she tried to play the harp, plucking sound from strings she'd found hidden in the attic, and she came to him with a frankness, with a blunt and welcome ease, like dropping your clothes on the beach, none of that sideways, side-saddle nonsense some women went in for, flapping their fans, whispering with their friends, she came to him honestly, long-limbed as a boy, straightforward as a soldier, flexing her lengthy fingers, fingers mobile as a monkey, deft as a bookkeeper, fingers that flared with magic and pulled gold and music from the air, as if gold and music had always been there, and who will do the accounts now? Who will account for him now? By his word, he is loosed and falling, and they won't let him in the room, they won't let him in the room, and from somewhere he hears the rising wail of an infant, a baby they tell him is a girl, sir, a girl who looks just like her mother, sir, her mother, her mother, her mother, she so wanted to be a mother and they won't let him in the room to tell her, they won't let him in the room.

Afterwards

April, 1916
Four years earlier

They had boxed up Annabel. Put her in the crypt. There had been a funeral. He believed he had been there. But he also knew it was impossible.

Jasper knew that each day followed another day, but this too was impossible, as every day was the same day. There was a war going on in Europe. There was an empty space in his house. That was all.

They had printed her name in the newspaper alongside the dead infantrymen. He had sold the harp. Given the dogs away. Put the stuffed baby elephant in the attic, upended, its little wheels spinning in the air.

It all seemed quite fraudulent. It was incomprehensible that events kept happening and she was not there to see them. Sometimes, he woke in the dead of night, wanting to tell her something dreadful had occurred, to shake her awake and say, 'My dear, you simply won't believe this.' But there was no one there, only the whistling walls and the empty dark.

She would be back soon. Not on this long, empty day, but perhaps the next. He wished someone would shush that noisy baby.

She would be back soon.

The Vegetable

'Is everything all right?' says Willoughby, nodding at her stomach.

'I don't know,' says Rosalind. 'I felt something.' She cautiously puts her hand down beneath the sheets and discovers the bed is sodden. Glancing surreptitiously at her fingers, she notices the liquid is tinged pink with blood and feels a distant jolt of fear.

'I'll fetch Betty.' Willoughby pushes back his chair, moves away from the bed.

Betty arrives in the room surprisingly quickly. 'Is anything the matter, ma'am?'

'There seems to have been some sort of accident, Betty. The bed is wet. I don't know why, I –'

'Goodness, it means the baby's coming, ma'am. I'll call Maudie to fetch the doctor. Let's get you out of that wet nightgown.'

'It's coming now?'

'They come when they want, ma'am. Arms up, that's lovely.'

Rosalind allows Betty to move her about like a rag doll. She is dazed, still lost in the heady world behind her eyelids – and Willoughby gone, when they had been so close, his mouth so near to hers she could feel the warmth of his breath.

Betty dispatches maids to fetch clean towels and hot water. Boots clatter up and down the staircase. Mrs Hardcastle appears in the doorway, tapping her fingertips together, then vanishes. There are shouts outside, the crash of a bicycle dropped to the ground. Messages are sent to Salisbury where Jasper is visiting a racing stables.

'When will it happen, Betty?' asks Rosalind.

'The doctor will be able to tell you, I'm sure.'

'I've quite an ache in my back. Does it hurt as much as they say?'

'It can't be that bad, ma'am, or people wouldn't keep doing it.'

Doctor Rutledge arrives promptly, having been visiting a patient in the village, and Mrs Hardcastle escorts him into the bedroom. He listens to Rosalind's heart with a stethoscope and runs his hands over her bump, frowning. Then he asks her to lift her knees up and hold them open.

'I beg your pardon?' she says.

'Need to take a quick look,' he says. 'See what's what.'

Betty smiles reassuringly and begins folding up the bedcovers from the bottom of the bed to allow the doctor access. 'A quick look, ma'am. To check all's well.'

Between them, Betty and Mrs Hardcastle push Rosalind's knees up towards her chest and then Betty prises them apart. Rosalind has to look away, her hands fluttering about her face, as the doctor leans in, armed with some kind of steel implement.

'I see,' says the doctor, after a while. He returns to feeling her bump, his eyes casually wandering around the room as if examining the decor. 'I see.'

The women wait.

After some time, Dr Rutledge turns to Mrs Hardcastle. 'Difficult to tell where this baby is.'

'Yes, Doctor.'

'Strapping big baby too.' Dr Rutledge looks at Mrs Hardcastle for some time, adjusting his waistcoat. There seems to be an unspoken assessment going on between them. Finally, he says, 'If it is the wrong way round, it might not be plain sailing.'

'It has been traditional for the Seagrave heir to be born in the house,' replies Mrs Hardcastle.

'Wouldn't like to take any chances. Especially after.'

'Yes, Doctor,' says Mrs Hardcastle.

Betty places her hand on Rosalind's arm.

'Is Jasper due back soon, Mrs Hardcastle?' says Dr Rutledge.

'We haven't heard from him, Doctor.'

'Am I right in thinking Mr Willoughby Seagrave has a motor car?'

'We'll find him right away, Doctor.'

*

Betty and Mrs Hardcastle help Rosalind down the stairs, both talking to her, a cross-stream of encouragement and reassurance. Other staff hover nearby, hands clasped nervously in front of them. Rosalind has been dressed in a clean nightgown, dressing gown and slippers, which gives her the curious feeling she is a child allowed up past bedtime.

'Good luck, ma'am,' says Blythe, opening the front door.

Outside, Willoughby – one hand on the wheel of his open-top car, one hand lighting a cigarette – revs the engine. Mrs Hardcastle opens the rear door and helps Rosalind into the vehicle while Dr Rutledge heaves himself into the front passenger seat, smiling cheerfully and saying, 'Splendid machine. A Wolseley, if I'm not mistaken.'

'Four-cylinder engine, four-speed gearbox. She'll go for miles, this one,' replies Willoughby, patting the wooden dashboard. 'Is Mrs Seagrave all right?'

Rosalind notices that the day has become evening. Long shadows are falling across the lawn, and the trees at the lawn's edge are silhouetted against a persimmon sky. Beyond the trees, she can hear the sea's gentle back and forth. It would be a perfect evening to sit outside with a cocktail, laughing at some snappy witticism with your head thrown back, a string of pearls at your throat.

'Mrs Seagrave is doing marvellously,' says Dr Rutledge. 'Let's get her to the hospital.'

'A hospital?' Rosalind asks, but her voice is lost in the roar of the engine. As they accelerate away, she looks back to see Betty and Mrs Hardcastle standing outside the ivy-covered house: Betty with one hand in the air, Mrs Hardcastle with both hands to her mouth.

The car jolts down the driveway, past the stone pillars that mark the entrance to the estate. The pillars are topped with indeterminate heraldic creatures that Jasper once explained to her, but Rosalind cannot remember what he said. The iron gates that used to hang between them are long gone and only the stone creatures remain, green with age, totems of a previous civilization.

*

As the car steams through the village and up over the Ridgeway, with choking belches of petrol fumes, the ache in Rosalind's back increases. She tries to tell Dr Rutledge, but he is having a shouted conversation with Willoughby about fuel consumption, and whenever he looks round at her, she feels obliged to smile politely. She attempts to lean forward to tap Willoughby on the shoulder, but the movement of the car and the awkwardness of her bump means she fails to make contact. It is easier to simply hang her upper body over the edge of the vehicle and take gulps of the evening air as the countryside flies past. She hadn't realized there was so much of Dorset. It looked much smaller in the pictures she'd seen.

The car suddenly comes to a halt, brakes screeching. The lane up ahead is full of sheep, their black faces emitting a cacophony of *baas*. A shepherd stands in their midst, staring open-mouthed at the vehicle. Willoughby swings the car into the hedgerow, reverses out and drives back up the lane.

'Try a left up here,' cries Dr Rutledge, gesturing towards a grass-covered track.

'There are no signposts anywhere,' says Willoughby, 'I could navigate better in the bloody Sahara.'

'Ah! By the stars, eh?' shouts Dr Rutledge, hanging on to his hat as they gain speed. He turns to Rosalind. 'All right back there?'

The pain in the lower half of Rosalind's body has worsened. It doesn't seem to be an ache any more, but something more purposeful. It comes in waves that tighten like an iron corset, until, at their peak, there is a moment where she feels ready to throw herself from the vehicle, then it fades and the world returns. She is not sure if this cycle lasts for minutes or hours. She hears the doctor reassuring her they will find the right road soon, but it is not possible to speak because it is coming again, the tightening. With each exhalation of her breath, she makes a moan like a cow. As long as she can fill her head with the moaning noise, she can still breathe. As long as she can stay hanging over the edge of the car, she can get through it.

Then they are pulling over to the side of a lane near some farm-land, and Dr Rutledge is clambering across the leather seat towards her. She is half aware that he is reaching between her legs, but this is no longer something she is able to worry about.

'Thought so,' he says. 'It's coming. On to your back, Mrs Seagrave, on to your back.'

Between them, Willoughby and Dr Rutledge manoeuvre her, so she is positioned lying along the back seat, propped up on Willoughby. Dr Rutledge has opened the rear door to give himself more room, and stands half out of the vehicle, feet balanced on the running board as he unbuttons her dressing gown.

'Do you have anything we could give her? A shot of morphine?' asks Willoughby.

'Too late for that.'

'Nothing at all?'

'It's nature's way. Follow my instructions, Mrs Seagrave. Let's have no fuss.'

The doctor rips open her nightgown with a practised air and Rosalind sees her own legs smeared with blood. She is suddenly weeping, furiously and copiously, like a child.

'Don't try to get up, Mrs Seagrave,' says Dr Rutledge. 'When I tell you to push, you must push with all your might.'

'But I don't want to,' she says.

Willoughby takes her hand. 'You're in it now, darling. I'm afraid there's only one way out.'

'Mrs Seagrave, I need you to push. Right now,' says Dr Rutledge, rolling up his sleeves and crouching between her knees.

Rosalind tips her head back to look at the sky and sees it miles above her, like the surface of the ocean. It is not possible to stay inside her body with all that is going on, it seems likely that she will die if she stays there, of pain and shame, and so she leaves it, and swims upwards to the blue film of sky, hearing her own curious lowing echoing out across the fields below her. Willoughby is gripping her hand and in some far distant part of her, she strains to rid herself of a boulder wedged in the structure of her body.

'That's it,' cries Dr Rutledge.

Willoughby wipes her hair from her face. 'Come on, soldier.'

When Dr Rutledge next tells her to push, Rosalind roars through gritted teeth, trying to heave the boulder out of her body. She heaves and heaves and thinks it will never be done, but suddenly it is done, and the doctor is lifting up a purple-faced infant, saying, 'It's a girl, a girl.'

Its fists are clenched and its toothless mouth is straining open like a baby bird gaping for a worm and its yellowy eyes are unfocused in the wandering way of the blind and when Rosalind looks at it, the moment is silent and empty.

'Good grief, the child's the spitting image of Jasper,' says Willoughby, his voice unexpectedly shaky.

'Never fear, Mrs Seagrave, the next one will be a boy,' says Dr Rutledge, tucking the baby into the crook of his arm. 'You popped this one out marvellously. We'll tidy things up and get you home. Shift yourself on to the picnic blanket, there's a good girl. Don't want to stain the seats.'

Dr Rutledge uses his handkerchief to carefully wipe the baby's face as it lies in his arms, and then smiles at Willoughby who is reaching out to touch the child's clenched fist, as if they two were the proud new parents.

'Hello there,' says Willoughby. 'How do you do?'

All Off

September, 1920

Cristabel wakes before dawn and doesn't know why. Then she hears it: the cry of a baby. She scrambles out of bed, pulls a cardigan over her nightgown and is about to race down the attic stairs when she sees Maudie, already dressed in her maid's uniform, frizzy hair escaping from her white cap, climbing towards her with an oil lamp.

'The brother –' Cristabel begins, but Maudie cuts her off with a shake of her head.

'It's a girl. Big one.'

Cristabel sits down on the wooden stairs, frowning. 'Are they sure?'

'Face like your father's, but it's a girl all right. Mrs Seagrave hasn't taken to it. Says it looks like a vegetable.'

'You said they'd try again if it wasn't a boy.'

'They will. That's why she's here.'

Cristabel sighs. It isn't what she had hoped for. The letters for the brother will have to be retrieved from under his pillow. The stones with faces too. It is a grievous blow, but despite this, she does feel some measure of sympathy for the vegetable baby disliked by the new mother. Surely sisters must be beneficial in some way. They know how to do weaving and how to cook simple warming fare. Sometimes they look after aged parents, when everyone else has left. Sometimes they are chained to rocks and offered up as sacrifice. She could probably find a use for that sort of thing.

Maudie looks at her thoughtfully. 'I know you was wanting a brother.'

Cristabel nods. 'But I have a sister.'

'Half-sister,' replies Maudie. 'She's no mother of yours, that one. You'd be wise to remember that.'

Rosalind is glad to get back to Chilcombe, where she can return to her bedroom sanctum and put the indignities of the motor car episode behind her. She is tended by devoted Betty, who brings her strengthening meals of liver and heart. Betty helps her bathe in scented water hot enough to return her to herself and, afterwards, binds Rosalind's stomach with a long piece of linen, to regain her figure.

Lying in bed, Rosalind runs her hands over the tight layers of fabric. She feels rather wounded by everything, rather taken apart, and the bindings are a protective casing, a comfort. Outside, it is becoming autumn and the wind is moving through the trees like a rumour. The seasons are on the turn.

Sometimes, Betty will ask if she wants to see the baby, but Rosalind will say no, the child is better where it is. Betty will nod understandingly. She has seen her sisters go half mad trying to look after screaming babbers. It is not the kind of work a delicate lady like Rosalind should do. A nanny is employed. Rosalind's mother writes to express her satisfaction that Rosalind has succeeded in *her primary and most blissful duty as a wife*.

Late one afternoon, Rosalind wakes to see Jasper standing at her bedroom window loudly blowing his nose into a crumpled handkerchief, his many-chinned profile startlingly reminiscent of the baby dispatched to the attic. A baby born in a car. How déclassé. She suddenly feels a clarification of her feelings towards her husband, as if everything up until that point had gathered together and hardened.

He speaks without looking at her. 'Betty tells me you are fond of the name Florence for the child. After the celebrated nurse, I presume. I would be happy with that choice.'

'I might call it Vegetable,' she says. 'It looks like one.'

Jasper turns to her, perplexed. 'What are you saying? Don't you like it?'

80

Rosalind does not answer. She stares back at him. He has caused this, and he has had to do none of the horrible bits. She feels the kind of impotent crossness she felt as a child.

Jasper continues, 'Harold Rutledge said you might be upset it wasn't a boy. Next time it will be.'

Rosalind says nothing; the silence is a small weapon for her to use. She carefully straightens her bedcovers. She needs to start making some lists. She wants to hold a birthday party for Willoughby in November.

Jasper frowns. 'I was delayed. On the day. Didn't want to worry you.'

'I wasn't worried,' she says.

'Willoughby said you were a trouper.'

'Did he?'

'You can call the child whatever you like. I'm just glad you're all right,' he says and crosses the room towards her, with his hands outstretched in a strange half-pleading gesture, as if carrying an awkward weight: a rolled-up rug; someone else's coat; an old ill dog.

'I'm perfectly all right,' says Rosalind, tucking her hands under the sheets. The thought of him touching her brings on a shuddery feeling. 'Could you ring the bell?'

'Can I get you something?'

'I want Betty.'

'Of course.' Jasper obediently presses the button on the wall that summons a maid.

'The name. Florence. It isn't because of the nurse,' says Rosalind, after a pause. Under the covers, she is running her hands over the bindings, adjusting them where they feel loose. 'Why should I care about some dry old stick of a nurse? No. I saw a film. When I was in London. *The Woman in White*. It was about a beautiful woman called Laura who falls in love with an art teacher, but an evil old man called Sir Percival tricks her into marrying him instead. What he doesn't realize is there's another woman who looks like Laura. Then – well, it's complicated, but Sir Percival dies in a fire so Laura and the teacher can marry like they should. Ah, Betty, come in. I was telling

Jasper about a film. Betty loves to hear about films. She desperately wants to go to a picture house, don't you, Betty?'

Betty nods. 'I do, ma'am.'

'It was the actress in the film, Jasper. Her name was Florence La Badie. I will always remember her.'

'I see,' says Jasper.

'My child may look like a vegetable, but at least she will have a film star name,' says Rosalind. 'Or is that worse, do you suppose? To be a dowdy girl with a glamorous name.'

'No daughter of yours could ever be dowdy, ma'am.'

'You are a dear, Betty. I almost want to take you to a picture house myself,' says Rosalind. 'Was there anything else you wanted, Jasper?'

Jasper blows his nose again. 'Only to give you my best wishes,' he replies, formal as a retiring judge.

Rosalind observes her husband as he crosses the room. Once the door has shut behind him, she lets out a breath. Then she gets out of her bed in her nightgown and walks barefoot to her dressing table, where she sits down on the stool, positioning herself in front of its triple mirror in order to see herself and her two pleasing profiles: a triptych of reassurance. Betty stands behind her, running one hand down her mistress's long hair, which shines in the glow of the softly sighing oil lamps.

Rosalind says, 'You will see a film, Betty. I will take you to London and give you the afternoon off specially.'

'That would be a treat, ma'am.'

Rosalind nods, then opens a drawer of her dressing table and takes out a photograph from a magazine, which she passes back over her head to the maid. 'While you're at the picture house, Betty, I will have my hair cut in that modern style,' she says. 'In a London salon.'

Rosalind waits to catch Betty's gaze in the mirror, then, using both hands, lifts her hair and holds it folded against the back of her head, so it appears shorter, a jaw-length bob. 'Like this,' she says. 'All off.'

Things

October, 1920

Cristabel, aged four and ever after, would place a great deal of importance on logic.

She is not allowed to have new boots because she spoiled her old ones by throwing them into the sea to serve as an anchor. She must wear the salt-stained pair until she has learnt her lesson. This is something she can understand. There is a followable logic to it. But there is one issue that does not seem understandable, however much she thinks about it. The issue of the things that boys have.

She had first noticed it when she came across a fisherman's wife playing with her infant son on the beach, letting him sit in the shallows at the water's edge. The naked boy, who was hitting the water with his plump hands, looked like the baby Jesus in the stained-glass windows in the village church. Slightly disgruntled, with a domed head. But between his legs there was a peculiar thing: a fleshy periwinkle curled on a wrinkled skin pouch of marbles. That – she later learnt from Maudie – was a thing that made him a boy, and boys were what the new mother was meant to be providing.

Cristabel did not have a thing. She had checked. Therefore, she was not a boy. She was not what was wanted. The vegetable baby also did not have a thing. Maudie confirmed this. Ergo, the vegetable baby was also not wanted.

Once alerted to the existence of these items, Cristabel kept a watchful eye on any she saw, to see if they did anything of interest. They never did. The things she sighted on the village boys when they went swimming in the sea were simply longer versions of the one seen on the baby on the beach.

What the things were called was a puzzle. Betty responded

crossly to this question, saying, 'Never you mind, madam,' and took away Cristabel's breakfast before she had finished. The fisherman's wife just laughed. Maudie, usually so blunt in her responses, pulled a face and said, 'I only know words your stepmother wouldn't like.'

They seemed such insignificant things but were protected by this peculiar anonymity and brought their owners considerable advantages. Boys with things were allowed to wear trousers and go to school. People ruffled their hair; threw them apples; gave them amusing nicknames; praised them for gumption. They didn't have to have petticoats or husbands. They kept their own surnames and drove motors.

The brother would have a thing too, and the brother would be the heir, and the heir was what everyone wanted. Cristabel thought 'heir' was a strange word. It looked like a mistake and was pronounced *air*, like the noise people make when they don't know what to say.

What heir meant was similarly confusing. You could be born an heir but also named one, if there was a sword. 'I name you Air,' said Cristabel to the umbrella stand shaped like an Indian boy, tapping her wooden sword on his shoulders. She would no doubt find out more when the brother arrived. He would probably share being heir with her. They were going to share everything, except jam tarts and the sticks that belonged to Cristabel.

Before she had known about the things, she had thought it likely that she might be a boy. She had qualities and ambitions well matched to boyhood. An interest in snails and maps and warfare. A roving disposition. Nobody told her that she wasn't. When they found her constructing a chariot out of a wheelbarrow and two croquet mallets, it was something typical of Cristabel. Eyebrows were raised. Punishments were half-heartedly discussed, then forgotten about.

It was only after the new mother started growing a baby in her stomach that people remembered Cristabel wasn't actually a boy, and that stricter standards of behaviour should be enforced. They started saying she must 'behave herself, like a big girl'. There was a distinct lack of logic in these new rules, but when she pointed this out, she was told to stop acting like an uppity little madam.

When the vegetable baby was christened (Florence Louisa Rose Seagrave – Cristabel's suggestion of 'Cristabel the Younger' sadly ignored), Uncle Willoughby bought Cristabel a dress and some squeaky shoes to wear for the church ceremony. The dress was a mass of bows and flounces, and she had to stand in front of the full-length mirror in the new mother's bedroom as they put it on her. There was much tightening and fastening, and she felt it as a kind of tethering, an impediment.

Her body was no longer something amenable that transported her rapidly about the place, like an excellent rickshaw; it was something forced to be stationary, something to be looked at.

'There,' said Betty, tweaking the ribbons on the dress, glancing between the real Cristabel and the reflected version. 'There you are.'

As if she hadn't been there before.

One evening, in the attic with Maudie, who is reading her *The Iliad* in return for one of Cristabel's pencils, it occurs to Cristabel that everyone interesting in *The Iliad* is a boy. They are all owners of things. The only girls in it are sad wives, sad servants or sad beautiful women who cause wars.

It is a dark, drizzly night. Wind sighs down the chimney. The sound of the sea comes and goes. Maudie, in her black and white maid's outfit, sits cross-legged on a rag rug in front of the fireplace, carefully following the words with her finger, slowly intoning. '"Unarm'd if I should go, what hope of mercy from this vengeful foe; but woman-like to fall, and fall without a blow."'

'What does it mean, "woman-like"?' asks Cristabel, who is tucked up in bed. The slanting room is lit by a few guttering candles on the mantelpiece.

Maudie thinks for a moment, then replies, 'It means Mr Homer never met me. Or Betty Bemrose, for that matter. You'd have a job to knock her down.' She carries on reading while Cristabel considers this.

'Maudie –'

' "... pent in this sad palace, let us give to grief the wretched days we have to live ..." '

'Why aren't there interesting girls in the stories?'

' "Still, still for Hector let our sorrows flow, born to his own, and to his parents' woe." '

'Maudie, why are all the best characters men?'

Maudie closes the book with a *clllump*. 'We haven't read all the books yet, Miss Cristabel. I can't believe that every story is the same. Bedtime for you.'

A Hunter's Moon

November, 1920

Jasper eats a late lunch alone. Sinks a full bottle of Bordeaux. Starts on a second. He hasn't seen Rosalind at the dining table in months and Willoughby doesn't often show his face, not even for dessert. Jasper grimly spoons lemon syllabub through his beard, while idly wondering – with no real hope or expectation – if he and Willoughby will ever attain an affectionate, brotherly relationship. It is a matter of regret to him they still slip into the well-worn grooves of ancient quarrels and petty bickering. Willoughby's a flibbertigibbet peacock, with more hair than sense, but he's brave. Dauntless. He's heard Willoughby's fellow officers talk about him with admiration. Jasper would like to be able to call his brother a friend. That would be something.

By the time he rises from the table, after a silent four-course meal eaten at a table set for three, it has become evening and dark outside. Jasper walks through the ground floor of his home, where servants are hurrying about, making everything ready for the guests who will soon be arriving to celebrate Willoughby's birthday. As Jasper opens the door to his study, he notices moonlight falling through the window like an invitation.

These days, he is more inclined to close the curtains and share the solitary lamplight of his desk with a decanter of brandy, but as a youth, he'd never been able to resist a moonlit night. He would steal down to the beach, book in one pocket, pork pie in the other, sole witness to a world lit up in eerie whiteness.

Even on that awful night when he'd broken his ankle, and was sprawled on his back crying, he had still kept gazing at the moonlight on the sea. And of course, the times with Annabel – the two of them swimming in the glittering ocean, so light in the water he could lift her like a bride – what a miracle that had been, what a gift. How he misses her. His love. His wife.

He hears a crash from somewhere upstairs in the house. Probably Willoughby dropping another bottle of wine he hasn't paid for. Jasper opens his desk drawer, pulls out a hip flask, tucks it into his jacket pocket, heads through the Oak Hall and out into the night air. He walks along the edge of the lawn, lifting his head to look at the moon.

For the last few nights, whenever he's gone out to talk to the horses, he has been captivated by the sight of a huge moon rising over the trees that surround the house. A giant disc, toenail yellow, heaving itself slowly into the night sky. Such effrontery in its bare-faced blankness. A Hunter's Moon, the villagers call it. After the autumn harvests have been gathered and there's nothing but stubble in the fields, a full moon comes in November to light up all the soft scurrying creatures with nowhere left to hide. The predators given a night of their own. The last killing of the year.

There has been too much killing. Whenever Jasper looks out across the front lawn, he remembers the summer of 1914 when war was declared. The Chilcombe Mell men who had joined up gathered in front of the house before leaving for France. There was a lunch provided. Ginger beer. Bunting. All very jolly.

His father would have known how to talk to them, that half-proud, half-shy bunch, shuffling about on the grass in their stiff new uniforms. But whenever Jasper looked at them, familiar faces kept catching his gaze, distracting him: little Albert who brought the post; Tom Hardcastle, head groom and devoted husband of Ada the housekeeper; Frank and Clive from the stables, standing with their father Sidney; spotty Reg the blacksmith's son, and Peter, the youngest footman, still wearing his wire-framed glasses. The following day, they would all be packed on to the London train from Dorchester, off to begin the fight.

Jasper, too old and lame to sign up for the Big Show, was downright envious. It was sickening to be out of it, to be a civilian in wartime. It gnawed at him, this static uselessness. If only he could do something that counted, to prove he wasn't what his father called a 'snivelling hands-upper'.

He wanted to inspire courage in the men, so had scoured his well-thumbed copy of *The Iliad*, looking for a way to ignite the stirring emotions he experienced when reading about gallant Hector, stepping out from the walls of Troy to face the warrior Achilles, despite the pleas of his family. Jasper looked for a suitable speech from that moment, but found there was a great deal about 'perishing', which seemed less than apt. There were other marvellous sections though, which he rehearsed, quietly, in the lavatory.

So then Jasper: standing at the doorway to Chilcombe, flanked by servants, faced by soldiers. (Suddenly, a rushing awareness: hadn't he always imagined a moment like this? Hadn't he always been travelling to this point?) He began. ' "Without a sign, his sword the brave man draws and asks no omen but his country's cause." So said Homer and so say I.'

He heard rooks cawing in the trees, saw Peter the footman carefully taking off his glasses to wipe them, watched Reg turn to Clive and say, 'What's he on about?'

'Buggered if I know,' muttered Clive.

Jasper cleared his throat. 'One would wish to join you, of course.' (The disappointing sound of his own voice; the men leaning forward, straining to hear.) He tried again: 'Of course, one would wish to join you.'

But they didn't want to hear about him, it was their day. He knew that, damn it, he'd considered it in the lavatory. Then from behind him, a clear voice came ringing out, like a fork striking a champagne glass. 'Naturally, my brother Jasper wishes he could do his bit, but we won't need any help. The only people in need of help are those poor devils who will be up against us!'

Laughter, cheers!

'By God, I'm sure that each and every one of you will stand alongside me, Willoughby Seagrave, and do your duty, for King and country, and for Dorset, this beautiful county and her beautiful women.'

Knowing laughter, cheers!

'You know me, boys, and while we're over there fighting the good fight, my family will ensure your families are well cared for, as we have always done.'

Murmurs of assent, sniffles from watching female servants.

'When we come home victorious, we'll meet again on this very spot, and Jasper will be here to welcome us back.'

Cheers, cries of agreement!

'Won't be long, boys – because the Boche don't stand a damn chance!'

The red and white bunting flapping in the trees, the sunshine on the dappled lawn, the joyous faces hurrahing, Willoughby in his officer's uniform, opening his hands to them all, and Jasper standing outside the walls of Troy, knowing he volunteered for a doomed encounter because he was too frightened to be thought cowardly.

'What do you say, chaps, a swift drink before we go?' Willoughby cried, bounding across the lawn to join the men.

Jasper retreated into the house. He hoped there might be some apple cake in the kitchen. He wished he hadn't worn a ceremonial sword. It clanked awfully.

Albert. Frank. Clive. Tom. Sidney. Reg. Peter. Willoughby. Only Frank, Reg and Willoughby came back.

Jasper continues to meander across the lawn, drinking from his hip flask. He can hear the hush of the sea, the tremulous hoot of a tawny owl; all else is silence. He looks back at Chilcombe, sees the shadows of servants flitting past windows, doing Rosalind's bidding, no doubt.

Lamps are lit on the ground floor, but the rest of the house is in darkness. Jasper hears the wail of a baby high in the attic. He finds the crying of children physically painful. He wishes he didn't ever have to hear it. Beyond the house, there is the Ridgeway, implacable and unlit. Beyond that, more hills and more darkness and towns and cathedrals and England and so on, all piling up behind it.

He is tired. Gone at the knees. Holed below the waterline. The newspapers say 'war weariness' has drained the nation's collective nerve power, allowing deadly Spanish Influenza to spread. Appalling, of course, that so many are dying from it, but the thought of a feverish descent is rather attractive – a sudden virulent end possessing the body as swiftly and irrevocably as love. He finds himself to be a heavy load. A sandbag of a man. He takes a swig from his hip flask, ambles round the corner of the house towards the stables, stumbling slightly on the lawn edge.

It is a comfort to him, the rich hay smell of the stables. The snorts and snickerings of the horses. He makes his way to faithful Guinevere's stall, rubs her velvet nose. She'd carried him through every ride with the hunt. It had been on her broad back that he'd first set eyes on Annabel Agnew. When had he last ridden out with hounds? Why didn't he have that in him any more? Yet another thing put down somewhere and forgotten about.

He unlatches the stall, leads the horse out. Finds a saddle, a bridle, and clumsily puts them on, murmuring alcohol-scented apologies into Guinevere's twitching ears. He pulls up a stool, balances precariously on it for a moment, before heaving himself into the saddle, shoving his feet into the twisted stirrups. Best foot forward. Once more unto the breach. Off we trot.

Animal and man move ponderously out of the stables, heading round the house, through the trees, and down the path that leads to the coast. The night is frosty and still. The moon hangs low over the sea: a vast, pockmarked sphere. Jasper closes one eye and squints at it. It is the tarnished light of ancient metal, of fallen shields and broken swords. It stares him down.

Beneath the saddle, the shifting of Guinevere's bones jerks him from left, to right, from left, to right, as the elderly horse carefully picks her way across the hard ground. Guinevere knows this route well, so Jasper lets the reins drop, allows his bulk to be tipped inelegantly from side to side. He closes his eyes, lets his head tip forward, his body still jolting about, as if assailed from either side by invisible opponents. It would be bliss to sleep. His hands pat about himself for his hip flask and it is as he is doing this – this childlike *pat-pat-patting* of his own stomach – that Guinevere catches a hoof in a rabbit hole and lurches forward, pitching Jasper out of the saddle.

It would have been all right if he had been holding the reins. It would have been all right if he hadn't had his weak foot tangled in the stirrup, which meant that his body was swung downwards in a perpendicular arc and his forehead hit the ground first, smashing against a large rock with considerable force. As it was, his brain was severely rattled inside his skull and the urgent signals travelling through his synapses to warn him he was injured never reached their destination, and the crushed cells of his brain began dying in overwhelming numbers, flickering out like stars disappearing from the night sky, so his last thought wasn't really a thought at all, more a sense of something rushing past him, and an image he had been picturing in his mind in the moments before he fell, of a woman in the sea silhouetted against an argent moon.

Loyal Guinevere regains her footing. Snorts. Waits for instructions. When none are forthcoming, she continues on her usual route, following the paths she knows of old, dragging the body of Jasper behind her.

Maudie Kitcat's Diary

party tonight. all sorts arriving.

Mister jasper gone wobblin off on a horse. he's proper drinky. Mister willoughby says never be the most sozzled person at a party, unless it's an awful party. then he winks. Betty says to watch him he's a rascal. other times she says Maudie you watch too much. she should make up her mind.

winks are secrets. little hooks. there are clasps on Mrs Rosalind's corsets called hooks & eyes. that is winks. little clasps only some see.

grandfather told me servants in this attic used to wink lights off and on to smugglers. most folk dont notice whats under their noses. i can be at the window in nothing but my slip and none of them downstairs knows.

Mister willoughby winks to make me blush but i dont care. i do it too. winked at a village boy & kisst him in the woods. i am 15 tomorrow. got meself gifts as they wont will they.

one of Mister willoughby's hankerchiffs from the laundry basket smells of him
box of matches
glass marbel with bubbles inside

on my birthday i am going to kiss someone else. dont mind who.

ACT TWO

1928–1938

Whale Fall

March, 1928

She reaches skyward, feeling for a handhold. Beneath her fingers, the surface is smooth and slippery. There is nothing to grab on to. At roughly head height, there is a wooden tent peg she has laboriously hammered into place using a rock. It has a skipping rope knotted around it, which she grips and pulls, testing her weight. The peg wobbles but holds. She will have to heave herself up using the rope, then use the peg as a foothold to get to the top.

Before she commences her attempt on the summit, she looks out across the bay: a lively teal sea beneath a cloudless sky, with the Isle of Portland on the far horizon. After a night of thunderstorms, the air is as fresh as clean laundry. The chilly mist that has swathed the county for weeks has been swept away, lifting like stage curtains to reveal the coastline in its spring colours, the cliffs covered with yellow gorse, busy birds bouncing from bush to bush. An untouched morning: her dominion.

The sun has been up for half an hour already and interested gulls are appearing overhead, swooping and calling. She doesn't have much time. She adjusts the items strapped across her back, leans on the skipping rope and begins her ascent of the great mound. Best foot forward. Onwards and upwards. Near the top, the gradient levels out and she proceeds by dragging herself forward on her stomach, using her grandfather's ivory-handled hunting knife for leverage.

Finally, she reaches the peak. She eases herself to her feet, pulls a home-made flagpole from the bindings on her back, and stands on tiptoe in order to give herself enough height and momentum to plunge the sharpened end of the flagpole into the carcass of the dead whale, the leviathan that is stretching more than sixty feet along the beach, reeking of the dark green depths of the ocean it traversed, before a storm washed it up on her beach, where she could claim it for herself: Cristabel Seagrave. She lets go a mighty war cry, hears it bounce around the bay, the bay, the bay.

Cristabel stands for a moment, holding her flagpole – a sharpened broom handle – as the disappointingly shallow wound she has made in the whale's rubbery hide begins to ooze a clear liquid and a faintly bacon-ish smell. She looks back down the creature's curving spine to its flat tail. The night before, when she had escaped from the house to watch the storm and discovered the dead whale washed up on the pebbles, its dark skin had been as glossy as wet lacquer. Now, out of its element, it is starting to dry out: wrinkling, paling. She can see white patches of barnacles on its back.

There are a few small wooden boats setting off from the next cove, about a mile to the west. She can hear the faint creak and plash as the fishermen row out from the shore, their sounds travelling low over the water like skimmed stones. They will have heard her cry. They will know she is waiting for them.

From behind her comes the sound of someone careering down the steep path on to the beach. It is her half-sister Florence, known to almost everyone as 'the Veg'. She is out of breath, her round face flushed, wearing a dressing gown, one unbuckled shoe and an expression of high alarm. 'I came as soon as I got your note,' she says. 'Goodness, I didn't think it would be so big!'

The creature is a long tubular shape ending in an enormous mermaid's tail. It is slumped on its side, with one flipper the size of a dining table flopped uselessly on the pebbles. At its highest point, where Cristabel is standing, it is seven feet high, a dark grey colour fading to a pale cream on its underside, which has a curious pleated texture. Its huge head is almost entirely made up of its bottom jaw; the upper jaw appears only to be a flat lid perched on top. The thin line of the whale's mouth is downturned and a small eye, still open, is tucked in the corner of the mouth, almost as an afterthought. It is – thinks the Veg – like a giant button-eyed sock puppet, the kind she and Cristabel use in their cardboard theatre, and its great size makes its glum expression most affecting.

'How sad,' whispers the Veg, tears filling her eyes.

'Pull yourself together, Veg,' says Cristabel. 'He was dead when I found him last night, and he was still dead when I came with my equipment this morning.'

'He?'

'I don't know. Hard to determine. Where's Digby?'

'I'm here, I'm here,' and a slim, dark-haired boy in shirt, shorts and plimsolls comes scrambling down the path. He has a checked tea towel knotted round his neck that flies out behind him as he pelts past the Veg. He only stops running when he is at the base of the whale, directly beneath Cristabel, then gives an admiring whistle. 'What a beauty.'

'Isn't he,' grins Cristabel.

'It's like I'm having a dream, only I'm awake. A whale on our beach. Did you claim him, Crista? Oh, you did! You took the flag!'

'Remembered in the nick of time, Digs. Tell me, what's afoot back at the house? Are your parents awake?'

'The situation remains uncertain,' says Digby, who is six years old. He is Cristabel's long-awaited brother, even though he isn't actually her brother.

'I woke Digby soon as I found your note. We came as fast as we could,' adds the Veg, who is seven and a half. 'You're very high up, Crista.'

'There's some fishermen,' cries Digby, pointing out to sea.

The girls turn to look, shielding their eyes with their hands. The morning sun is sharp white light on the ocean and the fishermen approaching in their wooden boats are silhouettes against the brightness. As they get closer, they rest on their oars and push back their caps, squinting towards the children and the whale.

'What have you got there?' shouts one.

'A mighty leviathan,' shouts back Cristabel. 'I have claimed it.'

'Is that right?' There is laughter from the boats, which rock gently, waves slapping against their sides. 'Are you Miss Cristabel Seagrave, by any chance?'

Cristabel stares at them, holding her flag tightly.

'It'll start to smell soon,' calls another of the fishermen.

'That's my concern,' she says.

'We'll see what the Coastguard has to say about that,' comes the reply.

The Veg calls out, in her high voice, 'Cristabel found it.'

'Thought that was you, Miss Cristabel,' says the first fisherman. 'You mind yourself up there.'

Cristabel straightens her spine and nods: a mute acknowledgement. 'Decent sorts, fishermen,' she says to the younger children. She has just turned twelve; there isn't much she doesn't know. She has read nearly all the books in the house and learnt a great deal more from men such as these.

She likes fishermen, gamekeepers, blacksmiths, butchers. She enjoys both their company and their useful skills, for she admires things done in an adept manner, in the same way she covets tools that can be snapped shut and pocketed. When the local men teach her practical skills, like tying knots or baiting fishing lines, and she is then able to carry them out by herself, it gives her the same feeling as having said, 'Now, look here all of you, listen to me.' The feeling of having written out some rules and handed them round. The feeling of being up in front on her own, as she is now, high on her whale, looking down at Digby and the Veg.

But someone else is approaching. Mr Bill Brewer, Chilcombe's land agent, a former London debt collector, spotted in the Army Service Corps by Willoughby's friend Perry who has an eye for a useful man, and now ambling down the path accompanied by his spaniel, which begins circling the whale, sniffing excitedly. 'Well, well,' says Mr Brewer. 'Who wants to explain this to me?'

'Mr Brewer, I need you to alert the authorities,' says Cristabel. 'I have claimed a whale for the Seagrave family.'

'So I see, Miss Cristabel. Do you have any plans for it?'

Cristabel and Digby exchange glances. 'We will preserve it for the annals of history,' says Cristabel.

'We will make famous the name of Seagrave,' adds Digby, patting the whale appreciatively.

'We will examine its innards for science.'

'We will put it on display so all may come and wonder.'

'We will hang its bones from the ceiling of the Oak Hall.'

'Yes! We will have an enormous skeleton inside our house!'

'Forming an exhibit of national importance.'

'Poor whale,' says the Veg, under her breath.

Mr Brewer peers at the whale. 'I'm not sure Mrs Brewer will let you bring that in on her clean floors.'

Cristabel cautiously lets go her flag, relieved that it stays upright, then crouches down to hiss to Digby, 'He's not playing ball. We will need to alert the authorities ourselves. Can you run back? We'll have to send a telegram.'

'To who?'

'The authorities. I'll stay here. Stand guard.'

'Righto.' Digby sprints off, pulling the Veg with him.

The two of them dart up the steep path that leads from the beach to their house. It is – as the Veg has often observed – the kind of path you would be nervous about going up if you didn't know where it went. It has – as she says – a trespassy feel about it. It twists and turns its way up the cliff, with gorse and blackthorn leaning in from either side, tangling their spiked branches together, so there is no way of seeing where it leads.

At the top is an old wooden gate in a dishevelled hedge, with a sign that warns: PRIVATE PROPERTY. Digby and the Veg crash through the gate and run on, following the path through dense woodland. Branches snap underfoot; wood pigeons take flight from the bracken with a panicky flapping; swords of sunlight slant downwards through the trees. The woodland thins out as the path widens and becomes more established, leading eventually to the edge of a large lawn. The children sprint across the lawn to the front entrance of Chilcombe. They push open the heavy door and, turning to shush one another, step carefully through the entranceway and into the Oak Hall, where light from a new glass cupola embedded in the ceiling falls the height of the building and lands on the pieces of a broken whisky bottle a maid is on her hands and knees sweeping up.

'Leave it, leave it,' says Willoughby, walking barefoot down the curve of the main staircase, tucking a stained shirt into crumpled trousers. 'More bottles will be broken, I'm sure. Might as well get used to treading on them. Breakfast is the main thing. I am desperate for breakfast.'

'Yes, Mr Willoughby, sir,' says the maid. 'And your wife, sir? Will she be requiring anything to be brought to her room?'

'Rosalind has renounced all solid food stuffs for Lent. She is enjoying a purely liquid diet.'

The children watch as, on the gallery, a door opens, and Rosalind appears, smudge-eyed, wrapped in a peach silk peignoir. 'I can hear you, Willoughby. Your voice is very booming. I'd like tea and toast. You know I would like tea and toast. My cigarette case is missing.'

Willoughby, reaching the maid, stage-whispers, 'Bugger the tea and toast. I'd like my breakfast outside on the lawn. Can you do that for me?'

'My silver cigarette case,' calls Rosalind. 'The one you gave me.'

'You should check Perry's trouser pocket. You most certainly had it when you were sitting on his lap.'

'You made me sit there, Willoughby. You always talk as if you had nothing to do with anything.'

'I am in need of eggs,' says Willoughby, still addressing the maid. 'What's your name – are you Lucy or Elsie? I lose track.'

Rosalind pads rapidly down the stairs in her satin slippers, tightening the belt of her gown and saying, 'Lucy left months ago and there's never been an Elsie. Leave the girl alone. Whatever she's called, she's to bring me my tea.'

'Why your tea not my breakfast? What is it you want, Rosalind?'

She is next to him now and her hands are busy about his waist, pulling at his shirt, laying her thin fingers on the flesh of his stomach. 'I didn't hear you get up. I woke up and you'd gone. You left me there alone.'

'I'm fairly sure I'd performed my husbandly duty. I was hungry, woman. Still am.'

'Digby!' cries Rosalind, suddenly noticing the children. 'What are you doing? Have you been outside? What have you got round your neck?'

'A fine goatskin cloak, Mother.'

'It looks like a tea towel. Put a coat on. Remember when you had that terrible spring cold? You aren't as strong as your father.'

'His father is hungry and is going to eat eggs if someone will ever bring them to him.' Willoughby walks past the children, ruffling the Veg's mousy hair as he passes.

The maid darts quickly in the direction of the kitchen.

'Our guests will be expecting their breakfast too, Willoughby,' says Rosalind. 'How many people were here last night?'

'Seven? Ten? That dreadful woman with the turban definitely hasn't left,' he replies, his voice echoing in the stone entranceway.

'She's an American poetess. Much admired.'

'How unfortunate,' comes Willoughby's voice from the bright lawn.

Rosalind sighs. 'You could at least talk to her.'

The Veg nods encouragingly at Digby, pushes him forward.

'Mother?' he says.

'Yes, darling.'

'May I send a telegram to the authorities?'

'Is this one of Cristabel's silly schemes?'

'It's not a silly scheme. It's a matter of national importance.'

'You mustn't let her bully you, darling,' says Rosalind 'I know she's older than you but she's not your big sister – just a cousin. She's lucky to be living here, all things considered.'

'Crista would never bully me, Mother.'

On the gallery, more bedroom doors are opening, and more dressing-gowned people with bleary, bloodshot eyes are appearing. One of them, a thin man with a ginger moustache, is wearing a turquoise turban at a jaunty angle.

'Perry!' cries Rosalind, lifting her arms so that sunlight from the cupola catches her sleeves like butterfly wings. 'You are naughty. You should take it off before anyone sees.'

'A military man is never without the appropriate headwear,' he replies. 'My God, I feel rotten. I hope there's a hair of the dog down there for me.'

'Darling, of course. Come, come. We'll breakfast on the lawn.'

'Mother?'

'Ask Mr Brewer, Digby. I haven't time for whatever it is you're talking about.' Rosalind starts towards the staircase to meet her descending guests, then turns back to the Veg. 'What are you wearing?'

'My dressing gown, Mother. And one of my shoes. I left the other in –'

'You're managing to appear even less appealing than usual. Have Maudie brush your hair, what little there is of it.'

'Yes, Mother,' says the Veg.

Digby takes the Veg's hand, squeezes it, and pulls her away. They head through the hall and downwards to the windowless world of below stairs, where they run along a corridor lined with a row of labelled bells – DINING ROOM, DRAWING ROOM, STUDY, MAS-TER BEDROOM, DRESSING ROOM, SECOND BEDROOM, GUEST ROOM 1, GUEST ROOM 2 – two of which are jangling neurotically, insistently.

On either side of the corridor are storerooms, cold rooms, pantries, wine cellars. These underground caves are crammed floor to ceiling with produce: tins, pots, jams, hams, butter dishes, biscuit jars, smoked fish, cold cuts, fruit cakes, and bottles of champagne stacked in a rack, like a glass honeycomb. At the far end of the corridor is the main kitchen, its tiled walls hung with copper pans, filled with a great black range with ovens on either side, and thick with bustling staff and the sizzle and spit of breakfast: kippers, eggs, black pudding. By scuttling through the kitchen, the children can leave the house by the back door, which leads to a courtyard surrounded by brick outbuildings. Mr Brewer's quarters, where he lives with his wife and young son, are here, above the laundry.

'Mr Brewer has a telephone up in his office. I believe we could use that to send a telegram,' says Digby, as they arrive at the door that leads to Mr Brewer's home. 'Do you know how to operate a telephone?'

'No,' says the Veg, 'and we can't go into his office without asking. That would be burgling.'

'It's not burgling if we need to alert the authorities.'

'Need to alert them of what?' asks Betty Brewer, née Bemrose, opening the door. 'What are you two up to? Where's that trouble-some Cristabel?'

Digby and the Veg exchange glances; they are unsure of Betty's loyalties. Even now she is housekeeper at Chilcombe and married to the equable Mr Brewer, they suspect her first report is always to Rosalind.

'Good morning, Mrs Brewer,' says Digby politely. 'We're not up to anything.'

Betty frowns, hangs a large set of keys on to a loop at her waist. 'Don't have time for nonsense today. I've eight hungry house guests and their staff to feed.'

'Cristabel found a dead whale and we need to alert the author-ities,' blurts the Veg.

Betty adjusts her dress, shifts her wide, authoritative bosom, pulls the door firmly shut behind her so that it locks with a click, and sets off towards the kitchen with a bustling step. 'Miss Florence, I believe I said I don't have time for nonsense.'

Digby and the Veg look at each other.

'We'll have to go back to the beach and tell Crista we've met with unforeseen difficulties,' says the Veg.

Digby pulls a face.

'Come on,' says the Veg. 'She'll know what to do.'

The children set off round the side of the house, heading once more for the woods, but are interrupted by a statuesque woman with dyed blonde hair, in a patterned robe, who is striding across the lawn with a cigarette holder and a champagne glass. 'Oh, hi,' she says, her voice a curiously elongated drawl. 'Are you scampering squirrels the heirs to the estate? Can you tell me where I find the sea? I find it invigorating to commune with the ocean before I break-fast. I can sense it's nearby – there's a breath of salt in the air.'

The Veg points towards the path through the woods. 'That way.'

'I thank you. But tell me, why the headlong rush?'

'There's a dead whale and –' says the Veg, breaking off due to a nudge from Digby.

'You're kidding.' The woman has a long expressive face, both solemn and humorous, and appears to have drawn on her own eyebrows. She turns and shouts back towards a group of people gathering at a table outside the house. 'These children say there's a dead whale. Is this a common occurrence?'

Digby cries, 'Good morning, everyone. Crista has claimed the whale for the Seagrave family. There's no need for fuss.'

'Too late, Digby old chap. If there's a whale on the beach, it already has an owner,' calls a man in a turban, who is Willoughby's army friend Perry, such a frequent visitor to the house that the children know him as Uncle Perry.

'An owner? Who?'

'The King, dear boy. Anything washed up on the beaches of England belongs to the monarch by right. Whales, dolphins, porpoises. If they wash ashore, they're "fishes royal". A law that dates back to Saxon times, if I remember rightly.'

'Really truly, Uncle Perry?'

'Upon my word.'

The blonde woman claps her hands together. 'I will never tire of these eccentric English laws. Why would you even have a law about whales? Oh my. So beautiful in its absurdity.'

From the table, Rosalind calls, 'Myrtle darling, don't waste your time with the children, come and have breakfast. I want to hear more about this Russian you met in France.'

The woman glides across the grass, turning in circles, half-dancing, making the breakfast party laugh.

The Veg puts her hand on Digby's arm. 'You will have to tell Crista about the King.'

Digby turns his wide brown eyes on his half-sister. 'Oh golly, Flossie,' he says. 'She won't like it. Not one bit.'

On the beach, Cristabel sits cross-legged on top of the whale, holding the flagpole upright, while her flag, an old handkerchief bearing an inky version of the Seagrave coat of arms – a crowned lion rampant – flutters in the breeze. Her face beneath the straight line of her fringe is resolute, determined. The whale is now surrounded by curious onlookers, local fishermen and people from the village, who are poking it and exclaiming loudly, while children clamber up its tail and pretend to ride it. Mr Brewer and his dog are still there, together with a few more Chilcombe servants. There is talk of a man from the Coastguard attending, and possibly a newspaper photographer.

Digby and the Veg push through the crowds.

Cristabel catches Digby's eye. 'What is it, Digs?'

He shakes his head. 'Bad news, I'm afraid. Uncle Perry says you can't claim it. He says it belongs to the King.'

'Belongs to who?'

'The King. Perry says King George owns all the dead whales.'

'But it's mine. I found it. King George doesn't even know it's here.'

'Perry says there's a law. I'm sorry, Crista.'

'How on earth can there be a law about dead whales?'

'I suppose if you're King you can have laws about whatever you like,' says the Veg.

'That is the most damnably unfair thing I have ever heard!' says Cristabel, yanking her flagpole from the carcass and throwing it down on to the pebbles, where it is gleefully captured by Mr Brewer's spaniel.

Mr Brewer, calmly retrieving the pole from his dog's mouth, says, 'Not much in life is fair, Miss Cristabel. Will you be coming down now? Must be time for your breakfast.'

Digby adds, 'Shall we have breakfast then, Crista? Aren't you ravenous? We could come back later.' He leans companionably on the whale and peers up at her.

Cristabel closes her eyes and places her hands on the creature beneath her. She feels the spring breeze on her face, hears the waves hitting the pebbles. She is tired, dizzily so, after being up nearly all night. She lifts her mind above the babble of the people surrounding her, and summons the memory of early that morning, when she had first clambered aboard the whale, and it had been hers: something she had found and claimed. This hulking beast, her deserved treasure, now taken from her by ridiculous old rules.

She hears the Veg far below saying, 'We could dig a moat around the whale, Crista.'

Cristabel's eyes flick open, and she slides down the side of the whale, landing neatly on her feet. She walks swiftly past Mr Brewer and the gawping, slack-jawed crowds. The Veg and Digby run to catch up with her as she strides up the cliff path, her fists clenched.

She speaks without looking at them. 'It might be his, but it shouldn't be his. Rules should always be fair. That's the English way. I'm going home now because I am hungry, but it is still my whale. By which I mean to say: it will be my whale. I've merely got to figure out how, and if I have to talk to the King directly, so be it.'

The Arrival of the God Poseidon

March, 1928

The sloping ceilings of the attic give Cristabel an Alice in Wonderland feeling, as if she were too big for the room. Lying on her narrow bed, she imagines her legs growing until her feet poke out the window. It is sunny outside; the rooks are nattering away in the trees. She wishes she was on the beach with her whale. She wonders which foolish king made up the whale rules. She wonders about the man who wrote the Alice in Wonderland book. He can't have been very sensible either.

'Stay still, Miss Cristabel, for heaven's sake,' says Maudie, who is crouched at the foot of Cristabel's bed trying to lace her boots.

With her head on the pillow, Cristabel can reach up and place her hands on the ceiling, where it slants downwards to touch the floor. Both walls and ceiling have recently been covered with a bold striped wallpaper in red and white, patterned like a circus tent. It is, according to Rosalind, quite the latest thing.

Many things are now the latest thing. Cristabel doesn't care for any of them. The chromium bathtub. The glass-fronted cocktail cabinet. The blue baize billiard table. The giraffe-hide footstool. The latest things arrive at Chilcombe in crates carried by sweating delivery men, and there is a general flapping about, as if this latest thing will make everything different, but each item, once put into position and subsumed into the quotidian, quickly loses its promise. The latest things are not the latest for long. Whether too modern to fit into the ancient house or not modern enough to avoid replacement, they are soon items of dissatisfaction, receding into the background or seeming to find their own way out.

'Up you get,' says Maudie, now a young woman of twenty-two,

with strong limbs, thick eyebrows and a mass of frizzy brown hair barely constrained beneath a maid's cap.

Cristabel is pulled to her feet, straightened up and brushed down. Her black hair is dampened with water and briskly combed into its usual square-edged bob: a series of hard borders around her unsmiling face. Then she is forced to eat a bowl of gelatinous porridge before she and the Veg are sent along the attic corridor to the schoolroom for French lessons with their latest governess, Mademoiselle Aubert.

Mlle Aubert is the girls' sixth French governess. Rosalind is insistent they must have a French governess, despite their efficient dispatching of each one that comes their way. Although Cristabel will freely admit to hastening their departures, she is of the opinion that Rosalind's own erratic behaviour is largely to blame for the rapid turnover of staff at Chilcombe. Cristabel has heard talk below stairs of drunken displays, outrageous demands. The servants say Rosalind is spending every last penny of Jasper's life insurance on home furnishings and entertaining, but rarely remembers to pay their wages. Cristabel has said as much to Uncle Willoughby. 'Rosalind does not inspire sufficient respect in the staff.'

'Cristabel, sweetheart, you know very well she would rather you didn't call her Rosalind.'

'You can't honestly expect me to call her Mother.'

'I suppose not. Auntie? Don't glower at me.'

From her desk in the attic schoolroom, Cristabel can hear the steady purr of Uncle Willoughby's newest vehicle, a sporty Daimler, as it heads off down the drive. He will be out all the bright day, speeding through the lanes, the world turning away beneath him like a spun globe.

'Attention, Miss Cristabel, *s'il vous plaît*,' says Mlle Aubert, a dour young woman with a face dotted by dark moles. 'You will be leaving the globe alone. It is for Master Digby when he is learning the geography.'

Cristabel gives the schoolroom globe a final spin, watching as the countries blur into a multicoloured mass, dominated by the pink sprawl of the British Empire, which contains natives and tea plantations and ancient civilizations where Grandfather Robert suppressed uprisings and opened tombs and shot lions. Nobody ever tried to stop him from claiming his great treasures. She wonders if he ever had to reason with a king. Also: would it be possible to stuff a whale? Cristabel makes a mental note to ask Digby's latest tutor, who is rather a sissy but useful in terms of providing scientific information.

In the airless schoolroom, there is only the squeak of Mlle Aubert's chalk on the blackboard as she writes out the verb *être*; the buzzing of a bluebottle battering itself against a window; and the regular *bump, bump, bump* of the Veg's boot swinging against a chair leg. Far below, Cristabel can hear the opening and closing of doors as the maids go about their business. Somewhere else in the house are Digby and his tutor, endeavouring to patch up Digby's ragged education before he heads off to boarding school in September.

It is stuffy up in the attic. Always too hot or too cold. There is only one small fireplace in the girls' bedroom, screened off by a wooden fire rail where the children's damp clothes hang steaming, and faced by a rocking chair where nannies have soothed generations of fractious Seagrave infants, the runners creaking against the floorboards.

'Do you think we should rescue that fly?' asks the Veg.

'*Non,*' says Mlle Aubert. 'We are doing verbs until you can say them in the proper way.'

'Verbs? *Alors!*' cries Cristabel, throwing up her hands in a Gallic gesture. '*Pourquoi?* Poor *moi.*'

The Veg giggles.

'Very clever, Mademoiselle Cristabel,' says Mlle Aubert, examining her cuticles. 'Clever girl to laugh at lessons.' Phlegmatic Mlle Aubert is proving a formidable opponent. She has already outlasted all her predecessors, primarily because she has no desire to be liked. She regards any sign of friendliness as something of a weakness in those foolish enough to approach her pleasantly. Willoughby has observed that Rosalind has employed the only objectionable French girl he has ever met.

Cristabel says, 'You must hate verbs too.'

Mlle Aubert folds her arms. 'French verbs are simple. English verbs are difficult. If you had to learn English verbs, you perhaps have a reason to be complaining.'

'Why did you bother?'

'Because I am not a lazy oaf. You, Mademoiselle Cristabel, will be like the English ladies who go to Paris to buy fancy hats and shout at shop girls in English and do not hear when the shop girls tell them in French they are going to charge them double for their fancy hats. They do not understand because they were too lazy to learn their verbs.'

'I detest fancy hats.'

'But if someone is saying you have the face of the donkey, you perhaps want to know.' Mlle Aubert raps the blackboard. '*Être.*'

'What's donkey in French? Is it *baudet*? How do you say you have the face of the donkey?'

'*Être.*'

'*Vous visage de baudet?*'

'Without the proper verbs, your donkey insults will always be weak.'

Cristabel lays her head on her desk for a moment. Then, in a muffled voice, 'Very well. I will do the verbs. But only in order to insult people correctly.'

Inscrutable Mlle Aubert gazes out of the window, slowly rolling up an exercise book. '*Être,*' she says, then dispatches the buzzing bluebottle with an efficient thwack.

After many interminable hours, it is lunchtime. Over a tepid meal of stewed brisket and boiled potatoes, followed by milk pudding, Cristabel tries to engage the Veg in a debate about time travel. Could a scientific inventor create a machine using levers and clockwork that might return them to yesterday?

'I didn't like yesterday,' says the Veg, 'there were prunes.' Her round face is serious, frowning.

'I didn't like it either, but it would be in the interests of furthering knowledge,' says Cristabel. 'Imagine, if you went back to yesterday, you might meet yourself.'

'Meet myself?' The Veg looks alarmed.

Cristabel continues, 'Or you could go back to the time of the Saxons and demand the rules about whales be rewritten because they're unfair.'

'Enough nonsense stories,' says Mlle Aubert, who considers most stories to be nonsense.

'What's the French word for whale?' says Cristabel.

'*Baleine.*'

'What's the French word for injustice?'

'Eat your pudding.'

After lunch, the girls have their afternoon walk. Following Mlle Aubert, they make their way downstairs and through the Oak Hall, which, under Rosalind's jurisdiction, is now full of expensive fur rugs, curving armchairs made from cream fabric and bright inlaid wood, and circular side tables holding decorative lamps, magazines and ashtrays. The ancient brass candle holders have been removed from the walls and replaced by spherical glass electrical lights. Where there once were tapestries of battles there are now elaborate mirrors. The grand piano has been moved into the middle of the room and is topped by framed photographs of people in tennis outfits, alongside a fluted glass vase filled with faintly carnivorous flowers.

But while the space no longer resembles a medieval hall at ground level, its remote upper reaches, with their dark wood panelling, still retain an austerity. The daylight that comes in through the new glass cupola seems to take an age to fall on to the modern furniture, in the same way that a column of sunlight is slowed when it passes through the depths of the ocean, in the same way as a change in the law is stalled in its passage through the House of Lords.

Outside, it is a beautiful day. Mlle Aubert adjusts the Veg's hat to keep the sun off her face and they set out across the lawn: Cristabel leading at a martial pace carrying a bucket; the Veg tagging along singing to herself; Mlle Aubert bringing up the rear. They take a circuitous route, as Mlle Aubert insists they avoid the path that would bring them on to the beach opposite the rotting whale, because the sight of it makes her *seeek*.

★

The whale's stay in Dorset has not been an easy one. A few days after it washed up, a very uniformed official from HM Coastguard came from Portland to stand alongside the whale's head and announce he was annexing it for the King. But it soon became apparent – after terse telegrams exchanged with palace staff – that the King would not be collecting his newest acquisition.

The uniformed official then announced he would be auctioning the whale on behalf of the King. There followed some vocal protests from Cristabel, who was taken back to the house by Mlle Aubert, whereupon she began writing letters to the King, in which she compared herself to England's greatest explorer, Captain Scott, who had heroically fought his way to the South Pole, only to find that the conniving Norwegians had placed their flag there already. She received no reply.

Cristabel was disgusted to hear from Mr Brewer that bidding at the auction was lacklustre, but the whale was eventually sold off to a retired schoolmaster from Affpuddle for thirty pounds. The schoolmaster told the local paper he would display its skeleton in his garden and give lectures on the mightiest of God's creations. Carpenters were then brought in, with shears and saws, to debone the creation, and the Seagrave children joined a crowd gathered on the beach to watch the grisly proceedings.

It was an unnerving spectacle. Men in rubber boots crawling about on top of the whale, sawing their way through its sleek body as if it were a giant ham, its blood streaming downwards, staining the pebbles. However, it soon transpired that the retired schoolmaster had not discussed his ambitious plans with his wife, and there would be no new home in Affpuddle for the whale after all. The post-mortem was ceased and the men in rubber boots retired, grumbling, to the pub. Local boys were paid to transport any loose pieces of whale back up to the village in wheelbarrows, where the blubber was taken by cart to Dorchester market to be sold for soap, while the organs went to local hunts to feed their hounds.

Despite an increasingly gaseous odour, what was left of the partially dismembered whale remained a popular curiosity. Students of zoology visited and identified it as *Balaenoptera physalus*, a fin whale.

An older male specimen, far from its usual hunting grounds. They were puzzled by its unorthodox stranding but hypothesized that it was hit by a ship. Its ongoing decay had caused the whale's head to deflate and its jaw to fall open, revealing a bristly fringe in place of teeth. The students said this material, which resembled closely packed quills, was called 'baleen' and acted as a filter for seawater in the same way as a gentleman's moustache served as a strainer for soup.

The students told them strips of baleen were used to make the stays in Victorian corsets, and the children found this a delightful concept: to use a soup strainer from the mouth of a whale to tighten the waists of women. Old photographs of Seagrave grandmothers were now seen in a different light – beneath their high-necked dresses, they had mouth parts strung about their midriffs like cannibals.

As the students continued their explanations of the whale's by-products and how they have been integral to man's advancement through the ages, Cristabel quietly laid a hand on the side of her broken creature. With its small eye placed redundantly on the side of its bulky head, she couldn't imagine how it could ever see where it was going. Its eye was like a porthole for a passenger on an ocean liner, just a place to peer out at things as they passed by.

She dreamt about the whale almost every night. In her dreams, she was again the discoverer triumphant; the whale, whole and beautiful, lying becalmed at her feet. Sometimes she dreamt that her whale was alive, and she would ride on its back as it crested the ocean, ruler of the seas, rightfully resurrected.

Cristabel is thinking thoughts along these lines, about whales and dreams, when she, the Veg and Mlle Aubert finally reach the shore. They can make out the remains of the creature around a low head-land, half a mile away.

Mlle Aubert, the afternoon sun etching dark lines on her face, sits on the beach, leans back against a large rock, and closes her eyes. 'Find things to put in bucket, girls. Collect shells for Madame Rosalind.'

This is their chance. Experience has taught them that Mlle Aubert can fall asleep within seconds of closing her eyes so, if they go quickly, they can get to the whale before she wakes up. 'Let's run,' hisses Cristabel, discarding the bucket and grabbing the Veg by the hand. They put on speed, the pebbles creaking and twisting dangerously beneath their boots.

But rounding the headland, the Veg pulls Cristabel to a halt, because there are children climbing over their whale. Four or five children scrambling over its carcass like crabs, and they are naked as savages, their bare flesh shining in the sunlight. Cristabel glares fiercely at them. It is painful to see her whale commandeered in such a way, like seeing pirates aboard a British naval vessel. One of them squats on his haunches, balancing on the whale's ribcage, and glares back. They are all dripping wet, with dark hair hanging in strands around their shoulders, and they clamber about as nimbly as the famous Apes of Gibraltar.

The Veg, red-faced and astonished, whispers, 'What are they doing?'

But there is more astonishment to come. For at that moment, they hear a booming voice coming from the sea. A bearded man is standing in the surf, and he too is missing his clothes. He is shouting, 'It is divine, the water!'

For a moment, Cristabel believes it is the god Poseidon, come from the briny depths to take them away in his chariot, but she hears answering voices, and turns to see two women capering on to the beach wearing shorts and shirts. They are carrying towels and one of them has a hamper, which she drops with a crash, shouting, 'Not as divine as champagne, I'll bet!'

'Ha!' cries Poseidon, his deep voice bouncing off the sea. 'Very good!' He falls back, his arms outstretched, to float on the clear water.

One of the women starts towards Cristabel and the Veg, waving a hand. 'Hullo,' she calls. 'Not sure we've had the pleasure.'

The Veg is only able to squeak like a mouse so it falls to Cristabel to announce they are the Seagrave children.

'Do you live here?' says the woman, brushing back her hair, which is short like a boy's.

'We live in our house, Chilcombe,' says Cristabel.

The other woman calls over. 'Did the child say Chilcombe? Isn't that where Rosalind Elliot pitched up? Mother told me, I'm sure.'

'Rosalind Elliot? This far from London?' says the first woman. 'Inconceivable.'

'Darling, that's exactly what I thought.'

'What on earth does she do out here? Open bazaars?'

At the mention of her mother, the Veg finds new courage, announcing, 'Rosalind is my mother.'

'What a turn-up for the books,' says the first woman. 'We must pay Ros a visit. Find out why she's gone native. One can only imagine she'd run out of options.'

'You are wicked, Hilly,' says the other. 'As is the smell from that rotting whale, my God.'

'Don't stand downwind, darling. Come hither.'

Now that the women are closer, Cristabel can see they look almost identical. Both are slim and flat-chested, all corners and clavicles, with cropped blonde hair swept back from angled faces. Women made of straight lines, like the illustrations in Rosalind's magazines.

There is a crash as Poseidon exits the ocean, stumbling on the shingle. Much of his broad body is covered with curly hair; there is a line of dark fur running down his stomach.

'Halloa!' he cries, waving his arms in the direction of the Seagraves. 'What is these we have here?'

Cristabel is stumped, being unfamiliar with the protocol required to greet a hairy naked man. The Veg solves this dilemma by covering her face with her hands and saying, 'We are Florence and Cristabel. How do you do?'

Cristabel, prickled the Veg has answered before her, decides to look at the man's beard and nothing else. When she looks up in order to locate the beard, she finds it heading directly for her.

'This child has such a face,' says the man, 'I think for a moment Anna Akhmatova has followed me here.' He reaches out a hand, damp from the ocean, and it encircles Cristabel's jaw, like a bandage for toothache. 'I should paint you,' he says, and, for a moment, she believes he means to redecorate her, to cover her with glutinous paint until she is an eyeless statue. In the distance, she hears the plaintive mosquito-like summons of Mlle Aubert.

'We have to leave now,' says the Veg, from beneath her hands, starting to back away. 'That's our governess. She's noticed we've gone so you mustn't try to capture us.'

The naked man smiles benevolently and holds up his hands in an expansive gesture. 'It is always the way, no? As soon as we meet, we part.' His black hair is both swept back and receding, revealing a prominent forehead and dark eyes tucked deep in his skull. He has a boxer's square cheekbones and a bullish neck.

'I beg your pardon, but this is our beach,' Cristabel says. 'This is our beach and those children are standing on my whale.'

'That's your whale?' says one of the women. 'Could you do something about the pong?'

The other woman says, 'Don't worry, girls, we know your mother. We'll pop over for a visit. Ros will have kittens.'

'Won't she, though,' says the first woman, looping her arm around her companion's waist so they stand linked together. Behind them, the savage children bounce on the whale. One of them sticks out its tongue.

'Rosalind is not my mother,' says Cristabel, ignoring Flossie tugging at her sleeve.

By now, Mlle Aubert has rounded the headland and is fast approaching, her sturdy legs carrying her across the stones. '*Alors! Criiistabel! Floorrence!* Get away from the stinking whale!'

The man, who has picked up a towel and is wrapping it around his waist, looks up with interest. '*Bonjour,*' he cries, adding in thickly accented French, 'What pittance do they pay you to chase their children for them?'

Mlle Aubert snaps back in her mother tongue, 'Pardon me, but that is none of your business, monsieur.'

'All that much, eh?' says the man, still speaking in French. 'Ah, but it is a privilege, no? For a servant to chase the children of the rich on a glorious day such as this.'

Mlle Aubert approaches, out of breath. 'I am no servant, monsieur. I come from a good family.'

'I don't doubt that, mademoiselle. I too come from a good family, with a beautiful house in the finest city in Russia, and last year, my brother was driving a taxi around Paris while I made portraits of rich men's wives on the banks of the Seine, and neither of us could tell you if our parents are alive or dead. It is the way of these modern times, no? That we find ourselves here, washed up on the beaches of the English.'

Mlle Aubert frowns at this curious stranger who speaks her language, and reverts to her slow English. 'You know Paris?'

'As I know the bodies of my lovers,' he replies, also in English.

Mlle Aubert's frown deepens. 'It was my home.'

'Then we must talk together of Paris. It is the only city, is it not?'

Mlle Aubert folds her arms. 'For you, perhaps. No longer for me.'

'But why?'

Mlle Aubert scowls.

The man looks at her intently. 'Let me guess. Your family is not what it was. There were hard times.'

She nods.

He continues, 'Before then, a life of pleasure. A fine house.'

Mlle Aubert laughs bitterly. 'In Faubourg Saint-Germain. Fresh flowers every day of the year.'

'Faubourg Saint-Germain? And now chasing children. *Ach*. What terrible fate befell the house of flowers?'

'That, monsieur, is not your concern.'

'It is not,' he replies cordially.

Mlle Aubert's jaw shifts from side to side. 'Do not take me for a fool.'

'I do not.'

'The house was not lost from foolishness.'

'Who would think that?'

'My father died at Marne a hero. He never believed he would die.'

'Heroes never do.'

'Now my mother lives above a shop on the Rue des Rosiers. Takes in sewing. She is hopeful a wealthy man will marry her so our family may be restored. But she is old and ruined.'

Cristabel and the Veg stare at Mlle Aubert. This is the most they have ever heard her say. Previously, they have seen her as a solid impediment in an unflattering black dress, not really a person at all, certainly not a person with a story. How intriguing to hear of people living in fine houses in Paris, and ruined mothers taking in sewing, for France is a country they know only as the place where soldiers of the Empire bravely gave their lives in the Great War, and where Rosalind and Willoughby go to get away from the children, neither of which suggests any kind of native population doing anything interesting.

'The clock moves slowly for those waiting for the past to return,' says the man, and holds out his hand. 'I am Taras Grigorevich Kovalsky. It is an honour to meet you.'

Mlle Aubert, her eyes shrunk to assessing pinpricks, ruminatively strokes the mole on her upper lip, then holds out her hand to Taras Grigorevich Kovalsky and does not seem in the least surprised when he bends to kiss it. 'I am Mademoiselle Aubert,' she announces over his bowed head, 'Ernestine Aubert.'

One of the blonde women, seeing the Veg's wide-eyed expression, says in a loud aside, 'Everybody ends up telling Taras their life story, darling. Normally before they agree to take their clothes off for him. He's a crafty beast, you'll see.'

Mlle Aubert glares at the woman, then grabs the Veg's hand and marches back up the beach, saying, '*Au revoir, Monsieur Kovalsky.*'

Monsieur Kovalsky, the god Poseidon, the painter of portraits, the crafty beast, waves at Mlle Aubert and the Veg, then turns to smile fondly at Cristabel, and it is as if this smile were entirely usual, merely a continuation of a line of previous smiles. He leans down and nods at the whale. 'I have come for this creature. I want to paint a picture of it. You say it is yours.' His eyes are black and shining.

'I discovered it, monsieur,' Cristabel says.

'You have a claim to it.'

'Precisely.'

'May I have your permission to paint its portrait?'

She thinks for a moment, then says, 'All right then. *Oui.* I give my permission. But make those children get off it. They should treat it with respect.'

'It will be done.' He puts his hands together. '*Merci*.'

'*De rien*,' says Cristabel. 'I hope it is an excellent portrait.'

Monsieur Kovalsky turns away, saying, 'I hope our paths will cross again, keeper of the whale.'

Cristabel runs after the Veg and Mlle Aubert. She looks back only once to glimpse Monsieur Kovalsky drinking from a champagne bottle with his head tipped back, and the two women pulling off each other's shirts. Then Monsieur Kovalsky bellows at the savage children and they disappear from the whale as if blown by the force of his voice.

All through afternoon lessons, Cristabel continues to see Monsieur Kovalsky in her mind; she holds his image like a shell she has collected. Mlle Aubert – Ernestine! – is similarly distracted. Cristabel and the Veg catch her gazing from the window, humming an unfamiliar tune under her breath. She asks them to provide answers to the questions: *How far to the Métro station?* and *How much for the beautiful tulips?*

The blonde women had spoken of Rosalind and talked of visiting Chilcombe. But Cristabel will not share this knowledge, this possible meeting, with the magpie Rosalind, because Rosalind will want Monsieur Kovalsky and his strange companions to be her latest things. Rosalind with her cocked head, her claws. No, Cristabel will hold this treasure, this shining discovery, as long as she can. It is a seashell kept carefully hidden between her palms; the shape of her clasped hands like someone waiting to applaud.

Welcome to Chilcombe

April, 1928

It is too warm to stay indoors. Mlle Aubert has the afternoon off and is writing letters, presumably of complaint, so Cristabel and the Veg are walking up the chalk headland that marks the eastern edge of their known world: Ceal Head. This is a 500-foot-high outcrop at the far end of their beach that stretches out into the ocean, resembling the long-nosed profile of a sleeping dragon. The dragon's sloping flanks are covered with green and brown vegetation; patches of white chalk show through like old bones.

Groups of schoolboys sometimes visit Ceal Head to tap at rocks with hammers in the pursuit of scientific knowledge. The rock formations here are of interest to those with an interest in rock formations, and Digby's tutor. He is now – the tutor – rummaging at the bottom of the cliff looking for fossils: a bent matchstick figure beneath the chalk face of history. Digby is standing listlessly behind him with a bucket.

The Seagrave girls follow a curving path up Ceal Head, staying close to the edge, looking down on to the undercliff, a tangled strip of wilderness that runs along the base of the headland, where they can hear wood pigeons communing with their insistent *coo-coo-coo*ing and busy wheatears with their *snip-snip-peep! snip-snip-peep!* Sometimes they spy linnets, songbirds balanced precariously on the uppermost branches of gorse bushes, pouring out rippling music.

As Cristabel and the Veg climb higher, there are fewer trees lining the path, and those that remain are wind-bent and wiry. Trees in exposed locations do well to keep their sails trimmed, thinks Cristabel. She approves of things that fit their purpose. Looking behind

122

her, she can see a group of adults picnicking on their beach, a safe distance from her whale. Their beach is known locally as Chilcombe Mell Beach, but the Seagrave children do not know any other beaches, so have no need to name it. Cristabel can make out Willoughby and Perry. She does not care to identify the others. She wants to walk until they have shrunk to nothing.

'Quick march, Veg,' she says. 'When I was your age, I used to run up this hill all by myself.'

'That tutor guy, he's no slouch,' says Myrtle the American poetess, swirling her drink, and peering along the beach towards the scrabbling tutor. 'Rocks all look the same to me.'

A picnic lunch has been consumed, mainly by the men of the party, along with several bottles of champagne. More bottles are lolling half-buried in the shingle at the water's edge. It is a humid day, and the ocean is glassily still. The sky and sea are translucent grey, merging into each other at the horizon, creating a flat wall of sameness; there is nowhere to get to.

Willoughby, lying on his back in a striped swimming costume, says, 'Tell me, Myrtle, are you wearing gentlemen's pyjamas? Have you raided Perry's wardrobe?'

'She's far taller than me,' says Perry, swatting at sandflies. He is a lean, ascetic figure, gingery and pale, with the fine hair of a duckling and a slight whistle to his 's's.

Myrtle laughs. 'Willoughby, you're a tease. These are silk beach pyjamas. I acquired them in Nice.'

'When were you in Nice?' asks Rosalind, a soft voice from beneath a parasol.

'I keep a villa on the coast, so I go whenever I crave that exquisite light,' says Myrtle, her lengthy arms cantilevering outwards. 'But it's getting so crowded now. I'm considering Italy next. Somewhere less *en vogue*.'

Rosalind nods. 'Quite half the people in Cowes last year were foreigners. Where in Italy might you go?'

'Venice, Rome, Verona. My heart leads me, and like a dog I follow.'

'You must read us more of your poetry, Myrtle. Perhaps this evening.'

'You are too kind, Rosalind. I would be honoured to share my words with you.'

Willoughby rolls over, buries his face.

Reaching the summit of Ceal Head, Cristabel and the Veg look out at the sea. It is mill pond still. If they peer over the edge, they can look down on to a kestrel, and it too is hanging unmoving, close to the cliff face.

It is something though, to be higher than hawks. They can see for miles. To the east, the coastline dips and lifts its way into the distance; there are secluded bays and chalk stacks, and Cristabel has vowed to conquer them all, as soon as she is allowed to go further than Ceal Head. To the west, the view is less spectacular but more familiar. They spy the chimneys of Chilcombe and, scampering up the coast path towards them, Digby escaping from his tutor.

Beyond Chilcombe lies much unexplored terrain. On the far horizon is the seaside town of Weymouth and the Isle of Portland, tethered to the mainland by a pebble causeway and made (the girls mistakenly believe, after overhearing a conversation about the island's famous quarries) entirely of stone: a barren, moon-like place.

In the absence of any kind of systematic education, the Seagrave children's knowledge of the world has been patched together from disparate sources to make an occasionally workable Frankenstein's monster of information. They know the names of most butterflies (Perry); how to skin a rabbit (Maudie); not to eat blackberries in October when the devil spits on them (Betty); and the quickest way to the village pub (Willoughby). But they do not know anyone in the village (Rosalind thinks it inappropriate) or what it is like to live in the village (they only ever pass through it while fetching Willoughby from the pub) or what lies over the Ridgeway, apart from London, the King and a tea room in Dorchester, where Willoughby takes them for sticky buns on their birthdays.

As for the rest of the globe, they could tell you that France is across the Channel, along with the icy wastes of the Antarctic, the Wild West, and the Hanging Gardens of Babylon, but they have not much idea of what goes on there. Digby will occasionally pass on truncated lessons from his tutors, but these isolated islands of education are quickly forgotten; foggy outcroppings of Latin or algebra, uninhabited, left to the birds.

However, their sparse factual education has a hefty coating of fiction. Their most treasured possessions are their books, most of which were liberated from the study by Cristabel in the glorious months of freedom after her father's death, when everyone was preoccupied, and she had the run of the house.

As well as their beloved Greek myths and Henty adventure stories, they have a copy of *Alice's Adventures in Wonderland*, left by a departing governess, and the girls have been named co-owners of a *Tales from Shakespeare* and an illustrated edition of *The Tempest* that Digby received at Christmas from his mother. They use them to stage productions in their cardboard theatre, with a sock puppet cast, as well as acting out scenes in the attic, using a bed sheet pegged along a clothes line as a stage curtain. *The Tempest* always stars Digby as Ariel the sprite and the Veg as Miranda the romantic lead, with an impressive turn by Cristabel as Caliban. She enhances her performance as the grotesque slave creature by stashing walnuts in her cheeks to fill out her face in a bumpy and drooling manner.

'Hold your horses, you swinish lords,' cries Digby, as he comes panting up the hill to join them.

'You'll do well to keep a civil tongue in your head, you insolent cut-throat,' replies Cristabel, pulling a tall teasel from the ground and brandishing it.

Digby stops to tighten the tea towel around his neck. 'How dare you address valiant Robin Hood in such a manner?' He runs to the Veg and grabs her by the hand. 'Fair Marion! Come hither to the smugglers' path! We fly to freedom!'

Their most-loved books have been read so many times, they only have to look at the covers to know how it feels to be enclosed within them. But the worlds contained within the books do not remain between the covers. They seep out and overlay the geography of their lives. The children feel sure a cliff path on Ceal Head is one used by smugglers in the book *Moonfleet*. (*It starts where the undercliff dies back again into the chalk face, and climbs by slants and elbow-turns up to the top. The shepherds call it the Zigzag, and –*)

' "Even sheep lose their footing on it, and of men I never heard but one had climbed it," ' says Digby, in a fervent whisper, pulling the Veg along.

'I don't want to, Digby,' says the Veg. 'It's slippy.'

'Then stand sentry at the top and use your musket well, my girl,' says Digby.

Moonfleet, with its tales of maddened seas and ships dashed to pieces on a shingle bank, is also responsible for Cristabel's notion that the pebble causeway that stretches between Weymouth and Portland is the only thing holding back a storm-tossed ocean raging on the other side. She likes to imagine what might happen if the causeway were breached, how the waves would come roaring across the bay, a thousand-strong army.

On wild nights, she will go to the window of the attic, and say to the Veg and Digby, in a voice heavy with foreboding, 'I can hear the waves tonight. We can only hope the causeway will hold.' When she says this, she can believe it is true, and it is a terrible thrill that runs through her, a powerful excitement, heightened by the sight of the Veg shutting her eyes and putting her hands together to pray.

'You should try to sleep,' Cristabel will say. 'I'll keep guard.'

Digby will nod solemnly, buttoning up his pyjamas. 'I'll take the next watch, Captain.'

The smugglers' path on Ceal Head is near a row of red-brick coast-guard cottages, perched high above sea level, determinedly facing every weather front blowing in from the Channel. The retired coast-guard who lives in one of the cottages is in his garden, a pair of binoculars in his hand. He and Cristabel exchange nods.

'Spotted something might be of interest to you, Miss Cristabel,' he says, as Digby and the Veg come running to join them, Digby's cloak now tied around his head.

'What's that, Jim?' says Cristabel.

'Man with a foreign-type beard heading towards your house. Didn't look like your pedlar kind, but I ain't seen him round here before. Had some women with him. In trousers. Afternoon, Master Digby, Miss Florence.'

'Good afternoon, Jim,' says Digby. 'How is your wife?'

'Improving, Master Digby, and that's to be thankful for. What's that on your head now? You playing Crusaders again?'

'It's a masterful disguise,' whispers Digby.

'When did you see this man, Jim?' says Cristabel.

'No more than five minutes ago, I reckon.'

Cristabel glances back down the cliff to the beach. The adults are still there, sprawled like fallen bodies. 'I'm much obliged to you, Jim.'

'No trouble at all, miss. I was planning to show you them reef knots, but I won't bother you if you're going on now.'

'My apologies, Jim, but this appears to be a matter of some urgency,' says Cristabel. 'Come on, Veg, look lively.'

'Why must there always be running?' says the Veg. 'Why can't we ever sit down for a bit? There's a lovely sitting spot over there.'

'No time for malingering,' says Cristabel. 'It's Monsieur Kovalsky. He's coming to Chilcombe.'

'Let us away!' cries Digby, sprinting ahead, his every third stride a skip or a hop or a wild leap over a bush.

Down on the beach, Perry asks, 'Are those your children up there?'

Rosalind peers at the cliff from beneath her parasol. 'Hard to tell.'

'They're coming down that path at quite a pace. I think it is the three of them.'

Willoughby, still face down in the shingle, says, 'Come now, Perry – you know Rosalind only has one child. A boy called Digby. Those girls have nothing to do with her.'

'I confess, I lose track of which child belongs to who,' says

Myrtle. 'Is the younger girl yours, Willoughby? The smiley one? She's a peach.'

Willoughby gets up and begins walking into the sea. 'Fancy a bathe, Perry?'

'Love to, old chap,' says Perry. 'Insufferably close today.'

Rosalind says, 'Myrtle and I will go back to the house to dress before dinner.'

'I think it was the children, you know,' says Perry, standing up and brushing the shingle from his legs. 'I can't see them any more.'

Willoughby disappears beneath the water.

Halfway down the cliff path, Cristabel, Digby and the Veg take a sharp right to follow a short cut. They clamber over a stone wall and are dashing through the woods that surround Chilcombe, when they hear a distinctive laugh.

'Front lawn,' says Cristabel, breaking into a gallop. 'Monsieur Kovalsky is on the front lawn.'

And he is, entirely, on the lawn: sprawled flat on his back. The two short-haired women are at the outdoor table drinking and smoking, clad in matching mannish clothes: striped tops and wide trousers. Blythe, holding a soda syphon, is standing nearby with Maudie, wearing expressions of mild concern and intense interest respectively.

'Hurrah, the children are here. They'll vouch for us,' says one of the women.

'Master Digby, Miss Cristabel, Miss Florence, these visitors are here to see Mrs Seagrave. They say they have already made your acquaintance,' says Blythe.

'Terrific,' says Cristabel. 'They have. Thank you, Blythe.'

Hearing Cristabel's voice, Monsieur Kovalsky rises to a sitting position. He is wearing an open shirt and loose corduroy trousers. His bare feet are covered in splashes of paint. 'The child is here,' he says. 'The keeper of the whale with the Akhmatova face.'

Cristabel lifts her chin and walks across the lawn towards him. She extends her hand, and, when he puts his broad hand in hers, shakes it firmly. 'Cristabel Seagrave,' she says. 'Welcome to Chilcombe.' She has rehearsed this moment many times in her mind and it is perfect that it happens exactly as it should. It is hardly marred at all by the arrival of Rosalind and Myrtle, as, at the moment they appear, Monsieur Kovalsky is holding Cristabel's hand, and this means Cristabel – for all eternity – will have always known him first.

'Rosalind,' she says, 'this is Monsieur Kovalsky. He is an artist from Russia who has spent time in Paris, in the country of France.'

Rosalind, uncharacteristically flushed after the walk back from the beach, is momentarily mute. Then one of the blonde women shouts, 'Ros! Yoo-hoo, darling! Surprise!'

'Philly? Philly Fenwick? Is that you?'

'The very same,' says Philly, lifting her drink. 'Why don't you join us? I do believe you live here.'

Rosalind approaches the table, handing her parasol to Maudie. 'Philly, my goodness, how long has it been?'

Philly half stands to embrace her. 'Absolute aeons. What's that scent you're wearing? Mitsouko? My, that takes me back. You must know Hilly. Hillary Vaughan. She and I met at the Slade. Been insep-arable ever since. Philly and Hilly. Well, it just had to be.'

'Couldn't prise us apart. Delighted, I'm sure,' says Hilly.

'What brings you to Chilcombe?' asks Rosalind.

Philly gestures towards the lawn with the two fingers holding her cigarette, as if waving a smoking gun. 'We're with that disreputable wretch. Became entangled in Paris. Hilly was modelling; I was tak-ing art classes. Both of us heartily sick of the debutante life.'

'Nauseated,' says Hilly. 'Endless lunches where you do nothing but talk about lunches. All our lovers and brothers dead. What did we care for lunch?'

'He found us in a Montmartre nightclub dancing the Ki-Ki-Kari, wanted us to pose for him as twins. We drank fantastic amounts of absinthe and moved into his studio on that apocalyptic night. Quite the adventure.'

'We followed Dionysus,' says Hilly, her eyes on Taras.

'We followed a great artist,' says Philly. 'He's the genuine article, Ros. His paintings are like nothing you've seen. We're on our way to Cornwall. Thought we'd drop by.'

'Taras wanted to paint the famous whale,' adds Hilly.

'I say, it's delightfully quirky you still have a butler. An ancient retainer,' says Philly. 'Do you have a grotto too?'

'Taras? Taras Kovalsky?' cries Myrtle. 'Oh my! This is the Russian artist I told you about, Rosalind. Monsieur Kovalsky, so fortuitous to encounter you again. Myrtle van der Werff. We met in Antibes.'

Taras Kovalsky, who has been sitting on the lawn smiling at Cristabel, looks at Myrtle. 'We have not met.'

'It was a pool party hosted by a couple from Florida. You had a crowd of devotees, but we spoke intently about sculpture. Its elastic qualities.'

Taras hums a little. 'No,' he says again. 'But we meet now, on this green lawn.'

'I did a reading,' says Myrtle. 'A piece about a fisherman's net.'

'Myrtle is a poetess,' says Rosalind. 'Very acclaimed. We met skiing in Switzerland. She's reading for us this evening. Perhaps you could join us, Mr Kovalsky? For dinner and poetry. You too, Philly, Hillary. Nothing grand. Lobster salad. Scallops. A light *mousse au café.*'

Taras stands and approaches Rosalind, takes her hand in his paint-splattered paws. 'Call me Taras. I am grateful for your kindness. Today, I am weary. I paint, I paint, but nothing comes.'

'A good meal may restore your artistic vigour, Mr Taras,' says Rosalind. 'Do you enjoy lobster?'

'Whatever you wish to share.'

'Maudie, please inform Betty we have extra guests for dinner. Where are you all staying?'

Philly laughs. 'We're bohemians, darling. Gypsies. We've been holed up in grubby farmhouses.'

'We knock on doors to beg for rooms for the night,' says Hilly.

'Doesn't your mother mind?' says Rosalind. 'You'll stay here, I insist. At least for a few nights.'

'It's rather splendid actually, Ros,' says Philly. 'Once you learn to embrace life without fretting about money, you open yourself up to fate.'

'Even in the smallest of villages, we can find lodgings and a local woman to come in and cook for us. We want for very little,' says Hilly.

'There are always those who believe in art,' says Taras, as he lifts Rosalind's hand to his mouth. 'You are generous. I bring with me others. There are children.'

'We have plenty of room,' says Rosalind.

At that moment, Willoughby and Perry appear in the garden, with towels slung about their necks, followed by Digby's tutor carrying a bucket of rocks.

Rosalind waves a hand at her husband. 'Good swim, darling? We have visitors.'

'So I see,' says Willoughby.

Rosalind turns back to her guests. 'Shall we say eight o'clock for dinner? With poetry to follow. What a charmingly impromptu salon. Tell me, Mr Taras, do you ever paint portraits?'

'My subjects choose me,' he says.

'We have wonderful works of art here at Chilcombe. Perhaps I could give you a tour?' Rosalind gestures towards the house and Taras makes his way inside. She scuttles rapidly after him, saying, 'If you'd like to turn left, you'll find –'

But Taras is already across the hall and up the main staircase in his bare feet, passing the paintings that line the stairs with hardly a backward glance. 'Horses, horses, dogs. What is that, a boar? The English and their animals. It is unnatural.'

'I keep the more modern paintings on the ground floor, Mr Taras,' says Rosalind in pursuit, 'although there is a fine view of the cupola from the gallery. I had it installed. There's a zodiac motif.'

Taras pauses to look over the gallery bannister to the hall below, where the children, Digby's tutor, Myrtle and Perry have gathered. Willoughby has sloped off to the drawing room for a drink, followed by Hilly and Philly. Taras points at Cristabel, his downward hand as portentous as Michelangelo's God. 'Where do they keep you, child? Where do you and your French servant sleep?'

'In the attic,' replies Cristabel.

'The traditional family nursery,' says Rosalind. 'Tell me, Mr Taras, how do you know we have a French servant?'

'Children and servants always in the roof. So much revealed by what is hidden in the tops of houses,' says Taras. 'Cristabella, show me the way to your attic.'

Cristabel runs up the stairs and guides Taras along the length of the gallery, past the adults' bedrooms and Digby's bedroom, to where a wooden door conceals a windowless corridor that leads to a narrow staircase that climbs further upwards. They are followed by Perry, Myrtle, Digby in his tea towel headdress, Digby's tutor, the Veg, and a rigidly smiling Rosalind, all strung out in a line like mountaineers.

Up in the cramped attic, Taras has to stoop. With his broad shoulders and bare feet, he seems a giant at the top of a beanstalk, shrinking each room he goes into. The girls' bedroom, with its striped wallpaper and cardboard theatre, seems fit for a doll's house, while Maudie's room beneath the eaves, with a broken teapot by the bed to catch drips from a leaky ceiling, is nothing but a cubbyhole.

The children are used to visitors circling the interior of the house as slowly and respectfully as underwater divers, so it is exhilarating to see Taras entering the places guests never go, banging open doors without ever stopping to ask.

The door at the far end of the attic, which leads to Mlle Aubert's room, is locked and the space behind it is stiff with the kind of silence produced by someone standing still and listening hard. Taras noisily tries the handle, then moves on to an adjacent smaller door that opens on to a low-ceilinged storage space containing crates, trunks, suitcases and an ivory model of an Indian palace.

One crate has tipped on to its side, spilling out swagger sticks, scimitars and spears. Paintings and tapestries are stacked haphazardly against the walls, alongside cracked glass cases of stuffed grouse and quail, while the mounted heads of antelope lie on the floor, staring blankly upwards. At the very back, a stuffed baby elephant on wheels is balanced precariously against a Victorian child's cradle and, in a cobwebbed corner behind the cradle, there is a tower of books topped by an apple core, a notebook, and what looks to be a hand-drawn map, held in place by a turquoise stone figure.

'What is all these?' Taras asks.

'I don't come up here often,' says Rosalind, raising a handker-chief to her face. 'I believe many items were collected by my husband's father, Robert Seagrave, a great traveller.'

'Collected?' says Taras. 'As if all these were waiting about like baggage for him to take home. I suppose it belonged to nobody until the grandfather came to find it.'

'I'm not sure I follow you,' says Rosalind. 'Many of those objects are antique. They weren't lying about.'

Taras clambers into the roof space, knocking over an antelope's head on his way to pick up the turquoise stone figure from behind the cradle. There is not enough room for him to turn round so he returns backwards, like a large bus reversing, brandishing it. 'This – this creation – she is an Egyptian goddess to be worshipped. Who worships her here?'

'That's a goddess?' says Cristabel.

'Should we give her back?' says Digby.

'Is it valuable?' asks Rosalind. 'We could move some of the more valuable items downstairs.'

'You want it now it has a price,' says Taras.

'I don't know anything about its price,' Rosalind laughs, a dry, forced sound.

'If you're that keen on it, Mr Kovalsky, why don't you make an offer for it?' says Perry. 'You must sell your paintings, after all.'

'Money is the great destroyer of art,' says Taras.

'Is it?' says Rosalind. 'Many artists I know consider money to be a great gift.'

'A gift that gets heavier and heavier,' says Taras, who is tenderly wiping dust from the turquoise sculpture, a seated figure with the head of a lion.

'I'm sure every family has boxes in the attic. Family treasures packed away for a rainy day,' trills Rosalind.

'Are not most days in England rainy days?' replies Taras.

'This is all very fascinating,' says Rosalind, 'but I must speak to Betty about scallops. If you'll excuse me, the children will be pleased to show you about, I'm sure.' Her neat footsteps tap away across the wooden floor. The crowd in the attic pull back to let her pass, then gather in again.

'I say, Mr Taras,' says Digby's tutor, 'did you say that item was a goddess?'

'The Egyptians knew her as Sekhmet,' says Taras. 'Goddess of fire and war. She protected the pharaohs in battle and on their journey to the afterlife.'

Myrtle peers at Sekhmet. 'I have a similar *objet* from Dutch New Guinea. Primitive art is compelling.'

'I didn't know it was a goddess,' says Cristabel.

Taras turns to her. 'But you were drawn to her, no? You kept her in your place. That is your place in there, is it not?'

'What have you been doing in there, Crista?' says the Veg.

'Nothing. I go in when I want to,' says Cristabel.

Taras nods. 'The unconscious guides us to mystical symbols and we must translate them. Children have a powerful connection with this instinct. What else do you do in there, Cristabella?'

'Nothing. I draw maps. I write plays. Stories.'

'How long have you been doing this work?' asks Taras.

Cristabel frowns. 'It's not lessons.'

'You have begun the work of an artist. This is how it starts. Attics. Secret corners,' says Taras. 'It is your soul's work.'

'I'm not an artist,' says Cristabel.

'You doubt yourself?' says Taras.

'No,' she replies.

'Good.' Taras brushes dust from the goddess, then hands her to Cristabel. 'Keep this one. She has called to you.' Then he pulls himself up and announces, as if bringing news from a distant kingdom, 'I am hungry.'

There is a general shuffling about among the people crowded into the attic, and they are beginning to make their way towards the stairs – except for the Veg, who is squeezing herself into the storage space – when Taras turns back to Cristabel. 'Whose child are you, keeper of the whale? You are not of that Rosalind. I cannot believe that. And you are not of the red-haired man with the womanly mouth.'

'Mr Willoughby Seagrave,' supplies Perry. 'Your host.'

'My parents are dead,' replies Cristabel.

'I saw nobody like you in the portraits,' says Taras. 'Except perhaps the one with the rhinoceros.'

'Grandfather Robert,' says Cristabel. 'I have his hunting knife.'

'But he does not have your ferocity. Perhaps only a woman can have such ferocity. Where are the paintings of your mother?'

'There aren't any,' says Cristabel.

Perry interjects smoothly, 'Perhaps I can be of assistance. I believe the portraits of Annabel, Cristabel's late mother, were returned to her family estate after her death.'

'Where is her family estate?' asks Taras.

'It no longer exists,' says Perry. 'Cristabel's mother had two brothers, both killed in the war, and a pretty younger sister who went off to India to get married, so the Agnew estate went to some distant cousin in Suffolk, if memory serves. Heard he sold off both home and contents to cover some sizeable death duties. A sad tale, but not an unfamiliar one.'

'Nothing left for the daughter of a dead daughter,' says Taras.

Cristabel is staring at Perry. 'This is my family estate,' she says. 'Chilcombe.'

'Of course,' says Perry, then claps his hands together: the flat, single sound of an Englishman restoring order. 'I don't know about anyone else, but I could do with a drink. Shall we?' He offers his arm to Myrtle.

'It is hot as hell up here,' says the poetess, and the party troops off, leaving the children in the attic.

The Veg, cobweb-strewn and sweaty, reappears from the storage space pulling the stuffed baby elephant behind her. Digby helps her drag it free, then turns to Cristabel, saying, 'Did Mr Taras say your goddess looked after people in the afterlife? Maybe it came from a tomb.'

'Probably, Digs. Might well be cursed,' says Cristabel.

The Veg looks up from affectionately patting the head of the elephant. 'I am feeling mystically drawn to this elephant. Doesn't he have an agreeable face? I shall call him Edgar.'

Digby steps closer to his cousin. 'Crista, did you mind about Uncle Perry –'

'Uncle Perry knows this is my family estate,' says Cristabel. 'He was talking about another place, that I never even think about. I never even think about that.'

'You don't,' agrees Digby.

'You poor unfortunates might want to forget all about your mother,' says Cristabel. 'She's going to make a fool of herself in front of Monsieur Taras. You know she goes swoony for an artist.'

The Veg nods. 'She's always wanted her portrait painted.'

'We found him first, Veg,' says Cristabel.

'He definitely likes you, Crista,' says Digby. 'He wants to paint your whale.'

Suddenly, the door behind them opens and Mlle Aubert steps out of her room. The children quickly blurt out their obligatory *bonjours* and she replies in her brusque manner, then adds, with a sly expression on her face, 'You know, *mes enfants*, Monsieur Taras speaks good French. Perhaps you might want to work on your own lessons, *non*? Then we could all talk together. As a conversational exercise.'

Cristabel remains poker-faced until Mlle Aubert has left the attic, then turns to the others. 'Does your mother understand French?'

'*Non*,' says the Veg, wiping the dust from the elephant.

'So if we learnt French to talk to Monsieur Taras, she wouldn't be able to tell what we were saying?'

'She only knows the names of perfumes,' says Digby.

'*Formidable*,' says Cristabel. 'A secret code.'

'When did you find this place, Crista?' asks the Veg, looking into the storage space.

'After Uncle Willoughby married your mother. She kept throwing my things out. I needed somewhere safe.'

'Why didn't you tell us about it?' asks Digby.

'You were babies. Babies can't be trusted. Besides, every ship's captain needs his own quarters,' Cristabel says, before heading to her room to stand the goddess Sekhmet on her bedside table.

Facts Learnt by the Children

When They Creep Out of Bed and Conceal Themselves Behind
the Coats in the Small Cloakroom Behind the Main Staircase
in the Oak Hall During that Night's Dinner Party

1. It can be very warm in April, at night, if you are concealed behind coats in a small cloakroom.

2. Adult voices increase in volume after each course of dinner, apart from Perry's, which remains a controlled, level murmur: a calm river snaking through the mountains and valleys of conversation.

3. Servants repeatedly dispatched below stairs to fetch cigars, champagne and port can and do swear in many fascinating ways under their breath.

4. Monsieur Taras considers art to be the only sane response to an insane world.

5. Willoughby thinks this is absolute arse.

6. Willoughby believes that the finest minds were lost in the war. What's left, he claims, are the ridiculous so-called Bright Young Things bed-hopping around London wearing each other's clothes and buggering each other.

7. There is something called buggering.

8. There are Russian people called Lenin and Trotsky that Willoughby and Perry only ever refer to with the appellation 'that': 'that Lenin chap', 'that Trotsky fellow'.

9. Rosalind wonders if Hilly or Philly has ever met any of the so-called Bright Young Things or been to their parties.

10. In Russia they believe an empty bottle brings a curse upon your family.

11. It is possible to tell when Myrtle has begun reciting her own poetry as the poem will begin with three or four words proclaimed loudly and ringingly at the same pitch and pace, as if she were banging the words together: 'BLUE ATLANTIC OCEAN LIGHT', 'HEART BLIND, I STUMBLE', 'OH, THIS CALLOUS WORLD'.

12. Taras went to France to be a painter, as he could not paint as he wished in his own country. He asks his fellow guests to remember that they do not live in a country that regards painting as an act of defiance.

13. You can identify the owner of a coat by its smell.

14. Taras has a Russian accent, which means that he places unusual EMphasis on unexpecTED syllables while his vowel sounds roll and yaw. Some words are stretched almost beyooooooooooooond endurance while others are pushed. Out. With. Dis. Gust.

15. Rosalind believes it is wonderful England is a free country and wonders if anybody at the table knows how to shimmy.

16. Taras says that in England freedom is measured out in silver spoonfuls to those who can afford it.

17. The sound of breaking glass can, after a while, cease to be startling.

18. Perry wonders whether anybody ever wrote to Annabel Agnew's family, to let them know how Cristabel was getting on.

19. Rosalind believes Jasper was worse than useless at any kind of correspondence and that he was probably supposed to do it but never did.

20. Rosalind says if she could find a way to dispatch such an impertinent child to another family, she would.

21. Rosalind says she is joking.

22. Willoughby will not permit jokes at his niece's expense.

23. Philly keeps a little something in a cigarette case that peps people up if they start to flag.

Things the Children Would Have Learnt Had They Not Fallen Asleep in the Very Warm Small Cloakroom Behind the Main Staircase in the Oak Hall and Been Taken Upstairs to Bed by Maudie Kitcat and Mr Brewer Who Had Been Alerted to Their Whereabouts due to the Veg Snoring

1. Some dinners go on so late that, after pudding has finished, the guests can demand they now be served breakfast by shouting EGGS-EGGS-EGGS-EGGS.

2. Rosalind has spoken to Mr Brewer and arranged for Taras and his entourage to stay in an empty cottage on the edge of the Chilcombe estate by the sea.

3. Rosalind has not consulted Willoughby about this.

4. At the end of dinner parties, people start having the same conversations they had at the beginning, only louder and over the top of each other.

5. Willoughby believes that three in the morning is a jolly good time to take his new car for a spin and that a beguiling plate of eggs should go with him.

6. Sometimes adults will cry while at the same time saying they are perfectly all right.

7. Perry's full name is Colonel Peregrine Aubrey Blomefield Drake.

8. Servants can sleep leaning against walls.

9. After a dinner party, people will go to their bedrooms, and there will be successive rounds of door openings and closings: firstly, the brisk openings and shuttings of people efficiently using bathrooms and lavatories; secondly, the more subdued closings of people going into their bedrooms, locking their doors and turning off the lights; thirdly, the discreetly spread-apart clicks of locks carefully being unlocked again, followed by the creaks of doors slowly opening, accompanied by tiptoed footsteps, barely audible knockings, and a hush of whispered closings, and this third round of sounds will go on and on, like an echo caught in the corridors, all the way to morning.

Through the Bluebell Woods

May, 1928

April is blown away by another round of storms, thunder rolling about the bay like a wooden skittle ball, then May steps in with a curtsey, and Dorset blooms with a giddy enthusiasm, like a young girl at her first county ball spun about the dance floor by a strong-handed farmer. The hedgerows take up motion, cow parsley quivering delightedly every time Willoughby roars past in his Daimler; Chilcombe's horse chestnut trees gladly wave their ice-cream cone flowers, and the buttercup meadows are all swaying invitation. Bring a picnic, bring a rug, bring a lap to lie on, a head to lie upon your lap.

The woods to the west of Chilcombe, mostly elegant beech trees with a few oaks and pines, now stand in a sea of bluebells, a flood of flowers lit by sunlight filtering through new leaves. Here and there are clumps of geometric bracken and the white pompom bursts of wild garlic flowers, filling the air with their profligate scent.

The three Seagrave children, wending their way through the trees, find they are carrying with them a careful silence. It is mid-morning, a Tuesday in the first week of May, and since entering the woods, their conversation has fallen away. They are all listening, although they couldn't tell you what they are listening for. They know these woods well, but the bluebells have altered them; they now seem charged with a strange expectation, the kind of silence you can hear yourself breathe.

The bluebells go on as far as the children can see, and the lines of beech trees – both the vertical trunks stretching upwards and the diagonal lines of the trees receding into the distance – repeat and cross-hatch and overlap until it is hard for their eyes to follow them.

The vanishing point vanishes, the defined becomes the undefined, and the trees become an endless wall. They cannot see through it. That there is a world beyond the trees seems doubtful. There is only the wood and the stillness of the wood. Cristabel imagines Robin Hood and his Merry Men hiding in the trees; she thinks of the peasant warriors of La Vendée who could merge so silently into the bocage, it was as if they melted away.

They are making their way down a sloping path to an old cottage on the edge of the estate where Taras and his entourage have set up home. Betty has often warned them of the dangers of mysterious gentlemen found in fairy-bell woods, but they are going to meet Taras beyond the woods, and believe this will be safe. Cristabel is also largely unconvinced by fairy talk, particularly in daylight hours, though the Veg secretly hopes she will encounter someone magical – a Puck or Titania – and Digby would welcome anyone at all.

The children walk as a solemn procession in descending height order: Cristabel leading with a frown, the Veg twirling a spiral of hair, Digby casting his wondering gaze from side to side. The girls are in plain cotton frocks; Digby in shorts, shirt and tea towel cloak. All wear long greyish socks that have concertinaed their way down pale legs, and sensible lace-up boots. The Veg's straw sunhat has been pushed from her head and is hanging down her back on its yellow ribbons. Cristabel's hat hangs in a bush half a mile back. She has replaced it with a handkerchief, tied and knotted like a buccaneer. She carries with her a stick, for swiping, and her grandfather's knife, to score the trunks of trees.

Just as Cristabel starts to believe they will be walking through the bluebells until their dying days, she notices that the trunk she is scoring does not belong to a beech, but to one of the blossomy hawthorns that mark the wood's ragged border. The trio move into open sunlight with a sense of relief and a smaller, quieter sense of loss. The woods seal themselves off behind them. Cristabel, familiar with the shifting ways of trees, piles a few stones at the roots of the hawthorn so they will know where to go back in.

★

They follow a grassy path to the cottage, which has lain empty since the last tenants left to find better-paid work elsewhere. It is tucked into the curving arm of the bay where Ceal Head slopes down to sea level, a few hundred yards east of the whale. Honeysuckle smothers its porch, while overgrown hollyhocks and hydrangea cover the ground-floor windows. Butterflies sun their wings on its walls, while squabbling seagulls hop along the roof, yanking straw from the thatch. It is a house of flora and fauna; half consumed, half alive.

Facing the cottage is an old stone barn with a thatched roof and wooden doors. The doors are currently open, revealing Taras, barefoot in stained overalls, holding a palette and painting animatedly on a three-foot canvas propped against an upended lobster pot. The children can make out either Hilly or Philly swathed in a sheet and reclining on hay bales in the shady interior.

The space between the barn and the cottage is repeatedly crisscrossed by the savage children they saw on the beach, who are now wearing a disparate selection of adult clothes – an embroidered blouse, a waistcoat, rubber fishing boots – and shouting at each other in a mixture of French and other unknown languages. A dark woman in a headscarf occasionally appears from the cottage to shout at the children and shake a mop at them, like an angry cuckoo from a clock, and every now and again, Taras turns to bellow at them in Russian. It is during one of these outbursts that he notices the Seagraves.

'Ah, Cristabella! Have you come to save me from these terrible people who do not know how to close their mouths when a great artist is working?' he says.

On his canvas, the children can see a rough figure and green hills, as simple as hills drawn by a child, one curved line on top of another. Everything is cheerfully coloured and flattened out. It is not at all like the paintings that hang in Chilcombe, with their muscular horses and epic horizons.

Cristabel moves closer, pulling off her handkerchief headpiece and nodding to the savages. One of the smallest – a girl, she thinks – smiles back and is consequently thumped on the arm by a larger one sprinting past. The child stops smiling but does not cry.

'Gosh, that must have hurt,' says the Veg, wincing. 'I don't think they have a nanny.'

'That one's got a toad,' says Digby.

'They are playing. It is a fairy story, I cannot remember,' says Taras. He shouts in Russian, and the children run off to the beach.

'We pretend like that,' says Digby. 'Pretending is my favourite thing to do.'

'All children love the theatre,' says Taras, swiping his paintbrush across the canvas.

'We've never been to an actual theatre, Mr Taras,' says the Veg, 'but we have a very good cardboard one.'

Taras nods. 'In Paris, I painted stage sets in the theatres for bread money. Lies! I painted for wine money. Then I would hide in the wings to watch the performance.'

'You painted stage sets?' says Cristabel, then turns to Digby with her eyebrows raised.

Digby searches her expression until he sees something that makes him nod very fast.

Cristabel turns back to Taras and says in a voice slightly louder than her own, 'We've often talked about putting on a real play here at Chilcombe. There's been many expressions of interest.'

'Ever so many,' adds Digby.

Cristabel continues, 'But it has been hard to find a suitable scenery painter. Here. In the rural countryside.'

A corner of Taras's beard twitches. 'You are thinking that perhaps I could paint sets for you?'

'Oh, let's put on a play,' calls the model in the barn. 'It would be a hoot.'

'Theatre is not, as you say, a hoot. It is an art,' says Taras.

'I would die to be in a real play, Mr Taras,' says Digby, hopping with excitement.

'Mother would adore it if we did a play that everyone came to see,' says the Veg.

Taras smiles. 'Clever Miss Florence, you are correct. The lady Rosalind has taken me in like a stray tommy-cat in the hope that great art will happen. We cannot disappoint her.'

Philly – for it is Philly wrapped in a sheet on the hay bales – calls, 'What a jolly troupe we shall be! I've always wanted to play the Dane.'

Hilly, who has emerged from the cottage wearing a man's shirt, hands Taras a drink and says in her cool voice, 'The Dane? Or a pantomime dame?'

'No whispering, darling,' calls Philly, adjusting her sheet.

'Because Philippa Fenwick never whispers, does she?' says Hilly.

'Enough,' says Taras sternly, though he has his arm about Hilly's waist and is patting her fondly with the hand that still holds a paintbrush. Behind them, the mop-wielding woman hurls a bucket of dirty water into a hydrangea.

Hilly says, 'I rather suspect Rosalind will want to be centre stage once she hears there's a show on.'

'Rosalind can't act,' says Cristabel.

'Oh, I think she can,' replies Hilly.

'What play shall we do, Taras?' calls Philly. '*Romeo and Juliet*?'

Taras faces the children. 'Cristabella, tell me. Do you have a favourite story? One you tell yourself in bed at night. I was a lonely child in an attic. I know how it is to tell yourself stories.'

Cristabel doesn't hesitate. '*The Iliad*. I tell it to Digby and the Veg too.'

'Perfect,' says Taras. 'We will create for you a Troy and a wooden horse for you to hide inside.'

Cristabel is so pleased by this development that she manages to stop herself from reminding Taras that the Trojan horse doesn't actually appear in *The Iliad*, it is in Homer's other great work, *The Odyssey*, but she cannot *not* say anything at all, so she steps briefly to one side and issues the correction to a confused Veg in a low voice.

'The wooden horse what?' says the Veg.

'There is a big picture of a horse on a hill not far from here,' Digby is saying to Taras, 'it's made from chalk. They made it for the King. But the King was cross because they did him riding away from the seaside when he should have been riding towards it. So the poor man that drew the horse hanged himself from a tree.'

'Betty says he haunts the woods to this day,' adds the Veg.

Taras laughs, a noise like the booming of a bull seal. 'Artists and patrons. It does not always end well. Let us try not to displease the lady Rosalind. I do not wish to swing from trees.' He turns to his canvas and paints a swift outline of a horse on one of the hills. The children are delighted to see their conversation so casually included in his work.

'We will work like billy-o on the show, Mr Taras,' says Cristabel, turning her hands to fists and placing them stoutly on her hips.

'What fun,' says Hilly, her voice flat as a pond.

Philly heaves herself up from the hay bales. 'Hilly, do you have a ciggie? I'm all out.'

Taras turns, waving his brush. 'I do not release you,' he shouts, '*back, back, back, back, back, back, back!*' His voice is so loud it makes the children jump, but they have never seen an artist at work before, and assume it is part of the process.

Taras then returns to jabbing at his canvas, as if the children were no longer there. His lack of interest in them means they can examine him properly, their first real artist. From the front, he is commanding: black eyes, dramatic beard. But from the back, he is workmanlike and oblong. There is a weightiness about him, an accumulation of meat over muscle, and his hefty arms hang like joints in a butcher's window. If the front of Taras is the artist-entertainer, the back reveals the lifter-labourer – the graft behind the artistry. The combination is something akin to a circus strongman.

The Veg points at the painting, whispers, 'Is it meant to be Miss Philly? It hasn't got legs.'

Taras says, 'You want legs? A machine can do legs. Art comes from within. From dreams.'

' "We are such stuff as dreams are made on," ' quotes Cristabel.

Taras nods. 'You have it. These others? *Psh.* Now I must work.' He flaps a hand at them.

Cristabel accepts the dismissal and walks away, Digby and the Veg following. She is glad to be on the move as the idea of doing a real play of *The Iliad* is an expanding bubble of excitement in her chest and she wants to take it away before anyone can burst it.

Up until now, she has had limited resources when putting on

plays. Only socks, bits of cardboard, and the Veg and Digby, occasionally supplemented by pliable servants or Betty and Mr Brewer's young son, a solid child who looks so like Mr Brewer they call him Small Bill, and who, being preoccupied with boxing techniques and knocking things over, is not much use. She and Digby have long talked about putting on a show one day, but she had never imagined it happening at Chilcombe, with a real artist and a real cast with adults in it. It is as if her private imaginings have inflated and burst their way free from the attic, like Alice in Wonderland after drinking a potion.

As they head into the woods, Cristabel's mind turns to the savages, their unruliness, how the older one had whacked the younger one. She would never hit a girl. Not even the Veg. But she appreciated the effectiveness of the blow. There was a fierceness about the savages she rather admired, and she would need ferocious warriors in *The Iliad*. She would need warriors and gods and spears and shields and bravery and betrayal and cowardice and loyalty. Cristabel looks into the bluebell woods, senses their humming vibrancy, the silent drawing back of quivering bowstrings. These she will bring forward. These will be on her side.

Two weeks later, and at the end of a sun-filled alcoholic afternoon, Rosalind and Myrtle are following the same path through the bluebells.

'My word, this is idyllic,' says Myrtle, swaying along in a straw sunhat, her American voice astonishingly loud in the hushed woods.

'My shoes are ruined,' says Rosalind.

Myrtle sighs – a great prairie wind through the trees – and says, 'If I lived here, I would walk these woods in the moonlight. With a lover.'

'Walk about at night?'

'Did your handsome husband never lead you into the woods, Rosalind? In the halcyon days before he was your husband. Spill a little.'

Rosalind shakes her head, wrapping a shawl about herself. 'There weren't any woods. It was simply something that happened. We turned to one another for comfort, after the death of my first husband. Like many do.'

'Death inspiring the sex impulse. How very Freudian.'

'Most things are, I'm told. Although Willoughby wouldn't have any of that.'

'Willoughby who married his brother's widow,' says Myrtle.

The two women are one behind the other. Rosalind leading, head bowed, dropping her conversation towards her feet; Myrtle following, chin lifted, letting her words rise.

'Sometimes I think he believes I arranged it all,' says Rosalind. 'Isn't that ludicrous?'

'How so?'

'We had been together, he and I. The night of the accident. It was Willoughby's birthday. There were silly games. But I certainly didn't intend it.'

'You woke from your widow's grief to find Willoughby – and to find him beautiful,' says Myrtle. 'He is rather beautiful. That flaming hair.'

Rosalind smiles automatically. She often receives praise from women on behalf of her husband, like diplomatic gifts. 'Do you think so? You wouldn't be the first.' She pulls at a tree branch, then adds, 'It wasn't solely grief, you know. There was an understanding between us. Before.'

'Before? You surprise me.'

'I'm sure I don't. You've been to all sorts of funny places.'

Myrtle laughs, lifting one hand so the bangles on her arm rattle downwards.

Rosalind continues, 'You think me inhibited because I don't talk about – shall we say, "intimate relations" – the way you do. Don't you find it rather spoils it, if you're always examining everything and having discussions?'

'*Au contraire*. I find the mystery only deepens.'

They walk in silence for a while, then Myrtle says, 'You're so alone with yourself here. In the city, everything distracts. But in the country? Listen. Nothing. Only your heart. And all its attendant terrors.'

'It can be very quiet.'

'I'm telling you, Rosalind, spend a weekend at an English country house and you die a thousand deaths. The longest hours of your life spent sitting waiting for someone to bring you a cocktail. Of course, when they finally do arrive, holding your drink and wearing a well-cut Savile Row suit, you fall desperately in love with them. Because what else is there to do? Why else do we go to these big houses with their infinite lawns? All these perfectly manicured empty spaces – they demand we find some way to fill them, some meaning to justify the empty hours.'

'It did feel empty here. After the accident. Willoughby couldn't get away fast enough.'

'Men do like to leave at speed.'

'He bought himself an aeroplane. Vanished for weeks. Couldn't bear the thought of being trapped at Chilcombe. I couldn't either. But I had no choice.'

Myrtle picks a bluebell, tucks it behind her ear. 'What brought him back? Willoughby the runaway brother.'

'I sent him a telegram. We were to have a son.'

'Digby.'

'I knew it would be a son. Willoughby says I couldn't possibly. But I did.'

'A changeling child. Those innocent eyes.'

'I gave him a son and heir. The Seagrave line would continue. There was no reason at all for him to be cold with me.'

'They don't always need a reason,' says Myrtle. 'I got married once. Isn't that comical? He was a writer. We met in Greenwich Village. Married soon as we could.'

'I didn't know that.'

'I went home to Boston to tell my parents, to break my daddy's heart. When I came back and walked into our apartment, I was crying my eyes out. I so wanted to be embraced but my new husband didn't even look up. Simply held out a dirty coffee cup and said, "Be a dear."'

'What did you do?'

'I went into the kitchen and washed it.'

'I rather thought you were going to say you left him.'

'Three years later, I did,' says Myrtle. 'Love is stubborn.'

'What do you mean?'

'I mean, even when you're standing in the rubble, you can usually convince yourself it's habitable, that with a good rug you could make it homely,' Myrtle laughs. 'We're still married, but I don't often disclose it. Men treat you differently if they know.'

'I try not to talk about money,' says Rosalind. 'It makes every-thing unpleasant. Willoughby doesn't like to think his money is actually mine.'

'Is it?'

'It's Jasper's life insurance and my inheritance. But he's my hus-band, so of course it's his.'

A pause in the conversation. The stillness of the woods swallow-ing all sound. The silence a kind of erasure. When the women look behind themselves, the path has vanished.

'Chilcombe is hardly my native milieu, but I do my best,' says Rosalind. 'He doesn't even notice.' A bramble catches her hem. Tugging it free, she wobbles forward in her delicate shoes, saying, 'I hope this won't end up in a poem, Myrtle. You could leave things out though. If you were to write about me.'

'Peregrine said much the same yesterday. That he liked poetry, but he preferred it without people. Landscapes not portraits.'

'Do you like Perry? He's ever so rich.' Rosalind flicks a quick look over her shoulder.

Myrtle pulls herself up to her full height. 'Darling, I'm ever so rich. My daddy didn't work all his life for nothing. I might have dis-appointed him, but I'm still his little girl.'

The women find a scene of bustling industry. Hilly and Philly have propped pieces of hardboard against the barn wall and are painting them to look like castle ramparts. The woman in the headscarf is sitting in the cottage porch sewing a long gown. Taras is in the mid-dle talking animatedly to Cristabel. He sees Rosalind and throws his arms wide. 'Ah! Never let it be said that the gods do not listen. Per-haps we will have a Helen.' Even from a distance of twenty yards, Rosalind can hear Cristabel sigh.

'Do you need some assistance?' says Rosalind, walking towards him. 'How fortuitous. That's why we're here.'

'Eager beaver volunteers,' says Myrtle, with a Boy Scout's salute.

Cristabel, who is wearing a sheep's wool beard, beckons Taras. He leans down to confer with her, stroking his own beard thoughtfully.

Rosalind feels the tight annoyance she knows as Cristabel rising in her chest. 'Is something the matter?'

Taras says, 'Cristabel says you can play Helen, but you will not need to learn any lines. She says you are to be a mute witness to bloody scenes of horror that you have brought about.'

'I assumed you would be overseeing the production, Mr Taras,' says Rosalind.

The Veg appears at Rosalind's side with a pillowcase belted around her middle. 'Are you to be Helen, Mother? Her face sank a thousand ships! Cristabel is Zeus. I'm Hector.'

'A man?' asks Rosalind, caught between her usual disparagement of her daughter and her keenness that her daughter should not reflect badly on her. 'What about you, Mr Taras? What part do you play?'

'Achilles. I come to burn the city. Inside the walls, Helen hides with her lover Paris.'

'Who's Paris?' asks Rosalind.

Taras points to the beach, where Digby, in shorts and a paper crown, is pacing to and fro, occasionally stopping to gesture. 'Et voilà. The boy prince, learning his lines.'

'Isn't he a little young?' says Rosalind.

'It is perfect,' replies Taras. 'Everything is said by the portrayal of Paris as a child of privilege.'

'Inspired,' murmurs Myrtle.

Philly steps forward, waving her cigarette. 'I'm the Greek soldiers, darling. We're very cross about the whole thing. Hilly is the Trojans. All besieged and moany. Typical Hilly. We're going to have identical costumes in different colours. Little tunics. Up to here.'

'Identical because there are no differences in war,' says Hilly. 'All sides equal in their futility. Particularly Philly's.'

'Is the play set in Greece?' asks Rosalind.

'Almost, darling. Thereabouts.'

'So my costume could be something flowing, in white or cream,' says Rosalind. 'Like in the paintings. Which reminds me, how is your art coming along, Mr Taras? I hope this isn't distracting you.'

Philly exhales a plume of smoke. 'His art is going marvellously, Ros. He has a new model. Apparently, she's the cat's meow.'

'Gosh, who's that?'

Taras rubs at the corner of his mouth. 'Ernestine has been kind enough to sit for me. Work is – it is progressing. It is work. It is slow.'

'Who is Ernestine?' asks Rosalind.

'Mademoiselle Aubert,' says the Veg. 'We all practise our French together.'

'Mademoiselle Aubert!' says Rosalind. 'I'm not paying her to have her portrait painted. Is she here?'

'You can't really tell it's her in the painting,' adds the Veg. 'It's all pink.'

'Hardly appropriate,' says Rosalind, and her hands lift to pat her newly shingled hair.

'We talk of Paris,' says Taras. 'The tree-lined boulevards. As we talk, I see it again. *Je reviens.*'

'Do you have any other models in mind?' says Rosalind. Again, the hands lift and pat.

'They choose me,' he says, and walks away.

Rosalind has a powerful urge to run after him and push him over, send him scrabbling on to the dusty floor of the barn, and to rip the paint-stained shirt from his back.

'We're rehearsing tomorrow, Mother,' says the Veg, 'I could go through the script with you.'

'I don't need help,' says Rosalind. 'Bring it to me. I'll look at it.'

Taras's voice comes from inside the barn. 'The giantess can be Ajax.'

'Guess that's me,' says Myrtle.

Cristabel nods. 'Ajax has a shield made of seven cow skins.'

'Who doesn't?' says Myrtle. 'My, would you look at that incandescent sky!'

Rosalind deploys her automatic smile, casting it blindly about herself. 'You must all come for drinks soon. We can play boules on the lawn.' Then she turns and heads back along the grassy path. She can hear Myrtle rhapsodizing, the insinuating murmurs of Hilly and Philly, and the children's babble. She enters the wood. Leaves them all behind.

Rosalind Seagrave walks through the dappled trees. The sunlight has stretched across the woodland floor throughout the day, across the celandines, anemones and dog violets. And this light will go on into the night, because the sky, on these shining spring days, does not want to go black. Even after the sun has gone, there remains a strip of amber across the horizon, and above that, a pale wash reaching upwards to a band of aqua and above that, a deep blue that is the colour of the very edge of space, and then and only then, high up and forgotten, the indigo black of the night sky, waiting in the wings, carefully holding the golden bauble of envious Venus.

Black Flag

May, 1928

The evening is mild, a fuzz of soft greys and greens. Mist has sidled in from the sea and draped itself across the hilltops, cutting Chilcombe off from the rest of the world. It is gone nine when Cristabel steals out of the attic. The adults have left for a party in Somerset, leaving the house to those who are confined to it: servants and children. Nobody is eating or drinking or making demands, so most of the servants are asleep in their beds or playing cards by candlelight down in the kitchen.

Cristabel creeps down the main stairs into the Oak Hall, which is lifeless as a crypt, dim light falling through the cupola on to the grand piano. The piano is rarely opened. Despite Rosalind's oft-stated wish that the children should 'be musical', nothing has been done to further this aim. One of the governesses offered piano lessons, but only the Veg persevered long enough to pick it up, and only the Veg sits at the piano to practise, determinedly plonking her way through melodies until she has mastered them, changing direction with each wrong note, like somebody blindfolded colliding with furniture.

Cristabel collides with nothing. She deftly crosses the hall and slips out of the front door into the misty night, where she spies the narrow shape of Maudie rounding the side of the building. For a moment, they stare at each other through the murk like alley cats, then Maudie nods and vanishes. Cristabel knows she is released, sight unseen. She also knows that whatever Maudie is doing is not something to be enquired about.

Stealthy as a poacher, Cristabel hurries across the garden. She is wearing her lace-up boots and her coat done up over her nightgown.

She carries with her a handkerchief dyed black and tied to a stick: a black flag – the international symbol for parley. Even pirates recognize the black flag. It means they are being offered a chance to sit and talk, man to man, weapons put to one side. She also carries a chunk of sponge cake and a silver trench lighter, two peace offerings shoved in her coat pockets, and her grandfather's hunting knife concealed in one of her sleeves as protection.

She reaches the edge of the lawn and is about to dart into the trees, when she hears a noise behind her. Digby. Barefoot in monogrammed pyjamas. Rubbing sleep from his eyes. Wavy hair standing up from his head. 'I heard you go past,' he says. Digby's bedroom is on the first floor, though he sleeps there only occasionally, preferring to stay with the girls in the attic. 'Where are you going? Why didn't you wake me?'

'I'm going to talk to the savages. Thought it best to go alone.'

He frowns. 'Why?'

She waves the black flag. 'I'm going to seek a parley.'

'You never do things without me.'

'Only one person seeks a parley.'

'I can help,' he says. 'I'll be your squire.'

'Very well, but I'll talk to them by myself. You're to stay in the woods.'

'In the woods?'

'Keeping watch,' she says. 'As soon as I need you, I'll give you the signal.'

'All right,' he says. 'Race you there.'

They spring through the woods like athletes, hurdling tree roots, making sure that any fears lurking in the shadows are outdistanced. When the cottage comes into view, Digby hides himself behind a hawthorn and draws back an imaginary bow and arrow. Cristabel nods at him, then leaves the woods, her heart pounding in her chest.

The flower-covered cottage by the sea is quiet, but it is a different kind of quiet to the staged and weighty stillness of Chilcombe. The cottage has all its doors and windows open. Candles wedged into empty wine bottles flicker on the window sills. Interesting smells are exuded: spicy food, turpentine, tobacco, and something else, rich and heady. Cristabel can hear low voices inside and is moving forwards to hear what is being said, when a twig breaks behind her.

She turns to find the tallest of the savage children, wearing nothing but a pair of shorts. He has come out of the barn. The others are scrabbling down from the hay bales to gather behind their leader, numerous as rats.

Cristabel waves the black flag, then puts it on the ground. She reaches into her pockets and holds out the cake and the lighter. The tall savage grabs the cake and tosses it over his shoulder to the smaller ones. He then takes the lighter, turning it in his hands to examine it. Carefully, Cristabel reaches out to spin the file wheel with her thumb, sparking it into life. 'It's a decent lighter,' she says, 'my Uncle Willoughby had it in the desert.'

The savage is so close to her, she can smell his skin. His shadowy face, lit from beneath by the lighter, is sharply angled, fiercely browed. He is a head taller than her and holding a cigarette in the corner of his mouth like a cowboy. Skinny and broad-shouldered, with shoulder-length dark hair and the wispy beginnings of a moustache. She thinks he must be about thirteen; old enough to consider himself an adult. She can hear the sea close by, its hiss and rattle on the pebbles.

She says, 'I come to offer you parley. I need people. For my play. For *The Iliad*. I know you like pretending. I've seen you do it. You dress up.'

He leans towards her. When he speaks, and it is the first time she has heard him speak, it is with a mixed-up accent and elongated vowels. 'Go home, little girl.'

He tries to put the lighter back in her hands, but she resists, pushing it towards him, saying, 'I'll make you an offer. If you appear in my play, I'll teach you to fight with a sword.' She raises her voice so the younger ones can hear. 'All of you. I'll teach you to fight like warriors. My uncle taught me. I know how to do it.'

The savage laughs. 'I know how to fight, little girl. The only thing I would do with a sword is rid myself of the blonde whores in my father's bed, *comprende?*'

For a moment she is confused. 'Blonde whores?'

He nods at the cottage.

'Wait,' says Cristabel, 'your father is Taras? He doesn't act like your father.'

The savage gives a snort. 'How does a father act?'

Cristabel is stumped. Over his shoulder, she can see the savages watching her. They all have black hair. 'Don't tell me he's father to all of you,' she says. She had assumed Taras's entourage was made up of disciples, not relatives.

The boy throws his cigarette to the ground. 'Why do you think we are here? We are children of the great Taras. Perhaps we will get a blond brother soon, eh? Maybe two. My mother can look after them like she looks after the rest of his bastards.'

'Who's your mother?' Cristabel suddenly remembers the woman in the headscarf. 'Do you mean the one that does the cleaning?'

The boy pulls back sharply. 'My mother is his wife.'

'I didn't know Mr Taras was married.'

'Why would he tell you? He prefers to forget.' The boy hoicks up a mouthful of saliva and spits it, a quivering froth, to the ground. 'But I can tell you something, little girl – one day, we will be rid of those blonde devils, and we will go home.'

'Do you mean Hilly and Philly?'

'They are not the first devils. There was one in Nîmes. One in Bruges. Sometimes, we collect the children. My mother becomes their mother. You understand?'

'I'm beginning to,' Cristabel says. 'Hilly and Philly are blonde devils, and you believe they are usurpers.'

The boy frowns.

'Usurpers,' she says again. 'They have taken your mother's right-ful place.'

He nods.

'I didn't know,' says Cristabel. '*Pardonnez-moi*. Do they make you sleep in the barn?'

'We choose the barn,' he says. A hysterical shriek of laughter comes from inside the cottage, as if to explain why. The boy tenses his jaw.

'How does your mother stand it?' asks Cristabel.

The savage shrugs. It is a complicated feeling, the one she has at that moment. There is something in the boy's expression she recognizes; something about what it is to be burdened with adult foolishness – and she will always be on the side of the usurped, the powerless. However, she cannot bring herself to be against Taras, her god from the ocean, the artist bringing her theatrical dreams to life. There is much that requires consideration. But there is also a task in hand. She has a play to produce, and she needs these half-naked foreigners to make up the numbers. She remembers a line from a Henty book: *An Englishman must always somehow or other put his foot down and square his shoulders in a way that a Frenchman never could.*

Cristabel clears her throat. 'I came to parley. To strike a deal. Tell me, are you French?'

The boy shakes his head. 'Half Belgian, half Russian.'

'But you speak French.'

'French, Russian, Flemish, English. Do you have a favourite?'

'English, naturally. Let me be clear: I need a cast for my play. I want you and your brothers and sisters to be in that cast.'

'Do you not have little friends to play with?'

She considers her answer for a moment before opting for the truth. 'No. We do not have friends. That is why I require you. In return, I will teach you to fight. Or I could get you things from the house. What do you want? Cigarettes? Chocolate?'

The savages whisper 'chocolate' among themselves like an incantation.

The boy says, 'Why should we trust you? You could steal for us, then call us thieves.'

'I give you my word of honour,' says Cristabel.

'I know nothing of your word.'

Cristabel thinks for a moment. Then she reaches out and flicks on the lighter, which the boy still has in his hand. She flattens her own hand and holds it above the flame. 'Watch,' she says, 'this is my word.' She lowers her hand towards the lighter, keeping her eyes fixed on his as her eyelids begin to flutter with pain.

The savages edge closer. The boy waits until Cristabel is holding her shaking hand very close to the flame, furiously blinking back tears, before he moves the lighter away and pockets it. Cristabel clenches her hand to her chest, taking deep breaths.

'Cigarettes, yes. Chocolate, yes,' says the boy. 'One more thing. I want to learn to drive a motor car. You fix that, we talk about plays. *Oui?*'

Cristabel nods. She is not yet in control of her voice.

He watches her for a moment, then says, 'We also do not have friends.' Cristabel is not sure if it is a statement of empathy or of threat.

She strides towards the woods, managing a shaky, 'Monsieur, I will consider your terms.' She has left her black flag on the ground.

He calls after her. '*Bonsoir, mademoiselle. Je m'appelle Leon.*'

Digby is in the trees waiting for her, shivering in the night air. She manages a smile, then sniffs, wipes her eyes. 'Burnt my hand.'

'You didn't give me the signal,' he says. 'Does it hurt?'

She nods.

'Did the savages do it?' Digby asks.

'No,' she says, 'I did. To prove my worth.'

'You did it?' he says. An owl hoots in the woods and Digby shivers again. 'Why didn't you signal me, Crista?'

'I knew I could do it, Digs.'

He is silent for a moment then, in an actorly voice, says, 'We must hasten to the castle to tend your wounds, my liege.' He leads the way through the trees, occasionally glancing at her over his shoulder, as they make their way home.

In the darkness of his bedroom above the laundry, Mr Brewer lights a cigarette as Maudie pads down the stairs and out into the night as silently as she had arrived. Weekends when his wife and son are away, Maudie has taken to slipping in and out of his bed like a cat.

It wasn't something he remembered trying to arrange – there were old acquaintances of that sort in Hammersmith he could visit if he felt the urge, grateful women who called him Billy, who remembered him as an ambitious young man, well known in the pubs of West London, a man who made it his business to make it his business – but it hadn't been entirely surprising when Maudie appeared late one night, materializing in the dark like something he'd dreamt up.

She hadn't ever offered him a reason for her late-night activities, she didn't talk much at all, which Bill Brewer – a man who navigated the world by anticipating demand and minimizing damage – appreciated. Ask no questions and all that. Only once, in a moment of idle curiosity, had he said to her, 'What are you doing here then, Maudie?' and she had eyed him assessingly from her preferred position, looking down at him, her hands resting on his chest as it rose and fell, and said, 'Practising.'

Rehearse

June, 1928

[SCENE: *A tumbledown cottage by a pebbly beach. A thatched barn full of half-painted canvases and a stuffed baby elephant on wheels. A stage set depicting a castle wall. A rehearsal.*]

TARAS: [*drawing a line on the ground*] The audience will be watching from here. The lights go up. Cristabella, now you begin your production.

CRISTABEL: Enter Achilles.

ROSALIND: Achilles is Mr Taras?

CRISTABEL: A thousand times, yes. The narrator starts our story.

DIGBY'S TUTOR AS THE NARRATOR: Me now? Very good. 'Achilles' wrath, to Greece the direful spring of woes unnumber'd, heavenly goddess, sing! That wrath which hurl'd to Pluto's gloomy reign the souls of mighty chiefs untimely slain; whose limbs unburied on the naked shore . . .' Oh, what's next?

CRISTABEL: 'Devouring dogs and hungry vultures tore.'

[*Enter savage children on all fours, snarling and barking*]

CRISTABEL: The Greeks gather to make the case for war against the Trojans.

PHILLY: [*waving a painted sign that says WAR*] War. War.

HILLY: A little more oomph, darling, come on.

ROSALIND: Where should I be?

THE VEG: Over here with me, Mother. We're in Troy.

TARAS AS ACHILLES: 'Why leave we not the fatal Trojan shore, and measure back the seas we cross'd before?'

THE VEG: [*whispering*] Achilles doesn't want to fight, Mother. He wants to go home.

CRISTABEL: Can we have the people creating the sea effect on now?

[*Betty Brewer, Maudie Kitcat and Mlle Aubert, backstage assistants, costumiers and goddesses, run on trailing blue ribbons*]

DIGBY'S TUTOR AS THE NARRATOR: 'The goddess-mother heard. The waves divide and like a mist she rose above the tide; beheld him mourning on the naked shores . . .' Naked shores again? Is that right?

CRISTABEL: Goddess, centre stage. No, we decided we didn't need the fish.

[*Savage children enter and exit with fish*]

MYRTLE AS AJAX: 'The limbs they sever from the inclosing hide; the thighs, selected to the gods, divide.' It's not my line, but I adore it.

MLLE AUBERT AS GODDESS: 'Shall Troy and ze adulterous spouse, in peace enjoy ze fruits of broken vows?'

ROSALIND: Why is she looking at me?

THE VEG: You're the adulterous spouse, Mother.

ROSALIND: She needn't look at me quite so hard.

PERRY AS NESTOR, KING OF THE GREEKS: 'Who dares, inglorious, in his ships to stay, who dares to tremble on this signal day; that wretch, too mean to fall by martial power, the birds shall mangle, and the dogs devour.'

WILLOUGHBY: [*lying on the ground in the middle of the audience space*] Bravo, old chap.

DIGBY'S TUTOR: This play is full of dogs.

[*Savage children bark*]

CRISTABEL: [*banging scenery*] No more barking!

LEON THE SAVAGE AS PATROCLUS: [*gesturing at savage children*] Quand allez-vous faire les choses, vous écervelés fils de putes? Zut alors.

CRISTABEL: Paris is snatched away by Venus. Mrs Brewer, that's you. If you can't lift your arms in that costume, just beckon with a finger.

ROSALIND: Do I do anything here?

CRISTABEL: No.

TARAS: But you must show through your face that you know the man you love is a dilettante. A man who chose beauty over wisdom.

WILLOUGHBY: I'm going back to the house for a drink. You're all doing marvellously.

The Mysterious Travelling Ways
of Voices at Night

June, 1928

She gives him the signal after supper – an earlobe tug, a sniff – and that means: up. Tonight, we go up. They meet in the girls' attic bedroom. Then, using a chair shoved under the window as something to stand on, and employing the Veg, who does not like high places, as corridor lookout, they heave each other out of the window, working like acrobats, each pulling or pushing in turn.

Once on the roof, they rest against the gable for a moment, before beginning their monkey clamber up the tiles to the apex, sending clumps of moss flying off the roof edge. Their destination is the group of chimneys at the roof's highest point. Between these altitudinous columns, Cristabel and Digby have made their nightly nest.

Sitting side by side, they occupy the same air space as bats, owls and moths: fellow travellers on the night air. The rapid swirl of bats, thrown rags of flapping chaos; the ghost float of white-faced barn owls in their Elizabethan ruffs; the soft thumps of bumbling moths against the attic windows. Occasionally, they can make out someone far below, like Perry wandering the lawn with his pipe, a circle of thinning hair on the top of his head. 'Nobody ever looks up,' Digby says, resting his chin on one hand. 'I must always remember to look up.'

A biscuit tin wedged behind a loose chimney brick holds cigarette cards, a French dictionary and a notebook. Digby and Cristabel leave letters for each other there too, so it serves as a private postbox. A candle stub jammed between roof tiles gives enough light for reading or writing, and Digby's tin soldiers are lined up in the guttering along the roof edge: a thin line of defence. Sometimes they hear people calling their names, and how delicious it is to remain silent and fugitive together.

Cristabel retrieves two apples from her pocket and hands one to Digby, being careful not to use her burnt left hand.

For some time, there is nothing but companionable apple-crunching, then Cristabel says, 'I've been imagining the first performance. Over there. Beyond the trees.'

'Everyone watching,' says Digby.

'Hector stepping out from the walls of Troy to defend his home.'

Digby carefully rolls his apple core down the roof edge into the guttering, then hugs his knees and says, 'Flossie does that scene perfectly.'

They pause for a moment, to listen out for the snores of their faithful lookout, their noble Hector, who always, without fail, falls asleep at her post in the attic corridor, often with one of her music books open on her lap, as she likes to practise the piano even when not at the piano, her small fingers dutifully making their way along invisible keys.

Other sounds from Chilcombe's inhabitants float up to the roof-top like balloons. Rosalind's voice, just then, as high and ringing as a handbell: 'Wind the gramophone, Philly darling.' Willoughby, his warm baritone adorned with the clink of heavy-bottomed glasses: 'Need a top-up, old chap?' Myrtle following Perry around like a rumour, her invocations all treacle: 'Peregrine, won't you dance with me.' The mysterious travelling ways of voices at night.

Digby continues, 'Flossie told me she imagines she's defending Chilcombe, not Troy. Isn't that splendid? We will always defend Chilcombe, won't we? When it's ours.'

Cristabel spits out an apple pip with a rapid *ffit*. 'Your mother says Chilcombe will be all yours. I imagine she'll have me and the Veg sold for scrap.'

'I would never let that happen,' says Digby. 'That would be a travesty.' He leans against her to find her hand, laces their fingers together, then bumps this single knotted hand on his knee.

He has never got out of the habit of holding her hand. If it were anyone else, Cristabel would think it mimsy, but his natural affection reaches across her straight-backed reserve (just as, nearly forty years before, the amiable toddler Willoughby would constantly grab the hand of the awkward adolescent Jasper), and once Digby has her hand, it is as if the annoyances and impediments that restrict her are loosened, and things are simpler, more possible, and it is no bother at all to lean together, knocking knees: brothers, outlaws, mountaineers, castaways. It is easier when it is the two of them.

Digby says, 'Think of all the plays we could do, if we were in charge. We could hire renowned actors.'

'We don't have to wait till then, Digs. We should do plays now, while Taras is here,' says Cristabel. She is crunching her way through her apple core until there is nothing left but the stem. 'I've an enormous amount of ideas. Brilliant ideas. This is my soul's work.'

Digby says thoughtfully, 'It isn't always the people you think will be good at acting who are good. I thought Mother would enjoy it, but she doesn't.'

'People have unexpected qualities,' says Cristabel. 'I thought Uncle Perry would think it was silly, but he's terrific.' She efficiently flicks away the stem of her apple, then pulls her cardigan down over her knees. The rooftop air, even on this summer night, is cold and celestial. The sky above them is full of stars.

'Crista,' says Digby, 'I noticed something at the cottage. There's only two bedrooms.'

'Yes?'

'The savages sleep in the barn and the dark woman goes in one room. But that only leaves one bedroom for Hilly, Philly and Taras. They must all sleep together. Crista, do you think that Hilly and Philly want to be boys?'

'What?'

'The clothes they wear, their hair. Perry says they look like Etonians. He says if he'd had a fag like Hilly, his school years would have been very different.'

'They might find trousers more practical. I might wear trousers soon.'

'Sometimes they wear dresses,' says Digby. 'Remember the ones with the glittery beads? It's as if they dress up as different people.'

'I did actually see them once,' says Cristabel. 'Taras and Hilly and Philly. I meant to tell you. I had gone through the woods.'

'You went without me again?'

'Digs, it was important. I had to meet with Leon to finalize our agreement.'

'I don't think he's a very good actor,' says Digby. 'He never remembers his lines.'

Cristabel bumps him with her shoulder. 'I'm telling you what I saw. In the cottage. Two blonde heads, one dark. Lots of legs. Hard to tell what was what.'

'In one bed?'

'Yes.' Cristabel remembers the tangle of limbs, the casual inter-twining of anonymous bodies lit by flickering candlelight, and a sickly pulse thumping in her chest. This was somehow linked with the memory of Leon's voice in her ear – *those blonde whores in my father's bed* – and then meeting him on the beach with no one else around, to promise him Uncle Willoughby would teach him to drive. She had even sought out Willoughby when he was at his most drunk and cheerful, to make sure he would agree, and the calculat-edness of this made her chest thump harder.

'Why do you think they do that, Crista?' says Digby.

She shrugs. 'I don't know.'

In truth, Cristabel feels she does know some of why the trio in the cottage share a bed; she has the outline of it. There were jokes she'd heard Willoughby make, muttered comments from village boys, certain sections in books Myrtle left on the lawn. But much was unclear. Even Maudie, their frank if erratic guide to the adult world, was reluctant to be drawn on the subject, simply smiling and pulling at strands of her own hair. Cristabel thinks again of the three bodies: their closed eyes, their absence from themselves. All the windows of the cottage open, as if it had been abandoned, as if they had gone on a journey.

Digby knocks his knee against hers. 'What do you think it will be like?'

'What?'

'Our play.'

'Oh. Nerves giving you trouble, Digs?'

'No, I'm trying to imagine it.'

'I can see how it should go in my mind and I think it probably will go like that and it will be a great success. The first of many.' She squeezes his hand. 'You're not to worry. I'll be there.'

In the house, a clock strikes midnight. As the night tips over into the small hours, the adult voices inside gain in volume but disintegrate in clarity. No longer gently rising balloons, they become shards and fragments, loud exclamations snapped in half by doors slamming and bursts of brassy music on the gramophone.

'I smell bacon,' says Digby.

'Bacon and eggs, I'll warrant, for those still up. Did you know if you throw an egg from this roof on to the lawn it won't break? I've done it ten times in a row before.'

'No!'

'I'll show you tomorrow. We should get some sleep.'

'Can I go in with you, Crista? I don't want to go back to my room.'

'Long as you don't kick me.'

So they snuff out their candle and slither and slide down the bumpy roof to the window and throw a blanket over their snoozing sister and jump into bed to close their eyes and let the night sky turn and wheel about without them.

The Iliad

To Cristabel, Chilcombe and its environs had always been a place of constancy. The sun followed the same course every day, arching over her head like a well-struck cricket ball. The pebbles on the beach clacked ruminatively as the tides moved in and out. There were fields, rounded fields, and ancient trees upon which she and only she had carved her initials. A reliably quiet place – which was always the first thing visitors remarked upon after the noise of their car engines died away. 'Gosh, isn't it quiet?' The answer was invariably, 'Yes, do come inside,' as if being exposed to such a large amount of quiet was somehow unwise.

However, on the morning of their performance of *The Iliad*, when Cristabel opens her attic window, she feels a new air come rushing at her from many miles away, flying across the glinting sea, fast as the shadow of an aeroplane. It is here. The day. Her day.

Nothing is as it usually was. There is a wriggling knot in Cristabel's stomach like a nest of mice. Eating breakfast seems nonsensical. The Veg is mumbling her lines while chewing her porridge, her woolly beard already hung round her neck, and Digby is bouncing about the attic on one foot. There are sounds of frenetic activity elsewhere in the house. Food being delivered. Chairs carried to and fro. Trestle tables arriving from the village.

This unusual bustling continues all day, with Rosalind at its heart, overseeing decor and catering, accompanied by Betty with her mouth full of pins to make any last-minute adjustments to costumes. Blythe and Mr Brewer are dispatched to decorate the path through the woods with Chinese paper lanterns and, by early afternoon, the cottage itself has been transformed by Taras, Hilly, Philly and Myrtle. Lengthy pieces of fabric are draped from the upper windows and pegged into the ground, creating a tent for Greek war leaders, and a large painted flag flies from the chimney pot. In front of the barn stand the plywood battlements of the besieged city of Troy, decorated with seashells by Taras. Coloured glass bottles holding candles mark out the front of the stage area.

All the weeds and brambles have been removed, the grassy area between the buildings has been mown, and borrowed wooden chairs and deckchairs fill the audience space. Cristabel carefully places one of her handwritten programmes on each seat, while the Veg, following Rosalind's orders, puts a cut rose from the garden on each programme, with a pebble to hold it in place. On the beach, a driftwood bonfire stands ready to be lit in the final act, so that the last scenes will play out against a backdrop of rising flames. Everything is poised and ready; an empty church awaiting its congregation.

But will they come? Cristabel had delivered all the local invitations herself. She borrowed a map from Mr Brewer, commandeered a bicycle from the butcher's boy and – after a painful afternoon teaching herself to ride it – spent a week whizzing through the countryside carrying invitations to the great and the good of South Dorset.

It had been thrilling to seek out addresses, following a map like an explorer. She had never known there were so many villages tucked away in the valleys. Osmington, Sutton Poyntz, Chaldon Herring, Tyneham. The thick summer hedgerows hung so far over the narrow lanes that, from a distance, they looked impassable, but as Cristabel approached, with her brakes squealing, the way through was revealed, like a series of concealed passageways. The warm evenings stayed light as she freewheeled past fields full of cows solemnly masticating, the cuckoo's echoing call following her through the dusk.

Rosalind may not have known anything about Helen of Troy, but she did – Cristabel reluctantly conceded – know something about how to put on an event. There was an admirable cunning in how she gathered what she needed. She had recruited a dressmaker friend of Philly's to design costumes and sweet-talked the vicar into lending her practically everything he owned. Rosalind even wrote the invitations herself, saying, 'The personal touch is everything, if you want the right guests.'

Myrtle, smoking in her battle gear during a pause in rehearsals, had replied, 'I'd certainly want to come along.'

'Darling, they all want to come along,' Rosalind had said. 'People are dying to meet Taras. But won't this be a novel way to introduce him? The great artist in a theatrical production with the children.'

Now the big day is here, and the time written on the invitations – *7 o'clock for pre-performance cocktails* – is ticking ever closer. Cristabel sits down under a tree and waits. There is nothing more to be done.

She hears their voices first. The voices of people walking up the driveway. Mr Brewer guides them on to the lawn, where maids with olive wreaths in their hair wait with trays of cocktails. Cristabel sees a few men who know Mr Brewer making jokes about his bare legs and leather tunic. Friendly winks and insults. She has never seen Mr Brewer behave in such a jovial way before. Then cars start arriving. One after the other, crunching up the gravel. Rosalind's high call of greeting floats across the garden, like the triumphant cry of the peacock.

A crowd begins to gather on the lawn, holding their cocktail glasses. They are all eyes, swivelling about, taking in the ancient house, the secluded garden, the other guests, and even occasionally examining Cristabel herself. She recognizes a couple of Uncle Willoughby's land-owning friends, porcine and bristling, along with a few straight-backed chaps he and Perry knew in the army. A group of intense young adults, with interesting haircuts and skinny wrists, she decides must be Hilly and Philly's art school friends, who Philly says all live in bedsits with gasrings on the floor, surviving on boiled eggs and frantically copulating to keep warm.

There are grand elderly women, weighty with the jet-black jewels of a previous age, talking loudly about Taras and his ART, and she assumes these must be the patrons he refers to as 'English old ladies with big purses'. She also catches the tail end of some of

Rosalind's gushing introductions and divines there is a 'celebrated restaurateur' and a 'modern sculptress' among those milling about. Nearly fifty people, if not more.

Ten minutes till curtain up. Cristabel runs down to the cottage. She needs to put on her costume and make her final preparations. Meanwhile, Blythe begins to lead the audience through the woods. It is a quite magical experience, they will all later agree, to wind through the trees on a midsummer's eve, following a path decorated by paper lanterns. When they arrive at the cottage, they realize – why hadn't they realized this before? – that it is in an idyllic spot, nestled in a grassy dip of land by the beach. House martins and swifts swooping in circles. Exhalations of honeysuckle sweetening the air. The lulling sound of waves on the shore. Barely a whiff of whale. They take their seats and pick up their programmes.

A hand-drawn picture on the cover depicts a furious man waving a spear at a castle. Below this, in inky letters, is written:

TONIGHT THE SEAGRAVE ESTATE IS PROUD TO PRESENT THE FIRST PRODUCTION EVER STAGED IN THE COUNTY OF DORSETSHIRE OF THE RENOWNED STORY OF *THE ILIAD* BY NOBLE MR HOMER

DIRECTED BY MISS CRISTABEL ELIZABETH SYLVIA SEAGRAVE ESQUIRE (ZEUS)

ART DIRECTION BY MR TARAS GRIGOREVICH KOVAL-SKY (ACIIILLES)

PLEASE NO TALKING OR INTERRUPTIONS

Cristabel Elizabeth Sylvia Seagrave, now backstage and peering through a slit in the walls of Troy, studies the audience as they look at her programme. Ordinarily, she doesn't like unknown people, but she is beginning to feel a fondness for her audience. It rises in her as an approving warmth that has to do with their willing acquiescence; how they are paying her programme due attention and leaning towards each other to point out features of the scenery.

She leaves her viewing place to go into the barn to pull on her costume. In contrast to the quiet expectation of the audience, inside the barn is a frantic, overexcited place, repeatedly rocked by explosive emergencies that run through the assembled cast like fire. *Patroclus has lost his shield! Hector's got her thumb stuck in her beard!*

Taras, the still point in the eye of the hurricane, sits on an upturned lobster pot, sipping vodka, in a short tunic that reveals his incredibly thick legs, each the size of a child's torso, and covered with black curly hair like a satyr. Hilly and Philly flit about him, slim as reeds in their soldiers' costumes, with their hair slicked back and eyes encircled with kohl. Perry, pale and upright in the suit of armour, stands nearby. His decades of military life, normally well concealed, are now curiously visible, as if the role of Nestor has allowed him to lift some kind of internal veil to reveal Perry the colonel, Perry the man at home in warfare. Mr Brewer too has resumed his soldierly bearing: a calm, tucked-in competence; the faintly amused fatalism of the capable lower ranks.

There is the Veg pacing solemnly back and forth with her wooden sword, very like her father in her beard, her tubby roundness never more affecting; she makes Hector a brave barrel of a man, valiant despite the odds. Myrtle, tall as an Amazon, fitting her helmet over her bleached hair while leaning casually against the elephant. The younger savages darting about, shaking their spears; Leon carrying a bucket full of rabbit's blood for the final battle (parasols are to be handed out to the front row during the interval). Digby, the beautiful prince, a loop of flowers in his dark hair. Rosalind, a trembling column of white. The three female servants in their draped goddess costumes: Betty all overflowing bounty; Maudie a wild-haired wood nymph; and Ernestine Aubert, solid and immovable as destiny.

Cristabel loves her cast. She realizes that now. She loves them as the gods love mortals: benignly, and with forgiveness. They had been infuriating in rehearsals, utterly rage-inducing, but now, by some mysterious alchemy, they are perfect. She takes a breath and begins to climb the stepladder propped against the side of the barn that will allow her to appear above the city of Troy, as if floating in the sky, at the moment of her first line, approximately ten minutes into the first act.

From her concealed place near the top of the ladder, she can see

Digby's tutor, the narrator, as he steps out on to the stage, the first performer to appear from behind the wooden ramparts. A hush falls over the audience. A few discreet coughs. A gull cawing, then –

> Achilles' wrath, to Greece the direful spring
> Of woes unnumber'd, heavenly goddess, sing!

It has begun.

At first, Cristabel keeps her attention firmly on the narrator, reciting his lines in her head as he goes along, but as he becomes more confident, she turns her attention to other members of her cast. She watches each of them step on to the stage, sees each begin to find their way. Quavering voices become stronger, nervous gestures more defined. Perry even exchanges a few dry asides with the audience. Eventually, Cristabel is able to turn her gaze to the crowd and take in their rapt expressions.

It pleases her immensely that she has created this. It reminds her of playing with the cardboard theatre in the attic, how her favourite part was lying on the floor, doing the voices, making the characters interact, and watching Digby and the Veg lying on their fronts, faces propped in their hands, transfixed by the story, as if it were unfolding all by itself. It was a conjurer's magic, a divine power.

She would never tell Digby and the Veg that when her time came to say her first lines as Zeus she felt true fear, a blood rush of terror that ran through her from head to toe, spinning her heart like a mill wheel. But as soon as she starts to say his lines, she is Zeus, king of the gods, and she knows how to be that.

Although her audience pays her polite attention, she, as a good director, can see there are more natural performers emerging from her cast. Perry, for example, with his knowing and easeful air. But their favourite by far is Digby. Even when he isn't saying anything, she notices their eyes seek him out. Nudges and nods ripple through the crowd whenever he appears.

She catches his eye once and sees that her own Digby is very far back. It is Paris who returns her gaze. While performing in front of grown-ups makes Cristabel feel a little hot and awkward, fearful she might be laughed at, for Digby, who sees no difference between himself and anybody else, it is as straightforward as breathing. His natural honesty means there is nothing between him and the part he plays, no complicating barrier of self-consciousness.

Then there is Taras as the warrior Achilles. When the other characters are onstage, there are moments of complicity between audience and cast, a sort of warm acknowledgement they are muddling along together. But whenever Taras appears, there is no interaction. His Achilles is a killer. A man aware of all the souls that must be sacrificed in order for him to obtain immortality, and exactly how they must die and the sounds they will make as they do so. He takes this awareness and lays it on those watching, with no quarter.

The performance flies past. The final scene – fallen Hector/Veg dragged behind her elephant, with the beach bonfire aflame – even has members of the audience dabbing their eyes with handkerchiefs, fluttering white flags of surrender. Then *applause, APPLAUSE*, the most wonderful sound, rushing around them like waves as they take their bows, rising in crests as Digby steps forward. And again for scene-stealing Perry. And again for the great Achilles. And again for Betty, nearly falling out of her bounteous outfit. And again for all of them. A held note of *clapping, clapping, clapping* that Cristabel hopes will never end.

Afterwards, the performers hurry backstage, slapping each other on the back. They keep breathlessly going over the play, re-enacting it to each other, the parts that had nearly gone wrong – *I almost forgot to kneel!* – and the parts that had gone well – *You did that speech better than ever!* – as a way of keeping it alive, tossing it between themselves like something that cannot be allowed to touch the ground. They garland each other with praise, clasp hands, spin about like dancers. Audience members find their way into the barn too, to congratulate them and shake their hands; slow-moving civilians meeting the glamorous dramatists. Cristabel has never had so many people talk to her, never heard so many people say her name.

Eventually, the audience and cast begin to make their way back up to Chilcombe. Leaving the barn, Cristabel catches Leon's eye. He is stained with rabbit's blood, his grinning face caked and filthy. He holds up a packet of cigarettes and nods towards the bonfire. She shakes her head. She wants to be at the house now. She finds the Veg and Digby, and together they sprint through the woods in the twilight, still half costumed, flowers flying from Digby's hair like moths.

Rosalind is already there, greeting each member of the audience as they return. She has a comment for each one, her manner tailored to fit each guest. For the rich old ladies, she is a gracious debutante; for the easily flattered old buffer from the neighbouring estate, she is a sparky coquette; for the weak-chinned vicar, a demure mother. Cristabel notes, with some frustration, that Rosalind seems perfectly capable of acting when not onstage.

The house itself forms a perfect backdrop. All the windows are wide open, the front door too. Chilcombe has been creakingly prised open like a doll's house, revealing an interior lit with bowls of floating candles, glowing and flickering like a treasure cave.

As the children file past, Cristabel hears her stepmother say, 'Your production has received positive reviews, Cristabel.'

Digby and the Veg continue into the house. Cristabel stops.

Rosalind speaks without looking at her. 'If there were to be another play, it should be done differently.'

Cristabel says nothing.

Rosalind waves at someone across the garden, then says, 'There should be strings of electrical lights in the trees, and the stage itself should be lit. Mr Brewer can arrange this. The costumes should be professionally made. There's a woman in Hampstead, I have her details.'

A pause. The hubbub of guests, of champagne, of success. The rooks cawing in the trees.

Rosalind continues, 'I won't be in it. I have too much to do. But Taras must be involved, Digby will have the main part, and it will happen by the end of the summer. The Veg can perform something on the piano in the interval, Myrtle tells me she's rather good, but none of that fiddly music she likes. Something everyone will like. We will invite people from the newspapers too.' She glances at Cristabel to check she's been heard, then adds, 'Tell Digby to mingle. Everyone's desperate to meet him.'

Cristabel says, 'I have some ideas.' Like Rosalind, she speaks into the air, as if musing out loud. 'Ideas of my own.'

'I'm sure,' says Rosalind, in her hostess voice.

'Perhaps I will write a list for you,' says Cristabel, and waits, unmoving. She doesn't often stand near her stepmother and is pleased to discover that there is no longer much between them in height.

Rosalind purses her lips, like a gambler mulling at a card table, then says, 'Very well.'

Cristabel nods, then joins the throng pouring into the house. She notices, with some surprise, that her entrance into the Oak Hall causes a stir. She hears whispered comments, mentions of her father's name. A few people even smile in her direction. She gives brief nods in return, offers a handshake here and there. It is, she supposes, important to greet people. Make them feel welcome. Things of that sort.

She spots Digby and the Veg eating chocolate cake by the fireplace, which Rosalind has filled with an exotic floral display, and heads towards them, slipping Myrtle's unattended cigarette case from the top of the piano into her pocket as she passes.

'Your mother wants us to do another play,' she tells them.

'That's terrific!' says the Veg, in an explosive scattering of crumbs. 'I'm so delighted! This has been the most perfect day in history! Look at all these people!'

'The greatest news I ever heard,' says Digby, shaking his head. 'We could do one of our Shakespeares, Crista.'

'We could, Digs, we could,' she replies, taking a chunk of cake from his plate. As she eats it, she examines the people looking at them, smiling in their best clothes, holding their cocktails, and she thinks about *The Iliad*. She thinks about what happened afterwards, in the next story, when the cunning Greeks finally made their way into the city of Troy to win the war.

After the body of brave Hector had been burnt on a pyre, the

Greeks constructed a huge wooden horse, to be presented to the people of Troy as a gift. A mighty stallion on wheels, hollow on the inside, and they had filled it with silent soldiers, packed together, gingerly stretching cramped limbs, and carefully running their thumbs down the sharpened blades of their swords.

If you find a way to give people what they want, they let you in, thinks Cristabel. If you make a creature to hide inside, they open the doors and pull you through.

Noises Off

A bedroom in the cottage by the sea

HILLY: You were the best, darling.
TARAS: Yes.

A guest bedroom at Chilcombe

MYRTLE: You were the best, darling.
PERRY: Please, Myrtle. Enough.

The main bedroom at Chilcombe

ROSALIND: Digby was the best, don't you think, darling?
WILLOUGHBY: Left my ciggies downstairs.

*A field halfway between The Shipwreck pub
and the Chilcombe estate*

PHILLY: I wondered which of us you would choose. My London
friends had a wager. Good old Hilly was the favourite. Odds on,
apparently. They didn't think I was your type.
WILLOUGHBY: Darling, you're not.
PHILLY: You say such awful things so charmingly. One could
almost believe you have no malice in you at all.
WILLOUGHBY: I don't believe I do.
PHILLY: Why do you carry on in such a way? All the women, the
affairs.

WILLOUGHBY: I wouldn't call this an affair. Besides, you're besotted with that Russian ogre. You're only here because it's Hilly's turn tonight.

PHILLY: Taras likes to drive women mad because he believes madness is a supreme form of expression. What's your excuse? I believe you secretly despise women.

WILLOUGHBY: You all seem to loathe each other quite enough as it is. Never understood why women can't get along. Always bitching about everything. Making life complicated. Cigarette?

PHILLY: Why even make love to me?

WILLOUGHBY: You talk as if I dragged you here by your hair.

PHILLY: Do you have a light?

WILLOUGHBY: [after a pause] If you've been doing something for a long time, it becomes a habit, I suppose. When I was in the army, there were things I did every morning without fail. Boots, buttons, hat. After a few years, I didn't even notice I was doing them. They simply got done.

PHILLY: A perfect definition of the unconscious drive. How easy it must be to be you.

WILLOUGHBY: Nobody ever says no, darling. Whose fault is that?

To London

July, 1928

It was Perry who suggested it, at dinner. 'Why don't you take the children to the ballet with you? They're becoming rather feral.'

'Feral?' Rosalind had said. 'Do you find them disagreeable, Perry? The girls have a degree of backwardness, I'll admit, but Digby has beautiful manners. We could take Digby.'

'A jaunt to the capital would be good for them all. Civilizing,' Perry replied. 'I'm in London next week, I'll meet you there. Treat them to afternoon tea at The Ritz. My grandmama used to take me when I was a boy.'

Myrtle draped her long hand on Perry's arm like a napkin. 'What an inspired idea, Peregrine. The children's eyes must be opened to the forces of enlightenment.'

'Must they?' said Rosalind.

'Oh, Rosalind,' said Myrtle. 'It'll make them more interesting at parties, if nothing else. Frowning like that will give you lines.'

'I rarely frown,' said Rosalind. 'It's simply the thought of Cristabel galumphing about the streets of London. She mustn't take the sword.'

'Has it occurred to you that Cristabel might be less of a galumpher if she visited London more often?' said Perry. 'Has she ever been there? Has she ever been anywhere? Astonishingly, it won't be that long before she'll be a debutante. She needs to learn how to behave. Nobody minds a spirited girl from the shires. A practical sort. But they will mind if she won't use a fork.'

'Surely she uses a fork?'

Willoughby laughed. 'I'm afraid not, my dear. She's taken to eating off her hunting knife. Like a pirate. I rather enjoy it.'

'You both know about this,' said Rosalind.

The two men, handsome in their evening wear, smiled at her rue-fully across the dining table, blameless and assured.

Cristabel gazes up at the locomotive engine and whistles appreciatively. 'A magnificent beast. Look at the size of the thing!'

The Seagrave children, much to their surprise, have been dressed in their best clothes and taken by car to the railway station at Dorchester where they are now waiting to board the 8.15 to Waterloo with Myrtle, Taras, Hilly, Philly and a strained-looking Rosalind on a sunny Wednesday morning in July 1928.

The station is bright and smart, bedecked with hanging baskets of red geraniums, while the train – olive green and shining – is the most impressive machine the children have ever seen. The highly polished cylindrical engine. Six smart carriages. It basks in the sunshine like a lizard, giving off a potent whiff of hot metal.

They are off to the Princes Theatre on Shaftesbury Avenue for a matinee performance by the legendary Ballets Russes during the last week of the company's summer season in London. Myrtle has a costumier friend who has arranged it and Myrtle is hopeful that Taras will meet Sergei Diaghilev, a man she describes as 'the company's famed impresario' as if she were reading it from a brochure.

She is saying this again, loudly, as a porter heaves the party's bags on to the train. 'And Diaghilev – the company's famed impresario – is said to be in town this week. Such a fortuitous opportunity, Taras. You'll adore him, he'll adore you, and *voilà*! You'll be the artist designing his next wonderful production. They say he holds court in The Savoy after every show, so that, darling, is where we'll go.'

'That, darling, is where Hilly and I will be during the show,' says Philly. 'We saw the Ballets Russes in Paris aeons ago. They were truly avant-garde then.'

Philly and Hilly are cutting quite a dash at Dorchester Station, in vivid emerald and saffron drop-waist dresses with matching headscarves. Myrtle, alongside them, wearing her turquoise turban and a Chinese fringed shawl, looks like an elongated genie.

Hilly, in saffron, says, 'Nowadays, Diaghilev peddles popular nostalgia for the masses.'

'He might as well work in advertising,' sniffs Philly. 'All those onion-domed churches applauded by people with no understanding of the Russian soul.'

Taras gives one of his bull seal laughs. 'Women! They want their artists to be poor and unsuccessful.'

'A true artist will always succeed,' says Hilly. 'But Diaghilev is a money man before he's an artist.'

Philly adds, in a lascivious tone, 'I've heard he's mainly interested in the contents of his male dancers' tights.'

Myrtle clutches her necklace of Venetian glass beads. 'I don't blame him. The thighs on Nijinsky. Eye-watering!'

'He's awfully short, Myrtle. Dwarfish. You'd crush him like a snail.'

'Diaghilev is interested in what?' enquires Rosalind.

'Enough of this chitter,' exclaims Taras, who is sporting a wide black hat and an embroidered shirt for his trip to the capital, along with checked trousers and lace-up shoes without socks.

As if in agreement, the waiting train lets out an irritable hiss of steam, and the women of the party shriek and laugh. The two other passengers waiting at the station – a farmer's wife and a shop girl – politely ignore them.

The station master blows his whistle, and the children climb aboard, making their way into the First Class carriage. The compartment they are to travel in is like a little room, with a door and windows and velvety seats with embroidered antimacassars that smell faintly of tobacco. Cristabel immediately busies herself working out the correct way to operate the window that allows access to the exterior door handle, so she will be able to properly exit the train when they arrive in London, while the Veg fiddles nervously with her hat. Digby is so overwhelmed he can only stare at the overhead luggage rack. The adults head further up the train to the dining car, where they plan to have scrambled eggs and champagne for breakfast.

Cristabel is saying, 'I like this window very much. Look. You pull down on this leather strap to open it,' when the train makes a sudden lurch to announce its imminent departure. There is a great *ffffffflump, ffffffflump,* like the sound of an immense mattress being turned over, as the engine starts to heave its way forward; a triumphant *hoo-hoooooo* from its whistle as it leaves the station; and then the *rickety-tack-rickety-tack-rickety-tack* of the carriages clattering over the railway lines at increasing speed. The children rush to lean from the open window so they can gaze along the long snake of the train, which is interspersed with the heads and upper bodies of fellow window occupants, fresh-air enthusiasts holding on to their hats and grinning.

'I wish I had a whistle,' shouts Cristabel, over the noise of the engine. 'I've asked for one every Christmas.'

They rocket through the countryside, white smoke pouring from the train's chimney. Sometimes, when the train rounds a bend, the angle of the track gives the children a glimpse into the engine cab where the grimy fireman is frantically shovelling coal into the glowing firebox, the ravening industry powering the huge machine, and how thrilling it is when they plunge into a tunnel, the smoke swirling about them, an enveloping blackness roaring in their ears.

'Are we still in Dorset?' asks the Veg, after a while, settling herself back on her seat. 'Or are we somewhere else?'

The children look at each other.

Digby shrugs, 'I don't know how to tell.'

'Probably over the county bounds by now. I'll check with the guard for you,' says Cristabel. 'Heavens, look at all those cows. You only ever seem to see cows side-on, have you noticed? Very rarely face-to-face.'

The countryside continues to hurtle past, vast acres of it. Orchards, farms, beehives. Shepherds with sheepdogs. Children balancing on gates, waving hankies. Passengers get on and off the train at every station, and each station has a different name. Wareham, Hamworthy, Parkstone. Sometimes, other trains come into sight, travelling in the opposite direction, and the sound as they approach is a relentless galloping that builds and builds until they pass each other in a rapidly screaming blur, the noise a terrible sundering.

Brockenhurst. Southampton. Winchester. There are bungalows, hospitals, churches, boating lakes, docks, many-funnelled ocean liners, lamp posts, schools, cricket pitches, cinemas. And people. So many people. It has the effect of subduing the children: the rushing mass of it all; its impassive busyness. It is hard to believe it has always been there, going on without them. There is so much of it.

When Cristabel imagined the train to London, she had thought of it as simply that: a train that would leave Dorchester and pass through some countryside that looked much like the countryside she knew and then reach London. But it transpires that there are many places between Dorchester and London. The line between Dorset and the capital is not a single sweeping stroke, but a wiggly squiggle, full of pauses and interruptions. There are countless towns and villages she has never heard of, and all seem to be populated by people merrily going about their business, unconcerned by the mysterious unknownness of their locations. Whatever could they all be doing? What was there to occupy the inhabitants of Beaulieu, of Sway, of Hinton Admiral? They weren't in any books. Nobody had ever mentioned them.

There was another peculiar thought that niggled at Cristabel: none of them knew her. None of them knew her name. Even the guard on the train didn't know her name, and she had rather expected he might.

After some time, the guard pops his head into their compartment to say they are approaching London. They look out of the window in anticipation, but it is as if they are coming into the city through its backstage area, as the view is a succession of unattended functional places: blackened industrial buildings, scrubby yards, outhouses, tangled fences. But the buildings pull themselves up, increasing in size and grandeur as they near their destination. They catch a glimpse of Big Ben, and then Waterloo Station itself appears round a corner, a huge open-ended warehouse, its roof a latticework of sooty glass and cast-iron arches, with sparrows and pigeons flying around inside, and a great clock hanging from the interior ceiling.

The train wheezes up to the platform, pulling up alongside others of its kind. Then carriage doors bang open and there are porters shouting and trunks being unloaded, and flower stalls and newspaper sellers, and people on the platform waving and calling. The Seagrave party disembark, and Hilly and Philly immediately set off at the brisk pace adopted by many of their fellow passengers.

'Toodle-pip, darlings,' calls Philly. 'We're lunching with Hilly's parents. Duty calls.'

'We can't take Taras,' adds Hilly. 'Last time, Daddy tried to stab him with a toasting fork. See you at The Savoy.'

The children are shepherded through the busy station by the unlikely duo of Myrtle and Taras, the tall American and the sockless Russian, with a sweating porter carrying their bags and Rosalind trailing behind, murmuring uncertainly, 'When was I here last? I can't remember the last time I was here.'

At one point, Taras turns to them, his eyes wild above his black beard, and shouts, 'Breathe in the restless city, children of the big house! Let it enter your veins.'

They do. There is an open-top car waiting outside Waterloo for them – Myrtle has arranged this – and, as it drives them through the noisy, fume-filled London streets, the children gulp in everything they can. The towering buildings; the policemen in white gloves directing the swarming traffic; the countless red motor-buses, each with a curving staircase on its rear end to take passengers to the top deck, staircases that twist upwards like decorative sashes bearing single, incomprehensible words: DUNLOP. CUSSONS. SCHWEPPES. As the car crosses a bridge over the Thames, the children can see working cranes lining the water's edge; tugboats chugging industriously about, and barges piled with black coal ploughing their way along the river.

Myrtle takes them to a clamorous restaurant, the interior of which is decorated with reflective surfaces: mirror, silver and glass. Every time the children look up from their pork cutlets they see multiple images of their fellow diners, fractured and scattered about. They have never eaten with adults before, and it is a disorientating experience.

Rosalind is glancing about, saying, 'I don't think I've been here before. No, I don't think I have.'

'You should insist that Willoughby take you to London,' replies Myrtle, from over a cairn of oysters. 'The spirit withers if left too long in the countryside. Too much scenery; not enough theatre.'

Taras, through a forkful of potato, adds, 'The modern city is a fuel. A petroleum.'

'Willoughby doesn't take me anywhere,' says Rosalind.

'Leave the man alone,' says Taras, adding a slosh of wine to his mouthful of potato. 'You are always under his feet like a cat, tangling yourself about.'

'Could somebody tell me,' says Cristabel, waving her eating knife to attract attention, 'what an "impresario" is? Like Mr Diaghilev.'

'He is the person in charge of a theatrical company, Cristabella,' replies Taras. 'He finds the money, decides the productions. He is the locomotive.'

'I don't think I like wine,' says the Veg, pushing away her glass.

'Add more water,' advises Taras, pushing it back.

'You know, Taras,' says Myrtle, who has moved her oysters aside and is smoking from a jewelled pipe, 'the more I think about it, the more I believe I might be useful for you. And you for me.'

'Is that so?'

'My poetry will always be my life's work, but I have a vision: a poster on the wall of a Tube station advertising a new exhibition by Taras Kovalsky brought to you by the kind patronage of Myrtle van der Werff. No! Brought to you by the Van der Werff Society for the Arts. Oh, but my daddy would just love for me to have a Society.'

Taras smiles. 'I would be delighted to help you spend your daddy's American dollars.'

'Well that,' says Myrtle, 'is what I was hoping.'

There follows much dull adult conversation of galleries and opportunities, but also good puddings: baked bananas served in rum with thick dollops of cream.

After lunch, they adjourn to the Belgravia home of a friend of Myrtle's so they can change their clothes. When they arrive at the

Princes Theatre, numerous taxi cabs are pulling up in the street outside, depositing people dressed in glamorous evening wear, even though it is a sunny afternoon. They crowd through the entrance into the theatre's tiled lobby area, which is ringing with the expectant voices of those waiting to be seated.

The children, under Myrtle's wing, are guided to their places at the front of the circle. They watch as the multitude of theatregoers find their places in the stalls beneath them. Beyond the stalls and the orchestra pit, where the musicians are warming up with a see-sawing cacophony, a red stage curtain hangs from ceiling to floor. The curtain is lit from beneath. It glows.

Then the house lights dim and the murmuring audience quietens. The conductor raises his baton, the violinists tuck their instruments beneath their chins, and everyone breathes in. They wait. Rosalind coughs. The curtain goes up.

From the wings, a long-haired figure comes running, leaping high as a deer, arms raised, legs fully extended, a body in the air at full tilt. Through the small binoculars she has found in front of her seat, Cristabel watches intently. She can see puffs of dust rise from the stage boards as the dancer thumps down to earth.

The conductor gives a flourish, and the orchestra begins to play. The dancer, a muscular figure in a skintight costume, responds to the music with exaggerated movements that extend through every sinew. Some movements are graceful and arching, but some are jagged and functional. Movements that implore, soothe, reach; others that deny, stomp, insist.

More dancers run on from the wings. Lit by the stage lights, they fling themselves about, their faces emphasized by dramatic make-up. Through her binoculars, Cristabel decides some must be women as they are wearing diaphanous dresses and dancing on the tips of their toes. She has never seen people move in this way before, and none of them seem embarrassed by what they are doing. The stage set is also intriguing. There are patterned shapes arching in from either side to create a forest bower, but when the lighting changes colour, the shapes resemble other things: a church nave, the beams of a workshop, the belly of a ship.

She trains her binoculars on the first dancer again. Despite the transparent costume, it is not immediately apparent as to what lies beneath, but she is fairly confident that the bulge at the top of the muscular legs indicates a thing that indicates a man. It is fascinating, almost shocking, to see a body so outlined and revealed. He looks naked. Cristabel glimpses drops of sweat flying from his forehead as he spins, but his face never betrays the effort he is making.

His face is bold. His eyes ringed. He is a man, but not one like Perry or Willoughby, closed off and wry. He is expressive, sensual, his arms outstretched, his mouth ajar. Occasionally, his hands frame his own face like an actress posing in a magazine. His jumps seem physically impossible – he can leap straight upwards from a standing position like a cat. He reminds her of the slender sprites that climb trees and make mischief in the Arthur Rackham illustrations in *Tales from Shakespeare*. Puck from *A Midsummer Night's Dream*. Ariel from *The Tempest*. Neither good nor evil; male nor female. Something else entirely.

Cristabel hears Rosalind whisper to no one in particular, 'I don't know quite what to make of that one.'

The music swells and there is a sustained note from a violin that floats high in the air and a cello part that sways underneath it, and the dancers lift each other and spin in unison and all the moving parts suddenly seem to be tied together, and there is an uprush of emotion in Cristabel's chest, which takes her by surprise. She doesn't know how to describe what she is feeling or how she has been made to feel it. But whatever it is, and however it is done, it appears to be contagious, because, glancing to the side, she sees the enraptured faces of Digby and the Veg staring at the stage, eyes shining.

She looks again at the performance, at how everyone involved is concentrating on the same aim, from the principal dancer spinning centre stage, to the unseen man high in the rafters controlling the spotlight, to the patient percussionist counting out the empty bars of space before his single soft *tink* on the triangle. It moves her the way that stories about soldiers uniting to go into battle move her, a collective endeavour in service of a single cause. She would like very much to be a part of that. No. She would like very much to be in charge of that.

After the performance, when the audience are all filing back out on to the street, blinking in the sunlight, there is a kind of milling about where they keep looking at each other's faces, as if trying to see if the show has left a mark. Cristabel frowns at her feet. She does not want to be examined.

Myrtle is swollen-faced and exultant, blotchily streaked with her own make-up. She grabs hold of Digby's hands and exclaims, 'The ballet always moves me to tears – oh, I drown! Did you love it, beautiful boy?'

'Ever so ever so much,' says Digby. His eyes have widened to dinner plate proportions. 'I could jump like that, if I practised.'

'We'll make a dancer of you yet,' says Myrtle.

'Some of the dancing was divine,' says Rosalind, cooling herself with a lace fan, 'but the music was a little coarse.'

Taras offers his arm to the Veg as they begin to stroll southwards towards The Savoy. 'Tell me, Miss Florence. Did the ballet move you?'

The Veg says in a quavering voice, 'Goodness me, Mr Taras. I feel as if my heart is bursting out to pieces at the seams. The orchestra was so wonderful – and the magic toy shop story! To see the dolls come to life like that! *C'était très bien.*'

'What are you saying? The one at the end? With the puppets?' says Rosalind, who is walking behind them.

'Yes, *La Boutique Fantastique*, Mother. The dolls loved each other so much they couldn't bear to be parted,' sighs the Veg. 'I was thinking though, Mr Taras, because their love was so strong, they might meet in the afterlife. Like how in the Greek stories, people don't actually die, they go and live with the gods. Do you think dolls get to go to the afterlife?'

'It is entirely possible, Miss Florence,' says Taras, in the oceanically deep voice that reminds her that he came from the sea and is familiar with gods and love and all else unknown.

Digby, who is bounding his way along the pavement in a series of

189

leaps and pirouettes, adds, 'Flossie, remember, they have to do it again tonight. And tomorrow. And the next day. So they will be together again and again.'

'Also true,' says Taras. 'The doll in the story, Miss Florence, did he love with all his heart?'

'He did!'

'But what enables us to know that he loves? His dancing. That is what we will remember, long after love is gone. Art will outlive us all.'

'Ah,' says Myrtle, 'but what inspired his art? His love. Love inspires art. Without love, there is no dancing.'

'You are too soft,' says Taras, not unkindly. 'It is your poems that will suffer.'

'I believe that's The Savoy over there,' says Rosalind. 'Has my hair survived the journey?'

Taras pauses to direct the Veg's attention towards her half-sister, who is walking behind the rest of the party, scowling at the floor, her closed-off face furrowed and intent. 'Look at Cristabella. She is already at work. Picturing her future productions. The American is right to say love inspires art, but not only love. Art inspires art. Anger, hatred, hunger – these can also inspire. But whatever it is, however it comes, there always is the work. The work of art is never done. Even when my hands are empty, I am still painting.'

The Veg nods thoughtfully. 'Cristabel is very good at puzzling away at things. For ages.'

'Many people give up,' says Taras, 'but it would surprise me if she were to be one of them.'

At The Savoy, the children are left to linger in the lobby, waiting for Perry to arrive and take them to The Ritz, while the adults head further inside, to where Mr Diaghilev sits behind a piano surrounded by admirers. The children catch a glimpse of a round man with a neat moustache and melancholy downward eyes, a dapper walrus patiently accepting compliments while expertly noodling on the piano. Gathered around him are smartly dressed men and darkly sparkling women with the tightly strung calves of dancers, and their conversation is like a song in which the verses are sung by the visiting Russians, low and rumbling, and the choruses are sung by their eager followers: the extrovert laughing Americans, the politely applauding English. *A ha ha ha! A ha ha ha! A ha ha haaaa quite right.*

It is a relief when Perry heaves into view in his colonel's uniform, hat tucked under one arm. The pale gingeriness that makes him so translucent in civilian life is eradicated by his military outfit, which fills him out, makes him a reassuring presence.

'I see the acolytes have found their target,' he says, ushering them out. 'I can't stand bohemians en masse, all shouting their radical opinions over the top of one another. Let's see how long it takes for Rosalind to notice you've gone.'

'We shouldn't upset Mother,' says the Veg.

'I'll leave a message with a bellboy,' says Perry, and hails one like a cab.

Entering The Ritz alongside Colonel Drake and being guided to a table in the Palm Court – a yellow and gold room of chandeliers and potted palms – is like the parting of the Red Sea. Chairs are pulled out for them; napkins flourished; enquiries made about the health of Colonel Drake's parents; benevolent smiles bestowed by staff and diners alike. A tiered cake stand arrives, bearing dainty sandwiches and scones to be eaten with clotted cream and straw-berry jam. Perry orders champagne, saying that his grandmama believed every visit to The Ritz deserved champagne, and they each have a glass. Its sneeze-making fizziness makes them giggly and emboldened.

'I don't think I will ever go to school,' proclaims Digby grandly.

'This is a very sophisticated place,' says the Veg. 'I wonder, Uncle Perry, do you think Mr Taras will marry Hilly or Philly?'

'Hillary,' replies Perry. 'There's cold marital steel in her eyes and, unless he marries her, she's no different to all his other girls. Although, Kovalsky will have to get shot of his cumbersome first wife before the nuptials proceed.'

'Mr Taras has a wife?' says the Veg.

'That's right,' says Cristabel, knocking back her champagne. 'The woman with the mop. Leon told me. She's his mother. They lived in Brussels. But she's actually Belgium. Comes from Flemish.'

'Other way round, dear girl. The wife is Flemish. Comes from Belgium. Quite a talented artist in her own right, I'm told,' adds Perry. 'Or she was before she married Kovalsky and started popping out Russian babies.'

The Veg looks perturbed. 'I hope when I fall in love with my husband, he doesn't have a wife.'

'Don't be a ninny, Veg,' says Cristabel, through a mouthful of scone.

'I'm not being a ninny.'

'You are being a ninny, you ninny. If he has a wife, he can't be your husband. Leon believes Hilly and Philly are usurpers, and he's right.'

'I'm not being a ninny. There is such a thing as a second marriage, isn't there, Uncle Perry? Mother had two marriages. She says only the uneducated disapprove of true love. And do you know what,' says the Veg, who is becoming flushed, 'I don't think I want to be called Veg any more. It's not a pretty name. It's not even my name.'

'It isn't,' concurs Digby.

'Digby never calls me Veg, so I don't see why the rest of you can't do the same.'

'You're Flossie,' says Digby and takes her hand.

'I am.'

Caught off guard, Cristabel flounders for a moment, chewing her scone.

'Flossie suits you very well,' supplies Perry.

'It does,' says Flossie, blinking rapidly. 'I think it does.'

'Who would like to hear about the time I won a medal in India and rode an elephant?' says Perry, while simultaneously indicating to a passing waiter that he would like a whisky and the bill. 'I had to steer it with its ears.'

After the elephant anecdote, the conversation turns to the other medals and stripes on Perry's uniform and what they mean and where they came from – the brushes with death, the hair-raising escapades and the bravery of soldiers who defend the Empire. Then he tells them it will soon be time for them to catch the train home and asks if any of them can remember the name of the train they arrived on.

'Did it have a name?' asks Cristabel.

'They usually do. And a number. Can you remember what colour it was?'

'Blue,' says Digby.

'No,' says Cristabel, 'green and gold.'

Perry nods. 'It is a useful habit to cultivate, remembering the details of trains. A good memory exercise. Next time, I will expect you to know the name and number too.'

After that, Perry sends for a car to take the children back to Waterloo. It is driven by a uniformed soldier who salutes the children as they climb in and again as they climb out at the station, which is emptier and echoing now.

Their train is waiting for them at the platform, so they run to it, and it sets off almost straight away. It has been such a treat to go to the ballet and The Ritz and have champagne and be driven through the city by a soldier, but now they are heading home, and it all seems to have come to a rather sudden end. Perry has told them he will arrange for Mr Brewer to pick them up at Dorchester, so there is nothing left for them to do but sit on the train as it gathers pace, heading away from the city and back towards Dorset. It is dark now. The day has ended.

When they had left Dorchester in the morning, the noise of the train had been regular and companionable – a mechanical horse, cheerfully galloping forth. But now they are leaving London and the train noise has become a desolate roar. It is a monster. It is a factory. Its black windows show only the reflections of those on board, looking tired and haunted.

Digby watches his own image carefully, lifts his chin, holds his hands to the sides of his face like the dancer, then shifts his gaze so his reflection looks back at Cristabel. She studies him, examines their monochrome side-by-side faces, then turns to her half-sister, who is reading the ballet programme for the third time.

'I will, you know,' says Cristabel.

'Will what?'

'Call you Flossie. If you like.'

'I would like that. If it's all right.'

'You should have said.'

'I have now.'

After a pause, Cristabel says: 'Perry's elephant story was first rate. You like elephants, don't you?'

Flossie nods. 'I do like elephants.'

Cristabel turns and looks out into the darkened countryside. She can see a few isolated lights in the distance like ships out at sea. Cars, she supposes. Farms. Things carrying on.

Somewhere between Southampton and Bournemouth they all fall asleep, rocked by the motion of the train, shivery with tiredness and huddled beneath a woollen blanket loaned to them by the guard. Cristabel in the middle with a protective arm round each of her charges: the softly snoring Flossie; the deeply dreaming Digby.

Maudie Kitcat's Diary

22nd July, 1928

Mister Willoughby off in his aeroplane again so Mrs Rosalinds in a blather. Maudie do this Betty do that. filling the house with orders. Betty is my seam straight. Maudie stop staring.

You can't miss nuthin but you can't get caught watching. Like how Bill never looks at me when his wife's around but I know what he hides behind his closed door face.

Bill keeps saying, you be careful, Maudie, but no one cares what i do. they'd only care if i got a bun in the oven. that won't happen now Bill got those things. Mister Willoughby has some too. inside pocket of his dinner jacket. don't seem to notice when some go.

they forget I turn out their pockets. they forget I empty their slops & wash their bed sheets. they forget me altogether. i see them asleep sick drunk bare as babes but when they wake and find me lighting the fires, they act surprised, pulling their sheets up all modest.

apart from mister Willoughby, he dont care. Splayed out shameless as a cat in sunlight. Like that tiger they had at the circus in Weymouth. opens his eyes and doesn't say a word. watches me work. watches me look.

Picture It

As the summer goes on, the children slip through the widening gaps in their timetables. Mlle Aubert becomes increasingly laissez-faire about lessons, while Digby's tutor is distracted by the pursuit of fossils, and Rosalind preoccupied with her guests. Everyone has wandered away from what they were meant to be doing. It's that time of year. The July sun rests on its laurels in a wide blue sky, comfortable and unthinking. Any other weather is very lightly done, just casual wisps of high cloud.

Into this unattended golden space comes Flossie, pulling her wheeled elephant and leading a group of savage children down to the beach. She is developing a game called 'our school' in which she is a kindly teacher, providing singing lessons and rides on Edgar. Cristabel and Digby are also passing through the sunlight. Whenever they grow tired of planning theatrical productions, they visit the barn where Taras paints. Sometimes, they talk to him in French, but mostly they sit watching him work, while he pays them the compliment of ignoring them entirely.

When Taras is painting, he frequently stops and shuts his eyes, as if trying to picture something or remember something. Cristabel and Digby notice this can happen when he is away from his work: his eyes suddenly close, mid-meal, mid-stroll, as if something has surfaced within and demanded his attention. Even when open, his eyes are often inaccessible, furtive black currants. They tightly seal off the workings of his mind, but Digby and Cristabel are conscientious observers.

They have seen that, although Taras cheerfully agrees to Rosalind's frequent requests to go up to Chilcombe to meet visitors, he rarely returns from the house empty-handed. Not only does he seem adept at acquiring useful items, like teaspoons for the cottage or the details of a man who supplies oil paints, he usually comes back with something else too: subject material.

Familiar faces begin to surface in his paintings – the vicar and the local MP – along with images found in the portraits of ancestral Seagraves, suggesting that when he grows tired of the people talking to him, he turns his attention to the silent ones on the walls. His lazy geniality begins to appear more like that of the crocodile lying in the shallow water with its great jaws smilingly open. The children like him all the better for this.

They also admire his ability to always be Taras. They are frequently obliged to become cleaner, politer versions of themselves, but Taras never changes. He addresses everyone in the same manner, wears whatever he likes, and is always stained. Paint embeds itself under his fingernails, soaks into the lines on his palms, and splatters his rolled-up shirt cuffs. He carries his work with him, along with the liquorice smell of turpentine. While most people zigzag through their days, trundling between obligations and meals, desires and interruptions, thinking about politics or pilchards or whatever else is coming along next, Taras follows a single path, that of Taras the artist.

One by one, he takes members of the household off to the barn, saying, 'But now I must make your portrait.' They don't know how to say no. There doesn't seem to be a way to do that. Sometimes they arrive to find a canvas already half filled, or a selection of props waiting for them, which gives them the simultaneously pleasurable and unnerving sensation they have already been thought about. For Mlle Aubert, there is a kitchen knife. For Mr Brewer, a handful of coins.

When Taras brings in each new model, he places them inside the barn, where they are framed by the doorway. Then there is a series of adjustments, as he positions and repositions both easel and subject. When he finally begins painting, his attention becomes disconcertingly inconstant – focused not on the person in front of him, but circling round them, repeatedly checking the light, the sky, the light, the sky. The children watch intently, hoping to pinpoint how it happens: the transfiguration of their lived reality.

Sometimes, Taras is frustrated by his work before he even starts. Once, when Mr Brewer had arrived for a sitting, Taras had punched his fist through a blank canvas, placed it on the floor, then walked calmly across the barn to pick up a new one.

'Everything all right, sir?' said Mr Brewer.

'The many times I will get this wrong,' said Taras, 'already tire me.'

Mr Brewer scratched his moustache. 'Whenever you're ready, sir.'

'No need for sirs,' replied Taras. 'We paint a little then have a drink, you and I, yes? I am Taras, you are Bill. Let us proceed, my friend.'

The children observe this too: his ability to acknowledge futility yet have a go anyway. To set off optimistically even if you soon find yourself back at the start. They are accustomed to all their attempts at anything being marked with a definite cross or a tick, but Taras does not appear to mind a cross. He even gives them to himself. It is a topsy-turvy way of thinking, but there is an intriguing ease to it, a widening of space. It seems a good way to do things, especially now, in this summer of laxity, this time of slack water.

Occasionally, Taras will go to the beach to do charcoal sketches of the whale, and Digby and Cristabel tag along. He is drawn, he says, to the bones of the creature, which are becoming ever more visible as scavengers pick away the flesh. He asks them to look at the bones and tell him what they see. Bones, they say. No, he says. Again. The ribs are a basket; the spine, a piano; the jaws, a wish bone. Better, he says. Again. The ribs are hands praying; the spine, a crenellated castle wall; the jaws, a pterodactyl's beak. Better, he says. But always again.

As they walk back to the barn, Digby asks, 'When you paint Hilly or Philly, why do you chop their heads off?'

'So I don't have to listen to them when I am working.' Taras laughs, then adds, 'A woman's body is majestic. I celebrate it.'

'You celebrate the bit without the head,' says Cristabel.

He shrugs. 'Perhaps I enjoy to chop the heads off.'

He gives Cristabel a few pieces of paper and some charcoal and tells her to practise her portraits, while Digby climbs about on the hay bales at the back of the barn, pretending to be a cowboy. Cristabel draws Taras as a crocodile coming from the sea; she draws herself as a whale beneath the waves.

'What about Miss Florence?' Taras asks.

'A song thrush? No, a dormouse. No, a field mouse,' says Cristabel.

'Where is she living? What is her home?'

'She likes to be snug. A snug nest with soft jumpers.'

'Cushions to sleep on,' adds Digby, who is half listening. 'Woolly socks.'

'Show me,' Taras says, so she draws it for him. Then he asks, 'How do you draw your home, Cristabella?'

Home? She never thinks of the word 'home'; she thinks of an attic at the top of a house. She draws a thin shape for the attic, then a funnel beneath it, filled with a swirl going round and round like a whirlwind. She already knows what Rosalind is: a magpie. Willoughby: a sword. Flying things. She adds them to her drawing.

'You see,' Taras says, tapping the top of her head with the end of a paintbrush. 'You have it already. All you need. Don't forget to put your name on it.'

They work on their respective pieces in comfortable silence, Taras standing at his easel, Cristabel lying on her stomach on the grass nearby. After a while, she gets up and approaches Taras with her paper in her hand, saying quietly, 'I don't know how to draw Digby.'

She has tried, but every time she puts her piece of charcoal to the paper, she stops, because she immediately has it wrong. They both look over to Digby, who is lying on the hay bales, caught in a dusty shaft of light.

The trouble is, he is many things. The brother she wanted and the brother she has, two different notions entirely, and cousin Digby, who is not really her brother, and actual Digby, her most faithful and cheering companion. He is a drawing scribbled over and screwed up and unscrewed again and kept in a pocket always. His presence in her life like a dog sleeping on the end of your bed: a loyalty so fond and constant, you only notice it on the rare occasions when you wake up and it's gone, and then all you want to do is get up and find it, so you can go outside and play. Or perhaps he is simply too close to her for her to see him properly, like a mirror held right in front of the face.

'Do another one of me instead,' suggests Taras.

Digby turns to them excitedly. 'There's an enormous spider over here.'

Soon, it is Rosalind's turn to stand in the barn, holding a bouquet of roses provided by Taras. She desperately wants her portrait to be painted, particularly as sullen Mlle Aubert and flighty Maudie have already had theirs done, but finds posing an uncomfortable experience. It is frustrating to be unable to see how he is depicting her.

'Can I see it?' she asks, but whenever she looks, there is only the outline of her body and a swirly blur where her face should be. In fact, as the painting develops, the void where her face should be becomes more of a void, while the flowers in her hands are lavished with detail.

'When do you think you will do my face?' she asks, glancing at the sky to see what on earth he keeps looking at.

'I am doing it,' Taras says, with satisfaction in his voice, using his thumb to smooth out ridges in the paint. 'It is a polished surface.'

'When do you think it will be finished? Properly.'

She wants it to be finished and framed. She dislikes unframed paintings. Nothing but bits of canvas stapled to wood. She and Willoughby had once gone for dinner at a house full of unframed paintings by a fisherman that resembled drawings done by a simple child. The guests exclaimed rapturously over them, but Rosalind likes her art to be more accomplished and behind glass.

Unframed paintings remind her of when Hilly and Philly had taken her to a party in an artist's studio in Fitzrovia after they'd been to see the Ballets Russes. Finally, she'd thought, as they climbed a staircase to the studio, a chance to visit bohemia. But bohemia had proved small and messy. No furniture to speak of, and the space crowded with canvases covered with garish images of typewriters and escalators. Canvases were stacked on the floor and propped up along the walls, and people in shapeless clothes were leaning against them, covering them with wine stains and cigarette ash. Someone was singing a sea shanty; a Hungarian composer was banging a saucepan; the air was thick with incense; and a Welshman with a spittle-filled beard kept shouting into her ear about cubism. They all had loud opinions about art, and they all kept tripping over it drunkenly. It was as if they had gathered together to reassure each other they were the beating heart of everything, but then had a terrible feeling that they weren't, so kept doing noisy, careless things to cover up the gaping hole in the middle of it all. 'WHAT IS SO VERY POWERFUL IS THE SENSE OF A MALEVOLENT TECHNOLOGY UTTERLY BLIND TO HUMAN CONSCIOUSNESS,' bellowed the Welshman. I would like a chair to sit on, thought Rosalind.

As Rosalind stands in the barn in front of Taras, she has that thought again: I would like a chair to sit on. A triangle of sunlight comes through the open doors straight into her eyes. She remembers that Myrtle (who adores the faceless portrait of Rosalind and has asked Taras if she can buy it) knows an Italian artist who produces the kind of paintings Rosalind covets. Floor-to-ceiling portraits of women wearing gowns in Venetian villas. An artist who would make her look like a real person, but taller. It is frustrating that her artist, the one she is housing and feeding, will not look at her in that way. She can picture it clearly.

Wings and Bones

August, 1928

If you were, like Willoughby, flying above Chilcombe Mell in a single-seater aeroplane on a summer's evening, the view would be as follows: fields, hedges, cottages, a church, and then a thicket encircled by a crowd of raggedy rooks. Not a sign of the house concealed beneath the trees until you were directly above it, then a fleeting glimpse of chimneys and a snippet of lawn, before you shot out over the glimmering ocean.

Willoughby believes the view from an aeroplane accurately depicts man's general irrelevance. Seen from the air, human structures are foreshortened, merely the temporary perching places of birds. England is nothing but a Hornby train set, a model village: predictable, ticketed and neat. But beyond it lies the sea, the sky, the horizon: endless places as vast as Willoughby's beloved Egyptian deserts. A few lines of poetry from his schooldays float into his mind –

. . . Round the decay
Of that colossal wreck, boundless and bare,
The lone and level sands stretch far away.

– but waft away before he can remember who wrote them.

He adores flying in the realm of the white clouds; enormous structures, casting shadows big as citadels as they glide along, moving with the slow dignity of things that believe themselves to be immensely solid. When trapped in drawing rooms, Willoughby will seek out windows with views of skies and follow the clouds as they pass, remembering that he has moved among them.

Reluctantly, he descends to earth, heading for a farmer's field about half a mile from Chilcombe, where he can land safely, and a couple of obliging farm workers with a tractor will manoeuvre his aeroplane into a barn if the weather turns. He switches off the engine for the final section of his flight, leaving just the air whistling through the wires and, somewhere below him, the rooks congregating. Their varying cries – a harsh *caw*, a ruminative *aarrrrrk*, a jocular *akakakakaka* – echo about the valley. A constant call and response: ays and nays; a corvine filibustering. Jasper claimed there was a local legend that if the rooks ever left Chilcombe, the Seagrave family would fail. Cristabel feeds them buttered toast every morning.

Willoughby purchased his aeroplane in the dreadful time immediately after Jasper's death. Days when he would wake with a jolt before dawn, his head pounding, and it would all come rushing back: his birthday party, a game of sardines, hiding in a back room with Rosalind, the window seat behind the curtains, his hand over her mouth. Then the shouts from outside. The whinnying of a horse. Someone banging on the front door. Mr Brewer running in.

It was always four in the morning when he woke up during those fraught and funnelled weeks. The sudden start of the guilty heart. Sometimes, when he came to, he would be lying in Rosalind's bed, her body entwined around his, and that would give him a second start. He would slink back to his room, usually wretchedly hungover, to endure the interminable wait before daylight and his first allowable drink, which would lift him enough to get through to the next allowable drink. He would resolve not to visit her room again, but she would seek him out: her brimming eyes, her pleading need, her well-chosen nightwear. He was weak. He was the roguish brother. He might as well accept his part in proceedings.

Two weeks after Jasper's death, he bought his first aeroplane – a plucky little Sopwith Snipe, built in the final weeks of the war, too late to be called into service – and that lifted him higher. He called it *May*. His favourite month of the year and one of his most favourite words when used in conjunction with the word 'you'. *May I? You may.*

Perhaps it was bizarre he was even thinking of such things – aviation, women, what Jasper called his 'bachelor activities' – when Jasper had so recently died. But his mind seemed unable to keep company with the fact his brother had gone. It was desperate, laughable, and in the face of such nonsense, his mind kept jumping up and scampering off to its favourite haunts. Even as he was walking behind his brother's coffin with little Cristabel holding his hand, he was trying to remember the name of a lissom Italian actress he'd met in Covent Garden.

Like a crude jester with a stick of jingling bells, his mind would occasionally jab him with a reminder that he had been engaged in 'bachelor activity' with his brother's wife when his brother died. It seemed terribly unfair, that combination of events; something that could never be undone, a judgement, a branding. Particularly unfair, given that he hadn't approached his brother's wife in his usual way. It had come from somewhere else, yet ended up in the same place, only worse.

What was to be done? Poked by the stick, burnt by the brand, Willoughby fled. He crossed the skies in *May*. Spent Christmas gambling in Monte Carlo. Went skiing with an Austrian fencing champion called Gretchen. Filled a bath at The Savoy with bubbles and showgirls on New Year's Eve. As long as he kept moving, it was all right. On and on and on. His flight both resistance to and acceptance of the mark singed into his side.

Whenever he soared over Chilcombe on his way somewhere else, he would feel rather sorry for it, the saggy old heap, empty and ownerless. But it wasn't empty at all. It was full of females: a newly wealthy widow, a baby girl, an orphan daughter, a flock of agitated servants, and poor Blythe and Mr Brewer left holding the fort, two stalwart men drowning in a sea of women. It wasn't ownerless either: it was waiting for the sole remaining Seagrave to give up the game and come back to earth.

But every time he returned to England, it felt fusty and small. *May*'s wheels would bump down on the turf and there would be a tingle of something bitter at the back of his nostrils as he inhaled his foggy homeland. A damp dog smell. Sodden moss. The cold green-grey of ivy. Elderly England: familiar; unimpressed; chuntering along as ever. He would refuel as quickly as he could. Get up to the clouds. Wings on his heels.

When he finally did go home to Chilcombe, after receiving a telegram telling him he was to become a father, Rosalind had clutched at him and said, 'You came back for me. I was sure you would. Please don't leave me again. I couldn't bear it. I think I would die.'

She said, 'Perhaps it was meant to be all along. You and I.'

She said, 'We're to have a son. A Seagrave son and heir.'

She said, 'So who is "May"? Is she someone I know?'

That was that. The trap was sprung. The mechanism whirred into life. There was the story Rosalind told about them – the graceful love story, the blossoming discovery, the younger Seagrave brother and the tragic Seagrave widow *turning to each other for comfort, as so many do* – and there was an intricate machinery set to spinning beneath it. It wasn't that he didn't trust her. (Although, did he?) It wasn't that he didn't want her. (Although, now he had her, did he? Off and on, he did. Off and on.) There was merely something that niggled. Something he glimpsed sometimes, between her slow blinks; something in the way her long-toed feet reminded him of a monkey seen in a Cairo market.

In sharp moments, he suspected she knew he knew she was not all her saucer eyes proclaimed her to be, but it was easier for them both to go along with it. Her devotion was soporific. He was Odysseus to her Calypso: the adventurer ensnared by a sweet-voiced nymph on an island of pleasure. He was Paris to her Helen: the beautiful stealer of beautiful ensnared wives. It was better not to question where her devotion came from or what it wanted. It was better not to look at things too closely, as a rule.

After they married – a discreet London ceremony that took place quickly enough to claim Digby (a conveniently small August baby) was born unexpectedly early – he found his view of her changed again. She seemed to meld with Chilcombe itself, like a hermit crab, so that when he thought of her, she was part of the house and all its expectations. There was Chilcombe and there was Rosalind inside it, wanting things done, fussing with furnishings. The way she would rush to greet him with attention and questions, her hands seeking out the flesh at his waist, her fingers pressing, kneading, and tiptoeing up on to their sharpened ends, so he felt her nails digging in. A line of tiny smiling bites.

That she was his wife seemed rather unreal. Inconsequential. The fact he was married would occasionally pop into his mind during turbulent flights, when the slim possibility of his own death bounced into view; but rarely before, and never after. Even then, he only remembered it in a distant, *oh yes* sort of way, as if it was something he'd seen on holiday once – a waterfall; an ostrich.

So he returned to Dorset as the owner of Chilcombe, as husband, father and owner of the estate. He set *May* down in a field. Took off his flying hat and goggles. Then slowly followed the meandering path along the cliff edge, back to his waiting obligations.

As he does this, on a balmy August evening in 1928, he thinks that a decent summer's day in England goes some way towards redeeming the country's usual dispiriting weather. The long grass whispers and shifts. There is the *futz* of a bumblebee close to his ear.

Emerging on to the lawn, he sees, once again, preparatory activity for a theatrical production. The door to Chilcombe is wide open and Blythe and Betty are overseeing the movement of furniture, trailed by Betty's sturdy young son, while Maudie grapples with a box of floral decorations. A few rooks are pecking at the grass, but they take off as Willoughby approaches, with brisk wingbeats of air, an efficient sound like the brushing down of an expensive suit.

Digby, wearing something yellow and voile, gambols across the lawn towards his father, followed by Myrtle, barefoot in a cerise silk dressing gown, brandishing a cocktail glass, and Cristabel carrying a huge set of cymbals.

'Willoughby Seagrave, runaway brother,' says Myrtle, 'we were wondering if you would make it in time.'

'I promised Cristabel I would be here for the rehearsal, and here I am,' he replies. 'Somebody may have to remind me what part I'm playing.'

'You're Antonio,' says Cristabel.

'We're doing *The Tempest* by a fellow called William Shakespeare,' says Myrtle, turning in circles on the lawn. 'I presume you've heard of him.'

'Always have a copy of his latest to hand,' says Willoughby. 'I'm not going to ask about the cymbals, as I don't want to give anyone a reason to make a noise with them, but I would like to know why my son is wearing tights.'

'I'm Ariel, Father,' says Digby. 'A tricksy spirit.'

'You mustn't let the girls dress you up like a doll, Digby,' says Willoughby.

'I chose my costume all by myself,' says Digby.

'Can we hurry up, please?' says Cristabel, setting off along the path through the trees.

Willoughby offers Myrtle his arm – 'Shall we?' – and they follow the children.

'That's quite a costume you have on, Willoughby. Is that a leather flying jacket?' says Myrtle, bumping companionably against a tree trunk as they make their way through the woods. 'Please don't ask me to elucidate *The Tempest*. I haven't been paying a great deal of attention.'

'It has a wizard, I believe,' replies Willoughby. Cristabel is far up ahead on the path, marching briskly. Digby has disappeared from view.

'Prospero. He's trapped on an island. That's Taras,' says Myrtle, passing her glass to Willoughby so he can take a sip. 'Oh, and there's a usurping brother, I forget his name.'

'That old chestnut.'

'There's some drunken comic relief too. That's where I come in.' Myrtle takes an elaborate bow that allows her dressing gown to gape open, revealing bare skin beneath.

Willoughby glances at her swaying breasts in the benignly approving way he might look at a child's drawings. 'Myrtle old girl, you're giving me quite an eyeful.'

'Don't tell your wife. She'll have me flung out.'

Digby appears from behind a tree. 'Who's being flung out?'

'Nobody,' says Willoughby. 'Digby, when was the last time you had your hair cut? What with the wild locks and the tights, it's all rather excessive. You'll have to smarten up before you go to school, or you'll be eaten alive.'

'What does excessive mean?' says Digby.

'You know,' says Willoughby. 'Overdone. Loud.'

'Excessive!' cries Digby loudly. His voice echoes through the trees.

'My word, Digby, I think you're the first person to say anything loud in these woods,' says Myrtle.

'I like to be loud, don't you?' he says, then runs after Cristabel and grabs her hand.

'You don't need to hold Cristabel's hand any more either,' calls Willoughby. 'You're not a baby.' He glances at Myrtle and adds, 'My mother spoilt me rotten. I refuse to let Rosalind do the same to him. Tell me, is Perry here?'

'Unlike you, Peregrine is never late,' says Myrtle. 'Generally, he likes to arrive before you've even noticed he's there.'

'He would call that reconnaissance.'

'Even when dining at The Berkeley?' says Myrtle.

'Colonel Drake is never off duty, Myrtle. Surely you've noticed.'

Myrtle turns to him. 'Why isn't Colonel Drake ever off duty? There isn't a war on.'

'There's always a war on somewhere, darling. What is it now, Digby?'

'Father, I asked Cristabel about my hair and she said many brave warriors had long hair.'

'Cristabel, Digby needs to have his hair cut and that's that,' says Willoughby loudly. 'Nobody goes to boarding school with long hair. Nobody who wants to survive anyway.'

Cristabel pauses on the path and turns round, holding a cymbal on either side of herself, like golden chariot wheels. 'I thought only women cared about hair.'

'Schools have rules,' says Willoughby. 'Digby needs to fit in.'

'Says the man who arrived in his own plane,' says Myrtle, taking a slurp of her drink.

'So Digby has to have the same hair as every other boy or he'll be punished,' says Cristabel. 'That's a ridiculous rule.'

'I didn't make them, darling,' says Willoughby.

'You go along with them,' says Cristabel, 'and you make Digby go along with them, and if I went to school, you'd make me go along with them, but I'm not allowed to go to school, and that's ridiculous too.'

Cristabel turns back to the path, leading the party out of the woods and along the grassy path towards the cottage.

'Cristabel,' begins Willoughby, 'it's simply one of those unavoidable things, I – good God, what the devil is that?'

The scene at the cottage has once again been transformed. The performance space is now surrounded by professional stage lighting ordered by Rosalind, and there are rows of new fold-out seats. But in the middle of the stage area stands the most surprising transformation of all: the Chilcombe whale.

The large rib bones of the whale have been removed from its carcass, stripped of flesh, and positioned upright on the ground to form a curving space, six feet high, between the barn and the cottage. They resemble twin lines of giant elephant tusks arching upwards like the sides of a galleon. Behind them, the sea is shining gold in the evening sun.

The bones have been placed far enough apart that members of the cast can move in between them or huddle beneath them, as Perry, Mr Brewer and several others are doing now, pretending they are aboard the storm-tossed ship at the start of *The Tempest*. Digby and Cristabel run to join them. A couple of hikers in shorts and walking boots have paused on the beach, watching proceedings with puzzled interest.

'It's quite a thing, isn't it?' says Myrtle to Willoughby, as they stand side by side looking at it. 'In the love scenes, it is illuminated with pink lighting. Nothing says romance like a dead whale.'

'How on earth did they get those great bones here?'

'I'm hazy on the details, but your wife approved it.'

Willoughby takes out a cigarette case, offers one to Myrtle, and frowns. 'I heard some talk of an outdoor theatre at dinner, but I never imagined this.'

'Rosalind is hopeful it will attract more artistic types,' says Myrtle.

'Don't tell me you people are going to stay,' says Willoughby. 'Always leave them wanting more – isn't that what they say?'

'You don't like sharing the limelight, do you?' says Myrtle.

Willoughby turns to her, his cigarette held in his mouth. 'The same could be said of you, darling.' He takes both sides of her loose dressing gown, pulls them together, then reaches around her waist to find the belt.

'What do you think a psychiatrist would make of our infantile need for attention?' asks Myrtle, swaying slightly. 'There must be something very lacking, don't you think?'

'I don't need attention,' he says, tightening her belt briskly, then tying it in a bow. 'All these theatrics, I mean, it's all right for the children, but for adults – it's hardly a worthwhile occupation.'

'And what is it that you do, that is so worthwhile?' says Myrtle. They are roughly the same height; they stand eye to eye.

When he doesn't answer, Myrtle reaches out to straighten the collar of his flying jacket, with the careful tenderness of the drunk. 'I ask myself the same question,' she says. 'What do I do? Why do I do it? Why can't I settle down? That's what my mother says. Why can't you settle down, Myrtle?'

'I do what is expected of me,' says Willoughby.

'Do you?' She squints at him.

He smiles. 'No, I suppose I don't even manage that. I do very little, Myrtle, which is also expected of me.'

At that moment, Cristabel, carrying her cymbals, clambers up on to one of the new seats in front of her cast and demands, 'Again.'

'We're in this scene,' says Myrtle, heading towards the bones and pulling Willoughby behind her.

As the actors go through their scene, Cristabel stands on the seat and repeatedly crashes the cymbals together, to represent the waves of the storm. The sound is a bright metal shock followed by a shimmering reverberation.

'Where did she get those infernal things?' Willoughby says, rubbing his temples.

'The local Salvation Army band,' replies Myrtle, reclining against a rib. 'It's not the only thing she borrowed from them.'

At that moment, Digby appears from the barn, calling, 'I've found my flute, but lost my wings.'

'Flossie will find your wings,' says Cristabel. 'All right, everyone, now Ariel has his flute, can we return to Act Two, Scene One, where Ariel sends everyone to sleep with enchanting music.'

'My son has wings,' says Willoughby.

'Digby looks divine,' says Myrtle. 'As long as you ignore the hideous noise he makes with that flute, it's a captivating scene.'

'Like the screeching of an owl, almost,' says Perry.

'Uncle Willoughby, Mr Brewer has your lines on a bit of paper if you need them,' calls Cristabel. 'Places, everyone.'

ANTONIO (**Willoughby**): Thank you. Where do I start? Here? Something something hope something beyond. This writing is very small. 'Will you grant with me that Ferdinand is drown'd?'

Enter the Whale

By the end of August, the Seagrave children have shed their previous lives like snakeskins. Now they are wild creatures who live in the sunlight with the savages, rampaging through the woods in theatrical costumes. On the rare occasions they go back into Chilcombe, with its cool stone floors, it is like stepping into a dark pond. Green-black and stagnant.

On warm nights, Cristabel, Flossie and Digby sleep inside the whalebones, huddled together under scratchy blankets, sharing stolen biscuits. It reminds Cristabel of when she would lift little Digby from his cradle and carry him upstairs to her bed where she could read him stories, how they slept tangled like pack animals to share warmth. They wake to the sound of the sea and when they run to the edge of the glimmering water, they find it pristine, newly created, a bale of blue silk unrolled at their feet.

Every morning, Cristabel looks at her bones with pride and relief. She had come so close to losing them. As the whale decomposed, local officials kept appearing to poke at it. They talked of burying it or blowing it up. Cristabel had begun to wish she could drag its broken parts out to sea, to let them sink beneath the waves, where at least nobody could touch them. She knew she must find some way to save it.

Then one night, up on the roof of Chilcombe, eating a bun and flicking through a notebook, she had seen a drawing of the wooden horse of Troy done by Digby – a horse on wheels, like an enlarged Edgar the elephant, with little people inside – and on the facing page, a note in her own blockish handwriting, reporting that, according to the book she is reading, Mr Melville's *Moby-Dick*, the

Norse kings made their thrones from the tusks of narwhals. She had turned the page, then paused, turned back. The wooden horse. The tusks. The king.

She looked out across the trees to the ocean. Put down the bun. Picked up her pencil. Sketched lines on the page. Curved lines, like the scenery that arched over the dancers of the Ballets Russes. In between them, she drew people acting and dancing. Then she ripped out the page and clambered down the roof to find Digby.

The following day, they took the drawing to Taras, who, delighted by their ingenuity ('Ah! The jumping minds of children!'), did a more detailed sketch, incorporating wooden struts to hold the whalebones in place, and all they needed now was Rosalind's approval. In order to gain Rosalind's approval, the idea had to come through either Digby or an adult, as any approach from Cristabel was bound to fail. The children knew that leaving something so important to an adult was a risky strategy, but feared Digby may not be taken seriously, so asked Taras to put the idea to Rosalind.

Cristabel and Digby hid in the cloakroom under the stairs the next time Taras came to the house for dinner and so were able to listen in when, amid the chatter between the second and third courses, he suggested using the whale's skeleton to make some kind of theatre. It was breathlessly exciting, to have someone in that private room of adults secretly acting on their behalf. But hearing their proposal discussed was like watching a beachball being tossed about. It bounced among the dinner guests lightly, entertaining some, patted away by others, and, infuriatingly, Rosalind paid it no attention at all, instead repeatedly asking what people thought of the escalopes served with cucumber in a cream sauce.

Their idea seemed to drift away, and they thought it lost for good, but it unexpectedly floated back into view after pudding was served, when Philly joked that they should sell ice creams if they made a theatre by the seaside.

'If we do what?' asked Rosalind, and so Taras explained 'his' idea for the whale again, only this time with more enthusiasm, as the dinner had involved several bottles of wine.

★

It was fortunate that, when Taras talked about the theatre for a second time, Rosalind was savouring one of the moments in life she most prized: the coffee at the end of a successful dinner. Everyone aglow with good eating, flattered and replete, not yet tired or argumentative. The conversation expansive, humorous, fond.

'A permanent outdoor theatre?' she said.

'An avant-garde outdoor theatre,' said Hilly, 'created by an artist.'

'My dear old aunt used to put on pageants in the grounds of her house every Empire Day,' said Philly. 'We children would march about dressed as Boudica and Nelson.'

Rosalind suddenly remembered going to watch an outdoor performance of *Twelfth Night* at a Sussex manor. It was before the war, a time that now seemed sealed off from her. How taken she had been both with the elegant lady of the house and the perfect setting: the tiered lawn and landscaped gardens; the guests strolling beneath cedar trees. It was as if they had been given access to an enchanted place. She could remember little of the play but recalled the sound of the appreciative audience sitting on the grass, a warm collectivity that somehow mingled with the warmth of the summer evening sky. A calm and benevolent sky, overlooking human activity that was beautiful, in a beautiful place, and how rare that was.

'Your son does love to perform,' said Myrtle.

'Digby has quite a talent,' Rosalind replied, remembering too the heady sensation of seeing her son applauded.

'A gift for pretence is hardly a talent,' said Willoughby, leaving the table to fetch his cigarettes. 'There's no future for him on the stage, darling.'

Rosalind watched Willoughby depart and took a sip of her coffee. She was, she felt, somehow anti-future. It did nothing, as far as she could work out, but grip too tightly on the present.

She looked at Taras, who was leaning back in his chair, his collar undone, watching her. He never bothered to conceal his watching; he was, at least, transparent in his lack of morals. The Rasputin in her dining room.

'It wouldn't be ugly, would it?' she said. 'I don't want anything ridiculous, that people might laugh at.'

'It will be magnificent,' Taras replied. 'Besides, Hillary would never let me create anything ugly. She is fastidious.'

Hilly, at his side, smiled the faint smile of the assisting woman, then looked at Rosalind with her still gaze. 'It would not be ugly.'

'Very well then,' said Rosalind. 'Create a theatre.'

So it began: the transformation of the whale. A project nominally headed by Taras, but in reality carried out by Mr Brewer and his network of useful contacts, starting with an acquaintance on the parish council, who persuaded the local fire brigade to bring their engine down to the beach, pursued by a gang of giddy village children, where they used seawater to hose the bones clean. Mr Brewer then arranged for some men from the village – a blacksmith and a carpenter – to transport the bones to their new home by the cottage, helped by Leon and the larger savages. Once on site, they were varnished and put into position.

Cristabel oversaw these operations. She carried her sharpened flagpole with her but, while she enjoyed holding it and pointing with it, she no longer had any desire to use it as a weapon against an animal she had come to regard as her ward.

Similarly, while she composed a letter to King George to inform him she had moved the whale (mentioned in previous correspondence) on to her family estate, she couldn't bring herself to post it. She wasn't sure why. She didn't want to claim the whale any more; it was no longer a conquest, it was something else. Something better. She tucked the letter under her bed and left it there.

Mr Brewer and his team even managed to extract the enormous jawbones from the rotting whale's head, through Mr Brewer enlisting the help of the village butcher. The bones were flensed and cleaned, then placed halfway between the woods and the cottage, standing one on either side of the path that led to the theatre, forming a triumphal arch, a huge needle's eye to pass through: an entranceway.

The whiteness of the whalebones drew fluttering moths and gnawing fox cubs, and these were not the only creatures to visit. Every year, at summer's end, Betty and Maudie carried all the stuffed animals out of Chilcombe to let them air on the lawn for a day or two. But this year, Cristabel and Digby borrowed a few to serve as props and decorations. Then they took more and more, until the lawn was quite depleted and the scene at the theatre a taxidermist's ball, a cavalcade of badgers, otters and quail, dancing and fighting around the bones, occasionally toppling over like stiff-limbed drunks. One bird, a great auk, was propped on the cottage porch, while several of the tiniest songbirds were tied around the brim of a top hat that Leon had taken to wearing. He tucked his cigarettes under their wings.

One morning, Leon gathers up a long rope from the barn, coils it neatly, and sets off alone towards Ceal Head. Intrigued, Cristabel trails him and finds him halfway up the coast path, peering at a tall sycamore tree near the cliff edge. He has thrown the rope over a high bough and is tying a branch to its end to serve as a swing. Once this is done, he turns and hands it to her, with a challenge in his eyes.

Cristabel takes hold of the swing and backs up. When she has gone as far as she can go, she takes a breath and jumps on to the branch before she can change her mind. She flies past Leon, past the tree, past the cliff edge; clinging to the swing as it soars upwards on its long arc, carrying her out over the sea, which rolls and crashes a hundred feet below her. There is an exhilarating moment, when the rope goes slack and she is left hanging high over the ocean, weight-less as a bird, before swooping back to safety.

For the first few swings, Leon stops her when she returns to land and checks the rope, but once satisfied it is secure, he starts to push her, so she goes even higher. Every time she goes past him, he puts his hands to her back to speed her on. Then they swap so he can try it, and they continue through the afternoon, workers on the rope, with hardly a word said between them.

One night, the children decide to have a war party, like the Indian braves of the Wild West.

Cristabel says Indian braves must make a sacrifice. She retrieves her sculpture of Sekhmet the fire goddess from the attic so they can build a bonfire in front of her. They use driftwood as fuel, and it catches quickly, sparks flying upwards between the bones.

What now? they ask her, their faces expectant.

First, she puts on Prospero's robes. Then she ties a stuffed weasel to a stick using shoelaces around its front and back paws, and the children parade to the fire to lay it across the flames. The weasel burns slowly at first, giving off a faintly chemical smell, then the dry rags inside it ignite and it roars into flame.

Cristabel uses a spade to spread out the glowing fire, the weasel burning in the middle. Then she tells them they each have to jump over the sacrificial animal to prove they are warriors.

'I will go first,' says Leon, taking off his top hat.

'No,' says Cristabel. 'I want to.'

'I don't know if I can do that,' says Flossie.

'If you jump high enough, you won't touch the flames, Floss,' says Digby, taking her hand. 'We'll go together. You, me and Crista.'

So they do, three leaping bodies silhouetted over the bright fire, hands clasped. Then the savages follow, one by one, and they all like it so much, they burn another animal and do it again.

Sometimes, when the others are asleep, Cristabel will walk around her whale. It is most clearly her whale in the solitary blue light of night, as it was when she found it. The late summer nights are windless and still, the silver sea calm in the bowl of the bay.

When Cristabel walks through the jawbones, she remembers the whale's downturned mouth, its vulnerable eye. When she stands in its ribcage, she recalls how she had once placed her hands on the outside of its body, and now she is inside its body, in the space created by its absent life. When she looks up, she sees the bones arching over her head against the vast starry sky like roof beams, like the skeletal beginnings of a strange new home. Something she has made from what was washed up, unwanted; something created from what was left to her.

Cuttings Kept in a Scrapbook by the Children

DORSET DAILY ECHO, AUGUST 1928

An amateur performance of Shakespeare's *The Tempest* at Chilcombe Mell drew a considerable crowd.

Mrs Rosalind Seagrave served cream teas for those attending. Miss Florence Seagrave gave a piano recital.

WESTERN DAILY PRESS, AUGUST 1929

A Midsummer Night's Dream was this week performed at Chilcombe, one of Dorset's lesser-known country homes.

The play was presented in a structure created by artist Mr Taras Kovalsky from the remains of a fin whale and used by the Seagrave family as a theatre. The part of Oberon was taken by Col Peregrine Drake, returned from a diplomatic posting in Persia.

Picture shows Miss Myrtle van der Werff, Miss Hillary Vaughan and Miss Philippa Fenwick in costume as Hippolyta, Titania and Helena, alongside Master Digby Seagrave as Puck and an unknown participant wearing the head of an ass.

THE LADY, AUGUST 1930

Regular readers will know how we delight in young people's artistic endeavours, so it was a joy to watch *The Tempest* at Chilcombe, in which Ariel was played by nine-year-old Digby Seagrave, heir to the Dorset estate.

His proud mother, Mrs Rosalind Seagrave, was in the front row – and quite right too, for her son has a natural sensitivity. Mrs Seagrave is hopeful a dramatic work by Mr Noël Coward will be added to the fledgling company's repertoire.

Master Digby, who attends Sherborne School, was quick to inform us he believes his cousin, Miss Cristine Seagrave, aged 14, to be the 'brains' behind their production. However, we suspect the presence of artist Mr Taras Kovalsky may explain the more diverting dramatic choices.

SOUTHERN TIMES, AUGUST 1931

This summer's theatrics at Chilcombe included a production of *Measure for Measure* in the remarkable 'whalebone theatre' along with extracts from Molière's *Le Bourgeois Gentilhomme*.

The latter was performed in the original French on the lawn of the manor. The Seagrave children are fluent French speakers thanks to their governess Mlle Ernestine Aubert, who accompanies them on trips to her homeland.

Guests were also treated to a selection of French 'vol au vents' served 'en plein air', an occasion hardly marred by the inclement weather.

TATLER, AUGUST 1932

All eyes were on avant-garde artist Taras Kovalsky and new bride Hillary Kovalsky née Vaughan on their return to England this week after a honeymoon spent dazzling even the most dazzle resistant elements of New York society.

The sought-after newly-weds spent time in Dorset before heading to a suitably artistic bolthole in St Ives.

Sadly missing from this year's South Coast social hullabaloo was Philippa Fenwick, said to be sojourning in Switzerland. We wish her well.

DAILY EXPRESS, AUGUST 1933

Miss Cristabel Seagrave has returned from a year on the Continent to attend this year's Queen Charlotte's Ball.

The athletic debutante, as much of a whizz on the ski slopes of Europe as she is riding out with hounds, no doubt caught the eye of many a potential suitor.

But Miss Seagrave told our reporter she will be missing much of The Season as she plans to take up the reins of a production of *Macbeth* at her family's outdoor theatre. Tally ho!

Picture shows His Royal Highness Prince George arriving at the Queen Charlotte's Ball. Full details of royal engagements, page 4.

WOMAN'S JOURNAL, AUGUST 1934

The golden summer days draw to a close and that can only mean a jaunt to Dorsetshire, where Digby Seagrave took centre stage at The Whalebone Theatre as a captivating Henry V.

His cousin Cristabel Seagrave has recently returned from being finished in Switzerland. The ever-fragrant Mrs Rosalind Seagrave, fresh from cheering on her husband at Cowes, told us Cristabel relishes the foreign experience.

DAILY MAIL, AUGUST 1935

Our critic was somewhat bemused by an unusual production of Shakespeare's *Julius Caesar* at The Whalebone Theatre in Dorset in which Caesar was played by Miss Cristabel Seagrave, a young woman from a prominent local family.

However, the backdrop of the setting sun over the ocean was picturesque enough to offset any juvenile errors of theatrical judgement.

THE TIMES, AUGUST 1936

The Spanish political situation found itself reflected in a production of *Romeo and Juliet*, with Romeo depicted as a member of an 'International Brigade'.

The amateur performance in Dorset saw the cast perform in contemporary dress, following the current trend to make the Stratford Bard a modern man.

Digby Seagrave, aged 15, a charming Romeo, told our reporter he was inspired by British volunteers joining the battle for Spain. He added he hopes to take up a place at Cambridge alongside pursuing his theatrical ambitions.

The production also included elements of dance reminiscent of Mr W. H. Auden's experimental works for The Group Theatre, bravely accompanied by Miss Florence Seagrave on the piano and cymbals.

SOUTHERN TIMES, AUGUST 1937

A smaller crowd than in previous years attended the Chilcombe summer production.

The cast of *Antony and Cleopatra* battled against persistent rain showers but were perhaps also struggling against the appeal of comedy film *Oh, Mr Porter!* currently drawing record audiences to Dorchester's Plaza Cinema.

DORSET DAILY ECHO, AUGUST 1938

Work has commenced on Weymouth's new pier after judges decided on a winning design from a number submitted to an architectural competition.

Summer visitors have enjoyed seeing the foundation blocks of the attraction being moved into place.

Further along the coast, visitors have also been entertained by a production of *All's Well that Ends Well* on the Chilcombe estate.

ACT THREE

1939–1941

Parties

Rosalind opens the front door as wide as it can go and the house inhales: a gasp of wind rushes along its hallways; the fires in the downstairs rooms bulge outwards to meet it and the candle flames leap and quiver – eager, oxygenated movements that are reflected in dancing glints along the silver trays of cocktails and the framed photographs on top of the grand piano, and on the piano itself, which is as black and slick as onyx.

Rosalind, standing in the doorway, pictures herself standing in the doorway. A slim silhouette against a rectangular glowing space. She adjusts her fox-fur stole; waits. From elsewhere, they are coming. Powering towards her in their expensive cars, headlights like torch beams funnelling through the evening darkness.

It gets dark earlier and earlier now. In the daytime, the autumn sunlight is low and rich, the countryside ablaze with trees in amber, umber and ochre. The trees on the estate stand proudly as their leaves change colour, the way people hold their heads high in front of a firing squad. But when the sun drops below the horizon, the chill is very sudden and very quick.

The grandfather clock in the Oak Hall strikes the hour. Soon Rosalind's guests will arrive, and she will have her party. Her parties have not ended. Not yet. But here comes Mr Brewer telling her they must draw the blackout curtains because the house is lit up like a target again.

'I know, Mr Brewer. I simply wanted everyone to see Chilcombe as it should be seen. We've gone to an awful lot of bother to hide ourselves from German bombers when there don't seem to be any.'

'Better safe than sorry, Mrs Seagrave.'

'The parcel tape across the windows is so very ugly, I'm sure it will scare off any invading force all by itself.'

'I'll draw the curtains, Mrs Seagrave.'

'In a moment.' Because there is a car coming up the drive and her guests are arriving. She should have a cigarette in her hand. 'Willoughby!'

Willoughby, sunk in a wingback armchair in the drawing room, rocks the whisky in his glass. He watches as Maudie empties a rumbling shovel of coal on to the fire, extinguishing the flames with a steaming hiss, then crouches beside it, puffing at it with a set of bellows until it flickers back to life. Willoughby hears a little huff of annoyance in each sigh of the bellows. Maudie has a gift for animating the inanimate, making the tools of her trade speak for her. She has never learnt to remove herself as the other servants do, even after twenty years working in the house. She is always very much there, drawing the eye.

In a corner of the room, a jazz record rotates on the gramophone, repeating its scratchy sentimental songs. Nearby, Flossie is also circling, practising dance steps and peering out into the hall at the arriving guests. She is wearing an embroidered pink dress two sizes too small. Willoughby wonders whether Rosalind deliberately dresses the poor girl badly, or whether her outfits are an unfortunate collision between nineteen-year-old Flossie's love for shepherdess dirndl and her mother's belief that a woman's clothes should wrap her as tightly as a gift from Harrods.

Willoughby stretches his legs out in front of him, props his feet on a footstool. He's never been fond of the start of parties. 'I've never been fond of the start of parties,' he says, as his wife calls his name again. 'Dull exercises in obligation. Maudie, do you like the start of parties?'

'I've never been to a party, Mr Willoughby sir,' she replies.

'Liar. Course you have. Even in those miserable Hardy novels, the villagers sometimes go to a party. Toast each other with *zoider*. Sing songs about courting till fate intervenes and crushes all hope.'

'Never been to your sort of party, Mr Willoughby.'

'They're overrated. You'd hate them,' he says, scrabbling at his hair. 'Maudie, I'm sorry – I'm not in the best of humours. I went to report myself at Winchester today, to offer my services to my country, but they told me to go home. Suggested I might like to organize the Local Defence Volunteers instead.'

'Betty told me she's carrying a pepper pot in her apron to defend herself against the Hun,' says Maudie. 'She might need some organizing.'

'Thank you, Maudie.'

'Are you too old to fight now, Mr Willoughby?'

'I bloody well am not. Still in my forties, until next month. Perry simply needs to have a word. He'll make sure Digby does all right too. Could you wander over to the drinks cabinet and find the whisky?'

'Master Digby couldn't fight anybody.'

'You don't get to choose when it comes to war. He'll do what he must.' As he says this, Willoughby can hear disconcerting echoes of his father in his voice. He finds he cannot look at Maudie and instead keeps glancing at his lap as if expecting to find a newspaper there, while his non-drink-holding hand has raised itself up in a splayed finger gesture that means it's out of my hands / it's been arranged.

With each guest that arrives, there is a draught that blows through the house, disturbing the fires in the fireplaces so they make a noise like rippling flags. Flossie, hovering in the doorway, reports, 'The Cunninghams are here. Her dress is beautiful.'

Willoughby offers up his glass to Maudie. 'Little more.'

'She has a white feather in her hat,' continues Flossie. 'Do you think that's a radical statement?'

'Your mother's friends often make their feelings known through headwear,' says Willoughby.

'They were married in Venice last month,' says Flossie.

'Is he the one they found in Green Park with a guardsman? I expect they've come to some arrangement.'

Flossie, adjusting her neckline, says, 'Crista says the rich never look at each other once they're married.'

'Not if they can help it,' says Willoughby, eyeing a glamorous photograph of his wife on a side table. 'Any sign of Perry?'

'Not yet,' says Flossie. 'There's an older man in a raincoat arriving now. Perhaps he's the exiled journalist from Poland. Mother says he's seen horrors beyond compare.'

'Your mother says many things. Often. Over and over.'

'He does look troubled.'

'Why don't you introduce yourself, Floss? You could cheer him up.'

'Maybe.'

'This might be the last party we have for a while,' says Willoughby. 'Best make the most of it. Do you want a drink?'

'No, thank you. There's Perry now.'

Flossie darts across the drawing room to examine herself in the mirror over the fireplace. She has spent the last few hours sitting in front of a mirror in the attic, with a grim-faced Maudie trying unsuccessfully to curl Flossie's hair with a pair of hot tongs. Betty normally does it, but they are short of kitchen staff, so Maudie had to step in. Flossie was forced to watch her own reflection repeatedly wincing every time the hissing tongs singed her hair; her face creasing with embarrassed smiling as if trying to fold itself away.

She looks at her hair. Bits of it are pointing outwards in peculiar ways, like someone giving confused directions. Her mother always tells her to tuck it behind her ears, but Flossie is aware her ears stick out a little, so prefers to keep them hidden. In this, as in much else, she feels her state of being is a series of unsatisfactory concealments, each of which reveals something else that should not be shown. To tuck back her hair reveals her sticky-out ears. To highlight her waist emphasizes her wide hips. To show off her ankles means displaying her sturdy calves. It is a series of feints and misdirections, in which she is both the magician waving the coloured handkerchiefs and the assistant with the fixed smile holding up the white rabbit by the scruff of its neck, and somehow also the rabbit too, limply dangling, proffered up; all of which has the effect of making her permanently anxious she has somehow come loose of herself, that the doves have escaped from the hat.

Flossie's self-consciousness is not helped by Rosalind's tendency to exacerbate her daughter's most vulnerable moments. 'That weight must come from your father's side,' Rosalind says pityingly, whenever she sees Flossie struggling to button up an outfit. Or, 'You look pretty, darling. Imagine how much prettier you'll be when you lose the puppy fat.' Pricking remarks Flossie must silently absorb, just as the maids remain mute as they attempt to make her presentable, emitting only quick intakes of breath as they heave on her girdle. Her appearance seems a matter of constant effort, on all their parts. No wonder her clothes leave angry marks on her.

In the drawing room mirror, her face is shiny with exertion. Perhaps it would be better if she put on her newly issued gas mask for the evening. Over her shoulder, Cristabel appears, unblinking as a hawk.

'Crista. You gave me a start,' says Flossie. 'The Cunninghams are here and a troubled journalist. Not really any suitable candidates for my ongoing husband hunt.'

'Beggars can't be choosers,' says Cristabel, still unblinking. She has the blankly assessing gaze used by children to size up other children on first meeting; mannerless and unconcerned. Her hair has not been curled. It is jaw-length and blunt. She is wearing a thin-strapped dress that used to belong to Rosalind and doesn't suit or fit her. Her strong shoulders are hunched forward as if she were caught outside in her nightgown. She frowns at Flossie. 'Have you finished your tinkering now?'

'I wasn't tinkering. I was being saddened by my reflection,' replies Flossie.

'I've never had much time for mirrors,' says Cristabel. 'You and your mother check them constantly. Why is that? It's not as if much will change from one moment to the next.'

As if summoned, Rosalind appears in the doorway in a fluid gown of regal purple, her high heels rapping on the floor. 'Chin chin,' she says jovially, raising her cocktail glass to someone else. 'Why are you girls hiding in here? I've invited lots of charming young men. So dashing in their new uniforms.' She is vivid, heavily scented: nails painted; hair set.

'I was reviewing my hair,' says Flossie.

'Nothing can be done for it,' says her mother. 'Come and mingle. That Communist writer you like is here, with her companion who wears breeches and useful shoes. The lesbians.'

'You always say that word as if you were holding it with tweezers,' says Cristabel. 'Everybody knows what they are, including you.'

Rosalind waves a hand. 'People change their minds all the time. I wouldn't be surprised if they were manning the defences soon. They're rather formidable.'

'I might join them,' says Cristabel. 'Do my bit.'

'Good idea, darling. You could join the WAAF or something. You might find a boyfriend there,' says Rosalind, taking a sip of her drink. 'Now Flossie, a word of advice, stay away from the puddings. The only women who should eat puddings are those who look like they never do. Then it's charming. But if you look like you regularly wolf down puddings, practically on the hour, then it's no longer charming, it's a lack of discipline.'

'Are there puddings?' says Cristabel, starting for the doorway. 'I'll have some before dinner. I'd rather a pudding than a boyfriend. There aren't many men in the WAAF anyway. What do you think the "W" stands for?'

'I know what it stands for,' says Rosalind. 'Where's my husband? He has my cigarettes.'

'I'm here and I don't,' says Willoughby, a voice from deep within the armchair.

Flossie turns to the mirror, puffs her cheeks out so they become inflated, then turns back to her mother and gives a little clownish shrug. Rosalind raises her thin eyebrows and leaves the drawing room. Flossie puts her hands up to her face and pats her balloon cheeks thoughtfully, enjoying the small drum noises they make, then slowly squeezes the air back out.

Cristabel consumes treacle tart, apple pie, gooseberry fool, then paces the halls like a zoo animal. There is a young man from a nearby estate at the party. A young man she has spoken to about books at a previous party. A young man she had hoped would arrive as she would like to talk to him at dinner, a fact which makes her feel so mortified and ridiculous she almost stalks out of the house and off the cliff. Through an effort of will, she forces herself to sit next to him and glowers at the tableware, eating sugar-coated muscat grapes one by one. She manages conversation in short bursts. Makes mention of her theatre. Makes mention of fascism. Little machine-gun rattles of effort.

She becomes cautiously optimistic that he is interested in her opinions, even though she keeps finding herself putting her hands into pockets that do not exist and making a sort of useless scooping gesture. She is even persuaded to dance with him after dinner and thankfully doesn't tower above him too much. Then, just as she is admiring the sight of his laughing face in the candlelight, he mentions, in passing, a woman's name. He mentions, in passing, an engagement.

Her disappointment is familiar. Handed this bracing draught ('I know you're not the marrying type, but I hope you won't be too appalled by the idea, Crista old girl'), there is nothing to do but gulp it down in one ('Don't be daft, Ralph. Overjoyed for you both') and put her blithely unconcerned expression back on. How sterling she is. How used to this she is becoming. It doesn't seem possible for it to be any other way.

Why is it that other young women are considered worthy of romantic attention when she is – well. She is twenty-three now. Perhaps she shouldn't bother at all. It is a language she does not seem able to learn. She sees the Communist writer and her companion in breeches heading towards her, no doubt keen to discuss tyrannical Franco and the situation in Spain, but she is suddenly too tired to make conversation. She leaves the house, heads for the lawn.

She folds her arms, cold in her thin dress, and looks up at the sky. She isn't even sure she wants a romantic relationship. Certainly not one that requires squeezing her feet into uncomfortable shoes like Cinderella's ugly sisters and standing about waiting to be asked. She cannot bear to wait to be asked. It fills her with such fury that agreeable chit-chat becomes impossible. Chit-chat! Even the phrase is infuriating. Offering inoffensive pieces of conversation to bachelors as if they were babies who needed their food chopped up. Surely there must be some other way to proceed, a more honest way, with none of this pandering.

Most days, she hardly thinks about it, or rather, she mainly thinks about it in terms of the relationships in plays, like that between Cleopatra and Mark Antony, which are far more fascinating. But then her stepmother will have one of her parties, and Cristabel is wheeled out and displayed like a piece of furniture left at an auction.

That she continues to take part is largely due to a perverse desire to prove Rosalind wrong in her belief that nobody will find her attractive, and a vague sense that it would be useful to have a partner to talk to, to have someone to escort you to events like these, so you didn't have to spend the evening being rebuffed. But to actually become someone's wife, to give up her name and her home and her theatre – that has always appeared to her a kind of bowing out.

Besides, the newspapers say there's been a rush of war weddings, young couples marrying before they are parted, so any available men are most likely being taken. War will probably make most of their decisions for them now, and in that, if nothing else, she feels it is almost a relief.

Digby, strolling over the lawn towards her – eighteen and slender in a dinner suit – says, 'You look glum, chum.'

'It's parties, Digs,' she says.

'I know, Crista. You can't stand them.'

'How can you stand them?'

'There's always someone to talk to. People are usually interesting, don't you think? And when I get bored of people, I come and find you.'

'You're much better at it than I am,' she says. 'I wish everyone would go away, Digs.'

'They will soon.'

'Thank goodness I have you,' she says, tucking her arm in his.

He looks at her. 'Shall we go up on the roof for a smoke?'

They go inside and make their way up to the attic, where Cristabel and Flossie still have two single beds in their cramped bedroom.

The oppressively striped wallpaper is now covered with glossy post-ers for art exhibitions arranged by Myrtle and hand-drawn posters advertising performances at The Whalebone Theatre. The stuffed baby elephant is serving as a makeshift desk, with its back covered with books and a stool tucked under its stomach, while the goddess Sekhmet reclines against a glass ashtray on the window sill. Digby, as the heir-in-waiting, sleeps in a grander bedroom on the floor below whenever he is back from school, which he likens to being kept in the Tower of London ahead of your execution.

Cristabel grabs a woollen jumper from the floor and pulls it on over her dress, then kicks off her shoes in favour of a pair of Digby's old plimsolls. They clamber out of the window and up the mossy roof tiles to the chimneys, where cigarettes and a hip flask await them. The surrounding hills are entirely black. There are no lights to be seen.

'Crista,' says Digby, lighting her cigarette, 'I have to tell you some-thing. I'm going to go. Maybe tonight.'

'What do you mean? Go where?'

'I'm going to join the army.'

'The army? But Uncle Willoughby –'

'I know. Father wants me to join the RAF. But he likes aeroplanes, and I don't. I want to be a regular soldier, like the men in the village. Like an ordinary person.'

'Your mother would say that you aren't an ordinary person.'

'But I could be, don't you think? I missed my chance to join the fight against fascism in Spain. I don't want to miss this one.' He sud-denly smiles at her, wide and joyful, as if he were talking of parties, not war.

'Bloody hell, Digs.' Cristabel takes a fervent drag on her cigar-ette, puts an arm around him and pulls him close. The thought of Digby going off to the army makes her stomach lurch with fear. She can feel the narrow bones in his shoulders, the restlessness beneath his skin. He might be old enough to enlist, but he is still a wriggly, excitable boy to her, his skinny legs bumping against hers. She says, 'I don't think this war will be like the one in Spain. You've never been able to beat me in a duel, let alone the Germans.'

'I've played lots of soldiers onstage,' he says, taking her hand in his before proclaiming, ' "When the blast of war blows in our ears, then imitate the action of the tiger!" '

'It's not a play. Why don't you look for something closer to home?'

'Should I volunteer to entertain the troops in Dorchester?'

'No, just something less –'

'Something less like a war?' he laughs. 'Crista, you of all people should know that we don't get to choose our battles.'

Cristabel flicks ash from her cigarette. 'I've seen Nazis. I told you what they're like.'

'You also told me that we've gone past the point where we can stop Hitler by talking about him. You said Nazism made pacifism impossible. You've always been very clear I should listen to you.'

Cristabel growls.

'I simply can't stay here,' says Digby.

'Why not?' she says. 'I do.'

'Be fair, Crista,' he replies, 'you go skiing in Austria every year.'

'That's because I have to spend the rest of my time here, with your mother,' Cristabel says, more harshly than she intends.

'You could live somewhere else,' says Digby, after a moment. 'Father would help you do that, I'm sure.'

'And leave our theatre to run itself?'

Digby gazes out across the trees towards the coastline. 'Look here,' he says, 'I don't know what will happen to any of this. But I do know that I want to go.' He pauses, then adds in a lighter tone, 'Besides, Father always tells me I am too like Mother. Too inclined to the dramatic. Perhaps I can show him I'm not. He respects a military man.'

'He won't respect you for being stupid.'

They sit in silence for a moment. The noise of the party continues beneath them.

Cristabel says, 'I'm sorry, Digs. Are you set on it?'

He leans his head on her shoulder. 'I am. I'm sorry too. You're cross, aren't you?'

'Trying not to be. You better write to me every bloody day.'

'Every day.' There is a pause, then Digby adds, 'I didn't think you were afraid of anything.'

'How dare you. I'm not.'

'Then you mustn't be afraid for me.'

'I bloody won't be,' Cristabel says, exhaling smoke and absent-mindedly stroking his head.

In the house below, someone drunkenly begins to sing 'Land of Hope and Glory'.

Flossie, downstairs, seems unable to find a way to insert herself into the evening. There are closed groups everywhere she turns. She has run out of introductory conversational titbits. Her hair hurts. She hasn't been asked to dance. She would like to play the piano, but there are people in the way. The party swirls about without her.

She wanders through the Oak Hall as the grandfather clock strikes midnight and sees, through a gap in the door, Willoughby still lounging by the fireplace in the drawing room. The fire has died down to an orange glow between the coals. There are men in evening dress leaning on the mantlepiece, drinking port and smoking cigars. Flossie pauses for a moment to listen to the coded murmur of gentlemanly talk: things to be spoken of only in certain circles; things to be spoken of only in a circular, allusive way.

She imagines opening the door to join them. But she knows that even just the sight of her – a young woman – would cause their voices to tighten and rise up like drawbridges. She would be admitted with a wry, tongue-in-cheek deference ('Ah, the younger Seagrave girl come to grace us with her presence'), but then the conversational allusions would become further angled, until all was inference. She would never get to hear what they really meant. She would never hear the way they talked without women.

As it is, eavesdropping outside the door, she can half hear the conversation as it circulates with the cigar smoke, although it is difficult to tell who is saying what. That is Perry, she is almost certain, making a disparaging comment about the French forces. And that is Willoughby, surely, saying that the only thing you can rely on in France are the good ladies of the Blue Light Café in Le Havre, no, those amenable mademoiselles never lose their heads, despite their national fondness for the guillotine.

Laughter. The clink of glasses. The rasp and fizz of a struck match.

Perry, again: 'Remarkably short-sighted, removing the heads of those in charge.'

Willoughby: 'They are rather short though, the French.'

Someone else now, with a booming tone: 'One is always thankful there's water between them and us, what? Frankly, if I were the Führer, I'd be tempted to invade them myself.'

Then someone else, equally booming: 'Get Willoughby to take you over in his flying machine.'

A crotchety, elderly voice: 'It'll be over by Christmas. I can't believe the Germans have built up an army. My son tells me those tanks they put on parade are made of cardboard. Is that correct, Peregrine?'

'Not at all,' replies Perry, as carefully measured as ever, a spirit level of a man.

Willoughby adds: 'Cristabel saw some Nazi parades when she was in Europe.'

'Did she now?'

'She was appalled by what was going on over there.'

The crotchety one again: 'Damn shame we lost David to that terrible American adventuress – Wallis or whatever she's called – he could have shored things up.'

'Wallis Simpson. Heard she learnt a few tricks in Shanghai that rendered the poor boy incapable.'

'Two marriages behind her, she'd have picked up more than a few tricks.'

Laughter, laughter. The syrupy glug of port. Cries of 'down the hatch'.

'The Bavarians have backbone. There's no arguing with that. They've a right to rebuild their country.'

'What else would you do? Considering the threat from the East.'

'Quite right. A matter of national pride.'

The booming voice: 'It's greed that's brought us all to this point. Pure greed. Always been the Jewish weakness.'

'But did you read that piece in *The Times* this morning?'

A hubbub. A symposium. A war room.

Then Perry, his assured quietness: 'Whilst one does always hope for the best, I believe our most pressing issue is that we've always believed the fellows we were up against would play fair. This belief has been held even within the intelligence services, which we've reduced to the extent they're now in a most parlous state. I'm not convinced that such things apply any more. Gentlemen, this will not be a gentleman's war. Look at Guernica – a purely civilian target. To be frank, I'm not sure we've left ourselves time to –'

Suddenly, Rosalind sweeps past Flossie to push open the door of the drawing room, flapping her hands at the wreaths of cigar smoke, and exclaiming, 'Here you all are. Surely we haven't finished dancing yet?'

D to C

19th October, 1939
Kent

Dearest Crista,

It's surprisingly easy to sign up to kill people. Or be killed, I suppose. Three train journeys, several injections, a strange half-hour where I had my teeth inspected, and now I'm a private in the British Army. Private Seagrave, Second Battalion, Grenadier Guards.

A man at the recruitment office said, 'Digby Seagrave? Willoughby's boy?' in a startled manner. I couldn't help but think of that Auden poem we all adored at school: 'You've got their names to live up to and questions won't help.'

I replied, in my best Lady Bracknell voice, 'Never heard of him, I'm sure.'

Now I'm at a training barracks with a kitbag (heavy) and a uniform (itchy), along with around 100 other chaps, joking about how long we might have left to live. It's oddly like being back at school.

When I arrived, a Scots sergeant major saw me walking in and unleashed a volley of foul language in my direction, which — roughly translated — told me I looked too much like a pretty little miss to be of use to anyone and I should get used to cleaning the latrines as that's all I was good for. It was marvellous. Like standing in a hurricane.

Some things I saw from the train I thought you might like: a sheepdog leaping a high fence, flying with its feet tucked up. Clumps of sooty steam from the engine hanging in trees, like trapped clouds. Geese flying in a V-formation, keeping pace with the train. An elderly gentleman in a back garden constructing a bomb shelter alongside his vegetable patch. Men in uniform standing on station platforms, with their families waiting to say goodbye. The women somewhat pinched.

The children wide-eyed, as if they knew something was happening, but weren't sure what.

I saw one man wearing navy uniform standing by himself smoking, and I wondered why he had no one to wave him off. I hope he will find some friends when he's at sea. Going past them was like travelling along a wonderful tableau. Everyone costumed up, ready to step on to the stage. I wonder where we will be when the curtain falls.

I suppose it is rather sad that I am not up at Cambridge now. A room in a college, with a gas fire for making toast. Having conversations with kindred souls. I think that version of Digby is a happy one. But here I am in an army camp bed with a straw pillow, writing to you, and this Digby is a happy one too, as it turns out. C'est la vie!

The man on the next bed is a terrific fellow from Hull called Groves. We hit it off instantly and were soon talking about how vital it is that the coal mining industry is nationalized. All the men in his family have worked as miners. He was rather surprised to find I knew something about it.

There is — as I hoped — a true egalitarianism among the regular soldiers. My new uniform is quite the best costume I've ever worn. When Groves and I go to the local pub, the landlord greets me in the same matey way as he greets Groves. There's none of that deferential nonsense you get if you're wearing smart clothes.

Write to me soon. I'm dying to hear how my departure was received. I hope Flossie wasn't too heartbroken. Tell her I miss her terribly and I'm sorry I crept away without a proper goodbye. But it did feel splendid to do exactly not *what was expected of me.*

Tomorrow we will be practising murdering sandbags. If that's all the Germans have got in store for us, then I feel confident I will be home by Christmas. Groves thinks it's likely we'll be sent to France in the meantime.

Wherever we go, I remain —

Yours,
Private Digby Seagrave

PS: I've lent Groves your copy of How Green Was My Valley. *He'll look after it, I'm sure.*

C to D

23rd October, 1939
Dorset

Dear Digby,

Such scenes after your departure! A country house drama par excellence.
Your father was furious and is now deep in the wine cellar, drinking his
way through the rarest vintages. Your mother, after some grandiose Greek
tragedy wailing, has announced she will be decamping to Mayfair next
month to stay with Myrtle. She says she wants MERELY TO MAKE
HERSELF USEFUL, but I've no doubt she will be spending her time
lunching at The Ritz and going to the cinema to goggle at Clark Gable and
Fred Astaire. (Flossie also smitten with Mr Astaire but has to travel to
Dorchester to see him at The Plaza, and you know how she can be about
buses on her own.)

(Flossie also hopelessly dejected at your departure. I will cut this scene
from the final production as I don't think you will like it, Digs. She could
hardly speak for crying. Do write to her soon.)

Of course, I could hardly bear it either. In fact, I couldn't at all. The more
I thought about it, the more it seemed ridiculous that you should go off to
fight while I stayed behind, so I decided to take up your mother's suggestion that I join the WAAF. One of the few times I have followed her advice.

I asked Perry to lend me the train fare and he was decent about it. Gave
me more than enough, and now I am on a bench at Dorchester Station
with my battered old suitcase. Not much in it. Bedsocks and books mainly.
Hard to know what to take. At the last minute, I popped in that little statue
of Sekhmet. Taras said she was the goddess of war, so I thought she'd like to
come along.

Perry told me to tell the officers in charge that I've got French and
German and I'm good at maths, so they make me a 'Clerk Special Duties'.

I reminded him I've never had a single maths lesson, and he said, 'You're a bright girl, you'll pick it up.'

He's gone back to London now. Apparently, he has recruited Leon, of all people, to serve as his driver, although I suspect that's not all he will do. I can't imagine Leon being a deferential chauffeur, can you? Last I heard, he was working on ships and getting into fights.

I had a letter from Myrtle saying London is as quiet as a cathedral because all the children have been evacuated. Peculiar to think of a city without children playing in the streets. She says everyone is going about their business as usual, trying not to notice the soldiers digging trenches in Hyde Park and rolling out barbed wire along the Thames.

Cities across Europe must be falling quiet now. Places we know. Streets we've walked. All the towns in Normandy where we escaped from Mlle Aubert. The Austrian resorts where I skied. Even that beautiful village in Provence where Myrtle took us for my birthday. That hotel with blue shutters. Floss in raptures over the tarte au citron. *Now all empty and barricaded.*

When I left, Flossie said she hoped the war wouldn't be as bad as people think. I reminded her of the Nazis I saw in Austria. Absolute HORRORS. It's only the fact that I am off to do my bit that makes me feel any better, though it was a wrench to leave Floss alone at Chilcombe. I made Bill swear to protect her for me, and the theatre too. Small Bill has gone off to join the navy and Betty is in a terrible flap, as you might imagine.

I have had an idea, about doing The Tempest *next summer – Prospero should be a charismatic dictator, with Ariel, Caliban and Miranda in matching uniforms as his subjects. The island as fascist state. A backdrop of black and red banners. Or is that too obvious? One doesn't want to bash people over the head with it all. Although, one rather does.*

I'm glad you have made a friend in Kent, although I have little interest in discussing domestic politics these days. We can jaw about democracy all we like, but the fact of the matter is that if Adolf wins, our country won't survive, and nor will we. Do everything your instructors tell you, Digs. Pay attention.

My train is here! I'm off to war! Damnation to Hitler! Write to me!

Crista

D to C

29th October, 1939
Kent

Dearest Crista,

Thank you so much for your letter. I'm thrilled right down to my muddy boots that you are off on an adventure. You were born for adventure.

The weather is filthy here. We've had downpours hammering on the corrugated roof all week and we keep having to go out in it. We've started six weeks of training with long marches and drills. It will, I'm told, 'kick us soft lot into shape'. We must do everything carrying our kit on our backs, which is extraordinarily uncomfortable, especially in cruel rain and ravening winds.

Kent has bigger skies than Dorset. It feels more exposed. It's as if the weather must travel across greater distances to get to us, and it rather resents this. I told Groves I felt persecuted by Mother Nature and he said in his wonderful Yorkshire accent that I don't half say some peculiar things. We were slogging our way across a sodden field in a gale at the time — I thought of King Lear wandering the storm-tossed heath and proclaimed: '"As flies to wanton boys are we to the gods; they kill us for their sport."' Groves said he would refer me to his previous comment. I am very fond of him already.

When we were out in the unending torrent yesterday, we saw a man taking down the signs at the railway station that say 'Canterbury'. He told us they're removing all the place names at stations to confuse the Germans if they invade. I said I imagined the Germans might have maps and compasses, not to mention guns to point at people to make them tell them where they are. The man snorted and got back up his ladder.

Last weekend, there was a dance in a nearby village hall. I chaperoned Groves. He adores dancing. He was telling me he and his friends save up to go to big dance halls that have sprung floors and orchestras and there's 'nowt' (nothing) better. He was swinging girls about the dance floor soon as we arrived, a huge grin on his face.

We only had gramophone records at our dance, no orchestras. But they played one of those slow Louis Armstrong songs at the end of the night — the kind Mother likes. I can't remember what it's called, but it's all about thinking of home, and I thought of her (most likely swaying about to her gramophone, dear Mother) and Father and Flossie and you and Chilcombe and everyone there.

You all seem much further away than you are. By which I mean, I could jump on a train and be back in a day, if I wanted. But that seems rather implausible. And how would I find the right station now they're all nameless?

Anyway, I leant against the wall of the Ickham Village Hall and had a sentimental cigarette, while Groves sashayed elegantly past me, partnered by a plump and beaming WVS girl with a ladder in her regulation stockings.

I do miss you all. I talk to you every day. I hope you can hear me.

Your Digby

PS: I find your Tempest idea most interesting and have decided I will play Prospero next summer, Germans allowing. Don't tell me I'm not old enough. War will age me perfectly, I'm sure.

C to D

10th November, 1939
Gloucestershire

Dear Digs,

Snap. We're both in barracks now. Mine's a Nissen hut with iron beds and a wooden floor. There's a temperamental stove in the middle with a chimney through the roof. I'm sharing it with fifteen other recruits, and we spend much of our time trying to keep the accursed stove alight.

We're woken at six every morning, then carry out brisk ablutions in an open-ended shelter that the wind simply howls through. There's an interesting mix of characters here – I sleep between a barmaid from Lincoln and a violinist from Cardiff – but we look rather pulled together once we're in our uniforms.

It is smart, Digs. Air force blue. Peaked cap with a brass winged badge. A tunic with brass buttons and a belt with a brass buckle. All the bits of brass must be polished every day – an enjoyable task. You should see how good I am at tying a tie now.

We do a great deal of marching about while being barked at by petty tyrant NCOs. Saluting and inspections and so on. Packing and unpacking our kit endlessly before heading off to queue for cabbagey meals clutching our tin plates and tin mugs (what we call our 'irons').

It is no doubt useful to have this ritual obedience drummed into us, but frustrating to have little time for myself. That said, we're kept so busy, I fall asleep soon as my head hits the pillow.

Some of the girls here have never been away from home before. A girl called Edna from Warrington was snivelling in her bed all last week. I asked what the matter was, and she said she couldn't sleep for worrying about her family. Convinced they'll be gassed by the Germans.

I told her the best thing she could do for her family was to defeat Hitler, and that keeping active is the perfect cure for an agitated mind. That, and making plans for the future. Talking of which, I may let you play Prospero next summer, but ONLY if you agree to have the whole thing lit by flaming torches. I'll explain another time.

Anyway, yesterday Edna and I were ferrying stuff around for one of the wing commanders. I was telling her about my time in Austria and I did an impersonation of Adolf – I have the spittle-filled voice down to a tee – and the wing commander must have heard this as he came in asking if I spoke German. I told him I spoke German and French, and although I had never learnt maths, I could pick it up and would subsequently make an excellent 'Clerk Special Duties'. He gave me a rather Perry-ish look – narrowed eyes / twitching moustache.

Turns out, things move fast if the military thinks it might have a use for you. I've been told once I've finished basic training, I'm to undergo further training for – guess what – 'Special Duties'!

Had a letter from Floss yesterday. She's had a flying visit from Myrtle, who is finding war extremely enlivening – isn't that funny? Apparently, she's rounding up exiled artists to tuck under her majestic wings, and hosting receptions for stateless politicians. She told Flossie she'd had a brief but SOUL SHATTERING affair with a Norwegian submariner and couldn't look at a pickled herring without weeping but was otherwise very jolly about the whole thing.

One of Taras's cryptic postcards has somehow made its way to me here too. Rather tattered, like it's been round the censor's office a few times. A picture of the Statue of Liberty with a sketch on the back of a hybrid creature. Do you remember how we used to pore over his postcards? Looking for symbols, like trying to tell our fortune in tea leaves.

Strange to think of everyone we know being in new and unexpected places. It's as if the war has shaken the world like a set of dice and we're all tumbling off in different directions. Which is an apt place to sign off, and say that I hope you are well, wherever you are. And wherever you are, my thoughts go with you.

Your Crista

Blackout

November, 1939

The attic windowpanes are damp with condensation. Flossie wipes them with her cardigan sleeve. The day outside is lightless and indistinct – the mist-covered sun resembles a sickly full moon, gauze-wrapped and ailing. Blustery gusts of wind hurry crowds of leaves across the lawn, while the bare branches of trees reach and wave.

There is a kind of skitteryness about November, thinks Flossie. It is a month both ominous and nervous. The crisp displays of October, all its smart oranges and yellows, have been spoiled and scattered about as November rushes in, dragging winter behind it like a trail of rattling cans.

Cold wind shakes the windows, but the house itself is quiet. Digby gone. Crista gone. Many of the staff gone. No house guests. Taras and Hilly have sailed to America, while Philly is with her parents in their Scottish hunting lodge, and Perry, Leon and Myrtle are in London. Only Willoughby and Rosalind remain, but Rosalind will soon be leaving for the capital, and Willoughby is so preoccupied, he may as well not be there at all. Down in the village, evacuee children are arriving to be billeted with local families: pitiful creatures wearing labels and clutching gas mask boxes, come to fill the empty rooms left by departing sons and husbands. Mr Brewer has been organizing their distribution.

Flossie turns back into the attic where the glow of her bedside lamp and the flickering fire in the fireplace console her. As much as she worries about her missing siblings and all that war might bring, part of her still enjoys the annual descent into winter: the battening of hatches; the tunnel leading to December and the fairy hollow of Christmas, her favourite time of year. She probably shouldn't think about such frivolities, but it feels miserly not to, especially when things seem so bleak. She remembers the Prime Minister's subdued voice on the wireless when he told them they were at war with Germany. How tired he sounded. Poor Mr Chamberlain. He wouldn't mind if she thought about something cheering.

She plants herself in the rocking chair by the fire, tucks her feet up, pulls a blanket over her lap, and tries to imagine the sparkling lights of Christmas, as if it were a distant inn on a windswept moor or a lighthouse glimpsed across a stormy sea. It is a poignant sensation, as if she were telling herself a story; a magical scene glimpsed through a pinhole camera.

Flossie often feels a romantic wistfulness beside a fire. She can see it in other people too: they build up a good blaze, then sit back and contemplate it with a faraway expression. She finds it pleasant to indulge this feeling without interruption from Cristabel ('What are you moping about now?') or Digby ('Floss, come and play Charades with me'). She has her book, her diary, her knitting – everything she needs. She could have Maudie bring up something on a tray for lunch, so she doesn't have to go downstairs. She could do a jigsaw. She could read her book right through to the end.

Flossie watches the flames and listens to the quietness, which, after a while, seems to become a tangible presence in the house. Something that rests calmly outside the attic, waiting for her to become used to it.

Two floors below, in the dining room, Rosalind watches her husband push aside a half-eaten plate of food in favour of a glass of wine and a crumpled copy of *The Times*. She is struggling to think of something to say. It is a curse, the way every conversational topic is now weighted down with war. The weather: war. The children: war. The estate: war. Willoughby himself: why he should be fighting the war. Or why it is important she understand why he should be fighting the war. Or why the war he should be fighting is so tremendously complicated that it is far beyond her comprehension. This last point is completely acceptable to her. It is impossible to understand.

Most conversations are now concluded by the snap of a shaken-out newspaper held before her husband's face. Men and their newspapers and their wars. Rosalind has been here before. It seems to continue quite happily without her, whatever she does. The way they talk about it with such relish, as if it were a subject for debate, as if it didn't mean dead boys. Thousands and thousands and thousands of dead boys, all over again.

'I wonder what Digby is doing,' she says.

Willoughby noisily turns a page. 'Training. Drills and so on. He'll need it. Suspect they'll be sending him to France soon.'

'He'll be all right, won't he? I couldn't –'

'How many times, Rosalind? We know what war requires. It requires courage. Sacrifice.'

But why, she thought, should war always get what it wanted?

'Willoughby, do you remember when Digby was a baby? His eyelashes –'

'Look at this,' he says, prodding the paper with a finger. 'Russia is invading Finland. The situation in China is appalling. The world is descending into barbarism. We don't have a choice.'

Surely they had a choice. They always had a choice. They chose extravagantly and at length. Fabrics, perfumes, tables in restaurants. People waited for their choices; praised their choices.

But her husband continues to sound forth on incomprehensible things: Belorussia, Maginot, *Reichstag*. Capital letter words. Head-line words. Rosalind suspects there must be similar conversations happening in dining rooms across the country: a buzzing swarm, incessantly circling above Britain at a furious pitch. Whenever you tried to swipe at them, they simply shifted into a million disparate parts and reformed.

She waits for a servant to appear and, when this doesn't happen, pours herself more wine, sloshing a little on to the tablecloth. The stain spreads as she rubs at it with a finger. She says, 'Well, darling, you said it yourself – it'll make a man of him.'

'Ridiculous of Digby to join the army. Even more ridiculous not to go in as an officer.'

'It was ridiculous.' Rosalind takes a sip of wine, then rounds the table, heading to the seat at her husband's side. 'Although, you said it would knock the nonsense out of him.'

'What you learn when you fight alongside other men, when you live and die together, there's nothing like it,' says Willoughby.

'Please don't talk about dying.' Rosalind leans forward to place a hand on his leg, but his eyes are still on the newspaper. Digby's eyes are never so preoccupied. They are always with you as if seeing you for the first time. Her sweet, beautiful boy. Gone to be a soldier. She hopes fervently that Perry will find him some kind of special position sooner rather than later.

She waits for Willoughby to notice her. His face is often long gone from her, these days. She receives only glimpses from his profile, the thinnest slivers of attention.

'He'll be grateful for it in the long run,' Willoughby says. 'Best thing I ever did.'

'I'm sure.'

'He needs to buckle down.'

'He does.'

Rosalind has a desperate feeling she will be echoing his words for ever. She is a parrot; she is a cave. She needs him to look at her to make it stop. It is in the word 'buckle' that she sees an opening. She slides her hand up his thigh.

'Willoughby, I have one of my heads coming on,' she says, trailing her hand further upwards, giving merely the tiniest tug on his belt. 'I might go upstairs, darling.'

There. The lift of an eyebrow shows she has snagged a forgotten corner of his interest. The newspaper is lowered. With that, she stands and walks out of the room, trailing an invisible thread behind her, a fly fisherman sending out a long whisking cast after a legendary pike.

Flossie, up in the attic, hears footsteps on the stairs far below, then the house falls silent. Maudie has been in to top up the coal scuttle, but Flossie barely noticed her or the fact it is getting dark outside. She is deep in her latest romance novel from the Boots lending library – *Nobody Asked Me* – following the intertwining paths of the orphaned heroine and the strangely distant hero. Alison loves Julian, Julian loves another, another loves Alison; she pines, he pines, we pine. His *firm, uncompromising mouth*, his *bruised and burning kiss*, his *half-indifferent, half-caressing voice*. Flossie traces the pattern of their story, as looped and neat as a bow.

At some point, a meal arrives on a tray, appearing as if by magic (which is almost true: Maudie has carried it up three flights, and the bread pudding contains raisins Betty had to go all the way to Dorchester to find, travelling on her son's bicycle because the bus service has been reduced on account of the petrol rationing), and Flossie eats mechanically, her eyes never leaving the page. By not allowing any interruptions, she can remain safe in the cocooning cinema of her mind. Her *flood of furious tears*, her *unsteady lips*, her *wild and useless impulses*.

One floor below, Willoughby rolls over. Where did he go, when he did that? Rosalind wonders. Where did he go when he turned away and raised the wall of his shoulder to her? There was no way of knowing then if his eyes were open or closed. The back of his body was so adamantly uninterested in her, it seemed possible he no longer had eyes at all. To tap his shoulder as they lay in bed together made her feel like a storybook mouse, an interloper with minuscule paws. *Pat, pat, pat.*

'What is it?' he would always say. But why did it have to be something? Why couldn't it simply be a little chat that would tell her she wasn't in some way repulsive to him now, that he was grateful for her efforts, rather than distractedly bothered by her, as if he were trying to get off a train and she were a stranger attempting to tell him he'd left his hat behind. Excuse me, sir, I'm awfully sorry to bother you, sir. What is it? It's just your hat, sir. It's just your wife, sir. *Pat, pat, pat.*

Rosalind cannot imagine feeling so immovably solid in the world. To feel someone else's attentions as inconsequential flutterings you could brush off. The desperate feeling rises again. She reaches for the pot of sleeping pills on her bedside table.

★

There is a knock at the front door that nobody answers. Betty and Maudie have gone to a meeting in the church about air raid warnings. Mr Brewer is rounding up more evacuees. There is a pause, then more knocking, louder this time.

Up in the attic, Flossie lifts her head. Why isn't anybody answering it? She puts down her book. There it is again, a banging echoing about the house. Feeling suddenly nervous, she stands up and patters down the stairs in her stockinged feet, buttoning up her cardigan. It seems a long way to the front door. 'One moment,' she calls, and her voice is ribbon thin – a silly affectation.

Opening the door to peer out into the night, she sees the butcher's wife with a bicycle. 'Sorry to trouble you so late, Miss Flossie. I've been round the back but there was no reply.'

'That's perfectly all right. How can I help?'

'Well, Miss Flossie, we haven't had payment for the last two weeks.'

'Oh, goodness. Who usually pays you?'

'That would be Mr or Mrs Brewer.'

'They've been ever so busy. I'll speak to them as soon as I can.'

'Very well. Do you know if it will be pork or beef for you this week? Miss Cristabel usually does the orders. We have missed our talks with her.'

'Crista's gone off to be in the Women's Auxiliary Air Force. Everyone's doing their bit, aren't they?'

'Certainly are, Miss Flossie.'

'Well, we've got to, haven't we? All mucking in!' Flossie's voice has become the jaunty voice she keeps finding herself using. A slightly mad way of talking. Brisk phrases batted back and forth that serve as a kind of mutual bolstering. 'When do you need the meat order by?'

'We'd need to know this evening, Miss Flossie. If we was going to get it to you by Sunday. There's a lot of deliveries to be done. Everyone's stocking up.'

'Of course. Pork or beef. Pork or beef . . .' Flossie pauses, and for a terrifying moment, meat in all its varieties becomes an abstract concept, entirely beyond imagining, but thankfully, before she starts

251

to panic, her brain rights itself, like a happy canoe, and she says, 'Pork, please. I've never really liked beef.'

'Thank you, Miss Flossie. Pork's my preference too,' says the woman, then pedals off down the drive.

As the sound of the bicycle diminishes, the darkness surrounding Flossie seems to intensify. She walks along the drive, wondering if she will still be able to see the woman, but the bicycle has disappeared into the night. The cottages in the village are usually visible through the trees, but Chilcombe Mell has also vanished beneath the blackout, as completely as the butcher's wife.

Everyone has gone into hiding. The animated lights of houses and shops and vehicles that used to dot the valley now seem as inconsequential as glitter. There is only black: the black silhouettes of trees, and the black Ridgeway looming above them, a featureless wall against a clouded sooty sky. Flossie remembers Taras saying the most important ingredient of black paint was the charred remains of animal bones. 'Bone black', he called it. How fragile normality is, she thinks, how easily reduced to nothing.

She hears the husky yelp of a fox in the woods, and turns to walk back to the house, quickly at first, on account of a fearfulness that has begun to scrabble at her heart, but then more slowly, steadying herself. She tells herself she has nothing to be afraid of, but a voice inside says she does have a great deal to be afraid of – just about everything, in fact.

Flossie looks at the house as if she were a stranger arriving on a lonely night. Chilcombe is lifeless, sealed up, emitting nothing but a thin needle of light from Rosalind's room, where the curtains are not properly closed. If Flossie knocked on the door, nobody would come running down the stairs to open it. She is on her own. And there are decisions to be made.

Postcard

19th November, 1939

Dear Father,

I know you must be busy, but I wanted to send you a postcard, in case you hadn't seen my last letter. As you can see from the picture, I'm in Dover and you will know what that means. Morale is good. We are keen to get going, although I wish I had time to visit Dover Castle. We have a perfect view of it from the docks and it looks glorious! I believe you would like to see me here, in my uniform, although I know you had a different uniform in mind for me. Many officers I meet remember you from the last war and tell me what a fine soldier you were. As I said before, I think of you and Mother every day, and I hope to make you proud.

Your son,
Digby

Note on Pink Notepaper with a Box of Turkish Delight

22nd December, 1939
Mayfair

Dearest Flossie,

I pray you are not lonesome in that aching old house beneath the rook-filled trees. Did you receive the Harrods hamper? I helped your mother pick it out. She sends Christmas wishes, and so do I.

London is haunted and watchful with the lights off. We wander the pitch-black streets, calling out to one another, while above us, silver barrage balloons float in the night air like giant tethered fish. I wear a full-length white fur coat, so am immensely visible and glide like the ghost of a queen.

Sweet Flossie, I will raise a glass to you tonight. But first: a Beethoven concert at the National Gallery – what bliss! They've taken down the paintings and filled the empty rooms with music, so we gather there, tinkers and tailors and soldiers and sailors and even Americans. Then to The Berkeley, where we will dance and spin till the darkness lifts. Oh, this unimaginable life!

Myrtle x

PS: I saw Cristabel last week. Her imperious face all furious angles. Perry will find her something important to do, never fear.

Christmas Card

23rd December, 1939
Middlesex

Leon,

Generous though it was of you to offer to relieve me of my virginity before Adolf kills us all, I'm afraid you have made several assumptions that cannot go unchallenged. One: that I still have it. Two: that if I do still have it, I would share that information with you. Three: that if I do still have it, I wish to dispense with it. Four: that if I do still have it and wish to dispense with it, I would consider you a suitable candidate. Although there may be foolish women who fall prey to your swarthy Belgian brute routine, please remember I knew you before you learnt how to wear clothes. Can you tell Perry that his suggestion worked and I'm now in Special Duties, based not far from London? And can you or he take me out for lunch? UTTERLY sick of military slop.

Cristabel

PS: Tidings of the season

C to D

20th January, 1940
Middlesex

Dearest Digs, wherever you may be,

I intended this letter to be a summation of my ideas for The Tempest thus far but must confess it is hard to proceed with theatrical plans without you. I confess too that the possibility of us putting on a play at Chilcombe this summer seems ever more unlikely. Flossie says the land at the cottage is being dug up so they can plant vegetables. Potatoes are to be grown in The Whalebone Theatre. Perhaps they will prove more popular than my recent productions. But we should plan for after the war. A victory performance, naturally.

It is IMMENSELY frustrating not to be able to talk to you. I feel I am repeatedly serving tennis balls over a net with nobody to return them. But anyway, here's an idea: wouldn't it be something to have the audience for The Tempest arrive by boat?

Ah, the long silence; the pock, pock, pock of the unreturned ball bouncing into a dusty corner.

There are many silences in my life now. I am being trained as an 'Operations Plotter', so I exist in basement rooms filled with cigarette smoke where the only sounds are brusque orders. We are being taught to translate radio signals on to a large plotting table, where little metal pieces representing aircraft are pushed around by WAAFs holding long rods. Similar to how I used to move characters around in our cardboard theatre, but with significantly less dialogue.

Thus far, we have only been doing training exercises, but if Hitler gets his act together and sends bombers over, we will do it for real. The hours are long. Sometimes when I come out of our burrow, I have no idea if it will be day or night.

I'm starting to think military training is largely a way of stopping people talking. I said as much to Perry – he and Leon took me out for lunch – and he replied, 'Dear girl, think of it as strategic. Silence gives us more time to consider our next moves.' He told me I should emulate the patient angler, who learns to let the river run by.

I countered by saying that lives could be lost if we spend our time staring at rivers. Perry said lives will always be lost in war, adding, 'It becomes a question of numbers.'

You can imagine how I growled at that. Leon did too. But Perry merely smiled and said anger is only useful if deployed strategically. He told Leon that an untrained dog will get itself shot, then told him to stop baring his teeth and take me to the Café Royal.

I wondered if Leon might take offence, but he simply laughed in his Blackbeard buccaneer way. Sometimes I forget he is Taras's son, but he has the same volcanic quality. You never know how he will react.

We went to the Café Royal and Leon was entertaining, albeit in a rather vulgar way, for several hours. Told me about his rackety adventures in the merchant navy and how Perry is teaching him useful things like how to strangle people with piano wire. He started to show me but had to take off at pace after he got a message from Perry. He would make an excellent Mercutio, don't you think?

Bother it, Digby. It is SO peculiar to not have you to talk to. Perry says I may not see you for months, years. An inconceivable idea. I can't face it. But I must.

Write to me, write to me, come back, come back. No, don't listen to me. Stay and fight and be as brave as you can. I'm counting on you to do that.

I will too.

Your Crista

Notebook Pages

France, somewhere
May 26th, 1940

Dear Crista,

I doubt I will be able to send this, but it comforts me to write to you.

We're in retreat. Became separated from our battalion somewhere near Arras. It was horrible. Only five of us left now, including Groves and me. We're running from the Germans, heading back to the Channel.

Never been so tired but I can't sleep. Can't remember the last time I took my boots off. I'm shaking all the time — look at the state of my handwriting! I find myself going over and over peculiar things. Speeches from Shakespeare. The items in my bag. The names of our men.

We march for miles, then sit in a ditch and wait because we aren't sure what to do next. Sometimes we meet other British troops, and we look at each other expecting somebody to have a better idea of what's going on, but nobody does.

We dug a shelter yesterday and turned up the skeleton of a German soldier from the last war. We could see the metal buttons from his uniform, lying about in his bones like loose change. Seems absurd we should be back in France trying to kill each other all over again.

I'm still not used to seeing dead bodies. Not even those from twenty years ago.

May 27th

We spent today hiding in our shelter while the Germans relentlessly shelled a copse 500 yards away, trying to hit a British anti-aircraft gun and its crew. The noise of shells is abominable: a shrill shrieking, then crunching explosions that rattle the teeth in your head. The chap next to me shouted, 'How many times do they need to bloody kill them?'

We plan to head off across the fields tonight. It's easier at night. In the day, the roads are clogged with hundreds of French people heading who knows where. Vehicles and carts piled high with luggage and furniture. Old men bent double under sagging bundles. Mothers in headscarves dragging along crying children. I saw one woman carrying a baby that was so motionless and blue I wasn't sure it was still alive.

I can hardly believe it, but apparently German planes have been flying low over the roads and gunning people down. Targeting unarmed civilians. Groves said, 'They've got that much spare ammo, they can use it up killing children.'

The French people didn't want to look at us. I found that hard.

May 28th

Yesterday we were lost in a forest until Groves spotted a couple of trees scored with knife marks. It was exactly how you used to mark our route through the woods at Chilcombe. The trees led us to a trail, littered with cigarette ends from troops who'd already passed through.

We stopped for the night in an empty house, only recently deserted. Two glasses of vin rouge on the table. Half a loaf of bread. The oven still warm. I found some candles, and we sat about the table in our filthy uniforms, tearing off hunks of bread, feasting like thieves. Groves has never had wine before. He said he could develop a liking for it.

We took turns to sleep in an upstairs bedroom. Groves and I went up together. As I was taking my pack off, we heard German bombers flying overhead. We watched through a gap in the curtains, like children peering up for Father Christmas.

Groves said it gave him the shivers to think they might be heading to England, so I put my arm around his shoulders. Felt such a long way from home.

May 30th

Hard to describe how it is here. Hard to believe that only a few weeks ago, these were ordinary towns, with gardens and families, and children going off to school. It is like a great machine has rolled through France, crushing the life out of it. The roads are littered with burnt tanks, dead horses, dead people. Flies everywhere. We march past, trying not to look.

The men keep asking me to do 'some of my Shakespeare' to take our minds off things so I have become a one-man travelling theatre troupe. I recite soliloquies as we trudge along. Strange to remember that, not so long ago, the theatre was all I thought about. Henry V proving popular. I tried a little Auden on them too. They liked him more than you do.

We have been leaderless for days now and the men seem to look to me, despite the fact I am as inexperienced as they are. I might even be the youngest of the five of us. Groves says it's because of my 'fancy wireless voice'. I asked if he minded my voice and he said he didn't at all.

His voice is rich and earthy. Full of humour. Every morning he pretends to take a breakfast order from us all, as we lie about in a pile, muddy and exhausted. 'The usual for you, sir? Smoked haddock? Fresh coffee?' Somehow, it's funnier because he does it without fail every day.

Slept in a pigsty last night. Lice crawling all over us. 'Least someone's eating well,' said Groves.

June 1st

We're not stopping any more. We must get to the coast.

We are buoyed whenever we see a cheerful British officer, waiting by a bridge to point us in the right direction, saying, 'You'll be home in time for last orders, lads.'

There seems to be a type of good humour that arises in some people at the most trying times. Groves has it too. His spirits never flag. He says we have to get out of here because he's smoked all his cigarettes and nearly all of mine, and he can't abide the French variety.

As we march along, the men chant a song. It starts, 'I don't want a bayonet up my arsehole, I don't want my bollocks shot away,' and goes on from there. I am grateful the French people we pass probably don't understand what the men are chanting, but I understand why they are chanting it. It doesn't seem to be a grand war that we are fighting, simply something we want to get out of with bollocks intact.

June 2nd

We are on an edge. Behind us is a town on fire. In front of us, grey sea.

To the left and right, thousands of men on a long shoreline. Every now and then, German planes come over and reduce our numbers. We are, as Groves says, absolute sitting ducks. I've stopped counting the number of dead bodies I've seen.

A beach full of fighting men, but we spend most of our time sitting in sand dunes, smoking with trembling hands. Yesterday morning, a German plane came screaming over and the man in front of me shot himself in the head, to save them the bother. Behind us, we can hear their artillery getting closer. There is nothing to do but wait. That is a heavy feeling.

Sometimes we see big British destroyers anchoring offshore. They can't get near to the beach as the water is too shallow, so smaller boats pick up a handful of men at a time and ferry them out.

We file obediently into the sea, watching as those at the front of the queue get taken off to where we long to be with every fibre of our beings. The water is full of wreckage and so glossy with oil, it looks like consommé. Then the destroyers leave for England without us, and we trudge back to the beach, shivering in our wet uniforms.

We've been here for two days now. The nights are the worst. The darkness and fire. The Germans have bombed something that held petrol and it belches poisonous clouds over the beach. Last night, poor Groves couldn't stop coughing. He buried his face into my shoulder, and I put my arms about him to try to shield him and wished us away from this place more than I have ever wished anything.

June 4th

It was about midnight. We saw a small boat going past the beach so a
pack of us rushed into the sea. It was a Norfolk fisherman with his sons.
They already had a crowd of soldiers on board.

The boat was moving away, but we hung on to the edge, begging them
to take us too, being pulled out deeper and deeper. I kept going under and
the fisherman leant over shouting, 'Grab my hand, son.'

The pack on my back was weighing me down as the fisherman tried to
heave me out of the water, then Groves was beside me, shoving me upwards. As
I tipped in, I saw one of his hands on the edge of the boat, gripping the
wood, his knuckles white. When I scrambled to my feet, it had gone. I tried to
see over, but other men were being hauled in, and the boat was moving faster.

I shouted at the fisherman that there were men in the sea, but he
pushed me away, saying they had hardly any fuel left. As we headed off, I
could make them out — men in the black water, slipping under the surface,
their eyes and mouths gaping wide open as if they couldn't believe it.
Their faces. Their tin helmets. Then just their hands, still reaching.

I shouted his name. I kept shouting his name until a British naval officer
told me he'd happily shoot me if I continued to impede the evacuation.

It seemed quite ludicrous, given all the trouble the Germans were going
to, trying to bomb us and shell us, for our men to die in such a simple way.
To open their mouths to the water and go down without a peep.

I don't know if he saw me or heard me.

I was very sick on the boat on the way back across the Channel.

We came ashore at Ramsgate where women from the Women's Institute
greeted us as if we'd been victorious. They gave us hot Bovril and clean socks.
I was given a postcard to send to my family to let them know I am all right. I
am all right. I am on a train full of filthy soldiers asleep on each other. It is
a sealed train. They have locked the doors so we can't run off now we're back.

Here are some things I have seen from the window: wounded French
soldiers lying on stretchers singing the Marseillaise; a turning windmill in
an open field; a poster advertising the film Pack Up Your Troubles.

I keep thinking of him. Drifting in the sea, a hundred yards off a
French beach. Bumping into the legs of other drowned men. He would be
so surprised to find himself there.

Incomplete Letter

Chilcombe
25th June, 1940

Dear Crista,

Of course I packed up your books before putting the evacuees in the attic! There was no need for a telegram. I don't think they would touch them anyway. They are very sweet but terrified of everything, especially cows. Betty says the ones her sister has are riddled with nits so we should count ourselves lucky.

I told them my beloved stuffed elephant was there to guard them, but this made them cry, 'on account of its insides coming out', so I have dragged Edgar and his leaking innards down to Mother's room, where I am sleeping. Both his eyes fell out en route, which gives him a rather beggarly look, the poor dear.

Did you know Mother has silk pillowcases? Betty says they do wonders for your complexion. I have been lolling on them indulgently and will have an entirely new face by the end of the week.

Digby left to go back to his barracks this morning. What a pity you couldn't get leave at the same time. I think he misses his friend Groves. He showed me a photograph of them in Kent. He believes he will be sent to North Africa next, and they will train him up as an officer.

He was terribly upset by the fall of France. We all were. Maudie says Weymouth is full of refugees from the Channel Islands, who have brought their tomato crops rather than let Germans eat them. Everyone thinks we will be invaded next. Do you believe that? Mr Brewer says our backs are to the wall and, as we've left most of our weapons in France, we will have to fight the Nazis off with saucepans.

Army lorries have been trundling through the village all week, taking sandbags and barbed wire down to the beach, and the Local Defence

Volunteers are doing drills in our woods. Once they've practised killing each other with chair legs and wooden rifles, they come in for a cup of tea and sit round the kitchen table cheerfully saying things like, 'We're for it now,' and, 'We're next on Hitler's list.'

It is dreadful to think we are readying ourselves for battle, but I suppose we are. We've wrapped the table lamps in brown paper and taken all the paintings off the walls, so we don't get crushed by a falling ancestor if a bomb drops. Mr Brewer has removed the glass cupola, so it's just a hole in the ceiling covered with tarpaulin now.

The wireless is on constantly, so the voices of important people echo about the place. I don't like being shouted at by Herr Hitler, but it is reassuring to hear our new Prime Minister. They say it has given our troops a lift to have Mr Churchill in charge. We've even had a telephone installed in the study 'in case of emergencies', though I must say it feels rather like an emergency already, and nobody seems sure who we should ring if matters get worse.

Mother rang yesterday from The Savoy looking for Uncle Willoughby, but he's gone to stay with Lord Someone-or-Other in Ireland. He sent me a postcard saying they still have decent whiskey in the pubs there, so he was going to do his bit for England by drinking them dry. I didn't tell Mother that.

We don't ever seem to have proper meals any more. It's as if we can't stop, because if we stop, our fears might catch up with us. Do you ever feel scared, Crista? I sometimes think I am the only one –

Flossie thoughtfully chews her fountain pen. It is always difficult to write to Cristabel. She wants to appear brave and resourceful, but worries she sounds like one of the briskly cheerful Government posters pinned up outside the village church.

POTATOES Feed Without Fattening And Give You ENERGY!
Help Win the War on the Kitchen Front: Above All Avoid WASTE!

She doesn't know how to address her sister. She wants to ask her if she too has convulsive moments of terror so sharply powerful that she has to sit down and weep. She wants to ask if Cristabel fears for Digby as much as Flossie does, but it seems like a breach of decorum, as to admit the possibility of fear admits the possibility of Digby hurt, of Digby shot, of Digby blown up, of Digby never coming home, and that cannot be done. That would be pulling a stone out of the wall that might bring the whole castle tumbling down.

Keep it under your hat! CARELESS TALK COSTS LIVES.

Flossie puts down her pen and puts the letter in a drawer. A postcard will do instead. A brief message saying only the essentials and none of the things that matter.

C to D

16th September, 1940
Bentley Priory, Stanmore

Dear Digs,

Not much time to write between shifts. We are on a four hour on, four hour off pattern and I must get some sleep. It's been relentless since bombs started falling on London. After so long spent wishing the war would hurry up and start, it's now not going to give us a moment to take a breather.

Our quarters are decent. I'm at Fighter Command, based in Bentley Priory, the type of grand house your mother always aspired to. Nothing like decrepit old Chilcombe. There are a few people here with an interest in the theatre. We talked about putting on a show in the concert room. I proposed Henry V, but then the senior officers got wind of it and decided they want to do comical skits dressed as women. I'm unsure why this should be comical, but they've put me in charge of lighting, so there we go.

I rather suspect this letter will be one I can't post, as the official line is that we don't tell anyone what we do here, but I want to talk to you about it, so I will keep this for when you are next back on leave.

It is very hush-hush. Us WAAFs have become adept at saying vague things about 'working with wirelesses' when asked, then changing the subject. There's an occasional advantage to the assumption that if you are a woman, your work must be trivial.

It's not trivial at ALL. We are tracking German aircraft as they come over the Channel, plotting their routes on a table map using coloured counters like tiddlywinks. Senior officers look down at the map from viewing balconies, like wealthy people in boxes at the theatre. They monitor what's going on and dispatch RAF fighters to meet the incoming Germans. Air raid warnings go out from here too.

It's easier if I pretend they are tiddlywinks in a giant board game. If I think about the fact there are real people involved, I can't concentrate. Some girls wear headsets and can hear the crackly pilots' voices over the radio. That's all right when they're saying 'Tally ho!' and 'I've got him!' but it's not all right when you can hear them screaming.

On one of my first shifts here, I had quite a start when I realized twenty enemy raiders were heading straight for Chilcombe. For a moment, I couldn't think what to do. It was a sunny morning, and there I was, using a stick to push counters over the sea, closer and closer to home. Floss would be there, I thought. Probably with her nose in a Mills & Boon book, completely bloody oblivious. For a moment, I considered trying to get a message to her, but one cannot desert one's post.

Then it came in over the radio that the Germans were attacking a Royal Navy ship in Portland Harbour. More than a hundred men died, but all I could feel was a sort of flattened-out gratitude. It's ghastly when you are thankful that other people are dead, rather than your people.

Flossie told me later they heard explosions and thought the invasion was starting. Apparently, Mr Brewer and others have hidden weapons up in a burial mound on the Ridgeway, as part of some sort of secret defence scheme. He says he didn't run from the Germans the last time and has no intention of doing so now, even if they drive their tanks on to our lawn.

When I was a child and I imagined defending Chilcombe, I always pictured myself charging down the drive on a horse, waving a broadsword. I thought about that a lot, you know. Everyone in danger – Cristabel to the rescue! Sometimes, I would lie in bed and imagine that everyone I cared about was dying and only I could save them. (Then I would have a creeping fear that I was going to make them die, because I was foolish enough to imagine it, and thereby somehow inviting it. That was a chilling feeling.)

But now my country is being attacked and I cannot charge at anyone. Only this morning, the officers on the balcony were looking down at my corner of the map, where I was inching my lethal tiddlywinks closer to Sussex, and it seemed very wrong that such things should occur, and my only role should be to show it happening.

I must have become slow in my movements because an officer behind me muttered, 'Still with us, Seagrave?'

'Yes, sir,' I said, and hurried my counters along.

I must be able to do more, Digs. Being here is no doubt a privileged position, rather like an overseeing god, and I am trying my best to be that kind of god, the aloof type that wisely lets events unfold. But I cannot help but feel I am more like those other impetuous gods, that fly down to the battlefield and intervene in the world of mortal men.

Perry says you're probably sweating in a tank in North Africa. Do be careful. We're in the thick of it now, aren't we?

Your Crista

A Nightclub in Piccadilly

March, 1941

There is a fervency to these dangerous Blitz nights. This one especially – a moonlit Saturday, a hint of spring in the air, and, despite everything, people heading out into the streets. The authoritarian darkness of the blackout makes their activity seem a forbidden escape, a midnight feast. It's after lights out, as Rosalind's mother used to say. The city is as tall and shadowed as a forest and they run between its legs like children.

Thousands of Londoners go down to the Tube stations to shelter there every night, whether bombs are falling or not. They tuck themselves under blankets, play cards, sing songs and knit. But there are others who make for different underground haunts: the basement grill at The Ritz; cellar bars in St James's where jazz bands play until the early hours; discreet nightclubs beneath the West End pavements that never stop serving. Places accessed via steep unlit steps, their clientele descending into the black earth to find caverns alive with laughter and light.

Rosalind has lived too long to join patriotic singalongs in grimy Tube stations when she could instead have a chilled glass of something, and she has always preferred the few to the many. A couple of gins to steady her nerves and she is high-stepping along the debris-strewn streets, broken glass crunching beneath her heels, navigating by means of the white lines painted on the kerbs, joining those going out on the town.

Every route through the lightless city is now an unpredictable one. It is a shadowy moonscape and the bombs change its shape every night. Landmarks evaporate, streets are roped off, and dust falls over everything. Air raid wardens in helmets and overalls poke long poles at the smouldering remains of buildings until the debris shifts and tumbles like coal, acrid smoke drifting along the roads like fog.

The plinths of famous statues stand empty, they have taken down Eros and boarded up the fountains, and the facades of bombed-out buildings are just that – facades with nothing behind them, no floors or ceilings or inhabitants. Houses hang open, sliced in two; bedrooms, bathrooms, all the intimate spaces exposed to public view. Nothing is sacred. It is a production set, and the scenery keeps changing. It is a production set, and the cast are here one day, gone the next. Only the sky is lit up, criss-crossed with movie-star searchlights while air raid sirens slide up and down the scale.

Rosalind is going to meet Myrtle in Piccadilly, but it doesn't matter if she's persuaded to stop in at a bar or two on the way. It's different now. Not everyone is in formal evening wear and there are so many in uniform. Flying Johnnies and Navy Jacks, as Myrtle calls them. Officers, aircrews and guardsmen. Does she know how to jitterbug? Yes, she does. Is she married? Yes, she is. But Willoughby hasn't looked at her for such a long time, and perched on a twisting bar stool, she can turn to have her cigarette lit in such a way that the green silk of her dress pulls tight across her thighs; see the men's eyes fall thankfully upon them. It is a mutual exchange. One more cocktail, the ice cubes knocking in the glass, and her face in the mirror in the ladies' room is high and triumphant. There are attentive men waiting for her to return to their company. Her husband is absent. Her mother is dead. She knows how to jitterbug.

When she and the men walk out together, rough women call from shadowy doorways, shouting for the men to come back for them later, saying they can't go off to fight Hitler without a bit of fun first, saying, come on, dearie, don't leave me lonely. Rosalind cannot disapprove, even though she should. She feels it as a communal benevolence, a blessing for the brave boys. She hopes they never have to resort to such things, but who could deny them their indulgences? It is as if everyone is living as she has always lived: in a dance towards pleasure as a means of distraction. They have joined her, with drinks in their lifted hands.

★

They go to the Café de Paris nightclub, nodding to the doorman as he pushes open heavy doors to let them in. They hurry down two flights of stairs, and she catches herself in a gilt-framed mirror lit from beneath and notices the sinews in her neck, taut as twin cable lines. She pauses, looks closer, wipes away a lipstick smudge at the corner of her mouth. She is always grateful for unscrupulous lighting, the kind favoured by medical professionals and stage actors: those who know the face is a canvas. She believes women should be objective about their appearance; too many will sail past mirrors if they are enjoying themselves, foolishly assuming that happiness somehow transforms them. One must unlearn such fond indulgence of oneself.

Men can turn away from you so easily. They can talk among themselves and forget you are there, and it is nothing to them. She cannot blame them. They are strong and male and prepared to die for their country and she is a woman in her forties with a décolletage that is starting to look like crêpe paper. She has a smile ready for the times they discard her – a winsome smile and a charming way of clasping her hands together that allows everything to continue. She couldn't let them feel awkward, even though it is nothing to them. It is not nothing to her. All she has ever wanted is to be wanted, but not in a coarse way. She is a parrot, a cave. She is weary of trying to be all the things they might want her to be, but what else is there to do?

From across the city comes the wail of the evening's first air raid siren. They are used to it now. Bombs have been dropping on London for months. They are so far underground, it is perfectly safe, and the owner has stockpiled champagne so they will never run out. The men head to the bar.

The nightclub interior has been designed to look like the ballroom on the *Titanic*: a polished dance floor surrounded by tables with white tablecloths and stylish lamps, overlooked by a curved balcony where Rosalind catches a glimpse of Myrtle waving a hand to indicate she has found them a good spot. A broad moustachioed man wearing many medals is sitting in front of her, sipping whisky.

On the other side of the dance floor is a sweeping double staircase, where glamorous dancers in feather headdresses are waiting to descend. The famous band in their dinner suits are tucked beneath the staircase, tuning their instruments, adjusting their music stands.

As Rosalind is handed a drink, the band starts up. A little shuffle on the cymbal – ta-*tah*, ta-*tah*, ta-*tah* – and the trumpets' swaggering answer – pa-*PAAH*-pa! pa-*PAAH*-pa! – and the audience start tapping their feet and nodding their heads even before the rest of the band comes swinging in, because they've all heard this one on the wireless, it's 'Oh Johnny, Oh Johnny, Oh!' and you can't help but want to dance. The band leader is swaying like Fred Astaire as he waves his baton, effortless and light, an elegant young Black man with a white bow tie. The dancers on the stairs have their hands up by their faces and are moving side to side in unison.

Somewhere overhead, the distant throbbing of enemy bombers and the rattling barrage of London's anti-aircraft guns.

One of the soldiers takes Rosalind's glass from her hand and puts it on a table in order to twirl her smartly on to the dance floor. Finding her body up against a broad chest in a khaki uniform, she is suddenly reminded of Willoughby the young officer pulling her close, as if he had every right to, even while she was still married to his brother. Such a treat to acquiesce, to drop all the effort of not making an effort, and to be claimed by him. The most longed-for surrender. The most handsome of men. She closes her eyes, and they sway together, and the evening is just beginning.

Outside, German aircraft are following the path of the Thames, which shines like a silver ribbon in the moonlight, leading them into the city. They drop bombs as they go. Cylindrical high-explosives fall from the bellies of the planes and descend at whistling speeds on to Barking and Limehouse and Whitechapel and Blackfriars and one dropped above Piccadilly comes plummeting down and

down and

down and

down and

down and

down

through a

small
exposed
ventilator shaft
which carries
it cleanly
twenty feet
underground
into the
gallery
above
the
resident
band
of
the
Café
de
Paris
where it
explodes
in a gas-blue flash
sending a shock wave of air
hot as a furnace blast
punching across the space
carrying before it cymbals and
chairs and sheet music and feathers
and instrument cases and musicians and parts of
other musicians and silk gowns ripped from dancing bodies
a high-velocity mosaic of glass shards stilettos forks oboes
ashtrays lacerating through the aircrews and their dates and the
waiters with plates just arriving at the tables until the nightclub
and its contents are a hurricane-blown dandelion clock
hurtling out to the edges
all single things now in flight and intermingled
part of
everything.

The decision of the bomb is final: there will be nothing here but air, and the clear space left behind. The lights go out. The ceiling collapses on to the dance floor. The Café de Paris is open to the night sky. Smoke rises from the rubble.

Note on Pink Notepaper
with a Bouquet of Roses

17th March, 1941
Mayfair

Darling Flossie and Cristabel,

'Women should always leave first – men like you better when they think you're on your way.' Rosalind told me that. She said the best method she knew to catch Willoughby's attention was to walk out of a room. She excelled at it. Such sinuosity. That statement returned to me today when I saw her funeral notice in the newspaper. She left first, the poor sweet. Although I believe she may be relieved by that. She never wanted to grow old.

I tried to live by her words for a while. I endeavoured to plan my exits well, to synchronize my movements in accordance with the potential interests of men. But I don't have time for that now. The world doesn't have time. War has compressed us – and we ignite. Besides, I have never wanted to leave rooms. I enjoy being in them: talking, drinking, proclaiming my verse!

I won't be able to attend Rosalind's funeral, though I know you won't be burying any of her in that cold church. I'm sailing to New York tomorrow, with crates of paintings I hope will be safer there, and meeting Taras and Hilly for a new exhibition of Taras's work. I'll also try to persuade America to hurry up and join the damn war. But I'll be back at Christmas, with armfuls of nylons and oranges.

You know, the strangest thing about the Café de Paris was the silence. The fireman who pulled me out told me if you are very close to a bomb, you don't hear it. One moment I was raising a toast to dear Winston, then there was a jolt of energy, as if time itself had shuddered, and everything stopped.

When I looked again, my companion for the evening was dead, although decent enough to remain seated at the table, and there was grey dust falling over everything like the fluttering ash of Pompeii.

Give my sincere condolences to Willoughby and Digby. Think of Rosalind with fondness and forgiveness and keep her picture on the wall, but remember there is more to life than being looked at. Vanity is a small box of mirrors. Let none of us squander these days. May we all leave last.

With love,
Myrtle xx

Exhibition Catalogue

KOVALSKY IN ENGLAND

Thursday May 15th to Saturday July 5th, 1941

The van der Werff Gallery, New York

7 cents

Proceeds to the American Red Cross

Preface by Myrtle van der Werff

So often the cry comes: what good is art in war? The galleries of Europe stand empty. Paintings are burnt by those who deem the modern element 'degenerate'. Now is the time for battle, not art, say the voices of reason.

We raise our voices in reply: art is our weapon! That artists in Europe suffer demonstrates how much they are feared by the Nazi menace we must oppose. To let fascists crush art beneath their jackboots, to fail to protect those who move us most profoundly, this would be a loss to humanity.

Among those who have fled persecution is Taras Kovalsky. Mr Kovalsky trained in France as part of the 1920s 'School of Paris' – émigré artists that included Messieurs Modigliani and Chagall.

Although two of the works displayed here appeared in London's International Surrealist Exhibition in 1936, Mr Kovalsky prefers not to align himself with any particular movement. However, it is right to say that among the Surrealists he found brother artists. Those who break down the barriers entrapping civilized man. Those who prize the irrational plumage of dreams, the rainbow lights of gasoline.

Visitors to this exhibition will be greeted by *Woman of the Roses*, an arcane image of the unconscious. Its faceless figure deftly undoes the conventions of portraiture. And how fine the roses, how blood-like, as compared to the ghostly pallor of the hands!

Cristabella the First shows a girl fiercely rendered in textured oil paint. With a wooden sword in her hand, she is not one of Mr Gainsborough's quiescent children with a beribboned hoop. This tangled tomboy is a feral Huckleberry Finn of the fairer sex. *The Burning* is born of similarly dark portents and dynamic colour (that inexhaustible orange! that viscous black!).

At a time when Europe is again enduring the spasms of war, these ominous images from an artist sprung from the crucible of conflict carry a formidable power – it is a rallying cry we cannot fail to answer!

TITLE	DATE	MEDIUM
1. *Woman of the Roses*	1928	Oil
2. *Mademoiselle Aubert Takes Up Arms* (lent by the Galerie Mouradian, Paris)	1928	"
3. *Maudie at Chilcombe*	1928	"
4. *Zeus Encounters the Whale*	1931	"
5. *The White Horse that Displeased a King*	1930	"
6. *Miss Florence* (lent by Willoughby Seagrave, Esq., Dorset)	1929	Drawing
7. *Bones by Moonlight*	1931	Gouache
8. *Infinity Found in the Seashell*	1933	"
9. *Bill* (lent by the Zwemmer Gallery, London)	1929	"
10. *Cristabella the First* (lent by Willoughby Seagrave, Esq., Dorset)	1929	Oil

11. *Altercation in the Memory*	1935	Photographic collage
12. *The Burning* (lent by the Zwemmer Gallery, London)	1934	Oil

OBJECTS

13. Dorset hag stone
14. Fossil
15. Burnt weasel

ACT FOUR

1942–1943

Captives

They see her coming across the field and still their movements. The sun is bright. Their eyes are shadowed beneath work caps. They wear regulation shirts and trousers. Some have twine for belts, some have the letters 'PW' stitched on to their sleeves. They have been camped in the field for three days now, but this is the first time Flossie has been to see them.

She notices their cautious, neutral silence as they watch her approach; how the warm air seems to solidify until she struggles to move through it, stumbling on the rutted earth.

A stout figure wearing British uniform removes his hat. 'Miss Seagrave,' he says. It is Sgt Bullock, his face florid in the heat.

'Good afternoon, Sergeant. I have come to collect the men who will be working in the stables,' says Flossie, wiping her hair from her eyes. 'Mr Brewer had to go to London.'

'Very well,' says Sgt Bullock. He turns to the German prisoners of war: five men who are living in a camp on the estate while being sent out to work on the nearby farms, where they are short of labour. Some of the men are to look after the few remaining horses at Chilcombe, which are also being put to work in the fields.

The prisoners are living in a large tent surrounded by wire fencing. They are guarded by Sgt Bullock and a pair of young British soldiers who have been billeted in Chilcombe Mell vicarage. Flossie does not know where the Germans have come from or what they did before they were taken captive, but she notices one has burns on his face and wonders if they were pilots.

Sgt Bullock, who is in charge, signals for two to step forward. As they do, they lower their heads and remove their hats: one is dark, the other blond, his hair almost white in the sun. 'They've been thoroughly checked,' says Sgt Bullock, as if the men themselves were horses.

'What are their names?' Flossie says. 'What are your names?'

The dark-haired man looks at her, his expression wary. 'Mattner,' he says.

The blond one is slower to raise his head but, when he does, he has a slight smile. 'I am Hans Krause,' he says, carefully pronouncing each word.

'I am Miss Seagrave,' she says.

'Miss Seagrave,' he says, and her name is unfamiliar in his accent.

Sgt Bullock scowls at the prisoners. 'One foot out of line and there'll be trouble.'

Flossie leads Sgt Bullock and the two Germans back across the field, over a stile, and towards the stables at the rear of the house: a strange parade. Approaching Chilcombe, she imagines her mother watching her – the way Rosalind would lean against the landing window, cigarette in hand, gazing flatly at the outside world. It is a curious thing to picture. Rosalind has been dead for over a year, although her bedroom still holds her scent. Betty says it is trapped in the upholstery fabric.

Whenever Flossie used to creep into her mother's bedroom as a child, it was always so suffused with perfume, she could feel its stickiness at the back of her throat. She would play with the make-up on the dressing table or open the wardrobe to run her fingers along the silky rainbow of dresses hanging inside. On a shelf above the clothes were hat boxes and a voluminous lace wedding veil that was a Seagrave family heirloom; Rosalind's clothes hung beneath its delicate netting like shimmering fish. After she died, Flossie donated Rosalind's best dresses to a second-hand shop in Dorchester and gave the rest to Betty, to be cut up and reused. They were too small for anyone else. She kept the veil.

Flossie leads Sgt Bullock and the Germans to the stables. Inside, the horses snicker for attention, their nostrils flaring. Sunbeams slant in through half-circle windows, columns of hayseed and dust.

'Have you worked with horses before?' asks Flossie.

Mattner nods. Krause grins. He has a gap in his front teeth. He reaches out to the nearest horse in its stall. 'My father has farm,' he says. His hands on the animal are expert, calm; it noisily gums his palm.

Flossie says, 'You will need to clean out the stables and make sure the horses are fed. We had two men who did this for us before, but they are – they had to leave us.' It seems oddly gauche to have to explain to the Germans they are short of staff because the staff are away fighting the Germans. She also isn't sure how much English they understand.

'These animals will need to get used to dragging a cart behind them,' says Sgt Bullock, dabbing his face with a handkerchief. 'You're lucky to still have them. The authorities have requisitioned most hunting horses. No room for luxuries when you're fighting a war.'

'I think my Uncle Willoughby had a word with the authorities,' says Flossie. 'He knows most of them.'

Sgt Bullock sniffs.

'Krause, Mattner, if you have any questions, do ask,' says Flossie. 'I can't speak German, but I'm sure we can muddle along together.'

Krause looks up from the horse and says, 'My English not good. But horse, for me, is home.' He claps one big hand on his chest, roughly where his heart is, and smiles at her.

'Thank you, Krause,' she says. 'I think this will work out most amenably, don't you, Sergeant?'

'That remains to be seen, Miss Seagrave,' says Sgt Bullock. 'These prisoners have proved themselves competent workers in the fields. They may be of some use here.'

His words are designed to remind the men of their limited range. It offends her somehow, his reduction of their capabilities. 'I'm sure they'll be marvellous,' she says, and hears her own English voice, high and girlish, echoing in the vaulted roof.

'You two, wait outside,' says Sgt Bullock. 'Miss Seagrave and I have other matters to discuss.'

'Do we?' she says, as the Germans leave.

He turns to her. 'I was led to understand that quarters were to be provided for myself inside of the main house. Earlier today I took the liberty of finding a suitable bedroom and have established myself in the unoccupied room above the dining room.'

'That's Digby's room.'

'It appeared to be wholly vacant.'

'It is now, Sergeant Bullock, because Digby's with the army in North Africa. But he will come back.'

'I believe in other parts of England the country houses adjoining POW camps have been entirely taken over for the war effort. I am sure we can come to some less formal arrangement. Please, call me Terence.'

Krause and Mattner come to the stables every morning. After the first few visits, Sgt Bullock does not accompany them, preferring to oversee the prisoners working in the fields from the comfort of a fold-out canvas chair before returning to the house in the evening, where he has taken to sitting at the dining table, smoking cheroots and helping himself to Betty's home-made parsnip wine while listening to the wireless. He is prone to making sweeping pronouncements about 'the Yanks' and 'the Boche' whenever they are mentioned, as if the BBC broadcasts were merely a prompt for him to provide his more knowledgeable opinions. Any dissenting viewpoint is met by blustery guffaws.

Flossie avoids him. He is a noxious, toad-like presence, squatting in her home. Whenever he sees her, he stands up and makes a movement towards the drinks cabinet, saying, 'Can I offer you anything by way of refreshment, Miss Seagrave?'

She waves him away, a gesture she recognizes as her mother's – not one she ever imagined she would need – saying, 'Sergeant Bullock, if you're going to smoke those things, I'd be grateful if you could open a window.' Her tone of voice, she notices, is also borrowed from Rosalind.

'He isn't bothering you, is he?' asks Betty, when they are drinking tea in the kitchen. 'No funny business?'

'No. I simply wish he weren't here,' says Flossie.

The irritation of Sgt Bullock's presence is exacerbated by the fact both Mr Brewer and Maudie are absent – and it is only their absence that reveals what unexpected allies they have become. Mr Brewer has always been busy with the Home Guard, as well as running occasional mysterious errands for Perry, but now it is his profitable sideline in discreetly supplying expensive restaurants with unrationed eggs and poultry that takes up most of his time. Meanwhile, Maudie has gone off to Weymouth on fire watch duties, where she is spending her nights stationed on the roof of a building with a whistle (although Betty has made dark remarks about Maudie's interest in defending Weymouth being more to do with the influx of sailors into the town than any kind of civic duty).

The evacuees have returned to London and so only Betty is left in the house. Now in her mid-forties, Betty has become a round hen of a woman, always clattering in the kitchen or complaining about her kidney troubles or fretting about her son being in the navy.

After Rosalind's death, Betty seemed to descend immediately into middle age, almost as an act of protest. The common sense she had as a young woman solidified into pessimism, and the war and its tribulations have only served to reaffirm that life is disappointing, the newspapers full of lies, and nothing she does will make a blind bit of difference.

Flossie finds this sour fatalism exhausting, not to mention Betty's inability to leave a kettle alone. There is Betty fussing in the bottom of the house, Sgt Bullock pontificating on the ground floor, and all that is left to Flossie is her mother's bedroom (too full of her mother and too hot) and the attic (too full of her much-missed siblings and even hotter). She picks up her spade and heads outdoors.

Every morning, Flossie walks through the woods to The Whalebone Theatre, following the path through the trees. But the theatre is no longer a space for performance – it now overlooks a large vegetable plot, created and tended by first Betty, assisted by Maudie and Flossie, and now Flossie alone. Several of the bones are entwined with sweet peas, which twist their green tendrils around the whale's ribs like ribbons round a maypole.

Flossie finds it hard but fulfilling work, nurturing her plot of earth. Betty was a no-nonsense but effective teacher of agriculture, having overseen the house's kitchen garden for many years, and Flossie soon began to relish the satisfaction of seeing her own amateur efforts become edible. Her garden does not have the neat uniformity of Betty's, which, despite no longer having gardeners to tend it, holds determinedly to its methodical Victorian design, with soldierly rows of terracotta rhubarb forcers and espaliered apple trees trained to grow flat against the walls. But Flossie's garden, with its wayward mix of useful vegetables and sentimental flowers, is all hers.

It is peculiar, but the theatre has become a home from home for her again, as it was when she was a child, but now it is one she inhabits by herself. If the weather is decent, she will spend the whole day working outside, sitting in a comfy spot at the base of one of the bones to eat her packed lunch. If it rains, she will shelter in the barn, and if she wants a cup of tea, she will go into the cottage, where the kitchen is just about useable.

Both the barn and the cottage are still cluttered with miscellaneous pieces of theatrical equipment. Costumes and props. Dog-eared scripts. It gives the place a rather ghostly atmosphere, as if a performance had been abandoned halfway through, which, thinks Flossie with a guilty twinge, is not so far from the truth.

It had been getting harder and harder to find people willing to perform in Cristabel's productions. Harder still to find audiences who wanted to watch an amateur Shakespeare play in the rain when they could see Errol Flynn or Gracie Fields on the big screen in Dorchester. Digby was due to head off to university, to start a new life in Cambridge, and Flossie wanted to get married. She cannot imagine Cristabel without her theatre, but what is a theatre without a cast or audience? Then the war came, and everything was stopped, and nobody knew if it would start again.

Which is why gardens are so useful, thinks Flossie. You don't have to think about all the questions that hang over them. You only need think about digging and weeding the patch of soil at your feet.

★

When she has finished her toil, Flossie will walk back to Chilcombe to feed Mr Brewer's chickens, who are living in one of the smaller outbuildings that used to belong to the gardeners. The head gardener's old wooden desk is now covered by roosting birds; flowerpots and seed packets are scattered among feathers and eggs. The latter she will collect in a basket.

It is when she is here, at the back of the house, that Flossie will often see Krause and Mattner. Sometimes it is jarring to remember that they are the enemy, especially as Krause is so friendly. He always waves or lifts his work cap. She seems to see him more than she sees Mattner. Perhaps because he has lighter hair.

When she is passing the stables, she will sometimes see Krause working, his broad back bending as he checks the horses' hooves. Sometimes he turns, from that bent position, and smiles at her. There is an informality in this, somehow. Because looks should be returned face-to-face, upright, and yet here he is, grinning over his shoulder, a horse's hoof in his hand. She can't help but smile back.

'Miss Seagrave,' he will say, and it is like a joke between them, though she is not sure why.

'Krause,' she will reply, somehow incapable of saying anything else or doing anything other than smiling and drifting away, looking down at the eggs in her basket as if they had materialized out of thin air. Such curious objects: both beautiful and alien. When she touches them, they are still warm, newborn. She can't remember what she is meant to be doing beyond laying her fingertips on the speckled shells of the eggs.

She is similarly befuddled one morning when Krause comes to help her with a heavy wheelbarrow. She can only wave her head slightly from side to side by way of thanks, as if she were the one with limited language. It is such an odd reaction, this failure to converse. She decides it must be a form of social anxiety; a dumbshow occasioned by the fact he is an enemy prisoner, making etiquette challenging.

When Sgt Bullock suggests that Krause, with his farming knowledge, could occasionally work at the vegetable patch, Flossie is so keen to signal that she is capable of coping with this unexpected proposal that she finds herself insisting upon it, in a haughty tone that surprises them both.

Sgt Bullock quickly agrees that yes, of course it must happen, although later that day, he becomes more pressing in his request that she listen to his after-dinner political monologue, and she feels these things are somehow connected, a form of realignment, so is unable to refuse.

When Krause first arrives at the theatre, Flossie has a sudden panic she has made a terrible mistake. She can hear Cristabel in her mind, furiously roaring about enemy aliens. But Krause, who is escorted by one of the British soldiers, is intrigued by the bones, and explaining about the theatre in a way he can understand, given the limitations of her German and his English, proves such an entertaining diversion, she soon forgets her doubts. The soldier seats himself in the cottage porch, half-heartedly watching them while practising card tricks.

Krause gets to work pulling up weeds with enthusiasm. 'I always belief I would work on farm, but I did not belief it would be England,' he laughs.

Flossie laughs too. 'It is funny how things work out.'

'How did you belief you would be?' he asks.

'Well, I didn't think I would still be here, to be frank,' Flossie replies. 'I thought I'd do the usual things, you know. Be a debutante. Do you know what that means?'

The German shakes his head.

'Well, debutantes are presented to members of the royal family and get proposed to by eligible young men, but I didn't get to do that because of the war.'

'Ah,' says Krause, looking none the wiser.

Flossie mimes putting a wedding ring on her finger and tries again, a little louder. 'I thought I would find a husband. A kind one. Go and live in his house. Have children.'

'Now vegetables,' says Krause.

'Yes,' says Flossie, surveying her plot. 'Not what I expected, but I do like them. I suppose I never imagined I would be the only one left at Chilcombe. The theatre really belongs to my sister. But it's not a theatre any more, is it?'

'Garden,' says Krause cheerfully.

After being introduced to the vegetables, Krause comes striding down to the bones every few days, trailed by the bored young soldier with his pack of cards. Pleasingly, it transpires that Krause and Flossie work well together, establishing a shared language of smiles and nods over trowels and twine. Working side by side means Flossie does not have to look at his face often, so is able to keep her strange shyness in check, although she is very aware of the nearness of his face, in profile.

Krause knows more about practical tasks than she does but is considerate in showing her what needs to be done, rather than trying to take charge. He even politely pays attention when she shows him the 'Dig for Victory' leaflet, though it must be largely gibberish to him. She has carried it in her coat pocket since it was issued by the Ministry of Agriculture at the start of the war, as it includes a useful table stating when crops should be planted, and advice on how to have 'health-giving vegetables every week of the year', concluding: DIG WELL AND CROP WISELY. Although mystifying at first, it has proved invaluable.

Flossie even plucks up the courage to get the bus to Dorchester to buy some shirts and overalls, so she is properly outfitted for her labours. The woman in the shop says approvingly, 'You look like a Land Army girl, Miss Seagrave.' And she does. The practical clothes suit her far better than the flouncy garments her mother used to buy for her. The Flossie in the changing room mirror looks freckled and strong. Sleeves rolled up. Hair tied back in a headscarf. A Land Army girl.

Flossie looks again at her reflection. She seeks out mirrors more frequently these days, but it is not in order to find her flaws, as it always used to be. Beyond her enjoyment of her new clothes, there is something else: a seriousness in her gaze that her eyes keep wanting to meet, as if she and her reflection were engaged in some kind of ongoing silent exchange.

★

One afternoon, when she and Krause are digging a new bed for lettuce, they hear the noise of a fighter plane. It is a throaty purring, like a large lawnmower, that comes and goes on the wind. They look up and see it coming over the Ridgeway, smoke pouring from its tail.

Though fighter planes in the skies above Dorset are no longer as common as they were at the start of the war, some still occasionally appear, and every time she sees one, Flossie is astonished by how close they come – flying low across the valley like Willoughby used to do, sending the rooks fleeing from the trees. This one now, a Messerschmitt with its engine guttering, passing so closely over their heads that Flossie can see the two crewmen in the cockpit. She watches as the plane heads out to sea, losing altitude rapidly. She hears Krause sigh, and wonders if they will be the last people to see the men alive.

Once, in the summer of 1940, she had been walking on Ceal Head when a German bomber roared overhead, pursued by a Spitfire. Both flew out of sight and then, a short while later, she saw the Spitfire return, and the pilot did a victory roll across the bay, turning effortlessly in the sky like an otter corkscrewing through water. It was as if he were performing his celebration just for her, and she jumped and waved at him. At that time, when everything had been so dark and precarious, it had been a moment of pure joy. She isn't sure she would feel the same now.

'Were you a pilot?' says Flossie. She points up.

Krause shakes his head, points down, and makes a gesture like a wavy sea. 'U-Boot.'

'A submarine. Gosh. Did you like it?' she asks.

He laughs and shakes his head again, before putting both hands over his head and ducking down, in a gesture indicating a cramped space.

'Yes,' she says, 'you are tall.' She reaches her hand up above his head, as if measuring his height. They both laugh. He holds his hand out over her head, and gives a shrug, to indicate that she is not quite so tall. They laugh again. But then there is something about the fact they have drawn attention to the whereabouts of his head in relation to hers, that makes them suddenly embarrassed, and they turn quickly back to their work.

He is German. He is the enemy. Cristabel's voice in her head frequently reminds her of this. She remembers too Rosalind's insistence that she only socialize with nice young men from good families. Krause, the son of a farmer, would not be acceptable. But if he wasn't, how would it be?

When Flossie pictures herself and Krause under other circumstances, she imagines meeting at a railway station somewhere, or in a restaurant. She spends a great deal of time considering what she might look like, stepping off a train or pushing open a restaurant door, and walking towards him. In these imaginary scenes, she does not summon up his face or his body, she sees only herself, as seen by him. He exists in these daydreams as an audience member, an admirer.

But there are other times when he comes into her mind unbidden. Sometimes, very early in the morning, before she has properly woken up, she will have the sense of him there, behind her closed eyelids. An outline against sunlight. His back and shoulders. She can't remember if she has ever seen this in real life, but it is as vivid as if she had. More vivid, in fact, as it carries with it a dream's strangely breathing weight, as if it were a living moment unlocked in the shifting time between sleep and consciousness.

She is grateful they cannot have much conversation as, increasingly, she does not want to have much conversation with anyone. When she and Krause finish their work, he is escorted by the British soldier back to the camp for his evening rations: soup with bread and margarine. After he has gone, Flossie will delay going back into the house in favour of wandering to the edge of the lawn, where she will sprawl in the shade beneath the trees, with an open book she does not read but uses as an occasional defence against Sgt Bullock or Betty.

Flat on her stomach with her chin propped on her elbows, Flossie will watch the dusk fall. From her low angle, the unmown lawn is a dense jungle, the house barely visible through the greenery, like Sleeping Beauty's castle. With nobody to prune them, the roses by the front door are overextending themselves, and the formal hedges have gone haywire, having a hundred silly ideas at once, multiple branches springing loose from their preset shapes. Insects zip about unchecked, drawing freehand vectors in the last of the light.

Flossie rests her head on her arms and squints into the setting sun, her eyelashes flickering at the edge of her vision. Her own flesh is very present and close. The cool softness of her upper arm against her mouth, her breath in the cave of her arms. She presses her open lips to her skin to see how it feels, closes her eyes. The shifting whisper of long grass. The rapid beating of a blackbird's wings as it suddenly takes flight.

Flossie's Diary

1st

Worked at vegetable patch all day. Sgt Bullock filling house with smoke from his revolting cheroots like a satanic mill until Betty persuaded him to go to the pub.

2nd

Very hot. Dug onions. Mr Churchill said on the BBC that we are 'still fighting for our lives'. Resolved to dig more onions. Sgt Bullock keen on The Shipwreck and will be taking his evening meals there from now on. A nation rejoices!

3rd

Mr Brewer back from London with a box of tinned peaches. Air raid on Weymouth last night. Thought of Maudie on her rooftop and said a prayer. Betty says I shouldn't worry as Maudie has more lives than a cat. The German word for sunshine is 'Sonnenschein'.

5th

Teaching Krause about The Wizard of Oz. Told him I've seen it five times. Entertained ourselves by trying to sing 'If I Only Had A Brain'. Krause slightly handicapped by not understanding the words, though this made him rather Scarecrow-y.

9th

Beautiful Schumann concerto on the radio. Tried to play it on the piano afterwards. Most of my favourite composers are German. I said as much to Mr Brewer and he raised an eyebrow in that 'well, well, well' way of his.

11th

Got the gramophone from Mother's room to play Schumann records in the kitchen. D and G are my favourite keys. One yearning, one reassuring. Betty says it all sounds the same to her.

12th

Cary Grant got married again. I lit a candle and had a moment of mourning. Letter from dear Myrtle. She says there is no fruit left in London, only cardboard bananas in the shop windows. Imagine! She intends to wear some as earrings.

13th

Sgt Bullock, Mr Brewer and Betty went to the pub, so I had a bath in Mother's bathroom. Took the gramophone with me. Arranged some roses in a jar on the window sill and they caught the evening sun perfectly. Strange to have lovely moments during a war. Never used to like being in the house on my own, but I do now. Sometimes.

16th

Radishes for Mr Churchill. The German for freckle is 'Sommersprosse'. Hans knows the English words for freckle, sunshine, rainbow and scarecrow. He can say 'There's no place like home' like a Teutonic Judy Garland.

17th

Betty suggested we sell some vegetables to her cousin who is a greengrocer in Dorchester. At first, we couldn't think how to get them there, but clever Hans pointed out there is an old horse-drawn carriage at the back of the stables. Mr Brewer retrieved a dead mouse from inside it and said, 'Maybe you shall go to the ball, Cinderella.'

20th

Postcard from Digby! Such joy to have even a few words from him. I cried. Sometimes I forget how much I miss him. I know it's ridiculous, but I do wish he could meet Hans. They'd get on so well.

24th

Hans tried to tell me a German joke about cabbage today. He was laughing so much he could hardly speak. I didn't understand any of it but couldn't help but laugh too. It does make the day go quickly when you can laugh. Runner beans have come on wonderfully.

25th

Betty has spoken to her cousin and he will buy our vegetables! We are open for business! Hans and I spent the day loading the carriage for our inaugural delivery trip. Our soldier chaperone is coming with us. Useful to have another pair of hands. Betty said when Mother and Father were married, they arrived at Chilcombe in the carriage. How romantic!

26th

Well, we made it to Dorchester and back. It was not what I expected. I've become so used to Hans, I had forgotten that some people might not like to see a German. He took it much better than I did.

30th

I must try to keep up my diary. I've never known how to fit a day into a few lines. Words are quite inadequate, such a lot of the time.

Tempo Rubato

All day they have been working outside in the heat. The sky a relentless blue. When the sun finally starts to set, they walk back through the woods pushing a wheelbarrow full of radishes and runner beans, trailed by the soldier. The footpath is cracked and dusty. Although there are a few weeks left of summer, the countryside is already drying out. The fields around Chilcombe are pale as straw, the hedgerows full of papery seedpods and feathery grasses; things are coming apart from themselves, fraying at the edges.

As they arrive at the front lawn, Flossie allows herself to remember that the house is empty. Mr and Mrs Brewer have gone to the cinema to see *One of Our Aircraft Is Missing*, and Mr Brewer invited Sgt Bullock to join them. Sgt Bullock said he would be grateful for an evening's entertainment and off they went.

There had been a look during that conversation. Mr Brewer had looked at her for a moment. It was a look notable only for its perfect blankness. It said nothing at all. There is, Flossie realizes, a power in saying nothing at all. She is becoming more familiar with silences, learning there are many different kinds.

Flossie and Hans take the wheelbarrow round to the outbuildings at the back of the house, where nettles are sprouting from cracks in the flagstones. Together they wordlessly load the vegetables into the wooden crates waiting in the carriage. Tomorrow, Flossie and Mr Brewer will be taking the carriage and its cargo to Dorchester.

Then Hans goes into the stables to check on the horses, while Flossie goes into the kitchen to wash her hands in the old Belfast sink that is as big as a cattle trough and filled with unwashed sauce-pans. The soldier sticks his head through the door and says he's going to nip down to the village for a pint. He has taken to doing this most days and she had hoped he would today.

'It's been such a hot day, you probably need a drink,' says Flossie, in a voice that seems too loud for the kitchen. She peers into the ancient mirror that hangs on the wall. The glass is dull and grease-stained, but in its murky depths she spies herself: rosy, suntanned, her hair tied back in a yellow headscarf.

She runs the tap and fills two tin mugs full of cold water, then goes to the back door. When Hans emerges from the stables, she holds them up and makes a movement with her head that means: come in. He frowns slightly, then, wiping his hands on his trousers, follows her into the kitchen. She hands him a mug, saying, 'The house is empty. They've all gone.'

She watches as he looks around. It is a room he has never been in before: a cavernous tunnel filled with black ovens and decorated with a ragged Union Jack flag Betty has pinned to one wall, along with patriotic photographs from the picture papers. A pile of grubby tea towels lies on the flagstones, waiting to be laundered, and the feathers from a plucked chicken drift about the floor. The big kit-chen table is covered with magazines, books, tobacco tins, gramophone records and an old wine cooler filled with onions. The copper jelly moulds that used to line the high shelves now balance by the sink, holding soil and seedlings.

Flossie puts the mugs on the table and gestures to say he should sit down. She finds bread and a jar of shrimp paste and makes thick, amateurish sandwiches, which they eat in contented quiet. She sees him look at the clock. She does not want to get him into trouble, but she would like to show him the main house, so, after they have eaten, she beckons him to follow her along the corridor and up the narrow stairs to the Oak Hall, and he does.

Hans enters the hall, eyeing the fireplace and the wood panelling, looking up at the tarpaulin covering the hole where the cupola used to be. He is frowning but does not appear overawed. He glances at her, and she realizes that his concern is not whether he should be allowed in the house, but whether she is doing something that might reflect badly on her.

'I thought you might like to look round,' she says.

Hans walks to the grand piano, running his hand along it in such a familiar way she suddenly knows there is a piano somewhere in Germany he is touching now. He points at the piano and says, 'You?'

She nods.

He points at it again and she laughs. He does it again, and she laughs even more, then she pulls out the piano stool and sits down, saying, 'Well, why not?'

Hans looks shy for a moment. 'I hear,' he says.

'I beg your pardon?'

He mimes playing a piano then points towards the back of the building. 'In the stables. I hear you play. Is good.' He cups one hand behind his ear and nods encouragingly. They are formal in this echoing hall in a way they have not been before.

She opens the piano lid. She has, once or twice or ten times, imagined playing in front of him. How strange to find herself doing it in reality. The grandfather clock ticks like a metronome.

For Flossie, playing the piano involves an element of willed forgetting. She finds it different to acting. Whenever she performed in her siblings' theatrical productions, she would be constantly going over her lines, because if she stopped thinking about them, she would lose them for ever. It is the same anxiety she feels when holding a birthday cake with lit and melting candles: that there is a rapidly closing window of opportunity for things to work out well.

But while acting required all its component parts to be dragged into her mind and forcibly held there, music requires blankness. Whenever she is ready to play a piece, she will sit at the piano, rest her hands on the keys, close her eyes and wait until she can feel nothing. Pure emptiness. Then she can begin.

With nothing in her mind, how does she know where to begin? (She just does.) How do her hands move without instruction? (They just do.) She does not look at her sheet music when she plays, and reproducing what it transcribes is not an act of memory, it is something else. In fact, if she finds herself consciously trying to recall the music as written, she will invariably hit a wrong note. Instead, with one foot tapping gently to keep time, she angles her head to one side, as if waiting to hear it somewhere in the distance. It is like that, if it is like anything: a listening; an admittance.

She closes her eyes. There is something beating in her ribcage that is high and fluttering and she calms it with her breath, waits till it comes.

Throughout her life, the piano has been a friend to Flossie. A place to sit when she could not settle. A place to go when she had no other place. As a child and as a young woman, she could often be seen perched on the piano stool, playing music to herself.

A few weeks before she died, Rosalind, wearing a white dress that clung to her like pouring cream, had found Flossie there. 'Playing the piano in an empty room is rather tragic, darling. Why don't you come through to the drawing room? There's quite a crowd this evening. Myrtle's going to recite some poems about the end of civilization.'

It was February. Heavy rain had rattled noisily against the windows.

'I'm all right,' Flossie said, pressing down on a single note. She could never play properly in front of her mother.

'You're playing very quietly.'

'I'm not really playing anything.'

'I remember my mother always told me to "keep myself up to concert pitch",' said Rosalind, straightening one of the photographs on top of the piano. 'I didn't even play an instrument.'

'I'm all right,' said Flossie.

'If you're sure.' Her mother's voice was somehow insubstantial. The sound of the rain teeming down outside seemed clearer: its consistency and thoroughness. Rosalind belonged to the murmur of exclusive rooms with cleverly positioned lamps and curtains drawn against the weather, where women would arrange them-selves and men would watch. A closed circuit.

For a moment, Flossie considered offering to play something for her mother's guests. Long enough had passed since the last time she suggested it that Rosalind might think it an entirely new idea and therefore novel enough to be included in her evening. The words reached Flossie's mouth but went no further. She tapped her finger-nails quietly on the ivory keys.

Rosalind glanced at her, as if Flossie had said something, and for a second, they eyed each across their respective silences until Rosalind turned to look at her reflection in the surface of the piano, then left without a word, leaving Flossie to the piano and the rain.

When she reaches the end of the piece, Flossie plays the final chord, then lifts her hands. The music hangs in the air, leaving a silence that thrums slightly, charged by the sound that has travelled through it. When she looks at Hans, his eyes are shining. 'Bach,' he says, his voice shaky.

It occurs to Flossie that the music she adores may contain other places and times for him. When she thinks of Germany, she sees lines of troops goose-stepping across cinema screens, but some-where behind that must be the Krause family farm – where his father keeps horses. She imagines an older man with broad shoul-ders like Hans, carrying hay.

'I didn't mean to make you sad,' she says, grimacing apologetically.

He mimes playing the piano. 'My grandmother.' Then he puts one hand on his heart and pats, as if reassuring it.

Flossie closes the piano. There is an entanglement around her then, made up of competing impulses, the most insistent of which is telling her to be a gracious hostess, to escort her guest to the drawing room and offer him a drink. But that is what the house expects her to do, and already they are somewhere outside what is expected, and she does not want to go back.

She does not see him as a guest to be charmed. Nor does she see him as a prisoner to be controlled or feared or shouted at in the street. She sees him as someone who, through no fault of his own, has found himself at Chilcombe and is trying to make the best of it – as she does. She sees Hans Krause, who helps her with the vege-tables, who is kind to the horses, who sings like the Scarecrow, who makes her laugh.

'Let's go out,' she says and goes to the front door, feeling a twinge of regret that she must always be the one who leads. It is with this in mind that she pauses in the doorway to allow him to catch up with her, and then deliberately walks at his side, matching his pace as they cross the lawn. The afternoon has become evening, golden and full of birdsong, and they head through the dappled woods, taking the route they always take.

On the narrow path, they walk side by side, and occasionally bump arms, at first accidentally, then deliberately, jokily; then deliberately, fondly; then deliberately, quietly, until the only thing left is for the hands that keep brushing past each other to seek each other out and hold on. With hands clasped, they continue to walk along the path, looking straight ahead, as if unable to admit to their hands' odd behaviour. Their hands, however, have no such compunctions – they squeeze each other and intertwine their fingers, as familiarly as old acquaintances.

Having become joined in this way, it is easy for Flossie to pull Hans past the bones and the vegetables, and down to the sea. She has no reason to make him go there, but there is a pleasure in pulling his hand, in taking him somewhere. The beach is empty, and a fresh breeze comes off the water. In contrast to the straw-yellow, sun-parched land, the sea is a deep, vivid blue. From all around the bay comes the plunge and fizz of waves reaching the pebbles then sliding back into the ocean.

Coils of barbed wire have been put along the top of the beach, running behind a row of upturned fishing boats. Up on Ceal Head there is a new brick pillbox, a lookout position usually occupied by a man from the Home Guard. They both glance towards it, then Flossie taps Hans's arm, to remind him of the faded letters stitched on to his shirtsleeve: PW. He covers them with his hand, then, with a curious courtesy, turns away from her to pull his shirt over his head. She is startled for a moment, until he nods at the sea. Then she understands: they are a couple from the village, stealing down to the beach for an evening swim.

His chest is ghostly white compared to his tanned face and forearms. With an impish grin, he quickly pulls off the rest of his clothes – dusty boots, work trousers, greying underwear – and runs

303

naked across the pebbles to the sea. Flossie is too surprised to be outraged. His spontaneous whoop of joy as he crashes into the water makes her laugh out loud, then she holds her hands to her face and looks around. The beach is still empty.

Hans splashes happily about like a dog, then swims away from the shore, before turning to look at her from the water. It is as if the change of element has released him: his open face, always quick to smile, has a new expression. He is no longer earth-bound, no longer on English soil. He beckons her.

Once again, it seems her hands have a measure of independence. She is still looking at Hans in the water, feeling astonished by his daring, but her fingers have begun unbuttoning her blouse from top to bottom. All her buttons are dealt with in this way, clasps and zips too. If she doesn't look down at herself, it is easy to take the undone items off, one by one, and allow them to drop to the beach.

Keeping her underwear on, she steps gingerly down the shingle to the water's edge. She has never swum naked, not even as a child. Digby and Cristabel always did, but Flossie was more modest. (Although, it occurs to her as she wades into the sea, it seems unlikely that either Digby or Cristabel have ever been swimming with a naked German prisoner of war.)

The water is colder than she expects. She finds herself on tiptoe, gasping, but forces herself to submerge. She swims briskly out to where Hans stands, calling, 'I can't remember the last time I swam in the sea!' as if they were on a day trip. He gestures at her head, drawing her attention to the fact she is still wearing her headscarf. She tries, ineffectually, to untie it, while standing in a slightly huddled position in the water to keep herself under the surface, until he bends down to her height and reaches around her neck with both hands to gently unknot it.

Once again, it seems easier, as his arms are already encircling her, for him to simply rest his hands at the nape of her neck, one thumb softly stroking the skin it finds there. And as their faces are now so close, it seems natural for him to lean in quickly, as if ducking under something, to press his mouth to hers.

They stay in this position, their bodies carefully held apart, as the

304

sea moves around them, but their kiss too has its own momentum, and it impels them to inch their feet closer until their bodies meet underwater and above. Flossie presses herself against him, firstly, to conceal herself, and secondly, later, because she wants to.

After some time, he hands her the headscarf. 'I might as well have kept it on my head,' she says, and finds her voice superfluous. Conversation, language, English – it seems unnecessary now. She has another way. A language-less language in which she wants to tell him many things. She touches his chest, his neck, his face; runs her fingers along his mouth.

They swim further out, then bob in the water like seals, looking back at the shoreline. The beach appears very far away, in the same way that their bodies seem distant when seen underwater. How easy it is to separate, from the land, from the shape of yourself. England is an unprepossessing layer of beige and green; it hardly seems worth fighting over. They move together and he holds her face in his hands as they kiss. The lavish freedom of the sea. Its lifting freedom.

But the sun is sinking, and they must go back. She can see it in the set of his jaw. She can feel it in the tight ache in her chest. She smiles at him and taps an imaginary watch on her wrist. When they return to the shore, he helps her up the steep rise out of the water, then steps back to look at her as she stands there, with the sea behind her. He holds up an imaginary camera. She does not fold her arms across her chest, as her internal voice is telling her to; instead, she places her hands on her hips and raises her chin. There, she thinks. For you.

'Schöne,' he says.

Then the moment is gone, and they are scrambling up the pebbles and hastily pulling their clothes on to wet bodies and squelching damp feet into recalcitrant shoes. They head back through the woods, solemnly holding hands like a couple going to a railway station to say goodbye. At the edge of the lawn, he strokes smooth one of her wayward pieces of hair, and it is the most loving way anybody has ever touched her. Then they let go of each other's hands and Flossie walks back across the lawn to the house and Hans takes the path that leads to the fields.

The Sun and the Moon

September, 1942

Somehow, it is never a surprise to look up and see Colonel Peregrine Drake. He has the rare quality of being able to materialize expectedly. Cristabel, having tripped on an unlit staircase and broken her wrist, is skulking about the gardens of Bentley Priory on a sunny day in early September, ineffectually raking leaves with her left hand, when she glances up to see him strolling towards her.

'Good afternoon, Section Officer Seagrave,' he says. 'Never had you pegged as a gardener.'

'I'm not,' she replies. 'Only doing it till this gets better.' She waves her plaster cast at him.

'How long till they let you back to work?'

'It's a straightforward break.'

'Of course it is.'

'Should be healed after four very dull weeks.'

'How about a trip back to Chilcombe?'

'I would need to book leave.'

'I've already spoken to your commanding officer. He agreed an angry and wounded Cristabel Seagrave is better off spending a few days in the country than stamping about here. Leon's waiting round the front with the car. Grab your things.'

The car is a military staff car, a khaki-green Humber, with a long bonnet and large mudguards. The engine is running: an efficient rumble. As Cristabel approaches, she sees a uniformed Leon smoking in the driver's seat, while Perry is in the passenger seat, rifling through a file of documents. Cristabel opens the rear passenger door, throws her kitbag on to the back seat, then clambers in.

306

'Off we go,' says Perry, closing his file, and the vehicle accelerates down the drive in a swirl of leaves.

Cristabel looks out of the window as they travel through the neighbouring villages. It is the civilian world, preoccupied and unknowing, no longer one they inhabit: a place of ration books and tiled fireplaces and raffles for the local Spitfire Fund.

She catches Leon looking at her in the rear-view mirror. She returns his gaze directly, with eyebrows raised, before turning purposefully to the window. When she glances back, some moments later, he appears to be watching the road, but then flicks his gaze to the mirror, to let her know he knows she has looked. His half-smile is infuriating. She is aware of the peculiar inequality of being a woman transported in the back of a car, with two men in the front. She wants to fold her arms, but her plaster cast makes it difficult.

'Digby's at Chilcombe,' says Perry, turning to face her.

'What? He's back from Africa?'

'In one piece too.'

Cristabel lets out a breath. 'Thank heavens.'

Perry turns back to the front, saying, 'Lieutenant Seagrave has been in England for a while actually, but we've kept him busy. Additional training. He'll be coming with me tomorrow, but I thought you might like to see him first.'

'Thank you,' she says. 'What sort of training?'

'Additional,' Perry replies, with a smile in his voice.

They drive through Middlesex and Hampshire, then descend into the winding lanes of Dorset. Cristabel is aware that Leon looks at her occasionally but does not mind so much now. They head south, passing thatched cottages, post offices, army camps. Three years of war has made the county look weary: the paintwork on pubs is peeling; outdated War Office posters flap from telegraph poles. There are hardly any other vehicles on the roads, just the odd bus or military truck and, once or twice, a horse-drawn wagon piled high with hay.

When they come up over the Ridgeway, it is late afternoon. Sheep are scattered along its high top, grazing on the burial mounds, while calling gulls pass overhead. The sloping fields are a gently rolling eiderdown, and the sea in the distance is hazy and shining, appearing to evaporate upwards into a sky that is sherbet-striped in pink, amber and blue.

They swoop into the valley and through the village and up the winding driveway to Chilcombe where Mr Brewer, in a greatcoat and bowler hat, is waiting for them outside the house. Leon turns off the engine and gets out of the car to open the door for Perry, while nodding at Mr Brewer.

Perry collects his files, saying, 'How peculiar to arrive at Chilcombe with no Mr or Mrs Seagrave to greet us.'

'I'm here,' says Cristabel, extricating herself from the back of the car before Leon can open the door for her.

'Colonel Drake,' says Mr Brewer.

'Always a pleasure, Bill,' replies Perry.

At that moment, Flossie appears in the doorway carrying a bundle of firewood and wearing canvas dungarees tucked into an old pair of riding boots. 'Is that Crista?' she says. 'Oh, it is! It is!'

The firewood is dropped and Cristabel finds herself unceremoniously pulled into the arms of her half-sister, who is saying, 'I know you don't like emotional scenes, but I can't help myself, you'll have to put up with it. Oh, you feel skinny, Crista, are you eating properly? Is your arm all right? I'll stop squeezing now. Come inside, come inside. The fire's lit in the kitchen. Hello, Perry. Hello, Leon. Gosh, don't you look smart in your uniforms.'

They file into Chilcombe, which Cristabel notices has reversed from its previous state. Before the war, the working elements of the house were kept out of sight downstairs, while the rooms above were opulent scenes of leisure. But now the main rooms have become dark storage spaces full of unused furniture and sacks of potatoes, while the heart of the house has sunk to the servants' kitchen.

Betty is there to welcome them, wearing a floral apron and fussing with the kettle, while Mr Brewer shoos a chicken outside, then gestures for the new arrivals to sit at the cluttered table. There is the scraping of a chair as Sgt Bullock attempts to get to his feet with a sloshing glass of parsnip wine in one hand; Hans is waiting at the back door with a bucket of apples, and they are all haughtily observed by a tabby cat perched by the sink. Flossie lights a candle squeezed into an empty brandy bottle, and this throws its flickering half-light around the subterranean kitchen on to the current inhabitants of Chilcombe: a makeshift, make-do-and-mend scratch band, holed up at the perilous edge of England.

'Where's Digby?' says Cristabel.

'Gone for a walk up the Ridgeway,' says Flossie. 'He'll be thrilled to see you. We didn't know you were coming too.'

Perry takes the seat nearest the range as Sgt Bullock, who has managed to become vertical, salutes.

'Sit down, man,' says Perry. 'No need to stand on ceremony.'

'An honour, Colonel Drake,' says Sgt Bullock, reseating himself.

Leon has found a wall to lean against, where Mr Brewer seeks him out. They shake hands, offer each other cigarettes. Watching them, Cristabel realizes that, despite their differences, they are of a type: middlemen, fixers. Both have found their way into the armed forces, where their particular skills could be polished and legitimized: Mr Brewer was Perry's batman in the first war; Leon fulfils a similar role now.

She tries to imagine the confidences that pass between them, the nature of their work. Leon, a cigarette held rakishly in his mouth, senses her watching and turns his eyes on her. She gives her blue WAAF jacket a tug with her left hand to straighten it out, then stands behind Perry's chair with her arms behind her back.

'You must be one of the prisoners,' says Perry, as Hans is turning to leave. It is a very Perryish manoeuvre, to find the person trying to depart and to pin them, like a butterfly, in place. Perry switches smoothly into German to say, 'I hear you've made yourself quite indispensable.'

Hans begins to back away, saying in German: 'Thank you, sir. I'm merely trying to repay the kindnesses that have been shown to me.'

'He'll be returning to the camp now,' says Sgt Bullock.

'Krause is a harmless lad,' says Mr Brewer.

Perry gestures to the seat next to him. 'Why don't you join us, Krause?'

'I won't have enough food if the German's staying,' says Betty.

'Leon, pop back to the car – there's a box containing some

309

provisions for Mrs Brewer,' says Perry. 'We can take tea in the kitchen. Won't that be novel?'

'We always do, these days,' says Flossie. 'I can't imagine eating anywhere else. The dining room seems miles away.'

'Food was always half cold by the time we got it there,' says Betty.

There is a convivial moving around and organizing, while places are taken, and tea is served. Hans sits down next to Perry and the tabby hops on to his lap. Hans strokes the cat as Perry quizzes him genially on whether he ever hears from his family in Germany, while Betty loudly gives her opinion of that unspeakable man Adolf Hitler. There then follows an exclaiming over and sharing out of the edible goodies Perry has brought with him – fruit cake and chocolate bars – followed by Betty insisting that Perry accept a basket of fresh eggs in return, which Perry holds politely on his lap until Leon takes it out of his hands.

Amid general conversation and cake sampling, Cristabel hears the German say to Flossie, 'The cat sleeps again, Flossie,' and sees her sister laugh, and she wonders at this familiarity with a member of the enemy forces.

'Where did the cat come from?' Cristabel asks.

'He turned up in the stables,' says Flossie. 'Hans feeds him scraps from his rations. We're going to call him Toto.'

'Miss Flossie always did have a soft heart,' says Betty, putting a knitted cosy on the teapot. 'Remember how she would look after that awful elephant as if it were a living creature.'

Flossie laughs. 'It's true. I would put food in his mouth, and it would go all rotten and I'd have to take it out again.'

Leon, in his dark voice, adds, 'I had to pull that elephant around for hours when we did the plays. It was a horse and it was a camel and it was a ship and it was a dragon.'

'Sometimes Digby would be riding on it,' says Flossie.

'Sometimes Cristabel would be standing on it giving orders,' adds Perry, looking at her.

'I'm going to walk up the hill to find Digs,' says Cristabel.

'I'll come,' says Flossie.

*

Flossie and Cristabel walk out together. They leave the estate, circle the edge of the village, then head towards the steep footpath that leads up to the Ridgeway, Flossie striding ahead in her boots. 'Watch that stile, the bottom plank is loose,' she says at one point, comfortably at home in the countryside in a way Cristabel has not seen before.

The footpath zigzags through gorse and brambles as it rises up the steep escarpment and, when they look back, the evening sunlight is doing thoroughgoing work, lovingly picking out the lines of strip lynchets on the fields below – marks left by those who farmed the valley thousands of years before. The path itself is ancient, a chalk footway engraved on the land.

They climb high enough that they can look down on a mob of rooks pursuing a kestrel round the valley: a swooping avian dogfight. At the top of the path is a prehistoric burial mound, a ten-foot-high grassy lump the shape of an upturned bowl, on the summit of which lies Digby. He is lying flat on his back, so still and tranquil he must be asleep.

Cristabel scrambles unceremoniously up to him, ending up on her knees by his side as he rests there, his eyes closed. Flossie follows but waits a little way back. For here is the brother. The deeply dreaming brother. He is narrower, stronger. His dark hair military short. He is wearing his army boots together with some old clothes of Willoughby's: baggy flannel trousers and a loose white shirt, sleeves rolled up to reveal tanned forearms. He has one hand flung above his head, as he did when sleeping as a child. He lies beside a small cairn of cigarette ends, and the rich light of the setting sun casts him in bronze.

'Digs,' says Cristabel. He stirs and opens his eyes, and there is no moment of surprise, just a faithful look of recognition, as if he had always known she would be there when he woke. He pushes himself up and they hug each other like sailors, with a side-to-side motion, slapping each other on the back, Digby receiving some awkward thumps from Cristabel's plaster cast. She can feel him bury his face in her shoulder for a moment, hears him exhale a muffled 'Crista'. Then Flossie is there with her arms around them both, squeezing them furiously, before they all pull apart and look at each other, and suddenly Digby's face is changed and there is an elusiveness in his expression, a tired squint.

'Oh, my sisters,' he says. 'Crista, have you hurt yourself? What's wrong with your arm?'

'It's nothing,' she says. 'Tripped over.'

'You look wonderful in your uniform,' he says. 'It suits you perfectly.'

'Isn't Digby brown?' says Flossie. 'Betty says he looks like an Arab.'

'Very brown,' says Cristabel. 'Tired too. Those are sizeable bags under your eyes, Digs. Are you sleeping all right?'

'Hard to sleep in the desert,' he says, then smiles. 'I've thought about coming home so often and now I'm here, it doesn't seem real. Let's lie down for a moment. It's heavenly to watch the seagulls flying overhead.'

The trio lie down alongside each other and look up at the sky.

'Do you remember when we all had measles?' Digby says.

'I was just thinking that,' says Flossie. 'They let us share one of the big beds.'

'I liked that,' he says, taking a hand from each of them.

'Three spotty dormice curled up together,' says Flossie.

'My eyes were too sore to read so Crista read us *The Iliad*,' says Digby, 'and Floss sang her favourite Christmas carols.'

'"God rest ye merry gentlemen, let nothing you dismaaaaay,"' sings Flossie in her sweet contralto.

They lie in contented silence, Cristabel occasionally glancing at Digby. It is such sustenance to see him. The actual him. After so many months.

'How peaceful it is,' says Digby. 'I haven't been in a peaceful place for a long time. When I was walking up here, I saw some smoke coming from the village, and I assumed it must be something on fire. An aeroplane or a tank. It was only a bonfire.'

'What was it like over there, Digs?' says Cristabel.

'Hot,' he replies, pulling a crumpled pack of cigarettes from his shirt pocket. 'Sandy. Beautiful. Everything shimmered and moved. Sometimes I could see why Father loved it, but sometimes it was hell.'

'Hell?' says Flossie.

'My men were burnt alive in their tanks. I could hear them. I couldn't do anything about it.'

'Goodness, how awful.'

'I don't mean to be gruesome, Floss, but that's the truth of it. I wish it wasn't.'

'The BBC say the Allies are winning in North Africa,' says Cristabel.

'Hard to tell when you're there,' says Digby, lighting his cigarette. His voice is airy, strangely nonchalant.

Cristabel looks at him. 'Perry says you've been doing extra training. Has he got you some sort of special position?'

'You know, Mother always wanted Perry to find me a "special position",' says Digby. 'Although I think when she said "special", she actually meant "safe".'

'What kind of special position?' asks Flossie.

'Oh, never mind about that,' says Digby, tapping his cigarette pack with his lighter. 'Where did you get those handsome boots, Floss?'

'I found them in the stables. I think they were my father's. Stuffed the toes with newspaper. Rather smart, don't you think?' Flossie clicks her heels together.

'Did your German friend teach you that?' says Cristabel.

Flossie blushes. 'Don't be like that, Crista. He's not one of those.'

'Krause's been nothing but charming to me. If Floss likes him, so do I,' says Digby. After a moment, he adds, 'I keep expecting to hear the church bells ring, but they don't any more, do they?'

'They haven't rung for years,' says Flossie. 'Have you been away that long? They'll only ring if we're being invaded or if it's the end of the war, though I don't know how we'll tell which is which.'

'Did you have a funeral for Mother in the church?' says Digby. 'I know you wrote but I can't remember.'

Cristabel nods. 'Flossie and I were there. Perry too. I sent you a copy of the service.'

'Did Father go?' asks Digby.

'He stayed in Ireland.'

'Anybody know what he's doing there?'

'They still have horse races in Ireland,' says Cristabel.

'And whiskey,' says Flossie.

'I went into Mother's bedroom yesterday,' says Digby. 'I almost expected to see her come swaying towards me with a drink in one hand, saying something like, "So many people are doomed to fall in love with you, darling!"' Digby changes the pitch and intonation of his voice to perfectly mimic his mother's, making it high and breathy.

'She never said anything like that to me,' says Flossie, laughing unconvincingly.

'Oh, Floss-chops,' says Digby, leaning his head on her shoulder. 'She said all sorts of silly things.'

Cristabel pushes herself up with her good arm and sits looking out across the valley. She is puzzled as to why Digby seems to have forgotten the details of his own mother's funeral, when she had taken such care to share them with him. It reminds her of his odd reaction to the news of Rosalind's death, how he hadn't seemed to take it in. It is also irritating that Rosalind can still upset Flossie, even when dead. She wants to say something about these matters but is aware her previous attempts at sisterly wisdom have often emerged as strict instructions, rather than kindly advice, and it seems important she should guide her siblings now, at this rare meeting.

'You know, Floss,' she begins carefully, 'you shouldn't worry about that.'

'About what?'

'What other people say about you. It gets in the way. It's like walking through life with an umbrella up.'

'An umbrella?' says Flossie.

'You don't need an umbrella.'

'I don't often have one,' Flossie says. 'It's only when I think about Mother, I suppose.'

'You're the lady of the manor now, Floss,' says Digby.

'The house is a state,' says Flossie, 'but my vegetables are thriving. I will have to show you.'

'You must,' he says.

'Only if you tell me about this special position,' says Flossie, kicking his foot.

Digby laughs. 'I'm not supposed to tell anyone. Loose lips sink ships and all that.'

'You don't have to tell us,' says Cristabel.

'I'd asked Perry to keep me in mind if anything interesting came up,' says Digby. 'I was sick of tanks. He got in touch in July. Said he'd been asked to wheel up some extra bodies for a friend. Sent me to a place in Northumberland Avenue. Lots of sandbags outside. People dashing about. Had an interview with a couple of chaps. One asked if I was afraid of death. I said I didn't think about it much any more. He said that made me very suitable.'

'Suitable for what?' asks Flossie.

'They're vague on the details, but that appears to be the way of things. It's freeing, somehow. Not knowing. They did a fascinating thing with a piece of paper. Wait, I'll show you.' Digby stubs out his cigarette, then rummages in his trouser pocket and finds a folded square of paper. He unfolds it to reveal an ink blot which has been pressed together to make a symmetrical shape. 'Tell me what you think it looks like. Don't consider it too much.'

'A heart?' says Flossie.

'I couldn't make up my mind,' he says. 'At first, I saw a butterfly. But turn it this way, and look – a dog.'

'What does it mean if you see a dog?' says Flossie.

'I don't know,' says Digby, folding up the paper. 'I'm not sure what they were looking for, but whatever it was, they must think I have it.'

'What do they want you to do?' asks Flossie.

Digby peers up into the sky. 'I can't let you in on the details, Floss, but the general idea is to make life difficult for the Nazis in France.'

'Digs, if it is secret, then you shouldn't tell us anything about it,' says Cristabel, feeling increasingly concerned.

'Crista, I can only speak French – they're not likely to send me to Greece, are they?' He sits up between the two women, looks across the valley to the ocean. 'Last time I was in France, we found an abandoned house in some woods. Groves and I drank wine by candlelight.' He opens his cigarette packet and lights a new one. 'Every time I look at the sea, I think of dear Groves. "Of his bones are coral made." Cigarette?'

'You're smoking a lot,' says Flossie, with a glance at the pile of stubs beside him.

Cristabel studies Digby. She sees his jaw is moving slightly, his fingers tapping themselves together. She realizes now that the breezy postcards he has sent from North Africa have told her very little. Bright brave faces. Beneath his deliberately casual tone, she can sense a jitteriness inside him, an erratic energy, like a fly trapped in a glass. He doesn't seem able to meet her eyes for long. If he were still a boy, she would put her arm around him, but he is twenty-one years old now, a young man who has spent nearly all his adult life at war, and the hunch in his shoulders tells her he does not want to be calmed or comforted, however much she wants to comfort him. She scratches the skin around her plaster cast, considers another tactic.

'I'm sorry about Groves,' she says. 'War can be cruel.'

'When you lose friends, it's more than cruel,' says Digby.

'Losing people is part of life, sadly,' Cristabel replies, instantly regretting her vicarish tone of voice.

Flossie says quietly, 'That doesn't mean you stop caring about them.'

'I didn't say that,' says Cristabel, more crossly than she intends. There is a sense of strain, of the distances and demands that pull between them.

Digby says, 'Do you think I don't know about war, Crista? Or do you think I can't do it without you?' There is a glassy sharpness in his voice she has never heard before.

'I think nothing of the sort,' she replies. 'I know very well how brave you are.' It is strange, because, although she is saying it to reassure him, she realizes she does know how brave he is, but has never told him so. Perhaps she hasn't even admitted it to herself. She couldn't risk him not relying on her. But he has never faltered, not even as a toddler, gamely following her into bramble bushes and freezing streams.

'Do you?' he says.

'I do,' she says, and it is like a relinquishing.

He looks at her and he is fully there for a moment then gone again, fiddling with his lighter, flicking it on and off. 'I am a good soldier. I am. At first, it was because I wanted Father to see I could be, but now it's for the men. I can't let them down.'

'You won't,' says Flossie.

'When I had my interview in Northumberland Avenue, they asked whether I would be looking over my shoulder if I was sent away. You can see what they were thinking. They don't want a distracted fellow.'

'What did you say?' says Cristabel.

'I said I didn't want to look back.'

'Well, that's something,' says Flossie.

'Let's look forward then,' says Cristabel, gesturing clumsily at Chilcombe with her plaster cast. 'To next summer, when you've won a medal, Digs, and we've won the war and we put on *The Tempest* and you play Prospero.'

Digby laughs. 'Hitler is doing a much better job of performing Prospero than I ever could. What is happening to the world has come entirely from his mind. The power of that!'

'All right, we'll do *Twelfth Night*,' says Cristabel.

'I think about that a great deal,' says Digby. 'The fact this is somebody else's dream. It explains perfectly why none of it seems real.'

She puts a hand on his arm. 'Hamlet, Digs. We haven't done him yet. We could go up on the roof and discuss casting tonight.'

Digby exhales a plume of smoke. 'Plenty of time.'

'Look,' says Flossie, 'Mr Brewer's flashing a torch to tell us dinner's ready.'

'Jolly good,' says Digby, getting to his feet. 'I'm famished.'

The trio head back down the path into the valley: Digby leading, Flossie and Cristabel following. The setting sun is on their right, glowing pink as it sinks behind the line of hills. As soon as the sun has gone, the air is colder, and the world a few degrees less glorious. On their left, an almost full moon rises over the fields into a pale sky.

D to C

18th September, 1942

Dear Crista,

Well, here I am. At a training school hidden on a large estate deep in a forest. Perry and Leon dropped me here on their way to London.

When Perry left, he said, 'If you see me again, you must never mention that you saw me here. This place does not exist. Colonel Drake works for the War Office. That's all you know.' Then off he went. Oberon, King of Shadows, disappearing into the forest with a car boot full of Betty's eggs.

You'll notice he said 'if you see me again' not 'when you see me again'. He is careful to be correct, isn't he? Once upon a time, I imagine that would have hurt my feelings, but now it feels as close to the truth as one can get. I am at a place that does not exist, and soon I may not exist — and if I cease to exist, will anyone know how or why or where? I might be one of those poor evaporated souls labelled 'missing in active service'.

One might imagine that the more precarious things become, the more sombre I might feel, but I find a pleasure in this double life. A relief, almost. I suppose it might work to my advantage that I have always been acting, in some form or other.

Some chaps find it hard to take it seriously. Last night, the instructors dressed as Nazis and interrogated us, and it was rather ludicrous, but isn't everything, if you stand far enough back? The fact we are being sent to France with made-up names and radios designed to look like biscuit tins is ludicrous. The fact we are at war is ludicrous!

One of the most popular instructors here, Rufus Hendricks, was an actor before the war. He says when all this is done, he will put me in touch with some decent agents. He teaches us about disguises. How a few adjustments to your hair and the addition of a limp can mean you go into a café as one person and come out as someone else.

He personally is always very smart. A man of neat lines: neat parting, neat moustache, neat fingernails. Careful hands. He taps on his desk with a cigarette to make a point.

Today he told us that our cover story is the life we will outwardly lead in order to conceal our real purpose. He said, 'If questioned, stick to your cover story. Do not be clever. Do not be fast. Do not let them think this is a game of wits, because why would it be? You are a dull, honest citizen.'

Next week we are being sent off to nearby towns to practise being dull, honest citizens who happen to have secret missions they must carry out before the clock strikes twelve — a scenario designed to test what we have learnt in the classroom.

I feel apprehensive at the thought of rejoining the outside world. It reminds me that it exists. I start to wonder about Father and Flossie and you. I have been avoiding thinking about you as, whenever I do, I can hear you telling me I should not be writing this down.

Ah, here you are again. I'll stop now.

Yours both here and not,
Digby

Blank Piece of Paper

Left on the desk in Digby's room,
that when held in the steam from a kettle revealed the following:

While demonstrative of a certain amount of ingenuity, it is not entirely surprising to find a letter hidden under a loose floorboard during a routine room check at this particular training school. I've put it in the wood burner to save you the trouble of having to do it while being berated by the security officer. Remember that you are under surveillance here too. Be thankful that it was delivered to me. Listen to your sister.

RH

Vignettes

September, 1942

The two men look into the night: side by side; driver and passenger. They are silhouetted profiles in the darkness. The only lights inside the car are the glowing tips of their cigarettes.

'How long were you in the cellar for?' says Hendricks, who is driving.

'About six hours, sir,' says Digby. 'It didn't occur to me the door might lock behind me.'

'You were unlucky the barmaid called the police,' says Hendricks.

'If only she'd been calmer. All rather embarrassing.'

'You're not the first of our students to end up in custody.'

'Thank you again for coming to get me, sir.'

The narrow dots of the car's taped-up headlights reach tentatively into the blackout, catching the trees that line the roads: a pale casting of branches, ghostly capillaries. Once or twice, the glassy eyes of a deer at the roadside.

Hendricks says, 'Let's imagine for a moment that you had been found by the Nazis instead of a nervous barmaid. How would you have explained being in that cellar?'

'I would have said I was leaving, and I'd taken a wrong turn, sir.'

'Most people leave a pub through the door they came in.'

'I suppose I acted on impulse when I saw I was being tailed.'

'A good operative is prudent, not impulsive. We'll leave it there for now.' Hendricks changes the subject. He asks about Digby's family, his past.

In the cocoon of the car, it is easy to talk. Their voices are disembodied, ownerless. They share the outlines of themselves, vignettes of who they were before.

'I imagine my family may seem unusual,' says Digby.

'Rather like the organization you are involved with now,' replies Hendricks.

'Perhaps that's why I like it. When I was at Sherborne, the difference between my family life and my school life seemed so vast, I felt I was going about in disguise.'

'Aping the enemy's manners,' says Hendricks, 'learning his language.'

'Exactly. The only place I felt comfortable was on the school stage.'

'How did you find it in the army?'

'Not unlike school, ironically,' says Digby, lighting a new cigarette off the end of the one he is smoking. After a moment, he adds, 'Dunkirk was difficult.'

'Heard it was a dreadful scramble.'

'I lost a friend there. Groves.'

Hendricks nods, makes a sympathetic noise.

Digby says, 'We joined up at the same time. Thought we would go through the whole thing together, then he was gone. In the first act. I still can't believe it. I was so close to him. I could have reached out.'

Hendricks nods again. After a while, he says, 'I have a friend. A radar operator. He's stationed up in Orkney. I miss him very much.'

The ordinariness of the statement is disarming. Digby feels something is enclosed within it, but it is uttered so casually, it resists the suggestion of enclosure. He cannot find a reply to match it.

Hendricks says, 'What was his name? His first name, I mean. Your friend.'

'Sam. Sam Groves. He was from Yorkshire. Loved dancing.'

'Sam Groves,' says Hendricks.

The night moves past. It is three in the morning and starting to rain. The car's windscreen wipers squeak across, revealing and concealing the blurred world outside. They drive through silent villages with not a single light showing in the windows.

'Do you know the Kipling poem about smugglers?' says Digby. 'How you must not peek out when they pass?'

Hendricks supplies the lines, in a suitably dramatic tone. '"Them that ask no questions isn't told a lie. Watch the wall my darling while the Gentlemen go by."'

'You remember it perfectly,' says Digby.

'Interesting they're described as "gentlemen",' says Hendricks. 'Nobody would call us that. I've heard our organization described as the Ministry of Ungentlemanly Warfare. They say our operatives are no better than assassins.'

'But we aren't assassins, are we?' says Digby. 'I simply want to do something that makes a difference. I'm sick of feeling helpless.'

The windscreen wipers squeak past a few times, then Hendricks says, 'It does take a certain kind of person to do this work.'

'What do you mean?'

'Our most effective operatives rarely make mistakes because they leave no room for them. They would leave people behind if they had to, without a second thought.'

'I've done well in training. Apart from tonight.'

'You have,' says Hendricks. 'I can see exactly why they recruited you. You are so nearly very good at this.'

'I can be useful in France, sir.'

'There are many ways to be useful. It's easily arranged. They'd transfer you to another branch of the service with no adverse marks on your file. I think they rather respect those who admit they're not up to it – and not many of us are. It's a cold, unflinching business.'

'I'm not going to let anybody down.'

Hendricks glances at him. 'Digby, you should not consider a lack of suitability for this work to be a failure. It is not a failure. War might depend on people who don't flinch, but humanity rather relies on those who do.'

The car veers slightly, bumping across rough ground, but Hendricks quickly recovers. In the darkness, it is hard to make out where the road ends and the verge begins. Digby looks out of the side window.

Hendricks says, 'It's not just your own life you risk. Last month, we sent a wireless operator to Brittany. He stayed with a farming family.'

'You don't have to tell me this,' says Digby.

'The Germans tracked him quickly. They made the children watch as they killed their dog. They made the parents watch as they beat the children. They tortured the father until his heart gave out, but left the mother alive, so there was someone to share what they'd done. Then they took our man away, for their sport. We don't know where he is. We don't know where the children are either. They ran away. Two girls. Six and four years old.'

'You don't have to tell me this. Tell me what you've been doing today.'

'I've tried to be useful,' says Hendricks, after a moment, and he turns up the long drive to their destination.

Outgoings

September, 1942

Flossie finds the letter informing her she is required by law to make herself available for vital war work buried in a heap of post on the kitchen table, covered by unpaid bills. It is several months old. Flossie suspects she may have deposited it there, during one of her periodic attempts to restore order to the house by shaping the chaos into little piles.

She takes the crumpled letter with her on the bus to Dorchester, where the Women's Land Army has an office in one of the council buildings, and is there interviewed by a preoccupied middle-aged woman her mother would have described as 'very county'. There is a poster on the wall that reads: 'JOIN THE VICTORY HARVEST!' with a picture of a young woman holding a pitchfork and smiling at a sunset.

'It'll be thoroughly vile work,' the woman says. She is sitting at a desk behind an ancient typewriter, a stack of forms, and a framed photograph of a spaniel. 'Have you ever got your hands mucky? Are you sure you wouldn't prefer something secretarial? Most girls your age do.'

'I'm quite decided,' replies Flossie. 'I want to be a Land Army girl.'

'Well, you look a hearty type. As long as your medical is satisfactory, I'm sure we can find a use for you. Have you experience with cows?'

'No, but I do have some chickens and a large vegetable plot.'

The woman snorts and writes something on a form.

Flossie adds, 'As big as an allotment, if not bigger.'

The woman turns the form over as if to examine the other side.

Flossie says, 'There are German prisoners working on my estate and they were asked to assist me with my vegetable plot. That might give you an idea of how large it is.'

The woman looks up. 'Your estate?'

'Chilcombe. Do you know it?'

'Why, yes. It has the outdoor theatre.'

'The Whalebone Theatre,' says Flossie. 'Have you been?'

'I'm sure I must have.'

'It's my sister Cristabel's creation. Full of vegetables now, but once the war is over, I've no doubt it will start up again.'

'Do you know,' says the woman, 'I believe I recognized you when you came in, Miss Seagrave. Perhaps we have met. You said you had Germans working for you?'

'Five of them.'

'How do you find that? I could hardly bear to be near them.'

'They've been useful, actually. Most hard-working.'

'If you leave, who will be at the house to keep an eye on them?' says the woman.

'That's a good question,' says Flossie, frowning. 'There would only really be our housekeeper Mrs Brewer there. She doesn't like to have anything to do with them.'

The woman rolls her pen in her fingers. 'I believe this could be resolved.'

'Do you? That is a comfort.'

There is a shuffling of forms on the desk, then drawers are opened, and new forms are produced. The woman says, 'There are some Germans being sent to Southampton to build houses, replacing the ones their countrymen have dropped bombs on. There's a gentleman in an office along the corridor dealing with it. Perhaps yours could join them.'

Flossie smiles weakly, but says nothing, momentarily uncertain of her voice.

The woman continues, 'As for the Land Army, we do have some girls stationed here, in lodgings in Dorchester. They go out to work on farms in the area, then return to their quarters in the evening. If you were to join them, you could feasibly get back to Chilcombe now and again. Might that allow you to keep a watchful eye on that estate of yours?'

'I suppose it would,' says Flossie.

'However, we still have the issue of your vegetable plot, Miss Seagrave. We can't let it go to waste. But that is easily rectified. It simply needs to be added to this form,' says the woman, brandishing a piece of paper.

'What does that form do?'

'This form identifies Chilcombe as a property requiring the assistance of Land Girls. Chilcombe hasn't been on this form before, but once it is on this form, it comes under my jurisdiction.'

'Does that mean I'd be sent to work on my own estate as a Land Girl?'

'Heavens no. That veers perilously close to favouritism. We would send a couple of other girls, keep things ticking over. Besides, I'm sure you'd prefer to have British girls working on your estate rather than sinister Nazis. What say you?'

'They're not all sinister,' says Flossie.

'We've got to stick together, haven't we?' The woman fits the form into the typewriter and begins noisily winding it into place. 'We're not in the business of making people's lives difficult.'

'No, quite,' says Flossie, standing up and extending a hand for the woman to shake. 'You must come to Chilcombe one day. I'm afraid it's not what it used to be, but you would be most welcome.'

The woman stands and returns the handshake fulsomely, with both hands, as if she has been awarded a rosette.

On her way out of the building, Flossie finds a lavatory at the end of a corridor. She quickly locks herself into a cubicle, where she closes her eyes and takes some calming breaths. Having Hans sent to Southampton was not at all what she intended when she came to join the Land Army. The thought fills her with dismay. Obviously, she hadn't expected him to stay for ever but she hadn't really considered him leaving either.

How can he be sent away when she imagines him with her most

places? He is there with her today. She has chosen him a perfect out-fit, a linen suit with a pale blue tie to bring out his eyes. They are going to stroll round Borough Gardens then go to an imaginary tea room for salmon sandwiches and other things you can't have any more. It doesn't even need to be salmon. It could be ham. Anything rather than queuing up at one of the Ministry of Food's British Restaurants to be served something brown and dispiriting from a large tureen by a harassed volunteer in a stained apron.

It is no doubt a good thing to have restaurant meals supplied by Government initiatives, but, thinks Flossie wistfully, wouldn't it be lovely to have an ordinary meal, in an ordinary way. No ration books or powdered egg. Choosing whatever you fancy. Saying yes, let's have a pudding, why not?

Flossie has a pang of longing for the ordinary. Its unremarkable freedoms. Being able to keep the lights on. Leave the curtains open. To pick up a newspaper without a feeling of dread. It is such a slog, at times, to keep trundling on. They might all be in this together, but this has been going on for ages, and she doesn't particularly want to be in it any more, with lots of other people, everybody tired and fed up. She wants to be somewhere there isn't a war on, in a clifftop restaurant as the sun sets, with charming waiters bringing many dishes, and no time limits and only one person.

She sighs. She wishes it could be like that, but it isn't. Ever since their time at the beach, something has changed between her and Hans. Whenever she sees him at the stables, they smile at each other, but their mouths stay closed and their eyes say they are sorry, though she is not sure what they are sorry for.

Sometimes, when she is on her own, she feels a pressing, panicky urge to find him, to throw her arms around him – and what? What happens then? Do they run away together? Where would they go? No, it is more simple and more impossible than that. She wants to throw her arms around him because she wants to throw her arms around him. The panicky feeling is due to the fact she can't. In a sharp, clear moment, she can feel how that panic could grow unmanageable enough to make a woman want to give up everything.

She looks at the leaflet in her hand welcoming her to the

Women's Land Army, assuring her in emphatic capitals that she is IN THE WINNING TEAM. FEED THE NATION, it exhorts, WHILE THE MEN ARE AWAY FIGHTING. She thinks of Digby. She must be brave too.

Looking up, she sees a mass of graffiti on the back of the cubicle door. Insults, jokes and declarations of love, authored and annotated by those who have passed through the building. She reads 'Try Sheila at The Old Ship, she's easy' and 'Captain Barnes has 12 inches', followed by 'And no bleeding clue what to do with it!!!' It makes her smile, despite herself, this scrawled conversation between strangers.

She rummages in her handbag, finds a lipstick, uses it to write her initials on the door and draws a heart around them. Then she steps back and admires her handiwork. There she is: FLRS. Florence Louisa Rose Seagrave. One of the gang.

A reverse charge call arrives from Weymouth a few days later. It is Maudie.

'Bill said you got Germans at the house.'

'Good evening, Maudie,' says Flossie, standing by her father's desk in the study. 'Yes, that's right. Are you in a pub?' She can hear raucous laughter, a jangly quickstep played on an out-of-tune piano.

'Red Lion,' says Maudie. 'You're not going to get yourself in trouble, are you?'

Startled, Flossie blushes. 'I haven't – it's not like that.'

'Does anyone know?'

'Oh, gosh. I don't think so. Oh, Maudie, do you think I'm awful?'

'I don't care what you do, Miss Flossie. But I do know you can't keep a secret to save your life and it would be bad if people were to find out. For both of you. You'd never hear the end of it.'

'We don't. It's not like that,' says Flossie, utterly mortified.

'I heard you the first time, Miss Flossie,' chuckles Maudie. 'You might be more cheerful if it was like that.'

In the background, Flossie hears a woman shout, 'Has she got rid of him yet?' and an American voice saying, 'Tell Florence I think she has the kindest eyes.'

'Who's that?' asks Flossie. 'What have you told them?'

'Sally, works behind the bar, and Donald, he's from Missouri. His family do – what was it you said?'

'Poultry production.'

'He's keen to meet you. I've shown him your picture,' says Maudie, and then, in a low voice, 'looks like that Errol Flynn.'

'Why have you got a picture of me?'

'From when we was in the paper, doing the plays. No one believes me, less I show them the picture.'

Flossie hears a door banging open and the sound of more American voices. 'Sounds busy there, Maudie.'

'Not too bad. There's a dance over on Portland, Saturday, if you're interested. Plenty of GIs going.'

'Who would I go with?' says Flossie.

'Me,' says Maudie.

For a moment, Flossie is flummoxed. To go to a dance with Maudie the maid seems a ridiculous idea. Although, it then occurs to her that Maudie is someone she has known her whole life. Someone who has, in her own way, always looked out for her. She remembers Maudie's peculiarly unemotional caretaking when they were children, the food she provided when meals were forgotten, the way she would lie with them, arms folded, if they had nightmares. There had been nothing soft or maternal about it: it was an orphan recognizing the need of other orphans, with an orphan's lack of sentimentality.

And now here she is again, with her brisk dispersal of doubt and faff, with her straightforward invitation to a dance on Portland.

'That's very kind of you,' Flossie says. 'I think I would like that. I miss dancing.'

'Kiss the German goodbye, Miss Flossie. Then we'll go out and celebrate before they send you to the farm.'

'I picked up my Land Army uniform today. Betty's in the kitchen trying to steam my hat to make it look less like a pudding basin.'

Maudie laughs. 'Don't wear that. We have Americans to impress.'

'Cheerio for now,' Flossie says and puts the receiver down.

★

When Flossie walks back into the Oak Hall, she pauses by the piano. Maudie's talk of GIs and dances has made her feel she is betraying Hans somehow. She knows someone as practical as Maudie would tell her she doesn't owe him anything, but that seems a cold way of looking at it. Hasn't there been a series of exchanges between them? The sandwiches she made for him from her own rations. The sweet pea flower he gave her, now pressed between the pages of her diary. The way they touched. It wasn't much, but it was all they could give.

She cannot see how she can discount it, not least as it hasn't ended at all. It cannot end because it cannot start, so it is something that always might be. Something possible but inaccessible. Flossie thinks of Dorothy in her wooden house, whirled by the tornado to a magical land, then taken back home to Kansas, knowing Oz will always exist, even when she isn't there. Never entirely discarded.

(Just as Flossie's yellow headscarf will always be tucked in the back pocket of a hard-working German prisoner, when he is clearing bomb sites in Southampton and cropping sugar beet in Hampshire and lying awake in a cramped bunk in a draughty prison camp, trying to compose letters in a language he does not know and so will never send. ~~Frekkels~~, he will write. ~~Scairero~~.)

In the last week of September, the prisoners' tent on the Chilcombe estate is taken down and the camp dismantled as quickly as a travelling circus. All that's left is a pale patch of flattened grass, like a fairy ring. Flossie looks at it, reminding herself of what Maudie said about how horrid it would be for Hans if anyone were to find out. She would hate it if anybody thought badly of him.

Flossie is full of a jumble of feelings; she has avoided the camp and the stables for days. She is not even planning to watch the Germans leave, but when she hears the military vehicles start up outside the house, she finds herself sprinting across the lawn to catch them. She sees Sgt Bullock departing in a staff car, trailing cheroot smoke, then spies Hans sitting in the back of a truck. He is so pleased to see her that he shouts her name and stands up to wave, hitting his head on the low roof of the vehicle with such a bang that the other men laugh and reach out to hold him steady.

Flossie reaches the back of the truck as it starts to pull away. 'I'm sorry I didn't come to say goodbye before,' she shouts over the noise of the engine.

He shakes his head and smiles. 'It is nothing. You will feed the cat?'

'I will, I promise,' she says, suddenly engulfed in exhaust fumes as the truck moves off down the drive. 'Good luck, Hans. I don't know what I would have done without you.'

He smiles again. He is still standing, held in place by a scaffold of men. He puts one hand up, pressing it against the ceiling of the truck to steady himself, then places the other on his heart.

'Yes,' says Flossie, nodding. She puts one hand on her own heart.

As the truck gathers speed, Hans waves at her as fondly as if they were saying hello not goodbye.

'Goodbye!' calls Flossie, and she waves until the truck goes out of sight. Then there isn't anything else to do but go back to the house, where Mr Brewer is waiting at the front door. She walks towards him, saying, 'If I appear to be emotional, it's because I have never been good with goodbyes. Of any kind.'

Mr Brewer says nothing but offers her a cigarette, which she accepts, and he lights.

'Could you please talk to me about something?' she says with a sniff. 'I don't mind what. I just need things to keep carrying on.'

Mr Brewer is about to say something when Flossie adds, 'Maudie says out of sight, out of mind.'

'Sounds like Maudie,' says Mr Brewer.

'I don't think I can smoke this cigarette,' says Flossie, her face beginning to crumple. 'I don't even smoke.'

'Let me take that, Miss Flossie,' Mr Brewer says calmly, removing the cigarette from her hand and reaching into his pocket for a handkerchief. They stand together for a while, as she holds the handkerchief over her face. Then he suggests they go down to the kitchen for a cup of tea.

★

Two cups of tea and three digestive biscuits later, Flossie feels less forlorn. Toto has curled up in her lap and she is comforted by his soft, purring warmth. Mr Brewer has occupied himself with discreet tasks around the kitchen, so she has time to pull herself together. After a while, she feels well enough to talk to him, and they chat lightly about the Land Girls and where Flossie will be staying in Dorchester. Then Mr Brewer sits down at the table facing her and says, 'As a matter of fact, there is something I wanted to discuss with you, Miss Flossie.'

'Yes?'

'An opportunity has arisen. The pub in the village is for sale. Betty's father. He's selling up.'

'Oh yes,' she says.

'I've always considered acquiring a property, something to fall back on in my later years. When my son comes out of the navy, be nice to think he could work in a pub with his old man. They'd let us have it for a decent price.'

'Are you in need of a loan of some sort, Mr Brewer?' asks Flossie.

'I see it more as a mutual investment opportunity.'

'Oh. I don't know anything about that kind of thing. I don't have any money. That sounds silly, because I must do, but I don't know where it is. You pay all the bills.'

'I do,' says Mr Brewer. 'You were right too, if I may be so bold. You don't have any money.'

'Don't I?'

He nods his head upwards to indicate the main house. 'This place has been running at a loss for years.'

Flossie frowns. 'Has it?'

'You've got some hefty outgoings but no tenants. No farms. No capital interest. You're living off savings, but there's not much left.'

Flossie has never received any monetary education, but as Mr Brewer continues to talk, she quickly has a sense of her family's financial situation: a one-sided tale of grand outward gestures, with a finite point looming into view. She also has the sense that she is entirely the wrong person to be faced with this issue, which surely requires someone as purposeful as Cristabel.

'What do I do?' she asks.

'I can do my best to help you, Miss Flossie,' says Mr Brewer, 'but it might not be a pleasant experience. People get accustomed to things being a certain way.'

'None of those people are here though, are they?' she says. 'Nobody's here.'

'They aren't. You're in charge now. Which is why you might want to consider any available opportunities to help you balance the books.'

Flossie thoughtfully strokes the cat on her lap. 'Is that advice?' she says, after a while. 'Or is it what you want me to do? Because I feel that, if I read that statement in a book, I wouldn't be sure.'

Mr Brewer smiles at her slowly, and she has the sense that he has joined her in the conversation for the first time, that the polite Mr Brewer who does such a good job of making himself absent when required has been discarded. 'It's business,' he says.

On the day she is to leave Chilcombe to join the Land Army, Flossie walks down to the beach to sit on the shore, taking off her regulation boots and socks, and burying her bare feet in stones that clack like maracas, watching long-beaked cormorants floating on the sea. Every now and then, they dive beneath the surface, appearing minutes later some distance away, surfacing with brisk head shakes, eyeing her with haughty indifference.

It is a warm, hazy morning: one of the rare gift days strung through late September like jewels. A single breaking wave runs slowly round the semicircle of the bay, smoothly as a cymbal brush. The water close to the shore is a tinfoil turquoise; further out, a darker Prussian blue.

Flossie paddles at the water's edge. The sea is so clear she can see through to her feet. The pebbles by her toes are the same as those on the beach, but under the warp of water they are sealed off and remote, possessed of some mysterious, polished quality. When she reaches in to pick some up, they are further away than they appear – and her pale hand fumbling underwater is the disembodied arm of a puppeteer. But when she takes them out of the water and holds them in her palm, the pebbles seem disappointingly small, diminished. She drops them back.

She strips down to her underwear, undressing perfunctorily as if for a doctor, then wades in. She floats on her back, hearing the tinny slop of salt water in her ears, its buckety clank and slosh. All other sounds are muffled and distant. There is only the water and her breath and the weight of her body hanging in the water. It is something like illness, the way the sea forces the self very close to itself; a state you are sunk in.

She tells herself she has done the right thing by not letting matters go any further with Hans. She has been a sensible girl. She has protected her reputation. She tells herself that there will be other men, other loves, other swims. That there won't always be this ache in her chest, as if something vital had been stoppered up inside her.

Above her, the dome of the sky; below her, the pebbles on the sea floor. Bobbing between the two: Flossie breathing out, in, out, in.

When Mr Brewer comes down to the beach to call her, saying her lift has arrived, she walks out of the sea in her underwear, picks up her uniform and boots, and continues past him without saying a word.

Night Flight

October, 1942

After take-off, the Lysander flies at 5,000 feet. Inside, Digby and another agent asleep in sleeping bags. No cloud, a full moon. Perfect conditions for a flight across the Channel.

Beneath them,
                    gulls   gulls   gulls

Radio waves following them until they find the aeroplane then
                                                    bounce back
                                        towards
                            a receiver
                        on a tall mast
                    a red blip
                like a
            heartbeat
        on the screen
    of a drowsy
radar operator.

The night air thick with invisible communication, dots and dashes, Braille bumps in the atmosphere, messages for agents, or those pretending to be agents:

```
-.... .-.. .. . ...- . / .-. --- ... .. - .. --- -. / -.-. --- -- .-. .-. --- -- .. ... . .-.. / .-. . . .-. - /
-.... .-.. .. . ...- . / .-. --- ... .. - .. --- -. / -.-. --- -- .-. .-. --- -- .. ... . .-.. / ... . . .-. .. /
-.. .. .-- / ... . .- / .- -. .-.. / -.-. .-. .-. --- ... .-. .-.. / ... --- --- -. . ...
```

the static of radio stations, snatches of canned laughter, orchestras, news.

Cristabel awake

> The
> chalk
> edge of
> England   A fishing boat   The sea
>   scattered with
>   moonlight.
>
>   Below the waves, the ocean's
>   black vault: rusting submar-
>   ines, broken ships. Corpses
>   from Hamburg, Iowa, Oslo,
>   inside the vessels they sank in,
>   waving in the currents like a
>   ghastly crop, arms aloft,
>   semaphore messages,
>   unreceived.

A Sober Cannibal

October sinks into November sinks into December. The days contract. The sun hardly bothers. The grey sky descends on to the earth until there is only a narrow gap beneath it. People scuttle along, close to the ground, wrapped up in themselves. There is not much space left for anything else.

Cristabel walks the cliffs, the cold wind whipping at her coat, while the waves below rumble and crash. She has come back to Dorset to spend a few days of leave but finds it hard to be in the house. She strides up the deserted coast path to Ceal Head with her chin tucked into her neck, her hands shoved into her pockets: a single strut beneath a sagging canopy of cloud.

There has been no word from Digby for over two months, which means he has probably gone into Occupied France. A letter from his superior officer reassuring her that all is well sounds so much like a template letter, she is convinced her suspicions are right. Cristabel carries the thought of Digby working undercover with her everywhere. It makes her mute and tense. She cannot get used to the idea. Instead, it becomes more agitating, more awkward: a lumpen, wriggling child growing heavier in her arms. What if his French isn't good enough? What if he trusts the wrong person? What if the Germans find him, a British operative behind enemy lines – here her mind shuts down.

It is late afternoon. The daylight has faded. Rain is starting to blow in from the sea. Cristabel catches a glimpse of her whalebones standing at the edge of the fretful waters, like King Canute attempting to command the tides. She stalks home through the puddles, retreats to her attic eyrie to brood.

Betty briefly appears to stoke the meagre fire and offer tea, but Cristabel does not want tea. She does not want anything. She cannot even bring herself to light a lamp. She puts on her pyjamas, then lies rigid in her narrow bed, listening to the rain battering on the roof.

She tells herself they wouldn't have recruited Digby if he wasn't up to the task, but she has seen enough of military life to know this is not always true. Perry once said it was a question of numbers. She looks across the room at Flossie's empty bed, now covered with Cristabel's kitbag and clothes. She imagines Flossie lying on a camp bed in her Land Army lodgings in Dorchester; Digby hiding in a French farmhouse. Above them all, the sky teeming down. She turns her face to the pillow.

In the middle of the night, she wakes up and does not know why. There is only the wind and the rain. Then suddenly, the clatter of small stones hitting the attic window. Cristabel lifts her head. It happens again. Another handful of gravel hits the glass. Unmistakable; a deliberate summons. She quickly flings back the bedcovers and goes to the window to push it open.

She leans out and peers down through the darkness, which is paint-striped with the silver flurry of raindrops. Standing on the lawn at the front of the house is a figure in an army greatcoat, dark-haired, looking up at her with a hand sheltering his eyes. The tinsel hiss of the rain, the tumult of the wind in the trees, the spilling over of what she carries in her heart: for a single inhalation, it is her brother returned. But then he raises his other hand and salutes sardonically, and he is taller, broader. Leon.

She exhales and looks at him, he at her. She raises her own hand to her forehead by way of salute, gestures towards the back of the house, and then turns to pull on a tartan dressing gown, which flaps out behind her like a cloak as she heads downwards, padding through the house in her bedsocks, scooting along corridors to the kitchen, where she unbolts, unlocks and pulls open the back door, and in he comes, shaking droplets of rain from his black hair like a wet dog.

'Do you have any food?' he says, in his strange accent. 'I am hungry.'

'Why are you here?'

'Bread. I see bread. Is there cheese?'

'Leave it alone. Why are you here?'

'I am collecting an order for Colonel Drake. Bill is providing items he requires for Christmas. I think a pheasant and some wine and so on. I had a flat tyre, so I am late. Where might Bill store such things? I bet it will taste better than this dry bread.'

'I don't know where Bill stores things.'

'Yes, you do, Cristabel Seagrave. You know where everything is in this house. Colonel Drake will not mind if we have a little of his food. Come, we can eat a – what do you call it? A midnight feast.'

They look at each other. He is gnawing a hunk of bread and grinning. He is rain-soaked, unshaven, and his uniform is dishevelled: the collar of his coat is turned up on one side; his shirt open at the throat; his boots loosely laced. He has a damp cigarette tucked behind one ear and, about his neck, he wears a striped knitted scarf in unexpected colours: yellow, pink, green.

'I do know,' she concedes. 'In the wine cellar.'

He disappears. Cristabel hears the sharp meow of a cat startled then reassured, Leon murmuring to it in Russian. When he re-appears, he is carrying a pork pie and a bottle of wine. 'Is there a fireplace up in your attic?'

'Yes, but –'

'Come, come. It is freezing in here. We will go up. Like we did as children, eh?'

She shakes her head but picks up tin mugs and a couple of apples, squeezing them into her dressing gown pockets, and follows him up the stairs, saying, 'You're leaving mud everywhere.'

'You don't care about that.'

'I might.'

'You don't. What are you wearing, Cristabel?'

'It's my grandfather's dressing gown. It's perfectly serviceable. Did you knit that scarf yourself?'

'A kind old lady gave it to me in a café.'

'Did she mistake you for a proper soldier?'

'She thought I was charming. Why is it so dark in here? Do you not have electricity?'

'Only sometimes. How did you know it was me in the attic?'

'Bill told me Flossie is at a pig farm or some such.'

'She's in the Land Army.'

'Digby is away. It would only be you.'

'Why did you throw stones? You could have knocked at the door.'

'It's more romantic. Like Romeo.'

'It's nothing at all like Romeo. He doesn't throw gravel.'

'I can't remember,' Leon says, as they arrive at the attic where, with his hands full, he pushes open the door with one booted foot. He peers down the shadowy attic corridor, looks up at the sloping ceiling and says, 'The roof is lower.'

'You're taller,' says Cristabel, and he is. Tall and wide-shouldered as a swimmer, but still with a trace of his teenage skinniness. Back when they were young, he was nearly always bare-chested, faded shorts low on his hips, a stolen cigarette and a narrow-eyed gaze. Long-haired gutter boy. Artful dodger. Suddenly she can see the young Leon very clearly, peering up at a tree on Ceal Head, when he had thrown a rope over a high bough to make a swing that flew out over the ocean. She remembers him looking up at the tree, as he is now inspecting the attic ceiling, yanking the rope and then handing it to her for the inaugural flight.

Cristabel moves past him into the girls' bedroom and lights the oil lamp. Following her, Leon deposits what he is carrying on Flossie's bed, piling it on top of Cristabel's clothes. He takes off his coat and scarf, then sits on the bed to pull off his boots, glancing at a half-complete jigsaw puzzle on the bedside table.

'It's Flossie's,' says Cristabel. 'I hate jigsaws.'

'I remember. You used to cut the pieces with scissors to make them fit.' With his boots off to reveal much-darned socks, Leon throws a packet of Lucky Strike in Cristabel's direction. She sits on her bed, helps herself to a cigarette, and watches as he opens the wine using an enviable pocketknife with useful attachments. As she hands him the mugs so he can fill them with wine, she notices his knuckles are scraped and there is a new scar on one of his wrists.

He passes her a mug, then gets up to rattle the poker in the fireplace until the flames start up again. This done, he pulls a blanket on to the floor to serve as a picnic rug and settles himself down in front of the fire to carve up the pie. There is a practised efficiency to his movements, the sense of someone adept at setting up camp.

He notices the cardboard theatre on the floor and pulls it towards him. 'Do you still play with this?'

'I don't play with it. I use it as a model when planning productions.'

Leon carefully slides the paper backdrop – white clouds and blue sky – out of the theatre and looks at it. 'Is your theatre still standing?'

'Of course,' she says. 'Although at the moment, it holds vegetables rather than audiences.'

He smiles, slides the backdrop back into place. 'I am glad it is still there. It nearly killed me to drag those bones from the beach.'

'It works well, but it could be better.'

'How better?'

She clambers off the bed and sits next to him on the blanket, pulling the cardboard theatre towards her. 'The audience are all on one level.' She uses the two apples to serve as audience members. 'If you are sitting behind someone in a large hat, your line of sight is completely restricted.'

'Lift them up,' he says.

'How?'

'Like a Roman amphitheatre. Raise the audience so they can see more.' He pulls a pillow from the bed, puts it in front of the cardboard theatre and places an apple on top of it. 'There's an amphitheatre in Nîmes. We used to go for the bullfighting.'

'I didn't know there was bullfighting in France.'

'Only in the South. Maybe not now the Nazis have moved in.'

'I suspect that's the kind of entertainment they enjoy,' replies Cristabel. 'I had considered some sort of raised seating, but I didn't know how to do it.'

'Stones from the beach. Sand. You have materials. Find a spade and a wheelbarrow. Build it up.'

'Would it be resilient if it was made out of sand?'

'I believe so. A mixture of sand and stones,' he says, placing another apple on the pillow. 'I could build it for you if I wasn't collecting pheasants for Colonel Drake. I always like to build things.'

342

He taps one of the apples. 'These people. They have the best view. They pay the most.'

'Did you want to be a builder?' she asks. 'When you were younger, I mean.'

'Nobody asked me what I wanted to be. I ran away to sea, then Colonel Drake took me in, and now I collect his pheasants.' He picks up one of the apples and bites into it.

Cristabel thinks for a moment, then points to his scraped knuckles. 'You don't only collect pheasants.'

He laughs. 'No. Sometimes I collect people.'

'Where from?'

'Beaches, mostly. Late at night. Sometimes they want to come. Sometimes not.'

'Is that the kind of thing Digby will be doing? Perry sorted something out for him.'

'No, Digby is an officer. Speaks good French. He's probably in a chateau. They won't let me talk to anyone. My accent is too Russian. Everyone fears the Russians.' He says this with satisfaction.

'Do you know if Digby is in France?' she asks. 'Did Perry talk to you about that?'

Leon eats his apple. 'Colonel Drake knows I never listen.'

She nudges him with her elbow. 'Tell me.'

'I think it likely,' he says, eventually.

'Digby's French is good, but not perfect,' she says. 'I wish I was there instead.'

'Maybe you will go. There is talk of women agents. They are running out of men.'

'They're sending women into France?'

'It is easier for women. A young man attracts the attention of the Germans. A young woman? With a smile and a wave, she can go on her way.'

'Could I go?' says Cristabel. 'Would they send me?'

'Speak to Colonel Drake. I'm only a pheasant collector.' He gets to his feet and begins to heave Flossie's bed across the room, pushing it next to Cristabel's.

'Leon, what on earth are you doing?'

343

'These beds are the beds of children. I am making a bigger one,' he says, pushing the two beds together before lying down on top of the covers.

Cristabel frowns but then climbs up on to the bed next to him, putting her mug of wine on her bedside table. 'When are you seeing Perry? Tomorrow?'

'I believe so.'

'Could you take me with you? So I could speak to him.'

'Perhaps,' he says, closing his eyes. 'I am tired. I will agree to anything.'

She lies down, folding her arms and looking at the ceiling, occasionally glancing over at Leon. Her mind is whirring with thoughts of talking to Perry and persuading him to let her go into France. She chews her bottom lip. She cannot stop her feet from fidgeting.

She looks at Leon again, his long body next to hers. She has never been alone in the house with a man before. His shirt has come untucked from his trousers on one side, revealing a gap of skin. After a while, she says: 'Have you read *Moby-Dick*?'

'I am uneducated. I don't read.'

'You should. You would like it.'

'Tell it to me then. A bedtime story.'

'Well. At the beginning, there is a scene where the whaler Ishmael must share a bed with a tattooed savage called Queequeg, who sleeps with his tomahawk.'

'Sounds an interesting man.'

'They meet at a tavern and are forced to share a room,' says Cristabel, then adds, 'did you want to go to sleep?'

He opens his eyes, turns to her. 'I can't. Somebody is talking.'

'I was reminded of a scene in a great work of literature and thought I would share it.'

He puts his hands behind his head. 'What happens in the tavern?'

'They sleep together,' she says, after a moment. 'Ishmael says it's better to sleep with a sober cannibal than a drunken Christian.'

'I didn't think it was that kind of book,' he replies.

'It's not. But they do sleep in the same bed.'

'Does anything happen between them?'

'Hard to say.'

'Maybe it happens when they are at sea,' says Leon. 'It is often the way with sailors.'

'Ishmael does say that Queequeg puts his arms around him in a "bridegroom embrace".'

They look at each other for a moment, then Leon slowly reaches towards her to unknot her dressing gown.

'What are you doing?' she says.

'What you are asking me to do,' he says. 'What is this, a reef knot?'

'A double reef knot.'

'I might have to cut it with a knife.'

'You most certainly will not.'

He skilfully unties the cord of her dressing gown to reveal her stripy pyjamas. 'There,' he says. 'You are now free of your grandfather's ugly gown. You can take it off.' She opens her mouth, but Leon speaks first. 'Cristabel, if you want me to go downstairs and sleep in the cat's basket, I will. But do not try to tell me you are saving yourself for a husband or any of that, for I am too tired for speeches.'

'I'm not saving myself for a husband,' she says. 'Or anyone else.'

'Nor should you,' he says.

'Although, some men prefer women who keep themselves, you know. Not that I care.'

'What kind of women do you think I prefer?' he says.

'I have no idea.'

'I have sent you many postcards, Cristabel.'

'Most of them obscene.'

'Exactly,' he laughs. 'They were so funny. That one from Plymouth – do you remember the picture? The little husband and the big wife in the deckchair.'

'They were all awful,' she says, smiling.

'What's more, when I am in London, I take you out for meals whenever you instruct me to.'

'Meals paid for by Perry.'

'These are small details.' He tilts his head to one side. 'Are you nervous?'

'What do you mean, nervous?'

'Are you nervous to have a man in your room? Is that why you want to tell me stories?'

It is a taunt like those he goaded her with in childhood and she recognizes it as such. She knows how to proceed from here. 'How dare you,' she says, sitting up to take her dressing gown off. 'Do I look nervous?' There is something imperative inside her then, something bold, pushing her on. Just as she had once held her palm over a flame, she now starts to unbutton her pyjama top.

Leon props himself up to watch her, his face still holding his usual combative half-smile, but there is something different in his eyes now, something quieter. His smile is secondary to his gaze, which is travelling over her as she takes off her top. She is lit by moving fire-light and he reaches across to touch the skin of her collarbone, runs his fingers along it.

'Are you cold?' he says.

'No,' she replies. 'You won't be. You've kept your shirt on, after all.'

'So I have,' he says, sitting up to take it off.

Now they are matched: opponents stripped to the waist. Leon has a line of dark hair running down his chest. There is a purple bruise on his ribs, a blotchy tattoo on his upper arm.

Cristabel nods at it. 'You really are a savage. What is it?'

'A lost bet in a bar in Danzig,' he says.

'No, what's it meant to be?'

'It's a ship. Look, it has sails. A little flag. Do you need spectacles?'

'No,' she says, and reaches out to touch it, as casually as she can. 'This looks nothing like a flag.'

'What looks nothing like a flag?'

'This, here.'

'Touch it again so I can be sure of which bit you mean.'

They pause then, like boxers circling each other in the ring. She traces the outline of the ship, then the inky ocean it sails on. The fire throws its shadows round the room. Outside, the rain contin-ues to fall. Then Cristabel moves first, leaning over and pulling him towards her, before she loses her nerve.

Coffee, Tea

Cristabel surfaces slowly from sleep as if from a great depth. It is akin to the pleasure of waking up the morning after a long day at the beach; to gradually come to in a body well used and well rested. She stretches with satisfaction, raising her arms and curving her back, lifting her body from the mattress and extending the full long length of herself like a bowstring till she can lay her hands flat on the wall behind her bed, remembering as she does so that she found the same position during the night. The echo of the movement runs through her like a quiver.

She opens her eyes. It is early morning, still dark and raining solidly, but a low glow comes from the remaining coals in the fireplace, and some light comes through the open window where Leon is leaning on the window sill smoking. He has pulled on his trousers. She can make out the bare skin of his back, the line of his spine. How curious it is to know she has touched that skin, felt those shoulder blades shift beneath her hands. How satisfying to observe him, while aware of that knowledge. She has no desire to move. She is replete as a conqueror. She wiggles her toes.

He glances at her, smiles, then turns back to the window, saying, 'I am so hungry, if there were still horses here, I would kill one and eat it.'

'There are, but you can't,' she says. 'We have lots of eggs though.'

He fires his cigarette from the window, neat as a dart, pulls the window closed, and picks up his shirt and boots. 'Then why are we up here? Put some clothes on, Cristabel Seagrave. I must eat.' As he passes her, he leans down and presses his mouth to hers, an urgent, rough kiss, his stubble prickly against her skin, and suddenly

347

everything they have done and newly discovered is with them again. She reaches up to push her hands into the thick hair at the nape of his neck as he glances at the clock on her bedside table and, with his mouth still open to hers and their breath passing between them, he says, 'We have half an hour before we need to leave.'

Breakfast is dry bread eaten in the car with a flask of black coffee they take turns to swig from. Cristabel is driving, as Leon claims he is too weak from hunger to turn the wheel. Once in the passenger seat, he adjusts his position to look at her, saying, 'Besides, I always like to watch you drive.'

'What do you mean?' she says, grappling with the gear stick as they head up the Ridgeway.

They are both back in their military uniforms: Cristabel's has been washed and pressed by Betty; Leon's has not. The car is Perry's sturdy military staff car, the khaki Humber. Their kitbags and the box of food and wine for Perry are piled in the back seat.

'When we were younger, that summer when Bill taught us to drive,' Leon says. 'I liked to watch you. You would get so furious with your mistakes.'

'I thought you just liked laughing at me.'

'I liked that too,' he says, brushing crumbs from his stripy scarf.

'That old car was a bugger to drive. Heavy as a tank. I don't know how we ever learnt anything.'

'You weren't even meant to be learning. Bill was only meant to teach me.'

Cristabel laughs. 'Oh, yes. I had forgotten that. I had arranged it, then thought to myself, "Hang on a minute, why's he getting to learn, and not me?"'

'Poor Bill. Going up and down the drive with us for weeks.'

'I had to sit on a cushion to see over the steering wheel.'

'I tell you though, if you learn to drive a car that size as a child, military vehicles are no trouble at all,' says Leon. He holds two cigarettes in his mouth to light them, then hands her one.

'Let's hope so,' she replies, and accelerates.

After a while, Cristabel says, 'Where are your brothers and

sisters now? Your mother? Are they all right? Do you hear from them?'

He exhales a wobbly smoke ring. 'One brother dead. One missing. One in Spain. Two sisters alive, I think. My mother, I don't know. She was in Ghent when the Germans arrived.'

'That must be a worry. Do you hear from your father?'

'I see from the newspapers he is alive and well and fighting the Nazis from the safety of New York City.'

'Myrtle still sees him. If you wanted to get in touch, she could pass on a message.'

'I could get a message to him if I wanted to.'

'Of course,' she says, then, 'I'm sorry about your brothers.'

'I am too,' he replies, then pulls a piece of leftover pork pie from his pocket and eats it between drags on his cigarette.

It is overcast and rainy. The empty roads are covered with puddles, potholes and the odd stray sheep, mud-sodden and full of grievance. Five days before Christmas, but the country is low-lit and undecorated. Each Christmas of the war seems a shadow of the one before: less food, less drink; more empty places at the table.

The war and all its deprivations seem relentless, but for Cristabel, there is a strange and guilty thrill running through it, for it is exactly this thinning of the ordinary that allows the unordinary through. How can it be that she loves this murky, blighted and pockmarked England more than she loved its peaceful green predecessor? Because she can drive a car through it, in a uniform; because she can be with a man in it, without marriage; because she can die for it, if she can persuade Perry to let her try.

'Tell me,' she says, for she wants to talk about everything now, 'where did you get those things – the, what did you call them, "johnnies"?'

'I get mine from the Americans. Theirs are bigger, you understand. Why do you want to know?'

'In case I need more.'

'Was that your first time, last night?'

'Why do you want to know?'

'I already know. I am asking to be polite.'

'You're never polite.' She glances at him. 'Yes, then. It was. The way I've heard it talked about, I thought it would be something of a horror show. Bloodied sheets and all that. But it wasn't like that at all. I wish somebody had told me. Have you been with a lot of women?'

'Not as many as I would like,' Leon says, then swears in Russian as the car bumps into a pothole, sending ash from his cigarette all over his lap.

'That was a good curse,' says Cristabel. 'I haven't heard that one before. What does it mean?'

'Life is screwing me,' he says, brushing ash from his trousers.

'You swear in Russian and talk to cats in Russian,' she says. 'And now I know you speak Russian in bed too.'

'Cats prefer Russian. Some women prefer French.'

'How many women have you been with?'

'I don't count.'

'I would count. Are they all different?'

'It is early in the day to have this conversation, Cristabel.'

'Are you embarrassed?'

'Not embarrassed. Mainly hungry, a little tired.'

'Very well then. Explain to me how women are different in bed. What do they like?'

'I will show you later,' Leon replies, wrapping his scarf about his neck. 'I'm going to sleep. Wake me in an hour and I will take over driving.'

'I didn't say goodbye to Betty,' says Cristabel, after a moment.

They get to London in the afternoon and find Perry in the unexpected environs of the café at Fortnum & Mason, where well-to-do women take tea after shopping in the department store. Perry has meetings there, explains Leon, because he finds people are less argumentative in the presence of cake. At a piano in the corner of the room, an elderly man in a dinner suit is playing Christmas carols; paper decorations hang limply from the walls.

As they arrive, an angry-looking French general in full uniform is leaving the table. Leon and Perry exchange glances and Leon follows the man out. Perry turns to Cristabel and gestures towards a three-tier cake stand, as if he had been expecting her. 'Help yourself, my dear.'

Cristabel takes off her hat. 'We didn't mean to interrupt your meeting.'

'It had finished,' says Perry. 'Sometimes, it's hard to remember that the French and the English are on the same side. We spend a great deal of time fighting each other.'

'About what?'

'They want to be more involved in our work, but they're impetuous, the French. Prone to playing both sides against the middle. It's tidier if we keep our activities separate,' he says, shaking out a napkin. 'Please, sit down. To what do I owe this honour?'

'I want to do more for the war effort,' Cristabel replies, sitting at the table. 'I'm sick of pushing tiddlywinks about.'

'What you do is vital. Tea? Plenty left in the pot. My French friend is not a fan.'

'I could do more. I've heard women might be used undercover in France.'

'Who on earth could have told you that,' he says, lifting an eyebrow as he pours tea, adding, 'I hope you aren't thinking you might find Digby there.'

'Not unless I was instructed to.'

'You would not be instructed to.'

'Does he need to be found?'

'No good agent needs to be found. Milk?'

'Yes.'

'Sugar?'

'Three, please.'

Perry carefully deposits sugar lumps into her tea with a pair of silver tongs, then says, 'Cristabel, let me state for the record that, officially, we don't use women in any combat role.'

'Other countries do. Did you see in the newspapers about that Soviet girl sniper? She has over three hundred kills. They invited her to the White House.'

'A useful piece of propaganda,' he says, passing her a cup and saucer.

'You don't believe it?'

'I imagine she has some skill, but she is clearly of more use as a newspaper story – why else would she be at the White House? Besides, we are English, not Russian. There would be uproar if we sent wives and mothers to the front line.'

'I'm not a wife or a mother. Do you think I might have a chance?'

'You're a capable girl. They'd investigate your background, of course. I hope they wouldn't find anything alarming there.'

'They wouldn't.'

'Your stepmother had some interesting friends, but I had Koval-sky checked out myself, and he's a dinner party revolutionary, nothing more.'

'You had Taras checked?'

'Better safe than sorry,' he says, pouring his own tea. 'Besides, it was useful for me to know what sort of family my chauffeur comes from.'

'Would you get rid of Leon if Taras was involved with something iffy? That's hardly fair.'

'Not necessarily. Leon has useful qualities. Speaks many languages. Not afraid to get his hands dirty, and, most importantly, has no desire to have my job.' Perry looks at her for a moment, then adds, 'He doesn't seem to have any ambition at all, beyond seducing my secretaries.'

To her surprise, Cristabel feels a twinge of jealousy, deep in her body, but lifts her eyebrows in what she hopes is a nonchalant manner and says, flatteringly, 'Someone like Leon could never do your job.'

Perry stirs his tea, then says, 'If I were to recommend you for certain confidential tasks, Cristabel, I would suggest that you be stationed a long way from your brother. To lose both Seagraves would be – what's that line from the Wilde play?'

'"To lose one parent may be regarded as a misfortune; to lose both looks like carelessness."'

'I knew you would know it,' he smiles.

'Is it likely that we would be lost? Be honest.'

'I am not one to speculate,' Perry says, 'but I am given to understand the odds of survival for an agent in France are roughly fifty per cent. One in two.'

To demonstrate, he pulls a coin from his pocket and spins it on the table. It rotates so rapidly it becomes a globe, then he quickly lays his hand over it before it falls.

He says, 'Cristabel, have you given any thought as to what you might do after the war?'

'Happily, the war seems to have removed the necessity of considering that,' she replies, revolving the cake stand to examine its offerings.

'In many ways, war is fought to determine what happens afterwards,' says Perry. 'The general I was speaking to when you arrived, for example, has strong opinions on the large number of Communists who have joined the Resistance since Russia came over to our side. He fears if the French are helped to victory by Communists, then Moscow will have a hand in their future.'

'If Communists want to join the fight, why on earth would we stop them?'

'They are rather overt in their methods. They want to draw others to their cause – a form of recruitment, if you will. Or a sign of insecurity.'

'Insecurity?' says Cristabel, helping herself to a chocolate eclair.

'Undercover operatives should need no applause,' says Perry, handing her a napkin. 'They should act like mosquitoes, delivering painful bites without ever being seen.'

'But winning is the main thing, surely? Pointless to tie ourselves up in political knots. Goodness, this tastes like real cream.'

'It is. And you are right: winning must be our aim. But even before the war began, men were considering how to be in an advantageous position at its end. I cannot believe that the formidable Cristabel Seagrave hasn't also considered her own future,' he says, adjusting his cup in its saucer. 'What it might be like to marry. To have a family.'

Cristabel scowls. She has always found this line of questioning tedious, a petulant tugging on her sleeve, and now, when they are discussing how to win the war, it seems wholly irrelevant. 'I don't have time to think about that.'

She glances at him and sees an odd expression flicker across his face, before he looks away from her, saying, 'Ah, here's Leon. I did not expect him back so soon. It would appear our French colleague did not require a lift back to his quarters.'

Leon arrives at the table and holds his hand out to Cristabel. 'You should not eat all of that cake. You should share it with me.'

'I drove us most of the way here,' she replies.

'Precisely,' he says, 'I need that chocolate item to recover.'

'How dare you,' she says, and takes a large bite, but puts the remainder in his hand.

'When do you have to get back to your duties, Cristabel?' asks Perry, who is watching them while pushing the coin on the table around under his finger, like a man considering a bet at the roulette wheel.

'This evening. Could Leon give me a lift back?'

'No, I don't think so,' replies Perry. 'It's not his car, after all.'

She looks at Perry across the table, but he does not meet her gaze. He says, 'I'll tell you what I'll do, Cristabel. I will make a call, on your behalf. I will make a suggestion that you are considered for some specialist work in the field. Beyond that, it is up to you.' He picks up the coin and hands it, smiling, to a passing waitress.

Captain Potter

January, 1943

The letter inviting her to attend a meeting with Captain Ebenezer Potter of the Ministry of Pensions is as deliberately innocuous as the room she meets Captain Potter in, at the back of a hotel in Whitehall. Judging from the floral curtains and patterned carpet, the room used to be a bedroom. It is entirely empty but for a wooden table – on which stands nothing but a packet of cigarettes and a saucer being used as a makeshift ashtray – and two wooden chairs, one of which is occupied by Captain Potter.

'Cristabel Seagrave,' he says, rising to shake her hand. 'Good to meet you. Did you travel to London this morning?'

'No, I stayed overnight with a friend.'

'Excellent. Do sit down. How are things at Fighter Command?' he says, and she sees he has no plans to conceal the fact he already knows a great deal about her.

'Busy,' she says.

Capt. Potter is middle-aged, wearing an army uniform, with dark Brylcreemed hair and a lively, watchful gaze. His mouth is held in a tight line, almost amused, as if holding something in. He says, 'Section Officer Seagrave, you've been asked here because we believe you may be of value in the war effort. We understand you are fluent in French and spent time in France while growing up.'

'My stepmother sent me there as often as she could.'

'She didn't go herself?'

'We went with our governess, Mademoiselle Aubert. We stayed in boarding houses in Normandy. She took long naps, while we roamed the streets like urchins.'

'By "we" you mean, you, Florence and Digby Seagrave. Cigarette?'

'I do. Thank you.'

'You then went to a Swiss finishing school, where you learnt some German.'

'I wasn't there for long. I have the basics but could never pass as German.'

'But you could pass as French?'

'I believe so.'

He lights her cigarette then his own, before switching into French to say, 'I hear you have an outdoor theatre at your home. Do you perform?'

She replies in French. 'As a child, I did, but as an adult, I prefer to act as director.'

'Even a director must take to the stage at the end of a perform-ance, to accept her bouquet.'

'I am uncomfortable with that custom, as it happens. I feel it diminishes the collective achievement of the cast.'

'You avoid the limelight?'

'I don't seek it out, if that's what you're asking.'

'Do you find it difficult to accept orders?'

'Not if they're sensible.'

'Can you ride a bicycle?'

'Yes.'

He leans forward on to his desk, switching back into English, to ask, 'Tell me, as an intelligent young person, what do you make of the Nazis?'

'I despise the Nazis and everything they stand for.'

'Then what do you think Herr Hitler's followers see in him?'

'Without wanting to sound facile, the Nazis I saw in Europe seemed most taken with their uniforms. Their parades. The grand display of it all. Even before we were at war, they could pretend they were warriors.'

'What young man doesn't want to be a mighty warrior?' says Capt. Potter.

Cristabel says nothing. There doesn't seem to be an answer to that question.

'What about the young women who are devoted to our friend

Adolf,' says Capt. Potter, rolling his cigarette between his fingers. 'What do you make of them?'

'I don't know what to make of them. I used to stay with a woman in Austria who was enamoured with the Nazis. Listened to all their speeches. I could never understand why.' She remembers it clearly: the cramped sitting room in her mountain lodgings; the wireless broadcasting the staticky roar of far-away thousands applauding; and the harsh German voice proclaiming that while *man gave to life the great lines and forms, it was the task of women to fill these lines and forms with colour*. How the woman had clapped. What was it that so delighted her? wondered Cristabel. Was it simply the word colour? Like a child pleased by bright flowers.

'How do you get on with other women?' Capt. Potter asks.

'I can get on with anyone if I have to. Why?'

'I'm building a picture of your character. Would you describe yourself as a political individual?' says Capt. Potter, though she doubts that is his real name, just as she doubts the existence of the Ministry of Pensions.

'I know right from wrong.'

'Your family situation is unusual,' he says. 'Your father died when you were young. I mention this because I believe a woman's loyalties invariably follow her father's. A little girl worships daddy, so if daddy is loyal to his country, then it follows she will be. But if she doesn't have a father –' Capt. Potter lifts his hands.

'I didn't have a mother either,' Cristabel replies.

'Did you ever imagine what it might be like to have had parents?'

She shakes her head. It has never occurred to her to picture an alternative upbringing. Her father was there and then he wasn't, and the solid shape of his death blocked out any other possibilities. Her mother, however, was never there, and Cristabel guards her indifference to this fact fiercely. It is an absence no one can touch.

'Captain Potter,' she says, 'there are many of my generation who lost parents. I cannot believe I am the only orphan you have come across.'

'Sadly, no,' he says. 'I am merely curious about how character is formed in the absence of parents. Before the war, I was a writer, so I think a great deal about character. You must too, with your interest in the theatre. What is it in our upbringing that shapes us?'

It is strange, but at that moment Cristabel thinks of Leon, as she had seen him that morning, in his bedsit at the top of a building near St James's Park. He was half naked, a towel tied about his waist, shaving at the sink in the corner, the razor blade scraping over his skin. His room overlooked rooftops and air vents, drainpipes and gutterings, and far below, a backstreet, home to hotels and members' clubs, quiet comings and goings, a doorman waiting in a top hat.

There was nothing of sentiment in his room. No books, no photographs. Only a wireless and a bottle of rum. He shared it with a man in the navy, who was away for long stretches at a time. They divided the room with a sheet hung from the ceiling. It was an empty, temporary space designed to be left easily. A backstage space; an overnight camp. It made sense to her.

She thought of how, having had no instructions to follow, no examples to live by, Leon had been left to raise himself, and had done so as a resourceful child would, using the tools to hand – and she had done the same: made a model of herself and set it to work in the world. They were rough copies, children's drawings; Mowglis who had taught themselves to walk upright and put on clothes.

Leon's dark eyes in the mirror watching himself become presentable, the practised running of the blade, its rough debriding. Waiting at the end of his single bed: their military uniforms.

'I don't believe parents are always necessary,' she says.

'Would you say then that being an orphan fostered a spirit of self-reliance?'

'Possibly. I was thrown upon myself a good deal, but never at a loss for things to do.'

'What would you say to someone who believes a young woman should not be called upon to fight a war?'

'If I can be of use to my country, then I should be made use of.'

Capt. Potter nods enthusiastically. 'I have great faith in the women I recruit. They operate more successfully on their own. Keep a cool head. Men are so used to being in the company of other men, they come to rely on it.'

Cristabel lifts her mouth in a smile, puts out her cigarette.

'What are your current domestic circumstances?' asks Capt. Potter. 'If I were to recommend you for further training, who would run your family home? Given that your cousin Digby is also on active service.'

She wonders how much Capt. Potter knows about Digby. She says, 'I believe my sister Florence is more than capable of managing the estate, which is curious, as I am not sure I would have said that before the war.'

'War is a great uplifter,' says Capt. Potter, slapping his hands on the table. 'For a fortunate few, war allows us to rise in ways that would otherwise be impossible. We can bring the very best of us to bear.'

She has the sense that he is enjoying the conversation and wishes to draw out the interview as one might extend a game of poker or a fencing match. There are men, she has observed, who enjoy this kind of interaction with women, but how to conclude the bout to attain the result she wants without offending him? Is he the type who would wish her to flourish her rapier and bounce coquettishly about for a while longer, or would he want her to go for his throat? She thinks for a moment, remembers how much she hates parlour games, and hears her Uncle Willoughby in her ear. 'Both hands on a broadsword, Cristabel.'

She says, 'Captain Potter, you talked about loyalties. I am loyal to my family. I am loyal to my country. But that is not why I am here. I am here because I cannot stand injustice. The thought of Hitler and his thugs marching across Europe as if they owned it thoroughly revolts me. It's arrogant bullying on the grandest scale and I hate it. I hate them and I hate it. I want to go to France as soon as I am able and, if sent, would do whatever is asked of me to defeat the enemy. Whatever is asked. Can you make that happen?'

Capt. Potter steeples his fingers; his eyes are very bright. 'Someone will be in touch.'

New Recruits

March, 1943

In the back of the car, Cristabel folds her hands in her lap. She doesn't ordinarily feel nervous.

She is wearing a new khaki uniform, that of a subaltern in the First Aid Nursing Yeomanry – a civilian corps, which, she has been told, allows her to be trained to carry arms. Women in the military are forbidden to take part in combatant duties, but, perversely, women civilians are less restricted. She is in an unmarked car, a huge Chrysler with black curtains covering the passenger windows, being driven to a manor house in Surrey that serves as a preliminary training school for undercover operatives. The driver is a young woman, also in khaki uniform.

Cristabel is not sure if she should make conversation. The peculiarity of being a uniformed woman in a car driven by a uniformed woman has underscored the feeling she has had since hearing Capt. Potter had selected her to be trained for confidential work: that she has stepped through the looking-glass. It is both exciting and disorientating, and she feels unusually jumpy, as if at the start of an opening night. She looks at her hands on her lap, checks her fingernails are clean.

The car slows to a halt. Cristabel pulls back the curtain. They have arrived outside an Elizabethan manor surrounded by pine trees. Its sloping tiled roofs and multiple chimneys remind her of Chilcombe, but there are uniformed people, young men and women, coming and going in the grounds: her first sighting of other new recruits. In the hotel where she met Capt. Potter, she had seen only the doorman who let her in; the rest of the building was disconcertingly empty.

She takes her bags from the driver, who wishes her good luck in a solemn tone, then walks to the main entrance, where she is let in by a staff officer who knows her name. There are timetables on the walls in the hallway, alongside maps dotted with pins. Cristabel heads automatically towards the main staircase, but the staff officer diverts her along a corridor to the narrow stairs at the back of the house, telling her she is to share a bedroom on the top floor with another woman, who is there when she arrives. A petite, dark-haired woman, patting Papier Poudré across her nose. She greets Cristabel enthusiastically, with a kiss on each cheek in the French style, saying, 'Welcome to the madhouse! I'll be in the bar when you're ready, ducks.'

Cristabel unpacks the few things she has brought with her, places the goddess Sekhmet on her bedside table, checks herself in a mirror. She draws herself up to her full height and lifts her chin, takes a deep breath, tries a smile, then a nod.

She goes back downstairs to find the bar. It is in what Cristabel imagines used to be the drawing room and now holds a mix of occasional tables, armchairs and a makeshift corner bar, behind which is the petite woman, pouring them each a Dubonnet and bitter lemon. She cries, 'Bonjour, chérie!' as Cristabel enters. Several uniformed men reading newspapers in the armchairs look up at the new arrival with curiosity.

'Isn't it a little early to be drinking?' says Cristabel. It is ten in the morning.

'They keep the bar open all day. It means they can weed out anyone with a reckless taste for booze,' replies the woman. 'They say they don't like it when their girls drink, but what they mean is they don't like it when their girls drink them under the table.' Her accent is a cheerfully haphazard mix of French and cockney.

'Don't start that again, Sophie,' groans one of the men. 'I've not recovered from last night yet.'

Sophie winks at Cristabel and hands her the drink. 'Here's to you, ducks,' she says. 'I'm Sophie Leray. Lovely to meet you. Try not to fall over.'

There are twelve new recruits, two women and ten men, and they train together. While training with the WAAF had been a series of drills repeated endlessly, training at the Surrey manor is curiously like being a guest at a country house, with group activities inter-spersed by regular meals.

Each day starts with an early-morning slog round an obstacle course, the women wearing borrowed battledress, followed by a cooked breakfast. Then they learn about codes and build Meccano models, or play variants of the memory game where items on a tray are concealed with a cloth then removed, one by one. After lunch, they throw hand grenades into a nearby chalk quarry, or swim in the chilly outdoor pool beneath the pine trees. In the evenings, they dine in full uniform, then walk to the neighbouring village to go to the pub, where they are eyed by curious locals.

'They didn't teach us this at school,' whispers Sophie one morn-ing, as they write out the Morse code alphabet.

'I didn't go to school,' replies Cristabel, her brain crowded with dots and dashes.

'You didn't miss nothing,' Sophie replies.

There are elements of the training which Cristabel tackles with ease – like climbing a tree and coming down it via a rope, Sophie at the bottom shouting, 'Saints alive, did you grow up in a jungle?' – and, having been hunting, she is familiar with firing a gun, although pistols are new to her, and learning to take them apart and put them back together is an enjoyable exercise. But some lessons are more challenging.

One morning, they are summoned out on to the lawns where mats have been laid out on the grass. A couple of conducting officers are already there, stripped to the waist like Ancient Greeks, their arms behind their backs. The PT instructor in charge, a muscular man with a Lancastrian accent, wastes no time in informing the recruits that they should pay attention, as what they are about to learn could save their lives.

Using the two half-naked men as demonstration models, the instructor rapidly runs through a series of wrestling moves. How to use your enemy's weight against him, how to throw him to the ground. He grabs one of the men, then flings him over so he lands on his back with a thump.

'Who's next?' he says. 'What about one of you girls? I've been told you want to go up against the Nazis.'

'Most men buy me a drink before they ask for a wrestle,' says Sophie.

'Most women know better than to think they can fight a war,' says the instructor, rolling his eyes. 'Hitler won't have time for your excuses, miss, and nor do I.'

Cristabel steps forward on to the mat. 'All right then.'

She hears one of the male recruits say, 'Go easy on her, eh?' So she adds loudly, 'But don't go easy on me.'

The instructor laughs, then approaches, hunched low, with his arms held out in front. Feeling self-conscious, Cristabel tries to mimic his actions, but as she is studying his footwork, he sweeps her legs out from underneath her, flipping her on to the mat with a smack that knocks the air from her lungs. Looking down at her, the instructor says, 'You're a lanky one. Got a long way to fall.'

One of the conducting officers pulls Cristabel to her feet, and she is about to leave the mat, but the PT instructor grabs her again. 'Try it with him,' he says, pointing to the conducting officer. 'Get lower this time. We've a war to win here, ladies.'

Breathing hard, Cristabel finds she has gritted her teeth. She crouches down, holds her arms out. The conducting officer approaches her and grabs her by the shoulders. 'Grab me,' he hisses, so she grabs his shoulders in return, her hands gripping his bare skin. His face is very close to hers, his eyes serious. He makes sudden movements, pushing or pulling her forwards and backwards. Once, he hooks a leg behind hers, but she kicks herself free. Knowing no techniques, she tries to rush him, to barge him to the ground, and he is knocked back a few steps, but quickly recovers, and she finds herself again hurled to the ground, this time with the conducting officer on top of her, pinioning her to the mat, his elbow across her throat. 'Sorry,' he says in a whisper. She can feel him breathing, the movement of his ribcage against her chest.

'Are you done yet, miss?' says the instructor, peering down at her.

The conducting officer lifts his elbow, so she can speak. 'No, sir,' she says.

The instructor smiles. 'That's the spirit.'

That evening, Cristabel sits in the bath examining the bruises on her hips, the grazes on her elbows. The session had improved as she had grown familiar with the techniques, but she was consistently caught out. The male recruits were quicker to get stuck in, they seemed to have no reservations about manhandling each other and rolling about in a tangle of limbs. Most of them must have learnt it at school. Even as young boys, they would have wrestled, played rugby, become familiar with the bodies of others. She had been taught to hold herself apart. Don't touch that. Hands off. Where are your gloves?

She looks at her hands. She could probably count the number of people she has ever touched on the fingers of one of them. Digby and Flossie. Leon. Maudie and the nanny who looked after her as a baby. She doesn't know if her mother held her. Wouldn't remember if she had. And now: the sweaty shoulders of a conducting officer; the muscular arms of the PT instructor ('Get a hold of the flesh, girl!'); the waists, backs, necks and legs of her fellow students. Sophie, who put an arm round her as they walked, exhausted, back to the house.

On her upper arm, she can see a line of red marks left by the fingers of one of her opponents, like a set of bloody fingerprints.

The instructors and officers at the house are familiar types – brusque military men or smooth Old Etonians – but the students are more diverse. They are British, French, Czech, Belgian, Mauritian, Canadian, or a combination. Only a couple have military experience, the rest have been selected for their language skills and whatever ineffable qualities Capt. Potter saw in them. They include a journalist, a teacher, a racing driver and an acrobat. Sophie, who has a French father and an English mother, worked in her father's dress shop in Hackney until she saw an advert in the newspaper looking for bilingual secretaries.

The nature of their work, what they are being trained for, is curiously intangible, and the conversations between instructors

Cristabel overhears in the bar are so vague, she suspects they must be deliberately so – that on this side of the looking-glass there is a purposeful smudging of the specific. This air of secrecy is infectious. Although Cristabel often wonders if Digby came through the house before her, she never asks about him. It feels important she concentrate on the task in hand. She pushes all thoughts of Digby to the corner of her mind that ruminates at three in the morning.

She has the sense that the recruits' role is a puzzle they are both part of and attempting to figure out. She is reminded of the scenes in films where a detective brings together the guests at a house party to inform them he is investigating a murder and the murderer is still among them: the deliberate lightness of the guests' responses – *oh heavens, surely not* – their eyes on each other.

As the weeks pass, she gradually uncovers that the organization she is involved with is a new venture set up to send agents into occupied countries. The French section is headed by a man called Colonel Buckmaster. She meets him briefly one day when he visits the manor, and he is as pale and unremarkable as Perry, lofty and murmuring, with the abstract air of someone consistently bothered by high-level things.

The organization is hidden beneath a blur of similarly unremarkable pseudonyms: the Inter-Services Liaison Bureau, the Joint Technical Board. Its official name is the Special Operations Executive, the SOE, which waggish instructors joke should stand for 'Stately 'Omes of England', given its frequent use of manorial buildings, but most simply refer to as 'the Org'. It sits outside the regular military forces and the established Secret Services and, like most untested new arrivals, is considered something of an amateurish gamble, not least because it is willing to use civilians as agents – and some are women.

A few of the instructors seem particularly disgruntled by the presence of female recruits and make their feelings known through sarcastic comments or jokes at the women's expense, especially after a few rounds in the pub.

'They think having women here will spoil their fun,' says Sophie, carrying their drinks to a table, ignoring the remarks coming from a couple of instructors at the bar. 'Wars have always been just for the boys. That's why they like them so much.'

Although Cristabel is disappointed by the juvenile jibes and a little stung by claims that she lacks a sense of humour, she resolves to ignore them. She is grateful for Sophie's companionship. To be the only woman among jeering men would be hard; a team of two, sharing a table and a pack of cigarettes, is a united front.

Besides, she has not much time to think about it. The fledgling agents' schedule is intense and at every stage they are observed by officers assessing them for suitability. Not all of them will make it through. Being watched adds an air of seriousness to proceedings. Each activity, however absorbing, is also a test. Every lesson completed, a tick in a box.

Cristabel finds this simplicity satisfying: it takes all her focus and allows for no margin of error; a system as pure as a machine. At the end of the day, she dives into the ice-cold swimming pool while the air around her is snapped into pieces by the sound of nearby pistol practice. The bang and gurgle of engulfing water. The crack and recoil of guns. When she gets into bed at night, sleep hits her like a punch.

The recruits are sealed off in the bubble of their strange new world. It is repeatedly impressed upon them that what they are learning is never to be shared. They have signed the Official Secrets Act; are forbidden to make telephone calls; and their letters are so heavily censored, it seems pointless to write any. Cristabel feels a little empty without her written monologues, her outlets for pronouncements and opinions, but also somehow new. Stopped in telling the story of herself, she is whoever she is when she wakes up. Quieter. Alone. Alone with others who are also alone.

'You can use the lav first,' says Sophie from the neighbouring bed, with a sleepy smile. 'I'm not getting up this early, however loudly they honk that bloody trumpet.' In the morning, without her make-up, she looks as young as a child.

Sophie had a fiancé, Bob, a fireman who died in the Blitz. A baby son called Paul is with her parents in Hackney. She has an American admirer now, who sends her Elizabeth Arden lipsticks from across the Atlantic: defiant reds. She applies the colour before they go to the pub, sharply outlining the contours of her mouth, as she tells Cristabel, 'Since my Bob went, nothing's seemed to touch me. I was in such a slump, then this came along. I was just glad to say yes to something. The sitting around was killing me.' She uses a tissue to blot her lipstick, pressing it to her mouth like a kiss.

In the pub, she continues, 'It's something different, isn't it? You and me, we'd never meet in ordinary life. Unless you came into my papa's shop looking for a frock.'

'I don't go into shops if I can help it,' says Cristabel, taking cautious sips of the fruit wine Sophie is insistent she try.

'You don't know when it's your round either,' says Sophie, giving her a friendly shove.

There is a lot Cristabel doesn't know, as it turns out. As she listens to her fellow students' tales of family meals and holidays, she realizes that her home life is uncommon. She watches Sophie – her chatty charm, her popularity – and feels, for the first time, the difficulty of being forged by a family that has left her strangely shaped. Unsure of the usual, its manners and textures.

However, there is one thing she knows: how to listen to a big house. The night the instructors creep into the students' bedrooms to test their reactions, Cristabel is behind the door, ready for them.

'How did you know they were coming, ducks?' asks Sophie, over breakfast.

'I grew up in a house like this,' says Cristabel, eating her porridge.

'But you didn't have people tiptoeing about in the dark.'

Cristabel thinks of her vigilant younger self, hiding up on the roof. 'It wasn't so different.'

'Blimey,' laughs Sophie. 'Remind me never to go to your house. Though I don't imagine I'd get an invite anyway, someone like me. Probably have to buy a ticket.'

Cristabel frowns. 'That won't be necessary. You'd come with me.'

'We'll do that then, shall we? When all this is done,' says Sophie.

367

Her tone is teasing but there is a query in it that Cristabel treats seriously.

'We will,' she says.

After three weeks in Surrey, the two weakest students are removed and the rest travel to Scotland for a month of further training – one instructor calls it 'a toughening' as if they were pieces of leather. They stay on the remote west coast in a granite Victorian residence. Located on the edge of a loch, tucked beneath a craggy mountain, the house has been chosen for its isolation and, like the manor in Surrey, has had its name removed and replaced with a number. The instructors here are hunters, mountaineers, polar explorers: men who will teach them the art of survival.

The recruits are sent on endless marches, tramping through mist and rain, eating only what they can kill. Cristabel is grateful for Maudie's long-ago lessons in rabbit-skinning. They make shelters from tree boughs, fires from dried cattle dung. Physicality, she finds, is levelling: they are all equally tired, equally sodden. In their struggles, they become a team, loyal to each other in a teasing, affectionate way. United against the instructors, the insects, the peat bogs, they talk of the nights out they will have in London, when it's all over.

It no longer matters who they are or where they come from. It does not even matter that some are male and some female. Cristabel is the best shot, a burly Czech man the best cook. There is a camaraderie among the recruits that Cristabel has never experienced before. She realizes that, for all she resents the unfair advantages given to the opposite sex, she does not want to be a man, she only wants it not to matter that she is a woman. She wants this. This friendship, this acceptance. To be valued for what she can do, rather than told what she can't.

Together, the recruits learn how to jump from a moving train, how to signal with an Aldis lamp, how to send and receive coded messages on a wireless set. Sophie, so fastidious about her appearance she curls her eyelashes every morning, proves an equally fastidious wireless operator, her nimble fingers several times faster than the rest of them, even in sheeting rain. They practise loading and firing weapons in darkness; learning to shoot from the hip in a crouched position, always firing twice, to make sure.

A pair of ex-policemen teach them methods of silent killing learnt in the backstreets of Shanghai. It seems ludicrous that one can be taught how to end a life in the classroom, that it can be reduced to a succession of simple steps. *A quick snap upwards and backwards.* There is a rumour that a student killed an instructor by accident this way. There are many rumours like this – warning fables of unwary agents and their fatal mistakes, or the minuscule errors that gave them away in the field: the one that sipped soup from a spoon not a bowl, the one that wore gloves with 'Made in England' stitched inside a finger, the one that looked the wrong way crossing the road.

One of the ex-policemen, an amiable man in his fifties, shows them how to use a lethal stiletto blade that has been specially made for them, designed to penetrate even the thickest military uniforms. Perfect, he says, for close-quarters fighting and 'sentry removal' – an interesting euphemism, thinks Cristabel, as if the sentry had been moved somewhere else, rather than left for dead with a hole in their ribcage.

'Anything can be a weapon,' says the ex-policeman, 'but this knife is a particularly good one.' He holds it up. They are in a downstairs room at the house, where long windows look out over the grounds to the deep blue loch beyond. The recruits are seated in fold-out chairs, each holding a knife of their own, while the ex-policeman is leaning against a desk alongside a straw-filled dummy in a suit and Homburg hat.

He continues, 'It's not for the faint-hearted. With a gun, you can shoot a man in the distance, easy as shooting a pigeon. With a knife, you need to get as close to him as you do to your sweetheart.'

He puts the knife on the desk, takes a sip from a teacup, and says, 'Pulling a trigger, anyone can do that. But if your brain starts getting in the way when you're holding a knife, that's fatal.'

'I don't think my brain's ever got in the way of anything,' says Sophie, to laughter.

The ex-policeman smiles politely. 'It's not always a tidy affair either. You might need to get your hands round his throat if the job is incomplete. Then you need to get away and forget him. That's the most important part.'

Cristabel holds her knife loosely across her palm, sensing how sweetly it balances between slender blade and brass handle. She looks away, allowing the feel of it to become something known to her hand, gazing out of the window over the sloping lawns, where there are windowless brick structures used to simulate solitary confinement, to the loch, where they will be submerged to test their ability to withstand cold. Each day gets a little steeper now, the path narrower, the oxygen thinner.

The ex-policeman says, 'Who can remember the most vulnerable parts of the target's body?'

Cristabel raises her knife.

Sometimes, they canoe along the coast, skirting rocky reefs and white sandy beaches. On clear days, the sea is an impossible turquoise, and when the sun sets, the sky is streaked with extravagant pinks and purples, lighting up the mountainous islands they can see from the shore. At these times, Cristabel feels an intense happiness; an almost painful awareness of being alive and breathing. The movement of the canoe through the water, the steady beat of her forward trajectory, the sunlight on the sea.

There are buzzards in the high peaks near the house. She sees them sometimes, rotating on the updraughts, drawing circles in the sky with long-fingered wings, their plaintive cries falling to earth. Once, on a morning run through the countryside, she had come across one standing on the ground, one yellow claw gripping a wriggling rodent. It was bigger than she imagined. A shaggy-coated king in a feathered cape of russet and cream, with a hooked beak and a powerful, undeviating stare. They had examined each other, and she felt its gaze as the assessment of an equal.

A whistle blew in the distance. The buzzard took off with its prey, its pale underwings flashing upwards, and Cristabel ran back to the house, hearing nothing but the sound of her own blood pounding in her ears, the rushing wind.

Full Moon

June, 1943

It is a humid June night. The house and its inhabitants are restless. Cristabel hears taps running, bed springs creaking, someone calling in their sleep. Lying on her bed, listless beneath the weight of unmoving air, she can hear sluggish raindrops falling outside. Her alarm goes off. It is 22:00 hours.

She puts on her dressing gown and goes for what they call an 'early breakfast'. She is the only one seated in the dining room beneath a fizzing electric light, where a tired female ensign brings her tea and toast. The windows show nothing but night and rain. As she is methodically eating, she sees Joan, a conducting officer from the Org, coming towards her.

'Chin up,' says Joan. 'The forecast is better for later. I bet you go tonight.'

'You say that every night,' says Cristabel, helping herself to another piece of toast.

She has been staying at the 'departure school' for a week. A Georgian mansion hidden in leafy Bedfordshire, it houses RAF personnel from a nearby airfield and agents waiting to fly out to Europe. Every night she has been driven out to the airfield, and every night her scheduled flight has been called off because clouds have covered the moon. The pilots require the moon to navigate, so have only a twelve-day window around each month's full moon to attempt their flights to France. Because of this, they are known as 'Moon Squadrons', and they stare up at the night sky with the fervency of astronomers, lovers.

'Let's get you dressed and ready,' says Joan.

*

Back in Cristabel's room, Joan helps her into the clothes of the character she will become in France: Claudine Beauchamp, a student of literature visiting relatives in the countryside to recover from a long illness. Claudine wears woollen underclothes and a winter vest – Joan says it gets cold on the flight – a beige blouse with a carefully fabricated French label inside the collar, a brown woollen jumper and a grey tweed suit. On her feet are lisle stockings and sensible black walking shoes, deliberately aged.

Claudine's hair is longer than Cristabel's used to be, and pinned up at the back, due to Sophie's insistence that she cannot go to France looking like a tomboy, a *garçon manqué*. In her jacket pocket, she has a pair of glasses, a book of French poetry, and a Lancôme lipstick which, thanks to Sophie, she can apply to her lips, if required. Cristabel puts her hand in her pocket to find its compact case. She likes the shape of it even if she is reluctant to use it.

The black Chrysler that carries her to the airfield purrs carefully along lanes slick with rain, past high hedgerows dotted with pale dog roses. The gated airfield has the feel of a temporary place, a few camouflaged Nissen huts standing in a soggy meadow. It is mainly active at night to avoid attracting German attention, its pilots taking off and landing in darkness. Large Halifax bombers, long-nosed shadows, wait on the concrete runways, ground crews huddled beneath them, carrying out mechanical checks in hooded waterproofs.

The airfield's secrecy is such that the building where the agents wait for their flights has been designed to look like a farmer's weatherboarded barn, but when Joan pushes open the door, the familiar military fug of cigarette smoke and male conversation drifts out to greet them. Cristabel takes one last look at the night sky, still covered with cloud, then steps inside.

It is a hollow building with no windows, full of aircrews studying maps, playing cards and drinking coffee from Thermos flasks. A Labrador dog lies sleeping in one corner. She sees the agent she will be flying out with, Henri, being fitted into his parachute suit. It reminds her of the barn at her theatre, where they changed into their costumes and waited to go onstage.

Henri is a Frenchman, one she trained with in Scotland, although he was not called Henri then. She knows his real name, his children's favourite games, his love of fishing, his quiet thoughtfulness, but that must all be packed away and left behind. He is only Henri now. She catches his eye and nods.

Joan takes Cristabel to a table and gives her a set of false documents – birth certificate, ration cards, travel permits – perfect forgeries in which her own solemn face looks back at her, with its new hairstyle and its freshly plucked eyebrows. She is even given a crumpled photograph of an older French couple: her new parents. Then Joan goes over the operational details of the mission.

Cristabel knows her mission inside out. After successfully completing her training, she had been summoned to London, to Org HQ – appropriately hidden in a building in Sherlock Holmes's Baker Street – and was there told that she was being sent to France to work as a courier. The Org has divided France into different areas called 'circuits', and within each one, there is an organizer, who is in charge, along with a courier and a wireless operator. Women are either couriers or wireless operators.

Cristabel is to work for an organizer known as Pierre, based in a circuit called Shepherd. Part of the Org's work is to arm existing secret forces, so Cristabel will be dropped into France alongside canisters full of weaponry to be distributed among Resistance fighters. She has her cover name, Claudine, and a field name, Gilberte, which is how she will be known by her fellow agents.

'Why does Pierre need a new courier?' she asked.

There had been an exchange of blank looks in the office.

She added, 'I only ask because, if he or she were caught because of an error, I wouldn't want to make the same mistake.'

They told her Pierre would fill her in, then she and Henri were taken to see Colonel Buckmaster, their head of department, who had regarded them with a curious rapid blinking before saying, 'Good luck to you, children,' and pressing gifts into their hands.

Cristabel's was a gold powder compact. She handed it to Joan as they left the office. 'I'll never use it.'

'You can sell it, if needs be,' said Joan, passing it back. 'Besides, a mirror can be useful for checking who's behind you.'

There followed a few days of kicking their heels in London before travelling up to Bedfordshire. Cristabel spent this time studying Michelin maps of France and memorizing the details of contacts. Once, Joan took her to the bustling Lyons Corner House on Oxford Street for lunch, and as they left, Cristabel saw Philippa Fenwick, arm in arm with a dashing RAF officer, coming out of a fashionable department store on the other side of the road. Philly glamorous in a red summer dress with a polka-dot scarf in her hair, exclaiming animatedly.

Cristabel almost lifted her hand to call out. She could imagine Philly's immediate response – 'Darling! What a thrill to see you! So noble in your uniform!' – but kept herself in check. She shouldn't want to be seen now. She stepped back into a doorway and watched Philly's bright figure disappear, her laughter echoing down the street.

One of the Halifax crew, the dispatcher, who is responsible for getting the agents out of the plane at the right time, approaches Joan and Cristabel in the barn, and gives them a thumbs up.

'Is the jump on?' asks Joan.

'Definitely clearing up,' he replies.

'That's good news, Gilberte,' says Joan, who is careful to use her charge's code name, even here.

Joan straps packages of French banknotes across Cristabel's body and helps her put on her pistol and holster, before zipping her into her camouflage jumpsuit. In its many pockets are Cristabel's knife, a flashlight, a compass, a fine silk scarf on which is printed a map of her circuit area, and a spade to bury the parachute. Joan then hands her a small box containing two cyanide suicide pills.

'You have to bite down on them before you swallow,' says Joan.

Cristabel wonders how they know this. 'I don't want them,' she says.

'Useful to have the option,' replies Joan briskly.

Cristabel puts the pills in one of her pockets, then sits down on a chair so Joan can bind her ankles to protect them. Looking down at the bindings, she thinks of the puttees worn by soldiers in the last war, those bandaged legs of upright men photographed outside their barracks, arms folded. She then waddles to the doorway of the barn to get some air, feeling as bulky as a badly wrapped parcel.

It is still raining. As Cristabel smokes a cigarette, a limousine with curtained windows pulls up outside and a tall figure in uniform steps out and heads to the barn, before stopping suddenly, and turning to her. 'Are my eyes broken or do we know each other?'

'We don't know each other at all. What on earth are you doing here, Leon?'

'What a surprise this is,' he says, looking her up and down. 'I have been sent here to collect someone. He is being brought back from where you are probably going, *n'est-ce pas?*'

'I won't be going anywhere unless it stops raining,' she says, offering him one of her new Gauloises.

'Your hands are not shaking though,' he says approvingly. 'I like this outfit.'

'This outfit is incredibly hot,' she replies, lighting his cigarette.

'Perhaps you might be better off –'

'Not now, Leon,' she says, but she is smiling.

'You will be grateful for it in the aeroplane,' he says. 'Do you know something I learnt this week, the Spanish call parachutes the white rose of death. Almost romantic, no?'

'Almost.'

'One moment.' He goes to the car, returning with a hip flask, which he passes to her. 'We must toast to your mission.'

She takes a cautious sip, grimaces.

Leon glances at his wristwatch. 'My guest will soon be arriving.'

Cristabel thinks of the pills in her pocket. 'Leon, just in case –'

He raises a hand to interrupt her. 'In Russia, we do not talk between the first and second drinks.'

'You've never been to Russia,' she replies, but takes another wincing sip from the flask before handing it back to him. 'Leon, I might not come back, you know.'

'Many will not,' he says, looking into the barn and waving to greet someone. Then he turns to her. 'You will come through this, Cristabel Seagrave. Your heart is strong.'

'I don't mean to be sentimental,' she says.

'When were you sentimental?' He places a hand on her chest. 'This is not sentiment. This is what will keep you alive.'

She lays her hand over his, rather awkwardly. 'I feel I should say something profound. Like in a book.'

'I don't want anything from a book.' He leans in and kisses her, holding it for a moment. 'Come and see me for a vodka when you get back.'

Cristabel looks at him, his thick black hair, his dark eyes, the way his mouth moves between expressions, never quite settling. She knows, very suddenly, the exact taste of his mouth, when it opens to her. Then she looks past him, up at the sky. 'It's stopped raining.'

The Halifax dispatcher appears beside her, nods at the moon, now almost fully visible through thinning cloud. 'Looks like you're in luck.'

Suddenly Joan is there too, and between them, they help her into her heavy parachute, fit its straps on to her shoulders and fasten her rubber jump helmet on to her head. They escort her and Henri through the puddles and across the runway to the plane, where the pilot and his crew greet them with handshakes before heading into the depths of the machine. Joan shakes her hand firmly and wishes her all the best. Cristabel looks back only once, sees a tall silhouette in the entrance to the barn, then she is hauled up into the belly of the Halifax.

Inside the fuselage, the aeroplane is a hollow tube, filled with pipes and metalwork, smelling of petrol. The seats have been taken out to make room for additional fuel tanks, so Cristabel and Henri must sit on sleeping bags on the floor, leaning back on their cumbersome parachutes, next to a stack of carrier pigeons in cardboard boxes, each box fitted with a mini parachute. The weapons containers that will be dropped with the agents hang under the Halifax in its bomb racks. The pilot has disappeared into the nose of the plane and the rear gunner has descended into his glass bubble at the back; Cristabel can hear the exchange of radio messages, preflight checks.

More suddenly than she expected, there is the rattle of the propellors starting up, one after the other, then the droning growl of the engines as the Halifax begins to move across the runway. 'I'd get some sleep if I were you,' says the dispatcher, draping a blanket over the pigeons.

Cristabel nods. She is unable to talk. She has been in an aeroplane before during her parachute training and found take-off a uniquely terrifying experience. Once up in the air, she can breathe again, but the machine's bumping, jolting transition from land to sky she finds gruelling.

'All tickety-boo?' asks the dispatcher, as they accelerate down the runway.

'Yes,' she manages, before closing her eyes and allowing the roar of the machine to lull her, the noise of its four engines like a swivelling fan, moving close then moving off, a circular hypnotic sound that shuts out everything.

The Halifax leaves England and flies over the Channel, gaining altitude to avoid flak as it approaches the French coast. The barrage of German anti-aircraft guns wakes Cristabel. The plane is climbing steeply and everything inside is sliding and shaking; she can feel its vibrations fuzzing through her hands, mechanical thuds and rattles, little wobbles of effort. The dispatcher is sitting nearby. 'They can't hit us up here,' he says cheerfully, and she wonders how many other agents have also woken at this point, startled to find themselves being shot at in their sleep.

She heaves herself up to peer through a small circular window, and catches a glimpse of the Channel far below, listing at a strange angle, its moving surface like the criss-crossed texture of skin, flecked by white waves. Then the plane veers sharply, the sea lurches out of sight, and there is the electric crackle of flak, puffs of black smoke. She sits back down, finds something to hold on to.

Once safely into France, the pilot flies lower to navigate by the moonlit rivers. The dispatcher opens the exit hatch to drop the pigeons in their boxes, each one carrying a piece of rice paper and a pencil, in the hope that messages will be sent back with them to Britain. Cold air rushes in with such a noise that the dispatcher must yell to be heard. 'If I got one, I'd put it in a pie!'

Cristabel can see straggly wisps of cloud passing beneath them and the shadow of the Halifax gliding over the fields and farmhouses like a dragon. She imagines people hearing it pass overhead. French people. German people.

It is three in the morning by the time they near the drop zone, the area where a reception committee should be waiting for Gilberte and Henri. The Halifax flies even lower, skimming across the land at 900, 800, 700 feet, close enough to the ground that the crew will be able to pick out the flashes of torches.

Suddenly, the aeroplane slows, banks around. A message comes through from the pilot on the intercom and the dispatcher opens the exit hatch again, beckoning the agents, saying, 'We've spotted them. Action stations.' He tightens their straps, then clips their parachutes to a static line in the fuselage, which will yank open the parachutes when they jump. He gives each a final pat on the shoulder, then crouches next to them as they wait by the hatch.

Cristabel looks at Henri's concentrated face as he stares down at the land. She wonders if he is thinking about his family, somewhere in the country beneath them. She puts her hand on his for a moment and squeezes it, and he turns to her, and they embrace awkwardly, saying, 'Bonne chance,' into each other's ears.

'The containers go first,' instructs the dispatcher, 'then Gilberte, then Henri.'

Cristabel nods. They always sent the women first during training to make sure the men would follow, and she prefers it that way. Less time to get nervous.

The Halifax steadily circles again. The light over the hatch flashes red and the agents peering through the hatch see the containers suddenly go whisking past on their parachutes. Cristabel edges closer, letting her legs hang over the edge. Then the light changes to green, the dispatcher shouts, 'Go!' and she goes without hesitation, out into space.

There is a rapid heart-stopping drop as she plummets into nothing, then a jolt as she hits the slipstream, the breathy swish of the silk canopy opening above her and another sharp jolt as the parachute catches and spins her, the stars flinging past in a whirling blur, a wild moonlit dance. Then the movement steadies and she is sailing serenely, and this is the part she loves the most, the part that never lasts long enough. The weightless exhilaration as she glides above the land, soaring like a hawk, the air whistling by.

All too soon, the ground comes rushing up to meet her and she lands with a thud. A second later, her parachute hits the ground behind her, with a great *fllllump* like a pile of bed sheets. She scrambles to her feet, and is disentangling herself from the harness, when she sees figures running towards her. For a second, she holds her breath, groping about for her pistol, then hears they are shouting in French, '*Bienvenue!*' The Halifax banks overhead, she catches a glimpse of the pilot in the cockpit peering down at her, before it roars away into the night, giving a farewell waggle of its wings.

Awake

Flossie lies in her dorm bed, listening to the thunder of German bombers flying over Dorchester. She closes her eyes, trying to pretend it is only a noise, aware that all around her, other girls lie stiff and silent in their beds, also feigning sleep – just as she imagines the pilots in the planes might only focus on their navigational instruments, blocking out thoughts of what they carry, or that they might die soon. All of them conscious; none of them wanting to be. Outside in the street, a dog barks madly: a sole protest.

How does it become normal for death to fly over your head? Flossie wonders. How does it become normal to carry on as if it were normal? She remembers how, when her mother was killed, it was at first a shock so immense that it seemed inconceivable. But now it is an old fact, a faded newspaper cutting. One absence of many. It is funny what you can get used to.

On her bedside table are photographs of Cristabel and Digby in their uniforms. A framed studio portrait of Rosalind balances behind them. The other girls often admire Flossie's sophisticated mother, although this no longer pleases Flossie as much as it once did. She remembers Myrtle saying that there is more to life than being looked at and thinks perhaps this is something else she is getting used to – the end of wishing that she could be like her mother. Beside the photographs, a pressed flower serves as a reminder of Hans, and other wishes.

Flossie finds that letting go of wishes is not always a relief, more a parting. The wish still exists, it has simply taken another road. She can sometimes see it, over in the distance, waving from a high hill. The trick, the task, is to continue on her path, even so.

The noise of the bombers diminishes as they fly further inland, heading to their targets. Flossie feels certain she will not sleep again, knowing that an alarm clock will be going off soon, to rouse her and the other Land Girls for their early start, but she does, fitfully.

The girls greet the alarm with groans, getting dressed under their bedcovers, pulling on jumpers and dungarees. They turn out into the morning, the only ones awake in the empty streets but for the air raid warden on his way home, and climb into a cart behind a tractor that takes them bumping out to the milking sheds, grumping companionably, leaning against each other.

'I didn't want to get out of bed,' says Flossie.

'It wouldn't be the same without you,' says Barbara, while Irene offers her a lemon sherbet from a paper bag. Shirley tucks her arm in Flossie's and begins to whistle. Flossie takes the sweet, looks back at the sleeping town as they head out to the fields, and thinks: I am so far from where I thought I would be.

But she is up and moving, awake early enough to see the morning countryside still folded into soft layers by the mist, the gentle weft of fields and water meadows, the river winding through, the sky growing light in the east, the first baby curls of chimney smoke from the farm cottages, and the birds already singing out from every hedgerow: still alive, still alive.

Claudine, Gilberte

June, 1943

Where she lands is not where she thinks she lands. Those that meet her give her the place name of somewhere a hundred miles away, to protect the location of their landing site. She does not discover this until several days later, and it stays with her – that even those who greeted her so warmly would also lie to her, cheerfully, if required. That is how it goes here.

The reception committee are members of a local Resistance group. Men and women, thin-faced and lean; the men dark with stubble, the women stockingless. They quickly round up the agents, their parachutes and canisters, bundle them into the back of a noisy truck running on charcoal, and carry them to an isolated farm-house, where an old woman in a headscarf serves them cassoulet and several glasses of rough red wine.

She, Gilberte, watches her hosts, reminding herself of how the French use bread to mop up their leftovers, how passionately they argue together. They talk of Charles de Gaulle, the exiled French commander in London, whose speeches they listen to on the BBC. They want to know what life is like across the Channel, what the British think of Stalin, when the Allied invasion might be – the long-awaited *débarquements*. Gilberte says she doesn't know. She has heard talk at HQ that the invasion might come as early as September but keeps this to herself. She lets Henri do most of the talking, saves her energy for eating.

After the meal, the canisters are opened as eagerly as Christmas presents. They contain cases of grenades as tenderly packed as Fabergé eggs, along with Sten guns and ammunition, cigarettes and chocolate bars, and a few folded notes from the women who packed them, encouraging words, drawings of hearts and flags.

Gilberte and Henri leave at dawn to walk to a railway station, where they separate to go to their respective circuits, with only the briefest of glances. Gilberte feels a lurch of sadness as Henri disappears into a train, as if he were all that is left of everything. But then her train arrives at the other platform, and she boards it quickly, carrying with her a canvas suitcase containing banknotes hidden in a secret compartment and a gun stashed in a tin of talcum powder.

Walking along the moving train to find a seat, she feels lit up in a spotlight, sure every other passenger can see immediately that she is a tall English girl wearing someone else's clothes. She has just taken a seat when she sees her first German: a Wehrmacht officer coming down the corridor.

She has often wondered how it might be when she meets her first German in the field – whether she will be filled with hatred or fear – but he is merely a man in a uniform with a shaving cut on his chin. He could be a bus conductor, a park keeper. He holds his hands behind his back and strolls along, in a self-inflated balloon of his own authority. The people on the train barely glance at him.

She stares out of the window as the officer nears her, watching the countryside pass by, its vineyards and villages, then feels him stop to look at her. She turns towards him, expecting to be addressed, but then sees that he is looking at all the passengers in that way, simply to show that he can. She drops her eyes to the floor. The officer walks on. She pulls the powder compact from her pocket to give herself something to do: Claudine Beauchamp looks drawn, a tightness around her mouth.

They are almost at their destination, when the train comes to a sudden halt outside a village station, its brakes screeching. She sees from the expressions of her fellow passengers that this stop is unexpected but not entirely unexpected. She presses her head to the window and sees, further up, waiting at the side of the train to board it, men in grey uniform and some in plain clothes.

She senses the woman in the seat opposite her, a housewife with a bag of shopping, regarding her with interest, so sits back in her seat. What, she wonders, would Sophie do? She would put on her scarlet lipstick and hold her head up, ready to smile.

Claudine is not that kind of woman, but she can be another kind: the studious kind that uses train delays industriously. She rummages in her jacket and pulls out her French poetry and her unflattering glasses. She puts on the glasses, rests her feet on the suitcase under her seat, looks up at the woman, gives a tiny lift of the eyebrows that does for, 'Eh, these checks, typical,' then opens her book.

By the time the men reach her carriage, she has read the same page at least twenty times. They are SS officers: more dangerous than the ordinary soldiers of the Wehrmacht. She can see the metal skull – the *Totenkopf* – on the black band of their hats. The men in suits and long coats are most likely Gestapo: Nazi secret police, more dangerous still. They greet the passengers and, in courteously formal French, ask to see their papers. She glimpses her unsmiling face in her forged documents as she passes them over. The men turn the papers in their hands with a disconcerting slowness, as if weighing their quality. One of the SS officers, thin and greying, says, 'What are you reading, mademoiselle?'

She realizes she cannot recall the title of the book without looking at it, so replies, 'Poetry, sir.' She has decided Claudine is shy and deferential. She does not speak much because her French does not have the local accent, although whether an SS officer would notice this, she does not know.

He says, 'I enjoy your French poetry. Verlaine. Baudelaire.' The men behind him are having a low conversation in German that she cannot make out.

He holds his hand out and she passes the book to him. He leafs through it. 'Do you read for pleasure?'

'I am studying them,' she says, her voice a dull monotone.

'Which is your favourite?' he asks.

She can only think of the poem she had been staring at when they arrived – something insipid about breezes – but cannot remember the title.

'I haven't read them all yet,' she says, and feels within herself the slight drop in confidence that accompanies a less than perfect answer.

He looks at her, then one of the others says, 'The next carriage.' Her book is returned, and the men move on.

Half an hour later, the train starts up again. Gilberte spends the remainder of the journey reading slowly to calm her nerves, choosing a few favourite poems to memorize, thinking all the time of Hendricks, the actor-turned-instructor at her final training school in the New Forest, who had insisted that their cover story could not be a mask they put on, it had to be a life, fully inhabited. There could be no gaps.

She remembers too the strangeness of meeting Hendricks, knowing he had taught Digby. How she had longed to ask about her brother but was determined not to mention him, lest Hendricks think she were only there because of him. How Hendricks had rescued her by mentioning Digby himself, a discreet aside in a quiet moment, a comment about Digby's acting ambitions. 'Yes,' she had said, 'he loves to perform.'

'Do you?' Hendricks asked, and she said no. She did not mention her theatre to anyone at the Org. Perhaps Digby already had, but she felt it inappropriate. It was slightly cumbersome somehow, embarrassing to explain, in this clipped, military world. There was no room for it. Hendricks had tapped a cigarette on his desk and nodded.

When the train finally arrives at its destination, a busy market town, she is directed into a queue where her forged travel pass is again inspected, this time by officious French police. She keeps her head down, speaks only when spoken to. She sees, in her peripheral vision, a family pulled from the queue, waiting anxiously in a pen of their own luggage.

After leaving the station, she makes her way through the town to the hotel where she is to meet her organizer. Unremarkable Claudine walks in a steady trudge, carrying her suitcase. There are Germans everywhere, eating at tables outside cafés, sauntering along the streets, as if they were tourists not occupiers. The Germans have cars, the French bicycles. The Germans browse in shops, the French queue outside.

On the walls, she sees faded advertisements for long-ago circuses overlapped by new posters calling enthusiastically for Frenchmen to work in Germany: images of muscular men with hammers, GERMAN WORKERS INVITE YOU TO JOIN THEM! She knows it is not an invitation: the Germans have introduced an order, the *Service du Travail Obligatoire*, requiring able-bodied men to work in the factories of Germany; it is partly this that has swollen the ranks of the Resistance, with young Frenchmen preferring to escape into the countryside than labour in the Reich.

The hotel is hidden in a backstreet. Run-down and unappealing, with faded paintwork. Carefully pushing open the creaking front door, she finds an empty reception area, but an old man mopping the parquet floor says quietly, 'Room six,' so she carries her suitcase up the stairs and knocks on the door. A young Frenchman opens it and lets her in. The room is dark, its shutters closed. Another person is inside, a man in his forties with a black moustache, sallow skin, and shadows beneath his eyes. He is sitting on the bed, holding a pistol in his lap, and watches as the first man questions her, until he is satisfied that he knows who she is, and that London has sent her.

Finally, Pierre gets up from the bed to shake her hand. 'I am glad you are here, Gilberte,' he says. 'You understand that we have to be careful.' His French accent is flawless. She knows he has been working undercover for over a year, and there is no trace of whoever he was before, except perhaps in the shadows under his eyes.

'You lost a courier,' she replies.

'We didn't lose her,' he says. 'They found her. You must keep moving.'

She does. She never stays in the same place twice. She sleeps on night trains, in haylofts, in wine cellars. She cycles hundreds of miles, carrying messages the length and breadth of their circuit area, her glasses and poetry tucked in her pocket. After a few encounters with German patrols, she never writes anything down, she commits it all to memory, and chants the messages to herself, as she pushes round the pedals on her bike. She gives Pierre her gun and her cyanide pills, deciding she would rather be discovered without them, if she is to be discovered. She keeps her knife. A woman can justify carrying a knife.

Pierre has also heard that the Allied landings may come in September and the activity in his circuit is increasing steadily, as the dogged Moon Squadrons provide more supplies for the fighters hiding out in the mountains and woods. He and Gilberte work constantly: contacting Resistance leaders; finding sites for parachute drops; collecting and distributing arms, equipment, food, money.

There is, she finds, a freedom in this unrelenting pace and purpose. This rapid, alien life that requires total immersion. In England, she had felt discomfort in all the places she was meant to be – drawing rooms, dining rooms, even those within her own home. English girls of her class were designed to be removed from their family homes by a husband; unremoved girls were a waste of resources; they required increasing amounts of resolution merely to exist within buildings that willed them gone.

Now she is self-propelled, nothing but necessary movement: a *fille anglaise* come to fight with the French, welcomed by a network of bakers and nuns and mechanics and railwaymen and the widows of soldiers, who give her a bed for the night and a glass of cognac, and send her on her way with a kiss on each cheek and the word *'courage'*.

One morning, she is sent to take money to the leader of a Resistance group hiding deep in a forest. It is a rainy day and the trees drip with a slow ticking. The forest is so dense, and the trees are so tall, the air feels immobile, thickened, as if the men were hiding in the weeds at the bottom of a lagoon. The occasional fighter plane passing high overhead is a faraway buzzing, a hoverfly seen from underwater.

The men – mainly local farmers and their youngest sons, wearing berets and hobnail boots, along with some war-weathered Spanish

Republican fighters – eye her with interest: a woman in their forest. She thinks of the Lost Boys in *Peter Pan*, making their homes in the trees. How she had loathed that play, with its suffocating clamour for mothers; petulant Peter bleating at Wendy to stay and do their darning, as if that's all she were for.

From a hidden section in the base of her rucksack, she retrieves a hefty brick of cash and hands it to the group leader, who has an ammunition belt strung across his chest like a Mexican bandit.

'You should have better security on the road into the forest,' she says in Gilberte's increasingly regional French. 'I saw your sentry long before he saw me.'

The leader counts the money, says nothing.

'I would like a receipt for that, please,' she says, then rummages in the bag to pull out a bottle of brandy. The men lean forward. She hands the bottle to the leader. '*Vive la France.*'

He pulls out the cork, takes a gulp, then hands it to the men behind him. '*Vive la liberté,*' he says, and beckons her into the camp.

Sous Terre

October, 1943

When the Shepherd circuit collapses, it happens very quickly. Their wireless operator is captured by the Gestapo in the attic above a pharmacy where he sends his coded messages to London, and the boy who works in the pharmacy runs a full five miles to inform Pierre and Gilberte.

The first forty-eight hours after an agent is caught are the most perilous. The wireless operator – manacled to a prison wall, battered and bleeding – is expected to hold out for that long without giving anything away, whatever is done to him, to give his colleagues a chance to scatter.

The last time Gilberte sees Pierre, he is in the yard of the farmhouse that serves as his base, throwing papers on to a bonfire, yelling at her to go. *Allez!* She heaves her bike from its hiding place in a cowshed and cycles away, stopping only to throw her glasses in a stream, untie her hair, put on some lipstick and roll her skirt a little higher. A German on a motorbike passes her and she smiles at him so brazenly, with all Sophie's outlandish charm, that he nearly drives off the road. She hates herself entirely for a moment, but pedals furiously on.

She has a contact in the next village, a hairdresser who takes her in, finds her new clothes – a floral dress and cork-soled shoes – and styles her hair, so it sits in a roll on the top of her head. When Claudine Beauchamp steps out into the world again, she is carrying a shopping basket and wearing a wedding ring, a young French housewife, with a photograph of her baby son in her purse.

She takes another train, and another, and another, only boarding at the last minute, carefully changing carriages to ensure she is not followed, sticking methodically to her training. She gets off the train at village stations rather than risking checks at the larger ones. She avoids hotels where she might be required to write her name in guest books. She hardly sleeps, she barely eats.

As the trains chunter steadily through the countryside, past lines of pollarded trees and slow canals, she reads her poetry book, placing her newly painted fingernail underneath each word to direct her tired eyes – following Victor Hugo as he tells her:

> *Je suis fait d'ombre et de marbre.*
> *Comme les pieds noirs de l'arbre,*
> *Je m'enfonce dans la nuit.*
> *J'écoute; je suis sous terre.*

> I am made of shadow and marble.
> Like the black feet of the tree,
> I dig into the night.
> I listen; I am underground.

When the train stops, she hears car doors slamming. A dog barking. Ordinary noises that might not be ordinary. In clandestine work, as in a play, there are no insignificant details. If you have a gun in the first act, it must go off by the third. Everything must be noticed, considered. Is the car a military vehicle? Is the dog large or small? In some shuttered-off part of herself, she is aware this ceaseless mode of thinking is exhausting, but believes it better to be awake and tired than asleep and dead. The barking dog is silenced by its irate French owner. The train pulls away from the station.

She returns to Victor Hugo, the engaging puzzle of translation. Does digging *dans la nuit* mean he digs through the night, or that he digs into darkness? Does *m'enfonce* in this context perhaps imply a covering of the self? Her brain is a spade that turns over everything.

Eventually, she makes her way to a village in the mountains, walking miles up steep, dusty roads to get there, her cork shoes crumbling, her feet blistered. A Resistance contact takes her to a wireless operator, hidden in a storeroom full of rabbit skins, who gets a message to London, and a message comes quickly back saying that London wants her to return by the October moon. The wireless operator tells her there are rumours that a large circuit in Paris has collapsed, sending Allied agents across France tumbling like a line of dominoes.

On a high plateau outside the village a week later, a Lysander aeroplane lands to drop off two new agents and to scoop her up, lifting her out of the game.

London is grey with fog. None of the grimy windows of Org HQ seem to close properly. Draughts whistle through. Radiators clunk ruminatively but remain cold to the touch. They have tea but have run out of sugar. One of the secretaries usually makes sure everything is topped up, but she hasn't come in for a week. The two uniformed men who are conducting Cristabel's debriefing look at the sugar bowl as if baffled by its emptiness. They offer her conciliatory words. They welcome her home.

'Have you heard from Pierre?' she says. 'Is he all right?'

They elide the subject of Pierre and move on to what they know of the situation in Paris: the collapse of the Magician circuit. It is this, they believe, that has led to the capture of agents in other circuits, including Shepherd, and the round-up of many Resistance groups. Magician was ambitious in its reach, its contacts numerous, its web spread far and wide.

The men have a folder in front of them, which they look through occasionally, as if checking details. Cristabel realizes she has not seen them in the office before. They tell her there were suspicions Magician had been infiltrated as early as July, when the wireless operator repeatedly omitted a security check, even after being reprimanded by London. A wireless operator should know the check must precede every message sent back to HQ.

'To omit the check would surely mean the operator was signalling they were in enemy hands?' says Cristabel, thinking of Sophie, who would never make such a mistake.

The officers nod. They say they have since, sadly, come to that conclusion.

Cristabel considers the word 'since'.

She says, 'Look, I don't know anything about Magician. But I can tell you about Shepherd. I know a good deal about that.'

Again, the men skate past her. They say that they believe one of the British agents in Magician, code name Gabriel, was not picked up by the Gestapo and is still at large in the city. They have received reports he has been sighted. But they have not received any word from him, nor does he seem keen to leave his blown circuit area. They are concerned – she notes the soft words, the kid gloves – that he may be compromised.

She waits for the question.

The men look at each other. It is, they say, unusual for an agent's identity to be revealed, but given the importance of security work at this pivotal time in the war effort, they believe it necessary. The agent known as Gabriel is her cousin, Digby Seagrave. Might she know if he had any contacts in Paris? Had he been in touch with anyone there, before the war? Is there anywhere he might go?

She is grateful at that moment for the mock interrogation she had undergone in the New Forest and the instructor who advised her to always answer the question in front of her, rather than appear to be anticipating what might come.

'Our governess was from Paris,' she says. 'Ernestine Aubert. I don't know if she is still there.'

'Did you ever go to Paris with your governess?' they ask.

'No,' she says. 'We went to Normandy.'

'Did you go to Paris with anyone else?'

'No. The only other place in France we visited was Provence. Our friend Myrtle took us there for my twenty-first birthday.'

'Any other family holidays?'

'None at all.'

That is helpful, they say. They write a few notes. They understand the situation might be difficult, given the family connection, but has her cousin ever given any indication that he might have – *sympathies* – no, perhaps it might be better to say – *doubts*. Had he doubts? Was there, did she know, any reason for him to fail to carry out . . . ?

The sentence peters out. She knows she is expected to fill in the gaps but chooses not to assist them with this. 'I am unsure what you are asking me,' she replies. 'I have had no contact with my cousin since last year. I don't know what he is doing in Paris. I cannot imagine what you think I would know. Surely this isn't why I've been brought back?'

The irritation in her tone is met by calm indifference. They say she was brought back for her own safety following the collapse of her circuit. They are looking for information because they are concerned that Gabriel may be contaminated, either through his own volition or through enemy interference.

One of the men moves a piece of paper from the folder and slides it in front of the other, who looks at it and then says, 'You spent some time in Austria. Is that correct?'

'Skiing,' she says, realizing then, at that moment, why she is being questioned by men from another department: it is because she is no longer part of her own team. She is related to a possible enemy agent. She is under suspicion.

Later that day, she catches a crowded train back to Dorset, squeezing herself into a window seat where she stares out at the evening sky as they leave London behind. Dark clouds are banked up over the countryside, solid as a battleship, and smatterings of rain trickle across the window. There is a single band of lemon light at the horizon, like a gap under a door. The leafless trees along the railway line are nothing but clumps of branches, skeletal witchy fingers pointing up madly, a thousand bare accusations.

She is so sunk in thought that, when the ticket inspector, making his way along a corridor packed with standing passengers, asks for tickets please, she automatically rummages in her coat pocket for Claudine's *papiers*.

A sailor sitting alongside her, kitbag balanced on his knees, stinking of beer, says amiably, 'I'm always losing my ticket. I'd lose my head if it wasn't screwed on.' His large body rocks against her with each bump on the rails. She has an urge to pull out her knife and stick it right in his face. But she doesn't have a knife any more, and she doesn't have her *papiers*. She has a single ticket to Dorchester. ('We'll be in touch if we need you,' the men in the Org had said, 'and if you have any word of your cousin, we'd be grateful if you would let us know. Immediately.')

Shadow Play

Sleeplessness is a hard habit to break. Awake at five, Cristabel walks down to the ocean, the only one alive but for the herring gulls and their mournful soundings: long calls, then repeated squawks. *Dash dash dot dot dot dot. Dash dash dot dot dot dot.*

The pre-human world before sunrise has a wild and rushing freedom. The sea is thick, momentous, a north-easterly wind pushing it high and hard. There is a sense of immense activity. The long grasses along the coast fold and shiver, fold and shiver, rippling in waves.

The pebbly beach under Ceal Head is deep in shadow, the cliffs black shapes against the sky. The first gold light of dawn will fall on the distant seafront buildings of Weymouth, before edging its way round to Chilcombe.

At the theatre, leaves are scattered across the ground. The vegetable plots have been dug over and covered with a layer of compost. Someone has taken down all the raspberry canes and tidily tied them with twine.

Pushing open the doors of the barn, Cristabel finds spades and wheelbarrows. She kicks them out of the way, clambers through to the back of the building where, underneath a pile of sacking, she finds a stack of wooden scenery, a jumble of stage lights and trunks full of costumes. A few fraying stuffed animals. A papier mâché wine goblet. She pulls things out, one after the other, brushing the dust from them.

By seven o'clock, the space between the bones has been filled with bits of scenery laid out flat – a castle wall, a tree, a gate – along with a few costumes, props and stuffed animals. The sun has crept over the horizon, blessing Weymouth with its first light, but the theatre is still in shadow, and she is cold. In the cottage she finds an old picnic kettle and a wobbly brass Primus stove that she coaxes into life, turning the sooty yellow flames into a hissing blue, then balancing the kettle on top. The resulting beverage is more rust than tea, but she fills it with sugar and takes it outside, sitting on the scenery and holding an old, chipped mug in her hands, watching as the sunlight inches towards her.

To the east, where the sky is growing light, she can see the patrician profile of Ceal Head in sharp relief, and the jutting headlands beyond it, a series of noble noses extending into the water, like the silhouette portraits of a Victorian family, father to child, receding into the future. The sea rolls in ridges towards them, and the sound of it hitting the land in the distance, and then at points closer, is a muffled battle; and its echoes, its effects and after-effects.

A high voice behind her says, 'I've never seen a lion before.'

She turns to find a boy aged about five, in woolly jumper and short trousers. He has a scrappy terrier on a bit of string and is standing by the mounted head of a lion, in the middle of her theatrical clutter. He says, 'Why is he only a head? Where's the rest of him?'

'He's only a head so he can hang on the walls of my house,' says Cristabel. 'My grandfather shot him.'

'Oh,' says the boy, stroking the lion's muzzle thoughtfully. 'I would like to put my teacher's head on a wall. Or Hitler's head. My mum says he's a devil. What's all this stuff?'

Cristabel takes a last, gritty gulp of tea and stands up, saying, 'We used to use it in our plays. A long time ago. Thought I might as well turn it out while I'm here. I've bugger all else to do.'

'I've never seen a play,' says the boy.

'I used to put on my own plays when I was your age,' Cristabel replies. 'We used to use a bed sheet as a stage curtain. Wait, I'll show you.'

She rummages among the costumes and pulls out a velvet cloak, then she finds some twine in the barn, which she strings between the whalebones. She is draping the cloak over the twine when a woman's voice calls, 'There you are, Norman!'

Cristabel turns to see a woman who looks like a tall Betty Brewer coming towards them. One of Betty's younger sisters, she feels sure. The one that married a farmer. The woman is wearing a tin helmet and a smart, faintly official coat, with an armband.

'Oh, it's you, Miss Cristabel,' the woman says. 'We had a report of some unusual activity on the beach. You aren't signalling anybody, are you?'

'No. Sorry. Nothing like that. Joyce, isn't it?'

'That's right, and I see you've met my Norman. I hope he isn't plaguing you. What is it you're up to now, Miss Cristabel? I thought you was off on service somewhere.'

'I'm in the First Aid Nursing Yeomanry. On leave at the moment.'

'First aid? That's sensible. You never know when you might need first aid. You must give us a talk at the village hall, if you've time. We're always looking for speakers.'

'Is that the new hall?'

'Certainly is,' says Joyce. 'We'll be putting on our first pantomime this Christmas, all being well.'

Norman pipes up. 'The first aid lady knows about plays.'

'Course you do,' says Joyce. 'You did them here, didn't you? I remember hearing about them. They said people would come all the way from London to watch.'

'Did you ever see one?' asks Cristabel.

Joyce laughs. 'Not the kind of thing I would be invited to. Although Betty – your Auntie Betty, Norman – she was sometimes in them. She was allowed to keep one of her costumes when she was a fairy, and it was a gorgeous thing. None of us can get into it now, more's the pity.'

'*A Midsummer Night's Dream*,' says Cristabel. 'We did sell tickets. You didn't have to be invited.'

'Well, if you have the time or the inclination, Miss Cristabel, we would be very grateful to have your professional opinion of our little pantomime. The Christmas committee meets Thursdays, after the whist drive, so do pop by. I'll let them know we've spoken.'

Cristabel smiles vaguely.

'If I come here again, can you do a play for me?' says Norman.

'Norman!' says Joyce.

'I will,' Cristabel says, 'so you should come here again.'

'Please don't put yourself out on his account, Miss Cristabel,' says Joyce, taking her son by the hand.

'What do you think should be in the play, Norman?' says Cristabel.

Norman thinks. 'Creatures that eat people?'

'Very well,' she says.

Cristabel watches them depart – Joyce in her helmet, Norman and his dog – then looks at the whalebones, half concealed by the crumpled cloak as if wearing a disguise. She shouldn't have said she would do a show for the boy. She can't do it all by herself. Although, if the cloak was a bed sheet, she could shine a torch through it and do some sort of simple shadow puppet performance. He might like that.

It's not an altogether bad idea. Perhaps she could use hurricane lamps, to cast shadows from different angles. Possibly some sound effects, like those in radio plays. She could put on the show at dusk, so the shadows stood out more clearly, and notify the Home Guard too, so she didn't get arrested. If only Digby was here, he could do some of the voices, and then the thought of him falls across her, eclipsing everything. She closes her eyes, waiting for the pain to pass. She isn't even sure if it is pain, it could be terror, it could be fury, but she cannot yet bring herself to look at it, to identify its separate parts.

After some time, Cristabel opens her eyes. The sun is above the cliffs now and moving slowly into the theatre. She must go back to the house soon; she has eaten nothing and is hollow with hunger. But first, a quick rummage in the barn, to see if there is anything she can use.

The Christmas Committee

December, 1943

Up at Chilcombe, Cristabel still sleeps in the icy attic though other bedrooms are vacant. On one particularly freezing night, she traipses through the house wrapped in a blanket, inspecting the other rooms. To enter Willoughby's room feels like trespassing, while Rosalind's old room now bears Flossie's mark: headscarves draped on a chair and a decrepit elephant waiting in a corner. Digby's room is dark and unwelcoming, the curtains drawn, dusty fir cones in the fireplace.

She even looks in the guest rooms, with their floral quilts and dried flower arrangements, mute and tidy as well-kept graves, but it feels ridiculous to sleep in one of those. In the end, she pulls an ancient army greatcoat of Willoughby's from under the stairs and sleeps wearing it, back in the attic.

Cristabel had seen Flossie, Betty and Mr Brewer when she first returned from London but has the sense that their lives only briefly diverted to greet her, and now continue without her. Betty and Mr Brewer are both busy with the village Christmas preparations, and Flossie is rarely back from Dorchester. Occasionally, she discovers the three of them laughing over cups of tea in the kitchen, sharing jokes and local gossip, and feels awkward in their company, aware of alliances, habits, formed without her.

She is increasingly conscious too of the pall of silence she carries with her, the fact that she can say nothing of where she has been or what she has been up to, and she certainly cannot share what she has heard about Digby or the churning mix of emotion his name now produces. It feels like a peg leg she drags behind her: a handicap they are all, in some way, aware of, but cannot bring themselves to mention. She is Ahab pacing the deck of his ship, with his *ribbed and dented brow*, his *unsleeping, ever-pacing thought*.

Any questions about what she has been doing on service are met with brusque dismissals: 'Nothing much.' 'The usual.' But they know her well enough to know that these snapped answers are a shield, even if they cannot fully imagine what lies behind them.

Her mind is riddled with thoughts of Digby. She feels sick with fear that he has been captured. To imagine the methods of torture she knows the Gestapo use – the ones she heard of in training – being administered to her brother, makes her frantic, almost frenzied. She fears she will go out of her mind purely to avoid staying in her mind with such imaginings.

But there is an anger within her too. Anger that her own war has come to an abrupt end. She knows Digby is loyal to a fault and would be mortified to know he had caused this, but whatever the reason, she has been sent home, and not because of anything she has done, but because of someone else. This injustice seethes in a tight knot in her chest.

It appals her to think there may be a question mark by her name. That Sophie or Henri or the other agents may hear of her return from France and wonder if she is a traitor, the worst of all possible things to be, when she had been determined to succeed. At night, she wakes herself up shouting in her sleep.

When she stalks the cliffs near Chilcombe, she can sometimes see, in the distance, peculiar military vehicles moving through the shallow waters off Weymouth Beach – amphibious machines, like a cross between a boat and a truck. There are increasing numbers of American troops setting up camp in the woods on the Ridgeway, and Mr Brewer says they are evacuating an entire village further along the coast to use the area for military training. They are preparing for the invasion of Europe, she feels certain, right on her doorstep, and she can only watch.

When Cristabel arrives at Chilcombe Mell's new red-brick village hall, she finds it full of children lined up along trestle tables, diligently painting newspapers to make paper chains and tying ribbons around sprigs of holly, overseen by several young women. A further group of about eight women, aged between thirty and seventy, are seated around a table near the stage, talking animatedly. Several are knitting, one is acting as scribe. She presumes this must be the Christmas committee.

Cristabel approaches the table and introduces herself. At the word 'Seagrave' they all begin to get to their feet. There is a fluttering of polite gestures: offers of seats, offers of tea. Someone scuttles off to find another chair. Cristabel, unwilling to take a seat, finds herself standing beside a table of women uncertain where to position themselves in relation to her. Eventually, Joyce sits back down, and the others follow her lead, apart from the one who departed to find an extra chair, who remains upright behind it, holding it with both hands like a footman.

'Joyce told me you were looking for some assistance, with your Christmas production,' says Cristabel, feeling like a teacher addressing a table of students. She notices they are glancing at her old trousers, her muddy boots.

'As I'm sure you know, Miss Cristabel is from the manor,' says Joyce to the committee. 'They have the outdoor theatre, down by the beach. She has experience in dramatic matters.'

The committee makes polite noises of interest. One of the older women says, 'I remember your father. He put on a show of fireworks one New Year's Eve.'

'Did he,' says Cristabel.

Another woman says, 'What brings you back to Chilcombe, Miss Seagrave? We heard you were away on service.'

'I was,' she says. 'I wish I still was. But I'm not.'

There is an awkward pause, then a younger woman asks, 'I don't suppose you have any costumes, Miss Cristabel? Nobody has any clothes to spare, these days. I mean, nobody in the village.'

'I found a few trunks of costumes only recently,' says Cristabel, trying to sound more agreeable. 'You must come and take a look.'

There are noises of grateful surprise, a note made on a list.

'Have you had your hair cut, Miss Cristabel?' enquires Joyce. 'There's a different look about you.'

'I did it myself. Rather a hatchet job, I'm afraid. It was getting on my nerves.'

'Very practical, I'm sure, for when you get back to your first aid duties. Norman! Those berries are poisonous.'

'Let me say to you all,' says Cristabel, 'I have no desire to interfere with your pantomime. I'm merely here to offer my support, as Joyce requested.'

Joyce chuckles. 'Oh, we don't need you to interfere, Miss Cristabel. Everything's ticking along. I simply thought you might have a few words of advice. But we don't expect you to bother yourself with a village pantomime, goodness no.'

Cristabel frowns. 'I didn't mean to imply that a pantomime was beneath me. I heartily applaud your efforts. Community theatre is to be celebrated.'

There is a silence. The women look down at the table, hanging determinedly on to their polite smiles. 'Costumes would be a great help,' says Joyce.

'I have stage lights too, if you have a power source – and you surely do, in this modern hall,' says Cristabel.

Another note is made on a list and Cristabel finds herself walking purposefully in the direction of the kitchen, as if to make an inspection of the hall's electrical wiring systems, and there finds Norman spitting holly berries into the sink, which provides her with a useful excuse to remain in the kitchen for a few moments, trying to think of a way to politely leave.

'Are you sure you don't fancy a peek at the script?' enquires Joyce, coming in to fill the kettle. 'We've gone with *Cinderella*, but popular songs, so there's something for everyone.'

'Sounds marvellous,' Cristabel replies.

'Perhaps you could do something at your theatre for the children, like you did for Norman.'

'Yes, perhaps,' she replies, making her way towards the door. 'Do let me know if I can be of any more help, Joyce. My sister Flossie is usually available too.'

'Oh, we know Miss Flossie,' says Joyce. 'In fact, you can tell her that my husband has found her an elusive ham, at long last. She had her heart set on having one at Christmas.'

Later that week, Cristabel is reading a newspaper in the kitchen, when Flossie comes in through the back door.

'Hello, Floss,' she says. 'Joyce in the village says they have found you a ham.'

'Wondrous news!' exclaims Flossie, who is in her Land Army garb, looking as corduroyed and rubber-booted as a young farmer.

'Don't we normally get one from the butcher?' asks Cristabel, putting down the paper. She is wearing a woollen hat and gloves, as the temperature has dropped below zero and even the kitchen is barely habitable.

'We don't have a butcher any more,' replies Flossie. 'He was called up last year. One has to scrape and beg to get any meat at all, these days.'

'Couldn't Perry sort you out? I was thinking of getting in touch with him, so I could ask.'

'Worth a go,' says Flossie, who has picked up the cat to nuzzle him. 'Betty and I have been dutifully saving our rations all year so we will have a few treats. Can't have Christmas without treats. Have you had a look in the larder?'

Cristabel walks out of the kitchen and along the corridor to the stone-flagged Aladdin's cave of the larder, where she finds shelves lined with home-made pickles and jams, glowing gems of jars, each one carefully labelled by Flossie with its contents and date of creation – *Summer Berry Jam, 15th August 1943* – as if the day itself, its light and life, were safeguarded inside.

'Haven't I been productive?' calls Flossie from the kitchen, where she has turned on the radio and is humming along with the music.

Cristabel carefully runs a finger along the lineage of preserves: *Quince Jelly, Rose Hip Marmalade, Damson Jam*. On the floor below are glass bottles containing blue-black liquid marked *Elderberry Wine*. She says, 'I didn't know you knew how to do all this, Floss.'

'Neither did I,' comes the cheerful reply, then Flossie singing the opening lines of 'Silver Wings In The Moonlight'.

'I'm going for a walk soon, if you want to tag along,' says Cristabel.

'Would love to, but Betty has bagsied me already – we're hunting mistletoe.'

'Righto,' says Cristabel. She straightens one of the jars, then leaves the larder, heading up the stairs to the main house, where she stands for a moment in the dusty pomp of the Oak Hall, next to the empty suit of armour.

She has, of course, spent time away from Chilcombe before the war, but had never envisaged she might one day return to her family seat and feel somewhat excluded, surplus to requirements. She shakes her head and walks into her father's study. She will write another letter to her superior officers, requesting again that she be sent back into France, reminding them of her excellent reports from training.

She will write the letter and run down to the post office, keep herself fit, keep herself ready. That is what she will do, she thinks, standing in the cold room, surrounded by pictures of horses and stories of battle.

Riven by a Tempest

December, 1943

Cristabel instructs the Brewers to spend Christmas Day with their relatives in the village, telling them there is no point in them being at Chilcombe because there is nothing for them to do. Flossie is attending a Land Girl lunch at a Dorchester hotel, and might come back in the afternoon if she is still capable of cycling, which seems unlikely, and Maudie is staying in Weymouth.

Before she leaves, Betty hovers in the kitchen doorway with a plucked chicken, watching Cristabel light a cigarette from the stove, and says, 'Are you sure you'll be all right?'

'How hard can it be?' says Cristabel, taking the chicken from her hands. 'I put it in the oven and take it out again.'

'I won't respond to that, Miss Cristabel, because it is the season of goodwill,' says Betty.

Cristabel rummages in her pocket and hands Betty a bar of French lavender soap, wrapped in decorative paper. 'Happy Christmas.'

'My word, I haven't seen soap like this for years.'

Cristabel has another bar for Flossie, which she puts on the kitchen table, thinking of the French woman who gave it to her, a young nurse who had sheltered her in the mountains before she left, pressing it into her hands saying it was a gift from France. She wonders if the woman is still alive – the newspapers are reporting the collaborationist Vichy Government in France is set on 'crushing the hooligans' of the Resistance.

On Christmas morning, Cristabel eyes the chicken, its white puckered flesh, then puts it in the larder where the cat can't attack it. The house is silent and cold. A solitary Christmas, she thinks, and the thought is almost pleasing, until she wonders what kind of Christ-mas Digby is having, and all the dark imaginings come rushing back.

She frantically shakes the thoughts from her head until she is surrounded by nothing but the sound of the empty house. The kitchen clock. The wind outside. She cannot imagine anyone else has spent Christmas alone in Chilcombe. The festivities of the past were probably grand affairs, filled with voluminous dresses and well-wishing and do-gooding, keeping up traditions, keeping up appearances. So many things must be kept up, and so much energy spent doing so, as if they were bearers carrying the house and its customs on a palanquin. It is a mercy that she need only do what she wants.

Cristabel picks up the radio and carries it to the Oak Hall. She wants to be able to hear it in the attic, where she is going to sort through old clothes to see if there's anything that might be of use to the women in the village. The furniture in the hall is now covered with old sheets, as the tarpaulin that covers the hole in the roof keeps flapping loose, letting rain blow in. She balances the radio on the shrouded piano, plugs it in and twiddles the dial until the sound of distant cathedral choristers comes crackling through.

When she comes back down, carrying a stash of clothing, the drums are rolling on the radio for the national anthem and then it is the King himself, in his grandfatherly voice, talking to the British Commonwealth and Empire, and its gallant allies. *Today, of all days in the year, your thoughts will be in distant places and your hearts with those you love.*

The weather outside is growing worse, gusting winds and heavy rain. Cristabel knows without looking it is two days until the full moon but suspects even the brave Moon Squadrons would not dare attempt a flight tonight. She unplugs the King and takes him down to the kitchen, where he resumes his speech. *Home and all that home means*, he says through a sudden cloud of buzzing static, *riven by a tempest such as it has never yet endured.*

*

When Flossie returns late that afternoon, she finds Chilcombe empty and a fuzzy radio loudly broadcasting Christmas messages from members of the services stationed in Ceylon. After a search of the house and grounds, she discovers Cristabel in the barn by the sea, covered in old sacks, a bottle of brandy at her side.

'What are you doing here, Crista? I've been looking for you everywhere,' Flossie says, shaking out her umbrella.

Cristabel opens one eye. 'Would you believe it's warmer in here than it is in the attic?'

'Why aren't you at home? It's Christmas Day.' The noisy rain on the barn roof is making Flossie's head hurt. She had been hopeful there might be hot food waiting for her at the house to soak up the alcohol she'd had at lunch.

'I've been sorting things out,' says Cristabel.

'Are you tipsy? You don't normally drink brandy. What's all this on the floor?'

'Shadow puppets. I've been making them. I might do a show for the village children. Don't worry, I won't let anyone touch your vegetables.'

'Are you all right, Crista? Have you heard from Digby at all? I thought we might hear from him at Christmas.'

Cristabel gets to her feet, staggers slightly. 'No, nothing,' she says, folding her arms. 'I was thinking, isn't it funny that we used to call you the Veg, and now you love vegetables.'

'I don't think that's funny,' says Flossie. 'Where's Betty?'

'In the village. I didn't think you would be back today.'

Flossie sighs. 'I'm not going to leave you on your own at Christmas, even if I have to cycle through a gale to get here, which I did.'

'I don't mind being on my own.'

'Well, I don't want you to be. There might only be us here, but that doesn't mean we can't have a lovely time,' Flossie says, putting up her umbrella. 'I'm going back to the house to eat ham. Will you join me?'

Cristabel rubs her forehead. 'I will. There's a chicken too. Betty left it.'

'I know,' says Flossie, tucking her arm in her sister's. 'I've put it in the oven. What have you done to your hair? You look like Joan of Arc.'

Across the bay, a storm is blowing in. On the far side of Chesil Beach, the side which takes the brunt of the weather, the churning water is marbled white and grey, roaring up the pebbles and seething back. These are big American rollers, come all the way across the Atlantic to hurl themselves at the beach in an extravagant tumble, a bruising, bullying bluster.

In Chilcombe's candlelit kitchen, the table is covered with the scattered pieces of home-made crackers and the carcass of a chicken. Cristabel, dozing in an armchair by the stove, drifts in and out of an elderberry-wine-soaked reverie.

When Cristabel dreams, she dreams of the whale. She dreams she stands on Chesil Beach, on the wet mountain of pebbles, above the turmoil of waves, watching as the whale approaches from the ocean, water streaming from its flanks in long white ribbons. She sees it dive beneath the bank like a submarine, and watches as its great barnacled back reappears on the other side, heading across the bay to where she sleeps and waits.

C to D

Boxing Day, 1943

D,

I have no reason to write this letter. I cannot send it anywhere. I simply have a pencil and a notebook, and when I have a pencil and a notebook, I write to you.

I sometimes feel I speak most clearly to you when I talk to you in my head as I am walking by the sea. Then, at other times, I feel I am only ever talking to myself, that I comfort myself by addressing a fictional you, as if I alone am rehearsing a play for two people.

This may be nonsense. I am monstrously hung-over.

I know you know I think of you always, because it seems to me you live in my mind and when you return, I won't need to tell you anything at all, because you have been here all along. Don't tell me that's not true. I won't believe it for a moment.

C

ACT FIVE

1944–1945

Higher Tiers

Cristabel is finally summoned back to Baker Street in the first week of the New Year. It is a bitter day in London, a few flakes of snow drifting from a heavy sky. Inside Org HQ, she is guided to a sparse briefing room lit only by a bare light bulb hanging from the ceiling and hears her stepmother's voice: *Lamps, darling, never overhead lights. So ageing. Practically mummifying.*

Her briefing is as polite and functional as she expected it would be. Had there been carpets in the building rather than cheap lino, she imagines a great deal would be swept beneath them. They tell her nothing has been heard from her missing cousin, but it is recognized that Gilberte is an efficient operator and there is no reason to further delay her return to the field. Their innocuous approach makes her suspect her return may simply be due to the fact they need more agents. She reminds herself that, as Perry once said, it's a question of numbers.

'You have already delayed my return to the field,' she replies, 'but needless to say, I'm eager to get started on whatever my next mission may be. I hope there are no question marks over my integrity.'

They shake their heads and talk of *protocols* and she recognizes in their stiff smiles the same sense of exasperation she feels, which suggests they too have exhausted the list of possible reasons for Digby's silence – Digby trapped and unable to communicate; Digby suffering some kind of injury or nervous collapse; Digby forced to work for the Germans under duress; Digby happily working for the Germans hoping for a Nazi victory – and come up with nothing concrete, so have turned to more pressing matters. She personally has dismissed the last option, but all else remains possible.

'Just so we're clear,' she says, 'do you believe my cousin might pose any risk to our operations in France?' It is easiest to discuss him in this objective way, as a professional issue to be assessed like any other.

They blink and say no, they are hopeful that is not the case. All reports from his training schools emphasized his loyalty to his fellow agents. Besides, there is *the bigger picture* to consider now. Cristabel nods, thinking of the increasing number of troops arriving in Dorset. She had noticed too, on her way to the briefing room, that there are camp beds set up in many of the partitioned offices, and the rooms containing the most high-ranking officers – the steely-eyed colonels and brigadiers – have a stream of visitors waiting outside. Those inside never come out, she hears only the occasional barked instruction: 'Come!'

A secretary is dispatched, and several cardboard files are brought to the briefing room. The secretary is asked to leave and to close the door behind her. A map of Northern France is unfolded on the table.

'The other possibility is that Digby has gone native,' says Perry, when they meet for a drink after her briefing. He has chosen a dark Victorian pub in Whitehall, filled with pipe smoke and coughing old men in black suits: MPs, civil servants, the dry machinery of power. A monochrome backdrop into which Perry in his uniform blends imperceptibly. Cristabel enjoys it, despite herself, this exclusive sense of being in among them, wearing a uniform of her own.

She had contacted Perry, ostensibly to ask about foodstuffs for Flossie, and ended up suggesting a New Year drink, thinking he might be someone she could talk to about Digby. Perry had suggested Digby join the Org, after all, and was someone who understood undercover work. She also suspected he might already know far more about the situation in Paris than she did, given his access to higher tiers of information.

Perry continues, 'Always a risk, using untrained personnel for covert missions. No surprise that some of them might go off piste. Invisibility can be intoxicating to the uninitiated.' His chalk-white face is lit by the winter light slanting through the frosted window; he seems more remote than ever, austere as a saint, a cipher of a man.

'We aren't untrained,' Cristabel replies.

'Four months, wasn't it? Between your recruitment and your deployment. Although I suppose it might do for the kind of short-term role the Org want you to perform.'

'It's no walk in the park,' says Cristabel. 'We have to liaise with an increasing number of Resistance groups, each with their own opinion of how the war should be won.'

'Another matter far too delicate to entrust to beginners. It's a basic rule of security that every time you increase your network, you increase your chances of discovery,' says Perry. 'Or, as my old mentor used to put it, three can keep a secret if two of them are dead.'

'You recommended Digby to work in France,' she says.

'He speaks French – he's what they wanted.'

Cristabel sips her drink. 'But you wouldn't use him yourself.'

Perry shakes his head. 'Digby is too much his mother's son.'

Cristabel has an image then, of the photograph Rosalind kept by her bed, of her and Digby, their fine-boned faces held together, twinned in beauty like a pair of cats.

Perry rocks the whisky in his glass. 'There are those for whom it is natural to identify all available exits as soon as they enter a room. I believe you may have become expert at this even before your current role, given your intense dislike of social engagements.'

'There's a double door at three o'clock to me that opens on to the street,' says Cristabel, 'and a door that leads to the loos at eleven. There's a service door behind me, at roughly seven o'clock, but I suspect that goes down to the cellars, and an archway behind the bar leading to a back room.'

'I cannot imagine that your cousin has ever thought to look for the exits, or consider why they might be prudent,' says Perry. 'His mother was similarly afflicted.'

'There was an instructor in Scotland who told us Churchill sleeps beneath a map showing all the possible invasion points of England, so his first thought on waking is to remember the threats we face,' says Cristabel.

Perry raises his glass. 'He's a stubborn bugger, but he knows how to fight a war.'

Cristabel drinks, then says, 'You wouldn't have suggested Digby if you thought he was a risk.'

'I believed he had a chance of succeeding,' says Perry. 'He has a certain charisma. Besides, he told me himself he wanted a change from tanks. With his love of the limelight, I thought he'd enjoy that noisy work your lot specialize in.'

'Noisy?'

'Blowing things up. Not how an intelligence organization should operate, in my view.'

'I imagine you are about to tell me how it should operate, and that will be based on the work that your lot do.'

'Quite right,' he says. 'We have people working undercover who will be there long after your lot have gone home to loud applause and newspaper articles. You will never know their names, but they are vital.'

'What do they do?'

Perry strokes his hand across the polished table as if smoothing it. 'They gather intelligence. Isn't that a beautiful phrase? Blueprints. Timetables. Paperwork. It is in the paperwork of an empire that we find its weaknesses.'

'What we do raises morale. It means the French know they're not alone.'

'Cristabel, it's all very well to have a gaggle of wine-soaked Frenchmen up a hill ready to fire guns when the Allies arrive, but unless we know the exact whereabouts of German coastal defences, the Allies have no chance of arriving.'

She concedes his point. 'Both, then. Both are important.'

'For now,' he replies, 'but the morale of the French peasantry is unlikely to be a priority after the war. Which is why your organization will come to an end once we are victorious. Somewhat ironic, to think you are working towards your own demise.'

'You don't know that.'

'It's been agreed. At the highest levels.' He gestures to the men sitting around them. 'There's no need for two intelligence organizations. Yours will go – and what will you do then?'

Cristabel looks around at the inhabitants of those rarefied levels. She cannot imagine they are often asked what they will do next.

Their ascendancy appears as simple as riding an escalator, from public school to Oxbridge to Sandhurst to the City or Parliament, grouse shooting, fly fishing, picking up a wife as one might collect dry cleaning, sons, port, cigars, the dark red rooms of self-interested decisions.

Whereas she is always stopped and queried. A series of roadblocks, identification checks. Reminders she is not where she ought to be.

'I don't think beyond the war,' she says. 'I think about my friends in France. The peasantry.'

Perry's mouth twitches. He has always been irritated by the French and this has been exacerbated by his dislike of de Gaulle, who – right on cue – he begins to talk about now, saying de Gaulle is impossibly arrogant, an exiled general who acts as if he had an army at his command, rather than a borrowed apartment in Mayfair and an occasional slot on the BBC.

Cristabel has more sympathy for the isolated Frenchman. She knows that an unwillingness to bend can sometimes be your best, your only, weapon.

'He gives them hope,' she says.

'He gives them an illusion,' sniffs Perry.

'Hope is an illusion,' she replies. 'That's why it's powerful.' She sees him look at his watch, and says quickly, 'Perry, your undercover people, might they know where Digby is and what he's doing?'

'France is not my department,' he says, and she sees he has somehow removed himself, shut himself off like an owl. She is aware then of an isolation in Perry, something he has always kept close to himself. Something small and once alive, held in a clawed hand that no longer registered it held anything.

She says, 'If I asked you, could you find out?'

He regards her. 'Are you going to ask me?'

Cristabel feels this is a moment he has been expecting and has already weighed up; she has a sense of him waiting on the other side of the question. She knows too, sharply, with a sensation that feels wrenching, that she cannot allow herself to be beholden to him, even if he can tell her about Digby.

'Why would I need to ask, Uncle Perry?' she says. 'I'm sure if your agents have any information about a British operative, they would share it with us, as a matter of course.'

His smile is milky as venom. 'Uncle,' he says. Then, 'Disingenuousness does not suit you, Cristabel.'

She says nothing, feels squirmily guilty, childlike.

He says, 'I have an appointment at White's. I would invite you, but I can't. It's a gentlemen's club.' He stands up, brushes down his jacket. 'Very particular about who it admits. Poor Master Kovalsky must wait outside, like a faithful hound. You'll be all right on the Tube, won't you?'

Cristabel makes her way down to the Tube to travel to the Bloomsbury hotel booked by the Org, where she will be staying until it is time to go to the airfield. The train is musty and half empty; a stout businessman dozes in the seat opposite her. She picks up his discarded newspaper and, as the train roars through its black tunnels, reads about the partisan fighters holding out, against expectation, in Yugoslavia and those harrying the Germans in Poland and the Balkans. She thinks of all those who are, at that moment, hiding in ruined buildings, holding borrowed guns in sweating hands, mouthing final prayers.

She scans the small ads. The births, marriages, deaths. Lost at sea. Killed on active service. Parents appealing for information of sons in POW camps. Coins and medals bought for cash. Frigidaires and fur coats for sale. A young widow seeks support for her children. A society clairvoyant hopes her friends and clients will have a peaceful and victorious 1944.

At the bottom of the page, an advertisement:

FUTURE REQUIRED
   Young Army Officer will require a situation on cessation of hostilities that calls for energy, resourcefulness and organizing ability
   Write Box M557, *The Times*, EC4

She realizes then what she should have told Perry. That speculating about the future is a luxury allowed to those who assume they have one. The train rattles into her station. She leaves the newspaper beside the sleeping businessman and heads to her temporary home.

My Dear Lads

Cristabel had always wanted her life to be a story. In every one of her beloved Henty adventure books, there had been an introductory letter from the author that began 'My Dear Lads'. It gave her the feeling of being in a club – a club bound for great things. Henty never talked down to his lads. They were as familiar with life's certainties as he was: that the British Empire was the finest in the world, but there was courage to be found on all sides, because, dear lads, we all have battles to fight.

Apart from Uncle Willoughby, Henty was the first person to address her with affection. He was the first to insist upon the importance of her own behaviour and the first to suggest that she could leave an impression on the world, which meant that she existed.

Because of this, whenever she now tucks her military pistol into its holster or zips up her camouflage parachute suit, she feels solemn and justified, as if she is finally inhabiting her rightful story. After all, the world Henty described was one that constantly seethed with wars, where a plucky lad need only hop aboard a brig and cross the ocean to find himself military attaché to the Prussian Army, or leading a musket platoon through the dawn mist, and young Cristabel had marched alongside them, wooden sword held high.

But alongside that feeling of rightfulness, there is an unease too, a slight embarrassment. She is discomforted by a nagging sense that by stepping into her story she might somehow be seen. Because the imagined place of the child within the story does not show the child herself. Because had the Duke of Wellington or Admiral Nelson ever looked down and seen that a small girl had joined their forces, that girl would have been sent home.

She has never doubted herself, and sees no reason to start now, but it is becoming clearer that she is where she is – sitting on the floor of a Halifax, bumping through turbulence over Northern France – only thanks to a series of time-limited loopholes. She is an anomaly. The parachute suit she is wearing is not designed for a woman: it is tight across the chest, long in the arms. She does not fit comfortably into this story, and she had always assumed she would, that it would be something she could join as easily as stepping in line with a parade.

That was how it had felt, during training in Scotland, and her first mission in France: that she was marching in line with others. But now, after seeing how quickly she could be discarded if the Org took against her, and after talking to Perry, she is not so sure. Perry is probably right to say that the Org won't exist after the war, and even if it does, it's hardly likely to keep her on, to let her climb the ranks, become a brigadier.

She wraps her arms around her knees and frowns. It is disconcerting to consider it like this, and equally disconcerting to discover that it hurts. But Uncle Willoughby always told her you should never bother yourself with what the top brass are up to, just worry about the man in front of you and the one behind.

As she pulls on her jump helmet, she wonders what Henty himself would have made of her, had they ever met. She imagines his slight puzzlement at the sight of a woman in military clothing, followed by a hearty greeting. He was, after all, from a time when men were referred to as giants and their way of addressing the world was to boom over its heads. How much she had wanted that sturdy voice; someone to tell her that she was right.

The dispatcher pulls open the hatch and lets fly with armfuls of British propaganda leaflets, whirling into the darkness like confetti. He shouts, 'Visibility's getting worse.'

Cristabel edges forward, so he can clip her parachute line to the fuselage, and peers down through the hatch on to a grey layer of cloud. She can see nothing: no roads, no fields, no reception committee. She will be jumping blind. Wind howls through the rattling plane and her fear rolls itself into a ball in her throat, which she swallows repeatedly, trying to push it back down.

The dispatcher has a shouted conversation with the pilot over the intercom, then shuffles towards her to speak into her ear. 'We can't see anyone down there, but we're not going to get a better chance. You want to give it a go?' She nods. She has already had one failed attempt to get into France in February, she doesn't want another. The dispatcher relays her decision to the pilot, the light goes from red to green, and she jumps before she can change her mind.

The cloud comes rushing up and she braces instinctively, knees up, elbows in, as if it were solid, but she slices straight through it. Her parachute opens with a *whoomph* as she tumbles through the cloud, a damp foggy mass that leaves her spinning and disorientated. Then suddenly, she is falling out the other side and a French hillside comes slamming up to meet her. She lies on her back, winded and gasping, grateful to have landed on earth rather than the roof of Rouen Cathedral. She looks up, but the plane is nowhere to be seen. Her story too has disappeared, and she is back on her own. She pulls herself to her feet.

It takes several hours of trudging through fields and along country lanes – leaping into a ditch every time she hears a car – before she reaches a railway station. From there, she travels to the small Normandy town where she finds the organizer who should have met her when she jumped. He is a no-nonsense Welshman, field name Antoine, and he barely registers her late arrival, leading her immediately out to a storeroom at the back of the garage where he is based. 'It's bloody relentless here,' he says, heaving an ancient bicycle from beneath a pile of cardboard, a man's racer with a high crossbar and drop handles. 'This is yours. Hope you've strong legs. Weighs a ton.'

'I'll manage,' she says. 'Why relentless?'

'Everyone's running out of patience. French and German. All very keen to know when the Allies might appear. We've a flood of new recruits, but none of them know how to hold a gun, and we're so short of wireless operators, our poor girl is sending messages for three different circuits. She never sleeps. Did you bring any uppers? Those tablets are the only thing keeping her alive.'

Cristabel nods. 'She can have mine.'

He rummages in his pockets for a few slips of paper. 'I need you to take some messages to her this evening. Mostly from me to London, and mostly furious. I've had it up to here with badly packed canisters that don't contain anything we need.'

'Where is she?'

He describes the address, then adds, 'I think you might know each other. She said I should look out for a tall English girl with a posh voice as you apparently owe her a few drinks.'

She finds Sophie – field name Sidonie – masquerading as a district nurse and living in a remote stone cottage surrounded by endless rows of apple trees. It is bizarre and wonderful to see a familiar face so far from home. Sophie has already outlasted the wireless operator's expected lifespan of six weeks by several months, but when she hugs her, Cristabel can feel how thin her training companion has become. She has the feverish intensity of someone on borrowed time.

'It's so good to see you,' Sophie says, her eyes shining. 'I can't wait for us to get back home and have that big night out. I think about it all the time. Seeing everyone again.'

'The invasion will come soon,' says Cristabel. 'They're ridiculously busy at HQ.'

'We've heard that for a while now, ducks,' says Sophie. 'The French think Stalin will get here before the Allies do. They say he's going to shout across the Channel to Winston to let him know it's safe to come over.'

'Do they really?'

'They do – and meanwhile, the Gestapo keep themselves busy. They're such bastards, I can't even tell you. But men never take rejection well, do they?'

'I've some messages for you from Antoine,' says Cristabel, rummaging in her pockets. 'They have to go to London tonight.'

Sophie leads Cristabel to an upstairs bedroom where her wireless equipment is hidden inside a narrow chimney. She says she normally works on the hoof, but there are so many messages now, Antoine found her a place to stay, where she can work uninterrupted.

'Been here since January,' she says, lifting the leather suitcase that contains her kit on to a desk. 'Home sweet home.'

'What are these?' says Cristabel, looking at a stash of envelopes tucked behind a clock on the mantlepiece.

'Letters,' she says, 'I thought it might look funny if I stayed here but never got any post, so I've been writing myself some letters. From an imaginary aunt. It's nice to have a bit of company. You can have a read if you want, but she's not much of a writer.'

Cristabel smiles. 'What does she write about?'

'Oh, she has this little son,' says Sophie, sitting at the desk, 'nearly two now, would you believe. She talks about him. What he's up to. That kind of thing. Let's have your messages then.'

Cristabel holds them out silently. Sophie snaps open the two metal clasps of the case, then takes the messages from Cristabel without looking at her.

The wireless is a metal radio set covered with black dials that fits snugly within its custom-made case. Sophie quickly sets it up, plugging in the crystal that determines its frequency and unravelling its aerial, which is a 100-foot length of wire that must be trailed out of the window. Then she takes Cristabel's messages and transcribes them into code, using a pencil and pad she keeps in a hidden compartment in the lid of the case.

This done, she puts on her headphones, pushes up one sleeve so her wristwatch is visible, looks at Cristabel and says, 'You staying?'

They both know that as soon as she begins to tap out a message on her Morse code key, she is putting them in danger. The Gestapo are so adept at tracking radio operators that Sophie must start, transmit, receive, pack up – hauling in the wire, winding it up, putting away the code pad, innumerable fiddly tasks that cannot be rushed – and hide the case in less than twenty minutes before detector vans can pinpoint her location.

Cristabel nods. 'Yes, I'll stay.'

423

Sophie pulls a pistol from a holster hidden under her blouse and hands it to Cristabel. Cristabel moves to the window and looks out over the orchard to the open countryside. A clear line of sight. She thinks of all the messages Sophie must send without anyone looking out for her and feels a spike of anxiety. She knows a wireless operator's work is dangerous, but it is one thing to know it, and another to see how isolated her friend is, how far from help.

Sophie puts her finger on the Morse key and begins to transmit Antoine's messages. Cristabel can hear, very faintly, the pizzicato beeping of code. During training, Cristabel had found the rapid dots and dashes impossible to follow.

'Don't count,' Sophie used to say, 'listen. It's like a song. *Dah dah didy didit.*'

Cristabel looks at her now. Sophie has closed her eyes to hear the code come singing through the airwaves, pencil poised above her notepad. The Org call their operators 'pianists' and the name suits them: it is delicate, vulnerable, listening work. Those skilled at it are so prized they are usually shuttled from place to place to keep them safe, travelling separately from their equally valuable sets, which are carried for them by couriers, and reuniting in anonymous locations, like forbidden lovers. But Sophie and her set have made a home here together. Cristabel notes the box of matches on the mantlepiece, the black papery ashes of burnt messages in the fireplace. She kicks at the grate to disperse them.

Sophie pulls her headphones off and passes Cristabel a decoded message as neatly written as homework. 'You best get going, ducks,' she says. 'There's a drop tonight. One person, five containers.' Then she begins the process of packing away her equipment.

'The WAAF girls in the receiving station compete to take your messages,' Cristabel tells her, as she helps Sophie fit the suitcase back into the chimney.

'Do they? That's nice,' says Sophie, looking pleased. 'I forget there's girls there. I only ever think of it as "London" – one person, doesn't say much, probably a bloke.'

'They say you have magic fingers,' says Cristabel, handing back the pistol. 'You never make a mistake.'

'Good to know I'm good for something,' Sophie says, tucking away the weapon, then giving Cristabel another fervent hug. 'Come a long way from Hackney, haven't I?'

'You have,' says Cristabel, nodding. 'You've done very well.'

Sophie kisses her friend on both cheeks. 'It's smashing to have you here,' she says. 'Now get going or Antoine will throw a fit. *À bientôt!*'

Cycling away, Cristabel looks back at the cottage, miles from anywhere, surrounded by the regimented lines of apple trees, growing shadowy in the dusk. She thinks of Sophie carefully burning the notepaper on which she writes her messages, a small flame held in her fingertips.

In the dead of night, Cristabel cycles to the landing site, flying along moonlit lanes on her racer like a breakaway rider in the Tour de France; standing up on the pedals as she climbs hills, hanging over the handlebars on the descent. Antoine has gone on ahead in a baker's van, and she finds him there, on the edge of a field in a group of beech trees, checking his watch, already angry. He says the plane is late and there are too many people waiting to greet it. Cristabel catches a glimpse of a group of young Frenchmen beyond the trees, smoking and talking, guns tucked in their waistbands.

'Why are there so many of them?' she hisses.

'Somebody in the village is bloody leaky,' he says.

By the time they hear the Halifax approaching – a low thrum that steadily becomes louder – the sky is already growing light in the east. Running out across the field in the grey half-light to signal to the pilot feels terribly risky. The white parachutes floating down, swaying leisurely, seem like giant billowing targets. The new arrival – a middle-aged Frenchman greeted enthusiastically by his countrymen – is similarly slow-moving. He cannot be an agent, she thinks, he seems perfectly happy to stand in an open field with a parachute strapped to his back. He even stops to pick up a handful of soil.

'On y va,' says Antoine. 'Vite!'

They hide the containers in the woods, because it is too light to risk taking them anywhere, then bundle the man and his parachute into the back of the baker's van so Antoine can drive him to the nearest railway station, the rest of them following on a motley selection of bicycles. Only Cristabel takes an alternative route and, when she arrives, is shocked to discover they are all still together, standing in a group on the platform. She scans the other passengers. There seem to be a lot of people waiting for this early train, some of whom do not appear to have any luggage.

'This is ridiculous,' she says to Antoine, opening her mirror compact as if to check her face.

He says in a low voice, 'They say they must stay close to him to protect him.'

'Who is he?'

'One of de Gaulle's lackeys,' says Antoine. 'On his way to Paris.'

'Do they want to put a sign around his neck to make sure everybody knows?' she says, snapping the compact shut and putting it into her rucksack.

'Let's get him to the safe house, Gilberte, then we can leave them to it.'

The train comes steaming into the station and the group board it together, heading for the First Class carriage. Antoine follows but sits apart from them, reading a newspaper. Cristabel stands in the corridor of the next carriage where she can see Antoine through the adjoining door. There is a clamour of alarm bells ringing in her head. She can hear herself breathing over the noise of the train moving off.

It only takes three things: the movement of Antoine's newspaper, as he lowers it with deliberate slowness; the fleeting glimpse of a figure in a black raincoat moving through the First Class carriage; and an irate Frenchman raising his voice.

Cristabel pulls down the nearest carriage window as far as it will go. The train is rattling through misty countryside, the sunrise an orange glow on the horizon. There is a shout in First Class, a barked instruction in German. *Hände hoch!* She sees trees coming towards her and grips the rim of the window with both hands, putting one foot up on the window ledge. Glancing back down the train, she sees another group of men pushing their way along the corridor towards her. She lifts her other foot on to the ledge, crouches for a moment, poised in the window like a long-limbed bird. Then a shot rings out and she takes flight.

She shouldn't have landed the way she did, awkwardly on one foot, turning over her ankle in a way that made her shriek with pain. She shouldn't have walked on that injured ankle. She shouldn't have gone back to the place they had just left.

She should have scattered. She should have fled.

She did at least avoid the skyline, hobbling and crouching across the rutted fields, biting her lip to muffle her involuntary cries of pain, lying flat beneath a briar hedge when a German patrol car passed, and staying flat, gripping the soil with her hands. She did at least, when they had moved off, crawl over the earth on her stomach, using elbows and knees, until she could finally make out Sophie's isolated cottage in the distance. And she did at least, when she was close enough to see the front door of the cottage hanging off its hinges, stop. She let herself look at it – a broken tooth in a punched mouth – and she let herself look at it again, then she made herself turn around and crawl away through the apple trees.

Les Enfants Perdus

Cristabel has an address, one she committed to memory sitting in a draughty office in Baker Street. A possible safehouse. A roadside bistro on the outskirts of Rouen that is part of an escape line that smuggles people out of France. She cannot walk all the way there on her injured ankle, the pain is dizzying now, so she takes a chance and waves down a boy driving a horse and cart, spins him an improbable tale of having fallen while out hiking, and offers money if he will give her a lift. He glances at her mud-covered skirt and blouse, but says nothing, just gestures with his head to say she can get into the cart.

As they bump along the narrow lanes, she sees dark smoke rising into the sky behind them: something is burning. The boy glances back, shakes his head, sets the horse at a trot. He drops Cristabel within hobbling distance of the bistro, a half-timbered building with window boxes of geraniums.

Inside, she finds an old woman cleaning glasses. Cristabel recites the meaningless code phrase – *I have visited the countryside with my Uncle Maurice* – and receives the coded reply – *I remember Maurice well* – and that is about all she can stand of conversation. The old woman hurries her through to the stockroom at the back of the bistro where Cristabel takes off her rucksack and sits among crates of empty cider bottles, feeling tears making their way down her face, though she herself stays still and does not make a noise. She leans against a crate, rests her head.

Later, the old woman brings her a dry hunk of bread and tells her that someone will come for her that night. He is a doctor so has a car and a pass that allows him to travel after curfew. When he arrives,

Cristabel is loaded on to the back seat of a small Fiat, told to lie down and covered with a blanket. The doctor, a short man in his fifties with curly hair and a greying beard, gives her a handkerchief and tells her that if they are stopped, she must bite her lip and spit blood into it.

The car journey is slow and steady, and even though Cristabel isn't ill, she feels the floating tranquillity of being a patient, watching the night sky go by from her recumbent position. When they are stopped – once at a Wehrmacht roadblock and once by French militia – and she spits blood, as instructed, the sharp satisfaction of the bite and the red stain on the handkerchief seem very true. The soldiers shine their torches at her in the back seat and she coughs and holds the handkerchief to her mouth so they can see the bloody evidence. She hears the doctor say in a grave tone that he suspects tuberculosis. The soldiers move away, the darkness encloses her, and the car rolls through the night.

At the doctor's house, she is helped inside and put to bed. The doctor gives her something for the pain in her ankle, which has swollen to double its usual size, and says it will help her sleep. She hears him say that a strong dose of painkiller is as good as being tucked up by your grandmother, but she has no reply and no voice to reply with, so closes her eyes.

When she opens them again, she sees wooden beams in the ceiling above her and shafts of golden light coming through gaps in shutters. The light is disorientating, it has the rich slant of evening, and she can hear convivial voices outside. She checks her watch: she has slept through the day. She heaves herself out of bed, hops across the wooden floor to the landing and gingerly makes her way down a narrow set of stairs. She is in a low, long house, with stone walls, large fireplaces and tiled floors. There are a few pieces of old furniture: a scrubbed wood table, a sagging bookcase, a brass lamp.

Stepping outside, holding on to the door frame for balance, she sees the doctor with a handsome woman in her forties, and a girl aged about seven. They are seated around a table underneath a walnut tree, which stands on the edge of a small meadow surrounded by woods. All rise to greet her. 'Come,' says the doctor, 'you must be hungry.'

'I must be going,' she says.

'You can't go anywhere on that ankle,' he says. 'Eat with us, and afterwards, I will look at it. But first, sit. Tell us what we should call you.'

'Claudine,' she says and allows herself to be helped to a seat at the table, which is covered by a white cloth and has a jar of flowers at its centre. The woman, who introduces herself as Wanda, the doctor's wife, busies herself making up a plate of bread and cheese, slices of peppery cured sausage, hard-boiled egg, lettuce, radishes. There is a glass of red wine, pungent and earthy, poured by the doctor – Édouard, he tells her, with a hand on her shoulder – and a toast proposed by Wanda to friendship and victory.

After the meal, Édouard lifts her foot on to a chair and gently examines her ankle. He frowns. 'It could be fractured,' he says. 'We need a splint, and you will have to rest it.'

'It's not safe for me to be here,' she says.

'You can stay in the attic,' he says. 'We keep the radio up there. You won't be the first person we have hidden here, Claudine.'

'Can you find out what happened to my organizer and our wireless operator?' she says in a low voice. 'Antoine and Sidonie. They are British agents.'

'I will make enquiries,' he says. 'But now you must rest. Or have more wine. Both are beneficial. Doctor's orders.'

A few days later, while rebandaging her ankle, Édouard tells her quietly he has heard Sidonie and Antoine were caught due to a local informer. Alerted to the existence of the British agents, the Gestapo had patiently waited until the parachute drop was carried out in order to capture Antoine, those arriving from England, and their useful containers. They then rounded up Sidonie, carried out a brisk series of reprisals – burning farms, shooting civilians – and took their captives to Fresnes, a prison in southern Paris.

Cristabel has heard of Fresnes: it is where they keep Allied agents and Resistance fighters, where they try to make them talk. Her

mind flinches at the thought of what might be done to her colleagues, for she thinks neither would give way easily, but at least
they are alive, for now. She wonders if the Gestapo were watching
Sophie's cottage when she visited. Had they seen her? Or worse,
was she the one who led them there? She feels nauseous considering
it. Was it possible she had let her security lapse?

'Our son also passed through Fresnes last month,' Édouard says
quietly. 'They caught him distributing Resistance leaflets at his
school.'

'Where is he now?'

'Somewhere else, we hope. We do not know. We can but pray.'

'It is hard, not to know,' Cristabel says.

He looks at her. 'It is hard.'

'What will happen to the informer?' she asks, after a moment.

'Nothing yet. I am told she will be taken care of.' His mouth
twists. 'I am never comfortable with that aspect, but they tell me it
is necessary.' He then continues winding the bandage around her
ankle, before adding, 'You should stay here for a while, Claudine.
Until you can walk. We will try to get a message to London to say
you are safe.'

Cristabel stays with them through April and into May. The weather
grows warmer. The first swallows arrive, scything in great arcs
about the house. They hear nothing more of Sidonie and Antoine,
but Édouard uses a contact to send a message back to London via
neutral Switzerland, letting them know that, although her circuit
no longer exists, Claudine has survived – and encouragingly, her
face has not appeared on any wanted posters, suggesting that she
survived unseen.

Despite this, Cristabel changes her appearance, as far as she is
able, dyeing her hair using strong-smelling chemicals acquired by
Wanda, ending up a streaky auburn colour. Wanda finds her different clothes too: summer dresses and cardigans left by a previous
fugitive, someone else who needed to shed their skin.

Hidden in the attic, Cristabel props herself up by the radio to listen to the *messages personnels* on BBC Radio Londres, broadcast

after the six and nine o'clock news. They are surrealist snippets that remind her of Myrtle's poetry – *My gold tiger walks at night, Natalie remains in ecstasy* – but hidden among them are coded messages meant for Resistance groups. These she passes to Wanda and Édouard to share with their network.

Cristabel also suggests that local *résistants* visit her if they require weapons training, and they come almost shyly, as if attending their first dance, with rusty pistols hidden in their satchels. Young farm boys, middle-aged teachers. She takes them out into the meadow, leaning on the wooden crutches Édouard has found her, and has them aim at ancient oak trees, bullets splintering the craggy trunks.

There are no other houses in sight, only cool, spacious woods, and the house itself has a calm, unhurried quality. It lies close to the earth, with a red tiled roof and blue-grey shutters. Swathes of rose-bay willowherb fill the garden, where chickens peck at the dirt. Every morning, Cristabel sees Wanda carefully setting the table for breakfast; Édouard serving his daughter with great tenderness.

Wanda is Polish. A few other émigrés who live nearby often visit in the evenings, sitting at the outdoor table to share scraps of news from their home country or reminisce about their old lives. Sitting in the sun-dappled garden, the war seems like a distant, unfathomable row. A spoilt child's monstrous game. Its thunderous throwing and stamping.

After meals, Édouard's daughter Annick climbs on to his lap, and he adjusts his position to accommodate her, one hand stroking her head, one reaching for his glass of calvados. Cristabel notices that, for both, this arrangement is so familiar as to be almost unconscious. Annick brings with her an old camera she wears round her neck, a battered black Leica, and gazes through the viewfinder as her father talks.

'My girl will be a photographer one day,' Édouard says. 'She wants to capture everything.'

'Or a detective,' Annick says. She turns the camera towards Cristabel.

'Oh, you shouldn't take a photograph of me,' says Cristabel, holding up a hand.

From behind the camera Annick says, 'It hasn't got any film in it. Father will get me a roll when there is some in the shops.'

Édouard catches Cristabel's eye over his daughter's head. 'You will have to come back another time, so she can take your photograph properly.'

'I will,' says Cristabel.

Annick says, 'Claudine fires guns. My brother could fire a gun.'

'He will come home to us soon, God willing,' says Wanda.

'Don't forget, Mama, he is a fast runner,' says Annick. 'The fastest in his class.' She grips the camera, squints through its little blind eye. The shutter closes, opens.

Édouard frequently encourages Cristabel to take part in their after-dinner discussions beneath the walnut tree. 'Tell us what you think, Claudine,' he will say, and although she usually comes up with an excuse as to why she prefers to listen to him, she will later lie in bed, having conversations with herself about what she does think, discovering it is less clear cut than she supposed. It helps take her mind off Sophie and Antoine. Digby too, although he often interrupts her internal debates with chatty opinions of his own.

If they talk about books, Édouard will sometimes leap up to run inside and pull novels from his bookshelf, saying, 'I cannot believe you have not read *Madame Bovary*!'

'I don't read romance,' Cristabel says, remembering the stash of romance novels by Flossie's bed, their gaudy covers. 'It seems so frivolous.'

Édouard cries, 'Frivolous! Romance is risk and passion and all the things that make a life.'

'Without passion we are only machines,' says Wanda, with a look at her husband.

Wanda's statement sounds like something Taras would say, and Cristabel hasn't thought of Taras in a long time. It is a surprise to find him here, at this table in a Normandy wood, although it is a place where he would feel at home. A place where exiles gather to talk of passion.

Cristabel cannot remember ever talking of passion, though she feels she might like to, if she could work out how to begin. She props her chin in her hands and finds that Leon appears in the back of her mind, as if waiting for her in the trees that circle the house. She remembers their closeness in the darkness, how she had felt she could ask him anything. Would she talk about passion to Leon? She tests the word in her mind. Imagines her mouth close to his ear. No, not passion. She would talk to Leon of want.

Looking up, she catches Wanda's gaze and feels flustered, as if uncovered. Wanda smiles.

The men and women who come to the house to learn how to fire guns are keen to do more than shoot trees, but with only a few weapons and no wireless, they are limited. However, Cristabel remembers an Org instructor saying *subversion is one of the most potent weapons to undermine the morale of the enemy* and instructs her band of volunteers in how to carry out small acts of insurrection, activities designed to impede, to slow up, to frustrate. To this end, they cut telegraph lines, puncture fuel tanks, block roads and sabotage railway lines.

But each act of rebellion comes with a risk, and when she joins Édouard, Wanda, Annick and their friends at the table in the garden, where they light candles as the night falls, she feels she is drawing danger towards them like a net.

One afternoon, when they are walking through the woods, Cristabel tells Édouard she is worried about staying with them. 'I don't want anything to happen to any of you.'

He shakes his head. 'No, you must stay.'

'I will find myself a new hiding place, if you don't.'

'You might have discarded your crutches, but you are still limping,' Édouard replies, but seeing her expression, adds, 'I will try to find something.'

They continue slowly in silence for a while, Cristabel hobbling along, until Édouard asks if she knows the French phrase *les enfants perdus* – the lost children. She shakes her head.

'I think of it often,' he says. 'It has a military meaning. It describes a small troop who volunteer to make a dangerous attack. To go first. In Dutch, it is *verloren hoop*. In English, *forlorn hope*. They were not expected to survive, but if they did, they were promoted. It was a chance for those with nothing to lose.'

Édouard looks up at the canopy of trees. 'When my son did not come home, I was sick. I suffered nausea, as one experiences in a boat. As if I could no longer move through the world without being sickened by it. My beloved boy. I became quite maddened by the idea of him walking through the front door. I used to sleep by it, in case I could hear him. In case he couldn't quite make it to the door. I could help him.'

He looks at her. 'I cannot help him, Claudine. But I can help you.' He reaches to grip her hand for a moment, then turns back to the path.

It is when she is sitting in the attic that she hears it. It is a warm evening. The roses that climb the front of the house have started to bloom; they are apricot in colour, many-layered flowers, with a somnolent scent that drifts in through the open window.

Annick is playing in the garden, while Édouard and Wanda are in the kitchen. BBC Radio Londres is softly intoning its nonsensical messages, and Cristabel is sitting cross-legged with her notepad and pencil, having put down *Madame Bovary* in order to concentrate. The bandages have been taken off her ankle, but it still aches, and she is rubbing it with one hand when the announcer says: *Les sanglots longs des violons de l'automne.* The six-word phrase from a poem by Verlaine that means an Allied invasion of Europe is imminent.

For a few seconds, she cannot breathe. She freezes, as if expecting the outside world to explode into rioting around her, but the woods stay silent, there is only birdsong. The radio announcer continues, unperturbed. Cristabel scrambles to her feet and hurtles downstairs. 'Édouard! Wanda! They're coming!'

Let's Face the Music and Dance

May, 1944

Flossie is in the old walled kitchen garden at the back of the house, one third of which is now occupied by a couple of young pigs Betty has acquired from her farming brother-in-law. Mr Brewer has fenced off an area for them to roam about in and constructed an ingenious domed shelter from corrugated iron. The idea is that they will permanently solve the Christmas ham problem, but Flossie, seeing them eagerly trotting to meet her, with their shy eyes and albino eyelashes, prefers not to dwell on this.

She has called them Fred and Ginger and, as she tips a bucket of potato peelings into their pen, she sings to them – tapping her feet in rhythm to the tune – and they grunt happily as they eat: throaty rumblings and little puffs of air. They take such satisfying pleasure in their food.

It is a bright, blowy Saturday in May and Flossie is once again an outsider in her own home. There are now six American officers billeted inside Chilcombe. They are attached to the infantry units camped in the woods on the Ridgeway, up by the burial mounds, where large signs warn:

CIVILIANS ARE FORBIDDEN TO LOITER OR TALK WITH TROOPS!

This does not deter the star-struck village children, who hang about the camp, hoping to be thrown a stick of gum or a packet of Life Savers sweets.

There are so many Americans now, it is as if Dorset has become a giant campsite and car park for the US Army. Despite ongoing efforts to widen roads and strengthen bridges, several large military vehicles have become wedged in narrow villages, and the spring hedgerows are covered with dust as heavy convoys grind up the country lanes.

In order to avoid being spotted by German aircraft, the Americans have covered their vehicles with camouflage netting and squeezed themselves – their troops, their tents and support units – into every available hiding space, every wood, every copse, every leafy lane. If any German planes do appear, all the anti-aircraft guns in and out of range open up with such an intense barrage of fire, the raiders either turn tail immediately or face a rapid immolation.

Flossie does not mind her American lodgers. Despite a tendency to always lean on or lounge across furniture ('It's like they've had their spines removed,' says Betty), they have made themselves popular through their willingness to share exotic treats like evaporated milk and tinned fruit. Their good-natured generosity often reminds Flossie of Hans, although it saddens her that they are made far more welcome than he ever was. They are treated almost as celebrities in the village and have even managed to convert Betty to the joys of AFN radio – the American Forces Network – igniting in her an unexpected enjoyment of the rhythmic jazz of Louis Jordan and Count Basie. ('It's got a bit of pep,' she says, tapping her hand on the kitchen table.)

There are Black American troops camped up in the woods too, although Flossie notices they are segregated from the white troops and carry out different duties. Whenever she cycles back to Chilcombe from her Land Army shifts in Dorchester, she sees them driving supply vehicles about. Betty has told her there have been fights in Weymouth between white and Black troops, and that white American soldiers visiting The Shipwreck tried to insist they should be served before some Black soldiers, but the locals were having none of it. ('Besides,' says Betty, 'the coloured gentlemen have beautiful manners.')

Flossie is conversing with Fred and Ginger when she hears it: the roar of a military motorcycle tearing up the drive. There are always people coming and going from the house, so she knows that if someone has arrived to see her, she will soon be called. After a while, she hears one of the Americans coming through the kitchen, saying, 'I'm sure she won't object, she's a doll. Why here she is, you can ask her yourself.'

The motorcycling visitor is in duffle coat and dark trousers, the type worn by officers in the navy. He is sturdy and fair, clean-shaven and square-faced.

'Ask me what?' says Flossie, turning to face them, wiping her hands on her dungarees.

'If we could use your lawns,' says the man. He has a Scottish accent and a steady gaze.

'Use them for what?'

'Games,' he says. 'Rugby. Football –'

'Baseball,' says the American.

'Tug of war. Anything really,' says the visitor. 'We're looking for a space where our men and the American troops can enjoy a little outdoor recreational activity. A way of keeping up morale. Any breakages, we'd be sure to pay for.'

'I don't see why not,' says Flossie. 'There are a few fields you could use too, if you could find someone to mow them.'

'We could get our boys to do that,' says the American.

'That would be kind,' says the Scottish officer. 'One more question. I happened to notice you have a gramophone in the hall upstairs.'

'I do.'

'I've been carrying around a set of records since the war began, hoping for an opportunity to put on a musical evening. I don't suppose you'd be willing to –'

'Lend you my gramophone?'

'I was thinking you might host it here,' he replies. 'If it wasn't too much of an imposition.'

Flossie thinks for a moment. 'We'd have to have a clean-up. The place is covered with dust and there's a hole in the ceiling.'

'Our boys could help with that too,' says the American.

'Very well then,' she says, and holds out her hand to the motor-cycling navy officer. 'Flossie Seagrave.'

He returns her handshake. 'George,' he says.

His accent, she thinks, might be a Highlands accent. It has a lilt to it. 'Just George?'

'George is what the men call me,' he replies. 'That or Padre.' And it is only then that she notices the white dog collar of a military chaplain tucked behind his duffle coat.

George comes roaring up the drive the following weekend with a box of records strapped to the back of his motorcycle, which he delivers to Flossie with a promise there are more to come. She is surprised to find they are not the popular big band songs that she expected, but Elgar, Haydn, Mendelssohn. George tries one on the gramophone and turns up the volume as loud as it can go, to test the acoustics, and swelling strings fill the full height of the hall.

'I've never tried it that loud before,' says Flossie. 'It sounds splendid.'

'What about the gallery, how does it sound up there?' he asks, and she darts up the staircase to stand on the gallery overlooking the hall.

'I like it here too,' she calls, 'rather like being in the gods at a theatre.'

'Perfect,' he says. 'I knew as soon as I came into this room it was made for music.'

Flossie comes back down the stairs, saying, 'We should make more use of it really, but it's awfully cold, even on a sunny day.'

'I'm very grateful to have the chance to listen to these again,' he says, patting his box of records. 'We don't have a gramophone on the ship.'

'You're on a ship?'

'Most of the time.'

'What do you do on board?'

'I'm a listening ear mainly,' he says, 'but I hold services too, up on deck, wearing my full rig and regalia. I've had to learn to preach over the sound of the ocean.'

'Who will be coming, to listen to the music?' she asks.

'Those that need it,' he replies.

★

439

The next day, a party of Americans set to work to make the Oak Hall habitable again. They attack their tasks with the enthusiasm of infantrymen in a state of peak physical fitness with not much else to do. They form lines to carry away unwanted furniture to stash in the outbuildings; climb on the roof to hammer planks over the hole in the ceiling; and clean the hall from top to bottom, even polishing the suit of armour until it too is battle-ready.

'Our main problem,' says Flossie to Betty, as they watch the Americans scrubbing the flagstones, 'is a lack of seating. I'm not sure how many are coming, and they can't sit on the floor. We should make it beautiful and comfortable for them, given that they – well, they won't be in Dorset for long.'

A young private from Milwaukee, wiping the floor near Flossie's feet, looks up and says, 'We're pretty used to sitting on the ground, ma'am.'

'I could find you a cushion, at least,' says Flossie. 'We have plenty of cushions. And pillows. And bedding. Actually, that might be a way to do it.'

She asks the private if he and his colleagues can round up every cushion in the house, along with any spare mattresses and bedding. The mattresses are arranged around the edges of the hall, topped with pillows and cushions, so the guests can sit on them, leaning up against the walls. More are scattered around the gallery so a further layer of listeners can recline up there. Eiderdowns and blankets are draped over the mattresses to make them look more enticing, and Flossie finds some candlesticks so the hall will be flatteringly illuminated. Betty is tasked with finding decent coffee to serve in the interval, and the Americans promise fresh doughnuts from their mobile canteen. Flossie even has the Americans chop her some wood so she can light the fire for the first time in years.

It is when she is standing in front of the fireplace, looking at the mirrors on the walls, that she thinks of her mother and realizes what else she should do.

George, who is turning out to be a resourceful man, manages to commandeer an army bus to bring the attendees of their first musical evening up to Chilcombe. The sun is beginning to set as they arrive, the rooks gathering noisily in the trees. Flossie, waiting in the doorway, watches them disembark. They are mainly Americans, in short bomber jackets with their hats worn on one side, with a few British Navy officers in dark double-breasted jackets. Some ordinary sailors too, in woolly blue jumpers. George, who has travelled on his motorcycle, is wearing a smart navy jacket over his shirt and dog collar. She sees the men looking up at the ivy-covered house, and then their eyes fall to her, where she stands with Betty and Bill.

It had taken a while to find it, given that all she wears these days are her gardening clothes, but found it she had, and Betty has adjusted it, so it fits her properly: a cornflower-blue dress she had once worn as Miranda in *The Tempest*, now transformed into an evening gown. A little Edwardian perhaps, with its square neckline and softly draped layers, more like the decorous tea gowns of the 1910s than the spinning dance frocks of the 1940s, but hopefully it will serve its purpose: to create an air of ceremony. Flossie believes that, if the men are to sit in the hall and listen to the records as attentively as she hopes they will, they need to enter it formally. The Brewers, on either side of her, are also smartened up: Bill in a three-piece suit and tie, Betty in a black dress with white collar.

She greets her guests warmly, one by one, as they file past her into the candlelit hall, holding their hats in their hands. Once inside, they make themselves comfortable on the mattresses, looking around at the paintings on the walls, or into the house's shadowy upper reaches. Betty moves among them handing out ashtrays. Their chatter, Flossie notes approvingly, has dropped to the level of an expectant theatre audience, and their faces are lit by the flames blazing in the hearth. The scene reminds her of a medieval castle or a Viking longhouse: men gathered about a fire in a tall dark room.

Flossie has positioned the gramophone on a table in the middle of the hall, next to a vase of tulips, so it will take centre stage from the start. She has been through George's records and added a few of her own to put together a programme to console and uplift, while making full use of the hall's fine acoustics. She walks to the table, waits for the men's conversation to subside, then carefully slides the first record from its sleeve and fits it on to the gramophone. She lifts the needle and guides it into place.

After the first night, it becomes a twice-weekly event. A core group of regulars develops, one of whom is a professional cellist from Chicago, who comes with requests for music he hopes one day to play himself, but the other clientele changes frequently, with George bringing new visitors.

Flossie wonders how George identifies those in need of music, or in need of whatever it is that music provides. She cannot see any common link between them. Most seem cheerful and untroubled, although some, she notices, have a nervous manner, a fidget to their hands. One evening, he brings three dark and handsome men who are part of the Free French Forces, so she plays a stirring Leclair concerto to provide a taste of their homeland, only to discover they are from Corsica, and have never been to France.

It is difficult too to gauge the men's reactions to the evenings. When the Americans come up in the daytime to charge about her lawn with footballs, they play-fight like puppies, teasing each other constantly. Nothing is allowed to be serious. It is, she imagines, an effective way of keeping their terrors at bay. But on the musical evenings, they are quiet, almost withdrawn. Some take off their boots and sit cross-legged in their socks, like schoolboys.

Looking at them, Flossie frequently thinks of Hans, how moved he was when she played the piano. She does not often play Bach to the men, as his music carries so much of Hans, but if she does, she will look around the room, observing their faces – tipped back with eyes closed, or staring up at the high windows, locked in their thoughts – and she will remember another soldier, missing his home and family, just as they do.

The men rarely look at each other as the music plays, there is a courtesy in allowing each man his space to listen, and some do not look at Flossie as they leave, although she always tries to end the evening with something light. But if they return, they might come with flowers for her, or something they have made themselves – a carved wooden bowl, a hand-drawn bookmark – totems of consideration. In return, she challenges herself to find a new outfit for every musical evening, racing back from the milking sheds of Dorchester to rummage through fading old costumes.

'They probably think the English dress like this all the time,' grumbles Betty, polishing her shoes.

'I know it seems silly,' says Flossie, pinning up her hair, 'but I want to make an effort.'

The men repeatedly request that she play Elgar's 'Nimrod', even though it appears to affect them powerfully. She finds it hard to watch them fight to maintain their composure as the kettledrums roll and the score ascends to its heights. It must cause them something close to agony. Perhaps, she thinks, that is what they require: something that allows them to follow their pain as it rises, in its most beautifully orchestrated form – one that insists on the inevitability of whatever will come, and then releases them, gently, with that knowledge. It is not comfort it gives them, she realizes, but acceptance; not an anaesthetizing of sorrow, but a clear articulation of it.

In the last week of May, one of the American officers tells her that the musical evenings must come to an end. The sailors are to return to their ships and the soldiers are to be sealed into their camps for their final briefings; the only place they will go now is France.

On the last night, she glances at George, who is in his usual place, sitting on the stairs, and sees that his hands are knitted together, his eyes closed, his brow furrowed. But as the music fades, he opens his eyes and slips automatically into his pastoral role, standing to put a hand on the back of a soldier making his way down the stairs.

As they go outside together, watching as the bus full of waving men makes its way down the drive, Flossie asks, 'What do you do now, George?'

'I go with them,' he says.

'What?' she says. 'You don't fight, do you? You don't have a gun?'

'No, I don't, which is a shame because I'm a crack shot. But I go with them, all the same.'

'Couldn't they let you have a gun just for this? Seems a little unfair.'

'I'll be on a warship. It has big cannons.'

'Well, make sure you stand behind one,' she says, and he laughs, although she feels immediately that her comment is flippant, inadequate.

'Would you mind keeping my records safe for me,' he says. 'Until I come back. And if I don't –'

'Oh, don't say that, George,' she says. 'I didn't get this ridiculous dress on just to sob all over it.'

'It is quite a dress too,' he says.

'Rather flamboyant, I know, but sometimes it's good to dress up.'

'I quite agree,' he says, lifting a hand to his collar.

Flossie laughs and says, 'It has been great fun, to be honest, to get out of my dungarees. To listen to your wonderful music. I've enjoyed it, very much.'

'The men won't forget it,' he says. 'This place. Your kindness. You. I won't either.' He gives her a quick smile, and looks at her for a moment, then straightens his jacket, nods smartly, and walks to his motorbike. She watches him kick the machine into life and set off down the drive, then she heads round the side of the house, in her trailing silver gown, to feed her pigs.

The Knight of Swords, The Star

June, 1944

Madame Camille, Weymouth's mystical psychic adviser to kings and queens, stands in her window watching men march along the harbour, laden with rifles and rucksacks. A tent has been set up by the Red Cross to hand out doughnuts to the Americans as they head to their boats – a sugared taste of home likely to soon be regurgitated on a bumpy Channel crossing. The wind has been gusting all day and the sea churns and rolls.

It has been good for business, she will say that. Having the Americans in town, with more money than they know what to do with. Every day, a new young man with a cigarette tucked behind one ear, asking about his future, trying to laugh it off.

She had hidden the Tarot cards they kept flinching at, the grislier images, and put those that looked like victory towards the top of the pack. The Knight of Swords. The Chariot. There's no truth in a doctored pack, but that's how she thinks of it: the act of a doctor. A spoonful of medicine. Off you go, boys. That'll see you right. It won't, of course. She's seen the cards that catch her sleeve, flip themselves upright. They speak of calamitous cost, slow struggle.

Madame Camille watches the troops filing into their vessels, moored one against the other across the harbour. She knows some souls never leave this realm for the next. She looks at the stubborn lines of grey faces beneath metal helmets, packed into their flat-bottomed landing craft like tinned sardines. They won't want to go.

Dusk. Maudie sits on her rooftop and looks out over the town. Weymouth is hushed. Expectant. The pubs and cafés are empty. The homes that billeted soldiers, took in sailors, now have a spare bed,

445

neatly made. Behind the town, there is a new field hospital, where doctors sit waiting, rolling bandages.

Maudie opens her diary. She's kept a list of all her men. Noted where she met them, if they came back with her, what they were like. They've swept in and out like the tides since the war began and brought their countries with them. From Austrian refugees playing waltzes in the tea rooms to Black Americans singing spirituals in the churches, and all of them swinging hard every Saturday night, when the big bands took the roof off the Co-op Hall.

One Black soldier told her when he first arrived, it was strange for him to look a white person in the face, that he had to learn to lift his chin. This, he says, lifting her chin, would be unthinkable. It is all unthinkable, but she likes to think about it. She pulls a pencil from her boiler suit pocket to add another.

5th June, 1944
Warren

smells of soap. Americans smell better. they can't hold their drink though & you can smell that on them too. you can learn a lot about people by their smell. you can learn a lot on the roof of a chip shop in Weymouth, though it's not called Weymouth any more. the papers call it a 'south coast town' so the Germans don't catch on to us. all the sticks of rock with Weymouth written in the middle have been disposed of like bombs.

names don't matter anyhow. names are just a peg for hanging things. i see a name in my diary & remember how it felt. sometimes a game, sometimes a fight. sometimes one when you thought it would be the other.

Warren means: his hands, his mouth. what he looks like out of his uniform, stretched out on a blanket on a rooftop by a radio playing Billie Holiday. he calls me a tall drink of water, but he is a river and i will lay myself along him.

he says if he makes it through, he will leave the Army. he says they're happy to use him, but they don't want him in the front for the photographs. he sees no point in working for white folks who don't want his handsome face in their photographs. he asks what i will do after and i wonder what

Warren reaches up, takes the pencil from her hand. He says he will have to go soon. He says let's not waste this.

When Maudie next opens her eyes, it is two in the morning, and she is alone. She looks up to find what has woken her and sees a steady stream of aircraft making their way across the star-filled sky. More than she has ever seen before. Bombers, troop carriers. Aeroplanes towing gliders. One after the other after the other after the other. An endless airborne convoy. A deep resonant hum. She kicks off the blanket Warren has covered her with and lies naked on the roof, watching them pass, letting the night air cool her skin.

The Americans

July, 1944

In the first week of July, Édouard takes Cristabel bumping along the lanes to the nearest town in his old Fiat, saying he has seen some Americans in a Jeep. 'They were enormous!' he cries, over the shrill whining of the car engine. 'And they were chewing gum! I thought perhaps they only did that for the movies!'

They find them – a three-man scouting party – in a hotel bar, where the town mayor has spread a map across a table and is pointing at it. The Americans are suntanned and dusty, in battledress, boots and helmets, with their hands on their hips. They are the first of the invading force to arrive in the town and seem like emissaries from another planet.

Cristabel approaches them and says, in her most English English, that she is a British operative working with the local Resistance. She suggests that if they doubt her credentials, they should contact Baker Street, London. The Americans look at her, taking in her badly dyed hair, crumpled frock and the tatty sandals loaned to her by Wanda. 'Do you speak French?' says the one who appears to be in charge, a first lieutenant.

'These people believe I am French,' she says, gesturing at the mayor and the hotel barman, as representatives of Normandy. A dismissive sniff comes from the barman, who is pouring cognac into three tulip-shaped glasses.

'We need a translator, who knows the area,' says the lieutenant. He turns back to the map. 'Tell me about this road through the woods.'

After the lieutenant makes a few phone calls from the hotel office to check her identity, Cristabel finds herself in the Jeep, giving the

Americans a rapid tour of the local countryside. She sits alongside an unsmiling soldier who has a machine gun balanced on the edge of the vehicle. Sometimes they stop and the lieutenant will fire questions at Cristabel to translate for a wide-eyed farmer. Where are the Germans based near here? How many are there?

Local people come to their front doors to stare at the vehicle as it flies past, uncertain what it signifies. They know that the Allies have landed on the beaches of Normandy, but they also know that the fighting has been fierce and the battle for France is not yet won.

The Americans drive through sleepy shuttered villages, with cobbled squares and dribbling fountains. Past sun-warmed stone walls and patchwork fields. Wide European skies. They even hurtle through a small town Cristabel once visited with Mlle Aubert, Flossie and Digby, a lifetime ago. They were lost, looking for a guest house. There was a bar where they asked for directions. A noisy ceiling fan. Mlle Aubert's yawning boredom.

'We might have another job for you,' says the lieutenant, after a while. 'Could you get into Paris?'

'Yes,' Cristabel says quickly.

'We're keen to know more about the strength of German forces in the city. We can't get close to it, and we have to head back to Saint-Lô tonight, but if you could –'

'Yes,' she says again. 'Tell me what you need. How to contact you.'

Édouard insists he will drive her as far as he can, using his doctor's pass. There are hardly any trains running. Most of the railway network has been put out of action, either by Allied bombing or Resistance sabotage, and as Édouard and Cristabel head towards the capital, they see British bombers flying overhead, dark lines of crosses in the evening sky. German military vehicles, covered in tree branches, sometimes race past in the opposite direction. Cristabel has her handkerchief ready to cough blood, but Édouard's Fiat seems of little interest to them now.

They are stopped only once, a few miles outside Paris, at a roadblock, where a single Wehrmacht soldier checks Édouard's pass, then nods them through.

'He looked barely older than sixteen, did you notice?' says Édouard, as they drive on. 'What a place for a boy to find himself.'

'They must be running out of men,' Cristabel replies, checking she has all she needs in her rucksack: papers, money, cigarettes, knife and Édouard's copy of *Madame Bovary*, which he has insisted she take.

Édouard pulls into a side street to drop her off. He leans over from the driving seat to kiss her on each cheek multiple times, and to give her a bag of turnips, telling her she should say she has been to visit friends in the country to get food.

'I must go,' she says. 'I don't want to be caught out after curfew.'

'Please be careful,' he says.

'I will come back,' she replies. 'I promise. Thank you for everything.'

He hugs her tightly and she hears him say, 'Dear child,' almost to himself, then he pulls away and nods. 'Go. Go, quickly. We will see you again.'

The Americans have given her a contact – an agent called Jules, someone they say is one of their most reliable operators in Paris – and a restaurant where the contact can be found. Cristabel finds a cheap hotel to stay in overnight. Even as an undercover agent in a grotty hotel in the middle of a war, it is exciting to visit Paris for the first time. She leans out of the window, listens to the city. Somewhere out there is Digby.

The following day, she pins a carnation to her blouse, as requested, and heads to the restaurant to find Jules. It is not the backstreet bistro she expected, but an expensive establishment on the wide avenue of the Champs-Élysées, where the outside tables are occupied by long-booted Nazi officers enjoying the sunshine. It is strange to see them so relaxed knowing that only a few hundred miles away, battle is being waged.

She goes in under the pretext of asking a waiter for directions, scans the clientele but sees nobody likely, and is about to leave when a hand reaches out from a nearby table and grabs her wrist.

'Didn't you see the newspaper?' says a woman in slow, regal French. 'I spread it out on the table most carefully.'

Cristabel turns to find the newspaper she had been told to look for, open on a table in front of an individual she had glanced at and then discounted, a rather grand woman in her fifties, in a fashion-ably striped skirt in grey and black with a matching jacket buttoned over a formidable bosom, and silver hair neatly set beneath a smart feathered hat. She has a broad-featured face and around her neck hangs a conglomeration of items: a cluster of beads, a pince-nez on a silver chain, and a silk scarf pinned with a horse-shaped brooch. On her strong hands are jewelled rings in dark colours: rubies, gar-nets. A fur stole hangs from the back of her chair and a crocodile handbag containing a small dog sits at her feet.

'I'm glad you're here,' says the woman, getting out of her seat. 'I'm quite desperate to leave. They've brought in a new chef, and it's been a disaster.' She picks up the stole and the handbag, pulls out a substantial bundle of banknotes from under the dog, and places the money on the table. As they head towards the street together, she pauses and takes Cristabel by the arm. 'But we must be glad to see each other.' She kisses her on each cheek, once, twice, three times. 'Now we go.'

Her name is Lieselotte de Brienne. She is, she tells Cristabel as they walk along the sandy, tree-lined paths of the Jardins des Champs-Élysées, half German and half American – 'a complicated mixture' – but has lived most of her life in France, having married a wealthy French industrialist, who is currently at their summer home near Avignon. 'He has never loved Paris as I do,' she says. Before the war, she hosted regular salons in her Paris apartment – gatherings of writers, artists, politicians – and has continued to do so throughout the Occupation, which is what brought her to the attention of the American secret services, who suggested she might invite some high-ranking Nazi officials, keen to mingle with French intellectuals.

'I'm just French enough to flatter their egos,' she says of her German visitors, 'just German enough to remind them of their mothers, and just American enough to make them think I'm a little foolish. That's the main thing, you understand. They think I'm only interested in caviar and gossip, so they say things they shouldn't in front of me. Or if not me, the sweet girl I bring in to top up their glasses. But I've talked about myself for long enough. What do you do?'

'I work for a British organization –' Cristabel begins.

'Not that. What do you actually do? Outside of all this,' says Lieselotte, extracting her dog from her bag to put it on the path, where it trots beside her.

'I'm not supposed to –'

'If you never relax your security precautions, I'm afraid our conversations will be very dull.'

'That's precisely the point of the precautions.'

'Tell me as much as you are able, and we will do what we can,' says Lieselotte, as they come to a halt in front of a decorative fountain that has stopped running, standing dry-throated in its empty stone bowl.

Cristabel pauses. 'I have a theatre.'

'A theatre? That's wonderful.'

'It's not. It could be. But it's not.'

'What do you put on there? What are your themes?'

'We did Shakespeare. I wouldn't say I had themes, although we once tried to introduce elements inspired by the war in Spain. One of my actors was keen on the idea. But, looking back, I think it was heavy-handed.'

'I am never convinced by political theatre. I do not like to be hectored,' says Lieselotte. 'Do you direct?'

'I do.'

'Well, that is perfect. An aspiring theatre director is exactly the kind of person I would take out for lunch. I was struggling to think of a reason why I would meet a consumptive art student or whatever they said you were pretending to be. Have you seen the new production of *Antigone*? At Théâtre de l'Atelier.'

Cristabel laughs. 'I haven't been to the theatre in a long time.'

'Then we will go. Everybody is talking about it.'

'I'm here to find out about German military readiness, not go to the theatre.'

'One does not preclude the other. Do we let them take all our pleasures? I think not,' says Lieselotte. She leans down to retrieve her dog and pop it back in her bag. 'We will try our luck at Lucas Carton. They can usually find me a table.'

She guides Cristabel out of the park and around the Place de la Concorde, an open square with a giant obelisk at its centre. Large black and red flags of the swastika hang on the imposing buildings overlooking the square and, at its corner, there is a road sign giving directions in German in an angular font, pointing out places for soldiers – *Soldatenkinos*, *Soldatenkaffee* – with a new one added at the bottom: *Zur Normandie Front*. The only vehicles that move through Paris are German: there is no petrol left for the French.

'I wanted to ask you something,' says Cristabel, as they walk to the restaurant. 'Two of our people are being held in Fresnes. Code names Sidonie and Antoine. If you can find out anything about them, we would be very grateful.'

Lieselotte nods. 'Where are you staying?'

'I'm in a hotel on the Left Bank.'

'There is a restaurant on Boulevard Saint-Germain where we can leave messages with the sommelier. I will give you the details,' says Lieselotte.

As they arrive at the entrance to Lucas Carton, a handsome Wehrmacht officer is coming out, accompanied by a young woman in a silk dress and high heels. Seeing Lieselotte, he greets her with extravagant courtesy, swooping to kiss her hand.

Lieselotte says, in German, 'Dear Herr Schulte, I hope we will be seeing you on Thursday, as usual.'

'I would not miss it for the world,' he replies, then gestures towards Cristabel, saying, 'Will your friend be joining us?'

'I hope so,' says Lieselotte. 'Claudine is a theatre director. I have been telling her about Anouilh's new production of *Antigone*, she's yet to see it.'

'Then you must let me get you some tickets,' says the German eagerly. 'It is a fascinating play.'

'Ah, but Claudine is doubtful about the morality of attending the theatre in a time of war,' says Lieselotte, in a teasing tone. Cristabel notices that Lieselotte's German is faster and more familiar than her French.

The officer smiles at Cristabel and says in careful French, 'The Ancient Greeks believed it was a citizen's duty to attend the theatre. I agree. I will buy for you some tickets.'

'You are too kind,' says Lieselotte, and he bows, before leading his companion away.

'I cannot accept theatre tickets from him,' says Cristabel, as they enter the restaurant. The elegant interior is lined with Art Nouveau wood panelling and curved mirrors, reflecting fashionable French diners and uniformed Nazis, served by waiters in white jackets. The two women are shown to a table in the window.

'You can and you will,' says Lieselotte, settling her dog beneath the table. 'We should take everything we can from him. It's not his, after all, is it? Nothing they have is theirs. In the meantime, you must accept something from me. I would like to buy you some clothes and send you to my hairdresser. I don't think I will take no for an answer.'

Lieselotte orders a bottle of champagne, then looks out of the window, at the Parisian women going past on bicycles, in white-rimmed sunglasses and red lipstick, their hair worn high at the front or tucked beneath turbans in bright fabrics, pedalling in wedge-heeled shoes with their skirts blowing high up their legs, flying like flags down the Boulevard Malesherbes.

'Look at those magnificent girls,' says Lieselotte, 'such defiance.'

Over the next few weeks, Cristabel regularly sallies forth on her own bicycle – one she steals from outside a shop, leaving a note of apology and a roll of cash, the going rate for a bicycle in Occupied Paris being almost the price of a car – and makes her way through the city and its outskirts, to surreptitiously investigate the where-abouts of German troops.

She locates the buildings where German units are based and ventures into nearby cafés and bars, tentatively seeking contacts who might tell her more about the strength of the forces. Any useful information she uncovers, she gives to Lieselotte to pass to the Americans.

Cristabel becomes practised in the art of asking neutral questions that might lead her to someone willing to talk. She finds that being seen to drink alcohol helps, so she can give the impression of being someone who has forgotten the need for caution. A gossipy drunk woman is irritating, but not suspicious, and there are plenty who are drinking their way through the war. A cheap brandy on an empty stomach rather takes the edge off it all too. Even Uncle Willoughby, who made war sound like the greatest adventure, was rarely without a drink in his hand, and now she sees why.

Her previous missions in France mean she is accustomed to the agent's heightened state of self-awareness, but now she feels doubly layered. For there is the work she is doing for the Americans and there is another part of her constantly scanning the city for Digby. It is not counter to her mission, but it is not her mission, and it gives her a slightly scrambled feeling, as if she were a radio switching between stations. She sets herself a limit of two drinks a day, determined to remain focused; she can play-act the rest.

Her dirty rucksack has been replaced by a smart satchel, and she wears an outfit provided by Lieselotte, a blue-and-white checked summer dress, and Oxford brogues with wooden soles, which she wears, like the Parisian women, with ankle socks. She has a matching scarf tied in her neatly trimmed, newly brunette hair and a pair of sunglasses, for it is hot and golden in Paris in July. The locals are lining the banks of the Seine, descending the stone steps that lead down from the city to the river, where they lie on the sun-warmed embankments beneath the rows of tall trees.

Time seems to be suspended in Paris; the population exists in a state of limbo. News of the Allies' advance is hard to come by, for neither the BBC nor the Germans will give details, and there are so many power cuts, it is hard to find a working radio. Sometimes, dark smoke blows all the way from Normandy, to float across the city, concealing the sun above the sunbathers like a huge, visible premonition, but of what, they are unsure.

455

The city is a stopped clock, a watched pot. There are queues outside the shops, lines of women leaning against walls, fanning themselves in the heat. Food, always in short supply, is now hardly supplied at all, and signs appear in shop windows listing all the things they no longer have in stock. There is a proliferation of signs and posters. Announcements about curfews, announcements about death sentences, and the garish *Affiche Rouge* – red posters with images of captured *résistants*. The Parisians stand and look and talk in low voices. Cristabel pushes her bike past, scanning the mug-shots, their bruised, staring faces.

There are rumours the Nazis have concealed dynamite beneath every bridge in Paris; there are rumours that someone tried to blow up Hitler himself. Guards appear at the doorways of hotels frequented by Germans. Streets are cordoned off by military vehicles. There are sporadic displays – the French march on Bastille Day for the first time in years, the Germans parade their troops down the main avenues – but nothing amounts to much.

Mostly, it is quiet. So quiet that when a German tank clanks through the city, it can be heard from several streets away. A mechanical monster, turning its turret with impassive slowness, pointing its gun at different buildings in turn: at a bank and a department store and a second-floor apartment, where they have chickens on the balcony. Like a child saying: *I'm going to get you, and you, and you.*

Cristabel cycles past as it sits in the middle of a tree-lined boulevard, an impassive metal monument. Restaurant owners come to their doors to look at it, then go back inside to wipe tables. She pedals onward, heading south, to the edge of the city. She keeps going until she finds a spot where she can see the massive Fresnes Prison in the distance: a grim row of stone detention blocks lined up behind a perimeter wall, overseen by a watchtower.

She can make out the lines of barred windows and imagines those inside. Young rebels like Édouard and Wanda's son. Captured agents like Antoine and Sophie. A prison full of the brave. She wonders what the Germans will do with them when the Allies arrive. It's me, she thinks. I'm here. Then she turns tail and heads back to Paris.

An Apartment in Paris

July, 1944

One thundery, humid day, Cristabel cycles to the north of Paris, to have a look at the Clignancourt Barracks, rumoured to house French volunteers in the SS. Though unable to get close to the barracks themselves, she sits in a nearby café for the morning and takes note of the type of military vehicles driving in and out, while eavesdropping on an interesting conversation about troop morale.

Afterwards, she cycles back through the city, taking a circuitous route to avoid the road closures. She stops briefly at a kiosk to buy a newspaper, and the newspaper seller says with a grin, 'Have you heard – the Allies have liberated Saint-Lô.'

The excitement of this news gives her renewed speed, and she is soon flying down towards the Seine when she notices a street sign – Rue des Rosiers – and comes to a halt. Rue des Rosiers was where Mlle Aubert's mother lived, above a shop. Where she had taken in sewing and hoped her family would one day be restored. It comes back to her in a rush. Chilcombe's stuffy attic schoolroom. Mlle Aubert's bitterness at her family's fall from grace.

Cristabel walks with her bicycle into the narrow, cobbled passage, peering along it. The buildings lean close together, they look older than other Parisian buildings. Some are boarded up or have broken windows. She sees scrawled graffiti, the word *Juif* painted on a front door. An old woman wrapped in a shawl sits on a doorstep. Cristabel offers her a cigarette and quietly asks if she knows a Mme Aubert who once lived in this street.

The old woman laughs, and her laughter sets off a cascade of throaty coughing. Eventually she says, 'She doesn't live here any more. She's gone up in the world. With her new friends.'

'Do you know where I could find her?' asks Cristabel.

'Why would you want to find her? We will find her, when this is done. You can tell her that.'

'I will tell her, if you tell me where she is.'

The old woman says nothing. Cristabel turns, as if to walk away, and the woman says, 'For the cigarettes.'

Cristabel hands over her cigarettes, and the woman says, 'Rue Beaujon. Near the Arc de Triomphe. Look for the best-fed concierge in the street. She's plump as a goose ready for pâté de foie gras.'

Cristabel is aware that it is not entirely advisable to try to find Mme Aubert, someone with a faint connection to her true identity, but she is curious, not least because she thinks there is a chance that Digby might also have been curious, had he ever seen the sign for the Rue des Rosiers.

Besides, it is a very faint connection, and the Allies might be here by next week. She feels the wind is behind her, and she feels this again when Mme Aubert proves extremely easy to find. She is standing in the street outside her *loge*, shooing away two jeering boys. She is a fleshy, sixty-something version of her daughter, with the same dark moles and unsmiling face, wearing a black dress, her grey hair knotted in a bun.

Cristabel shakes her head sympathetically. 'Typical children.'

'They show me no respect,' says Mme Aubert.

Cristabel looks along the street: a row of vanilla-coloured apartment blocks in the chic 8th arrondissement, an area she usually avoids due to its popularity with the Germans. The Gestapo have their headquarters not far away, in leafy Avenue Foch. Madame Aubert has done well for herself, and there are only a few who do well in wartime. She thinks of the threat made by the old woman in the Rue des Rosiers, her mention of 'new friends', and decides to take a chance. 'I don't suppose you are Madame Aubert?'

'Who wants to know?'

'My name is Claudine Beauchamp. I was given your name by my friend, Herr Schulte.'

At this, Mme Aubert guides Claudine towards the *loge*, saying, 'Herr Schulte? I'm not sure I recall a Herr Schulte.'

'He speaks very highly of you.'

'Won't you come in, Mademoiselle Beauchamp? You can leave your bicycle by the stairs.' Mme Aubert ushers her into her rooms, which are shielded from the street by net curtains. Along one wall is a set of cubbyholes for sorting post and a cork board on which to hang room keys. There is a desk covered with papers and a visitors' book. Through an alcove, there is a dining table covered with an old-fashioned tablecloth, and a large dresser holding a mass of crockery, in different shapes and styles. 'My family china,' says Mme Aubert, seeing Cristabel looking at it.

'Beautiful.'

They exchange further pleasantries, then Mme Aubert disappears into an adjoining kitchenette to make coffee. Cristabel quickly flicks through the visitors' book, wondering what name Digby might have used, and what he might have said, if he had been standing in this room. After a moment, she says, 'I was told you might be able to help find me accommodation, Madame Aubert.'

'I might,' replies Mme Aubert, from the kitchenette.

'I hear you're very discreet,' says Cristabel, scanning the pictures on the walls: family photographs, images of saints, and a framed portrait of Marshal Pétain.

Mme Aubert returns with rose-patterned china cups on a silver tray. Cristabel gestures at one of the photographs on the wall, which she is sure shows a surly Mlle Aubert. 'Who is this charming girl? She looks rather like you.'

'My Ernestine. She's a governess. Employed by many fine families. I only wish she was closer.'

'She doesn't live in Paris?'

Mme Aubert shakes her head. 'She's in Switzerland. Before that, England.'

'You must be very proud.' Cristabel sips her drink. 'My, this tastes like real coffee. That's hard to find these days.'

Mme Aubert smiles a little shyly.

Cristabel smiles back. 'We all need our indulgences. Whereabouts

459

in England did your daughter work? I visited England before the war. I wouldn't go there now. They say it's unrecognizable.'

'I am unsure where, but it was with a distinguished family, like my own. This —' she gestures at the surrounding rooms – 'is a temporary measure, you understand.'

'These are difficult times,' says Cristabel sympathetically. 'They say the English are being overrun in their own country. Swamped by the most undesirable elements.'

Mme Aubert shakes her head. 'Terrible.'

'If it carries on, there won't be anything left of decent society.' With a glance at Pétain, Cristabel adds, 'Thank heavens there are still those who take a stand.'

'Without him, we would be lost, and goodness knows, France has suffered enough,' says Mme Aubert, then looks at the clock on the wall. 'With regard to your accommodation, Mademoiselle Beauchamp, I look after another property on this road. Number twenty. There is an apartment on the third floor that has recently become vacant. Perhaps you would like to have a look?'

'Please, if I may.'

'I'll give you the key as I have to get to the butcher before he closes, but we could meet back here once you've looked round.' Mme Aubert stands to hook a key off the board, then hands it to Cristabel.

'Perfect,' says Cristabel, getting to her feet. 'How fortunate you have somewhere available.'

'The family who were there. They should never have been allowed in. It's their kind that have caused all this.'

'Perhaps it's for the best that they went.'

'If they hadn't done anything wrong, they wouldn't have been hiding,' says Mme Aubert, picking up a shopping basket. 'I used to see them. Coming and going at all hours.'

'How suspicious.'

'You couldn't trust them.' Mme Aubert pauses on her way to the door and adds, 'It's curious we should talk about the English. One of the family my daughter worked with also stayed in number twenty, up on the fourth floor. He had lovely manners. You could tell he was well bred.'

460

'Did he?' says Cristabel, her throat suddenly dry.

'He said I kept it so beautifully, it reminded him of home, which he told me was one of the most historic houses in England.'

Cristabel smiles, despite herself. Digby had lied to this woman just as much as she has. He didn't care at all about his home or its history. How funny it should only occur to her now.

'Is that apartment still available?' she says.

'I'm afraid not,' says Mme Aubert, heading out into the street.

'What was an Englishman doing in Paris at this time?' says Cristabel, as casually as she can.

Mme Aubert looks at her. 'I wouldn't know.'

Cristabel leans towards her in a conspiratorial manner. 'You know, I've heard a lot of the English can't stand Churchill. It wouldn't surprise me if some decided they might be better off on the other side.'

Mme Aubert smiles. She leads Cristabel down the road to number 20, then continues on her way.

Cristabel makes her way into the building, which is a typical Parisian apartment block, with a dark wooden staircase winding up to each landing. She climbs the stairs, with the key to the third-floor apartment in her hand, but doesn't stop on the third floor. Instead, she tiptoes to the fourth, and stands outside the door of the apartment for a few moments, for no reason she can explain. She touches her fingertips lightly on the door, and is almost tempted to try the key in the lock, but shakes her head, and makes her way back down to the third-floor landing, where she is met by a uniformed SS officer coming up the staircase who says, 'Claudine Beauchamp?'

She pauses, just for a second, then says, 'Yes.'

The officer is out of breath, but he smiles and says in French, 'Good. Madame Aubert told me you were here with the key. I have also come to see the apartment.'

She holds out the key towards him, but he shakes his head, saying, 'No, please. You first. You are the prospective tenant. I am only here to look at some of the items inside.' He gestures towards the door, which she unlocks, and he follows her in.

The apartment is full of light. It has windows stretching floor to

461

ceiling that overlook the street, and sunshine streams in on to the polished herringbone floor. The furniture is upholstered in pale yellow, and the high ceilings are white, with gilded decorative corners. On the walls are modern paintings and mirrors that send sunlight dancing around the room.

'Ah, Madame Aubert has cleaned it up well,' says the officer. He has taken off his hat and is fanning himself with it. He is a heavy-set man in his forties, with a wide leather belt stretching around his grey tunic, and a ruddy face. 'You will be lucky to live here.'

'I'm only looking,' Cristabel says, walking away from him as if to examine the view from the windows.

'It has always been my dream to have an apartment in Paris,' he says, putting his hat on a chair, then crossing the room to examine a painting on the wall. 'A foolish dream perhaps.' He moves to a second painting, looks at it closely, then takes it off the wall to set it on a coffee table.

'Yes,' says Cristabel, walking rapidly into the adjoining dining room, feeling the rapping of her wooden-soled shoes on the floor as small shocks running up her legs.

'I had even started looking around. To see if there was something I could buy.' She hears him laughing to himself.

Cristabel circles the dining table, then returns to the main living room, where the SS officer is examining a marble paperweight. He has gathered a selection of items on the coffee table. A few paintings, some porcelain figurines. He looks up as she comes in. 'I do envy you. With the way things are going, you will be in Paris far longer than I.'

She nods and heads to the other end of the apartment, where she quickly circuits the bathroom and the main bedroom, then goes into a smaller bedroom, which has two twin beds. It must have been a room for children, she thinks, as there is a series of pencil lines on the door frame, marking how they have grown.

She heads past the officer again, who is looking at another painting, and goes into the kitchen, which is at the back of the building. She is mechanically opening cupboards, when something catches her eye: a set of plates with the same rose pattern that had adorned Mme Aubert's coffee cups.

She returns to the living room and says, 'I must be leaving. Not long till curfew.'

He looks up from the painting. 'Somebody here had very good taste.'

The sunlight coming through the windows picks out something glinting on the floor under the coffee table, and Cristabel reaches down to pick it up. She finds a child's pair of glasses, one lens smashed. The officer watches as she puts the glasses on the coffee table by the paintings, the figurines, the paperweight.

'What do you think of the apartment?' he says, putting the painting with the others. He has a pistol, she notices, in a holster at his side.

'It's not quite what I'm looking for,' she says.

'Where do you live now?'

'On the Left Bank.'

'With family?'

'On my own.'

'What do you do?'

'I'm a student.'

'A student in new clothes who can afford an apartment like this,' he says, and she feels she has taken a wrong turn.

'My family have some money, inherited money,' she says, and begins to move towards the door.

He holds up a hand. 'When I arrived, you were coming down from the fourth floor. Why was that?'

'I'd gone to the wrong floor.'

'But the key to this apartment is carefully labelled.'

'I was muddled. I didn't sleep well last night.'

'May I see your papers?' he says.

She finds them in her satchel and hands them to him. He examines them carefully.

'May I see what else is in your bag?' he says, and she has the sense of a dead end.

'Just a book and a few things,' she says, knowing that in her bag is the notebook where she has written the details of the vehicles at the Clignancourt Barracks. It also contains the address of the restaurant where she can leave messages for Lieselotte.

'Could you take out those things for me and put them on the table so I can see them.' His voice is subdued, almost weary, as if he has said this many times.

Cristabel's brain is whirring like a coding machine, frantically trying out possibilities: he could look at the notebook, realize what the notes are and arrest her; he could look at the notebook, not understand what the notes are and release her – but what SS officer would see notes he didn't understand and assume they are innocent? Plus: the restaurant address could lead him to Lieselotte. Plus: he knows her cover name. Every way she spins it, there is no way past this moment. Even the way she is pausing now, delaying carrying out his request, is whittling down the possibility of her leaving the apartment safely. Every second of inaction is incriminating.

'Empty the bag,' he says.

'Of course,' she says. The coding machine clicks into place. There is no way past this. Even if she knocked him out, he would still wake up and know what she looks like.

She tries to take herself back to Scotland, to the training room with the straw dummy and the lessons about the target's body. But the room she is in seems full of her breathing, full of his. She can remember every step of the exercise about how to surprise a sentry from behind and cut his throat, but he is not a sentry facing away from her, and her knife is in her waistband not in her hand. It is obscene to think of combat in this sun-filled room, to consider attacking someone standing in front of her, so close she can hear the neat tick of his wristwatch, but she is thinking too much and a voice in her head says: *This is your job.*

She fumbles with her bag, drops it to the floor and bends to pick it up. He does too, and she comes up sharply beneath him, sending a hand palm first into his jaw, knocking him off balance. She grabs the marble paperweight from the coffee table, and, grimacing at the thought of the impact even as she does it, sends it crunching into his nose, his mouth. He spins, spitting blood, but shouts, lashes out, catching her with a thudding blow to the head.

She staggers back and sees him swearing at her through his

blood-filled mouth. She cannot have him look at her. She pushes the coffee table at him, and he falls on to his back, pulling his gun from its holster. She scrabbles over the table towards him, stamps on his hand with her wooden heel, kicks the gun spinning away across the polished floor beneath an armchair.

He scrambles after it on all fours and she goes after him. He swipes out furiously with a fist, hitting her hard across the chest, knocking her sideways into a bookcase, sending a landslide of books thudding on to the floor. He reaches the armchair before she does, and is groping underneath it, but she has pulled her knife from her waistband, and is clambering on to his back. Her hands are sweating, and she muffs her first attempt, the blade catching uselessly in the thick fabric of his uniform.

He rears up, trying to shake her off, shouting a coarse stream of spittle-thick invective, and this fires within her a sudden fury and she thrusts the long knife as high and hard as she can into his upper ribs, locking her left arm around his throat to pull him back on to it, as she has been taught. He makes a high, horrible noise like an animal, then collapses on to his stomach, writhing beneath her, his arm still reaching beneath the armchair, fingernails scraping towards the gun. She is wrapped around him, the knife held between their bodies, so they are pinioned together.

She hears him say, in choking, gargled German: *Please.* She hears her own muffled English. *Don't.* She yanks her arm tighter around his neck, drives the knife deeper. He bucks and rolls until they topple over, stuck together, interlocked like dogs, and she lies beneath him, holding him fast against her, her eyes open to the gilded ceiling, hearing the breath rattling in his throat, the wordless, tongueless sounds he makes that are like *mummmumumumu*, aware of the warm urine seeping through his uniform, the sharp stink of her own sweat, for all the long minutes that it takes for his mouth to stop moving, his body to stop convulsing, his weight to become deadweight, and his head to loll against hers like a baby.

Now there is only her own ragged breath in the quiet apartment, and the sound of it is unbearable. She desperately heaves him off her. Shifts herself away. Gets quickly to her feet and goes to the kitchen, shaking and unsteady. The sour taste of bile rises in her throat, and she swallows it back down, spits into the sink. She is emptied out. The violent rage that inhabited her has slunk away, leaving only shuddering disgust.

She wants, more than anything, to leave the apartment, but she must do something with the body. The machine in her brain is still working, slowly. She looks out of the kitchen window into the courtyard below: a steep-sided crevasse made of the back walls of different buildings, an undecorated space, with a collection of bins and piles of rubbish at its base.

She returns to the officer, who is slumped on his side, the brass handle of the knife protruding from his back, as if he were a wind-up toy. She feels a shudder of horror. She thinks of the ex-policeman in Scotland, who spoke of using the knife in such practical terms, as if it were like hunting: something necessary a man did then put behind him. How can she put this behind her? It lies in front of her: drooling and lifeless. Evidence of her ability to kill.

But Mme Aubert will soon be returning. Cristabel must be as methodical as a hunter. She goes into the bathroom, finds a towel and takes it to the German to put underneath him. Moving his body, feeling his soft weight, makes her retch. She coughs, shakes her head.

Once the towel is in place, she pulls out her knife, which exits the body with a slow suction, followed by a trailing string of blood. The wound seeps a little, staining the man's gabardine tunic, but does not bleed as much as she feared. She takes a deep breath, then yanks his boots off, one by one, using her foot against his leg as leverage, to stop him sliding across the floor. She unbuttons his sodden breeches and pulls them off. His pale flesh is still warm. He has hairy calves, a scar on his knee, a hole in one sock.

She works fast now, unbuckling his leather belt, pulling off his tunic, shirt, socks. Wristwatch. Wedding ring. She manoeuvres him about like a floppy dressmaker's dummy – a clammy, damp dummy – until he is left in only his underwear. She pauses for a moment, then pulls them off as briskly as a nanny pulling swimming trunks from a wet child on a cold beach, looking away at the windows.

Then she drags him into the kitchen, her hands under his armpits, his bare heels squeaking against the floor. It is an arduous task, he is almost too heavy to move, and she kicks at the furniture in frustration, wiping the sweat from her eyes.

Once into the kitchen, she opens the window as wide as she can, and heaves him towards it. The only way she can think of to get him over the window ledge, is to position herself beneath him and topple him over, so she wedges him against the wall, then crawls under his body, to raise him up on her shoulders in a cumbersome fireman's lift, groaning with effort, her hands pushing deep into his fleshy stomach, forcing his body through the gap, his wobbly head knocking against the frame, until he finally tips and goes, plummeting into the pile of rubbish with a clattering bang. She watches him fall. A naked corpse found by some bins might buy her a little more time than an SS officer discovered stabbed in a luxury apartment.

It is then that she notices a young girl standing in the window of a building opposite, her hands pressed to the glass, staring. They look at each other. Cristabel puts an unsteady finger to her lips.

She pushes herself on. Makes herself go back into the living room, where she repositions the furniture, rehangs the paintings. The German's wet uniform is still lying on the floor. After a quick search, she finds a neatly packed suitcase under the main bed. She empties its contents into a bedside drawer, then fills it with the officer's clothes and boots. She adds his gun and the bloodstained paperweight. Then she returns to the living room and uses the towel to mop the floor, before squashing that too into the suitcase. Before she leaves, she goes back into the kitchen and glances at the window opposite, but the girl has gone.

In the street outside, the evening light is radiant, and screaming swifts are darting between the buildings. She walks back to Mme Aubert's, lugging the heavy suitcase with her, and posts the key to the apartment through the letter box. She retrieves her bike and pedals away, wobbling slightly, the suitcase balanced precariously on her handlebars, wearing a jacket she found in a wardrobe buttoned tightly over her bloodstained dress.

Antigone

The following morning, she meets Lieselotte in a quiet café near the Jardin du Luxembourg to tell her she needs a new name, new papers, new clothes and a new address. Claudine Beauchamp is done. She has been compromised.

'Anything else?' asks Lieselotte, taking a bite of croissant, then grimacing. 'I'm not sure what they have made this with, but it is not flour.'

'I have a suitcase I need to get rid of,' says Cristabel, ordering a brandy. They are seated outside at a round marble-topped table, side by side on rattan chairs, looking out at the street. Cristabel is wearing sunglasses. There is a large bruise on her temple she has attempted to cover with make-up.

'A new identity, a suitcase you need to get rid of and a breakfast brandy. You have been busy,' says Lieselotte.

'I have been foolish. I took unnecessary risks.'

'I am sure your information about the barracks will be useful,' says Lieselotte. 'I will pass it on as quickly as I can.'

'Worth a life, do you think?'

Lieselotte breaks a piece from her croissant and gives it to her dog under the table. She is in green and white today, with elaborate earrings made from twisted silver, and a pillbox hat with green netting. She says, 'I can find you clothes and a place to stay, but papers will take longer. My contacts are all printing leaflets for the Resistance.' She looks at Cristabel, who is stony-faced, and adds, 'Last Bastille Day, the Resistance released leaflets in every theatre in Paris, all at the same time. It was beautiful. An act of theatre in itself.'

Cristabel says nothing. They sit in silence for a while, watching people go by. A group of children running into the gardens. A man carrying a laughing woman on the crossbar of his bike. A horse-drawn milk cart.

Lieselotte says, 'Claudine Beauchamp will have one more outing. She has a ticket for *Antigone* tonight. As do I. Arranged by Herr Schulte. To be left at the theatre door in our names.'

Cristabel shakes her head. 'I don't want to go to the theatre.'

Lieselotte signals the waiter for the bill. 'Well, I don't want to go alone. Be ready at six. I'll have some clothes sent round.' She picks up her handbag, turns to Cristabel. 'Did you expect this to be fair?'

There are no taxis left in Paris so Claudine Beauchamp and Lieselotte de Brienne travel to the theatre in one of the 'vélo-taxis' that have taken their place: wheeled carriages like rickshaws, just big enough for two, pulled along by a man or woman on a bicycle. Some have roofs to protect passengers from the weather, and some are powered by two people pedalling a tandem, but theirs is open to the summer sky and pulled by one man in a beret and shirtsleeves, baggy trousers tucked into his socks, who takes them rattling along the streets at a lively pace, thin wheels bouncing on the cobbles.

It is peculiar to travel so fast while being so low to the ground they could reach out and touch the knees of pedestrians. It is equally curious to travel in a contraption pulled by a human not an animal, but their cyclist is whistling, the breeze is refreshing, and Paris is lovely even from a low angle. They trundle along at kerbstone height, looking out at the table legs and chair legs of the café terraces, the crossed legs of customers, the suited legs, the fishnet legs, the intertwined legs, and the stray cats that wind among them.

The streets may be empty of traffic, the restaurants not as busy as usual, and the cinemas shut, but many Parisians who would normally depart for the coast in the summer remain in the city. Even if there is no food, there is usually some company and an ersatz beer to be found, and it is Saturday, the Allies are in Normandy, the Russians are taking the fight on to German soil, and the theatres are still open.

'Tell me about your theatre,' says Lieselotte, as they head northwards. 'Do you have a resident company?' Lieselotte is in a burgundy taffeta evening gown with matching cape, an avalanche of pearls around her neck, and holding a gold clutch bag too small to contain her dog, which has been left with the maître d' at Lucas Carton.

Cristabel, a pillar of black satin, shakes her head. 'Nothing like that. We had volunteers. People borrowed from the local amateur dramatic society. We're based out in the countryside, so somewhat limited.'

'Do you not have signs?' says Lieselotte, as their carriage rattles across the stately Boulevard Haussmann, where mannequins pose in the windows of grand department stores.

'Signs?'

'Signs, like a circus. To tell people you are there,' says Lieselotte, gesturing at one of the large swastikas hanging from a nearby building.

'No.'

'Do you have visiting companies?'

Cristabel shakes her head again, rummaging in her borrowed evening bag for cigarettes. 'It was only me, and some friends, and anyone I could force to do my bidding.'

Lieselotte frowns. 'Force? Why did you force them? Did they not want to do it?'

'Not like I did.'

'Then why use them? You must find those who care about it as much as you do.'

'Easier said than done.'

'Most things are. Do you care about it?'

'Of course.'

'You don't have to care about it,' says Lieselotte, 'but if you don't care about it, you should find what you do care about. This is the rule I have for my salons also. I do not care what your interests are – tennis or architecture or playing the bassoon – as long as you have one.'

'I do care about it,' says Cristabel.

'Forgive me, but from what I have heard, you are a theatre director who prefers to be called a student, who uses half-hearted amateurs as actors, who is disenchanted by her own productions, but does not invite other companies to visit, and will not put up a sign.'

'That's a little unfair,' says Cristabel.

'It is not. Do you want to create? To make something?'

'Of course.'

'Of course is not yes.' Lieselotte looks at Cristabel: her pale face, her bruised forehead. Cristabel looks away, lights a cigarette.

Their cyclist is working hard now, pulling them up the slope of the city through Pigalle, neighbourhood of artists' studios and after-dark entertainment, where German soldiers are lining up outside the cabarets.

After a while, Lieselotte says, 'In this city, it is impossible to make theatre. No power. No lights. No money. Every script must be approved by the Germans, the *Propagandastaffel*, so the writers must squeeze themselves into ridiculous shapes to have their work accepted. If they get their plays on to the stage, they will be berated by those who say it is treason to put on plays and they will be reviewed by those who want only to score political points. It is impossible. Yet look where we are.'

They have arrived in Montmartre, the closely packed hill village at the top of Paris, where the Théâtre de l'Atelier sits by itself in a cobblestone square, overlooked by spindly linden trees, and flanked on either side by apartment buildings and restaurants. It is a small theatre, painted white, with three arched double doors on the ground floor and three arched windows on the first floor, where there is a balcony and a bar, and it is surrounded by people waiting to go in.

Their cyclist helps them out of the vélo-taxi, and nods at the crowd. 'Busy tonight.'

Lieselotte replies, 'They say it is busy every night. Have you been?'

'In February,' he says. 'Nearly froze to death.'

'It was cold in February,' she says, pressing a large tip into his hands. 'Thank you, monsieur.'

Lieselotte and Cristabel join the people heading into the theatre and collect their tickets at the box office. There is a sign in the foyer with directions to the nearest air raid shelter, and instructions that theatregoers should stay out of the circle in case of bombs, so they make their way through to the stalls.

Inside, the theatre is dark, curved, intimate. The red seats of the stalls are close to the stage, so there is little distance between performers and audience. There are no lights in the building, so theatre staff stand by with torches to guide people to their places. Lieselotte waves at several people she knows.

Cristabel spots Herr Schulte, and her stomach lurches queasily, remembering she gave his name to Mme Aubert, who may soon be passing on that information to those investigating the murder of an SS officer, along with a description of a tall woman who goes by the name Claudine. Herr Schulte waves cheerfully. He is at the front of the audience, in evening wear, with a few other men who look German. Lieselotte tells her that the theatre must set aside a certain number of seats for the Germans in every production.

The evening begins with a short piece called *À Quoi Rêvent les Jeunes Filles* by a nineteenth-century playwright, which is immediately interrupted by the wail of an air raid siren. The audience, unperturbed, pick up their things and walk back out into the square, continuing their conversations. The sky over the city is peach now, streaked with the long clouds of sunset, and sparrows are gathering in the trees. Cristabel notices that the audience is mixed: older people in formal outfits, alongside young people in shirts and skirts, a group of whom stand near her, sharing one cigarette between five.

When the all-clear is sounded, they file back in to watch the rest of the first play. The lack of stage lighting somehow has the effect of bringing the actors closer, as if the audience were watching a rehearsal rather than a performance. Then they wait for the curtain to rise on *Antigone*.

'Do you know the story? It is a Greek tragedy,' says Lieselotte, who has put on her pince-nez to squint at the programme.

'I do,' says Cristabel.

'What is most intriguing about Anouilh's version,' says Lieselotte, 'is that nobody can agree on it. All the critics adore it, but for different reasons. Some praise it for being a Vichy play or a fascist play, others for being a Resistance play, even an anarchist play.'

'Anarchist?'

'Yes. On the opening night, when the curtain fell, there was total silence. Nobody could believe that such a play would be passed by the censors. But that's the strangest thing, the Germans want to see it as much as the French. Everybody is convinced that it speaks to them.'

As Lieselotte says this, the curtain rises on a bare shadowy stage, which is lit only by a column of natural light falling through a skylight. The back wall of the set looks like draped curtains, and the actors sit on a row of steps beneath it. The women in black gowns, the men in white tie and tails, with a few in raincoats and homburg hats. They are playing cards, chatting, as if they had just stepped out of a party.

One of them, a man in glasses and a bow tie, strolls towards the edge of the stage. He smiles at the audience familiarly and says, '*Voilà*. The people gathered here are about to act the story of Antigone. The one who's playing the lead is that skinny girl sitting there. Staring in front of her. Thinking. She's thinking that soon she's going to be Antigone. That she'll suddenly stop being the thin dark girl whose family didn't take her seriously, and rise up alone against everyone. Against Creon, the king. She's thinking she's going to die . . .' he pauses here and looks at the audience members closest to him '. . . although she's still young and, like everyone else, would have preferred to live.'

Cristabel leans forward.

The play moves swiftly. It begins with Antigone secretly trying to bury the body of her brother who has been killed in battle but denounced as a traitor. She is arrested by guards and taken to Creon. Creon tells her that nobody is above the law. He tells her that someone has to steer the ship. He says, 'The only things that have got a name now are the ship and the storm. Do you understand?'

Antigone says, 'I'm not here to understand. I'm here to say no to you, and to die.'

There is a ripple through the audience at this, a collective intake of breath, scattered claps.

Creon does not give up. He wants to save Antigone. He tells her it is easy to say no, that saying yes is the harder task, one that requires rolling up your sleeves and getting stuck in. There are nods in the audience at this, murmurs of agreement.

But the light falling through the skylight is fading, the darkness in the theatre is spreading on to the stage, and Antigone refuses to be saved. From there, the clockwork tragedy unfolds all by itself and death follows death follows death until the curtain falls.

There is a moment of silence, then the audience stands and applauds furiously, shouting *bravo, bravo*. Cristabel remains in her seat. Staring in front of her. Thinking.

She had followed Antigone closely throughout the play, sticking right on her heels – Antigone who gets up early to be the first one alive, Antigone who feels the whole world is waiting and is annoyed that it does not seem to be waiting for her. Cristabel had followed her like someone who has spotted someone they think they know. But Anouilh's play led her first one way, then the other, and left her somewhere in the middle, believing that although Antigone was right, she was also foolish, and that although Creon was at fault, he was not altogether wrong.

She can see how Antigone's martyrdom must appeal to the young Parisians in the audience, but what freedom does Antigone have? Her sole self-directed act ends in her death, offstage. She defends her brother, then handily tidies herself away, hanging herself in her own dress. Just as in Shakespeare's *Measure for Measure*, the defiant sister who defends her brother is tidied away into an unlikely marriage at the end of the play. What if, wonders Cristabel, there was a version in which they stayed? Stayed alive. Stayed themselves.

Cristabel looks across at Lieselotte who, with the rest of the audience, is clapping the bowing actors they can now hardly see. She sees Lieselotte's proud profile in the half-light, the exuberant mass of pearls around her neck.

The cast leave the stage and the theatre staff with torches reappear. The audience moves towards the exits, hurrying to catch the last Métro before curfew. As Cristabel follows Lieselotte along the row of seats, she sees two stagehands darting on to the stage, to pick up the few props left behind: a wine bottle, some playing cards. The smaller of the two catches her eye, and then the curtain comes down.

Outside the theatre, one of the street lamps that stands in the square has flickered into life. It is covered with blue paper, giving off an eerie, maritime glow. None of the other lamps are working; there are only a few low candles in nearby restaurant windows, where waiters are sweeping up.

Lieselotte's vélo-taxi has returned to take her home. Cristabel says she will make her own way, and watches as Lieselotte disappears into the night in her human-powered chariot. Cristabel then circles the theatre, looking for the stage door. Once she finds it, she waits in the shadowy doorway of a building opposite, watching as the cast come out, exchanging kisses, waving goodbye, until she sees the smaller stagehand, in pulled-down hat and turned-up collar, come through the door and make his way along the cobbled street.

She follows at a careful distance as he walks swiftly up the steep paths of Montmartre, stopping only to tie his shoelace. He turns a corner, and she increases her pace, but when she gets there, he has vanished. She moves forward cautiously, looking around. She is up high now, the wind is blowing, and she can see the dark city spread out beneath her, the thin scaffold of the Eiffel Tower in the distance. Then she hears a footstep, and a voice behind her says, 'Did you think they taught me nothing, Crista?'

We

She is so furious with him she cannot let him go. She holds him tight against her and swears copiously in a ferocious mix of French and English. He hugs her back, laughing, and saying, 'I know, I know.'

She pushes him away from her. 'Where have you been? Digby, where have you been?'

'I'm Denis here,' he says in French, 'and we should get off the streets before we're arrested. This way – I have a place nearby.'

He leads her to a small bistro. There is a door at the side of the building, which Digby unlocks, looking both ways down the street before guiding her inside. She follows him up a staircase to a tiny apartment that sits above the restaurant. It is dark inside, all the curtains are drawn, but she sees the flickering light of a candle coming from one room, and a male voice says, 'Denis?'

'I have someone with me,' replies Digby. He glances at Cristabel, then leads her into the room, saying, 'Jean-Marc, this is Cristabel, my sister. Cristabel, this is Jean-Marc.'

She sees a young Frenchman in glasses, with brown curly hair, sitting in a shabby armchair, reading a newspaper by candlelight. He is in vest and trousers, with bare feet crossed in front of him. He stands as she enters, looks at Digby. 'Your sister?'

'I should have known she would track me down,' says Digby, smiling.

Jean-Marc hastily puts down the newspaper and holds out his hand. 'It is such an honour to meet you, Cristabel. I've heard so much about you.'

'I'm Claudine here,' she says, returning the handshake firmly. 'What have you heard?'

'Only good things,' he says. 'Can I get you a drink? I would offer coffee but there is so little gas, it takes an hour to boil the water.'

'I'll get the wine,' says Digby, heading to the kitchen. 'Crista, take a seat. My God, we have so much to talk about. I can't believe you're here.'

Jean-Marc gestures to the armchair next to him, and Cristabel sits down for a moment, only to discover that she is too keyed up to make polite conversation, so follows Digby into the kitchen, where she finds him pulling the cork from a wine bottle.

'It's just a vin de pays –' he begins.

'Where have you been?' she whispers. 'I've been worried sick.'

'Did someone send you to find me?' says Digby.

'No, I spotted you because I happened to be in the audience while you were wandering about onstage.'

'It's my cover, I work there,' he says.

Cristabel looks at him, trying to take in what she is seeing. He is Digby but he isn't Digby. He looks entirely French. His dark hair is longer, worn slicked back like the young Parisians. He is wearing baggy trousers held up by a narrow leather belt, and a striped shirt open at the neck, with the sleeves rolled up. He hasn't shaved for a few days, and is thin and tanned, but his brown eyes are very bright. She has the strangest urge to run her hands over his face, to check he is real.

'You work for the Org,' she says, 'who are very keen to know where you are. I work for them too. I was in France last year, carrying out my own mission, and they called me back to question me about your whereabouts.'

'Did they?'

'I did not enjoy it.'

'No, that can't have been fun. Tell me everything you've been up to, Crista.' Digby puts a hand on her arm, adding, 'I've missed you so much. I like your dress.'

'Never mind about my bloody dress. Why haven't you contacted London?'

'Are you cross with me?'

'Nobody knows what the hell you've been doing, Digs. I thought

477

you'd been captured by the Nazis. I nearly went out of my mind.' Her voice seems very loud in the small kitchen.

He looks suddenly concerned. 'I'm sorry. I didn't think you would know anything about it. Does Father know? Or Floss?'

'Just me.'

'What did they tell you?'

'That your circuit was blown but you were still at large. They suspected you were compromised.'

He shakes his head. 'There's far more to it than that. They used us shamefully.'

'Who?'

'London,' he says. 'Last year, they kept telling us the invasion was coming. We took huge risks to get everything ready. But it was a deception.'

'A deception?'

'A trick they were playing on the Germans, to distract them. To make them think it would happen in September. We're convinced that's what they were doing. Jean-Marc says they used us like bait.' He turns to get wine glasses from a cupboard.

'I'm sure they had their reasons,' says Cristabel.

'I'm sure they did too, and they would be the same reasons they have for all they do: their own interests.'

'Agents in the field don't get told everything.'

He turns to her fervently. 'They lied to me, and I believed those lies, and I persuaded my friends to believe those lies, and they risked their lives on my behalf and most of them are now in prison or dead. Because they trusted me.'

She says nothing.

'What would you do in that situation, Crista? Should I go back to London, to those liars behind desks who thought the lives of our allies were disposable, or should I stay here and fight the war I signed up for?'

When she still says nothing, he pours wine into the glasses, hands her one. He says, 'If I could have contacted you, I would have. Let's go into the other room.'

Jean-Marc half stands as they reappear. Cristabel returns to the

478

spare armchair. Jean-Marc sits back down. Digby sits on the rug. There is a silence in the candlelit room, and in the city outside. Cristabel stares at the floor, considering what Digby has told her.

Jean-Marc turns to her. 'How did you find Denis?'

'I was at the theatre,' she replies.

'Did you come on your own?' asks Digby.

'I'm not going to go into the details,' Cristabel says, shifting in her chair. There are bruises on her body, and she cannot find a comfortable position.

'You can talk in front of Jean,' says Digby. 'There are no secrets here.'

'There probably should be,' she says, rubbing her eyes. She wishes she could talk to her brother without someone else there, and she wishes he would consider she might want to do that. She is immensely grateful to find he is still alive, almost dizzy with relief, but shaken by their sudden meeting, and confused by the situation she finds herself in. She feels the safest option is to stick to operational matters. She says, 'Denis, did you stay at an apartment managed by Madame Aubert? Near the Arc de Triomphe.'

He laughs. 'Oh, you found her too, did you? I tracked her down after our circuit collapsed. I was there till Jean-Marc found this place. Isn't she dreadful? She's on Jean-Marc's list.'

'List?'

'We are compiling a list of known collaborators,' says Jean-Marc, 'for after the war.'

'Something happened in that apartment block,' says Cristabel, without looking at them. 'An SS officer was killed. It would be prudent to assume that, even though the Germans are a little preoccupied, they will be seeking any possible suspects. Particularly those who told Madame Aubert they were from an English family.'

'I knew that was a risk,' says Digby, pulling a face, 'but it persuaded her to let me stay.'

'It would be wise for you to keep moving, Denis,' says Jean-Marc.

'I have a contact who is finding me a place,' says Cristabel, 'you could stay with me. If you want.'

Digby nods. 'All right. I'll need to get some things from the theatre.'

'We can go early tomorrow,' says Jean-Marc. 'You should take some of the new leaflets.'

'We've been creating a manifesto for revolution, to be distributed throughout Paris,' says Digby. 'Jean, you must read what you wrote yesterday to Crista. Go from the bit that starts: "Betrayed by our elders". I'll find us something to eat.'

Cristabel watches Digby as he heads to the kitchen. There is an energy to his movements. The jitteriness she saw when they were last together in Dorset seems to have gone, or rather, seems to have been focused and is now carrying him forward, buoyant as a sailboat.

Jean-Marc picks up a notebook from the floor, coughs politely, and reads, ' "Betrayed by our elders, the bourgeois pseudo-elite, we have found ourselves as outlaws in our own country. We have said no to the lies and we are brothers because we have said no." '

'Very stirring,' says Cristabel.

'That last line was inspired by *Antigone*,' says Jean-Marc. 'Did you see in the programme she is described as "the sister of all those who say no"? We have seen it so many times. Every time, it inspires us.'

Digby reappears empty-handed. 'I don't know why I went to the kitchen. I know we have no food. Tell me, how's darling Floss?'

'She's fine. In the Land Army.'

'Wonderful!' exclaims Digby.

Jean-Marc puts a finger to his lips. 'It is late.'

'Crista, you must be tired, I'm sorry – I'm being a terrible host,' says Digby. 'Jean, could we make up the camp bed for her?'

'Certainly,' says Jean-Marc, putting his notebook down, then heading into an adjoining room.

'We don't often have visitors,' says Digby brightly.

Cristabel feels suddenly overwhelmed by it all. She is tired and sore, resentful of being made to listen to revolutionary speeches, disgruntled by Digby's inability to notice her resentment, and now she is being put to bed like a child, and it makes her angry and frustrated and horribly close to tears.

'Did you really miss me?' she says.

'Yes. Why do you say that?'

She shakes her head, unable to speak.

He kneels on the floor next to her, his wide eyes concerned. She shakes her head again, looks away, her eyes filling. He leans forward, puts his arms around her. 'What is it? Tell me.'

'You don't know,' she manages, 'what it's like.'

'What do you mean?'

'Every morning, you wake up, and there's a moment when it's all right. A split second. But then you remember. You don't know where they are, you don't know if they're alive or dead, and that's all you can think about, for every hour of every day. It's bloody agony.'

He tightens his hold on her, kisses the top of her head. 'You're here now. And I'm here. You always did worry about me too much.'

'I have to,' she says, leaning against him. 'Nobody else does.'

'That's better,' he says. 'You sound quite aggrieved, like your old self.'

She laughs, wipes her nose with her sleeve. 'Who's Jean-Marc?'

Digby sits back and smiles. 'A Resistance leader and a fine one. We intend –'

'No, I mean, who is he to you? Is he why you're here?'

He looks at her again. 'We're here because it's the right thing to do. Why do you ask?'

'I simply wondered. A lot of your sentences seem to start with the word "we".'

'Isn't that a good way to begin?' says Digby. 'I like to think of being part of a we. I don't only mean those of us here, I mean all those who feel the same as we do.'

'You always did want everyone to join in,' says Cristabel, noting he has not fully answered her question. 'Always rounding up people to be in your games. Do you remember when you persuaded the postman to read the part of Lady Macbeth?'

Digby smiles and looks at Jean-Marc's notebook, lying on the floor. 'Crista, aren't you sick of always having to do it their way? It's so formulaic, so hidebound. The thought of us winning this war only to go back to the way we were before, it's unbearable.'

Jean-Marc calls from the other room, 'Can you help me with these blankets, Denis?'

Cristabel watches Digby go, finishes her wine. She can hear rain starting to fall outside. She thinks then of the two of them up on the roof of Chilcombe, when they were a big I and a little i who were a we, which seems no longer to be the we in which he wants to be.

Cristabel undresses in the box room she is to sleep in, climbing carefully into a fold-out canvas bed. The walls of the apartment are paper thin, and she can hear the opening of cupboards in the room next door, and Digby's murmured conversation with Jean-Marc, then the sounds of them getting into bed. There is something in their fond tone, and the sound of Digby laughing quietly, that tells her they are very close together. There is something childish and petulant in her that wants to creep out of bed and press a glass to the wall, to hear what they are saying, but they are whispering now, so she couldn't hear them even if she tried. She pulls a blanket over her head, then lies stiffly in her bed until she falls asleep.

They leave early next morning. Digby is carrying a bag of clothes while Jean-Marc has an empty suitcase holding an empty briefcase, both of which are to be filled at the theatre. Stepping out into Montmartre from the cramped apartment, stretching and yawning, feels like climbing out of a tent pitched high on a mountain. Below them, the sun is just appearing over the grey rooftops of Paris. As they make their way down the steep cobbled streets, the first beams of sunlight come jinking up the narrow gullies of the city to meet them, picking out apartment windows and painting them gold.

'It's so quiet,' says Cristabel, as they arrive at the square that holds the theatre. She is still in last night's evening gown and heels, and internally cursing, not for the first time, the impracticality of women's clothing, its limited uses.

'A city populated only by birds,' says Digby, gazing up into the trees where sparrows are chirruping. 'Imagine living in a city like that.'

She looks at him and her heart suddenly aches with knowing him. He has always had this hopeful way about him, a quality of elsewhere, a boy of treetops and light.

'Normally, the bakers would be up and about, but they have nothing to bake,' says Jean-Marc, unlocking the stage door.

'When the Allies get here, we will have bread again,' says Digby.

'With thick butter,' says Jean-Marc.

'Stop it, you're making my stomach rumble,' says Cristabel, following the two men inside. She finds herself next to an office containing pigeonholes for the actors' post and a few wilting bouquets of flowers. Jean-Marc locks the door behind them, and they make their way down a corridor, where the unplastered walls are covered with posters from previous productions. The corridor winds about the back of the building, passing cramped dressing rooms full of rails of costumes and cluttered dressing tables.

Digby takes the empty cases and heads off down a narrow set of stairs, saying, 'I'll be as fast as I can.'

'We'll meet you at the stage,' says Jean-Marc, leading Cristabel along a labyrinthine passage that brings them out at the side of the stage. It is the first time she has ever been backstage at a theatre. From where they stand, she can see the hanging layers of different backdrops, swaying gently, painted scenes of different places, multiple dimensions. Beside her is a complicated row of ropes, heading upwards into the roof of the theatre, like the rigging on a ship. She has the sense of being on the edge of something ceremonial, something larger than herself, as if waiting behind a curtain before an audience with an emperor.

Jean-Marc turns to Cristabel. 'It is wonderful to watch the production from here.' His voice is respectfully hushed, even though the theatre is empty. 'Denis tells me that, in England, this space is called the wings, like on a bird.'

'It is.'

'I like that. Here is the effort, you know, the beating of the wings, lifting the performers.'

There is a noise from somewhere underneath them. Then, a moment later, a wooden trapdoor in the middle of the stage is pushed open and Digby appears like a jack-in-the-box, proclaiming, ' "If we shadows have offended, think but this and all is mended: that you have but slumbered here, while these visions did appear!" '

As his voice echoes about the theatre, Cristabel hears his father in him – Willoughby's warm story-telling baritone – as if Digby briefly embodied an older version of himself. Having not seen him for so long, she now seems to be seeing different versions of him, some familiar, some strange. Past and present and future Digby.

'I'll pass the stuff up,' he says, then disappears below stage.

Jean-Marc walks to centre stage, and Cristabel follows, looking out at the rows of red seats. How exposing it feels to be there, even with nobody in the audience. The theatre doesn't feel entirely empty.

Digby appears from the trapdoor again. Looking down into it, Cristabel sees he is standing on an adjustable wooden platform. He hands up the leather briefcase, which is heavy now.

'What are you bringing?'

'Ink and paper mainly,' says Digby. 'You wouldn't believe how precious they are.'

'They're the best weapons we have,' adds Jean-Marc, 'especially as London won't send us any guns.'

'Jean-Marc keeps asking, but they ignore him,' says Digby. 'It's like writing to my father. Do you know what Perry said to me once, he said they were reluctant to give the French too many weapons as they might use them for mischief after the war. As if we were naughty children.'

Cristabel thinks of Perry, pouring tea in the café at Fortnum & Mason, telling her that wars are fought to determine what happens afterwards. Any pleading request from someone like Jean-Marc that landed on his desk would be neatly disposed of.

'Do you hear from him?' says Digby. 'Father, I mean.'

She shakes her head.

'Denis, we must hurry,' says Jean-Marc. 'The cleaners will be here soon.'

'I just need to pack the other case.' Digby vanishes beneath the stage.

Cristabel and Jean-Marc wait together. After a while, she says politely, 'Have you managed to keep the theatre open all through the war?'

'We closed when the Nazis first arrived,' he says. 'When we opened again, we were limited in what we could perform. Nothing too patriotic. We could only do myths, legends, nostalgic stuff. All the old theatrical ghosts. But the audiences came back.'

Cristabel wonders if it is ghosts she can sense when she stands on the stage. Roles waiting to be stepped into, reinhabited – like Antig-one at the start of Anouilh's play, waiting to become Antigone.

Jean-Marc continues, 'Last winter, it was the hardest we have had, people were so cold, so hungry, but the theatre was the busiest it has been for years.'

'Why was that?'

'Well, for one, it's warmer when you are around other people,' he smiles. 'But when you are struggling, you feel alone, then you come here, and you see others have struggled – like Antigone.'

'You see her courage.'

'Antigone dies alone. But we tell her story at Théâtre de l'Atelier. In here, we still have voices.'

'Even if you don't speak directly.'

'There are many ways to speak,' he says. 'Do you remember that line in *Antigone* – "Nothing is true except that which we don't say." We all know what that means.'

Cristabel looks out at the theatre space, curled in on itself like a seashell containing the echo of the sea. She imagines the audience, shivering in an unheated theatre, leaning against strangers for warmth. She thinks of the playwrights trying to find a way to reach them through the gagging layers of officialdom. Then she thinks of her own pre-war performances, which seem now to be a kind of pointless mumming, an empty masquerade.

'I imagine Denis found it hard to stay offstage,' she says.

Jean-Marc laughs. 'He did. He is a good man, your brother. We are lucky to have had him.' He pauses for a moment, then adds, 'The bruise on your head. It is recent, no?'

'Is it obvious?'

'No, I only noticed when we were outside, but we have stage make-up that will cover it better. I will find some.'

Digby reappears then, lifting a canvas suitcase up through the trapdoor, which Jean-Marc takes from his hands. 'What are you two talking about?'

'The theatre,' says Cristabel. She hopes Digby has not noticed the bruise. She does not want to talk about that apartment, with him or anyone.

From outside, they hear the sound of aeroplanes approaching. 'The Allies can only be days away now,' says Digby.

'My lazy old man will be getting out of his armchair for the first time since the war began, pinning on his rusty medals,' says Jean-Marc.

'We won't let the old men claim this one,' says Digby, smiling at both of them.

They listen as the planes roar overhead, then Cristabel says, 'Do you have any contacts in Fresnes, Jean-Marc?'

He nods. 'There is a man who works here who is a carpenter in the prison. If you come back tonight, you could speak to him during the show.'

'I need to go to my hotel to change,' she says. 'Is there somewhere Denis could stay? Just for today.'

Jean-Marc smiles. 'There is a woman not far from here who is happy to accommodate young men. She has the perfect cover. Nervous men come and go from her house at all hours. She tells the Germans she keeps the best girls for them, but she lies. She is a true patriot. The best girls are only for the French.'

'She's really such a lovely woman as well,' says Digby.

'Sounds ideal,' says Cristabel briskly, picking up the suitcase.

That evening, Cristabel returns to Théâtre de l'Atelier as the crowds gather outside, but this time, she enters through the stage door. Backstage is busy. As she passes the dressing rooms, she sees half-costumed actors, at the midpoint of make-up, their faces blank with thick foundation, no longer themselves, yet not quite their characters. They are chatting, smoking, singing. She even catches a glimpse of Antigone in her black dress, leaning towards a mirror to brush blusher beneath her high cheekbones. Jean-Marc, who is leading her through the building, turns and says, 'Did you see her?'

Cristabel nods, excited despite herself.

As they get closer to the stage, she hears a noise growing louder, a murmuring din, and realizes it is the audience arriving. She didn't know what a noise they made. Jean-Marc guides her along a passage that runs across the back of the stage, allowing the cast to cross from one side to the other during a production. It is a thrill to pass through here unseen, knowing the audience are taking their seats on the other side of the gauze backdrop. Cristabel is used to hiding in corridors and landings, all the furtive places of a house, but here, in the house of the theatre, life runs through its secret compartments.

Jean-Marc guides her to a space in the wings, tucked beside the props table, where she can watch, if she keeps out of the way.

'Don't step over that line or the audience will see you,' he says, pointing to a white line painted on the floor. 'The actors wait there until it's their turn to go on. I find Denis standing there sometimes. Habit is second nature, *non*? I will see you in the interval.'

Cristabel watches proceedings with intense interest. There are stagehands moving scenery, and two of the actors from the first play are having a whispered conversation about ration tickets while holding their wigs in their hands. The final call goes out backstage, a shout echoing down the maze of corridors. Out front, the chattering audience quietens. The actors finish their conversation, put their wigs on. A stagehand heaves on a thick hemp rope, pulling it hand over hand, and as the curtain sweeps open, Cristabel can hear its long sigh rushing across the stage. One of the actors steps up to the white line. He lifts his face, his mouth moving slightly, then he steps over the line, into the light.

In the interval between the first and second plays, Jean-Marc re-appears and points to a ladder bolted to a wall at the back of the theatre. It leads to a gantry, a platform suspended high over the stage to allow technicians access to the stage lighting. 'Up there,' he says, 'if anyone asks, we're checking the wiring.' They climb the narrow ladder into the darkness, hearing the sound of a pigeon trapped somewhere in the distant roof space above them, murmuring coos, the whisking of wings. Glancing down, Cristabel can see stagehands making the stage ready for the start of *Antigone*.

The gantry is small and wooden, precariously attached to pipes that run along the wall. It sways and creaks as Jean-Marc and Cristabel leave the safety of the ladder and climb on to it. The carpenter is sitting there already, an older man with a cigarette in his mouth, twisting a screwdriver in his hand. He nods at Cristabel, shakes Jean-Marc's hand.

'Fresnes,' says Jean-Marc in a whisper. 'She has questions.'

'I'm looking for two people,' says Cristabel. 'The Germans probably believe they are British agents.' She gives Sophie and Antoine's cover names and a brief description of what they look like.

'The woman has dark hair?' says the carpenter.

'Yes,' says Cristabel, 'she's petite. Smiles a lot. She's probably popular, even in prison.'

He nods. 'I have seen her. Not him, but her.'

'She's alive?'

'I think so.' He pulls a stray filament of tobacco from his lip. 'It is not always good to be popular in prison.' He looks from Cristabel to Jean-Marc.

'Can you get a message to her?' says Jean-Marc.

The carpenter looks down at the stage, where the cast are taking their places. 'Perhaps, but I cannot promise. They keep her separate.'

Cristabel looks at Jean-Marc. 'Is it worth sending a message?'

The carpenter hesitates for a moment, then says, 'If you have anything you want to say to your friend, you should say it now.'

There is something solemn in his voice that gives Cristabel a sense of unease. She holds on to one of the ropes at the side of the gantry.

Jean-Marc puts a hand on her back. 'What do you want to say?'

'I don't know what I can say,' she says.

'We must hurry,' the carpenter says. 'They are going to start soon.'

'Tell her you are with her,' whispers Jean-Marc.

'But I'm not,' she replies.

'She might want to hear that, even if you aren't,' Jean-Marc says. 'What would she want to hear?'

Cristabel can hear the noise in the theatre quietening. She whispers, 'Tell her that I'm close.'

The carpenter nods, tucks his screwdriver into his pocket, gestures to the ladder. 'Anything else?'

'Tell her we will have that night out in London,' says Cristabel.

Cristabel leaves the theatre before *Antigone* begins and walks back down the city through the summer twilight. The air is warm, uncomfortably so, and the streets smell of sewage and uncollected rubbish. There is only one day left in July and Paris is heading into the desert of August, with no food and not much water. Everything is running out. On the tin wall of a stinking pissoir Cristabel reads, in scrawled graffiti: *Vive les Soviets!*

As she crosses the Rue de Rivoli, she sees a German military staff car outside one of the hotels being hurriedly packed by several female staff members, in their grey Nazi uniforms. They are filling it with a peculiar mix of items: a box of files, a case of Moët et Chandon, a sewing machine. One of them is handing out packs of butter to puzzled passers-by, some of whom have stopped to watch. Walking past, Cristabel smells smoke, and looks up to see burning ashes, pieces of charred paper, falling from the sky like snow.

The Island

August, 1944

When Cristabel arrives at the restaurant to meet Lieselotte, she is already leaving.

'If you want to charge nearly a thousand francs for a Camembert, you should ensure your staff look after your customers properly,' she says loudly, handing Cristabel the handbag containing her dog. 'Hold him for me, while I adjust myself.' She pauses for a moment to put on her gloves and tilt her hat – a bright red geometric structure – to one side. 'There. Off we go.'

As they walk along the Boulevard Saint-Germain, Lieselotte takes back her handbag, saying, 'One must never stay in disappointing restaurants, Claudine. Life is short.'

She rummages beneath the dog and pulls out a set of keys and an envelope, which she gives to Cristabel. 'The keys to your new home. The address is in the envelope, along with some money and new papers. The apartment will be empty this evening, when my mother-in-law will have been removed from it. I have the pleasure of escorting her to Avignon, where we will be joining my husband.'

'You're leaving?'

'I am. My mother-in-law is infuriated by the inconvenience caused by the Allies, I miss my husband and, well, those of us who sound German will not be popular soon.'

'But you work for the Americans.'

'There will be many people claiming they work for the Americans. I would rather not be part of that jostling. Do you know if the Métro is working today?'

'I don't think so.'

'I will walk. So now we say goodbye.' Lieselotte stops in the middle of the pavement and kisses Cristabel on each cheek, then unexpectedly reaches out a bejewelled hand, which she places on the side of Cristabel's face. She puts her thumb under Cristabel's chin to push it higher. 'Like that,' she says. 'Keep it like that.' Then she turns and walks smartly down the tree-lined street, her heels rapping on the pavement.

Cristabel watches Lieselotte go, then enters a nearby church, a dark gothic building with a vaulted ceiling. She sits on one of the wooden chairs provided for the congregation, tucked behind a marble column, and carefully opens the envelope.

There is a roll of cash, which she tucks inside her blouse; a new set of identity documents, in which her occupation is listed as theatre director; and the horse-shaped brooch Lieselotte often wore, wrapped in a note. A few lines in an elegant hand – *If you do not want it, sell it, but make sure you get a good price for it. When you reopen your theatre, invite me* – and an address on the Île Saint-Louis.

An elderly priest appears beside her and politely asks if he can help her.

'I don't think so,' she says, 'but thank you all the same.'

In the middle of the Seine are two islands shaped like a whale and its calf. Both islands are reached by bridges, and Cristabel crosses one now to reach the smaller island, the Île Saint-Louis, where she finds Lieselotte's mother-in-law's apartment building in a narrow side street.

The entrance is a huge domed double door surrounded by stonework, a *porte cochère* big enough to let a horse and carriage through. One of the keys allows her to open a small door cut in the larger door, which takes her into a hall leading past the concierge's rooms, and then another key opens a door into the main building, where a wooden staircase with iron bannisters coils upwards. The air inside is cold, mournful, amplifying the noise of her footsteps.

Two more keys in two different heavy locks open the door to the fourth-floor apartment, which has the beeswax and velvet smell of old money. Antique wooden dressers. Bow-legged chairs covered with embroidered fabric. A bedroom sunk in ruffles. Tall French windows – *portes-fenêtres* – that wobble slightly as she opens them. The apartment is near the top of the building, looking out on to the island's sloping rooftops and the cream-coloured apartments across the street. Leaning out and peering right, Cristabel can see the poplar trees on the banks of the Seine.

The rear of the apartment looks down into a courtyard cluttered with the backs of other apartments. Many homes in Paris seem to be like this: formal at the front, gossipy at the back, where kitchen windows overlook kitchen windows, sinks and saucepans, air vents and arguments. There is no electricity, no working lights, and when she turns on the kitchen tap it does nothing for an age then dribbles rusty water. If the building is a body, it is an elderly one, full of coughs and gargles.

Still, she likes it. She's never had a place of her own. Her previous stays in Europe have been in dull French guest houses with Mlle Aubert, or in the Austrian lodgings where she stayed while skiing. In her Swiss finishing school, she had to share a dormitory with girls who only talked about marriage, and her few stays in hotels have been spent reading in her room, avoiding communal areas. Even in Chilcombe, she has never felt entirely welcome. More like someone holding out, against increasing odds. She takes her bag to the bedroom. Puts *Madame Bovary* on the bedside table.

When she goes to meet Digby, crossing the bridge from the island back to the mainland, she has the feeling of striding across the swaying walkway that leads from a ship to a harbour wall, with all the swagger and secrecy of the intrepid voyager.

Together, they hide Digby's cases beneath the floor in the apartment by prising up the wooden floorboards, then Cristabel spends some of Lieselotte's money on a selection of the meagre things left in the nearest grocery: prunes, macaroni, a hard corner of cheese. In the kitchen cupboards, they find a few miscellaneous tins, along with three withered onions, a dusty bottle of brandy and some candle ends. On their first evening, they sit themselves at the polished dining table, with the tall windows open to the sky.

'To our new home,' Digby says, lifting his glass.

'I don't think this macaroni has cooked at all,' Cristabel says. 'I didn't know how long to do it for.'

'Jean-Marc is always laughing at me because I have no idea how to cook anything. I didn't even know how to light the oven.'

She pokes at her food. 'Probably should try to eat it anyway.'

'About Montmartre,' says Digby, after a moment, 'I was thinking, it might have been strange for you.'

She shakes her head. 'Let's not.'

'He's not the reason I stayed, but he is a good man, Crista.'

'He says the same about you.'

'Does he?' Digby laughs. 'Well, we're agreed then.'

She looks at him. 'I'm glad. It was just a shock to see you.'

'And you were cross.'

'Bloody furious.'

He turns his glass on the table. 'I know it must look like I'm doing everything wrong, but I'm not. It's the opposite. I'm finally getting things right.'

There is a distant explosion that makes them both jump. 'Artillery,' he says. 'They're getting closer. Is there a radio here? There's meant to be an hour of electricity tonight.'

They hunt about the apartment for a radio and find one in the bedroom. They take it to the dining room and try to tune it in, twisting the dial backwards and forwards.

'You must have enjoyed working at the theatre,' she says, as the radio crackles.

'Adored it,' he says. 'Being part of the company is like being part of a family.'

Cristabel feels the slight pain of that statement as something like the distant artillery fire: muffled, dull.

He catches her expression. 'Crista. Not like that. I've imagined you and Floss here so many times. Coming to watch me onstage.'

She feels she is dragging something behind her: a cannon, cumbersome and slow. She says, even though she doesn't want to, 'So we'd have to come all the way here to see you.'

'Yes,' he says gently. 'You would.'

A burst of rapid jazz comes from the radio, then the stately French of BBC Radio Londres. The news announcer speaks in the diplomatic language of someone instructed not to give too much away, but the situation sounds promising. Allies gaining ground, Germans retreating. There is a brief mention of the British public waiting at home, and Cristabel thinks of Flossie, and Betty and Joyce, and all the women holding the fort in Chilcombe Mell. They will be listening to their radios too, pausing in their kitchens.

'We used to talk to Taras about theatres in Paris,' Digby says, topping up their glasses. 'Never thought I'd end up a stagehand in one of them.'

'We used to talk to Taras about doing our soul's work,' Cristabel says. 'How ridiculous we were. All our imaginings.'

'You mustn't say that.' He leans forward in his chair. 'Do you know what I love most about being at the theatre? It's a whole building filled with people and equipment and complicated bits of kit that big burly men operate, and its entire purpose is imaginary. Isn't that wonderful?'

'I suppose,' she says.

'When I'm there, I can talk to people about characters, about what acting means, whatever I like, and nobody laughs or scoffs or tells me I need to do something more sensible with my life. I can talk to them like I talk to you.'

He takes a packet of cigarettes from his pocket, finds a half-smoked one, lights it. 'Do you know, at school, we were discouraged from reading fiction. They confiscated my *Wind in the Willows*. I asked for a new one and Father gave me a cricket bat. Told me not to bother with stories. Told me to give up the stage. Everything I've liked has been taken away from me, and nobody could give me a good reason why.'

He exhales and continues, 'I suppose Mother was sympathetic, sometimes. She would come creeping into my room at night, when she was tipsy, with a prawn vol au vent wrapped in a napkin, saying, "I'll be in the front row every night, darling. You'll be the new Olivier. Is that his name? His wife is very pretty." But she'd forget all about it the next day.'

Cristabel smiles at his perfect impression of his mother, the way he makes Rosalind both very herself and somehow more likeable.

He continues, 'Without you and Floss, I would have been lost. You helped me hang on to it, you know, until I got here. But it's not a silly thing. It's not a dream. It's possible.'

'How can you be certain?'

'Because you made me certain,' he says, reaching across the table to hold her hand. 'I say this to Jean all the time. My parentage may have been rather lacking, but I had a splendid role model. The bravest, most determined sister.'

'Hardly,' she says. 'I've done things I'm not proud of.'

'Don't be like that. You can make anything happen. You're our dauntless leader.'

'I'm not, Digs. I wasn't even a leader when I was part of a circuit. I was a courier.'

'You could have been. You're more than good enough to lead a circuit, I'm sure.'

'I might well be,' she says, 'but we will never know, because the Org doesn't allow women to be circuit leaders.'

'Come over to the French. Bugger London. Bugger their silly rules.'

'How many Frenchmen do you know who would be keen to take orders from an Englishwoman?'

'I don't think they'd care. If you were good, and I know you would be, they wouldn't even notice you were a woman.'

'But that's the crux of it, isn't it? Either they notice I'm a woman, and they don't want me because of that, or I have to hope they somehow don't notice, which leaves me rather eradicated either way.'

'I think you're making it more complicated than it needs to be,' he says.

'I'm not making it anything. That's what it is. The only reason you think it's complicated is because you've never thought about it.'

'Hold on,' he says, letting go of her hand. 'I do know what it's like to not fit in. The boy who prefers sonnets to rugby doesn't always have an easy time at school.'

'At least you got to go to school,' Cristabel says, then sighs. 'Perhaps I am being unfair.'

'No, I'm sorry. Didn't mean to be touchy. Go on.'

'Ironically, I find it difficult to talk about, even to you.'

'Why?'

'I feel I'm moaning,' she says. 'One oughtn't to complain about one's lot. One should be grateful to be included at all. But that's how it works, isn't it? We had an instructor who said women were ideal wireless operators because they enjoyed stopping at home all day. Did I challenge him? No, because I didn't want to seem difficult.'

'That's understandable. Nobody wants to stick out too much.'

'Same applies to me running off to join the Resistance. They would use me as an example of why women are unsuited to this kind of work.'

Digby shakes his head, stubs out his cigarette. 'I don't believe that. I'm sure I'm not being held up as an example of why men shouldn't be used in the field.'

'Probably not, which rather proves my point. Although they might, if they knew about you and Jean-Marc.'

'That has nothing to do with it. My feelings about London and my feelings about Jean are completely separate things.'

'I know that, Digs. What you do after hours, so to speak, is your choice.'

He pauses for a moment. 'It's not a choice, Crista. It's who I am.'

She looks at him, and he continues, 'I've never wanted any of it, not really. I don't believe Father wanted it either, do you? Being lord of the manor.'

'I suspect he loathed it,' says Cristabel. 'Not sure he will ever come back to Chilcombe.'

'Why should he? Why do we keep forcing ourselves to do these things? To what end?' Digby laughs. 'I thought I was failing, because I didn't match up. What an enormous waste of time. There's no life for me back there, Crista. Not one I care for.'

'Well, I'm pleased you're decided.'

'You don't sound pleased.'

'I sound spiky, don't I?'

'You do.'

She holds her hand out and he puts the cigarette packet into it. She takes out a crumbling cigarette end and lights it, holding it carefully in her long fingers as she inhales. When she next speaks, her voice is hesitant. 'I suppose it just leaves me in a fix. I mean, I always knew you would head off to university, but I presumed you'd come back too. I thought the rest of it wouldn't matter so much, because we'd have our theatre. But now you've somewhere else to go, and I don't know what I have left. I never imagined it without you.'

'But you've always been so indomitable, Crista. You'll always find a way.'

'A way where? I don't fit anywhere. That's probably why I made the theatre, don't you think?'

'That's precisely what I'm saying,' says Digby. 'We don't fit their moulds.'

She passes the last of the cigarette to him. 'When you inherit Chilcombe, you should give it to Floss.'

'They made me write a will before I flew out to France,' he says. 'You and she get equal shares.'

'They made me write one too, but I didn't have anything to leave anyone.'

They both laugh. Outside, there is the boom of more artillery fire, then the wail of an air raid siren.

Digby says, 'I simply want to choose my own life. Don't you?'

'I have no idea what it would be,' she replies.

'Not knowing is by far the better option,' he says.

They talk late into the night, and the following night too. Of family, of theatre, of war. In the daytime, Digby goes to meet his Resistance colleagues. In the absence of Lieselotte, Cristabel is without a line of contact to the Americans, but Jean-Marc has sent some men cycling out of the city to meet up with the approaching Allied troops, so she decides to wait for them to report back.

The city is bright with August sunshine, but there is an exodus of Germans that is gathering pace: administrative staff leaving in requisitioned civilian cars, military lorries laden with furniture. Cristabel goes to cafés and sits close to the public telephones, where she can catch snatches of conversation. Place names are mentioned in excited whispers. *The Allies have reached Nogent-le-Rotrou! They're nearly at Chartres!* She notices a pair of Wehrmacht troopers sitting impassively at a nearby table and tries to imagine what they are feeling. The waitresses serve them in contemptuous silence.

In the evenings, she and Digby go back to their island quarters, to cook hopeless meals and make cigarettes from the remains of other cigarettes. She likes to pull an armchair close to the window, to look out at the opposite apartments as the evening draws in, their individual windows lit with candles, glowing like honeycomb cells. Then the curtains are closed, the blackout descends on the city, and the Île Saint-Louis must sail through the darkness like a ship on the river.

'Baudelaire lived on this island,' says Digby, who has found a history of Paris on a bookshelf and is leafing through it while lying on the sofa, 'and Chopin.'

'Flossie likes Chopin,' says Cristabel, thinking of her sister at the piano, playing the composer's circular patterns, like pebbles dropped in water. It feels like a scene from another world.

'Digs, I've been thinking,' she says, after a while, 'if I reopen my theatre, I want to do things differently. Watching *Antigone* made me think about whether I could take a play that's been done before and tell it a new way.'

'Go on,' Digby says, putting down his book.

'*The Tempest*, say.'

'How would you do it?'

'I would make it Caliban's story. Start with his birth. With his mother, the witch. Children like witches.'

'You'd do it as a play for children?'

'I might. I can picture it done with shadow puppets.'

'Is Caliban's mother a witch?' he asks. 'I never played him.'

'Perhaps that's just what they say she is. Maybe she isn't at all,' she says. 'You could tell the children they're going to hear a secret story, one that's never been told before.'

'Oh yes, I like that,' says Digby. 'I would do Ariel's story. When I think of him, I see him as a flame, a moving energy.'

'A dancer could play Ariel. A dancer with fire.'

'The whalebones like a cage around him.'

'Yes. Perfect. Is this the last of the brandy?'

'Let me investigate.'

Sometimes, they are visited by Jean-Marc. Cristabel is warming to him. There is an air of readiness about him, a focused commitment. His bouncy curly hair, his earnest face behind his glasses. Digby tells her that Jean-Marc likes to hike in the Pyrenees, and she can picture him there, in rucksack and boots, keenly assessing the wind direction. She notices too his concern for Digby, his insistence that Digby eat, sleep. He is the mountain guide, she thinks; Digby the high clouds that pass over.

There are moments too – when they think she isn't watching – that she sees them look at each other, sometimes with an intensity that feels almost intrusive to witness, sometimes with expressions that are quietly euphoric; prayers and answered prayers.

Occasionally, Jean-Marc has other *résistants* with him, young men and women, and she notices their fierce comradeship, how they rarely talk without a hand on another's shoulder. It reminds her of her team in Scotland, and how much she misses them.

'Most of the *résistants* are sure they will die,' says Digby, lying on the sofa one evening. They are drinking a syrupy peach liqueur found at the back of a cabinet. 'It is strange to hear them talk about it, but they are not unhappy.'

'No,' she says, thinking of Antigone. 'They have belief.' Although, she also remembers that Antigone lost her belief, right at the end, when the martyr's death she had longed for became a gruelling, physical task to be carried out, like forcing yourself to walk out to sea.

Some evenings, Digby will fall asleep on the sofa. Cristabel can tell without looking when Digby is falling asleep because of the change in his breathing. She will sit and listen to his breathing, while in the streets along the Seine, German tanks line up beneath the trees.

★

One night, she wakes with a shriek, fighting for air, the darkness somehow wrapped around her face, tight as a cloth, and Digby comes running into her bedroom, saying, 'What's the matter?'

She is only able to say she had a nightmare, the kind where you can't breathe. She doesn't mention the body in the dream, how it lay on her chest, an immense damp deadweight crushing the oxygen from her lungs, his eyes still open and pleading with her.

Digby brings her a glass of water. He tells her that in North Africa, the desert night would sometimes echo with the screams of soldiers having nightmares. He sits with her for a while, quietly, then puts a cigarette and a lighter on the bedside table and leaves her to go back to sleep.

One evening, in the middle of August, a boy comes running with a message from Jean-Marc to say that he may have news of Sophie and Antoine. Over a thousand prisoners have been taken from Fresnes and loaded into buses. It is rumoured that there are British agents among them, and they are being driven through Paris to a railway station.

Cristabel flies down the stairs, only pausing to walk slowly past the elderly concierge, then runs again to her bike. She pedals furiously through the city, passing chaotic streams of German cars and lorries, which seem to have multiplied like ants overnight. Some vehicles are packed with blank-eyed soldiers returning from the Normandy front, covered with battle dirt, still holding their weapons.

She notices crowds gathering in cafés, and screeches to a halt outside one, to find out what's going on. She can see people inside clustered around a radio. The news comes fast: the Allies have landed in the South of France, the Resistance have come out in support, the Germans are in retreat all across the country. Here in Paris, the police have gone on strike and are marching through the streets in their shirtsleeves. 'Freedom is on its way,' shouts a man, to the sound of cheers.

As Cristabel cycles onwards, she hears sporadic gunfire from the city suburbs. She heads to the Gare de l'Est, thinking she will try that first as trains go to Germany from there. Reaching the station, she throws her bike to the ground and sprints inside only to find it empty. A woman rushing past sees Cristabel's desperate expression, catches hold of her arm and says, 'The prisoners? I've heard they're at Pantin.' The woman jumps on to the back of a waiting motor-cycle, which roars off. Pantin is another station, north-east of the city. Cristabel gets back on her bike and forces herself to stand up on the pedals, pushing them round again and again.

When she finally reaches Pantin, panting and weary, she finds an uneasy stand-off. A train is waiting at the platform, sitting unmoving in the evening sun. It is made up of a long series of old-fashioned cattle wagons, each one guarded by an SS soldier with a machine gun.

On the platform nearby there is a huddle of Nazi officers, one of whom is holding a clipboard, and a large crowd of agitated women, who are pressing forward into a line of guards who keep pushing them back. There are a few representatives from the Red Cross, wearing armbands to identify themselves, who also move forward, only to be shoved back.

Cristabel makes her way into the crowd. Some of the women have notes in their hands, some food parcels and bottles of water. They are pleading with the guards to allow them through, to reach those in the wagons. The guards ignore them. The heat of the bodies packed together on the platform is stifling. Cristabel looks down to see a small boy beside her, holding his mother's hand.

'How long have you been here?' she says to the mother.

'Since lunchtime,' says the woman, her mouth set very tightly. Her hair at her temples is wet with sweat. Cristabel moves her body, so she stands behind the boy, to protect him from the jostling crowd.

Sometimes, a woman is let through to run along the length of the platform, banging on the doors of the cattle wagons, calling out the name of a son or daughter, husband or father. An answering shout from inside means the guards briefly unlock the wagon's wooden doors and slide them open, so a parcel can be pushed into someone's hands. When the doors open, those waiting on the plat-form catch a glimpse of the prisoners standing inside, packed tightly together. At this, there is a rise in shouts from the crowd – a cacophony of called-out names – and an answering rise in violence from the guards, who push the women back, fire their guns into the sky.

Just beside the nearest cattle wagon, Cristabel notices a girl aged about ten, standing next to the padlocked doors. She is dressed smartly, in a neat dress and cardigan, with polished shoes, and holding herself upright, like the impassive SS sentry who stands near her. The girl occasionally glances over to where her mother, a young woman holding a baby, is pleading with one of the Red Cross representatives, but for the most part, she looks upwards, to the tiny opening at the very top of the wagon, which is covered by a metal grille. There, Cristabel can see a man's face, his hands gripping the metal bars. He must be being held up by those inside, in order to reach the grille. He and the girl are looking at each other, steadily, though his hands on the bars are white-knuckled with effort.

Cristabel stands on tiptoe to peer at the Nazi officers, trying to figure out who is in charge, who to approach. There seems to be no logic in why they allow some women through, merely the whims of certain officers at random times. She asks the woman next to her, 'Are they letting anyone off the train?'

'I've heard they will let them out if you can prove they are ill. I have a letter from our doctor,' the woman replies, a crumpled piece of paper gripped in her hand.

Cristabel tries to edge her way towards the front of the crowd, but other women turn on her angrily when she tries to squeeze past them. Her mind is running through the maze of all possible solutions and repeatedly meeting dead ends. She considers trying to get a message to Jean-Marc, to suggest some kind of Resistance interception, a blockage further up the line, but she doesn't know where he is or what route the train will take. She also suspects that there would not be enough people available to attempt an attack on a well-guarded train. She has nothing she can give Sophie or Antoine. No food or water. Her best idea – trying to get close enough to the officers to bribe them with a discreet roll of cash – is ruled out when a woman in front of her tries it and is marched off by a guard.

All Cristabel's shouted entreaties to the officers prove useless. She tries claiming that Sophie is pregnant, that Antoine has an infectious disease, but gets no response. She cannot even think of a reason why she should remain there, but she cannot leave. As the hours pass, the women's shouts become less coherent; they are no longer calling out in the hope they will be answered, they are calling because there is nothing else to do.

The sky is growing dark, and the women are swaying against each other with tiredness, when there is a sudden clanking and hissing, as, with a sickening lurch, the engine starts up and the train begins to slowly move away. There are screams from the women on the platform, muffled shouts from inside the wagons. The crowd heaves forward in panic, several women split away from the group, to run alongside the slowly moving train, the guards shouting after them.

Cristabel waits for a second, expecting gunfire, and when none comes, takes a breath, roughly shoulders her way through the crowd, and also begins to run, glancing at the SS men as she passes. The front of the train has already left the station, the first cattle wagon too, but she lengthens her long stride and reaches the end of the platform in time to bang on the side of the second one. 'Sophie,' she shouts, 'Antoine, Sophie.'

She can see hands at the grilles, pushing out small notes. She can hear some of those inside the wagons singing the Marseillaise. Some take up her shout and call out for Sophie, Antoine. One wagon passes, then another. She bangs on their wooden sides, shouts and bellows, frantic now, furious with the other women on the platform who are shouting over the top of her. As the penultimate wagon goes past her, she hears a clamour inside it, then sees two thin hands on the grille, and a pale, haggard face. Sophie.

'Where are they taking us?' she says, her voice weak.

'I don't know, we'll find out,' says Cristabel. The train is moving faster, and Sophie falls from the grille as her wagon judders over the rails, then she reappears.

'Make sure my boy's all right,' she says. 'Only tell him the good stuff.'

'I will, I will, don't say that,' calls Cristabel. She is right at the end of the platform now and forced to come to a halt, as the train moves away without her. 'Don't say that,' she shouts after it. She sees a small hand waving through the grille, multiple voices shouting messages she can't make out, then the train blows its whistle, and leaves the station, lumbering slowly round a bend.

She can hear an SS guard barking orders at her as she watches the train head out of sight. She decides she will watch it until the last possible second, even if they shoot her for it. They will not move her from this spot. She straightens her spine, so that when they shoot her, she will be standing tall. The guard is shouting again, and he is closer now.

Then she remembers the notes thrown from the wagons, lying on the platform at her feet, and whatever it is that is so rigid and unmoving in her tears apart. She swears, swears and swears again, vehemently spitting her words down the empty railway line towards the vanished train, then she turns and raises her hands, so the guard knows she is obeying him.

Behind him, she can see the crowd of women splintering into pieces, distraught now, some running for the exit, some sinking to the floor. She picks up as many of the dropped notes as she can, then heads quickly back towards the station, passing the little girl in her smart dress, still standing upright at the platform edge.

Back on the island, she sprints up the stairs to her apartment, where she finds a scene of industry, despite the fact it is growing late. Jean-Marc and Digby are sorting posters into piles to be plastered across the walls of the city by willing runners – a group of teenagers are waiting by the door, each holding a satchel.

'There's a train,' she says, breathing heavily, 'just left Pantin. It's carrying the prisoners from Fresnes. Can we stop it?'

Jean-Marc glances at her. 'We can try to get a message to the Americans, but it is hard to contact anyone at the moment.' Then he turns and issues rapid instructions to the runners, while handing each a stack of posters.

'What about the Red Cross?' she says. 'Can we go through them?'

'You can try,' he says. He pulls on a satchel of his own and puts a hand on her shoulder. 'The faster we end this war, the better their chances.' He quickly kisses Digby on both cheeks, then follows the runners out into the night. Digby watches him go from the window.

'Where would they be taking them?' Cristabel says. 'The prisoners. I don't understand what they're doing with them. Most Germans want to leave as fast as possible, not bother with prisoners.'

'We might think they're losing, but they won't think that,' says Digby. 'Not all of them. They'll be following orders. Transporting enemies of Germany to the camps.'

'Camps? POW camps?'

'We've had some reports that suggest they're not POW camps,' he says. 'Not as we would understand them. Let's hope the Allies get there first. Sit down. I'll get you a drink.'

She slumps into an armchair in her sweat-stained clothes, feeling for the first time her aching legs, her sore feet. She kicks off her shoes. Accepts a drink from Digby. He blows out the candles so they can open the curtains, letting in the night air.

They sit together in silence for a while.

'You can always talk to me, you know,' he says, a voice in the darkness. 'About anything.'

'We have a telephone in the house now,' she replies, 'so I just might.'

'Whatever is the world coming to,' he says, and she can hear him smile.

In the last hour before curfew, they walk around the island, hoping to meet someone who might sell them a few cigarettes. There are steps leading down to cobbled walkways along the water's edge, where they find those who want to be close to the dark river. Anglers. Drunks. Runaways. Those who might talk themselves into a room for the night, and those who will slip beneath the waves before the dawn, the island sailing on without them, long lines of fishing rods trailing from its sides like harpoons.

August

August, Paris, 1944. Magnificent weather. Allies approaching from the east and the south. Afternoon gunshot in the streets, crackling through the heat like a grouse shoot. Cristabel cycles through the city, its avenues simmering in the sunlight, carrying messages for Jean-Marc.

She takes with her the notes thrown from the train at Pantin, passing them on to their intended recipients if she can. She has to open them to find names and addresses but tries not to look at the contents. From the few words she glimpses – *goodbye, my love! kiss my girls!* – it would appear those on the train do not expect to come back from wherever they are going. It makes her heartsick every time she thinks about it, imagining fierce Antoine and irrepressible Sophie, trapped and taken away.

Every few blocks, she passes groups of Parisians building barricades. Residents have begun piling up everything they can find: food trolleys, road signs, old beds, public benches. There is a festive, communal air, as if they were building bonfires. They are even pulling up the paving stones of their own streets.

Much of this activity is overseen by young men like Jean-Marc and his friends, with slicked-back hair and shirtsleeves rolled high like movie gangsters, swinging grenades from their suntanned fingers. Irregular forces, stared at by children, already fêted and immortal. A civilian guerrilla army which has materialized from the shadows, putting on armbands that read FFI: *Forces françaises de l'Intérieur*. The FFI posters promise that, in the battle to liberate Paris, everyone will get a Hun. The Hun tanks trundle into position, ready to prove them wrong.

Some roads are empty but for whistling bullets, as the two sides take casual potshots at each other, neither yet fully committed. Some are clogged with Germans, who continue to desert the city in a motley mix of vehicles: some cheerfully drunk; others shooting at passers-by. The Parisians wave toilet brushes at the departing convoys, hang home-made French flags from their balconies. In the formal gardens, stubble-dark soldiers sleep beneath statues. In the offices of diplomats and officials, terse telephone conversations at all hours.

It is like a carnival, with all its gaiety and danger. Nothing was happening and now anything might happen. All things are ending and beginning at once. Everything they have hoped for.

Early morning. Before sunrise. Digby shakes her awake, beckons her to the window. Cristabel looks out over the city: its zinc roofs, dotted with clusters of terracotta chimney pots and burbling pigeons; the soft new sky.

Peering down into the narrow street, she sees, huddled in entranceways, groups of men wearing armbands, holding weapons. One is staring at his watch. Others keep leaning out, glancing at him. Finally, the man with the watch nods and sets off running, his footsteps echoing down the shuttered street. The others follow him. More and more, appearing from doorways like children leaving their homes to follow the Pied Piper.

When she turns around, Digby is pulling a FFI armband on over his own shirt. He has retrieved his pistol from under the floorboards and is tucking it into his waistband. He pushes his hair from his eyes and looks at her.

'I've never seen you with a gun,' she says.

'I used one a fair bit in the army so I shouldn't make too much of a fool of myself,' he says. 'We're going to Île de la Cité, to occupy the police headquarters. The liberation starts today.'

'Have you got one for me?'

'A gun?'

'Yes, Digs. They trained me too, you know. I was the best shot in my class.'

'Are you sure?'

She puts her hands on her hips. 'Do you think I joined the Org to sit in an apartment?'

'No,' he says, sheepish. 'I just don't want you to get hurt. But look, once I know what's going on, I'll be in touch. I'll send someone back for you. With a gun.'

'Make sure you do,' she says.

He hugs her tightly and smiles. 'I will. I promise. We can fight side by side on the barricades.' Then he leaves the apartment. She hears him loudly taking the stairs, two at a time.

'Try not to draw attention to yourself,' she says to the empty room.

She waits in the apartment, trying to pass the time by finishing *Madame Bovary*, but the main character seems even more constrained than she is, and this merely adds to her impatience. Throughout the day, there is distant gunfire like the sound of fireworks. Sometimes she goes to the window, only to see the people in the opposite apartments also standing at their windows, arms folded. The streets below are empty, though occasionally an individual will hurtle through, as if pursued. Gazing out across the city, she can see puffs of smoke rising from distant parts of Paris but has no idea what they mean. Sporadic, unreadable gestures.

By late afternoon, the waiting has become almost unbearable. Then she hears the secret pattern of knocks at the door that means Jean-Marc. She quickly lets him in. He is wet with sweat, lugging a large bag, but beaming, exultant.

'We have taken control of the Police Préfecture,' he says, panting, 'but we need reinforcements. Ammunition, water.'

'Has Denis found me a weapon?' she says.

He pulls from his waistband a pistol. 'From Denis, for you. A Luger, taken from the body of a German officer, less than an hour ago.'

When she holds it, the handle is still warm from being against Jean-Marc's stomach. For a second, she imagines it is the heat of the dead German and feels faintly nauseous. She takes a deep breath and concentrates on the weapon lying across her open palm, feeling its weight. It has been months since she held a gun, but during training, she always took her time to get used to it, rather as she would offer a strange dog her hand to sniff, to give it a chance to take her measure.

Jean-Marc opens his bag to reveal several boxes containing rounds of ammunition, and a pile of empty wine bottles. 'Can you help fill these?'

She tucks the gun in her waistband and heads to the kitchen, where she and Digby have stored water in saucepans. She empties this into the bottles, filling each, putting the corks back in, then passing them to Jean-Marc to put into the bag. They stuff blankets into the bag to protect the bottles before he picks it up, staggering under its clanking weight.

'You can't carry that on your own,' she says. 'Let me get another bag.'

She finds her own rucksack and they split the ammunition and water between them.

'Ready?' he says, as she pulls the rucksack on to her shoulders.

'Ready,' she says.

Together, they make their way outside into the sunshine and head from Île Saint-Louis to the bridge that leads to the larger Île de la Cité, where the grand Police Préfecture sits in an open square, facing Notre-Dame cathedral. Cristabel has tucked her arm through Jean-Marc's, as if they were a couple. 'If we are stopped, we say our home has been damaged in the fighting and we are going to stay with my parents,' she whispers, as they stride along.

When they reach Île de la Cité, they pause for a moment beneath the shady awning of an empty café. The streets are deserted but there are several *résistants* cycling furiously towards the scene of the uprising, weapons slung round their necks, followed by a running photographer with a camera in his hand. From the direction of the Préfecture, she can hear loud singing of the Marseillaise. Why are they singing, she wonders, when the battle is not yet won? But Tricolour flags are already sprouting from windows, high flutterings of red, white and blue.

Jean-Marc cautiously leads her around the edge of the island to a place where they can see, in the distance, one of the other bridges that leads on to it. It is filling with Germans: marching soldiers and armoured cars, all heading towards the Préfecture. Her heart clamps up for a moment, fearing the singing *résistants* will be ambushed, then she sees flashes of defensive gunfire coming from behind the parapets that line the river, the deafening clatter of Sten guns wielded by FFI fighters, and the Germans throwing themselves to the ground.

She and Jean-Marc move quickly along a side street that leads towards Notre-Dame. They slow down as they reach the end of the street, then cautiously peer out around the last building, looking into the square. On their left is the cathedral, standing behind huge stacks of sandbags protecting its main front portals, and on their right is the Police Préfecture.

Cristabel can make out figures at the windows, the long shapes of rifles aiming downwards at a German tank that is sitting in the middle of the square, squat and unmoving as a toad. She can hear the sound of bullets hitting the metal body of the tank, a succession of ineffective pings, then the tank fires back, a deafening boom, and a huge cloud of smoke and dust billows from the Préfecture. She can hear crumbling stonework, a fire alarm going off, shouting voices. Flames appear, flickering in windows.

Jean-Marc starts to move into the square, just as a German motor-cyclist comes speeding past. 'Get back,' he hisses, and they scuttle back to safety. They try again, keeping low and staying to one side, where they are sheltered by a line of trees. They proceed in fits and starts, huddling in a narrow doorway when there is a volley of gunfire from the Préfecture, bullets whining past in pursuit of a German armoured car which briefly appears at the far end of the square, before heading out of sight.

From one end of the square to the other is a distance of less than a hundred yards, but it takes Jean-Marc and Cristabel twenty minutes to cover it. Finally, they are facing the Préfecture, where smoke is gusting from the windows. Now they only have to cross a road to dash through the grand arch that leads into its courtyard. Jean-Marc stops Cristabel and says, 'One at a time, from here. I'll go first, then I'll cover you.' He adjusts his bag, pulls his pistol from his waistband, then sets off running, his gun held up in front of him.

At that moment, a German lorry comes roaring round a corner, with a soldier hanging over its front mudguard, firing wildly. Jean-Marc cries out and falls to the floor, dropping his pistol, his bag hitting the ground with a crash. There are shouts from those in the Préfecture, the lorry's brakes screeching as it swerves into the square, gunfire ricocheting off the buildings. Jean-Marc is lying in the middle of the road, clutching his side, Cristabel still crouched by the building where he left her.

Two stretcher-bearers appear from the Préfecture, waving a small white flag. They begin to make their way towards Jean-Marc but run back to cover when the lorry reverses towards them at speed. The German soldier is still sprawled across its mudguard, spraying bullets. There is thick smoke drifting across the road. Jean-Marc is trying to push himself up. He is only five yards away. Ten at most. She can reach him. Pull him to safety.

As she sprints towards him, she hears bullets hitting iron street lamps. She drops to her knees next to him, covering his body with hers, and turns her gun on the moving lorry, firing once, twice, at the soldier on the mudguard, who slides off the vehicle, then once straight through the side window at the driver, sending the lorry veering into a tree.

There is the whistle of bullets passing very close by, striking sparks from the paving stones right next to her. She half stands, and turns about, peering through the smoke to see where they are coming from. Someone is running towards her, looking high above her, and as he reaches her, he spins her round so she is shielded as he fires upwards, and she realizes, too late, that there are snipers on the roof of the cathedral. She sees a dark shape outlined against the sky, hears the crack of a rifle, then another, then a silence, a flock of pigeons suddenly taking to the air.

She must be injured, she thinks, for Digby is holding her very tightly. 'Am I hurt?' she says. He is leaning heavily against her, pulling her down to the ground. He coughs, and it is a choking wet sound, and when she puts her hands to his back, his shirt is sodden. She sees one of the stretcher-bearers, a man wearing a metal helmet painted with a white cross, come running towards them. The man grabs Cristabel's hands and presses them against Digby's back. Then he turns and beckons to a woman who runs towards them holding the stretcher. They take Jean-Marc first, then return for Digby. There is no more gunfire from the cathedral, she notices. Digby must have got him. 'You got him,' she tells him, as they carry him on the jolting stretcher. He looks at her and smiles.

One of the large buildings on the edge of the square is a hospital. They have moved all the patients and staff down to the basement, to protect them from the fighting outside. There are no lights, so some of the nurses carry torches. There are about a dozen wounded people – civilians and FFI fighters – lying on wheeled gurneys in dark corridors, or on makeshift beds on the floor, and more are being brought in, the stretcher-bearers struggling up and down the steep stairs.

Jean-Marc is laid on the floor, where a nurse kneels next to him. He is still conscious, groaning with pain. Cristabel is moved to one side, pushed into a corner, as people in medical uniforms crowd around the body of her brother, who has been placed on a metal gurney. She can see his legs writhing. Then a doctor gives him an injection and his legs fall still. From outside, she can hear the clanging of a fire engine's bell.

She sees a doctor place a hand on Digby's arm. Then he says something to a nurse, before starting to move away down the corridor. She walks quickly after him, saying, 'Doctor, is he going to be all right?'

The doctor turns to her; he is a man in his sixties with grey hair and an agitated expression. 'We've given him morphine, to make him more comfortable.'

'That's good,' she says.

'But that is all I can do.'

'What do you mean?'

'They have left me with nothing,' he says. 'I am sorry. We will get you a chair.' He puts his hand on her shoulder, moves on to the next bed.

She follows him. 'There must be something you can do.'

'He has been shot through the lungs. His only chance would be an operation, but I have no equipment, no anaesthetic, nothing. The Germans took it all with them.' There is the loud crump of a powerful explosion outside, the sound of shattering glass in the building above. The medical staff all drop to the floor.

'What does he need?' says Cristabel, crawling closer to the doctor. 'I'll find it.'

'I would stay with him, if I were you,' he says, getting gingerly to his feet. 'He might not have long. Please. I must work.'

She gets up and stands for a moment, then walks back to Digby. His eyes are still open, his breath coming in ragged gasps and coughs. She feels guilty, somehow, almost panicky, that she knows what the doctor has told her, and he does not. She has never liked to keep anything from him. She goes to him and brushes the hair from his face. He is pale. His forehead damp with sweat. She sees him recognize her. He tries to speak, but only manages her name, then Jean's name.

'Jean's all right,' she says, 'they're looking after him.'

She sits on the wooden chair a nurse has brought to the bedside. She knows that, in films, those waiting by the bed usually tell the ones in the bed not to try to speak, but she feels strongly that he should speak, must speak.

She says, 'I didn't spot the sniper. I'm sorry.'

He shakes his head, then coughs and the cough is full of thick blood. He swallows awkwardly, gulps for air, and when he looks at her again, he is further away. His eyelids droop.

'Don't go anywhere, Digs,' she says, 'I'm here. I'm going to stay with you.'

His eyes flicker open. There: his familiar gaze. 'Never doubted,' he manages, then more racking coughs, blood-flecked spittle. His eyes shut and his head nods towards his chest.

She sits in the dark basement, where the nurses run back and forth as the guns rattle outside, and watches him. She feels as if he is going somewhere inside himself, to engage in a struggle that does not include her. From where she sits, the struggle appears strangely ordinary. Merely a man on a bed fighting to breathe, his chest rising and falling in jerks, little jolts of effort. She looks around for something to break apart the ordinary, some kind of prop. She doesn't even have a handkerchief. She cannot go and find one. This is all she has now.

His eyes flutter open once more, and look at her, then they close and stay closed. His breath is coming more slowly now. She is pinioned, caught in a double agony: both wanting this time to end and wanting it never to end. It is unreal, she thinks, what is actually happening. It is just behind her, huge and unreal and unbearable. She cannot look at it.

(But if she did, what would it be? If she could look her loss in the face, what shape would it be? What colour? Bright blue. Sky blue. Hope blue. A love as big as the sky. How bright and fierce it is. How impossible to extinguish. To think of it gone feels like screaming. He is her brother. He is someone she willed into being. He is inside her and outside her. And she would take all that she has ever had and throw it away in an instant, to be there on the gurney, to fight in his place. She would give away having ever known him to keep him from –)

She will not think of the words. There will be no words that imply an ending. She will not look behind her and she will not look at his shirt, so soaked in blood, or think of the sound of it, the steady dripping on the concrete floor. She will stay calm. She will stay with him.

She picks up his hand, knots their fingers together and says his name. She asks if he remembers when they used to go up on the roof, and his mouth twitches. She says that when he was little, she used to tell him stories until he went to sleep, and she feels the faintest answering squeeze of his hand. She tells him a story about a girl who wished for a brother and the brother who came to her, who was so loved by everyone, and the theatre they made, and the adventures they had, and she keeps telling him this story even when the story takes her right up to the point where she is now, with the brother in front of her, the deeply dreaming brother, his beautiful face so peaceful she could almost believe he was asleep, if she didn't know that he was going so far away, he would never be coming back, and if she hadn't seen that his chest had stopped moving, and so he is –

And so he has –

But perhaps it doesn't end if you keep telling it. Perhaps if she continues to hold his hand and carry on with the story then there won't be an end. She lays her head on the gurney by his head. She moves her mouth to tell the story, even though she seems unable to make any sounds. She stays there. Even when there is a kerfuffle because a nurse comes over and tries to cover him with a sheet, she stays there.

A porter appears with a pencil and a label in his hands and says, 'What's his name?'

'Denis,' she says, unmoving. 'He's with the Resistance. If you try to put a label on him, I'll kill you.'

The porter moves on. A nurse who has been mopping the floor nearby comes to the bed and says, 'Denis. A hero of France.'

Cristabel nods.

'Do you have somewhere you can go, my dear?' says the nurse. 'Do you have family nearby?' She is a middle-aged North African woman, with black hair tucked under her white nurse's hat and dark eyes. She looks tired but her voice is steady, courteous. She speaks French with a slight accent.

'No,' Cristabel replies. 'He is my family. This is my place.'

The nurse looks thoughtful. 'I heard you did not want to have him covered.'

Cristabel shakes her head. 'No.'

'I understand,' says the nurse. She stands looking at Digby, then she walks away. A little while later, she returns carrying a jug and a bowl, and several torn-up strips of fabric. She busies herself with these things in a calm, methodical way, pouring water into the bowl. She says, 'In my family, we bathe our dead, before we cover them. We make them ready together.' She dampens a piece of fabric in the water and passes it to Cristabel. 'Perhaps you could help me to do that.'

Cristabel holds the fabric, watching as the nurse gently begins to wipe away the blood from Digby's hand, turning it over carefully to wash clean the palm, the creases in his palm, his fingers, the spaces between his fingers. 'He has beautiful hands,' says the nurse.

Cristabel releases the hand she is holding and lifts it towards the nurse, so she can clean it too. Then she takes her own piece of fabric and slowly begins to wipe away the dirt on her brother's face. The salt sweat stains on his forehead. The grime smudged across his cheek.

She watches as the nurse takes a pair of scissors from her pinafore apron and cuts open Digby's bloodstained shirt, carefully lifting him a little, in order to remove it from his body. Cristabel stands up to help her, as the nurse covers the wounds in his back with a dressing. Then, together, they wipe clean his chest and stomach, his neck and arms. It is soothing, somehow, this task.

When it is done, the nurse says, 'Now, we must give him his privacy. Can you do that for him?' She has a white sheet in her hand, which she offers to Cristabel.

Cristabel nods. 'I can,' she says, taking the sheet.

When Jean-Marc finds them, late that night, Cristabel is sitting on the concrete floor of the basement beside a gurney that holds Digby's shrouded body, reaching up so she can still hold her brother's hand.

What Remains

September, 1944

When Flossie sees the telegraph boy in his smart little cap coming slowly up the drive on his bicycle, she knows instantly what has happened. She just has to wait to find out which of them it is. She feels sorry for the boy, who the villagers have nicknamed 'the Angel of Death', so when he hands her the telegram, she makes sure to thank him politely. He looks abashed.

She takes the piece of paper down to the kitchen without looking at it and puts it face down on the table. She is still sitting there with it when Mr Brewer comes in an hour later. She feels it is a bomb, sitting in her house. A very flat bomb. Mr Brewer sees it and he too knows at once what it is.

'Would you like me to get Betty?' he says.

'No,' Flossie says. 'I will look at it soon.'

He nods. 'Shall I leave you to it?'

'No, stay. Please.' She is worried that when she reads it, she might fly apart in a way that is irreversible. She taps her fingers on the tabletop. She wishes they were here with her, to help her with this bit. Either of them, both of them. 'I must be brave,' she says and pulls the telegram towards her. It is such a fragile thing. Then she turns it over and the words jump out in a muddle, so she has to blink and read them again.

Deeply regret.

Killed in action.

Digby.

When Mr Brewer asks what it says, somebody answers but it is not Flossie, as she is no longer there.

*

Grief takes Flossie away. It takes her for days and days. Takes her tightly, wraps her so entirely in herself, that she cannot be sure anything exists beyond the arms she has around herself, the ball she is curled in. Sometimes she is shaken by dry juddering sobs, but she has no tears. She is small and hard as a periwinkle. Just an empty shell taking her pain from place to place, hunched over it like a miser.

Like this, she moves through her days, or her days move past her. She doesn't often move. She observes the weeds multiplying in her garden but seems unable to do anything about them. She sits on the beach, watching as the waves come smacking in then draw back, leaving sea foam popping on pebbles, vanishing through the gaps, tiny lights going out.

She stays in this vacant state for over a fortnight, trailed by Toto the cat, who lies next to her whenever he finds her curled on her bed. Betty leaves corned beef sandwiches on the bedside table. Flossie ignores them until they go away. Mr Brewer appears with a piece of paper, asking her to check the wording of the death announcement for the newspapers, and she closes her eyes and nods blindly.

One day, Flossie opens her eyes to find Maudie sitting on the bed, holding a pile of post. 'All these have come,' says Maudie. 'You should read them.' Maudie is wearing her Fire Watch uniform: a dark boiler suit with solid rubber boots.

Flossie shakes her head. 'No thank you, Maudie.'

Maudie opens the first one and begins to read it out loud. A letter from Digby's old English teacher, talking of his enthusiasm, his imagination. The next one is from a classmate of his at Sherborne, remembering his kindness, his silliness, how he made them all dress up one night in pillowcases.

'Pillowcases?' says Flossie.

'That's what it says,' Maudie confirms, opening the next.

One from a soldier who had served with him in France, remembering how he entertained them with Shakespearean speeches. One from a tank driver who had been with him in North Africa, who wrote of his courage. Each letter is like being shown a different part of Digby.

'This one's from Miss Myrtle,' says Maudie.

'Oh, let me see it,' says Flossie, sitting up to take it from her hand.

Maudie puts the rest of the letters on the bed and stands up.

Flossie looks at her. 'Why are you here, Maudie? Aren't you needed in Weymouth?'

'Betty rang me. Said you needed someone to get you out of bed.'

'I've never been very good at getting up.'

'Like your father,' says Maudie. 'I'll give you the rest of today. Then tomorrow, we get you up and out. No use mouldering in here. All those letters need replying to, for one thing.'

Replying to the letters is not as onerous a task as Flossie first feared, because it is like having a conversation about her brother, and sharing lovely stories, which is something she always liked to do. She takes her replies down to the village to post them, and this means she gets some proper clothes on, and people come and talk to her, and say how sorry they are, and this is all right too, somehow; the pats on her arm, the sympathetic expressions. She supposes many of them have lost someone, and know what it is like to be so entirely hollowed out by sadness, you hardly exist at all, and have to be reminded to brush your hair because you have forgotten it's there.

She goes back down to her garden too, her space between the bones, and finds there is a great deal that needs doing, once she clears away the weeds. Carrots, runner beans and early potatoes, all ready to harvest. The last of the raspberries too, and then the canes need to be cut down. It is a comfort to have small things that require her attention.

As she works, she considers what she might do with her crops. Betty has a recipe for raspberry shortbread she could try, if she saves up her margarine rations. This imaginative pondering feels as if she is, if not exactly returning to herself, then arranging to meet herself, a little further on.

One day, in late September, she is sitting on the step outside the cottage with a dog-eared novel and a cup of tea, when Cristabel sits down next to her, puts an arm around her shoulders and they lean their heads together. They stay there until it starts to rain, then they go into the cottage, where Flossie puts the kettle on to boil, washes a few mugs. Cristabel walks round the house as if reminding herself of it. Neither speaks. They are quiet in the way people are after great upheaval, moving through what remains. Their actions are the tender brushes of archaeologists, carefully wiping away the dust.

Cristabel picks up the book Flossie is reading and looks at it. 'Have you read *Madame Bovary*? I think you would like it.'

'I haven't,' says Flossie. 'That one's very good though. I always go back to Jane Austen when I want to feel better about the world. She tidies things up for me.'

They take their tea to a small table in the cottage and sit down. After a while, Cristabel says, 'I was with him. When it happened.'

'You poor darling,' says Flossie. 'Was he – was he in a great deal of pain?'

Cristabel shakes her head. 'They gave him morphine.'

Flossie takes a deep breath. 'I might ask more about it another time, but I don't think I can now, if that's all right.'

Cristabel nods and they sit for a moment, listening to the rain outside growing heavier, more insistent. The sound of it hitting the sea is a crackly hiss, like spitting oil in a frying pan.

'What were you doing in France?' says Flossie. 'Were you doing the same kind of thing as Digby? The secret work?'

'Don't tell anyone, but yes. That sort of thing.'

Flossie nods, then says, 'It's ever so silly, but I keep thinking about the fact he just missed his birthday. It was only a few days later. He would have been twenty-three.'

'He would have liked a birthday in Paris,' says Cristabel.

'Oh, he would have adored that,' exclaims Flossie and sighs. After a while, she says, 'What did you do, Crista? Afterwards.'

'I picked up a gun,' Cristabel says, and her eyes are heavy and numb.

Cristabel tells Flossie how she fought with the Resistance until the Allies arrived. Crouching behind a line of sandbags, aiming a rifle down a long boulevard, existing nowhere but in the midpoint of her crosshairs. How it was pure and righteous to fire a gun then; every recoil of the weapon against her shoulder was an impact she needed.

How she and Jean-Marc had been among the crowds that thronged the pavements when de Gaulle marched into Paris, the tall General walking the streets with his arms spread wide like a mighty alba-tross. How people hung from balconies, climbed up statues, to catch a glimpse of him. How she felt like a pillar of silence, a pillar of salt, in an ecstatic city of noise.

How she had not wanted to leave Jean-Marc, who was so racked by his pain, she wasn't sure he wouldn't turn his gun on himself. How she sat up with him, through his sleepless agonies. How theirs was a curious companionship forged in hard, silent drinking, while the streets outside clamoured with celebration. How one night the power had suddenly come back on all over Paris, turning on every light at once, radios suddenly blaring from apartments across the city, and how this had been a terrible glare, a spotlight that showed them each other, wincing, huddled in chairs, like furtive things uncovered.

How one morning she woke up, hung-over and liverish, and went for a swim in the Seine, let herself sink until her lungs were burst-ing, and when she surfaced, knew it was time to go home.

She made contact with the American Army, who got her to a working telephone, which got her through to London, where a pleasant WAAF with a soft Devon accent promised to find her a place on the next plane home and a few nights in a hotel for a bit of a rest, as if she were booking a holiday, rather than returning from a battle. She flew home in a Lysander with two British commandos, one carrying a huge bottle of Chanel perfume. Debriefed in a hotel in Bayswater. Slept for twenty-four hours solid.

It was then that she saw Leon and used his body as something to fall into, over and over, until there was nothing left of her but the marks she left on him and he on her, but she does not tell Flossie this. There had been a dark oblivion at the edge of those nights, which Leon could allow, but she does not wish to bring it with her.

Cristabel instead tells Flossie how she had been given back her old civilian clothes – kept neat and folded by a secretary in the Org, her saggy stockings treated reverently as relics – then caught a train home to Dorset, thinking that somewhere, in a back office in Baker Street, there must be Digby's old clothes, still neat and folded and waiting.

'I haven't been into his room yet,' says Flossie.

'I don't believe I can go into the attic ever again,' says Cristabel. 'We might have to burn the whole place down. Would probably save us money in the long run.'

'Actually, Bill and I have some ideas on that front. We're making investments, in property, and we plan to advertise for paying guests. I'm sure you never thought I would be a career woman.'

'I met a man once who told me that war allows us to rise in ways that would otherwise be impossible. Although, I think you would have always risen, Floss.'

'Like dough,' says Flossie brightly.

They laugh together and Cristabel feels the weight inside her shift a little.

'Crista, I was thinking I would go back to the Land Army,' says Flossie. 'It would give me something to do.'

'That's a good idea. I might go to London. Stay with Myrtle. Or Leon, if he's about.'

'You'd stay with Leon? Are you and he . . . ?'

'No. No, no.'

Flossie raises her eyebrows. 'That sounds like one of *those* no's.'

'What no's?'

'The kind that don't feel confident on their own, that need a few friends around them.'

'No.'

'Another little friend.'

'Stop it.'

Flossie smiles and says, 'It's none of my business what you do, Crista. I do know these things aren't always straightforward.'

They look at one another for a moment, with fondness and interest, then Flossie says, 'If we go away, Betty and Bill could have some time off. Their son's in hospital in Plymouth. I know they'd like to visit him.'

'Yes,' says Cristabel. 'Let's shut the place up for a while.'

Cristabel travels back to London. She takes with her a book, planning to relish a train journey that can be enjoyed without anxiety, but doesn't read a word, simply sits looking out of the window as England rolls past: muddy farmland and stone cottages; woods where the leaves are starting to change colour.

At Winchester, two middle-aged women in expensive coats and hats board the train. They do not acknowledge her as they enter the compartment. Instead, they take their seats and continue a conversation that Cristabel senses has been going on for some time.

'I said as much to Hugh, they cannot expect us to go another winter without proper hot baths,' says the first, snapping her handbag clasp firmly shut.

'I worry we've quite forgotten ourselves,' replies the other. 'We've all made sacrifices, and gladly so, but at some point, life must return to normal.'

'You have it exactly,' says the first. 'Must we wait for every hamlet in Europe to be liberated before we fill the car with petrol?'

They laugh, then one turns to Cristabel and says, 'I'm sure you feel the same. Must be frightful to be young in such dull, penny-pinching times.'

Cristabel can see from how they examine her that they find her hard to place. Battered walking shoes, yes, but good quality. A decent skirt and jacket, but a foreign-looking blouse. A strong profile, but tanned as a workman, and a curious indifference in the way her long body is arranged across the seat. No handbag whatsoever.

As they regard her, they adjust their own clothes – a draped cashmere scarf, a fur stole – as if adjusting robes. With their upright posture and tight twists of silver hair, there is something of the judiciary about them. They consider it their right to inspect her, and she knows what they see. She is, after all, of their kind. Or was.

Ever since Paris, she has felt that whatever was once Cristabel is no longer there. Every part of her, her heart and her bones, from the tips of her ears to the tips of her toes, has crumbled. She has fallen away, a chalk cliff slumping into the sea. She is not what she was. She is a space where something once stood, a pile of stones and dust, waiting to be rebuilt.

Cristabel says, 'I do not feel the same.'

'Why ever not?' says the first woman, looking down her nose as if looking down a staircase.

Cristabel can hear the furious muffled shouting of her former self, desperate to inform these women that they know nothing of sacrifice. But that self is buried now, and she is tired. There are only so many battles one can fight.

These women belong to her dead life and are as ghosts to her. She will let them pass through her as the train is passing through England, flashing by in her peripheral vision: small houses, small fields, small houses, small fields. She stares at the women until they look away, then turns back to the window.

Cristabel returns to Baker Street. The building is as poorly lit and draughty as it ever was. Not as busy now, many of the offices are deserted: there is only the occasional clatter of the teleprinter from the signals room, and the odd messenger pushing a squeaking trolley down an empty corridor. She eventually finds Joan, her former conducting officer, packing things into a cardboard box.

Joan gives her a firm hug. 'Good to see you. How was it?'

Cristabel pauses. 'I don't know how to sum it up.'

'No, I imagine it must be a lot to contend with.'

Cristabel gestures to the box. 'Off somewhere?'

'Transferred to the Foreign Office. Not much for me to do here any more.'

'Good luck,' says Cristabel, then, 'Joan, I wondered if anything had been heard from Sophie Leray. I know she was captured, and then taken away in a train.'

'We hoped we would find our people in the prisons when we got to Paris, but it appears they were all cleared out. We're assuming the Germans are keeping valuable prisoners to use as hostages.'

'Will you let me know, if you hear anything?'

'I will,' says Joan. 'Good luck to you too, Gilberte.'

'Cristabel,' says Cristabel, holding out her hand.

Cristabel heads back down the corridor, towards the stairs that will take her out of the building, when she sees, through an office doorway, a familiar figure. Colonel Peregrine Drake, reclining in a chair, his hat on a desk, laughing at something someone on the other side of the desk has said. He senses he is being watched and turns his gaze on her. 'Cristabel.'

'Hello,' she says. 'How are you? I didn't know you would be here.'

'I pop in,' he says, then stands and approaches her, puts a hand on her arm. 'I was so sorry to hear about Digby. I hoped he would make it through.'

'So did I,' she says.

'But you came back,' he says, 'and I'm sure your family are enormously thankful.'

'I haven't seen Uncle Willoughby for years,' she says. 'I don't think he has any idea of what's gone on.'

Perry politely allows this to pass, then turns to the person on the other side of the desk and says, 'Cristabel Seagrave. One of the Org's girls. Went into France.'

Cristabel doesn't have to enter the room to know the type of man sitting there. A brigadier or general. Stiff moustache. Carpeted with medals. A sense of him being hunched over something, defending it, and angry to be interrupted in the act of defending it. She steps in anyway and salutes, a gesture that feels awkward in her civilian clothes. 'Sir.'

He is a brigadier. 'Good to have you back,' he says.

Perry says, 'But why are you here, Cristabel? Surely you should be at home. You must have missed it terribly.'

'I'm trying to find out if anything's been heard from a girl I trained with. She was captured.'

Perry nods. 'We're all keen to know more about those who are missing. The difficulty we face is that, if we circulate the details of women agents in an effort to find them, it means admitting they were there.'

'They were there,' she says.

'Not officially,' he replies.

'We're doing all we can,' says the brigadier.

Empty Houses

September, 1944

The telephone rings, its shrill summons echoing through Chilcombe, but there is nobody to answer it. The house is empty. There is just the *click* and *tunk* of water pipes. The uncoordinated chiming of unwound clocks.

Unread post piles up behind the door. Circulars and condolence cards. Letters from a military chaplain travelling across France.

A box of records waits by a dusty gramophone. Parched potted palms press themselves to unwashed windows. Heavy books in the study talk only among themselves, if they talk at all. Dust motes take flight on perilous journeys across vacant spaces.

In other valleys and villages, other houses, much the same. Unaffordable manors left bare, heirless; hollow mausoleums.

The dust motes alight on the grand fireplaces, where the cobweb-covered marble surrounds have a pattern within them: the tightly packed fossils of freshwater snails, who were making their way along the pebbly bottoms of streams, before time and weight and money brought them here, crushed and immobile, calcified structures so finely polished that it is easy to forget they were ever anything else.

Uniforms

October, 1944

The kitchen door is so swollen and stiff with autumn rain, Cristabel has to put her shoulder to it to force it open. Inside is gloomy and dark. There is a tap dripping into an empty sink. Flossie follows her in, exclaiming, 'Goodness, it's freezing in here.'

'There's an untoward smell,' says Cristabel.

'I fear Toto's been hiding dead things again,' says Flossie.

Betty bustles past them, heading determinedly towards the kettle. 'Cup of tea'll help.'

Bill is next, followed by Maudie and Toto the cat, his tail quivering with delight at the return of human company.

'I've found a couple of girls in the village who'll come in and clean the place next week,' says Bill.

'Then we'll be all ready for our first paying guests,' says Flossie, swiping away a cobweb.

'I'll go up and check the main house now,' he says.

Cristabel watches Bill disappear along the dark corridor, hears his footsteps heading upwards. She feels that she is as far into the house as she is able to go, that this underground bunker is reasonably safe, but above her, the waiting rooms are full of pain, strung about with danger like hidden mines waiting to be triggered.

'How many people are coming to stay, Floss?' she asks, opening a kitchen drawer, looking for candles and matches but finding only croquet balls and old dog collars.

'We've had five responses to our advertisement so far,' says Flossie.

Betty clucks and shakes her head. 'There are preservation societies,' she says, filling the kettle, 'that look after historic houses, so you don't need to have any old Tom, Dick or Harry staying in them.'

'I'm not giving Chilcombe to a preservation society,' says Cristabel, 'not my half, anyway. Floss might give them hers.'

'There are so many people who need somewhere to live, Betty,' says Flossie. 'There's a girl I know from the Land Army who just got married, but she and her husband can't find anywhere they can afford.'

'When I think of what it used to be like, with Mrs Rosalind and her lovely parties,' sighs Betty, taking the kettle to the stove. 'She always wanted everything just so. Hasn't been the same since.'

Flossie retrieves dusty teaspoons from a cupboard while Betty continues to reminisce about Chilcombe before the war. She feels disengaged from the older woman's nostalgia. As a child, whenever she crept down from the attic, eager to glimpse one of her mother's parties, it had never been the romantic scene she envisaged. It had been loud and careless. People falling over, arguing, spilling drinks.

Once, peering over the gallery, she had seen Rosalind, wearing a revealing harlequin costume, sprawled across the lap of a masked man, while Willoughby in a toga banged on the piano. Rosalind had tried to attract her husband's attention but succeeded only in falling out of her costume and slipping to the floor, while Willoughby glanced at her and glanced away again, as if it were something commonplace, a matter of no concern.

Flossie ran back to bed and pulled the covers over her head to shut out the sight of her mother so scandalously exposed. But in the morning, she had seen them both at the breakfast table, sipping tea, reading newspapers, as if everything had always been normal. It made her feel the night was an earthquake that opened a crack in the floor, sending everything sliding, plummeting, and then closed up again, so neatly you would never know. That she was, somehow, the one mistaken.

To preserve Chilcombe as it was then, feels dishonest to her somehow. It would continue that slippery feeling of nothing being as it seemed.

'Where's Miss Cristabel going to stay if there's strangers in her bedroom?' says Betty, now rounding up teacups as if they were disobedient children.

'I'll be at the cottage,' says Cristabel. 'I have work to do at the theatre.'

There is a silence in the musty room, then Flossie says, 'Are you sure?'

'Quite sure,' says Cristabel.

Flossie says cautiously, 'Might it not be time to try something else?'

'No, I don't think so.'

'Sometimes we stick at things because we feel we ought to,' says Flossie, carefully putting her clinking handful of teaspoons on the table, 'but you know, people say a change is as good as a rest.'

'I'm not interested in what people say,' says Cristabel, putting her hands in her pockets. 'You think I'm being stubborn, Floss, and you're right. But stubbornness has got me this far. Where I've been mistaken is in its application. I thought I should do the same old plays in the same old way. That's where I was wrong.'

'Once Miss Cristabel gets an idea in her head, she won't be dissuaded,' says Betty.

'Well,' says Flossie. 'I'm sure you'll find plenty to be getting on with.'

There is the sound of Bill's steady tread coming along the corridor, then he reappears with a pile of post. 'Letters for you,' he says, handing them to Flossie.

Flossie peers at them curiously, then opens the first, reading it quickly, before holding a hand to her mouth. 'Oh, poor George.'

'Who's George?' says Cristabel.

'A friend. He's in hospital in Brussels,' says Flossie, rapidly opening another letter. 'He had shrapnel in him, and they had to operate to take it out.'

'Imagine shooting shrapnel at a man of the cloth,' says Betty.

Flossie sits down, still reading. 'He says he's been thinking of our musical evenings.'

'What's this?' says Cristabel, pulling towards her a cardboard box that is sitting on the kitchen table.

Flossie looks up. 'Oh, Crista, that's Digby's clothes and books. From his room. I asked Betty to pack it up. I thought you might want to –'

Cristabel hastily pushes the box away from her. 'Seal it up, Betty. Put it away.'

Betty puts the teapot on the table with a sudden thump that surprises them all, and says in a tearful voice, 'I keep telling myself it's a blessing in disguise that Mrs Rosalind doesn't ever have to know she's lost her darling boy.'

The others are silent for a moment, while Betty hunts in her apron for a handkerchief, then Bill moves next to his wife and says, 'Miss Flossie, Miss Cristabel, Betty and I were wondering, has anyone spoken to Mr Willoughby? To let him know about Master Digby.'

Flossie and Cristabel look at each other. Flossie says, 'I put a notice in *The Times*.'

'There's no telling if he saw it,' sniffs Betty.

'We haven't heard from him for a long time,' says Bill.

'Not a peep,' says Betty, blowing her nose.

'He wasn't the most traditional of fathers,' says Bill, 'but to lose a son.'

'No, you're quite right,' says Flossie, 'we should find him. Does anybody know where he is?'

'Last I heard, he was trying to buy a seaplane somewhere near Limerick,' says Bill, 'but that was over a year ago now.'

'I don't even know if you can travel to Ireland,' says Flossie. 'Is it allowed? Who would go?'

'I'd go,' says Maudie. They all turn to look at her. She is leaning by the back door, half in and half out of the building, wearing rubber boots and her dark-coloured boiler suit, with a whistle hanging round her neck and an armband that reads *Fire Guard*. Her wild hair is tied back, and she has propped her tin helmet by the sink. 'It is allowed, but you need a passport and a permit.'

'How do you know that, Maudie?' says Cristabel.

'I had a lover from Ireland,' says Maudie.

Cristabel is surprised to hear such a sentence come from the maid, but Maudie doesn't look like a maid any more, this rangy woman in her thirties, dropping her cigarette end on the floor outside and grinding it beneath her boot. Cristabel wonders why

Maudie is in uniform, given that she's not on duty, but knows a uniform can be hard to relinquish. Her own civvy clothes – functional shirts and twill trousers – are as close to military dress as she can get, while Flossie still looks like a lady gardener, in floral headscarves and hand-knitted cardigans. Cristabel imagines a wartime uniform, with its anonymity and status, might be even more appealing if your original outfit belonged to a subservient role.

'I don't want your loose talk in my kitchen, Maudie Kitcat,' says Betty, 'you can keep that for those dirty sailors' pubs.'

'Betty, it's all right,' says Flossie. 'Maudie has boyfriends. Lots of people have boyfriends.'

'Wouldn't call them boyfriends,' says Maudie.

'I might be able to help you with the paperwork,' says Cristabel, thinking of the secretaries at the Org, who seemed able to summon official papers out of thin air. She moves towards Maudie at the back door. The October sky outside is grey and a fine rain is falling, but the fresh air is a relief compared to the stale house.

'I could give you a hand clearing out the cottage,' says Maudie.

'We could pop down now, see what needs doing, if you don't mind the rain,' says Cristabel.

'Tea'll be ready soon,' says Betty.

'Bit of mizzle never hurt,' says Maudie.

One month later. Late afternoon. Maudie. Stepping from Holyhead Harbour on to the gangway leading to a ferry that goes to Ireland. The first time she has ever left land. The first time she has ever left anywhere. She sees the choppy water slapping sullenly against the harbour wall beneath her, and it thrills her.

The ferry is crowded. Standing room only. Baggage piled up in the corridors, with children perched on top. Suitcases, trunks, cages full of chickens. Maudie is crammed on to the front deck, beside a family that tell her the journey is bad, but the customs officials in Ireland are worse. They'll confiscate everything, and you'll only get it back weeks later, if you get it at all. But it's a rare treat, they say, to leave the blackout behind and to sail to Dublin, where all the lights in the harbour will be shining on the water.

She is hardly listening. She is leaning on the swaying guardrail, feeling the boat come juddering to life beneath her, its thunderous propellors starting to turn. The ferry gives an ear-splitting blast on its horn as it chugs out of the harbour, escorted by gulls flying low over the water, leaving behind hilltops covered with cloud.

Maudie looks down at the churning ocean, the tumult of white peeling away from the bows, as the ferry makes its way out to the wild winter sea. There is a following swell, which lifts the boat and carries it forward, in long surges, as if it were being scooped up by a giant's hand.

She is no longer on dry land. She is no longer in any place at all. She is held up only by water, which is capricious and powerful and cares for nothing. She thinks of her grandfather, the smuggler, who even when he'd been bedridden for years, still felt the rocking of the ocean. She understands it now: once you know a life outside obedience, you keep it with you.

The wind is picking up and the sky darkening as the ferry ploughs its way into the Irish Sea, freezing spray from the waves blowing on to the decks. The passengers huddle together and watch with curiosity as Maudie opens the small suitcase she has with her, pulls out her maid's white apron, carefully ironed and packed by Betty, and drops it over the edge of the boat, a writhing pale spirit flying over the water. Betty had pressed the apron into her hands, saying it might come in handy, you never know, then unexpectedly clasped Maudie to her wide bosom like a mother with a child. How peculiar to be embraced by a woman. Warm and soft and peculiar. Maudie watches as the apron is swallowed by a wave. When this pitching ferry crosses to the other side, she will step off into the future as someone new.

Victory Pageant

May, 1945

'Can we try that again?' says the cameraman.

'Very well,' says the producer. 'Take four. Mrs Seagrave –'

'Miss.'

'Miss Seagrave, if you could stand on the lawn there and provide us with a brief explanation of what this wheelbarrow is for.'

'I told you. I used it to build up a raised section of my theatre, to create better seating.'

'I know that,' the producer replies, a slight edge to his voice, 'however, as I have said, we need to film you explaining how you did it for our viewers.'

'You've filmed me explaining at least three times already,' says Cristabel. 'How many do you need? I have things to do.'

'What we're trying to achieve here,' says the producer, pinching the bridge of his nose, 'is to give our audience a real sense of your theatre. How unusual it is. Such a unique venue for a celebration. One moment, let me write that down. "A unique venue – some may say rather eccentric –" No, hold on. "A rather eccentric but very British production, celebrating the end of hostilities in Europe, in rural Dorsetshire." Yes, that's it.'

'How long will this take?'

'We'll finish this scene, then we'll get footage of excited local people arriving. After that, we'll need shots of the performance itself, but we'll endeavour not to be intrusive. Can you remind me again what the show is?'

'It opens with a victory pageant performed by children from the village, dressed as those who helped us win the war. Soldiers, firemen, nurses and so on. They sing songs, led by my sister Flossie.

After that, I put on a show for the children, featuring creatures that eat people.'

'I remember you saying something about puppets?'

'Giant puppets. I created them using papier mâché and fabric on wire frames, and also through the adaptation of some stuffed animals we had in the house.'

'Yes, I did note that. You said you had a local lad we could film?'

'Norman. He's waiting there, dressed as a Frenchman.'

'Perfect. Over here, Norman. Those are splendid onions. How are you feeling on this special day?'

'Happy because Hitler is dead. Can you film my dog? He's got a ribbon on.'

'The telephone's ringing,' says Cristabel and leaves the camera crew, to go back inside.

It had taken a while to pluck up the courage, but Cristabel can go into the main house now, as long as she sticks to the ground floor. Once Flossie's paying guests were installed, Chilcombe felt different, more accessible. There is a brass letter tray, holding a pile of post for other people. A coat stand with many different coats. A variety of outdoor footwear marking the comings and goings of other people who have their own keys, who know it only as their new lodgings, who have questions about hot water and use of the gardens. The house has developed the stoic functionality of shared accommodation, with fraying rugs and chipped paintwork, although Flossie makes sure there are always fresh flowers on the piano.

Cristabel never ventures upstairs, but she knows Bill has cleaned out the attic for a young widow with four small children. She hears the children sometimes, galloping down the stairs, or plonking away on the piano, encouraged enthusiastically by Flossie if she finds them there. ('That's it, Martin! Hands together!')

The study is now an office, used by Flossie and Mr Brewer as a place to keep their rent books and meet with tenants. Flossie has installed a filing cabinet; the desk is covered with a mixture of utility bills and seed catalogues, and there are tomato plants on the window sill. When Cristabel goes in to pick up the telephone receiver, the first thing she hears is a torrent of static, then a familiar voice says, 'Cristabel?'

'Leon?'

'Oh, now you answer.'

'I answered straight away.'

'I try many times.'

'I only just heard it ringing. Where are you?'

'On my way to Berlin with Colonel Drake.'

'You're in Germany?'

'I don't know if you could give it a name any more. There is nothing left but rubble.'

'What's that noise in the background?'

'Americans. They are happy because everyone is pleased to see them. But you haven't asked.'

'Haven't asked what?'

'Why I have telephoned.'

'Why have you?'

'I saw your photograph in the newspaper, with Flossie smiling and waving a big flag. I liked to see the whalebones. Someone very strong must have put those up.'

'Gosh, you saw it too? Everyone seems to have seen it. There's some people here today from Pathé News, come to film us.'

'Was it your idea, to have victory shows at the whale?'

'Yes, although Floss helped out with the music, and we roped in some villagers to make costumes and props.'

'You should be glad, no? Is good publicity.'

'I am glad. Rather a surprise actually. The telephone's been ringing constantly, with people wanting to come along.'

There is a crackly silence on the other end that she recognizes as one of Leon's natural silences. One of the qualities she most likes about him is that he never feels obliged to fill pauses with politeness. She listens to his silence as it passes through the thin wires between them, covering hundreds of miles, existing both there, in the ruins of Germany, and here, with her, in this room. It is reassuring to listen to. She leans her head against the receiver.

'How is it, with you, now?' he says, after a while.

'All right if I don't look up.'

'You don't need to look up. Not yet. One boot after the other.'

'You'll come and see me for a vodka when you get back?'

'I will. And I will come to one of your performances, once we are finished dividing up Germany. But I am running out of money so –'

He is gone and the silence on the other end is empty. She puts the receiver down but stands in the study for a moment, thinking of the newspaper reports she had seen, describing the horrors the Allies were finding as they advanced into Germany, the camps full of starving prisoners. There were photographs she could hardly bear to look at, although she forced herself to, studying the skeletal faces, in case there was one she recognized. She wonders what Leon has seen, what he will see, whether he will be the same when he comes back, one boot after the other.

The drawing room at Chilcombe has remained a communal room, where tenants can congregate for conversation and board games. They were hesitant at first, preferring the informality of the kitchen, but since the weather has become warmer, they have gathered there more frequently, and several of them are there now, making polite conversation with some of the intriguing guests who have arrived to see the newest production at the theatre: a week-long run of performances celebrating victory in Europe.

'Oh, Crista, there you are,' says Flossie, already in costume and carrying a tray with some glasses and a jug of lemonade. 'Some children have run off with the bunting and I fear Betty will go berserk if we can't get it back. She spent all week sewing it. George has pursued them into the stables, but that only seems to have encouraged them.'

'To run from the priest in my village was always a great sport when I was a girl in Germany,' says Lieselotte, in heavily accented English. 'We would torment him until he was demented.'

'Are you being sufficiently looked after, Lieselotte?' says Cristabel. 'Have you had something to eat?'

Lieselotte nods. She is in a black-and-white checked dress, like a chessboard, with a black ostrich feather hat and a handbag that appears to be made from molten cutlery. The Chilcombe tenant who has been cornered by her – a nervous young dentist from Tavistock – has an expression somewhere between terror and awe.

'I believe I have had a Scots egg,' Lieselotte says, 'I don't believe I want any more. This young man has been kind enough to provide me with champagne. He has an interest in molars, he tells me, and gum health.'

'There's masses of champagne,' says Cristabel. 'We found bottles that had been stashed away at the start of the war. It's probably obscenely expensive.'

'This is as it should be,' says Lieselotte, smiling at the dentist. 'We are celebrating the defeat of an evil that would have ended us all.'

'Here's George with the bunting!' cries Flossie. 'Do you require lemonade, George?'

'No, thank you, Flossie, you're very kind, but I think I'll survive,' says George, a little flushed in his dark chaplain's outfit. 'I rather enjoyed the chance to have a look around while I was running after the children. I found this in the stables –'

'Oh, Crista, look,' exclaims Flossie. 'It's your wooden sword.'

'Then I must return it to its rightful owner,' says George, passing it to Cristabel with a smile, before turning to help Flossie put down the tray on a side table. Then he and Flossie turn simultaneously to welcome another tenant who is lingering by the doorway, to shepherd her into the room and provide her with refreshments.

Cristabel can see how well matched they are, already operating as a partnership, even though Flossie keeps blushingly insisting they are 'still getting to know one another'. Both possess a natural outward quality. It is not a quality Cristabel has. Or rather, it is something she has to remind herself of. Other people. Their feelings. She is always so focused on what she is doing, whereas Flossie will stop, and look around.

She tries it now, nodding at the newly arrived tenant, the harassed mother of the children in the attic, who is wearing a plain dress and old stockings and nervously holding a glass of homemade lemonade while staring at the oil painting on the wall beside her.

'Painted by a Russian artist who used to stay with us,' says Cristabel. 'He had an unusual way of seeing things.'

'Those funny animals with big heads,' says the woman, 'they look like your puppets.'

Cristabel laughs. 'I suppose they do.'

'My lot love being in your show,' says the woman. 'It's kept them out of my hair for weeks.'

'I'm glad,' says Cristabel.

'They're mad for those puppets too,' says the woman. 'They keep acting out the story when they're meant to be in bed. About the sprite and the monster living on an island. Did you come up with it all by yourself?'

'It's based on a play I already knew, with additional material provided by my friend Norman,' says Cristabel. She looks at the wooden sword in her hands, then says, 'I don't suppose your lot would like this, would they?'

'They'd like it very much,' says the woman, 'but they'd most likely break something with it.'

'That's what it's for,' says Cristabel, handing it to her. 'My Uncle Willoughby gave it to me a long time ago, and he would be keen that it continue to break things.'

She thinks of Willoughby then, as she often does, wondering how he is. There had been a telegram from Maudie at Christmas, reporting that she had found Willoughby and requesting that a photograph of Digby be sent to an address in Dingle, County Kerry. After that, only a card on Cristabel's birthday in March with a picture of a seaplane on the front and a message in Willoughby's looping handwriting saying he was raising a glass of Guinness to her, with a postscript adding that Maudie might one day make an admirable co-pilot, followed by a huge exclamation mark.

She can't quite believe he would take Maudie up in a seaplane. She suspects this is boastful bar talk. But she likes to imagine he might. She likes to imagine their seaplane soaring above the rugged coast of Ireland, heading out over the ocean. Both in flying jackets and goggles, maybe even flying down to Egypt; a pair of runaways. That is the story she conjures for him, while knowing that his reality may be rather more soaked in grief and alcohol, the slow dissolve of the grandiloquent drunk in the pub corner. Perry once said of Willoughby that there was a strain of Englishmen who could not bear to be in England. She knows he is happier elsewhere, not being heard from, held in her imagination. Her glamorous travelling uncle.

Flossie appears and says, 'It's nearly six o'clock. The audience will be arriving.'

The sisters step out on to the lawn and look up at the sky. It is one of those changeable, breezy spring days that could go either way. It had rained heavily early that morning, a sudden downpour as the bells in the village church rang out across the valley, and large clouds are still moving over the Ridgeway, but it might hold.

The camera crew, tired of waiting for Cristabel, have moved up the drive to film audience members arriving, a crowd of chattering people, dressed smartly for the occasion, men in suits or uniforms and women with bright lipstick on tired faces, holding babies with red, white and blue ribbons in their wisps of hair. They are heading towards the stone pillars, between which hangs Cristabel's new sign welcoming them to: THE WHALEBONE THEATRE.

She is pleased she managed to get it up in time for Lieselotte to see it when she arrived, the paint practically still wet, and she is delighted by the gaudy lettering in red and gold, with an image of a spouting whale, painted by a signwriter who works for travelling circuses. It has exactly the right amount of exuberance and ridiculousness: designed to excite children and to remind adults of the children they were.

Much of the same spirit has gone into decorating the route across the lawn, which is lined with stuffed animals painted cheerful colours, and where youngsters from the village dressed in an array of costumes – airmen, nurses, cowboys – are now handing out hand-drawn programmes. Nearby plants and bushes are decorated with old Christmas baubles and colourful strands of wool, like knitted spider webs.

Cristabel marches across the lawn in order to hurry through the woods before the audience. The path through the trees has been festooned with paper streamers and some old Chinese lanterns she found in the barn, which will light up like fireflies when it gets dark.

At the theatre, in the space where the seats once stood, there is now a raised section, like a wide set of stairs, made from sand and stones from the beach, with wooden planks to sit on. Early arrivals are already making their way up. They have brought Thermos flasks and picnics, treats put by for this long-awaited victory. Bacon and egg pie. Tinned grapefruit segments. Bottles of beer. Blankets and raincoats too, because you can never trust the English weather. In front of the raised seating stand the whalebones, draped with the flags of many nations, and illuminated by powerful searchlights borrowed from the naval base at Portland for one week only.

In the barn, Cristabel's giant puppets wait, lolling against the walls, along with those who will operate them: a trio of budding actors found by placing an advertisement in the local paper; a couple of acrobats discovered at the circus when she went to meet her sign-writer; and a young woman who was part of the Chilcombe Mell Sewing Circle until she heard Betty complaining about her sewing machine being used to create monsters, and came to join them.

Cristabel has made her home in the cottage by the sea, but she cannot enter it today, as Betty has been in there since dawn making trifles from packet jelly and old cake crusts, along with endless rounds of sandwiches, and is now loudly pointing out to anyone who approaches that, down in the village, it's street parties and sing-alongs, but she's slaving in a kitchen and you can hardly call that a celebration, while also refusing to leave her post, stubborn as a gun-ner, because she can't trust anyone else to do it properly. Cristabel recognizes these grievances as Betty's own song, to be sung proudly as an anthem at times of importance, and she dare not interrupt.

Cristabel stands by the whalebones for a moment, looking out over the sea. Huge clouds move across it, their shadows darkening the water beneath them. Along the curve of the coast, there are bonfires on beaches and clifftops, and groups of people splashing into the cold waves, while the battleships in Portland Harbour give occasional blasts on their mighty horns.

The Prime Minister had said on the radio that their task was not yet complete, but they should allow themselves a 'brief period of rejoicing' to mark the end of the war with Germany. Cristabel tries to summon some feeling of celebration, but it seems muted, as if happening somewhere in the distance. But she is glad it is happening and there are things she can do, useful things, so she turns her attention to the bones, to arrange the flags, and prepare the stage.

Flossie and George are ushering the last of the guests towards the path through the trees, when a military Jeep crunches up the gravel drive and out comes the imposing figure of Myrtle in a trailing red velvet dress, carrying her high heels and holding on to a red, white and blue paper hat, which threatens to take off in the wind.

Her voice resounds across the lawn. 'Flossie, darling!'

'So glad you made it, Myrtle,' calls Flossie. 'What a lovely dress.'

'My curtains, darling, sacrificed for fashion. Who needs curtains when the blackout's over?' says Myrtle, blowing a kiss at the departing Jeep. 'But look at you – is that gold lamé? You're proud and dazzling, like the Statue of Liberty.'

'I am the Statue of Liberty,' replies Flossie. 'I'm representing America in our pageant, although I've lost my burning torch.'

George is waiting politely nearby and Myrtle heads towards him, stepping gingerly across the gravel in bare feet, saying, 'I may need to lean on this man. It's bedlam on the trains, my sweet. Riotous scenes. I joined a party of Polish airmen so I'm slightly too well refreshed.'

'Myrtle, this is George,' says Flossie. 'Don't lean on him too hard. He was injured. He was with the troops on D-Day.'

'I'll let you know if I'm about to collapse,' says George.

'Beautiful and brave, darling. What a catch,' says Myrtle, stroking George's hair. 'Are you faring well, Flossie?'

'Sometimes,' says Flossie. 'Some days are better than others.'

'Digby would never want you to be woeful, my sweet,' says Myrtle.

'It's strange,' says Flossie, 'because this is such a happy time, but I weep whenever I see the children in their costumes. I keep forcing cake on them, and it's not even nice cake.'

'We must celebrate when we can, darling. It doesn't come around often,' says Myrtle and embraces Flossie. She smells of French cigarettes and heady perfume, and her make-up is smudged into the lines around her eyes. She looks older now, a little timeworn, but still extravagantly Myrtle, and when Flossie looks at her, she sees a refusal to be anything less. She wonders what George must make of Myrtle, although he seems unperturbed. Nor has he minded spending the day with a woman dressed as the Statue of Liberty. Perhaps a chaplain is more familiar with the peculiarities of human behaviour than most, which makes him surprisingly well suited to being part of her family, and although Flossie is aware that her romantic thoughts have, once again, got ahead of themselves, this time, she doesn't feel too far behind them.

Flossie looks at her watch and says, 'George, do you mind taking Myrtle to the theatre? I'll round up any stragglers, then follow you down.'

'Not at all,' says George, and as they make their way into the trees, she can hear Myrtle exclaiming over his divinely Celtic accent.

Flossie peers down the drive and looks round the garden, which is rather shaggy and overgrown, in need of some tidying, but also as green and blossomy as only a garden in May can be. She sticks her head into the house and calls out to check there is nobody left, but Chilcombe is dark and empty. There is just the solemn ticking of the grandfather clock. Then she pulls the door shut, and heads through the trees towards the sea, because the performance is about to begin.

Encore

C to D

I thought of the day you died today. I think of it most days. I thought of how I loved you before you even existed, and how I love you now, when you no longer exist. Which of course makes a nonsense of the whole idea of existence and leaves only love. This, dear brother, is the kind of sentimental flannel I am prone to now. Although, it also happens to be true.

People make many assumptions about women, most of them fatuous, and one is that we somehow lack clarity. That we are vague and silly. Personally, I consider certainty to be a kind of arrogance.

I knew EVERYTHING when I was twelve years old, and with each year of my life, I know a little less, and there is a freedom in that. You have space for a good deal more. I always find it instructive to talk to school parties who visit the theatre, to hear their ideas about how it might be used. There is always more to be done, you see.

I'm hopeful by the end of the year we will be able to offer week-long stays at Chilcombe, for students keen on the dramatic arts. Won't that be something? I have an idea that one day we could turn the house into some kind of permanent educational facility, to sit alongside the theatre, although I'm told making alterations to an ancient building is a Sisyphean task. I also have an idea for a version of Romeo and Juliet where the characters are insects, but I'll save that for my next letter as it requires drawings.

Had to have builders come and look at the tiered seating as it's crumbling at the edges. Still, it's lasted a good few years. Not bad for something I constructed myself. I always think of those seats as ones that I built with grief. It was after I came back from France, and it was something physical I could do that tired me out so I could sleep.

Flossie, George and the boys are coming for my birthday lunch tomorrow, so I will be attempting to operate the cooker. Édouard and Wanda can't make it this year, as their beloved boy just became a father. Édouard rang to tell me, bursting with pride. Their son still suffers from his injuries, but they are so devoted to him, I know they will help raise the baby as if it were their own. No Leon either, but he's promised we will go adventuring in the summer, on his new boat, which he claims is even faster than the last.

Which reminds me, I had the dream again. I am flying in an aeroplane, a Halifax. I recognize the noise of the engines, that deep rumble. I am wearing a parachute suit and I have a scarf tied around my neck, a silk one printed with a map, but I don't know what the map is of, or where I'm going. The hatch is open, and the night is rushing in. I think I am on my own in the plane, but I am not at all nervous. I know that, somewhere below me, in the dark, is the country where you are.

You know how it goes from there, don't you? Oh, I do miss it sometimes. Red light. Green light. Go! Then jumping through the hatch into nothing, and the wind and the parachute opening, lifting me up, up, up.

C

Acknowledgements

Thank you to all those who helped and encouraged me throughout the writing of this book.

Special thanks go to:

My thoughtful and enthusiastic editors Helen Garnons-Williams and Diana Miller; my wonderful agent Clare Alexander, for taking me under her wing; Poppy North, Olivia Mead, Alexia Thomaidis, Kyiah Ashton and the lovely team at Fig Tree, and designer Julia Connolly for creating the beautiful cover.

My wise teachers Susan Elderkin, Rob Middlehurst, Irene Flint, and most especially Francis Spufford, who deserves a volume of thanks all to himself.

My friends, for their cheerleading and kindness, Lucy Axworthy, Alison Freeman, Denize Creed, and my childhood companion in adventuring, Tamzin Hyde, who used to live with her mum Rosy in a remote house on the Dorset coast, where, together with my sister, we roamed the cliffs dressed as wizards, and where the earliest seeds of this story were planted.

Becky Steeden, for heartening lunches; Becky Pressly, for neighbourly support in the final stages; and Cathy Varley, for being the world's nicest landlady.

My family, in Dorset and Shropshire, for their support, particularly Nancy, Mum, Abs, Jamie, Luka, Amelie, Ian and Evie. I would also like to remember those family members we have recently lost: Chris Righton, Maureen Poulson, Anne Sargent and my dad, Anthony Patrick Quinn. All much loved and much missed. As a boy, Dad played with paper aeroplanes in a Birkenhead air raid shelter while German bombers flew overhead, and he remained interested in wartime history his whole life. It was, in fact, a book I bought for him, and later borrowed, that was my introduction to undercover agents in World War II.

I am grateful to all the books and publications that have informed this novel, and the libraries that enabled me to read them, particularly The Women's Library, where I browsed Rosalind's favourite magazines, and Dorchester Library, where their local history section (and their dedication to providing books during lockdown) was invaluable, as was the Imperial War Museum in London and its online resources.

I owe a special debt of gratitude to the historians and authors who taught me about the remarkable women agents of the Special Operations Executive, of whom their recruiting officer Selwyn Jepson once said, 'In my view, women were very much better than men for the work. Women, as you must know, have a far greater capacity for cool and lonely courage than men.'

Finally, an enormous thank you to my irreplaceable corner crew, Peggy Riley and Sarah Leipciger, who helped me carry this whale from beginning to end.